D1436578

Harriet
Imogen
Octavia

JILLY COOPER

Harriet
Imogen
Octavia

BCA

LONDON NEW YORK SYDNEY TORONTO

This edition published 1996
by BCA
by arrangement with Corgi Books

CN 2026

Typeset in Baskerville by
The Design Team, Ascot, Berkshire
Printed and bound in Great Britain by
Clays Ltd., St Ives plc.

CONTENTS

Harriet

To my niece Amelia Sallit with Love

Part One

CHAPTER ONE

It started to snow as Harriet was writing the last paragraph. Looking up she saw the flakes tumbling out of a sullen, pewter-grey sky, swirling and chasing each other, drifting into the branched arms of the trees. With a yelp of excitement she put down her pen and ran to the window. The flakes were small and compact. It was going to settle. Now they were belting down, and suddenly the towers of Oxford were encapsulated in a flurry of white flakes, as though someone had violently shaken a snow scene in a glass ball.

She went back to her essay, copying out the last two sentences with a flourish, then she wrote her name at the top of the first page: Harriet Poole, carefully closing up the Os, because she'd read somewhere that it was a sign of weak character to leave them open.

She had got up at six to finish her essay, having spent all week re-writing it. Anything to avoid the humiliation of last week's tutorial. Her tutor, Theo Dutton, who chain-smoked and showed no mercy, was famous for his blistering invective. When she had finished reading out last week's essay he had asked her three questions which entirely exposed the shallowness of her argument, then, tearing up the pages with long nicotined fingers, had dropped them disdainfully into the waste paper basket.

'That was junk,' he had said in his dry, precise voice, 'you merely copied out other people's ideas with varying degrees of accuracy. Read Shakespeare rather than books about Shakespeare. Look into your heart and write. You're trying too hard; relax; enjoy what you read or dislike it, but don't deaden it on paper.'

Her eyes had filled with tears. She had worked very hard.

'You're too sensitive, Harriet,' he had said, 'we'll have to raise your threshold of pain, won't we? A large dose of bullying each week until you build up an immunity.'

His hard, yellow eyes gleamed through his spectacles. He was smiling, but she wasn't sure if he was fooling or not. He always made her feel faintly sexy, but uneasy at the same time.

'Now,' he had said briskly, 'for next week, write an essay on which of Shakespeare's characters would be best in bed and why.'

Harriet flushed scarlet.

'But I can't . . .' she began, then bit her lip

'Can't write from experience? Use your imagination then. Shakespeare didn't know what it was like to be a black general or a Danish prince, did he?'

'Hamlet wouldn't have been much good,' said Harriet. 'He'd have talked too much, and never made up his mind to, until it was too late and one had gone off the boil.'

Theo had given a bark of laughter.

'That's more like it. Write something I might enjoy reading.'

Well, there was her essay, and it had taken her all week. She had read nothing but Shakespeare, and thought about nothing but sex. And she felt light-headed from exhaustion, a sense of achievement and the snow outside

She was also starving. No one was up. The landlady and her husband liked to lie in on Saturday. Downstairs among the letters scattered on the floor lay one from her boyfriend, Geoffrey. Reading it, she wandered into the kitchen, her jeans, too long when she wasn't wearing heels, swishing on the linoleum.

'Dear Harriet,' wrote Geoffrey, on office writing paper, 'I am really fed up. I can't get down this weekend, but I must finish this report and hand it in to the M.D. on Monday.'

Then followed a lot of waffle about pressure of work, grabbing every opportunity in the present economic climate and doing it for both their sakes.

'So pleased you have finally gone on the pill,' he ended up. (Harriet had a vision of herself poised like a ballerina on a tiny capsule.) 'I'm so fed up with being parked outside your bedroom every night like flowers in a hospital. I want you so much darling, I know I can make you happy. I'll be down next weekend, early Friday night. Meanwhile keep yourself on ice. Hugs and kisses and other things, love Geoffrey.'

Harriet felt a great wave of relief, then felt guilty. One really shouldn't contemplate losing one's virginity to someone one felt relieved one wasn't going to see. Virginity should be lost gloriously. Geoffrey wasn't glorious, just solid and very, very persistent.

Now that he wasn't coming down, she could lapse a bit, and not bother about dieting until Monday. She opened a tin of baked beans and put a slice of toast under the grill. After her tutorial with Theo, she could go to the library and get out a couple of trashy novels — she deserved a break after all that Shakespeare — and later go to the new Robert Redford film, and see it round twice, and eat a whole bar of Crunchie, and perhaps an ice-cream too. The weekend stretched out like the snow beginning to cover the lawn.

After eating every baked bean she felt fat, and decided to wash her hair in Theo Dutton's honour. There was no shower in the bathroom. It was either a question of scalding your head under the hot tap or freezing under the cold, which was much colder because of the snow.

As she alternately froze and scalded she pondered once more the problem of her virginity. All her friends were sleeping with their boyfriends, and she suspected that if she'd really fancied Geoffrey she'd have succumbed to him months ago. If Robert Redford, for example, came to Oxford in a play and bumped into her outside the theatre or met her at a party, she'd be his in a trice. She was conscious of so much love welling up inside her. If only she were beautiful and not so shy, she might attract some beautiful man to give it to. She couldn't be bothered putting conditioner on her hair after she'd washed it. Theo wasn't that attractive.

Dripping, she went into her room. Her papers and books were scattered all over the floor. She wished she were one of those people who could transform a room into a home with

13

a few feminine touches. But she loved her room, messy as it was, and even if she didn't have a great love in her life, the days at Oxford had their own happiness. Theo Dutton, when he wasn't being vile, calling her his star pupil to another don who'd dropped in to borrow a book, a muddled feeling she had of the importance of intellectual things, music, writing books herself, being reviewed one dizzy day in the *Times Literary Supplement*, 'Miss Harriet Poole in her first novel shows sensitivity and remarkable maturity.'

The snow was covering the lawn and the red roofs now. Two children, shrieking with delight, were scraping it off the top of a car to make a snowball. On the ledge of the window lay a moth. Harriet picked it up — she had read somewhere that human hands burnt insects' feet like hot coals. It was too cold to put it outside. Running out of the room, she parked it gently in her landlady's maidenhair fern on the landing. At least it would have something to eat. She spent so much time worrying about dogs being put out on the motorway, and horses being sent to the slaughter house, and children in orphanages. What on earth was she going to do when something really terrible happened to her — like one of her parents dying?

The snow had now nearly hidden a cluster of snowdrops that had courageously sprung out of the dark earth. Snow on snow, thought Harriet; perhaps she should write a poem about it. Crouching in front of the gas fire she got out a pen and began to scribble.

An hour later her hair was dry and she realized she was going to be late. She pulled on a red sweater because it brought some colour to her sallow cheeks, red tights and a grey skirt, which bagged slightly. She must get some new clothes, but her grant never went far enough

She tried on a belt, then took it off because it emphasized her spare tyre. She really shouldn't have eaten all those baked beans; perhaps it was being on the pill for a week that made her feel so fat. The red tights had a ladder, but her black boots covered that. Her duffle coat had two buttons missing. The snow, like life, had caught her on the hop.

Aware that she might want to brood over Geoffrey's letter

14

later, she put it with her essay in a blue folder. Outside the house, she caught her breath as the frozen wind cut through her like a knife. Her bicycle, its red paint peeling, lay against the ivied wall. The snow, now four inches deep, turned yellow where a dog had lifted its leg on her front wheel.

As she pedalled past the park snow was settling in the dead leaves and hollows of the chestnut trees. In the churchyard the stone angels had white mobcaps on their heads. The frozen puddles didn't crack beneath her bicycle wheels. As she headed towards the Banbury Road, the snow stepped up the pace, exploding over her in rockets, filling up her spectacles, blinding her.

Grimly battling on, she thought about Geoffrey's letter. So pleased you're finally on the pill. Oh dear, but that was next week. Who knew but the world might end tonight? She turned a corner. Suddenly a dark blue car came out of a side road, swerved frantically, made a dizzy glide across the road, caught the wheel of her bicycle, and the next moment she was flying through the air on to the grass verge, her glasses knocked off, her possessions flying. The car skidded to a halt. The driver jumped out. He had dark gold hair, and his face was as white as the snow.

'Christ I'm sorry,' he said. 'I should have looked. Are you OK.?'

Harriet sat on the verge, trembling and wondering if she was. The base of her spine felt agonizingly jolted. Her skirt was rucked up; her long red-stockinged legs in their black boots sprawled out like a colt; dark hair tumbled over her face.

'I'm all right,' she gasped. 'It was my fault. I should have rubbed the snow off my glasses. I couldn't see where I was going. I'm most terribly sorry.'

The words came out in a rush. Often, when she spoke, she had to hang on to a word to steady herself.

'No one usually comes down this road,' he said.

'It's a short cut. I was going to a tutorial. Oh God, where are my glasses?'

'Here they are.' He picked them up and polished them for her. 'Are you sure you're all right? You've gone awfully white. Can you walk?'

He took her hands and pulled her gently to her feet, and, when she swayed slightly, put his arm round her. Harriet put on her spectacles and, looking at him, suddenly realized it was Simon Villiers and blushed scarlet.

'Where's my essay?' she muttered.

He retrieved it from a hollow in the verge.

'Pity you had it in a folder! The ink would have run in the snow. Been a marvellous excuse not to hand it in. Look, I really think I'd better take you to hospital.'

'I'm all right. I must go to my tutorial.'

Simon looked at her buckled bicycle. 'Well you won't get there on that,' he said ruefully. 'I'll get the garage to come and pick it up.'

There were flakes of snow gathering in his blond hair.

'What you need is a slug of brandy. I've got some in my digs. Come back, and I'll ring up and say you're ill.'

He helped her into his car.

'You don't have to bother, really you don't.'

'Shut up,' he said gently. 'Women are always being silly about inessentials.'

Inside the car he lit a cigarette and gave it to her. Harriet thought this was such a smooth gesture, she hadn't the heart to tell him she hardly smoked. The cigarette was very strong and made her cough. The heat was turned up overpoweringly, so was the wireless.

'Do you really have to go to this tutorial?' he asked, when he'd finally got the car out of the snow.

She nodded.

'Where is it?'

'Hallerton Street, No. 44.'

'Theo Dutton?'

'You know him?'

'He tutored me my first year, until he realized I was past redemption. Not surprised he snapped you up; he always corners the pretty ones.'

He sat lazily beside her, driving with one hand. He was wearing dark grey trousers, a black shirt, and a pale blue velvet coat like Peter Rabbit. His eyes ran over her in an

16

amused, speculative, slightly condescending way.

'I wish you'd take your glasses off again,' he said. 'You're eyes are far too sexy to be hidden. I must say it's a most unorthodox way to meet, but I'm very glad we have. What college are you at?'

'St. Hilda's.'

She noticed he didn't introduce himself. He assumed rightly that everyone knew who he was.

'Why haven't we met before?'

'I've been working.'

'Theo keeping you to the grindstone?'

The car skidded slightly. Harriet jumped out of her skin. Simon laughed.

'Better keep my eyes on the road. Mind if I stop for petrol?'

As he got out to speak to the petrol pump attendant, Harriet surreptitiously turned the driving mirror and had a look at herself. Not too bad; thank God she'd washed her hair.

She couldn't believe it. Simon Villiers picking her up. She stole a quick glance at him, marvelling at the blond hair falling on the collar, the delicate aquiline features, the slightly cruel, beautifully shaped mouth, and tawny complexion without any trace of pink in it. Most amazing of all were his eyes, sleepy, and bluey-green with the dark lashes so thick and close together that they gave the illusion he was wearing eye-liner.

She was so dazed she forgot to put the mirror back and Simon nearly backed into a passing car.

'This journey's becoming pure Marx Brothers,' he said, replacing the mirror.

She didn't look at him, feeling that beastly blush staining her cheeks again.

'Come and have a drink after your tutorial.'

'Oh I don't . . . I mean you don't have . . .'

'There'll be other people there,' he said.

Oh God, she knew what they'd be like, models and actresses down from London. He read her thoughts.

'No one very alarming. I'll look after you. Please,' his

17

voice dropped, caressing and husky, 'let me make some reparation for nearly killing you.'

They drew up outside Theo's house.

'You'll come.'

'Yes, I'd like to.'

'Don't mention me to Theo. He'll give me a lousy press.'

As he drove off in a flurry of snow, she realized once again that he'd automatically assumed she knew where he lived.

CHAPTER TWO

As she walked up the snowy path, her feet made no sound. The wonderful softening of the snow gave her a feeling of great irresponsibility, as though her reactions were blurred by alcohol. Hoods of white lay over the yew trees and turned the lavender bushes into white hedgehogs. Snakes of snow lay on the branches of the monkey puzzle.

Her brain was reeling, that she should have met Simon Villiers in this way. Ever since she'd seen him playing Brick in the OUDS production of *Cat on a Hot Tin Roof,* she'd known moments of exquisite unfaithfulness to Robert Redford. She knew Simon was a playboy with buckets of money and a frightful reputation. She knew that even her friends at St. Hilda's, who happily slept with their boyfriends, still disapproved strongly of the Villiers Set. Harriet pretended to disapprove too, but she was secretly excited by their double-barrelled names, their fast cars, their frequent appearances in the gossip column, their ability to get chucked out of smart restaurants, their reputation for sexual ambiguity, and drugging and drinking.

'The downward path is easy, but there's no turning back,' she muttered to herself as she pulled the doorbell. Theo Dutton's children fell on her.

'Hullo, Harriet. Harry ate a lamb for breakfast. It's a joke: Harriet a lamb for breakfast.'

'I've heard it before,' said Harriet.

'What time is it when an elephant sits on your fence?' said the eldest.

'I don't know,' said Harriet.

'Time to get a new fence,' the children exploded with laughter.

19

She often baby-sat when the Duttons went out.

'We've made a snowman in the garden. Come and look at it. What does it remind you of?'

'It looks like your father,' said Harriet.

'Waiting for the BBC to ring,' said the youngest.

Harriet giggled.

'Isn't the snow lovely?' she said.

'Will you take us tobogganing this afternoon? Daddy's working on a broadcast, which means he'll go to sleep.'

'And Mummy's got a cold.'

Three expectant faces gazed at her.

Euphoria at meeting Simon overwhelmed her.

'All right. I'll come and pick you up at 2.30,' she said.

'This is much better,' said Theo Dutton, lighting another cigarette.

Harriet watched the snow thickening on the roof opposite.

'The style leaves a lot to be desired. I want to shake it and plump it up like a pillow, but your ideas are good. You've used your imagination.'

His shrewd, yellow eyes gleamed at her behind his spectacles. He tugged at his beard.

'You're very abstracted today,' he said. 'Someone's switched a light on inside you. What's happened? Boyfriend not coming down?'

Harriet laughed.

'Lack of sleep — and I just love the snow. I'm sorry if I seem a bit dopey. I got knocked off my bicycle on the way here. I didn't get hurt but it shook me a bit.'

She hoped she wouldn't be too terrified of the people in Simon's flat. She ought to go home and change into something better, but into what?

Theo looked at her speculatively, admiring the full breasts, the puppy plumpness, the long slim legs, the huge grey eyes with their heavy lids. One didn't normally realize the beauty of them hidden behind glasses. She was terribly shy, but through the shyness one could feel the vitality. She'll fall like a ripe plum any minute, he thought, with all

20

the wistfulness of the happily married. There was nothing like a young, full-blooded girl suddenly introduced to the pleasure of the bed.

He sighed. Harriet wondered if she ought to rush out and blow the last of her month's allowance on a new sweater. It would do her good not to eat for a fortnight.

'This week,' said Theo Dutton, 'we'll look at the sonnets. "With this Key," said Wordsworth, "Shakespeare unlocked his heart." When my mistress walks, she treads on the ground, and don't forget it.'

At a quarter to twelve he got out the sherry bottle.

'There are two kinds of sherry in Oxford: one you cook with, the other you use for drinking. Usually the two get muddled, but not in my house. I think after this, you'd better go back to bed — alone.'

He poured the sherry into smeared glasses.

'I promised to take your children tobogganing,' said Harriet.

She came out of Theo's house to find a long, dark green car waiting for her. A man got out; he was smoking a cigarette and had auburn hair and the wild careering good looks of a red setter. Harriet recognized him immediately as one of Simon's cronies, Mark Macaulay.

'Simon sent me to fetch you,' he said. 'He thought you might get cold feet; as if anyone could get anything else in this bloody weather. Are you all right?' he added, as she got into the car. 'Simon said he sent you for six.'

Physically and mentally, thought Harriet.

'I'm a bit sore at the bottom of my spine,' she said.

'Your coccyx,' said Mark and laughed rather wildly. He already seemed a bit high.

'Are there lots of people there?' she said.

'About a couple of dozen, including one or two predatory ladies who won't be at all pleased that you've appeared on the scene.'

He shot her a sideways glance and laughed again.

Harriet felt nervous and excited at the same time.

21

'Do you think I ought to go?'

'It's more than my life's worth if you don't. Not that it's worth a lot anyway,' he said, taking a bottle of brandy out of the dashboard and taking a swig. 'I'm going down hill faster than a greased pig as it is.'

'I wish I could go home and change,' said Harriet.

'Don't change a thing. What Simon likes is novelty and you're certainly different.'

'He's only being kind because he knocked me off my bike.'

'Simon,' said Mark, 'never does anything to please any-one except himself.'

CHAPTER THREE

Harriet had never seen anything like Simon's drawing-room — with its shaggy fur rugs, huge tropical plants, emerald green silk curtains and roaring fire which flickered on the French paperbacks — mostly plays and pornography — in the bookshelves. Invitations were stacked like a pack of cards on the mantelpiece. Signed photographs of famous actors and actresses looked down from the black walls. Glamorous people prowled about the room like beasts in a jungle. Then, most glamorous of all Simon, his blue-green eyes glittering, came over to welcome them.

He removed Harriet's coat, then her scarf, then her spectacles.

'I don't want you to see my imperfections too clearly,' he said, kissing her on the cheek. 'Isn't she sweet?' he added to Mark.

'Yes,' said Mark. 'Much too sweet for you. That's worrying me.'

A handsome Indian strolled up to them.

'I wish you hadn't painted this room black,' he said petulantly. 'I don't show up against it.'

'Go and stand in the snow,' said Simon.

He gave Harriet a glass of ice-cold white wine, running his finger caressingly along her fingers as he did so.

'That should cool you up,' he said. 'How was Theo? Did he like your essay?'

'He seemed to — for once.'

'What was it about?'

'Which of Shakespeare's heroes was — well — the b-best in bed.'

'Bloody old letch excites himself that way. I suppose

23

you're an authority on bed now?'

Harriet looked at her feet. There was a pause, then she glanced up at Simon and encountered a look that nearly took her skin off. Crimson, she turned to look out of the window.

'The snow's so beautiful, isn't it?' she said in a choked voice.

'We aim to please,' he said smiling at her. 'Sit down and enjoy the view. You don't need to meet any of these boring people.'

Harriet parked herself on a black velvet window seat trying to merge into the green silk curtains. She had never seen so many exotic people, and the room smelt so erotic too. Not only must every pulse spot of each ravishing creature be throbbing with expensive scent, there was also the smell of the apple logs burning in the grate, a faint whiff of incense, and the heavy fragrance of a huge bunch of rainbow-coloured freesias massed in a blue bowl on the table. There was another, sweet, clinging smell she couldn't identify.

Suddenly there was a terrific pounding on the door, and a handsome man with grey hair walked in. Harriet immediately recognized him as the leading actor at the playhouse this week.

'Simon darling, I just knew this was your room. You can smell the stuff all the way down the street. You'll get busted if you're not careful. Hullo baby,' he added to a stunning blonde in a white silk shirt, and, taking a cigarette from her lips, inhaled deeply. When he breathed out about two years later, he turned to two elegant young men who were following him.

'They're both called Jeremy,' he said to Simon. 'And they're madly in love with each other, which makes things a bit complicated.'

The two young men giggled.

'Jeremy and Jeremy,' said the handsome actor. 'You haven't met Simon.'

'We've heard so much about you,' said the young men in chorus. 'Quite the rising star, aren't you?'

'Simon,' said a sulky-looking redhead with a mouth like a

rubber tyre, 'can't we draw the curtains? All the plebs are looking in.'

'My friend here,' said Simon, giving Harriet a smile, 'enjoys the view, so we'll leave the curtains open.'

The redhead exchanged glances with the blonde in the white shirt.

'How's Borzoi, Simon?' said the actor taking another drag at the blonde's cigarette.

'Gone to the States,' said Simon.

'For long?'

'For good I hope,' said Simon, filling Harriet's glass.

The actor raised his well-plucked eyebrows.

'Like that, is it? Imagine she was a bit of a handful.'

'At least if she tries to come back, she's such a bitch she'll have to spend six months in quarantine,' said Simon.

Everyone laughed. More people arrived. Harriet watched the undercarriage of the gulls dark against the sky. The railings in the street were losing their shape now.

'I must do something about my hair,' said a wild-looking brunette.

'You could try brushing it,' said her boyfriend.

Simon, the actor and the two Jeremys started swapping such scurrilous stories of stars of stage and screen that everyone stopped their conversations to listen.

'Not boys, my dear, two girls at a time. His wife doesn't mind; she's got her own girlfriend anyway,' said the actor.

'I bet she minded her notices last week; they were ghastly,' said one of the Jeremys.

'Evidently in her costume she looks just like the Emperor Vespasian in drag,' said Simon. Harriet's eyes were out on stalks.

A rather ravaged beauty came through the door, wearing a fur coat and trousers. No one took any notice, so she went out and came in again.

'Deirdre,' everyone shrieked.

'I'm exhausted,' she said. 'I haven't been to bed.'

'Darling,' said the actor, kissing her. 'I didn't recognize you with your clothes on.'

Someone put on a record.

25

JILLY COOPER

'My very good friend the milkman says, that I am losing too much sleep,' sang Fats Waller.

Mark Macaulay came and sat down by Harriet, and filled up her glass.

'How's your coccyx?' he asked. 'I ought to work this afternoon, but I shan't.'

'What are you going to do after schools?' said Harriet.

'I thought of having a stab at a Dip.Ed.'

'I didn't know-you wanted to teach, Markie,' shrieked Deirdre. 'You *hate* children.'

'I know, but a Dip.Ed'll give me another year to look around. They don't work one very hard, and by the end of another year, one might have decided what one wants to do.'

'I've got an interview with a military publisher next week,' said a boy in jeans with flowing blond hair. 'I expect they're awfully straight. Have you got a suit you can lend me?'

'Simon has,' said Mark. 'You'd better get a haircut too.'

The snow had deadened the roar of the traffic in the Turl to a dull murmur. A little bunch of protest marchers were struggling down the street with placards.

'The acne and anorak brigade,' said Mark. 'What are they banning this time, reds or fascists?'

'More jobs for teachers, I think,' said Harriet, trying to see without her glasses.

'Aren't they just like Good King Wenceslas and his page?' said Deirdre, 'through the rude wind's loud lament and all that.'

'I'm sure Wenceslas had something going with his page boy,' said Simon.

'I wish I had principles,' said Mark, looking at the marchers.

'I like people better than principles,' said Simon, 'and I like people with no principles best of all.'

'Oscar Wilde,' muttered Harriet.

'Clever girl,' said Simon. 'Dorian Gray's my next part. OUDS are doing an adaptation.'

He'll be marvellous at it, thought Harriet, watching him move off to fill someone's drink. Even amidst the glittering

26

menagerie of tigers he surrounded himself with, his beauty made him separate.

Two girls looked out of the window.

'That car's been parked there for ages,' they said, 'let's go down and write something awful all over it.'

They rushed out of the door, and a minute later their shrieks could be heard, as, lifting their slim legs up like Hackney ponies, they raced across the snow.

On the wall opposite was pinned a poster of a beautiful girl with long streaky hair and cheekbones you could balance a tray on.

'Who's that?' she said to Mark.

'Borzoi, Simon's ex,' he said.

'Why did they split up?'

'Inevitable, darling. They both spent far too much time arguing with the mirror which was the fairest of them both. Borzoi's doing better than Simon too, at the moment, and that doesn't help. She's also extremely spoilt.'

He looked at Harriet in amusement. 'That's why he fancies you.'

'He couldn't.'

'Sure he does, and that's what's making Chloe so uptight.' He nodded his head in the direction of the sulky redhead who was flirting determinedly on the sofa with the handsome actor. 'She was convinced she was next in succession.'

Oh golly, thought Harriet, but the warm excited feeling inside her persisted.

Back came the two girls from the snow.

'I only got as far as "Bugg",' shrieked one, 'when a policeman came along.'

'Everything looks so white and virginal,' said the other, huddling by the fire.

'Don't know any virgins,' said the actor. 'Bit of a collector's item these days.'

'Moppet Wilson is,' said Deirdre. 'Never bares anything but her soul.'

'What's she saving it for?' said Mark.

'The man she marries. She thinks it something one gives him like a pair of cuff-links on one's wedding day.'

27

'I'd rather have cuff-links,' said Mark draining his glass.

'Virgins must be boring to go to bed with,' said Chloe, looking directly at Simon. 'They don't know first base from second.'

Harriet looked up. Simon was looking straight at her. He gave her his swift, wicked smile. He knows, she thought in panic, and felt herself going scarlet again. Oh why the hell had she worn red? She turned her burning face to cool it against the window pane.

'When I was a child I liked popping balloons, and fuchsia buds,' said Simon softly. 'I always like putting my finger through the paper on the top of the Maxwell House jar. I like virgins. You can break them in how you like, before they have time to learn any bad habits.'

There was a long pause. Harriet got up and stumbled to the lavatory. Her heart was thumping, but her thoughts had taken on a strange, sensual, dreamlike quality. In the bathroom was a bidet, which seemed the height of sophistication. She toned down her face with some of Simon's talcum powder.

As she came back into the room, the actor was leaving.

'Must go, darling. I've got a matinée. If I drink any more I'll fall off the stage. Come along Jeremy and Jeremy,' he added to the boys, who were feeding each other grapes.

'Do put in a good word for me to Boris,' said Simon casually. 'He was coming to see *Cat*, but he never made it. Tell him I'm doing Dorian Gray at the end of term.'

'Sure will, baby,' said the actor. 'We'll all have dinner one day next week.'

'He doesn't like the hours I keep. He suggests that you should marry me,' sang Fats Waller.

'Where shall we eat, Simon?' said Chloe. 'What about the Parisian.'

'I'm not forking out a tenner for a lot of old bones cooked in cream,' said Simon.

Chloe glared at him.

'I must go,' said Harriet hastily.

'We're just going to eat,' said Simon.

She didn't want to eat. She knew at last she had come face

to face with someone so fascinating that, if she allowed him to do so, he would absorb her whole being. She felt on the verge of some terrible crisis. She wanted to be alone and think.

'I promised to take Theo's children tobogganing.'

'Oh come on,' said Simon. 'They won't mind.'

'I promised.'

'All right then, as long as you come back later.'

'You'll be fed up with people by then.'

'Only of certain people. *We* haven't begun yet.'

He put her coat on, and as he flipped her hair over the collar he let his hand slide caressingly down its newly washed length.

She jumped away nervously.

'I'll drive you back,' he said.

'No,' she stammered. 'I'd rather walk.'

But as she moved away down the path, he caught the two ends of her red scarf and pulled her back till they were only a few inches apart.

'Promise you'll come back?'

She nodded. She could see the scattering of freckles on the bridge of his nose. The bluey-green eyes were almost on a level with hers. He had hardly to bend his head to kiss her. He tasted of white wine and French cigarettes. She felt her stomach go liquid, her knees disappear, as all the books said they would and they never had with Geoffrey.

Breaking away from him, she ran down the street, not even feeling the icy winds now. As she rounded the corner, she surprised two undergraduates with placards by bursting out laughing.

CHAPTER FOUR

Her manic high spirits infected the children. They drove up to Hinksey Hill yelling Knick Knack Paddy Wack at the top of their voices, and screamed with delight as the red and silver toboggan hissed down the silent hillside, throwing them into the drifts and folds in the snow. Then they got up and, panting, pulled the toboggan to the top of the hill, hurling snowballs at one another, the Duttons' cairn snapping at the snow with ivory teeth, until they were all soaked through but warm inside.

Simon Villiers kissed me, she wanted to shout to the white hilltops, and happiness kept bubbling up inside her as she hugged the children more tightly. They were reluctant to let her go.

'Stay to tea,' they pleaded. 'There'll be crumpets and chocolate cake and *Doctor Who.*'

'Harriet obviously has other plans,' said Theo Dutton, who opened the front door to them. 'Be careful, my sweet. Read your sonnets. Try to shun the heaven, if it's only going to lead to hell.'

Was it so obvious to everyone, wondered Harriet, as she galloped back to her digs through the snow. She passed the Robert Redford film without a twinge of regret. She'd got the real thing ahead of her.

Back in her room, she examined the picture of Geoffrey, smiling self-consciously and clutching a tennis racket. And that photograph makes him better looking than he really is, she thought. She glanced too, at the photograph of her elder sister Susie, looking ravishing on her wedding day and hanging on Peta Neave's arm. That was one of Harriet's problems, always being compared with a slim, beautiful sis-

30

ter who never got spots, and who had the kind of self control that never took too many potatoes, or betrayed too much interest in a man until she knew that he was hooked. Harriet knew how Susie had churned inside over the rich and glamorous Peter Neave, how she had waited all day biting her nails for him to ring, and when he finally did, had had the nerve to say, 'No I can't tonight, or tomorrow, or the next night, and I'm away this weekend,' playing hard to get for the next few weeks until she'd literally brought Peter Neave to his knees with a proposal of marriage. How could one ever believe one was attractive when one ate too many cream buns and lived in Susie's shadow, and frightened men off by getting too keen too quickly? She must try and be sensible about Simon.

What could she wear? Her grey shirt had a mark on the front; the maroon sweater had lost its elasticity in the wash so the polo neck looked like a surgical collar; she'd sweated lighter rings under the arms of her brown dress when she'd been nervous at a party. Her jeans were clean but they covered her legs, which were her best thing, and they were so tight they would leave marks all over her body when she took them off. But she was *not* going to take them off, she said to herself furiously. Soon there were clothes lying all over the floor. The water only ran to a tepid bath. She was in such a state she washed her face twice, cut herself three times shaving her legs, and then got back into the bath to wash between her toes in case Simon was the sort of man who kissed one all over. Then she rubbed her landlady's hand-cream all over her body and smothered herself in French Fern talcum powder.

In the bedroom, she examined herself naked in the mirror. Were the goods good enough? Her bust was much too big. But men didn't seem to mind that. Her legs were all right except for the bleeding, but everywhere else was a bit voluptuous. She took the mirror off the wall and, holding it above herself, lay down on the bed. Would she pass muster at this angle? Her stomach looked flatter anyway, and her hair fanned out nicely. Stop it, she said to herself furiously, you're only going to have a drink with him.

31

There was a knock on the door. She jumped up guiltily, grabbing a towel.

'Going out, dear?' said the landlady, Mrs. Glass, 'there's a nice piece of hot gammon if you fancy it.'

Mrs. Glass often grumbled how much her lodgers cost her, but she preferred the ones that stayed in. Miss Poole was a nice, quiet girl, and sweet natured too, if she wasn't so dreadfully untidy.

'Your poor mother wouldn't want you to starve yourself,' said Mrs. Glass, who thought everyone under eleven stone needed feeding up.

'I'm going to a party,' said Harriet. 'I'll probably stay the night with a girlfriend, so don't worry if I don't come back.' The glib way she could lie.

'Quite right not to trust young gentlemen driving on these roads,' said Mrs. Glass. 'Do you good to get out and enjoy yourself for a change.'

'I'll have a real tidy out tomorrow,' said Harriet, wincing as she put deodorant under her arms. Her leg was still bleeding; it must be all that excitement pulsating through her veins.

She put on a pair of black lace pants and a black bra with a red ribbon she had bought in anticipation of Geoffrey. The pants hardly covered her at all and the red ribbon was too much, so she tore it off.

There was her black sweater all the time under the bed. She could wear it with her red skirt. It was getting late. What happened if Simon got bored of waiting and went out?

For once, her hair obeyed her. She splashed a bottle of scent, a Christmas present from Susie, all over her. She hoped it didn't clash with the French Fern. How did French ferns differ from English, she wondered. Perhaps they were more sophisticated.

She galloped back along the streets. It was very cold now and the street lights gave the snow a curious pale radiance. Her breath crystallized in little clouds before her. The white nights, she said to herself; she was Anna Karenina smothered in furs hurrying to meet Vronsky, Natasha quivering with guilty expectation waiting for Anatole.

She felt more and more sick with nerves. Perhaps her mouth tasted awful; she stopped at the newsagents to buy some chewing gum. The windows of Simon's digs were black. He's gone, she thought in panic; one of those dazzling creatures has spirited him away. No, a thin beam of light trickled through the green silk curtains. A group of people were coming out. Oh, those echoing self-confident voices!

'I do think it's anti-social of Simon to throw us out when it's so cold. Chloe is going to be simply livid,' said one of the girls, scooping up a snowball and throwing it at one of the boys, as they all went screaming off into the night. Harriet threw away her chewing gum, it made no sound as it landed in the snow. The door was still open as she went up the path. Simon emerged from the darkness, his hair gleaming white in the street lamp.

'I thought you'd done a bunk,' he said.

'I got soaked. I had to change.'

He put his hand out and touched her cheek.

'You're frozen. Come in.'

Only three people were left in the drawing-room. Deirdre who was putting on lipstick, a blond man who was rooting around the drinks tray to find himself some more wine, and Chloe who sat on the sofa, huddled like a sparrow on the telegraph wires on a cold day.

'Oh poor thing,' thought Harriet. 'I'd mind losing Simon.'

'Come on chaps,' said Simon removing the bottle from the blond man, 'chucking-out time.'

Harriet went over to the fire. She felt miserably embarrassed. Chloe looked mutinous. Simon got her blond, squashy fur coat out of the bedroom and held it out for her.

'Come on, darling,' he said firmly. 'Beat it.'

Two angry spots of colour burnt on her cheeks. She snatched the coat from him and put it on herself.

'You're a bastard, Simon,' she hissed. 'And *you* won't escape unscathed either,' she added to Harriet, and, with a sob, ran out of the room down the stairs.

'We might all meet at Serena's party later,' said Deirdre, kissing Simon on the cheek. 'She is expecting you, Simon.'

'Not tonight, darling. Tell Serena I had a previous . . .' He shot a glance at Harriet. 'No, a *subsequent* engagement. Now goodnight, darlings.' And he shut the door on them.

He turned and shot Harriet that swift, devastating smile.

'One has to be brutal occasionally to get what one wants in life.'

'She was awfully upset,' said Harriet.

'She'll recover,' said Simon.

He chucked some logs on the fire, covering the flame and throwing the room into semi-darkness, and gave her a drink, the cold condensing on the outside of the glass. She held on to it to stop her hands shaking and took a huge gulp; it was a long time since the baked beans.

Simon disappeared into another room. She felt as though she was alone in some deserted woodland house, and that Indians or some invaders were slowly creeping through the undergrowth towards her — but she didn't know when or from where they were going to attack. Simon returned with the remains of a quiche on a plate.

'We never did have any lunch. Do you want some?'

She shook her head.

Simon helped himself to a slice.

'You're all right after the crash, are you?' he said with his mouth full .

'Just a few bruises, that's all.'

'I must look at them later.'

Her heart thumped madly; the firelight flickered on his face. She jumped as a log fell out of the grate.

'Relax,' said Simon. 'I've never seen anyone as terrified as you. What put that scared look in your eyes? Were you raped as a child? Did you have strict parents? Were you bullied at school?' He was making fun at her now, but his voice was like a caress.

She took another gulp of wine. Having eaten the inside of the quiche Simon was about to throw the pastry into the fire.

'We could give it to the birds,' said Harriet.

'We could, I suppose.' He opened the window, letting in a draught of icy air; the snow gleamed like a pearl. Simon put

34

a record on the gramophone. It was a Mozart piano concerto.

'You still look sad,' said Simon.

'I was thinking . . . about Chloe.'

'Not worth it. She's the most frightful scrubber. I only
took her out a couple of times. She's one of those girls like
scrambled egg, amazingly easy to make, but impossible to
get off the pan afterwards.'

Harriet giggled.

'That's better,' said Simon, 'now come and sit on the sofa.
No, next to me, not six feet away.'

She was still trembling, but the excitement was beginning
to take over. He picked up her hand and kissed it.

'I thought you were terribly good in *Cat on a Hot Tin
Roof*,' she said brightly.

'I know I was,' said Simon. 'So we've exhausted that subject.'

His hand on the back of the dark green velvet sofa was
edging towards her hair, but he didn't touch her. His timing
was so good, he held off until she was in a panic that he was
never going to. It was terribly hot in the room, she could feel
the sweat trickling between her breasts.

'You're so pretty,' he was saying in a low husky voice, and
then he kissed her. At first she kept her arms clamped down
by her side, but suddenly like the reflex action when one's
knee is tapped, they shot up and coiled themselves round
Simon's neck, and she was kissing him back with all her
might, and his hands were on the move all over her body.
Hastily she pulled in her spare tyre.

'I mustn't.'

'You must, you must.'

'You'll think I'm too easy.'

'I don't. I just think you're overdressed, that's all,' and he
took off her earrings and put them side by side on the table.
Then took off her shoes, and took the telephone off the
hook.

She sat back waiting for an attack on another front.

'You've got such a lovely body,' he said, filling both their
glasses.

'One should really take lessons at prep school in undoing bras. Oh, I see; it does up at the front,' he said a minute later.

His hands were warm on her bare back. He kissed her eyes, her hair, her mouth; she'd never dreamed he'd be so tender.

'No,' she gasped, leaping up as his fingers edged inside her waistband.

How could she explain she wouldn't be easy like this, if she didn't find him so overwhelmingly attractive?

'Sweetheart, stop fighting it,' he whispered. 'I refuse to be put outside the bedroom every night, like flowers in a hospital.'

Harriet gasped. 'You've read Geoffrey's letter!'

'I picked it up in the snow. I'm glad he's glad you've gone on the pill, but I'm even gladder.'

'You shouldn't read other people's letters,' she said furiously.

'One must, just to find out all the nice things they're saying about one. Tell me about Geoffrey. What does he do?'

'He's a marine biologist.'

'Oh well, we can't all be perfect.'

'He's clever,' said Harriet defensively. 'He's just come down from Plymouth.'

'One can't come down from Plymouth. One can only go up,' said Simon. He was attacking her waistband again.

'It's too soon,' she muttered, 'I don't even know you.'

'You talk too much,' he said. 'I've never heard so much fuss about something that's so nice.' He started to pull off her sweater and she was enveloped in a fuzz of black wool.

'It's got buttons at the back,' she squealed, as he nearly removed her ears.

'Don't be frightened,' he said, when she was finally freed, and he pulled her down on the floor beside him. The apple wood of the logs mingled with a trace of his lavender aftershave, and the animal smell of the white fire rug which scratched against her back. She had no will power. It's going to happen she thought in panic.

'Will it hurt?'

36

'You'll be so excited by the time I've got you revved up, you won't feel a thing,' he whispered.

In a few minutes the Mozart concerto jigged jollily to its ending, and the only sounds in the room were her gasps for breath and the soft crackling of the fire.

Later they went into the bedroom, and once in the night she got up to go to the loo, and gazed at herself in the bathroom mirror, searching for lines of depravity. She looked rather disappointingly the same except that her face was flushed, her eyes dazed. She wondered why she didn't feel more guilty, then realized it was because she loved him.

CHAPTER FIVE

'That was so gorgeous,' she said next morning when they woke up.

He grinned. 'You'll find it a perfect hobby, darling, and so cheap. I say,' he added, 'what's your name?'

She gave a gurgle of laughter.

'Harriet,' she said, 'Harriet Poole.'

'I've never had a Harriet before.' He lay back and laughed, 'Oh I'm just wild about Harriet,' and then he pulled her down on top of him.

For the next fortnight she had to keep pinching herself. Simon Villiers was her lover; the impossible had been achieved. They hardly got out of bed, except for the occasional excursion to the Randolph for breakfast, or an excursion to Hinksey Hill to see what making love was like in the snow. Harriet found it extremely cold, and nearly died of a heart attack when a cow looked over the fence and mooed at her.

Never in her life had she been so happy. Willingly she cooked for Simon, ironed his shirts rather badly, ran his errands, and submitted rapturously over and over again to his love-making.

'You really do ad-dore it, don't you?' he drawled in amazement.

The snow seemed here to stay. The ploughs came and scattered salt and sand on the roads, but the houses and the parks were still blanketed in whiteness. Harriet was doing absolutely no work. Simon had forbidden her to wear her glasses, so work gave her a headache anyway. She rang both Theo Dutton and Geoffrey and told them she'd got 'flu. The weight fell off her; she lost over a stone living on wine and love.

Never had she met anyone so witty, so glamorous, so glorious as Simon. Only one thing nagged her, at this supreme moment in her life: she felt unable to describe him adequately in her diary. There was an elusiveness about his character that she couldn't pin down; he seemed permanently to be playing someone other than himself, and watching himself doing it at the same time. Although books filled his flat, he never appeared to read, except theatre reviews in the paper or the odd stage magazine. When he watched television he was far more interested in the techniques of the actors and actresses, and in who was playing whom, than in the story.

It was only in the third week things started to go wrong. Simon had an audition in London with Buxton Philips. Not realizing it was early closing day, Harriet arrived too late to get his grey velvet suit out of the cleaners. She was shattered at the storm of abuse that broke over her when she got home.

'But you've got hundreds of beautiful suits,' she stammered.

'Yes,' hissed Simon, 'but I wanted to wear this one,' and he walked out of the house without even saying goodbye.

Harriet was supposed to be writing her essay on the sonnets, but she couldn't stop crying. In the end she gave up working, wrote a poem to Simon, and spent hours making a moussaka, which she knew he liked.

He came back from London on the last train, if anything in a worse mood than when he left.

'How did it go?' she said nervously.

'Bloody terrible! Buxton Philips didn't show up.'

'Oh no,' wailed Harriet. How could anyone stand up Simon?

'All I saw was some old bitch of a secretary. "Ay'm sorry, Mr. Villiers, but it's always wise to ring Mr. Philips in the mornin' to check he's able to make it, he's *so* busy." '

'Oh poor Simon.' She got up and put her arms round him, but she could sense his detachment.

'Fix me a drink,' he said, pacing up and down the room.

'In a few years' time, that bastard'll be crawling to me. "Ay'm sorry, Mr. Philips, Mr. Villiers is far too busy to see you." He'll regret this.'

'Of course he will,' said Harriet soothingly. 'You're going to be a big star, Simon. Everyone says so.'

She handed him a drink.

'I missed you so much, I've even written you a poem,' she said blushing. 'I've never written anyone a poem before.'

She handed it to him.

Simon skimmed through it, his lips curling.

' "Our love is like a rainbow arched in shuddering orgasm against the sky",' he read out in a deliberately melodramatic voice. ' "Orgasm" in the singular? I *must* be slipping.'

Harriet flushed and bit her lip.

'I also found this lovely sonnet, which describes exactly how I feel about you,' she said hastily, handing him the volume of Shakespeare.

'Harriet de-ah,' sighed Simon, as he glanced at it, 'if you knew the number of women who've quoted that poem at me! You're in danger of getting soppy, sweetheart. I don't mind women being romantic, but I can't stand soppiness.'

She tried once again.

'I've made some moussaka for supper,' she said.

'I'm bored with moussaka,' said Simon.

She was still crying when he came to bed. 'What's the matter?' he said. 'I love you,' said Harriet, in a choked voice. 'Well, if you love me,' said Simon softly, 'you must like the whip.'

He woke up next morning in a better mood, and they made love, sat drinking coffee and reading the papers in bed until lunchtime. Harriet had forgotten the insults of last night, aware only of a swooning relief that everything was all right again. Her euphoria was short-lived. She was looking at the horoscopes.

'It says I'm going to have a good day for romance,' she giggled. 'Perhaps I shall meet a tall dark stranger. I always dreamed I'd fall in love with someone tall and dark. Funny you should be small and blond.'

'I am *not* small,' said Simon icily.

40

She knew by the idle drumming of his fingers on the bed-side table that there'd be trouble, that he'd bide his time and then retaliate without scruple. He started to read a piece about some famous actor's sex life. When he came to the end he said:

'That's why I want to make it to the top. Apart from telling Buxton Philips to get stuffed, just think of the birds one could pull. Once you become a big star, you can virtually have any woman you want.'

There was a pause. Harriet felt faint at the thought of Simon having another woman. A great tear fell on to the paper she was reading, followed by another, and another.

'What's eating *you*?' said Simon.

She got clumsily out of bed; not wearing her spectacles and blinded by tears, she bumped into a table, knocking off a little Rockingham dalmatian that she knew Borzoi had given Simon. It smashed beyond redemption. Harriet was appalled.

'I'll buy you another, Simon, truly I will.'

'As it cost about £80, I think that's extremely unlikely,' he snapped. 'For God's sake stop snivelling. It's bad enough you breaking it, without making that Godawful din. I'm hungry. Go and put on the moussaka, and then have a bath but don't forget to leave the water in.'

Harriet lay in the bath, trying not to cry and wondering what it would be like to be married to Simon. "Harriet Villiers" had a splendid seventeenth-century ring. Could she cope with being the wife of a superstar? Some stage marriages she knew lasted for ever. She wouldn't be a drag on him; when he was away acting, she'd have her poems and novels to write; she might even write a play for him.

She could just see the first night notices:

'Simon Villiers's wife is not beautiful in the classical sense, but there is an appealing sensitivity, a radiance about this brilliant young playwright.' Unthinkingly she pulled out the plug.

Simon walked into the bathroom, yawning, hair ruffled, to find Harriet sitting in an empty bath, dreamily gazing into space.

41

'I thought I told you to leave the fucking water in.'

Harriet flushed unbecomingly.

'Oh God, I'm frightfully sorry. Perhaps there's some hot left.

There wasn't.

Even worse, she went into the kitchen and found that, although she'd turned on the oven, she'd put the moussaka into the cupboard instead, so when Simon came in, shuddering with cold and ill-temper, there was nothing to eat. The row that followed left her reeling. He really let her have it. She had no defences against the savageness of his tongue.

Once more she went and sobbed in the bedroom, and she heard the front door slam. Hours later when he came back she had cried herself to sleep. He woke her up.

'You're too sensitive, Harriet baby. You overreact all the time. Poor little baby,' he said gently, 'poor, poor little baby. Did you think I wasn't coming back?' Never had he made love to her so tenderly.

CHAPTER SIX

Harriet woke up feeling absurdly happy. True love could only be forged on rows like that. It was the first of March, her meagre allowance had come through. She got up, leaving Simon asleep. She cashed a cheque at the bank, and bought croissants and orange juice. In spite of a bitter east wind, the snow was melting, dripping off the houses, turning brown and stacked in great piles along the road.

It would be spring soon. She imagined herself and Simon wandering through the parks with the blossom out, or punting under long green willows and dancing till dawn at a Commem ball. All great love affairs had their teething troubles.

When she got back to Simon's rooms, she took his mail into his room. He was still half asleep, so she went to the kitchen and made coffee and heated up the croissants. She was worried about a large spot that was swelling up on the side of her nose. However much make-up she put over it, it shone through like a beacon; she must start eating properly.

When she took breakfast into his room, he had woken up and was in excellent form.

'Buxton Philips's written me a letter saying he's sorry, he's coming down to Oxford to take me out to lunch,' he said. draining a glass of orange juice.

'Oh darling, that's wonderful,' said Harriet.

Simon drew back the curtains. Harriet sat down on the bed, with the spot side furthest away from him, pouring out coffee.

'I think you'd better start packing, darling,' he said, liberally buttering a croissant.

'Oh God, is your mother coming to stay?'

43

He shook his head, his face curiously bland. 'I just think it's time you moved out.'

She looked at him bewildered, the colour draining from her face.

'But, why? Was it because I smashed your dog, and let out your bath water, and forgot about your suit, and the moussaka? I'm sorry. I will try to concentrate more.'

'Darling, it isn't that,' he said, thickly spreading marmalade. 'It's just that all good things come to an end. You should live a little, learn a bit more about life, play the field.'

'But I'm not like that, I'm a one-man girl.'

Simon shrugged his shoulders.

'W-when will I see you,' she was trembling violently now.

'You're making this very difficult for me,' he said gently.

She sat down.

'Mind my shirts,' said Simon hastily, removing the shirts she had ironed from the chair.

She stared at him. 'What did I do wrong?'

'Oh, for Christ's sake, you didn't do anything wrong.'

It must be a bad dream, it must be. She felt her happiness melting round her like the snow.

'Why can't I see you any more?'

'Darling, for everything there is a season. You're a lovely warm crazy girl, and we've had a ball together. Now I've broken you in nicely, you'll be a joy for the next guy, but it's time for us both to move on.'

'But I love you,' she stammered.

He sighed. 'That's your problem, sweetheart. I never said I loved you. I never pretended this was going to last.'

Her face had a look of pathos and stricken dignity.

'I don't believe it,' she whispered.

Simon was not finding this as easy as he had expected, rather unpleasant in fact. Oh God, why did women get so keen on one? He was nibbling the skin round his thumb nail. He seemed to Harriet to have shrunk in size; there was something about his eyes like an animal at bay.

She licked her dry lips. 'Will you find someone else?'

'Of course I'll find someone else,' he snapped, anger with himself making him crueller towards her. 'Borzoi's coming back. I got a letter from her this morning.'

'And so I get d-dumped like an unwanted dog on the motorway.'

Slowly it was dawning on her that his future didn't contain her.

He tried another tack. 'You're too good for me, Harriet.'

'I'm not,' she said helplessly.

'Yes, you are. I need a tough cookie like Borzoi.'

The sun, which hadn't been seen for ages, suddenly appeared at the window, high-lighting — the chaos of the room the unmade bed, Harriet's clothes strewn over every chair, the brimming ashtrays.

'Cheer up,' said Simon. 'At least it's a lovely day. Come on, lovie, get your things together; we haven't got much time.'

As he threw records, scarves, papers, make-up into her suitcase, she felt he was getting out an india rubber and carefully erasing every trace of her from his life. He was hard put to contain his elation. Even his goodbye was absent-minded. He patted her on the bottom and told her to behave herself. She could almost hear his sigh of relief as he shut the door and rushed back to tidy up for Borzoi.

She went straight home and dumped her suitcase. For a minute she lay on her bed and listened to the clocks striking all over Oxford. Only eleven o'clock. A whole day to be got through, a whole lifetime without Simon stretching ahead. She got up, turned on the gas and knelt down beside it; after ten seconds the meter ran out.

Mrs. Glass came in and started to shout at her for the rent, then she saw Harriet's face and stopped. 'White as a corpse, poor little thing,' she told her husband afterwards. ' 'Er sins must have catched up with 'er.'

Harriet got up and went out and walked round the town, the slush leaking into her boots. She didn't notice the cold even in her thin coat. She had nothing of Simon's. He had written her no letters, given her no presents. How crazy she had been, how presumptuous to think for a moment she could hold him. It was like trying to catch the sun with a fishing net. She walked three times round the same churchyard, then took a bus to Headington, looking at the trees, their branches shiny from the melting snow. She got off the bus and began to walk again, thinking over and over again of the times Simon and she had spent together, illuminated now in the light. Never again would she tremble at his touch, or talk to him or gaze at him. All she would hear was stupid people yapping about his latest exploits, that he'd landed a part in a play, that he was back with Borzoi.

It couldn't be true. Borzoi would come back, Simon would realize they couldn't make a go of it, and send for Harriet again. Wading through the cold grey slush, she walked back to her digs and fell shuddering into bed.

Everyone said, 'I told you so.' Geoffrey was magnanimous, then irritated that she wouldn't snap out of it, then furious that Simon had succeeded where he had failed, and made violent attempts to get her into bed. Her girlfriends, who had all been jealous of her and Simon, were secretly pleased it was over. Theo Dutton was vitriolic about the badness of her essay.

The child looked in terrible shape. She was obviously having some kind of crisis.

'Come on,' he said. 'Who is it?'

'No one, nothing,' she muttered. 'Simon Villiers.'

'Oh dear, oh dear. He was the nasty bug all my girl students caught last summer. I thought he'd gone out of fashion now. I must say I'm disappointed in you, Harriet. I thought you had better taste. He was one of the worst students I've ever had; his mind is earth-shatteringly banal.'

Then, like Mrs. Glass, he saw the stricken look on her face and realized he was on the wrong tack.

For days she didn't eat, wandering round Oxford getting thinner and thinner, gazing for hours at the river, wondering whether to jump, hanging around Simon's digs at a respectable distance hoping to catch a glimpse of him. Mostly she saw him come out and sit in his car, impatiently drumming his fingers on the steering wheel, revving up the car, lighting cigarette after cigarette. Then Borzoi would come spilling out, spraying on scent, trailing coloured scarves, her gorgeous streaky gold hair tumbling over her face. And they would drive off arguing furiously.

CHAPTER SEVEN

It was only after a month that Harriet started to worry but it was a worry that was nothing compared with losing Simon. Another week slipped by, then one evening she washed her hair and put on a black dress of Susie's that she'd never been able to get into before, but which now hung off her, and went to see Simon. She waited in the cold till Borzoi had gone out, almost biting her lip through as she watched Simon kiss her in the doorway. Then Borzoi drove off with a roar, and Simon went back into the house. He took a long time to answer the doorbell. For a minute she gazed at him close up; he was after all only a face. How could he have caused her so much unhappiness? Then suddenly all the old longing came flooding back.

'Hullo,' he said, hardly seeming to recognize her. 'Oh it's you,' he added politely. 'What can I do for you?'

'Can I come in?'

He looked at his watch. 'I'm going out in a second.'

'I don't want to hassle you, but it's important.'

'Oh dear,' he sighed. 'Well you'd better come in.'

The room was in chaos. There were ashtrays full of stubs everywhere and finger-smeared tumblers and cups full of old wet coffee grounds. Clothes, everything from fur coats to party dresses, lay piled high on every chair.

'Tidiness has never been Borzoi's strong point,' said Simon, picking some dead flowers out of their vase and throwing them dripping into the ashes of the fireplace. 'Thank God the char's coming in the morning.'

He put a cigarette in his mouth — not offering her one.

'Well,' he said, noticing her red-rimmed eyes. 'How are things? You've lost a lot of weight. Been dieting?'

47

Harriet took a deep breath. 'Simon, I'm pregnant.'

The match flared. Simon breathed in deeply. The end of the cigarette glowed. He threw the match into the fire.

'Are you sure?'

'Yes, I had the results of the test yesterday.'

'But you were on the pill.'

'I know; but I'd only just started taking it, and the night we first w-went to bed together, I was in such a state before-hand I think I may have forgotten to take it.'

'Bloody little fool,' said Simon, but not unkindly. 'Are you sure it's mine?'

She looked up horrified, her eyes full of tears.

'Oh yes, there's never been anyone else.'

'What about Jeremy or Gordon, or whatever he was called.'

'Geoffrey? Oh no, I couldn't. I didn't . . .'

She started to cry.

'Oh dear, oh dear,' said Simon. She was aware only of the terrible boredom in his voice. She might have been some mild inconvenience, a button off his shirt, a pair of dark glasses left in a taxi.

He went into the kitchen and put the kettle on.

'Well, you'd better go to London as soon as possible, and see Dr. Wallace.'

'What for?'

'To get rid of it of course.'

'B-but I couldn't.'

'It's not dangerous any more, darling. You don't want to listen to any of those old wives' tales. Dr. Wallace is a pro. They just suck it out with a Hoover these days.'

Harriet winced.

'Borzoi's been to him twice,' said Simon. 'So have Chloe and Deirdre and Anne-Marie and Henrietta. Honestly, he ought to give me a discount the number of birds I've sent to him.'

'But I don't want . . .' Harriet began.

'You might feel a bit depressed afterwards, but it's the end of term next week, so you can go home and recuperate.'

'But it'll be so expensive. I don't want to rip you off.'

'Oh don't worry about that, darling; I'll treat you. I'm not that much of a sod. Do you mind Nescafé? Borzoi insists on making real coffee, but it's so disgusting, and I can never get the coffee grounds out of my teeth.'

He poured boiling water into two cups and handed one to her.

'If you like,' he went on, putting two saccharine into his cup, 'I'll ring old Wallace now, and fix you up an appointment. The old bags on the switchboard give people they don't know rather a hard time.'

The scalding coffee burnt her throat but seemed to give her strength.

'Would you mind terribly if I kept it?'

'Oh be realistic, angel. You of *all* people are simply not cut out to be a one-parent family. I know people keep their babies, but they have a bloody awful time, unless they're rich enough to afford a lover and a nanny.'

Harriet sat in Dr. Wallace's waiting-room feeling sick, thumbing feverishly through the same magazine, watching girls go in and out. Some looked pale and terrified like herself, others obviously old timers, chatted together and might have been waiting for an appointment at the hairdresser's. Two models embraced in the doorway.

'Fanny darling!'

'Maggie!'

'Friday morning — see if you can get booked in at the same time, and we can go in together.'

Dr. Wallace was smooth, very suntanned from skiing and showed a lot of white cuff.

'You're certain you don't want to get married and have the child, Miss Poole? This is a big step you're taking.'

'He doesn't want to marry me,' whispered Harriet, unable to meet the doctor's eyes. 'But he's perfectly happy to pay. I've got a letter from him here.'

Dr. Wallace smiled as he looked at Simon's royal blue writing paper.

'Oh dear! Mr. Villiers again; quite a lad, isn't he? One of our best customers.'

Harriet went white. 'Fond of him, were you? Shame, shame, boy's got a lot of charm, but not ideal husband material, I wouldn't say. You're very young, plenty more fish in the sea. Not much fun bringing up a baby on your own, pity to ruin a promising academic career.'

'I know,' said Harriet listlessly.

'Just got to get another doctor to sign the form. Will first thing Friday morning be all right for you? You'll be out in the evening. There, there; don't cry, it'll be soon over.'

Her last hope was her parents. She caught a train down to the country. As she arrived one of her mother's bridge parties was just breaking up. Middle-aged women, buoyed up by a couple of gin and tonics were yelling goodbye to each other, banging car doors and driving off.

Harriet noticed as she slunk up the path that the noisiest of all was Lady Neave, Susie's mother-in-law.

'Goodbye, Alison,' she was saying, clashing her cheek against Harriet's mother's cheek with infinite condescension. 'Great fun! We're all meeting at Audrey's next week, aren't we, Audrey? *Hullo*,' she added, suddenly seeing Harriet. 'Are you down for the weekend? You must go over and see Peter and Susie. The new wallpaper in the drawing-room is such a success.'

What a gauche child thought Lady Neave, as she drove the Humber off in a series of jerks, narrowly missing the blue gates at the bottom of the drive. One could hardly believe she came from the same family as Susie, who although not quite what the Neaves would have liked for their only son, knew her place and was shaping up as a nice little wife.

Mrs. Poole, having made her farewells, found Harriet slumped in a chair in the kitchen, the cat purring on her knee. Why must the child look such a fright, she thought, that awful duffle coat with all the buttons missing, no makeup, hair unkempt. She was just like her father, always grubbing round in his silly old museum.

'I wish you'd warned me,' she said. 'I've only got sausages for supper. Are you staying the night?'

'Yes please,' said Harriet.

'That'll be nice — just the two of us.'

'Where's Daddy?'

'Away; gone to one of his dreary ceramics conferences.'

Harriet's heart sank. Her father was the only person she could talk to.

Her mother put some sausages on to fry, and started washing up.

'These bridge fours have become a regular thing,' she said, plunging glasses into soapy water. 'Elizabeth Neave's really a wonderful girl.'

How could anyone over forty be described as a girl? thought Harriet.

'She's really bullying me to get a washing-up machine; she says they're such a boon when one's entertaining.'

Harriet looked at the rubber gloves whisking round the hot suds — like surgeon's hands, she thought in horror, sucking a baby out like a Hoover. The smell of frying sausages was making her sick. Out in the garden the wind was whirling pink almond blossom off the trees.

Look at her just mooning out of the window, thought Mrs. Poole. Susie would have picked up a tea-towel and been drying up by now.

'How's the 'varsity?' she said. 'You look very peaky. Have you been working too hard?'

Harriet turned round:

'I'm pregnant,' she said.

'What?'

'Pregnant.'

The rubber hands stopped, then suddenly started washing very fast.

'How do you know?'

'I had a test.'

'It's Geoffrey,' said her mother in a shrill voice, 'I never liked that boy.'

'No it isn't. It's someone else.'

'You little tart,' hissed her mother.

Then it all came flooding out, the hysterics, the tears, the after all we've done for yous, the way we've scrimped and saved to send you to university.

'I knew this would happen with all those Bohemians with their long hair and petitions, and free love,' shouted her mother. 'It's all your father's fault. He wanted you to go so badly. Where did we go wrong with you? What will the Neaves say?'

On and on, round and round, repeating the same arguments with relentless monotony.

Harriet sat down. The cat, no respecter of crisis, rubbed against her legs, and then jumped on to her knee purring like a kettle drum.

'Could you please turn those sausages off?' said Harriet, suddenly overwhelmed with nausea.

'What are you going to do about it?' said her mother. 'I suppose the young man's ditched you.'

'He doesn't want to marry me, if that's what you mean.'

'He may have to,' said her mother ominously.

'Oh, Mummy, it's the twentieth century,' said Harriet.

'Look, it meant something to me, but it didn't mean anything to him. He doesn't love me, but at least he's given me the money for an abortion.'

Her mother took the cheque. Her expression had the same truculent relief of people who have waited half an hour in the cold, and who at last see a bus rounding the corner.

'Banks at Coutts, does he? Fancies himself I suppose. Isn't it against the law?'

'Not any more,' said Harriet, 'I went to a doctor this morning in London. It's all above board; they'll do it on Friday.'

'It seems the best course,' said her mother somewhat mollified. 'The young man does seem to have his wits about him.'

Harriet took a deep breath.

'Do you really want me to go ahead with it? Wouldn't it be better to keep the baby?'

Her mother looked appalled, as though the bus had turned out to be 'Private' after all.

'What ever for? Where could you keep it?'

It was as though she was talking about a pet elephant,

thought Harriet.

'You can't have it here,' her mother went on. 'Think what people would say — the Neaves for example. It's not fair on Susie and Peter. Where would you live? You haven't got any money.'

'You thought it was all right when Amanda Sutcliffe had a baby,' said Harriet.

'Everyone knows Amanda Sutcliffe's a bit potty. Those sort of girls are expected to get themselves into trouble. It seems callous, I know, but with your 'varsity career and all that the only answer seems to be to get rid of it.'

'It isn't an "it", its a her or a him; it's your grandchild,' said Harriet in desperation. 'You always wanted grandchildren.'

'But in the proper way,' said her mother, starting to cry. 'What would everyone say?'

'What does it matter?' said Harriet, and, rushing out of the room, ran upstairs to her own room and threw herself down on the bed.

Later her mother came up and sat on the bed and stroked her hair.

'I'm sorry I shouted at you, darling. It's just the shock. You must realize you can't just have a baby. It's a serious responsibility; having it's only the beginning. A child needs a stable family, parents, financial support. Once Friday's over, you'll be able to carry on with your life. You know how heartbroken Daddy will be if you don't get a degree. You need a holiday. We might all go to the Lakes this vac. I know you've always wanted to see Wordsworth's cottage.' She was smoothing her shoulder lightly but firmly now as though she were making pastry. Harriet found it dimly touching that her mother was trying to be nice, but only dimly. Since Simon had gone she found it very difficult to react to anything normally. She came down and watched television with her mother, who later said she was tired and went to bed. Harriet sat dry-eyed and stared at the horror movie which was about a huge tarantula spider. She hardly realized that the spider had been replaced by a vicar talking about resignation:

'For everything there is a season,' he began in his thin reedy voice.

And it reminded her so much of Simon that tears suddenly spurted out of her eyes. Growing inside her was the only thing of Simon's she had left. It was at that moment she decided to keep the baby.

Part Two

CHAPTER EIGHT

Mrs. Hastings closed the box file with a snap.

'I'm afraid I've nothing for you, Miss Poole,' she said.

Harriet felt desperation sweeping over her.

'But there must be something!' she said. 'I'll do any kind of work, as long as it's living in.'

'You said that last time, Miss Poole, before you took that post with Mr. Widnell.'

'I know I did. I'm sorry.'

Mrs. Hastings examined her long red nails, as though she'd just enjoyed tearing some animal apart.

'I should have thought a girl with your background, Miss Poole, would know how to keep a man like Mr. Widnell at a distance. But I suppose keeping men at a distance isn't quite your forte, is it?'

Harriet clenched her hands together. She could feel the sweat rising on her forehead. Keep calm, she told herself. Don't shout at her — it won't do any good.

'You must have something,' she repeated. 'I mean we won't survive unless I get a job.'

Mrs. Hastings's neon smile flashed on again. 'You should have thought about that before you left Mr. Widnell in such a hurry. Come back on Monday.'

Harriet was about to plead with her when the telephone rang. Mrs. Hastings picked it up.

'Mr. Erskine? Oh, not again! All right, put him through.' Her voice turned to honey. 'Hullo, Mr. Erskine. How's it all going?'

There was a pause. 'None of them will do? But I must have sent nearly a dozen girls along to see you. Well, yes . . . I fully appreciate your going to France tomorrow, Mr.

Erskine, but what can I do? I've sent all my best girls along. . . What about my worst girls? We don't have any of that sort on our books!'

Suddenly, her eyes lit on Harriet. 'Just a minute, Mr. Erskine.' Her tone became conciliating. 'How would you feel about a girl who's — I might say — rather tragically placed?'

Harriet squirmed with mortification.

'What sort of circumstances?'

The red-nailed hand rearranged the cacti on the desk. 'Well, I have a Miss Poole on my books who has a young baby . . . no, quite by chance she's not married. You'll see her?' The neon smile was really flashing now. 'Marvellous! You'll find her a charming person. Very quiet and refined, not at all the type you'd expect. She drives a car, cooks, she's got a degree in English, lots of experience with children.'

She waved away Harriet's exclamation of protest.

'All right, Mr. Erskine, I'll pop her in a taxi right away.'

She put down the receiver.

'Well, Miss Poole, you're in luck. That was Cory Erskine.'

'The writer?'

Mrs. Hastings nodded.

'I love his books,' said Harriet.

'He's obviously better at writing than getting it together with people,' said Mrs. Hastings. 'His marriage has just come unstuck.'

'Unstuck?' said Harriet in amazement. 'But he's married to Noel Balfour, isn't he? They're always being held up as a model couple. She keeps being interviewed in magazines on how to keep one's husband happy.'

'No one,' said Mrs. Hastings sourly, 'could keep Mr. Erskine happy. He's one of the most difficult men I've ever had to deal with. You won't get the job but, if by some miracle he does offer it to you, mind you take it. People in your position can't afford to be choosy. And do smarten yourself up before you go round there, and try to be a little bit more positive. His address is Number Nine, Chiltern Street.'

How can you smarten yourself up, thought Harriet dolefully, as she frantically combed her hair, when you've run out of cleansing cream, deodorant and eye make-up. When you can't afford to get your shoes mended, and you've taken the sheen out of your hair washing it in soap powder.

CHAPTER NINE

Number Nine stood out from the other houses in Chiltern Street, because it was painted cobalt blue with an emerald green door. Quaking with nerves, Harriet gave her last pound in the world to the driver and rang the bell. After some delay the door was answered by a tall angry looking man in a black polo-necked sweater.

'Yes?' he said unhelpfully.

'Mr. Erskine? I've come from the agency about the job.'

'Come in. I'm on the telephone.'

She followed him upstairs into a large, untidy room. Books covered the walls, littered a very large desk, and were strewn all over the rose-coloured carpet.

'I won't be long,' he said.

Lighting a cigarette, he picked up the telephone.

'Oscar? You're still there? Look, I don't give a damn if the Yanks do pull out, we'll raise the cash some other way, but I'm not writing another major character into the script!'

Poor Oscar, thought Harriet sitting down in a lemon yellow chair, hoping her laddered tights didn't show too much.

Then she studied some photographs on a side table. Two were of very beautiful children, a boy and a girl, with long blonde hair and dark slanting eyes. Another photograph was of a racehorse. Cory Erskine, she remembered, had once been famous as an amateur jockey. The fourth was of Noel Balfour herself, in a bikini, looking not unlike a sleek and beautiful racehorse — long-legged, full bodied, with the fine head, tawny eyes, classical features and wide sensual mouth that were so familiar to cinema audiences all over the world.

And what of the man Noel Balfour had been allegedly

happily married to for so long? Harriet turned back to look at Cory Erskine, examining the aloof, closed face with its dead-pan features, high cheek-bones and slanting, watchful eyes. He looks like a Red Indian, she thought, inscrutable and not very civilized at that.

As he came to the end of his conversation, a shaft of winter sunshine came through the window, lighting up the unhealthy pallor of his face, the heavy lines around the mouth, the grey flecks in the long, dark hair.

'Sorry about that,' he said, putting down the receiver. He picked up a half empty whisky bottle. 'Have a drink?'

Harriet shook her head. She hadn't eaten since yesterday lunchtime, and a drink the size of the one Cory Erskine was pouring into his own glass would put her out like a light.

When he offered her his cigarette case, however, she couldn't resist taking one, although she knew one wasn't supposed to smoke at interviews. Her hand shook so badly when he gave her a light that he had to steady it with his own hand.

He straightened up and looked at her for a minute. 'You're in pretty bad shape, aren't you?' he said abruptly. 'How long is it since you had the baby?'

'Three months,' said Harriet. 'I wasn't awfully well afterwards; but I'm fine now.'

'Who's the father?'

Harriet blushed.

'You can tell me,' he said. 'I don't make a habit of rushing round on roller skates with a megaphone, as soon as anyone tells me anything.'

'He was an undergraduate,' said Harriet, 'called Simon Villiers.'

Even after so long, the mention of his name made her mouth go dry, her throat tighten.

Cory Erskine looked up.

'Simon Villiers? Good-looking boy, blond? Loaded with money? Doesn't he want to go on the stage?'

Harriet started shaking. 'You know him?'

'I've met him. I had to give a couple of lectures on drama at Oxford last summer. Simon Villiers was allotted to look

61

after me.'

'How was he?' asked Harriet in a strangled voice.

'Extremely pleased with himself. Don't you see him now? Doesn't he help you?'

'He gave me a lot of money to have a proper abortion, but I funked it so I bought some contact lenses instead and kept the baby.'

'Does he know you've had it?'

'I wrote and told him. He didn't answer. I think he's probably abroad. He wasn't in love with me.'

'Won't your parents help?' he asked.

'Only if I have William — that's the baby — adopted, and I can't bear to do that.'

'Where's he now?'

'I've left him with a friend — but only for the afternoon.'

Her stomach started rumbling with hunger. She felt at a distinct disadvantage in his lemon yellow chair, her bottom much lower than her legs.

Cory Erskine shook the ice round in his whisky. 'And you want to look after my children?'

Harriet nodded, trying desperately not to appear too eager. He pointed to the photographs on the table.

'Jonah and Chattie, aged eight and five. Contrary to all the rubbish you've read in the papers about Noel's and my married bliss, they've had a very rough time. Ever since Jonah was born, Noel's been making her mind up whether or not to leave me. The children have been used as pawns. Now she's finally decided she wants to marry Ronnie Acland.' His voice hardened. 'And we're getting a divorce.'

'I'm abroad a lot. The children live up in Yorkshire in my old family home. Noel has never got on with any of the nannies. As a result, they've had a succession of people looking after them. They desperately need someone kind, loving, responsible and permanent to give them security.'

He looked at Harriet, taking in the pitiful thinness, the long legs sprawled like a colt's, the lank dark hair drawn back in a crumpled black ribbon, the irregular features, sallow skin, huge frightened eyes, full trembling mouth.

'Have you any idea what you'll be in for?' he said. 'It's a

dead-end part of the world. Nothing ever happens there. All the locals ever talk about is hunting. I go up to work there because it's more peaceful than London. Could you throw yourself into looking after two children? Because if you can't, there's not much point your coming. How old are you?'

'Nearly twenty,' said Harriet.

'But Mrs. Hastings said you've got a degree.'

'No, I dropped out when I got pregnant.'

'But you do have experience with children?'

'I've looked after friends' children a lot.'

'But I gathered you'd had a job, or was that just part of Mrs. Hastings's meticulous inaccuracy? How long did it last?'

Harriet shuffled her feet. 'Only one night,' she said in a low voice. 'It was a housekeeping job for a man in the country.'

'And?'

'He . . . he tried to rape me the first night.'

Cory Erskine raised an eyebrow. 'Quick work! How did he manage that?'

'He came into my bedroom j-just after I'd turned out my light and . . .'

'And you didn't feel it worth your while to capitulate. Very admirable.'

Harriet flushed angrily. If she had expected sympathy, she was quite wrong. Cory Erskine's face was without expression.

'And the baby,' he went on. 'Is he good? Does he cry much?'

Harriet took a deep breath. She might as well be honest, as she obviously wasn't going to get the job.

'Yes, he does; but I think babies are barometers. They reflect the mood of the person looking after them. I mean,' she floundered on, 'if I were happier and less worried, he might be, too. It's just that I haven't been very happy lately.'

Cory Erskine didn't appear to be listening. He was examining the page in his typewriter. He turned it back, and typed in a couple of words with one finger.

Bastard! thought Harriet. How dare he be so callous!

'Well, if he cries that's your problem,' he said without looking up. 'We'll put you both at the far end of the house and then no one but you will hear him.'

Harriet gave a gasp.

'You can cook and drive a car?' he went on.

She nodded.

'Good. You don't have to do everything. There's a house-keeper, Mrs. Bottomley. She's been with our family for years, but she's getting on and the children exhaust her. Jonah's a weekly boarder at a prep school, and Chattie goes to day school. You'd have to look after them when they're at home, ferry them to and from school, see to their clothes, cook for them, etc. I'm going to France for at least a month from tomorrow, but when I come back, I'm coming up North to finish a couple of scripts.'

'Do you mean you're really going to hire me?' asked Harriet in a bewildered voice.

He nodded. 'I only hope you won't be horribly bored.'

'Bored?' said Harriet slowly. 'That's like asking a drowning man if he'd be bored by a lifebelt.'

It was the first time Cory Erskine had smiled, and Harriet could suddenly see why Noel Balfour had once found him so attractive.

'I suggest you travel up on Sunday,' he said. 'There's a good train at twelve o'clock. I'll arrange to have you met at Leeds. Now, if you'll forgive me, I've a lot of last-minute things to do.'

'I can't begin to thank you,' she stammered. 'I'll do everything I can to make them happy.' As she stood up, she swayed and had to clutch at the edge of the desk to stop herself falling.

'You'd better start eating properly,' he said, getting out his cheque book. 'Twenty pounds for travelling, twenty-five pounds in advance for your first week's salary.' He handed her a cheque for forty-five pounds.

Harriet found herself fighting back the tears. 'I'm sorry,' she said, turning her head away. 'I'm just not used to getting breaks. You can't give me that much money.'

64

'I want you to look after my children properly, not just moon around the house. Now, I don't anticipate Mrs. Bottomley will try and rape you, so I'll see you again towards the end of February. You'll probably find it easier to settle in without my poking my nose in all the time.'

After she'd gone, still stammering her thanks, he sat down to work again. Then, a minute later, he got up and looked out of the window. Harriet was walking down the road. He watched her take the cheque out of her bag, examine it in amazement, hold it up to the light, then give a little skip of joy, so that she nearly cannoned into a passer-by.

Before she rounded the corner, she turned round to look up at the window, and waved at him timidly. He waved back.

I'm a bloody idiot, he told himself. I could have got any Nanny in London and I end up with a waif with a baby — which means four children to look after instead of two!

He looked at the photograph of his wife and his face hardened. He poured himself another stiff whisky before settling down.

CHAPTER TEN

Once the euphoria of landing the job bad worn off, Harriet grew more and more apprehensive. She had difficulty enough looking after one baby. What right had she to take on two children, who were probably spoilt and certainly disturbed?

I won't be able to cope, she kept telling herself as the train rattled through the Midlands the following Sunday. Each mile, too, was taking her further and further away from Simon, and the remote possibility that one day she might bump into him in London.

As promised, a car met her at Leeds station and once they were on the road, William, who had yelled most of the journey, fell into a deep sleep, giving the exhausted Harriet a chance to look at the passing countryside. It did nothing to raise her flagging spirits.

The black begrimed outskirts of Leeds soon gave way to fields and woodland then to wilder and bleaker country: khaki hillsides, stone walls, rusty bracken, with the moors stretching above, dark demon-haunted, Heathcliffe land. Harriet shivered and hugged William closer. No wonder Noel Balfour had run away from such savage desolation.

They drove through a straggling village of little grey houses and then the road started climbing steeply upwards.

'There's Erskine's place, up yonder ont' hill,' said the driver. 'The Wilderness, they call it. Wouldn't like to live there myself, but these stage folks have funny notions. I suppose you get used to anything if you have to.'

The big grey house lay in a fold of the moors, about half a mile from a winding river. Surrounding it was a jungle of neglected garden. Pine trees rose like sentinels at the back.

Harriet knocked nervously at the huge studded door, which was opened by a middle-aged woman with piled-up reddish hair and a disapproving dough-like face. She gave Harriet a hostile stare, but seemed far more interested in stopping a large tabby cat from escaping.

'Ambrose! Come here, you devil!' She just managed to catch the cat by the tail and pull him squawking into the house.

'Miss Poole?' she said icily, very much on her dignity. 'I'm Mrs. Bottomley.'

'How do you do?' said Harriet, trying to shake hands and clutch William and the luggage at the same time.

As she walked into the hall, two children rushed down the stairs, dragging a black labrador, and stopped dead in their tracks, gazing at her with dark, heavily lashed and not altogether friendly eyes.

'Jonah and Charlotte,' said Mrs. Bottomley, 'this is Miss Poole.'

'How do you do?' said Harriet nervously. 'This is William.'

'Did you have a good journey?' said the little girl in a formal voice. 'We're so recited to see you. Ambrose is on heat; that's why he's not allowed out. We thought he was a "he" when Daddy bought him.'

Mrs. Bottomley picked up one of her suitcases.

'I'll show you to your room,' she said coldly, starting up the stairs.

'Watch the string,' said Harriet in anguish, but it was too late. The string snapped and the contents of the suitcase — all the dirty laundry — her own and William's that she hadn't had time to wash before she left — cascaded on to the floor with a crash.

The children shrieked with laughter. Chattie went into hysterics of excitement. Nothing could have broken the ice more completely as they rushed round putting things back.

Mrs. Bottomley, frostier than ever, led Harriet along a winding passage to her room. The house, in contrast to its grim exterior, was positively sybaritic inside. Whoever had chosen the moss-thick carpets, the watered silk wallpapers, the brilliantly clashing curtains, had had an inspired eye for colour, if no regard for expense.

There were also looking glasses everywhere, in the hall, on the stairs and at the end of the landing. Harriet tried not to look at her worried, white-faced reflection.

'What a lovely house, and how beautifully you keep it,' she said, making a feeble attempt to remove the rigid expression of disapproval from Mrs. Bottomley's face. The housekeeper ignored her.

'You're in here,' she said, showing Harriet into a little grey and white room with yellow curtains and yellow flowered four-poster bed. 'The child can sleep next door,' she added coldly. It was as though she couldn't bear to acknowledge William's existence.

'Chattie and Jonah are at the far end of the passage, but there's a device you switch on, so you can hear if they wake in the night. I'll see them to bed tonight. Your supper will be ready in an hour.'

All this time she had not looked Harriet in the face. Oh dear, sighed Harriet, she really does resent my coming here.

Later, feeling more and more depressed, Harriet found a place laid for one in the huge green Victorian dining-room.

She looked at Mrs. Bottomley timidly:

'Won't you come and eat in here with me?' she asked.

'I have my meals in my own part of the house. I hope that will be all,' said Mrs. Bottomley.

But as she stalked majestically towards the door, she heard a muffled sob and, looking round, she saw that Harriet's face had disintegrated into a quivering chaos of misery, as she fished out her handkerchief.

Mrs. Bottomley's heart melted. She padded across the room and put an arm round Harriet's shoulders.

'There, there, my lamb, don't cry. You'll get used to it all in no time. I know it seems an out-of-the-way place for a young girl, but the children have been so excited, especially with you bringing the baby, and you'll be company for me. I get lonely of an evening.'

Harriet wiped her eyes. 'You don't mind about William, and me not being married?' she said.

68

'Never gave it a thought,' lied Mrs. Bottomley, who had been boasting in the village that she'd soon put the hussy in her place.

'You come and eat in the kitchen with me. You'll feel better when you've got something inside you. We'll have a drop of sherry to cheer ourselves up.'

From then on Harriet and Mrs. Bottomley were firm friends. The housekeeper bossed her, fussed over her, bullied her to eat, and gave her endless advice on how to look after the children.

CHAPTER ELEVEN

Even so Harriet often wondered afterwards how she survived those first few weeks looking after Cory Erskine's children. The day seemed neverending, rising at six, feeding and bathing William, getting Chattie off to school, by which time William's next feed would be due. Then there was endless washing and ironing, shopping, rooms to be tidied, meals to be cooked, beds to be made.

Night after night, she cried herself to sleep out of sheer exhaustion, to be woken a couple of hours later by William howling because his teeth were hurting.

Hard work alone she could have coped with. It was just the endless demands on her cheerfulness and good temper. Chattie, incapable of playing by herself, wanted constantly to be amused or comforted. She adored the baby and was a perfect menace, feeding him indigestible foods which made him sick, going into his room and waking him just after he'd fallen asleep.

Jonah, Harriet found even more of a problem than Chattie. He was obviously deeply unhappy and, when he came home at weekends, Harriet did her best to amuse him.

In between bouts of moodiness, he was very good company, but Harriet could never tell what he was thinking behind the aloof Red Indian mask he had inherited from his father. Often he didn't speak for hours and, although he never mentioned his mother, Harriet noticed that he always hung around when the post was due, and was hard put to conceal his disappointment when no letters arrived.

Cory wrote to them regularly, long letters full of drawings and wild, unexpectedly zany humour. Noel Balfour patently didn't believe in correspondence. Only one postcard ar-

70

rived from her in five weeks, and that was post marked Africa and addressed to Cory. On the front was a picture of a team of huge muscular Africans playing football. On the back she had written, 'Had them all except the goalkeeper, darling.'

Mrs. Bottomley's face shut like a steel trap when she saw the postcard, but Harriet, although dying to know more about Cory Erskine's relationship with his wife, was sensible enough not to ask questions. She felt that Mrs. Bottomley would tell her in her own good time. She was right.

They were sitting before supper one evening towards the end of February in the small den off the dining-room. Above the fire hung a huge, nude painting of Noel Balfour. She's so beautiful, thought Harriet, I can't imagine any man not wanting her.

'Who did it?' she asked.

Mrs. Bottomley puffed out her cheeks and went red in the face with disapproval, but the desire to gossip was too much for her.

'Master Kit did, and he never should have done, neither.'

'Who's he?'

'Mr. Cory's younger brother.'

'Goodness,' said Harriet. 'That's a bit close to home. It's awfully good.'

'So it should be,' said Mrs. Bottomley glaring at the lounging opulent figure of Noel Balfour. 'He took long enough over it. Mr. Cory was abroad at the time, and Master Kit rolls up cool as a cucumber "Ay've come to paint the magnificent scenery, Mrs. B." he says, but there was a wicked glint in his eyes. I knew he was up to no good.'

'What's he like?' said Harriet. 'Like Mr. Erskine?'

'Chalk and cheese,' said Mrs. Bottomley, helping herself to another glass of sherry. 'He's handsome is Master Kit. Tan and golden as one of them sun-flowers and enough charm to bring roses out of the ground in winter. But he always brings trouble. Drove his poor mother mad with worry. Magnificent scenery, indeed. He never moved out of Mrs. Erskine's bedroom, and she lying there totally nude, as though butter wouldn't melt in her mouth, and the central

71

heating turned up so high, you'd think it was a heatwave. And it wasn't just painting they got up to, neither.'

'Whatever did Mr. Erskine say when he got home?' said Harriet in awe. 'He must have hit the roof.'

''E did,' said Mrs Bottomley. 'You should have heard them. Mr. Cory, very controlled as always, but very sarcastic, and Mrs. E. in hysterics. You could hear her shouting all over the house: "Well, at least I kept it in the family, this time"!'

There was a pause before Mrs. Bottomley said, in a confidential voice, 'You see Harriet, Master Kit wasn't the first by a long way. Ever since Master Jonah was born, it's been one young gentleman after another.'

'But why does Mr. Erskine put up with it?' said Harriet. 'He doesn't strike me as being the permissive type.'

Mrs. Bottomley shook her head.

'He isn't,' she said glumly. 'He's tough in most ways, but where she's concerned, he's as weak as water. He loves her.'

'But how's he got the strength to divorce her now?'

Mrs. Bottomley shrugged her plump shoulders. 'Happen he won't. She claims she wants to marry this Ronnie Acland, but I reckon Mr. Cory will take her back in the end. She likes being married to him. It gives her respectability, and he makes a lot of money. She's extravagant, you know, wants the best of everything — and she likes having power over him, knowing he's still under her spell.'

Harriet understood so well how Cory felt. Now that she no longer worried about being able to keep William or where the next penny was coming from, all her thoughts centred on Simon.

Her longing for him grew no less with time. It hungered in her, night and day, engulfing her senses and her reason in an aching void. She tried to fill the void with hard work, to stupefy the ache by watching endless television, and reading long into the night, but her loneliness deepened round her as though she were alone in a huge cave.

Later that evening, after Mrs. Bottomley had gone up to bed, the telephone rang. Harriet answered it.

72

'Mr. Erskine calling from Dublin,' said the operator. 'Will you accept the call?'

'Yes,' said Harriet, wondering what Cory was doing in Ireland.

'Hullo, hullo, Cory. Can I speak to Cory, please?' It was a man's voice — slow, lazy, expensive, very attractive.

'He's not here,' said Harriet.

'Hell, I thought he'd be back,' said the voice. 'Where is he?'

'In Antibes still. Can I help?'

'Not really, darling, unless you can lend me a couple of grand. I've found a horse Cory's got to buy.'

'Do you want to ring him?' said Harriet. 'I've got the number. Who is it?'

The voice laughed. 'Kit Erskine, registered black sheep. Hasn't Botters been telling you horrible stories about me?'

'Oh no, not at all.' Even though he was miles away at the other end of a telephone, Harriet could feel herself blushing.

'Of course she has. Don't believe a word. It's all true.'

Harriet giggled.

'And you must be Harriet?' he went on. 'The distressed gentlefuck'

'What do you mean?' said Harriet furiously, immediately on the defensive. 'How do you know?'

'Cory told me or, rather, he issued king-sized ultimatums that I was to keep my thieving hands to myself where you're concerned. Is that your little baby making that horrible noise?'

'His teeth are hurting,' said Harriet.

'Why doesn't he go to the dentist? Any news of Noel?'

Harriet, rather indiscreetly she felt afterwards, told him about the postcard of the African footballers.

Kit laughed. 'Funny how she likes to keep an eye on Cory, and on me, too, for that matter. In fact, she's had her eye on so many men in her time, I'm surprised she hasn't developed the most awful squint. Everyone's laying bets whether Cory'll divorce her or not.'

'I think I'd better go and look after the baby,' said Harriet, feeling suddenly that she shouldn't be discussing her employer.

'Don't go,' said Kit. 'Are you as sexy as your voice is? What do you look like?'

'Scrawny and sallow-skinned,' said Harriet.

'Just my type,' said Kit. 'I've a portrait to paint up North next month. I'll come over and case the joint. Don't go shacking up with any of the local gentry before I arrive.'

Bitter, bitter, sweet, thought Harriet afterwards. Bitter because, in his gaiety, panache and directness of approach, he reminded her so much of Simon; sweet because, even over the telephone, it was nice to be chatted up once more.

Later still that night, Ambrose the cat decided to have her kittens at the bottom of the huge four-poster quadruple bed in Cory and Noel's bedroom. At six o'clock in the morning, having finally installed her, tired but contented, in clean straw in the kitchen with five kittens, Harriet finally fell into bed.

It seemed only a few minutes later that she was woken up by Chattie's voice telling her very smugly it was half past nine.

'Oh, my God!' said Harriet, leaping out of bed. 'And it would be Mrs. Bottomley's day off.'

Frenziedly pulling on her clothes, not even bothering to wash, she rushed downstairs, fed Chattie and Jonah bread and marmalade, packed Jonah's suitcase for the week, put William brawling and unfed into the car in his carry cot, and set off to drop the children at school.

It had frozen the night before and the road was like a skating rink. Harriet tried hard to concentrate on driving, but was distracted by Jonah fiddling with the door handle. The next moment, his hand slipped and the door swung open, nearly taking him with it. Narrowly missing an oncoming car, Harriet pulled him back, locked the door and gave him a ringing slap on his bare leg.

'Don't ever do that again!' she shouted.

Jonah said nothing, gazing in front of him, colour slowly draining out of his cheeks, as the red finger marks grew on his thigh.

Chattie, of course, was delighted. 'Naughty, naughty Jonah,' she chanted.

'Shut up, Chattie!' snapped Harriet, turning the car into Jonah's school gates.

Jonah grabbed his small suitcase and jumped out of the car.

'Goodbye, darling,' said Harriet her anger evaporating. 'Pick you up on Friday evening.'

Jonah was white with rage.

'Don't call me darling!' he said in a trembling voice. 'I hate you! I *hate* you! I wish you'd never come. I'm going to tell my father to send you away.'

On the verge of tears, Harriet dropped Chattie off at her school. William was bellowing his lungs out with hunger all the way home.

'William! Please!' she said, her voice rising in desperation. 'It won't be long.'

While she was heating up milk for a bottle she very hurriedly washed some of William's clothes and put them into the spin dryer.

Suddenly the telephone rang. William redoubled his howls. At the same moment, the milk boiled over and as she rushed to retrieve it, she realized she'd forgotten to put a bucket underneath the spin dryer.

'Oh, my God!' she screamed hysterically, as soapy water belched forth round her feet. 'Oh, shut up! Shut up, William!'

'You appear to be in some difficulty,' said a dry voice behind her. Aghast, she swung round. Standing in the doorway stood Cory Erskine.

His reactions were incredibly quick. In a second, as Harriet gaped at him, he had turned off the spin dryer and removed the milk from the boil.

'There's enough milk left for one bottle,' he said. 'I'll get the telephone.'

Oh, God, thought Harriet wretchedly, I've really done it now. He couldn't have come back at a worse moment!

'It's Jonah ringing,' said Cory. 'He wants you.'

'Where's he ringing from?'

75

JILLY COOPER

'From a call box. Take it upstairs. When he's through, tell him it might be diplomatic if he went back to school. Give the baby to me. I'll feed him.'

Jonah had rung up to apologize. His voice sounded high and strained. 'I just rang to say I don't want you to go away. I won't complain to my father about you, and I'm s-sorry, Harriet.'

She felt a great lump in her throat.

'It's all right, darling,' she said. 'It's lovely of you to ring. I'm sorry, too.'

Returning to the kitchen, she found William had fallen asleep halfway through his bottle, his mouth open, his long lashes sweeping down over his cheeks.

'He's a beautiful child,' said Cory, handing him back to her. 'What was Jonah on about?'

'We had a row this morning. He was apologizing.'

Cory grunted. 'That child's got far better manners than either of his parents. Wonder where he gets them from. How's Chattie?'

'Fine, in tearing spirits. I'm so sorry you had such an awful homecoming,' said Harriet. 'I'm afraid we all overslept, and things got a bit chaotic. Would you like some breakfast?'

Cory shook his head. 'I'm going to follow William's example and get some sleep. I've been driving all night.'

He looked absolutely played out — deathly pale, unshaven, his eyes bloodshot and heavily shadowed.

An appalling thought stuck Harriet. 'Oh, you can't go to bed yet. Ambrose had her kittens last night in your bed and I haven't changed the sheets!'

He must loathe coming back here, she thought, as she made up the huge double bed in the room he had once shared with Noel Balfour. It was such an ultra-feminine room. Everything stagily erotic — the thick, white carpets, the rose-strewn wallpaper, the huge canopied four-poster, the pink frills frothing round the dressing-table — must remind him so poignantly of her.

But if Cory minded, he gave no indication. 'It's going to snow,' he said, gazing out of the window.

As Harriet put on the pillow cases, pink from her exertions, she realized he was watching her, and was suddenly conscious that she hadn't even had time to wash her face that morning, and was wearing an old red sweater, drastically shrunk in the wash.

'You look better,' he said. 'You've put on weight.'

'Mrs. Bottomley keeps feeding me up on suet puddings,' said Harriet, blushing.

Cory surfaced about seven, and came into the kitchen, Chattie hanging on one hand, a large glass of whisky in the other. Chattie was also clutching a six-foot tiger balloon.

'Look what Daddy brought me,' she said. She turned to Cory. 'Harriet overslept this morning and made me late for band, so I had to play the triangle instead of the tangerine.'

'Tambourine,' said Cory. 'And don't sneak.'

Chattie ran to the window.

'Look how deep the snow is! Can't I stay up for supper?'

'No,' said Cory. 'You can show me Ambrose's kittens and then you're going to bed.'

'How are you getting on at school?' he went on. 'Have you got a best friend yet?'

'Everyone wants to be my best friend,' said Chattie. 'But they've got to learn to share me.'

At that moment Mrs. Bottomley walked in from her day off, weighed down with carrier bags, her maroon wool coat and felt hat trimmed with a bird's body covered in snowflakes.

'Mr. Cory,' she squawked. 'You 'ave given me a turn; you should 'ave warned us. If I'd known, I'd 'ave opened up the front room. Still it's very *nice* to see you.'

And he really was nice to *her* thought Harriet, taking her parcels, and teasing her about buying up the whole of Marshalls and Snelgrove, asking after her rheumatism.

'Mustn't grumble,' said Mrs. Bottomley. 'Having Harriet here's made a difference. Saves me a lot of work, 'aving a young pair of legs running about the house.'

Cory glanced at Harriet's legs.

'Pleased with her, are you?' he said.

'Well I'm not saying she isn't a bit dreamy at times, but

we've had some laughs, and she's a hard worker,' said Mrs.
Bottomley, unpinning her hat. 'Which is more than I can say
for some of those hoighty toighty misses in the past. And
how was Antibes?' she added, pronouncing it Anti-bees.

For a second Cory's eyes met Harriet's.

Then he said gravely, 'Anti-bees was very exhausting.'

'You look peaky, I must say,' said Mrs Bottomley, 'as
though you'd walked all the way home. Must be all that foreign food — frogs legs and ratty twee — you need feeding
up.'

Harriet was determined to redeem the morning's disastrous homecoming by cooking Cory a magnificent dinner,
but it was not to be. She went into the garden to shake the
water out of a lettuce, and stood transfixed. The pine trees
now carried armfuls of gleaming white blossom, urns filled
with snow were casting long blue shadows across the lawn,
flakes soft as tiny feathers poured out of the sky.

Memories of the first time she'd met Simon came flooding
back. Oh, God, she thought, in an agony of despair, when
will I ever see him? She didn't know how long she stood
there — five, ten minutes — but, suddenly, she realized she
was frozen.

When she got back to the kitchen she gave a shriek. Tadpole, Cory's labrador, had the steak on the floor, Ambrose
was sitting unrepentant on the kitchen table, tabby cheeks
bulging with the last of the prawns and the sauce had curdled past redemption on the stove.

At that moment, Cory walked in. 'For Christ sake, what's
the matter now?'

Trembling, Harriet pointed at Ambrose and Tadpole.
'The snow was so beautiful, I forgot I'd left the steak and
prawns on the table.'

Again Cory surprised her. It was the first time she'd heard
him laugh and, after a few seconds, she began to giggle.

'There's nothing in here,' he said, looking in the fridge.
'We'd better go out.'

'Oh, God I'm so sorry.'

'Stop apologizing and go and do your face.'

'But you can't take me!'

'Why not? Mrs. Bottomley'll baby-sit.'

'But, but . . .' Harriet began a stream of feverish excuses.

Cory interrupted her. 'I don't mind hysterics nor having my dinner ruined, but I can't stand being argued with. Go and get ready.'

He took her to a restaurant down the valley. Harriet, appalled by the prices on the menu, chose an omelette

Don't be silly,' he said irritably. 'What do you really want to eat?'

'It's all so expensive!'

'You should see the prices in Paris. Anyway I've just had a large advance so you might as well take advantage of it.'

At first, he kept the conversation on a strictly impersonal level, telling her about his trip to France, and the black mare, Python, he had just bought on Kit's recommendation, who was being flown over next week. 'If she's any good I'll just have time to get her fit for the point-to-point in April.'

By the time the coffee arrived, wine had considerably loosened Harriet's tongue.

'Well,' said Cory, re-filling her glass, 'how's it working out, looking after the children?'

Harriet smiled nervously. 'Fine, I'm awfully happy here.'

He didn't smile back. 'I've been watching you for the past two hours. You still give the impression of a girl who cries herself to sleep every night.'

'Black or white coffee?' asked Harriet, confused.

'Black, please, and don't change the subject. Sure, you think you're fine. You've filled out, you've got some colour in your cheeks, but your eyes are still haunted; you get flustered far too quickly. And you've torn that paper napkin you've been clutching into shreds.'

'I'm okay,' she muttered. Then added in a trembling voice, 'Are you trying to say you want me to go?'

If she had looked up then she would have seen his face soften.

'You don't know me very well yet,' he said gently.

'If I wanted you to go, I'd tell you straight. Tomorrow you're going to see my doctor for some tranquillizers and sleeping pills. You'll only need them for a few weeks. I don't

JILLY COOPER

want you cracking up, that's all. Now, I suppose you'd prefer I talked on impersonal subjects. How did you meet
Simon Villiers?'

Harriet choked over her coffee, then shrugged her shoulders. She so badly needed to talk to someone.

'I met him at Oxford. It was snowing like today. Simon
drove round a corner and knocked me off my bicycle. Of
course, I knew who he was. Everyone knew about the
Villiers set — all night parties, fast cars, models down from
London. I wasn't hurt, but he insisted on my going back to
his rooms. There was a party on. Later he kicked everyone
out. When we woke up next morning, he asked me what my
name was. You're not shocked?'

Cory lit a cigar. 'Not unduly.'

'It was the first time I'd been to bed with anyone. It was
like stumbling into Paradise.' She looked at her hands. 'I
thought it would last for ever. Then one morning we were
drinking coffee and he suddenly announced I'd have to
move out as his regular girlfriend was coming back that day.
I was so stunned, when I found I was pregnant, it seemed
un-important compared with losing Simon. The reason I
kept William really was because he was the only thing of
Simon's I had.'

She looked at Cory with huge, troubled, slate-grey eyes.

He smiled. 'Do you think Jonah's happy at school?'

She was intensely grateful that he realized she didn't want
to talk about herself any more.

80

CHAPTER TWELVE

Life became much easier for Harriet after Cory Erskine arrived. It was having a man to make decisions, to shoulder responsibilities, to shut up the children when they became too obstreperous and, most of all, to talk to.

Cory was, in fact, not easy to live with — aloof, peremptory, exacting, often extremely bad-tempered. But in a good mood, Harriet found him lovely company, amusing, never pulling intellectual rank on her, an inspired listener. Yet as weeks passed, she didn't feel she knew him any better.

He was very unpredictable. Some days he would bombard her with questions, what did she feel about this, how would she react to that. On other days he was so abstracted she might not have been there, or he would suddenly get bored with a conversation and walk out leaving her mouthing like a goldfish in mid-sentence.

He also kept the most erratic hours, working most of the night. Often when she got up because William was crying she would hear the faint clack of the typewriter against the gramophone pouring out Verdi or Wagner. Then he would appear at breakfast looking terrible, read the paper, drink several cups of impossibly strong black coffee, and go out and ride across the moors for a couple of hours.

After that he generally snatched a few hours' sleep on the sofa in his study (Harriet had a feeling he couldn't bear sleeping alone in the huge mausoleum of a double bed), and emerged at teatime absolutely ravenous, and often as not wolf all the sandwiches Harriet had made for the children's tea.

He was also drinking too much. Every day Mrs. Bottomley, her mouth disappearing with disapproval, would come out of his room with an empty whisky bottle.

He was obviously miserably unhappy. The drinking to drive out the despair would plunge him next day into black depression, which made him irritable and arbitrary. While he was working he hated interruptions. The children had to be kept out of his way. The telephone rang all the time for him, and he went spare if Harriet didn't catch it on the third or fourth ring. Always she had to make the same excuse:

'I'm afraid Mr. Erskine's working. If you leave your number I'll ask him to ring you back,' which he so seldom did that Harriet was on the end of a lot of abuse from people — mostly women — who rang a second and third time and were convinced Harriet hadn't passed on the message. He also made notes, as thoughts struck him, on bits of paper and telephone directories all over the house; and after the day, when she had to go through four dustbins to find the magazine Cory had scribbled a few lines of script on the back of, she learnt not to throw anything away again without asking him.

One afternoon in early March, however, Cory was sitting in the kitchen eating raisins absent-mindedly out of a packet and reading one of Jonah's comics. William sat propped upon a red rug spread out on the flagstone floor, beating a saucepan aimlessly with a wooden spoon, gurgling happily and gazing at the gleaming copper pans that hung from the walls. Harriet, who'd that morning read an article in a magazine about the dangers of an all-tinned-food diet for babies, was rather dispiritedly sieving cabbage and carrots, when the telephone rang. Glad of any diversion, Harriet crossed the room to answer it, but it stopped on the third ring, then just as she got back to her carrots, it started again, rang three times and stopped. Then it started again and this time kept on ringing:

Sighing, Harriet put down the sieve again.

'Don't answer it,' snapped Cory. He had gone very pale. 'It's only someone playing silly games.'

Then it stopped, then started the three rings stop, three rings stop formula again. Then kept on ringing for about three minutes. Harriet noticed the way his hands gripped that comic.

'I'm going out,' said Cory. 'And don't answer the telephone.'

Next minute she heard the front door slam.

The ringing kept on. It must be the secret code of someone he doesn't want to talk to, thought Harriet. It was getting on her nerves. She'd run out of bread, so she decided to walk William in his pram down to the village and get some. She enjoyed shopping; she was beginning to know all the shop people who made a tremendous fuss of William.

It was a cold, cheerless day. The only colour came from the rusty bracken and even that lay flattened by the recent snow. The village was deserted except for a few scuttling, purple-faced women in head scarves. Harriet came out of the bakers, warming her hands on a hot french loaf, and went into the supermarket opposite. She immediately noticed one customer, a girl with bright orange curls, wearing an emerald green coat with mock fur collar and cuffs, stiletto-heeled green boots, and huge dark glasses. Taking tins down from the shelves she was attempting to lob them into the wire basket she had placed in the middle of the floor.

'Loves me,' she muttered as a tin of lemon meringue pie filling reached its destination safely, 'Loves me not, oh hell,' she added as she also missed with a tin of dog food. A child with very dissipated blue eyes, and a pudding basin hair-cut was systematically filling the pockets of his waisted blue coat with packets of fruit gums. The shopkeeper, who was trying to find a packet of washing-up-machine powder for another customer, was looking extremely disapproving.

The girl in dark glasses looked up and peered at Harriet.

'Hello!' she said to Harriet, 'You must be Cory Erskine's nanny. I'm Sammy Sutcliffe, I look after Elizabeth Pemberton's kids across the valley; they're more or less the same age as Chattie and Jonah; we ought to get them together.'

'Oh that would be lovely,' said Harriet, suddenly craving companionship her own age.

'We've been skiing, or I'd have come over before,' said

83

the girl.

'You look terribly brown,' said Harriet.

'Yes,' said the girl, 'but it only goes down to my collar bones. Stripped off, I look like a toffee apple.'

She giggled and took off her glasses to show large, rather bloodshot, green eyes framed by heavily blacked lashes.

'The're to hide my hangover, not to keep out the sun,' she said. 'You never see the sun in this backwater.'

She put the lentils, which were spilling out of their packet, back on the shelf, took another packet and moved towards the cash desk.

'And put those sweets back, you little monster,' she screeched at the small boy, who was busy now appropriating tubes of Smarties. 'You've got the morals of an alley cat. He's a little bugger our Georgie,' she added to Harriet. 'Just like his Dad, except his Dad pinches bottoms rather than sweets.'

Outside she admired William.

'What a little duck,' she said. 'You must be knackered looking after three of them. Why don't you bring Chattie and William over to tea tomorrow and I'll fill you in on all the local scandal?'

'Gosh, thanks awfully,' said Harriet.

'Ours is the big house stood back from the river on the Skipton Road, just beyond the village,' said Sammy. 'You'll recognize it by the sound of crashing crockery. Don't be alarmed. It'll only be my boss hurling the Spode at her hubby. Actually I think Cory's coming to dinner tonight. She rather fancies him, my boss. Can't say I blame her. I think he's lovely too — looks straight through one in such a god-damned sexy way.'

Cory got home about eight. He looked terrible. He's been in the pub, thought Harriet. She accosted him with a list of telephone messages.

'Mrs. Kent-Wright rang. Could you open a fête in May, and if not could you find one of your show business friends to do it?'

'No,' said Cory. 'I couldn't.'

'A lady from *Woman's Monthly* wants to come and interview you next Wednesday at seven.'

'No,' said Cory, 'ring and say I can't.'

'And Elizabeth Pemberton rang to say they're wearing black ties this evening.'

'Oh, Christ,' said Cory bounding upstairs. 'I'd forgotten. Bring me a drink up in my dressing-room, would you?'

In twenty minutes he was gone, leaving the bathroom awash, five towels at high tide, and his five o'clock shadow in the basin.

Through her two-Mogadon-induced slumber Harriet heard ringing and ringing. Don't answer she thought, it's someone trying to get through with a secret code. She pulled the blanket over her head. The ringing went on. It was the door-bell. Cory had a key. Who the hell could it be calling at that hour? Burglars, she thought in terror, then realized they'd hardly be ringing the bell. It must be some maniac off the moor, bent on rape. Wearing only her short scarlet nightgown, her hair falling in tangled curls down her back, she turned on all the lights, and nervously crept downstairs. Tadpole emerged, frowsty and bug-eyed, from the kitchen and thumped his tail.

'You're a fine watch dog,' she said. The ringing went on. The chain was on the door. She opened it an inch.

'Who is it?' she said nervously.

'It's me, Cory.'

'Oh God, I'm sorry,' she said undoing the chain. 'I thought you had a key.'

He stood in the doorway, swaying slightly. He was deathly pale; there was a cut on his forehead where the blood had dried; his tie was crooked, his hair ruffled. He looked at her intently, trying to focus but squinting slightly like a Siamese cat.

'What have you done to your head?' she said, thinking irrationally of Elizabeth Pemberton's flying Spode saucers. 'Are you all right?'

'I am,' he said in a blurred voice. 'The car's a write off.'

He walked into the house unsteadily, heading towards the drawing-room.

'Oh my God,' said Harriet running after him. 'You poor thing, sit down at once.' She dived under the table, pulling her nightgown as far as it would go over her bottom, to put on the lights by the fire. 'I'm so terribly sorry. Shall I ring for the doctor?'

'I'm perfectly all right,' said Cory. 'I ran out of fags on the way home, which didn't help.' He took a cigarette with a shaking hand out of the green jade box on the table. Harriet found a match and lit it for him.

'I'll get you a cup of strong, sweet tea,' she said.

'You can fix me a drink,' said Cory.

'He's had far too much,' thought Harriet. 'You might be concussed,' she said aloud.

'I'm O.K.,' he said irritably. 'I walked all the way home from the other side of the village, following the white lines in the middle of the road admittedly; so I've had plenty of time to work up a thirst. So if you please . . .'

Harriet poured him a large whisky and soda. He drained half of it in one gulp.

'Why didn't you ring me?' said Harriet, 'I'd have come and collected you.'

'I'd spent my last 10p in the pub this afternoon,' he said. 'And that reminds me, I took a quid out of the house-keeping. Do you want a drink?'

Harriet looked at the clock. It was three in the morning. She'd have to get William up in three and a half hours.

'Go on,' said Cory.

She poured herself a small glass of white wine.

Tadpole scratched at the fur rug in front of the fire, circled twice, then sat down as near the dying embers as possible.

'Are you sure you don't want a cup of tea?'

'I just want someone to talk to for a few minutes.'

Harriet curled up on the sofa, trying not to yawn, tucking her long legs under her. She hadn't shaved them for months, not that Cory would notice in the state he was in.

'Was it a good evening?' she said politely.

'Bloody awful. "Just a few friends", said Elizabeth, and I arrive an hour late to find three couples and a battle-scarred thirty-five-year-old with a "for hire" sign on her forehead lined up specifically for me. She was called Geraldine or Jennifer or something. We were put next door to each other at dinner, with everyone surreptitiously watching to see how we were hitting it off, just like mating dogs.'

'Was she very beautiful?' said Harriet.

'Very — but she laughed too much, and asked too many questions about the ages of my children, and the script I'm writing at the moment, and didn't I adore ballet, because she simply adores it. I was lumbered with her after dinner too, and out of the back of my head, I could see Elizabeth mouthing to all her friends, "It's going frightfully well." "Frightful" just about summed it up. Then at midnight she asked me if I'd terribly mind running Jennifer or Geraldine back to her cottage in Gargrave.'

The pale mask of his face was expressionless. He finished his drink and put his glass very carefully down on the table.

'So I ran her home, and she gave me all the old crap about dropping out of London and leaving her stockbroker husband because he didn't want children, and anyway he was knocking off his secretary, and how much more genuine and sincere people are in the North. And tomorrow I shall get a bollocking.'

'Who from?' said Harriet.

'Elizabeth. For behaving badly.'

'What ever did you do?'

'Didn't try and pull Geraldine or Jennifer.'

'Mary Whitehouse would have been proud of you,' said Harriet.

'I know,' said Cory, 'it's a great source of consolation to me. Fix me another drink, there's a good girl.'

'Did she terribly want you to?'

'She wanted me to try. She's frightened of the future and she wants someone to blot out the loneliness and to describe as "the man in her life". She even put more scent on in the car going home, very secretively so I wasn't supposed to notice. She waited when we got to the house, wriggling down in the seat with her head tilted back but I need that sort of complication like a hole in the head, so I got out and opened the door for her, and she started to cry and fled up the path, and then the poor cow couldn't find her latch key until she'd turned her bag out. And I felt such a sod. Some sort of instinct of self-preservation made me put on a safety belt for the first time in years, and I drove off down the Fairmile slap into a tree. Hostesses can't resist a spare man.' He was rambling now. 'They're gold dust round here, a going spare man, a going-to-sleep-in-the-spare-room-every-night man. I got very used to spare rooms when I was married to Noel.'

His long eyelashes lifted, and his dark eyes frowned at her as though she was the one who had hurt him.

He must be pissed out of his mind, thought Harriet; it's the first time he's mentioned Noel since the interview.

'They want to get their own back on her for pinching their husbands,' he went on.

'Did she pinch them?' said Harriet.

'The one's she wanted, she did, and the wives of the one's she didn't were in a way more piqued that their husbands should be slavering over Noel and her not taking a blind bit of notice of them.'

He picked up Jonah's homework composition book which was lying on the table. 'People in India have no food,' he read out, 'and they often go to bed with no supper.' He laughed. 'And all the old harridan puts at the bottom of the page is "Try and write more clearly, and write out the word Tomorrow three times".'

He picked up a pencil:

'Tomorrow and tomorrow and tomorrow,' he said, writing with great care, 'creeps on this petty pace from . . .'

'Oh you mustn't,' cried Harriet in horror. 'Jonah's teacher will murder him.'

'I pay the fees,' said Cory. 'If Miss Bickersteth wishes to flip her lid she can ring up and complain to me. People in India have no food,' he repeated slowly, 'and they often go to bed with no supper. People in Yorkshire have a great deal too much to drink, and often also go to bed with no supper. Please get me another drink,' he said, 'and don't tell me I've had enough. I know I have.'

'You look absolutely exhausted,' said Harriet. 'You're the one who should be taking sleeping pills and eating regular meals.'

'Stop trying to mother me,' said Cory.

Harriet handed him a drink.

'It's a bloody weak one,' he grumbled.

Their hands touched. 'You're cold,' he said.

'I've got a warm heart,' said Harriet, flustered and wincing at the cliché. Cory didn't notice.

'My wife has hot little hands,' said Cory, 'but her heart is as cold as the grave. She's a nymphomaniac. I suppose you've heard that.'

'Well, something of the sort.'

'She's also the most beautiful woman I've ever seen.'

'I know,' said Harriet.

'Do you think the children look like her?'

'No,' lied Harriet. 'Much more like you.'

'Today's our wedding anniversary,' said Cory.

'Oh God,' said Harriet, stricken. 'How awful for you. I am sorry.'

'You really are, aren't you?' said Cory. 'All that messing around with three rings on the telephone was her trying to get through. It was our secret code.'

'You'll find someone else soon,' said Harriet unconvincingly.

'Easy lays aren't the problem,' he said. 'It's like pigs in clover working in the movie business; always plenty of pretty girls hanging about. Then you wake up in the morning, and it's the wrong head on the pillow beside you, and you can't get them out quick enough.'

He put his head in his hands, feeling gingerly at the bump on his forehead.

'I could have Noel back tomorrow if I wanted, but it's like being an alcoholic, one drink and I'd be lost.'

'It's that bit about shunning "the heaven that leads men to this hell",' said Harriet. She felt she was having a very adult conversation.

'That's right,' said Cory. 'If she came back she'd be all over me the first week or two. Then she'd get bored and start

89

looking for distractions. I couldn't even work properly when she was around. If she was at home she wanted constant attention. If she was out, I couldn't concentrate for worrying where she was. Show business's happiest couple indeed!'

He laughed, but the laugh had a break in it. She could see the chasm of his despair.

'Today's our tenth wedding anniversary,' he went on, his voice slurring. 'The bloody bitch was the beat of my heart for ten years. Being married to her meant drifting along from day to day on the edge of despair. Do you know what I did this afternoon? I went out and sent her six dozen roses. Imagine the smirk on her face when she gets them. My lost love is so utterly, utterly lost, but just the same I did it. All tough guys are hopeless sentimentalists. Jesus I'm wallowing in self-pity. I'm sorry.'

He was shivering now. I must get him into bed, thought Harriet.

He shot her a sideways glance. 'I'm keeping you up,' he said.

'No, no,' she said, gritting her teeth to hide a yawn.

She heard a faint wail from upstairs. 'I'll just go and see who that is.'

'Sometimes they go to bed with no supper,' muttered Cory.

Upstairs Chattie was lying out of bed, Ambrose curled up in her arms, her long white legs sticking out. Harriet tucked her up and replaced her blankets. William was sleeping peacefully too, and when she got downstairs she found Cory asleep as well, his elegant narrow-hipped length sprawled across the sofa, his half-smoked cigarette in his hand She put it out, loosened his tie and took his shoes off, then got the duvet and a blanket from his bedroom and covered him up.

'It's you and me babe,' she said to Tadpole, and suddenly felt very responsible and grown up, as she looked down at Cory's face. In sleep it had lost all its anguish.

CHAPTER THIRTEEN

The next day was catastrophic After two hours sleep, Harriet was walking round like a zombie. Matters grew worse as William regurgitated sieved carrot and cabbage over everything, the washing machine gave up the ghost, and in the usual rat race of rounding up homework books, pinnies and gymshoes, she realized there wasn't any dinner-money left for Chattie in the housekeeping. Mrs. Bottomley was away for the night and therefore not available for a touch. After rifling every pocket in her wardrobe, the only solution was to wake Cory — who was not best pleased at being roused from a heavy slumber to one of the worst hangovers in recorded history. His temper was not improved by the embarrassment of finding himself still in evening clothes and lying on the sofa.

'Why the hell can't you organize the bloody housekeeping?' he howled.

It was hardly the moment, Harriet decided, to remind him that he had filched the last of it himself.

When she got back from driving Chattie to school, he had changed into day clothes, was trying to keep down a glass of alkaseltzer, and in the sort of picky mood that soon reduced her to screaming hysteria.

How was he to find a pair of socks, he demanded, when the hot cupboard looked as though a bomb had hit it. Why didn't she ever put anything back where she'd found it? Was it really necessary to have toys lying all over the hall, nappies dripping over the kitchen?

'The washing machine's broken,' protested Harriet

'Well get it mended.' said Cory.

For something to do she busied herself opening a tin of

91

dog food.

'There are already three tins, two of them with mould on open in the fridge,' said Cory.

Chattie had demanded coca-cola for breakfast and Harriet had been too bombed to refuse her. Cory now picked up Chattie's half-full mug.

'Do you really want to ruin the children's teeth? Shouldn't they have milk occasionally?' he asked

'They usually do,' said Harriet through gritted teeth.

Before he could think of a crushing reply, she turned on the waste disposal to remove the remains of Chattie's Weetabix.

'For God's sake turn that thing off,' yelled Cory, clutching his head.

'What?' said Harriet, pretending not to hear.

The next moment he stalked out of the room.

Pig, pig, pig, she said to herself, keeps me up till three o'clock in the morning, banging on about his bloody wife, and then expects peak efficiency. And to relieve her feelings she went upstairs and cleaned the bath with his flannel.

By lunchtime she felt contrite. He really had looked very ill. He ought to eat something. She took great pains making a mushroom omelette, and taking it with a glass of freshly squeezed orange juice up to his study.

His hangover obviously hadn't improved.

'I didn't ask for anything to eat,' he said. 'I'm not hungry. Please take it away.'

'You ought to have something, just to blot up the alcohol,' she said brightly, putting the tray down amid a pile of papers.

Then she saw the expression on his face, and bolted out of the room before he could throw the tray at her. She and Tadpole shared the omelette.

'It would have been wasted on *him*,' she said to Tadpole who chewed it up with great, greedy, crocodile jaws. At least she, Chattie and William were going out to tea, so they'd be out of Cory's hair.

She was just getting ready when the telephone rang. Even running down the landing, clutching a protesting, half-dressed William, she couldn't reach it before Cory. He came out of his study, looking bootfaced.

'It's Elizabeth Pemberton's nanny,' he said. 'For you.'

Muttering apologies, Harriet fled downstairs to answer it.

'We've got problems,' said Sammy cheerfully. 'Elizabeth says she's got one of her ancient aunts whose just lost her husband coming over — at least that's *her* story. I've never known anyone change the sheets and have a bath in the middle of the day for an ancient aunt. Anyway she wants us all out of the way. She thinks it would inhibit poor "Aunt Barbara" to have all the kids hanging around. Can we come over to you instead?'

'Yes, of course,' said Harriet, wondering what the hell Cory would say.

Sammy arrived with Georgie, looking very done-up in a tight navy blue sweater, with *Come and Get Me* printed across her jacked-up bosom, drainpipe jeans, blue and yellow glove socks and impossibly high-heeled sandals.

'I do like your walking shoes,' said Harriet, giggling.

'Elizabeth hates them,' said Sammy. 'They make holes in the parquet.'

She reeked of cheap scent.

'It's called *Seduction*,' she said. 'Worn specially in Cory's honour. Is he here?' She looked round expectantly, patting her hair.

'He's working,' said Harriet, 'and not at his most sunny.'

'Hungover up to his teeth, I shouldn't wonder,' said Sammy. 'Elizabeth said he was as high as a kite when he arrived last night.'

Tadpole shambled in, wagging his tail, and promptly goosed Sammy.

'Good old Tadpole,' she said patting him. 'Never forgets a crutch.'

Chattie bore Georgie upstairs.

'There's ... Shirley Temple film on television,' she said.

'Well, don't disturb Daddy, whatever you do,' said Harriet.

'Do you mind if I bath William?' said Harriet. 'I didn't get around to it earlier.'

'Do you mind if I borrow a razor and shave my legs?' said Sammy. 'I'm going out with a new guy tonight, and one should always be prepared.'

'This is a much nicer room than mine,' said Sammy, lounging on Harriet's yellow counterpane, painting her toe nails with Harriet's nail polish. 'Noel spent fortunes having it done up in the faint hope it might help her to keep a nanny longer than three weeks. Admittedly she threw all the pretty ones out because she was convinced they were all after Cory.'

Her spikily mascara'd eyes softened as they lighted on William, splashing around in the water, chuckling with laughter, and waving his arms about.

'Don't you love him? Look at his lovely fat wrists,' she said. 'The folds always look as though they've got elastic bands on. I envy you really. I got knocked up last year, but it was too much hassle, so I got rid of it. You're very brave to keep him. I wouldn't have the courage.'

Harriet dripped water from a flannel on to William's round belly.

'The unmaried mother's home wasn't much fun; all those films on V.D. and drugs, and having to sew for charity and go to church,' she said. 'And it was awful in hospital. All the fathers coming to see the mothers, holding their hands and admiring the babies. One girl had a lover and a husband rolling up at different times; both were convinced they were the father. No one came to see me. But it was all worth it in the end.'

'What was the father like — no good?'

Harriet swallowed. 'That's him by the bed,' she said.

'Crikey,' said Sammy gaping at the photograph. 'Wouldn't kick *him* out of bed. Not surprised you fell for him.' She looked at Harriet with new respect. Obviously there was more behind that uptight, rather shy exterior than met the eye. 'Never mind, you've got Cory,' she said. 'I wouldn't mind sharing a house with him.'

'And Mrs. Bottomley,' said Harriet.

Sammy grinned. 'Can't say I'd fancy a threesome with her.'

She started a second coat of polish.

'I must say it's nice being here again. I got quite friendly with their last but one nanny. She liked Cory but couldn't stand Noel. Noel treated her like dirt, always trying to get her to bring up breakfast in bed, and lay out her clothes, and comb out her wigs for her. Can you believe it, she needed a nanny more than the children did. She's a friend of Elizabeth's,' she went on, 'or rather they both pretend to be, lots of kissing and darlings when they meet, and bitchy as hell behind each other's backs. Elizabeth doesn't need a nanny either. She just wants one for status, and to take the children off her hands when she wants to see one of her boyfriends. Honestly she's had more pricks than a second-hand dart board.'

Harriet laughed, but felt the conversation was getting a bit indiscreet.

'Are you going out with anyone nice tonight?' she said.

'Smashing! He's a Finn. His firm have sent him over here to build a factory outside Leeds. He's got a lovely accent and an island all of his own. I said I thought all Finns were very drunken and uncouth. He said Finns ain't what they used to be. I thought that was quite witty.'

Harriet sprinkled William with talcum powder, trying not to feel envious. It was such a long time since she'd had a date. In the same magazine that she had read about sieving carrots and cabbage had been a piece on bringing up children. 'All babies need the love of a father and a mother,' it had said, 'a background of security and a happy home.'

Oh dear, perhaps she ought to start looking for a father for William.

'Where does one meet people round here?' she said.

'Darling,' said Sammy. 'On the other side of the valley is Wakeley, with discos and bright lights and rich industrialists with loads of bread just waiting to spend it on you and me. There's even a singles bar just opened called the Loose Box. It's always packed with the most dishy single guys, people who've come up North on conferences and who've got nothing to do in the evenings. I picked up my Finn there. I'll take you there one evening next week.'

Harriet cuddled William, feeling his small solid weight against her left shoulder, his fat hands clutching her hair thinking how gorgeous he smelt. The Loose Box sounded rather too advanced for her.

The telephone went.

'I'll take him,' said Sammy, holding her arms out to William.

It was a Senora di Cuizano ringing from Rome. It was imperative to talk to Cory, she said. Harriet wasn't risking it.

'I'm afraid he's awfully busy at the moment. Can he ring you back?'

The Senora sounded extremely put out. Perhaps she ought to tell Cory? Then she heard the front door bang. He'd probably gone out to get some cigarettes. She went into the kitchen to get tea. Sammy came down and sat in the rocking chair, hiding behind her hair, then peeping out making William crow with laughter.

Ten minutes later she heard the front door open; he must have just gone down to the stables.

'I wonder what Chattie and Georgie are up to,' said Sammy, making no attempt to move.

'I'll just make the tea,' said Harriet, 'and I'll go up and see.'

'Oh look — walnut cake,' said Sammy, 'how lovely. Elizabeth's so mean we're never allowed anything like that for tea and when you consider the amount they spend on drink, and pouring oats down their horses. It must be quite a nice life being Elizabeth's horse.'

'Cory's nice that way,' said Harriet. 'He's not interested in how much money I spend. He's nice anyway,' she said, 'when he's not being nasty.'

She had spoken too soon. At that moment Cory threw open the door.

'Harriet,' he roared, 'will you get those bloody children out of my hair. Can't you manage to control them for five minutes. That infernal Georgie's been smoking my cigars, and sprayed water all over my script, and Chattie's scribbled over the walls.'

Sammy giggled.

'Oh God,' stammered Harriet. 'I'm sorry. I'll remove them at once. I thought they were watching television.'

'Who was that on the telephone?' said Cory.

'A Senora di Cuizano rang from Rome.'

'And what did you say to her?' said Cory, his voice suddenly dangerously quiet.

'I-er-said you were busy.'

'Jesus Christ,' said Cory. 'Don't you realize that was Zefferelli's P.A.? I've been trying to get hold of her all day. You've probably just lost me half a million bucks.'

Harriet fled upstairs and met Chattie and Georgie coming down.

'I don't like Daddy,' said Chattie, sniffing.

'Makes two of us,' muttered Harriet.

Georgie was looking very green.

'Where does Dracula stay in New York?' he said.

'I don't know,' snapped Harriet.

'The Vampire State Building,' said Georgie, and was violently sick all the way down the stairs.

Later she was telling Chattie a bedtime story.

'Who's been sleeping in *my* bed?' she said in mother bear's medium sized voice.

'Why don't Mummy and Daddy bear say, "Who's been sleeping in *our* bed",' said Chattie. 'Mummy and Daddy used to sleep in the same bed, although they don't now. They might again one day, I suppose.'

'And little baby bear said, "Who's been sleeping in my bed",' said Harriet, in a high voice.

'My mother's very famous,' said Chattie. 'She looks like a princess all the time. Georgie says his mother doesn't look like a princess first thing in the morning, only when she goes out. People are always asking for my mother's naughty-graph.'

Harriet decided she'd heard quite enough about Noel Balfour in the last twenty-four hours.

'And Goldilocks looked up and saw the little baby bear, and screamed and screamed.'

'Is Drackela in real life?' said Chattie.

'Oh Chattie,' wailed Harriet, 'can't you concentrate for one minute?'

Cory appeared in the doorway.

'Hullo, Daddy,' said Chattie.

Harriet refused to look up; her lips tightened; she was fed up with Cory.

'That's enough stories for one night,' said Cory.

Harriet got up, and walked straight past him.

She heard Chattie shrieking with giggles as he kissed her goodnight.

Downstairs, the tea things were still waiting to be cleared away. Harriet groaned. She felt absolutely knackered. Dispiritedly she started loading the washing-up machine.

Cory walked in and opened the fridge.

'I'm starving,' he said.

Serve you right, thought Harriet, you should have eaten that omelette.

He opened his mouth to speak, once again she turned on the waste-disposal. For a minute they glared at each other, then he laughed.

'Turn that bloody thing off. I'm going out to get some curry.'

Harriet's mouth watered.

'There's a movie I want to watch later,' said Cory.

'Really,' said Harriet, crashing pans.

'Will you *please* stop sulking,' said Cory. 'I'm sorry I kept you up half the night. I don't remember what I said, but I must have bored the pants off you.'

Didn't have any on, anyway, thought Harriet.

'I'm sorry I've shouted at you and bullied you all day,' he went on. 'It was entirely my fault. I was feeling guilty about wasting a whole work day yesterday, and then being in no condition to do any work today. You're a good girl. I've put on a bath for you, so go and have a long soak — by which time I'll be back with the curry.'

Totally disarmed, Harriet gave a grudging smile. One had to admit that Cory had his moments.

She was just getting into her bath when she heard crying. It was William. She'd only just put him to bed. She wrapped a towel round her and went into his room. Immediately, he stopped crying and cooed and gurgled at her. His nappy was quite dry, but as soon as she'd tucked him up, and turned off the light he started yelling again.

She was just about to go back into the room when Cory came down the passage with his car keys.

'Leave this to me,' he said. In amazement Harriet watched him go over to William's carry cot, wrap his arms into his shawl, winding it up tightly like an Indian papoose.

'They like to feel secure,' he said to Harriet.

William opened his mouth to bellow indignantly.

'And you can shut up,' said Cory sharply. 'Give your poor mother a bit of peace.'

William was so surprised he shut his mouth and didn't make another sound.

Out on the landing, Harriet blinked at him.

'You're absolutely brilliant with babies,' she said.

'Noel was never the maternal type,' said Cory. 'So I've had plenty of practice.'

They had a nice, relaxed evening, drinking red wine, sluttishly eating curry off their knees in the drawing-room, and throwing the bones into the fire. Harriet enjoyed the film, but, as Cory was an expert on movies, was determined not to appear too enthusiastic.

'It's quite good,' she said. 'Although some of the dialogue's a bit dated. Who wrote it?'

'I did,' said Cory.

Harriet was so glad the room was lit by the fire and Cory couldn't see how much she was blushing.

'Have some meat and mushroom, it's quite good too. I wrote it,' he went on, 'with a Hollywood Pro called Billy Blake. It's the last time I'll ever collaborate with anyone. It shortened my life, but I learnt a lot.'

'What was she like?' said Harriet, as the heroine took off her dress.

'Thick,' said Cory.

'And him,' said Harriet, as the hero hurled her on to the bed.

'Nice fag — lives with a hairdresser.'

99

'Golly,' said Harriet, 'I never knew that. If you know all these people, why don't you ever ask them up here?'

'Film people are all right to work with,' said Cory. 'But I don't want to go into their houses, and I don't want them here, talking the same old shop, movies, movies, movies. And I don't like the way they live, eating out every night in order to be seen. If you hang around with them you start believing you're a star, everyone treats you like a star, and doesn't act normally towards you, and you start thinking that's the way people really behave, and you lose touch with reality — which is lethal for writers.'

He threw a chicken bone at the fire, it missed, and Tadpole pounced on it.

'No, darling,' said Harriet, retrieving it from him, 'It'll splinter in your throat.'

Cory emptied the bottle between their two glasses.

'The script I'm doing now's a bastard,' he said. 'It's about the French Civil War in the seventeenth century.'

'The *Fronde*,' said Harriet.

'That's right. It needs so much research.'

He picked up two biographies of French seventeenth-century aristocrats, which were lying on the table.

'Instead of stuffing your head with novels, you could flip through these and see if you could find anything filmable.'

Harriet wiped her chicken-greasy fingers on Tadpole's coat and took the books. 'I could certainly try,' she said.

Cory's glass was empty. 'Shall I get another bottle?' she said.

'Nope,' said Cory. 'That's my lot for tonight. I'm not risking hangovers like yesterday any more. I'm turning over a new leaf. Bed by midnight, no booze before seven o'clock in the evening, riding before breakfast. Don't want to die young, I've decided.'

'I'll cook you breakfast,' said Harriet.

'That's going too far,' said Cory nervously. 'How did you get on with Sammy?'

Harriet giggled. 'She's staggeringly indiscreet.'

'I hope you never discuss me the same way,' said Cory.

'I s-said you were absolutely marvellous,' said Harriet,

her words coming out in a rush. 'Then you spoilt it by coming in and shouting about that telephone call from Italy. She's going to take me to the Loose Box one evening to pick up rich Finns.'

'Not sure that's a very good idea. From all I've heard about that dive, "Loose" is the operative word.'

He picked up a handout from Jonah's school that had been lying under the big biographies. 'What's all this?'

'The Parents' Association on the warpath again,' said Harriet. 'They want money for the new building, so they're holding a Parents' dance. Tickets are £3.50 and for that you get dinner, and a glass of wine. You should go. You might meet Mrs. Right.'

'Not if I'm going on the wagon,' said Cory. 'I can't allow myself lapses like that.'

CHAPTER FOURTEEN

Cory kept his word. He cut down smoking and drinking to a minimum and although occasionally she heard the gramophone playing long into the night, he was usually in bed by midnight.

Most evenings he would come downstairs and talk to her while she was giving William his last feed. They spent a lot of time together, gossiping, reading, playing records, and talking about Cory's script. Harriet was enjoying the research she was doing for him; it was the first time she'd used her brain since Oxford. She also found she was taking more trouble with her appearance. She was tired of saving up money for her and William's future. She wanted to buy some new clothes.

There were also two new additions to the household: Python, a little black mare who arrived from Ireland — Cory was delighted with her and immediately began getting her fit for the point-to-point — and Tarbaby, a lamb with a sooty face, whose mother had died on the moors, and who Harriet was trying to bring up with a bottle.

'Just like having twins in the house,' said Cory, as he watched her make up bottles for the lamb and William.

One Monday towards the end of March she was cooking breakfast and getting Jonah and Chattie off to school when Cory walked in. She still couldn't get used to seeing him up so early.

He threw a pair of underpants down on the kitchen table.

'I know you think I'm too thin, but this is ridiculous. These pants belong to Jonah.'

Harriet went pink. 'I'm sorry, I get muddled. I'm just putting eggs on for Chattie and Jonah. Do you want one?'

102

Cory grimaced.

'It'd be so good for you,' she said.

'All right. I suppose so.'

He sat down and picked up the paper.

'I haven't finished my general knowledge homework,' said Jonah, rushing in, one sock up and one sock down, hair unbrushed, waving an exercise book.

'Who was Florence Nightingale?' he said.

'She was a lesbian,' said Cory, not looking up.

'How do you spell that?' said Jonah.

'You can't put that,' said Harriet. 'Just say she was a very famous nurse, who looked after wounded soldiers in the Crimea.'

'She was a lesbian,' said Cory.

'Can I have sandwiches today?' said Chattie, 'We always have mince and nude-les on Monday, it's disgusting.'

'You'll eat what you're given,' said Cory.

'What has a bottom at the top?' said Chattie.

'I really don't know,' said Harriet.

'Legs,' said Chattie, flicking up her skirt, showing her bottom in scarlet pants and going off into fits of laughter.

'Oh shut up, Chattie,' said Jonah. 'I'm trying to concentrate. Why is a Black Maria called a Black Maria?'

'She was a large black lady who lived in Boston,' said Cory, 'who helped the police arrest drunken sailors. She kept a brothel.'

'What's that?' said Jonah

'Better call it a house of ill-fame,' said Harriet, 'Oh God, the toast's burning.'

She rescued it from the grill, and cut three pieces into strips, then unthinkingly cut the tops off three eggs, and handed them out to Cory, Jonah and Chattie.

'Toast soldiers,' said Cory, 'and no one's taken the top off my egg for years either.'

Harriet blushed: 'Sheer habit,' she said.

'What's a house of ill-fame?' said Chattie.

Harriet dropped off Jonah and then Chattie.

'Don't forget to feed Tarbaby,' shouted Chattie, disap-

JILLY COOPER

pearing into a chattering sea of little girls.

As Harriet walked out of the playground, she met a dis-traught-looking woman trying to manage three rather scruffy children, and a large grey and black speckled dog, who was tugging on a piece of string. Harriet made clicking noises of approval. The dog bounded towards her pulling its owner with it.

'What a darling dog,' said Harriet, as the dog put his paws on her shoulders and started to lick her face. 'Oh isn't he lovely?'

'We can't bear to look at him,' said his owner. 'Come on Spotty.' She half-heartedly tried to pull the dog away.

'Why ever not?' said Harriet.

'I've got to take him to the dogs' home, after I've dropped this lot.'

The children started to cry. 'I can't afford to keep him,' went on the mother. 'I've got a job, and he howls something terrible when I go out, so the landlady says he's got to go. They'd find a home for him.'

'But they may not,' said Harriet. 'They put them down after seven days, if they can't. Oh dear, I wish we could have him.'

Spotty lay his cheek against hers and thumped his plumed tail.

'What kind is he?' she said.

'A setter, I think,' said the owner, sensing weakness. 'He's only a puppy.'

Harriet melted. 'Hang on,' she said, 'I'll go and ring my boss.'

Cory had started work and was not in the mood for inter-ruptions.

'Er-Mr. Erskine, I mean Cory, there's this absolutely sweet puppy here.'

'Well,' said Cory unhelpfully.

'He's got to be put down unless they can find a home for him. He's so sweet.'

'Harriet,' said Cory wearily, 'you have enough trouble coping with William, Chattie, Jonah and me, not to mention Tadpole and Tarbaby. We haven't got rid of any of

104

Ambrose's kittens yet and now you want to introduce a puppy. Why don't you ring up the zoo and ask them to send all the animals up here for a holiday? Telephone Battersea Dogs' Home, and tell them we keep open house.'

'I'm sorry,' said Harriet, chastened.

'What's his name?' said Cory.

'Spotty,' said Harriet, 'and he's a setter.'

There was a long pause.

'Well, you'd better think up a new name before you get him home,' said Cory and rang off.

Harriet couldn't believe her ears.

'We *will* look after him,' she said to the woman, 'And he'll have another dog to play with.'

She was worried Spotty's owner might burst into tears, but she seemed absolutely delighted, and later, as Harriet drove off with the dog, she saw her chattering very animatedly to a couple of friends. Not so Spotty, who howled lustily for his mistress for a couple of miles then got into the front seat beside Harriet, and finally collapsed moaning piteously all over the gear lever, his head on her lap.

'I must think of a name for you,' she said, as they got home. She opened the A.A. book and plonked her finger down blindly. It landed on Sevenoaks.

'Hullo, Sevenoaks,' said Harriet. 'You've got a cattle market on Monday, two three star hotels and you're twenty-five miles from London.'

'Harriet,' said Cory, as Sevenoaks charged round the drawing-room, trailing standard lamp wires like goose grass, 'That is not a puppy — nor is it a setter.'

'Come here,' said Harriet, trying to catch him as he whisked past.

'He's fully grown,' said Cory. 'At least two and virtually untrainable.'

Sevenoaks rolled his eyes, charged past Cory, and shot upstairs, followed by Tadpole, who was thoroughly overexcited. Sevenoaks had already received a bloody nose from Ambrose, a very frosty response from Mrs. Bottomley, and tried to eat one of Cory's riding boots. Now he could be heard drinking out of the lavatory. Next he came crashing downstairs, followed once more by Tadpole, and collapsed panting frenziedly at Harriet's feet. She looked up at Cory with starry eyes.

'Look how he's settled down,' she said. 'He knows he's going to be really happy here.'

All in all, however, Sevenoaks couldn't be described as one hundred per cent a success. Whenever he wasn't trying to escape to the bitches in the village, he was fornicating with Tadpole in the front garden, digging holes in the lawn, chewing everything in sight, or stretching out on sofas and beds with huge muddy paws.

The great love of his life, however, was Harriet. He seemed to realize that she had rescued him from death's door. He welcomed her noisily whenever she returned, howled the house down if she went out and had a growling match with Cory every night because Cory refused to let him sleep on Harriet's bed.

The following Wednesday was another day of disasters. Cory was having trouble with his script and was not in the best temper anyway, particularly as William was teething and spent the day screaming his head off, and Sevenoaks had chewed up Cory's only French dictionary. Harriet botched up Chattie's lamb chops by burning them under the grill while she was filling in a How Seductive Are You quiz in a women's magazine, and she'd just finished pouring milk into William and Tarbaby's bottles when Ambrose came weaving along and knocked the whole lot on to the floor. She was also in a highly nervous state, having at last promised Sammy she would accompany her to the Loose Box that evening.

If was half past seven by the time she'd cleared up and got everyone to bed. There was no time to have a bath; she only managed to scrape a flannel over her face and under her armpits, pour on a great deal of scent and rub in cologne in an attempt to resuscitate her dirty hair.

At five minutes to eight the doorbell went. Sammy was early. Harriet rushed downstairs with only one eye made up aware that she looked terrible. Cory met her on the landing.

'Going out?' he said.

'Yes,' she said defensively. 'It's my night off.'

She opened the front door to two earnest-looking women with wind-swept grey hair. One was clutching a notebook, the other a rather ancient camera.

'I'm sorry we're late,' said the woman with a notebook. 'It's a very difficult place to find at night.'

Chattie wandered down the stairs in her nightgown. Visitors always meant a possibility of staying up late.

'And who are you, young lady?' said the woman with the camera.

'I'm Chattie. I had a pretty dress on today.'

'And I'm Carol Chamberlain,' said the woman with the notebook. 'We've come all the way from London to interview your Daddy.'

'Come into the drawing-room and I'll get you a whisky and tonic,' said Chattie.

Harriet went green, fled upstairs and knocked on Cory's door.

He didn't answer. She knocked again.

'Yes,' he said, looking up, drumming his fingers with irritation.

'I don't know how to tell you this.'

'Oh God,' he said, with infinite weariness. 'What the hell have you done now? Have all Sevenoaks' relations arrived?'

Harriet turned pale.

'I-um-I'm afraid I forgot to put off *Woman's Monthly*. They've come all the way from London. They're waiting downstairs.'

'Was he absolutely insane with rage?' said Sammy, who always enjoyed stories of other people's disasters. It was a source of slight irritation to her that Harriet got on so well with Cory.

'Absolutely insane,' said Harriet miserably. 'I may well have joined the great unemployed by tomorrow.'

They were tarting up in the Ladies of the Loose Box. Crowds of girls around them were backcombing like maniacs. One girl was rouging her navel.

Harriet was fiddling with her sweater.

'Do you think it looks better outside my jeans?' she said to Sammy.

'No,' said Sammy. 'Doesn't give you any shape. Let's see what it looks like tucked in. No, that looks even worse. Leave it hanging out. You look absolutely fantastic,' she added with all the complacency of someone looking infinity better.

She was poured into black velvet trousers and a low-cut black sweater, her splendid white bosom spilled over the top like an ice-cream over a cone. She was also wearing black polish on her toes and fingernails, and a black rose in her newly dyed mahogany curls.

No one's going to want to talk to me, thought Harriet as they went into the arena. All around her people were circling and picking each other up. Some of the girls were ravishingly pretty. It could only have been a spirit of adventure, not a shortage of men, that led them to this place.

Sammy was already leering at a handsome blond German in a blue suit.

'I'd just love a sweet Cinzano,' she said fluttering long green eyelashes at him.

The German fought his way to the bar to get her one. The next moment a pallid youth had sidled up to her.

'I work in films,' he said, which he patently didn't.

'Really,' said Sammy. 'I'm a model actually.'

Harriet had completely forgotten the hassle of hunting for men. She kept trying to meet men's eyes, but hers kept slithering away. Don't leave me, she pleaded silently to Sammy. But Sammy was on the hunt like Sevenoaks after a bitch, and nothing could deter her from her quarry.

'It's always been my ambition to go to Bayreuth,' she was saying to the handsome German.

The worst part of the evening for Harriet was that she wasn't a free agent. She couldn't split because Sammy was driving and she hadn't brought enough money for a taxi.

Sammy having downed eight sweet Cinzanos was well away with the German, and seemed to be having an equally devastating effect on his friend, who had spectacles, a nudging grin and a pot belly.

'Come over here, Harriet,' said Sammy. 'You must meet Claus.'

She pushed the fat, nudging grinning German forward.

'Harriet's frightfully clever and amusing,' she added.

Harriet became completely paralysed and could think of nothing to say except that the weather had been very cold lately.

'Ah but the freezing North brings forth the most lovely ladies,' said the fat little German with heavy gallantry. He was in Yorkshire, he told Harriet, for a textile conference and had lost 10 kilos since Christmas. Harriet didn't know if that were good or bad.

'Isn't he a scream?' said Sammy.

She pulled Harriet aside.

'They want to take us to The Black Tulip,' she said. 'It's a fantastic place; you have dinner and dance, and there's a terrific group playing.'

'It's going to make us frightfully late, isn't it?' said Harriet dubiously.

'Oh come on,' said Sammy, drink beginning to make her punchy. 'No one's ever taken me to a place like that before. It's the chance of a lifetime.'

Oh God, thought Harriet, I mustn't be a spoilsport.

The Black Tulip was even worse than the Loose Box. Harriet found her smile getting stiffer and stiffer as she toyed with an avocado pear.

'First I cut out all carbohydrates,' said the little fat German.

Opposite them Sammy and the handsome German couldn't keep their hands off each other. They were both getting tighter and tighter. Harriet wondered who the hell was going to drive her home.

'Then I gave up bread and potatoes,' said the fat German.

He must have been huge before he lost all that weight, thought Harriet, as she rode round the dance floor on his stomach. She suddenly longed to be home with Cory and William and the children. What would happen if William woke up? Mrs. Bottomley slept like the dead. Cory'd go spare if he had to get up and feed him. She wondered how

109

long he'd taken to get rid of *Woman's Monthly*.

'A new penny for your thoughts, Samantha,' said the handsome German.

'They're worth a bloody sight more than that,' said Sammy.

They all laughed immoderately.

'I also cut out all puddings and cakes,' said the fat German.

'I get no kick from champagne,' sang the lead singer. 'Pure alcohol gives me no thrill at all.'

You can say that again, thought Harriet.

Sammy was leaning forward, the fat little German gazing hungrily at her bosom.

'Shall we go for a drive on the moor?' he said.

'No.' said Harriet, violently. 'You all can,' she added. 'But could you drop me off first?'

'We're all going back to Heinrich's hotel for a little drink,' said Sammy, getting rather unsteadily to her feet.

'I must get back in case William wakes,' said Harriet desperately.

After some argument, Sammy relented. 'We'll get you a cab,' she said. 'Claus can pay. The only one going at this hour is driven by the local undertaker.'

Harriet felt as cheerful as a corpse, as she bowled home under a starless sky. She couldn't stop crying; she had no sex appeal any more, the world was coming to an end, she'd never find a father for William.

As she put the key at the door, Sevenoaks, who usually slept through everything, let out a series of deep baritone barks, then, realizing it was her, started to sing with delight at the top of his voice, searching round for something to bring her.

'Oh please, Sevenoaks, lower your voice,' she pleaded.

But as she crept upstairs, Cory came out of the bathroom with a towel round his waist, his black hair wet from the bath, his skin still yellow-brown from last summer.

'Did *Woman's Monthly* stay for hours?' she said.

'Hours,' said Cory, 'I had to throw them out. It must have been pre-menstrual tension I was suffering from before they

110

arrived.'

Harriet was feeling too depressed to even giggle.

'I'm terribly sorry,' she said.

Sevenoaks sauntered into Cory's room and heaved himself up on to Cory's bed.

'Get him off,' snapped Cory. 'That dog's got to go. He's been whining ever since you went out. Where have you been anyway?' he said in a gentler tone, noticing her red-rimmed eyes.

'To the Loose Box, with Sammy. We met some Germans, one was quite good-looking, the other one was awful. The good-looking one fancied Sammy, so did the awful one, but he had to put up with me. I tried to get out and find some people of my own age, but I don't think they liked me very much.' And with a sob she fled to her room.

When she turned down the counterpane and got into bed, she found her electric blanket switched on, and a note pinned to the pillow.

'Dear Harriet,' it said.

'Doesn't matter what *He* says, we think you're smashing, and so does he really, love from Tadpole, Ambrose (Miss) and Sevenoaks.'

Harriet gave a gurgle of laughter. Suddenly the whole evening didn't seem to matter very much any more. She lay in bed and thought about Cory. She felt like a child joining up numbers to discover what a picture was; she felt she hadn't managed to join up any of Cory's numbers at all.

CHAPTER FIFTEEN

Harriet was ironing in the kitchen when a car drew up.

'Come on, let's hide,' whispered Chattie. 'It's awful old Arabella. She only turns up when Daddy's at home.'

'We can't,' protested Harriet, watching a tall girl get out of the car. 'She's seen us.'

'Anyone at home?' came a debutante quack from the hall.

The girl who strode into the kitchen was in her late twenties, very handsome, high complexioned, athletically built, with flicked-up light brown hair drawn back from her forehead.

'Hullo, Chattie,' she said breezily. 'How are you?' But before Chattie could answer she turned to Harriet. 'And you must be the new nanny. I'm Arabella Ryde-Ross. Cory's spoken about me, I expect.' But before Harriet could answer the girl turned to William, who was aimlessly beating the side of his chair with a wooden spoon.

'What a darling baba. Not another of Noel's cast-offs?'

'No, he's mine,' said Harriet.

'Oh?' said Arabella. It was strange how someone could get four syllables out of that word.

'Doesn't your husband mind you taking a job?'

'I'm not married.'

'Oh, how amazingly brave of you.' Arabella paused and looked at William again. 'I must say Cory's a saint, the lame ducks he takes under his wing.'

'One, two, four, five. Bugger it. I've left out three,' said Chattie, who was counting Ambrose's kittens.

Harriet tried not to giggle. Arabella looked appalled.

'Chattie, don't use language like that. Run along and play. I want to talk to Nanny.'

112

'She's not called Nanny, she's Harriet, and I don't want to play, thank you,' said Chattie. Then a foxy expression came over the child's face. 'Would you like a sweetie, Arabella?'

'Aren't you going to offer Nanny one?'

'It's my last,' said Chattie. 'And I want you to have it.'

'That's very kind of you, Chattie,' said Arabella, popping the sweet into her mouth. 'I get on so well with children,' she added to Harriet. 'People are always saying I'd make a wonderful mother.'

At that moment Cory wandered in and Arabella flushed an unbecoming shade of puce.

'Hullo, Arabella,' he said. 'You look very brown.'

'It fades so quickly. You should have seen me last week. I've just got back from St. Moritz, or I'd have been over before. We're having a little party next Friday.'

Cory frowned. 'I think something's happening.'

'Well, we'll have it on Saturday then.'

How could she be so unsubtle? thought Harriet.

'No, Friday's all right,' said Cory. 'I've just remembered. It's Harriet's birthday. It'll do her good to meet some new people. Yes, we'd like to come.'

Harriet didn't dare look at Arabella's face.

'Did you like that sweet, Arabella?' said Chattie.

'Yes thank you, darling.'

Chattie gave a naughty giggle.

'Tadpole didn't. He spat it out three times.'

Harriet scolded Chattie when Arabella had gone, but the child shrugged her shoulders.

'I hate her, and Mummy says she's after Daddy. I hope she doesn't get him,' she added gloomily. 'She never gives us presents; she says we're spoilt.'

'She's got a point there,' said Harriet.

'She's just told Daddy he ought to give you the push, because we're so naughty,' said Chattie, picking up one of the kittens. 'But he told her to shut up, and we'd never been better looked after. Goodness, Harriet, you've gone all pink in the face.'

Trees rattled against her bedroom window. She looked at

the yellow daffodils on the curtains round her bed and felt curiously happy. William was getting more gorgeous every day. She was getting fonder and fonder of Chattie and Jonah. Sevenoaks lay snoring across her feet. She felt her wounded heart gingerly; she was not yet deliriously happy but she was content.

'Happy Birthday to you,' sang a voice tunelessly, 'Happy Birthday, dear Harriet, Happy Birthday to you.'

And Chattie staggered in with a breakfast tray consisting of a bunch of wild daffodils, a brown boiled egg, toast and coffee.

'Oh how lovely!' said Harriet. 'Shall I take the coffee off?' She put it on the table beside her bed.

'Daddy's just finished feeding William,' said Chattie.

'And he's coming up with all your presents. Oh, why are you crying, Harriet?'

'Harriet's crying, Daddy,' she said to Cory, followed by Mrs. Bottomley, as he came in and dumped William on the floor.

Cory saw Harriet's brimming eyes.

'She's entitled to do what she bloody well likes on her birthday,' he said. 'Get off the bed, Sevenoaks.'

'She'd better put on her dressing gown,' said Mrs. Bottomley, looking at Harriet's see-through nightgown. 'Happy Birthday, love.'

Harriet couldn't believe her eyes when she opened her presents. Ambrose and Tadpole had given her a rust silk shirt. Sevenoaks was broke and had only given her a pencil sharpener. Chattie gave her a box of chocolates, several of which had already been eaten.

'I just had to test they were all right,' said Chattie.

There was also a maroon cineraria from Jonah, which he had chosen himself and bought with his own pocket money, and a vast cochineal pink mohair stole from Mrs. Bottomley, which she'd knitted herself, because Harriet never wore enough clothes. Cory gave her a grey and black velvet blazer, and a pale grey angora dress.

'But they're beautiful,' she breathed. 'I've never seen anything so lovely.'

'Sick of seeing you in that old duffle coat,' said Cory.

'Daddy loves giving presents,' said Chattie, 'and he hasn't got Mummy to give them to any more.'

When she'd eaten her breakfast, she got up and went to look for Cory. She found him in his study flipping through the pages of the script he'd written yesterday.

Harriet cleared her throat.

'I just want to thank you for everything,' she said, blushing scarlet. 'For making me feel so happy here, and for those heavenly presents. I really don't deserve either, what with Sevenoaks and all the messages I forget to pass on and all that.'

And, reaching up, she gave him a very quick kiss on the cheek and scuttled out of the room.

'Sexy,' said Chattie, from the passage.

As the hour for Arabella's party approached, Harriet grew more and more nervous. She'd been a disaster in the singles bar. What likelihood was there that she'd be any better with the hunting set? She must remember to say hounds instead of dogs.

She was sitting wrapped in a towel, putting her make-up on, when Chattie banged on her door.

'Come on. I want to show you something. Keep your eyes shut.'

'It can't be another present,' thought Harriet, feeling the thick carpet under her feet as Chattie led her towards the stairs, then turned sharp right into Jonah's bedroom. She shivered as a blast of icy air hit her.

'Don't look yet,' said Chattie pushing her forward, 'Now you can.'

Through the open window above the elm trees, at the bottom of the garden, Harriet could see a tiny cuticle of new silver moon.

'Now wish,' said Chattie. 'It doesn't work if you see it through glass. Wish for the thing you most want in your life. I've already wished for some bubble gum.'

Harriet, listening to the mournful cawing of the rooks

115

suddenly felt confused.

For the first time in months, she didn't automatically wish she could have Simon back. He was the fix, the first drink, that would trigger off the whole earth-shattering addiction all over again. She didn't want her life disrupted. Her thoughts flickered towards Cory for a second, then turned resolutely away. Please give William and me happiness and security whatever form it takes, she wished.

She turned round and found Cory standing in the doorway watching her. She couldn't read the expression on his face.

'I hope it's a sensible wish,' he said acidly. 'Like making your dear friend Sevenoaks less of a nuisance. He's just eaten the back off my only pair of dress shoes.'

He kicked Sevenoaks who slunk towards Harriet, rolling his eyes and looking chastened at the front, but waving his tail at the back.

Chattie flung her arms round him.

'He's so clever, Sevenoaks,' she said. 'He's eaten your shoes because he doesn't want you to go out.'

'He's definitely an asset, Daddy,' said Jonah, who'd just arrived for the weekend.

'He's a very silly asset,' said Cory.

'Ryder Cock Ross to Banbury Cross,' said Chattie.

The Ryder-Ross's house was large, Georgian and set back from the road at the end of a long drive.

Women were clashing jaw bones, exchanging scented kisses in the hall. One of them, in plunging black and wearing so many diamonds she put the chandeliers to shame, was Sammy's boss, Elizabeth.

When Harriet went upstairs to take off her coat, the bed was smothered in fur coats.

She was wearing the dress Cory had given her for her birthday. She examined herself in Arabella's long gilt mirror. It did suit her; it was demure, yet, in the subtle way it hugged her figure, very seductive. Oh please, she prayed as she went downstairs, make someone talk to me, so I'm not a drag on Cory.

He was waiting for her in the hall — tall, thin, remote, the pale, patrician face as expressionless as marble.

As they entered the drawing-room, everyone turned and stared. A figure, squawking with delight, came over to meet them. It was Arabella, wearing a sort of horse blanket long skirt, a pink blouse, and her hair drawn back from her forehead by a bow.

'Cory, darling, I thought you were never coming!'

She seized Harriet's arm in a vice-like grip. 'I'm going to introduce Nanny to some people her own age.'

Whisking Harriet into the next room, she took her over to meet a fat German girl, saying, 'Helga, this is Mr. Erskine's nanny. Helga looks after my brother's children. I thought you might be able to compare notes.'

Harriet couldn't help giggling to herself. Nothing could have reduced her to servant status more quickly. It was not long, however, before two tall chinless wonders came over and started to tell her about the abortive hunting season they'd had.

Half-an-hour later they were still talking foxiana, and Harriet allowed her eyes to wander into the next room to where Cory was standing. Three women — the sort who should have been permanently eating wafer-thin mints on candlelit terraces — were vying for his attention.

He's an attractive man, thought Harriet, with a stab of jealousy. I wonder it never hit me before.

Suddenly he looked up, half smiled at her, and mouthed: 'All right?' She nodded, the tinge of jealousy gone.

'A brace of foxes were accounted for on Wednesday,' said the better-looking of the two chinless wonders. 'I say,' he said to Harriet, 'would you like to come and dance?'

He had long light brown hair, very blue eyes, and a pink and white complexion.

'Yes please,' said Harriet.

There was no one else in the darkened room as they shambled round the floor to the Supremes, but he was much too straight to lunge at her during a first dance, thought Harriet with relief.

'We haven't really been introduced,' he said, 'My name's

117

Billy Bentley. Haven't seen you before. You staying with Arabella?'

'I work for Cory Erskine,' said Harriet.

'That must be interesting,' he said. 'Frightfully clever bloke Cory, read so many books, very hard man to hounds too.'

He's certainly not very kind to Sevenoaks, thought Harriet.

'You ought to come out with us one day,' said Billy Bentley.

They shambled a few more times round the floor.

'Suppose I ought to get you a drink,' he said. 'But honestly you're so jolly pretty, I could go on dancing with you all night.'

Harriet felt quite light-headed with pleasure, but, as they came out of the room, Arabella drew her aside.

'Nanny,' she said, as Harriet crossed the room, 'could you give them a hand in the kitchen? They're a bit short-staffed.'

Cory was out of earshot so Harriet could do nothing but comply. As she came out of the kitchen, half-an-hour later, she heard a slightly blurred man's voice say, 'I see old Cory's surfaced at last. Looks better, doesn't he?'

'So he should, my dear.' A woman's voice, catty, amused. 'Pretty cool, I call it, bringing your mistress and passing her off as a nanny. Arabella says she's got a baby. I wonder if it's Cory's.'

Scarlet in the face, trembling with humiliation, Harriet carried the glasses into the dining-room, straight into Cory.

'What the hell are you doing?'

She lowered her eyes in confusion. 'Arabella said they needed help in the kitchen.'

'Like hell they do. Put those glasses down at once. You're shaking. What's the matter?'

'Nothing, it's nothing,' snapped Harriet, her voice rising. 'I was just upset at being treated as a servant.' She fled upstairs on the pretext of doing her face.

Returning to the drawing-room, still shaking, she was button-holed by a very good-looking man with greying blond hair and a dissipated face.

'Lolita! At last!' Harriet drew back. 'My name's Charles Mander,' he went on. 'You're not local are you?'

'Yes,' said Harriet, defiantly. 'I look after Cory Erskine's children.'

'How electrifying! Lucky Cory.' His eyes, alert with sudden interest, travelled slowly over her body, stripping off every inch of clothing.

'And have you met Noel yet?' Then he began to laugh. 'No, of course you haven't. She's not silly enough to let a pretty girl like you under her roof.'

'What do you mean?' said Harriet angrily.

Then Cory was by her side.

'Hullo, Charles.'

'Hullo, Cory, old boy. Long time no see.'

The greeting was amicable enough, but Harriet could tell that the two men hated each other.

'I've just met your charming little — er — friend. I congratulate you, Cory. Such a comfort on these long winter nights.'

Cory gave a cigarette to Harriet, selected one himself and lit them both before he replied, 'You always did have your mind below your navel, Charles.'

Charles Mander started to laugh again. 'It reminds me of that song we used to sing in the nursery. How does it go? Something about "God bless Nanny, and make her good". I must say, I wouldn't mind making Nanny myself.'

There was a frozen pause.

'If I were a gentleman, Charles,' said Cory, in a voice that sent shivers down Harriet's spine, 'I'd knock you down. But it would only give you the satisfaction of being a public martyr.'

He turned, deliberately looking at a fat blonde woman lurching towards them.

'Your wife's drunk again,' he added quietly.

Cory and Harriet didn't speak until they were nearly home. Gone was the easy cameraderie of the past few weeks.

Then Cory said, 'I'm sorry about Charles Mander. There's no point in beating about the bush. He used to be a

119

lover of Noel's, probably still is, so he can never resist bitching me up. I imagine you heard the same sort of remark as you came out of the kitchen.'

Harriet nodded.

'What did they say?'

Harriet's tongue seemed to be tied in knots. 'They said William was your child.'

'Charming,' said Cory. 'The hunting season's been so frightful they're very short on gossip. Doesn't bother me. But I should never have exposed you to that snake pit. I should have realized how vulnerable you are.'

'It was so lovely,' she muttered. 'Everything's spoilt now.'

'It needn't be,' he said as he turned the car into the drive.

Once inside, he followed her up to her room. Outside the door, she paused and stammered out her thanks for taking her to the party.

'I enjoyed taking you,' he said and, putting out a hand, smoothed back a loose strand of hair that had fallen over her eyes. 'I was watching you this evening. You had that lost wistful look of the moon when it suddenly appears during the day. I must say I've been wondering about you myself lately.'

Harriet looked up, startled. Cory's face was in shadow. Then suddenly they both jumped, as unmistakably down the passage came the sound of Sevenoaks drinking noisily out of the lavatory. The tension was broken. Harriet went off into peels of laughter.

'The enemy of promise,' said Cory. 'Go to bed little one, and don't worry.'

Harriet went to bed, but couldn't sleep. What had Cory meant that he'd been wondering about her lately? It seemed her relationship with him was something so fragile, a candle that she had to protect with both hands because everyone was trying to blow it out.

CHAPTER SIXTEEN

She felt staggeringly untogether in the morning. She had a blinding headache. It was as much as she could do to feed William. Chattie, recognizing weakness, started playing up.

'We're going to the meet with Daddy,' she said. 'Can I wear my party dress?'

'No, you can't,' said Harriet.

'Well my red velvet dress then?'

'Trousers are much warmer.'

'I don't want to wear trousers. I'm not a boy.'

'Oh Chattie, please,' she said in despair.

'You'll wear them and bloody well like it,' said Cory coming in tying a stock, his long legs encased in boots and tight white breeches.

Chattie tried a different approach.

'Can I have a two-wheeler with stabilizers?' she said.

'Only if you do what Harriet tells you. How do you feel?' he said to her.

'Frightful.'

'So do I,' said Cory. 'God knows what Arabella gave us to drink. Some fruity little paint stripper, I should imagine. One could almost hear the enamel dropping off one's teeth.'

'Why do you go on wearing a dinner jacket, Daddy,' said Chattie, 'if it always makes you feel sick in the morning?'

Harriet suspected he'd gone on drinking long after she'd gone to bed.

'Can Harriet come to the meet with us?' said Jonah.

'Oh please yes,' said Chattie.

'It's too much of a hassle with William and things,' said Harriet.

Cory, a cigarette hanging out of the corner of his mouth,

121

was filling up a hip-flask with brandy.

'You can leave William with Mrs Bottomley,' he said. 'Do you good to get some fresh air. There's a button missing from my coat. Can you sew it on?'

'Are you taking Python?' said Harriet.

'Yes,' said Cory. 'As a second horse. I'd like to see how she makes out.'

The horses went to the meet by box. Cory drove Harriet, Jonah, Chattie and the dogs by car.

The mist had rolled back from the hills to reveal a beautiful mild day. The ivy was putting out shining pale leaves; young nettles were thrusting through the green spring grass. Catkins shook in the breeze, the bracken burned the same rusty red as the curling leaves that still clung to the oak trees. The wet roads glittered and the stone walls gave off an almost incandescent whiteness in the sunlight.

'I'm hot,' said Chattie 'I could have worn my party dress.'

'Chattie I've told you a hundred times,' said Harriet.

'No you didn't, you only told me twice.'

'Don't be rude,' said Cory.

There was a pause.

'It's raining, it's pouring,' sang Chattie. 'The old man's snoring. He went to bed and bumped his head, and couldn't get up in the morning. The doctor came and flushed the chain and out flew an aeroplane.'

Both children collapsed in giggles.

'The doctor came and flushed,' sang Chattie.

'Shut up,' said Cory.

'Ouch. Sevenoaks is treading on me.'

'Can we stop for some sweets? There's an absolutely brilliant sweet shop in Gargrave,' said Jonah.

Gradually they caught up with riders hacking to the meet. Soon there was a steady stream of cars and horse boxes.

Cory parked on the side of the road.

'You can bring Tadpole,' he said, locking Sevenoaks in the car. 'I'm not risking that delinquent getting loose.'

'We must give him a bit of window,' said Harriet, winding it down.

Cory went off to find his horse box. Harriet took Chattie

and Jonah and walked along to the village where the meet was being held. Little grey cottages lined a triangular village green. A stream choked it's way through pussy willows and hazel trees. The churchyard was full of daffodils in bud.

Riders everywhere were gossiping and saddling up. There was a marvellous smell of trodden grass and hot, sweating horses. Anxious whinnyings came from the horse boxes. Hunt terriers yapped from the backs of cars.

There was Arabella looking considerably the worse for wear, Harriet was glad to notice, impatiently slapping her boots with her whip and looking round for her horse. And there was Billy Bentley, looking far more glamorous than he had last night, in a red coat, his long mousy hair curling under his black velvet cap, sitting on a huge dapple grey which was already leaping about as though the ground was red hot under its feet. Next to him, taking a swig out of his hip-flask, eyeing the girls, supervising the unboxing of a magnificent chestnut in a dark green rug, was Charles Mander.

Harriet tried to slide past them, but she had not counted on Chattie, who rushed up and said,

'Hullo, Charles.'

He turned. 'Hullo Chattie,' he said. 'How are you?'

'Fine,' said Chattie. 'Why don't you come and see us any more? He always used to come and bring us presents when Mummy lived with us,' she added to Harriet.

'Hullo, pretty Nanny,' said Charles.

Harriet tried to look straight through him, but only managed to look sulky.

'I'm five now,' said Chattie. 'I used to be four.'

'I used to be four too,' said Charles.

'My daddy's twenty-one,' said Chattie.

'I wish my children put out propaganda like that,' said Charles, laughing.

'I'm getting a two-wheeler soon with stabilizers.' said Chattie.

'I could do with some stabilizers myself,' said Charles.

He walked over to Harriet, the dissipated gin-soaked blue eyes looking almost gentle.

123

'Look, I've got rather a hazy recollection of what happened last night, but I've a feeling I bitched you up. I'm sorry. I can never resist taking the mickey out of Cory. He's so damn supercilious.'

'He *is* my boss,' said Harriet.

'Thank Christ he's not mine, but I didn't mean to take it out on you.'

Harriet stared at him, not knowing what to say.

She was rescued by a voice behind her saying, 'Hullo Harriet.' It was the haw haw tones of Billy Bentley. She was flattered he remembered her. 'You disappeared very fast last night,' he said. 'Saw Charles chatting you up and then you bolted. Can't say I blame you. Enough to put anyone orf.'

He brayed with laughter. He should just sit on his horse and look glamorous, thought Harriet.

'I suppose I better get mounted,' said Charles. 'We're friends now, are we?' he added to Harriet.

'Yes, as long as you're not foul to Mr. Erskine,' she said.

He shrugged his shoulders. 'That's old history. Perhaps you'd have dinner with me one evening, and I'll tell you all about it.'

'I say, hands off Charles,' said Billy Bentley. 'You're married. Leave the field free for us single blokes.'

His horse suddenly bucked and lashed out warningly at a nearby chestnut.

'This bugger's had too much corn,' he said. 'I wish we could get going.'

Charles Mander settled himself on to his horse. An earnest-looking grey-haired woman sidled up to him and pressed an anti-fox-hunting pamphlet into his hand.

'Thank you so much,' he said to her politely and, getting out his lighter, set fire to it and dropped it flaming at her feet. She jumped away and disappeared, shaking her fist, into the crowd.

'Bloody hunt saboteurs,' he said, riding off towards the pub. 'I'm going to get my flask topped up.'

Billy Bentley hung about, looking down at Harriet, trying to control his restless horse.

'Going to the hunt ball?' he asked.

124

'No I'm not.'

'Going away?'

'No, I'm just not going.'

'What a shame,' said Billy, suddenly turning pink. 'I say, I liked talking to you last night. Wonder if you'd come out one evening?'

'I'd love to, but it's a bit difficult,' said Harriet, turning pink too. 'I've got this baby, my own I mean, not Jonah or Chattie.'

'Doesn't matter a scrap,' said Billy. 'Bring the little chap with you if you like. Still got our old nanny at home; got nothing to do; love to look after him.'

Harriet was touched and wanted to tell him so, but next moment the whipper-in arrived with the hounds, who looked curiously naked without collars, tails waving frantically.

'They haven't been fed for two days,' said an anti-fox-hunting youth who was waving a poster saying, 'Hounds off our wild life'.

Grooms were sweeping rugs off sweating, shuddering horses; riders were mounting and jogging off in a noisy glittering cavalcade, with a yelp of voices and a jingle of bits.

Cory rode up on Python, black coat gleaming, eyes popping, letting out snorts of hysterical excitement at all the activity around her.

'I'll ring you this evening,' said Billy. 'Morning, Cory. That's new, very nice too.'

'Kit found her in Ireland,' said Cory. 'Had a couple of days on her with the Kildare.'

'Up to his weight, was she?' said Billy. 'Bloody good. Put her in for the point-to-point, will you?'

'I thought I might.'

'Cory darling!' It was Elizabeth Pemberton, wearing rather too much make-up, but looking stunning in a black coat, and the tightest white breeches. She caught sight of Harriet and nodded to her dismissively.

'You are coming with us on Friday, aren't you?' she said to Cory.

There was a pause, his eyes flickered towards Harriet,

125

then away.

'Yes I'd like to,' he said.

'I think we'll be about twenty-four for dinner,' she said.

Big bloody deal, thought Harriet.

The Master was blowing his horn up the road. Next moment Arabella rolled up on a thoroughly over-excited bay, which barged round, nearly sending Harriet and the children for six.

As the hunt rode down into the valley, the pigeons rose like smoke from the newly ploughed fields.

'Let's follow them.' said Harriet.

But when they got back to the car, she gave a gasp of horror. The back seat was empty; Sevenoaks had gone; he must have wriggled out of the window. She had terrifying visions of him chasing sheep, running under the horses' feet, or getting on to the motorway.

'We must look for him,' she said, getting into the car and driving off in the direction of the hunt, which had disappeared into the wood. Then followed a desperately frustrating half-hour bucketing along the narrow country lanes, having to pull into sideroads every time an oncoming car approached, nearly crashing several times because she was so busy scouring the fields for Sevenoaks.

The hunt were having an equally frustrating time; hounds were not picking up any scent. Riders stood around on the edge of the wood, fidgeting. Then suddenly an old bitch hound gave tongue, and the chorus of hounds swelled, and the whole hillside was echoing. Pa pa pa pa went the melancholy, plaintive note of the horn, and the next moment the hunt came spilling across the road. There was a clash as stirrups hit each other, a snorting of horses, and they were jumping over the wall on the opposite side of the road. From the top of the hill Harriet watched them streaming across the field. There was Cory blown like a beech leaf in his red coat, standing up in his stirrups now to see what was on the other side of a large wall. The next moment Python had cleared it by inches. Hounds were splaying out by a small wood at the bottom of the valley, then suddenly they turned and came thundering back in Harriet's direction.

'There's the fox,' screamed Chattie, and gave the most ear-splitting view halloo.

Ten seconds later the hounds came flowing past her. Suddenly in the middle Harriet recognized a familiar figure, dirty grey, pink tongue hanging out, galloping joyously.

'Oh look, there's Sevenoaks,' screamed the children.

'Come here,' bellowed Harriet.

For a second he looked in her direction and gave her a naughty, flickering, rolling look, then trundled on in the centre of the pack which swept in a liver, black and white wave over the hill.

All the pent-up emotion of the last twenty-four hours welled up in Harriet. She sat down on the bank and laughed until she cried.

Her elation was shortlived. The hunt was soon miles away. She must get back to William. She drove home feeling depressed — not merely because of the day's catastrophic developments. She tried to analyse why, as she got the children a late lunch, and fed William. Perhaps I'm just tired, she thought.

'I just landed on one of your hotels, and you didn't even notice,' said Jonah.

'Oh God, how much do you owe me?' said Harriet.

'£1,000,' said Jonah. 'It was jolly honest of me to tell you.'

'Jolly honest,' answered Harriet, wishing he hadn't.

'Here's £1,000,' said Jonah. 'Now we can go on for another half-hour.'

Harriet was dying for him to best her. Worried about Sevenoaks, she was finding it impossible to concentrate. There was no way she could win now; she wanted to get the game over as quickly as possible.

Fortunately Sammy arrived at that moment, bringing Georgie and Timothy, the Pembertons' elder child, who was a friend of Jonah's, so all four children disappeared to the attic.

Sammy and Harriet went back into the nursery where William was rolling around on the rug.

'How was Arabella's party last night?' said Sammy.

127

Harriet gave her an expurgated edition of what had happened.

'It was hideously embarrassing, but Cory was so sweet about it afterwards.'

'I think Charles Mander's rather attractive,' said Sammy. 'He's reputed to beat his wife. He's known round here as Rotation of Riding Crops.' She shrieked with laughter. 'Fancy old Arabella shoving you off to do the washing up.'

'She'd be quite attractive,' mused Harriet, 'if she didn't push so hard.'

'Must be getting desperate. I wonder how old she is. About thirty I should think. I hope I die before I'm thirty. It sounds so old.'

'Forty must be worse,' said Harriet. 'Mrs. Bottomley must be over fifty.'

They brooded silently over this horror.

'Cory's thirty-four,' said Sammy. 'It doesn't seem too bad for a man; but, just think; when you were born he was fourteen, getting all clammy-handed and heavy breathing over girls at parties.'

Harriet thought she'd rather not.

'Elizabeth and Michael didn't have much fun last night either,' said Sammy. 'There weren't any alkaseltzers in the house. We'd run out, but Michael came down in the night and had sixteen junior aspirins.'

'What's happening on Friday?' said Harriet.

'The Hunt Ball,' said Sammy. 'Everyone gets absolutely smashed and blows hunting horns, and rushes upstairs and fornicates in cordoned-off bedrooms.'

She picked up a cushion and peered round it at William, making him go off into fits of giggles.

Harriet was sorting out a pile of washing.

'Who else is going in Elizabeth's party?' she asked casually.

Sammy looked at her slyly. 'You mean who's she asked for Cory?'

Harriet went pink.

'I just wondered if any of the people I met last night are going to be there.'

'She's invited another of her glamorous, neurotic, divorced girlfriends called Melanie Brooks for Cory. I saw the letter Elizabeth wrote her:

' "Darling Melanie, So pleased you can make it. Try and catch an earlier train, as it's a bit of a rush on Friday night and you want to look your best because I've lined up a gorgeous man for you, a disconsolate husband whose wife's just left him, but very fascinating." '

Harriet winced.

'Don't worry,' said Sammy. 'She's ancient. At least thirty, and her legs are awful.'

'But those'll be covered by a long dress at a ball,' said Harriet gloomily.

The telephone rang. To Harriet's surprise it was Billy Bentley.

'Hullo,' she said. 'Have you finished already?'

'My horse went lame; not badly; he'll be all right after a few days' rest.'

'Did you have a good day?'

'Slightly chaotic actually. The Hunt saboteurs fed in an enormous black and grey dog which completely disrupted the pack. They ran right across the motorway — no one was hurt, thank God — and ended up in a council estate, cornering a ginger cat in an outside lavatory.'

'Oh goodness! Is the cat all right?'

'Got away, thank God,' said Billy. 'Or it'd be all over the papers.'

'And the big grey and black dog?'

'Well we whipped it out of the pack and Cory very kindly took care of it. He gave a man on the council estate a fiver to bring it back to your house. He's going to hold it as hostage until the Antis claim it. It's completely wild.'

Harriet thought she would explode trying not to laugh.

'After that we had a terrific run. Look, are you doing anything on Friday?'

'No, at least I don't think so. My night off.'

'Like to come out?'

'All right.' Damn it, if Cory was going to go gallivanting with gorgeous divorcées, she wasn't going to get in his way.

'It's the Hunt Ball. You won't mind that, will you?' said

129

Billy.

'Oh,' Harriet gave a yelp of alarm.

'We'll eat at home first. I'll come and pick you up about eight.'

'I haven't got anything to wear.'

'You'd look smashing in nothing,' he brayed nervously. 'See you Friday and bring William. Nanny's looking forward to seeing him.'

Harriet replaced the receiver very slowly.

'You lucky, lucky thing,' said Sammy.

'I'm sure Cory won't like it. He'll think I'm trying to cramp his style,' said Harriet. 'But Billy was so sweet about William.'

'Oh they're used to illegits in that family. Billy's sister's had two at least. Half of their ancestors have been born on the wrong side of the duvet. Now throw that photograph of Simon away,' she went on, 'and make a fresh start. Billy's lovely and stinking rich, and faint heart never won fair chinless wonder.'

'I've got nothing to wear,' said Harriet.

'I've got just the thing,' said Sammy. 'A fantastically long slinky orange dress I bought last year, in the hope that I might lose weight and get into it. I didn't, but it would look sensational on you.'

The noises above became wilder.

'I'd better go and turn the hot water up,' said Harriet. 'Cory'll go spare if he doesn't get a decent bath when he gets home.'

She couldn't bring herself to tell Cory she was going to the Hunt Ball. She washed and starched his dress shirt and brought the red tail coat with grey facings back from the cleaners and tried on Sammy's orange dress which became her absurdly well. But as the day grew nearer she put off telling him, because he was too abstracted to bother, or because he was in such a good mood and she didn't want to spoil it, or in a bad mood which she didn't want to make any worse.

On the pretext of buying Chattie tights, she went into

Skipton and found a flame-coloured boa to cover up some of the lack of dress. She failed, on the other hand, to find a bra to wear under it.

'Go without,' said Sammy. 'Live a little.'

'I'll fall out when I dance — if anyone asks me to.'

She spent the day of the ball surreptitiously getting herself ready, as she knew with putting the children to bed there wouldn't be much time later. She painted her nails and washed her hair, and put on a headscarf so it dried smooth. She was peeling chips for the children's tea when Cory came into the kitchen, carrying a couple of shirts.

'Don't do any more work, Daddy,' said Chattie, seizing his hand.

He opened the washing-machine door and was just about to throw the shirts in, when instead he drew out an old bunch of daffodils:

'Planning to wash these?'

'Oh dear, I'm getting so vague. I meant to put them down the waste disposal,' said Harriet.

'I suppose you also mean to put those chips down the waste disposal and the peelings into the pan?' he said. 'And why are you wearing a headscarf? Are you feeling all right?'

'Fine. Do you want a cup of tea?' said Harriet nervously.

'I want something stronger,' said Cory, pouring himself a large whisky.

'You ought to eat something,' said Harriet.

'I know, but I'll be eating again in an hour or two.' He cut a slice of pork from the joint, covered it in chili pickle, put it between two slices of bread and settled down with the evening paper. His eating habits drove her to despair.

Chattie scrambled on to his knee.

'Are you going out tonight?'

'Yes.'

'To the Ball? Will you take me?'

'No.'

'Are you going to dance with Harriet?' she went on, ignoring Harriet's agonized signals. 'She's going to wear an orange dress which shows all her bosoms.'

131

'Don't talk rubbish,' said Cory.

'She is,' said Chattie. 'Sammy lent it to her.'

He turned to Harriet.

'Is this true?' he said sharply.

She nodded, blushing, grating cheese so frenziedly over the cauliflower that she cut one of her fingers.

'Who's taking you?'

'Billy Bentley,' she said, sucking her finger.

'Didn't know you knew him.'

'I met him at Arabella's party, and at the meet.'

'I see. Who's looking after William and the children?'

'Well it is my night off, and Mrs. Bottomley said she'd baby sit, but if that's difficult Billy says their old Nanny can look after William.'

'Billy seems to have displayed more initiative than usual,' said Cory. 'Where are you having dinner?'

'With his parents.'

'You'll be poisoned before you get to the ball. They've got the worst cook in the West Riding.'

And he stalked out of the room, leaving the half-eaten pork sandwich and the glass of whisky. Harriet wondered if she should go after him and apologize. But what was there to apologize for, except she hadn't told him? It was entirely up to her what she did on her evenings off. Perhaps he didn't like downstairs mixing with his upstairs friends. Oh, why had she agreed to go?

She was getting ready, sitting in front of her looking glass, just wearing a pair of pants, when there was a knock on the door. She grabbed a towel; it was Cory. His dark hair sleeked down, wearing his red tail coat with the grey facings and black trousers.

'You do look nice,' she stammered. Privately she thought he looked stunning.

Cory shrugged. 'I'll have champagne poured over it before the night's out. Can you cut the nails on my right hand?'

As she bent over his hand, her hair in Carmen rollers tied up with a scarf, keeping the towel up with her elbows, her hand shook so much, she was frightened she'd cut him.

132

'You can leave William here,' he said. 'I've cleared it with Mrs. Bottomley.'

'You're sure you don't mind?'

'Been monopolizing you too much myself lately. Do you good to get out.'

'Yes,' she said, trying to sound more enthusiastic.

He glanced round the room. 'The light's terrible in here. Go and make up in Noel's room. I must go. I'm invited for eight. If any of the young bloods start pestering you, give me a shout.'

The mirrors in Noel's room showed her from every angle. It's like a Hollywood set, she thought, all those pink roses and ruffles. It's a mistress's room not a wife's, and quite wrong expecting Cory to sleep in it, like putting a wolf-hound in a diamante studded collar and a tartan coat. And how extraordinary to have so many photographs of oneself looking down from the walls: Noel sunbathing topless, Noel receiving a screen award, Noel arriving at a première smothered in ermine, Noel laughing, with Chattie, Jonah and Tadpole gazing up adoringly. That one hurt Harriet most of all. Trust Tadpole to suck up, she thought. Sevenoaks would be more discriminating.

She gazed in the mirror. She looked small and defence-less. She'd been rubbing olive oil into her eyelashes for at least a week now, and they didn't seem any longer. If only she could be a thousandth as beautiful as Noel tonight. The orange dress slithered over her head — it really was low; she took out the rollers and brushed her hair until it shone and stood back, for once pleased with her appearance.

She took the hair out of her brush, opened the window and threw it out; it promptly blew back again. Time was running out. Hastily she loaded up her evening bag, break-ing her comb to get it inside. Pinching some of Noel's loose powder to fill the little gold compact her parents had given her for her sixteenth birthday she wondered when she would ever see them again. Her sudden overwhelming wave of homesickness was only interrupted by the door bell.

133

CHAPTER SEVENTEEN

Dinner was much less alarming than she expected. Billy's parents were friendly in a bluff horsey sort of way, and even though there were twenty for dinner — mostly hunting types — they were much less glamorous and bitchy than the people at Arabella's party. There was only one really pretty woman there, a Mrs. Willoughby who had red hair and sparkling green eyes like a little cat.

Harriet sat between the joint-master and Billy's Uncle Bertie, who squeezed her thigh absent-mindedly and flirted with her in a gentle way.

The food, as Cory predicted, was disgusting. Fortunately a Jack Russell with beseeching eyes sat under the table and wolfed all her fish. The second course, Coq au Vin, was full of soot and quite inedible. Harriet toyed with hers for a bit then, when a maid came round with a large bowl full of bones, thankfully threw her chicken pieces in too. It was only when the maid moved on to Billy's Uncle Bertie on Harriet's right, who immediately picked up Harriet's bits and put them on his plate, that she realized with horror that the maid was handing round second helpings.

She also put up another black after dinner when the women were drinking coffee. 'Have you lived here long?' she said to Billy's mother, during a pause.

'Well quite a long time,' said Mrs. Bentley.

'About five hundred years,' whispered Mrs. Willoughby, out of the corner of her mouth.

Fortunately the wine had been orbiting the table pretty fast at dinner and everyone laughed.

Nice car, thought Harriet, as Billy's Ferrari roared along the narrow roads. She snuggled down under the fur rug. Perhaps it was its coating of dog hairs that made it so warm.

'Do you ride?' said Billy.

'No, I'm afraid I don't. I get taken for one occasionally,' said Harriet.

'You'd look super on a horse. I could teach you very quickly.'

'Do you really think you could?'

'We've got an old pony of my sister's. It taught us all to ride. It's as quiet as anything. Soon get you going on that.'

She'd soon be talking about running martingales with Arabella!

Billy swung the car between a huge pair of gates. Sneering lions reared up on pillars on either side; the curtains flickered in the lodge window as they went by. Ahead the big house was blazing with lights, floodlighting illuminated the blond walls. Drink had done nothing to still the butterflies in Harriet's stomach.

The car park was a quagmire from the recent rain.

'Up to my fucking hocks in mud,' bellowed a hunting lady in disgust, holding her dress above muscly knees. The wind plastered Harriet's feather boa against her lipstick.

She left her coat on a huge four-poster, it's rose pink brocade tattered with age. In the distance she could hear the sensual throb of the music. It was almost eleven; the ball was in full swing. Pale-shouldered women crowded in front of the gilt-framed looking glass, putting on scarlet lipstick and slapping powder over flushed-from-dinner faces.

The frayed banners hanging from the walls shivered in the heat; a pair of huge, blue chandeliers hung from the ceiling. On the landing a group of women laughed loudly. Elizabeth Pemberton in hyacinth blue was one of them. As Harriet went downstairs, clutching the curved banisters for support, she breathed in the sweet heady scent of a huge tub of pink hyacinths.

Billy was standing looking distinguished under some antlers. 'You're easily the prettiest girl in the room,' he said, taking her hand. Beyond lay the ballroom brilliantly lit. On tables round the walls champagne was plunged into ice

135

buckets. The Master's wife, heavily corsetted, stood in the door distributing largesse. The band had stopped; couples were drifting off the floor. There was Arabella her face looking glamorously suntanned for once against a floating white dress; and Charles Mander leaving his hand lingeringly on the bare back of a fast-looking beauty. She couldn't see Cory anywhere.

Harriet was instantly conscious that Billy was regarded as somebody. Seeing her with him lots of people who'd ignored her at Arabella's party said 'Hullo', and were obviously trying to remember where they'd seen her before. Billy found their table and the rest of the dinner party near the band, and after knocking back a few more glasses of champagne, asked Harriet to dance.

Surreptitiously Harriet was still searching everywhere for Cory. Then, as they reached the far end of the ballroom, suddenly she saw him and felt an absolute explosion of jealousy. He was talking to a beautiful, slightly ravaged looking woman with greeny gold hair, slanting eyes, high cheek bones and a beautiful green silk dress worn off one shoulder. That must be Melanie. She had the kind of mystery and sophistication that made Harriet feel as raw as a broken egg.

'Hullo Harriet,' said Elizabeth, who was sitting at the same table. 'Sammy's dress *does* suit you. Harriet's terrifyingly thick with my nanny,' she added to the ferret-faced man in a red coat sitting beside her. 'One shudders to think what they tell each other about us.'

Cory looked up suddenly and noticed them.

'Hullo, Cory,' shouted Billy, waggling his arms and legs so vigorously in time to the music that his mousy locks fell over his pink forehead. 'I'm taking good care of her,' he brayed with laughter.

'I'm sure you are, Billy,' said Cory, giving them both a rather wintry smile. He turned back to Melanie.

Harriet felt a great stab of disappointment. Suddenly she knew all the scenting and curling and orange dress had been directed at Cory, and he'd hardly glanced at her.

The ball grew more raucous. Young men were trying to lob ice cubes down the front of girls' dresses. In the kitchen a group were engaged in feeding a long string of cocktail sausages down the waste disposal, with shrieks of laughter. Harriet had danced with nearly everyone in the party, and drunk nearly a bottle of champagne, which only deepened her despair. Billy was doing his duty dance with his aunt. Mrs. Willoughby was as usual dancing out of her party. Everyone else was on the floor, except Harriet and two men in red coats who sat with their backs to her discussing a day out with the Quorn. Harriet tried to put on an animated 'I am-just-waiting-for-my-partner-to-return' sort of face. She was terrified Cory would see her being a wallflower. Billy's mother stopped at the table and whispered to one of the men in a red coat. He turned and looked at Harriet. 'Of course,' he said, in a long-suffering voice. 'May I have the pleasure of this dance?'

Harriet was so humiliated, she got all hot and flustered and said sorry each time he tripped over her feet. He never apologized at all. There was Cory dancing again with the beautiful Melanie. Oh God, don't let him fancy her too much.

The ball became wilder; upstairs the cordoned-off bedrooms were heaving with occupants. After a trip to the Ladies, Harriet saw Mrs. Willoughby emerge from a side-room, patting her hair, with Elizabeth Pemberton's husband, Michael. During a break between dances, a drunk poured a whole bottle of champagne over his wife, and then, picking up another, started to water the rest of his party. Two men in dinner jackets carried him bellowing out of the ballroom, his legs wriggling like a sheep about to be dipped.

Harriet was well on her way down a second bottle. She felt very above ground now and cannoned into several chairs when Billy asked her to dance.

'I've got you under my skin,' played the band.

I've got you under my lack of chin, thought Harriet and giggled, as Billy pressed her to his chest. Cory was dancing with Melanie yet again, her face pale and dreamy against his scarlet coat. They looked so beautiful together, quite separate from anyone else in the room. Harriet felt the music

137

and longing eating into her soul.

'He will not always say, what you would have him say, but now and then he'll say something wonderful,' played the band.

Harriet and Billy were passing Cory and Melanie now. Harriet looked up, and suddenly her eyes met Cory's and she found she couldn't tear them away. On and on they stared at each other, as the colour mounted in her cheeks.

Billy looked down at her, as though he could feel the current.

'Hey,' he said, 'are you still with me?'

'I'd like a drink,' muttered Harriet. She felt jolted and uneasy; her heart was thumping. She was just gulping down a second glass, when a soft voice said, 'Would you spare a dance for an old fogey?'

She turned expectantly. It was Charles Mander, his face flushed, his cheeks veined with red. It was twenty to two, only a few minutes and they'd all be posthorn galloping. Suddenly she wanted to dance so badly with Cory, she nearly wept.

The next minute she was being mauled to bits on the floor. The tempo was very slow now and Charles was breathing down her neck, peering down the front of her dress, one warm hand wandering over her back and neck, the other which was holding her hand, nudging continually at her breast.

How could Noel have ever fancied him, thought Harriet. The music stopped.

'Not letting you go so easily,' said Charles.

'I must get back to my party,' said Harriet desperately and, wriggling away, went slap into Cory.

'My turn, I think Charles,' he said.

And, joyfully, she melted into his arms. She was conscious of his height and strength, and in spite of being very drunk now, she tried to make herself as light as possible.

'Have you had a nice time?' he said.

She nodded, not trusting herself to speak.

He's my boss, she thought, and he loves Noel; but she felt herself curling round him like bindweed, lust leaping in her like a salmon.

Suddenly the contact of his body became unbearable; she lost her step. The music stopped to desultory clapping; several young men were galloping about the floor, kicking up their legs and uttering hunting cries. Across the room she saw Elizabeth Pemberton beckon imperiously to Billy and nod in their direction. Cory, however, held firmly on to her hand; perhaps after all he wanted her to stay. The band started up again. Reprieve, reprieve! Harriet's self-control went to the winds. She put both her arms round Cory's neck and smiled up at him.

'I've been wanting to dance with you all evening,' she said.

He laughed. 'You're pissed out of your mind.'

'Am I really?' she giggled, nestling against him. 'I've enjoyed myself.'

'Clinging to Charles Mander like a limpet?' said Cory.

'You mustn't have a hang-up about him,' said Harriet.

'I have not,' said Cory, extremely tartly.

'He's attractive, but not a millionth millionth as attractive as you.'

Melanie danced by with Michael Pemberton, trying to catch Cory's eye with a do-you-need-rescuing expression on her face.

Harriet glanced at her.

'She's not the answer for you either,' she said.

Cory raised his eyebrows.

'Since when did I give you permission to dictate my sex life?'

'Only tonight. I could supervise the whole world's sex life tonight. Sammy says she doesn't look nearly as hot first thing in the morning, and she'd got awful legs, and she asked Sammy to put a hot water bottle in her bed tonight, so she can't be expecting to give you her all this evening.'

'The nanny mafia' sighed Cory. 'You spend far too much time gossiping to Sammy.'

'Sammy says Melanie's marriage broke up because she didn't like sex. Anyway she's too old for you.'

'She's four years younger than me.'

I know. But she's too old inside. You need someone young and silly to stop you looking so sad.'

Her foot caught in her hem, and she stumbled and fell against him. His grip tightened on her; he laid his cheek against her hair.

'You talk a lot of nonsense,' he said. 'And you're going to feel terrible in the morning.'

'It's not morning yet,' said Harriet dreamily. 'It was the nightingale and not the lark that pierced the fearful hollows of thine ear.'

Suddenly there was a tantivy of hunting horns and view halloos, the sober fox trot tempo quickened, and broke into D'Ye Ken John Peel.

'Oh Christ,' said Cory, as a whooping line came thundering towards them.

What a noise of galloping feet! Harriet could feel the boards heaving as they rushed round the floor, one cavalry charge after another gathering up couples still trying to dance like fish in a net. With Cory protecting her from the scrimmage, Harriet was loving every minute, her cheeks flushed, dark hair flying.

Round and round they went until she was quite breathless. Suddenly they all slithered to a halt, stopped like statues, while the band played God Save the Queen. Just in front of them Charles Mander was patting Mrs. Willoughby's bottom while Mrs Mander snored peacefully in a chair with her mouth open. Harriet found her fingers curling in and out of Cory's, and looking up saw Elizabeth Pemberton glaring in their direction.

The band stopped. A fat woman executed a pirouette and collapsed on the floor with cackles of laughter.

Harriet watched fascinated.

'At least I'm not as drunk as her.'

'Nor are you going to be allowed to be,' said Cory firmly. Picking up Harriet's bag which was lying on the table, he extracted the cloakroom ticket and handed it to Mrs. Willoughby who was on her way upstairs.

'Annie, be an angel and get Harriet's coat while you're up there. She's much too slewed to find anything.'

Billy Bentley arrived, braying nervously.

'We got lorst,' he said.

'This child has had far too much to drink,' said Cory sternly.

''Fraid she hash; entirely my fault; take her home at onshe.'

'You're as bad as she is,' said Cory, dropping his cigarette into a discarded plate of fruit salad. 'Neither of you is in a fit state. Give her a ring in the morning, but for God's sake get someone to drive you home.'

'Or you might go slap into a tree along the Fairmile,' said Harriet and laughed.

Elizabeth came up to them. 'You're coming back for a drink, aren't you, Cory?'

Cory said he had to take Harriet home.

'Billy can take her,' said Elizabeth.

'Far too drunk.'

'Michael can run her back then.'

Harriet frantically pressed Cory's hand.

'He's too drunk too,' he said. 'It's late, and she *is* my responsibility.'

'I am, I am,' agreed Harriet, beaming.

'Thanks, Annie,' said Cory taking her coat from Mrs. Willoughby. 'I feel I ought to tip you.'

'I'd much rather have a kiss,' said Mrs. Willoughby, her eyes gleaming. 'You and Harriet,' she shot a sly glance at Elizabeth, 'must both come to dinner.'

Harriet had never seen anyone so cross as Elizabeth Pemberton.

Outside the rain had stopped; the clouds had rolled back like a blind on a clear starry night.

'Damn,' said Cory, going up to his car. 'I've left the lights on; the battery's flat.'

'As flat as Elizabeth Pemberton's chest,' said Harriet. Really she was behaving very badly; she must get a grip on herself.

'Having trouble?' It was Harry Mytton, one of the red-faced stalwarts in the Bentleys' party. Out of the corner of her eye, Harriet saw Elizabeth and her party bearing down on them.

'Quick,' she whispered.

'Battery's flat,' said Cory. 'Can you give us a lift? The garage can come and get it in the morning.'

Harriet leapt into the car as quick as a dog thinking it might be left behind. She found she was sitting on two riding crops and a dog lead. There was a sticker for the Aylesford point-to-point in the back window.

As the headlights lit up the bracken and the trailing traveller's joy, she was achingly conscious of Cory sitting beside her in the back. Mrs. Mytton discussed one of the drunks in their party.

'Kept a pack in some unlikely place like Haslemere,' said Harry Mytton. The huge stars seemed to be crowding in on them as they drove along the winding road. Harriet kept being thrown against Cory.

'Annie Willoughby's a damned attractive woman,' said Harry Mytton, 'magnificent woman across country you know.'

'She can even keep potted plants alive,' said Mrs. Mytton.

Another corner, another lurch across the back of the car. This time Harriet didn't bother to move away, nuzzling up to Cory like a puppy. Her head kept flopping forward. In the end Cory turned her over, so she lay with her head in his lap, and stroked her gently behind the ears, almost as he might have petted Tadpole or one of the children.

Looking up she could see the lean line of his jaw, above the white tie. Behind his head, out of the back window, Orion glittered in a sooty, black sky. Now he disappeared, now he appeared again as the car swung round the bends.

'What did Orion do?' she said sleepily.

'He was a mighty hunter who died of a scorpion sting,' said Cory. 'After boasting he'd rid the world of wild beasts. Then Zeus put him in the sky.'

'Who was that, Cory?' said Harry Mytton. 'Didn't he used to hunt with the York and Ainsty?'

Cory's lips twitched. Harriet started to giggle. He put his hand over her mouth. She started to kiss it. He shook his head, smoothing her hair back from her forehead.

Orion was moving back and forth again. Following his progress, Harriet suddenly began to feel very odd. She shut her eyes. Everything went round and round. She sat bolt upright.

'What's the matter?' asked Cory.

'I feel sick.'

'Serves you bloody well right.' Cory wound down the window, and shoved her head out. Icy blasts of cold made her feel better, but it was a relief when Harry Mytton turned into the Wilderness drive.

The owls were hooting in the garden. Mrs. Bottomley's thermos of cocoa was waiting for them in the kitchen. Cory unscrewed it and poured it down the sink.

'Don't want to upset the old girl.' he said.

Harriet fled upstairs, put on more scent and cleaned her teeth. Then, thinking Cory might smell the toothpaste and think she was trying too hard, rinsed her mouth out again. Then she turned off her electric blanket.

'Careful, Harriet, careful,' said her reflection in the mirror. 'This kind of behaviour got you into trouble before.'

Down in the drawing-room Cory had taken off his coat and tie and stood in front of a dying fire nursing a glass of whisky.

Harriet curled up on the sofa, watching the light from one lamp fall on the bowed heads of a pot of white cyclamen.

The telephone rang. Cory picked it up.

'No it's very kind, Elizabeth, but I'm absolutely knackered. Thank you for a tremendous evening.' There was a pause. 'As to that, I don't think it's any of your bloody business. Goodnight.' And he dropped the receiver back on the hook.

'Interfering bitch,' he said.

Harriet giggled. 'I bet she said, "That child's been hurt enough".'

Cory looked startled, then he laughed. 'That's exactly what she did say.'

For a minute he looked out over the silent valley, then he drew the curtains, stubbed out his cigarette and came towards her. Then he held out his arms, and she went into them like a bird out of the storm. As he kissed her she could feel the currents of excitement coursing over her. God, this is absolute dynamite, she thought, as her hands crept around his neck, her fingers twining into the thick black hair.

Suddenly the telephone rang.

'Leave it,' said Cory, his hold tightening.

'It might be important,' murmured Harriet.

'Can't be.'

'I'll get it. It might wake Mrs. Bottomley and we don't want that,' said Harriet, giggling. 'I'll say you're in a meeting.'

She picked up the receiver. She could hear the pips.

'It's long distance for you from America.'

'I expect it's MGM about the treatment,' he said, taking the receiver from her.

Suddenly the colour drained from his face. Someone must have died. She could see the knuckles white where his hand clutched the receiver. The conversation was very brief. Harriet collapsed on to the sofa. She had a premonition that something very terrible was about to happen to her. She looked at Cory and suddenly had a vision of pulling a wounded man up to the edge of a cliff, then finally letting him go so his body circled round and round as he splattered on the rocks below. Cory put down the receiver and reached automatically for a cigarette.

'That was Noel,' he said. 'She's finished filming and she's flying back to England tomorrow. She and Ronnie Acland are coming North next week. She wants to see the children so they're coming over for lunch on Wednesday.'

'But she can't,' gasped Harriet. 'It'll crucify you. She can't go round playing fast and loose with other people's lives.'

Cory glared at her, his face grey. He seemed to have aged ten years. The last hour might never have happened.

'They're her children as much as mine,' he snapped.

Harriet stepped back as though he'd hit her, giving a whimper of anguish.

'And don't stare at me with those great eyes of yours,' he said brutally. 'If Noel and I choose to behave in a civilized manner, it's nothing to do with you. You'd better go to bed.'

Harriet heard the cocks crowing. She looked at the photograph by the bed. She couldn't even be loyal to Simon's memory. Cory was a different generation; his world was in ruins; he merely regarded her as a diversion, because he was a bit tight and she was available.

Her mind raced round seeking comfort, but she found none. She saw her dishevelled clothes in the bedroom, the unstoppered make-up, the cellophane pack which had contained her new tights. She remembered the excitement with which she'd dressed. She'd been so sure, she'd even turned off her electric blanket. She crept between the sheets and shivered until dawn.

CHAPTER EIGHTEEN

As Wednesday approached Cory grew more and more impossible, snapping at Mrs. Bottomley, the children and, most of all, at Harriet.

On Tuesday night he was going to a dinner in Leeds and asked Harriet to iron a white dress shirt for him. She took considerable pains over it but, unfortunatdy, Ambrose, who had been looking for mice in the coal hole, walked all over it when she wasn't looking.

Cory hit the roof. 'Can't you ever concentrate on one thing for more than five minutes?'

Harriet lost her temper. She had been cooking all day for tomorrow's lunch and she had a headache.

'If you didn't make people so nervous, they might stop making a hash of things.'

'Go on!' he said glaring at her.

'I don't mind you shouting at me. But I don't see why you should take it out on Mrs. Bottomley and the children. It's not their fault your rotten wife's turning up tomorrow.'

Oh, God, she thought, as his face twisted with rage, I've really put my foot in it now.

'It would be as well if you remembered whose house this is, and who pays your salary!' he said, stalking out of the room.

Half-an-hour later she heard the front door bang and his car drive off with a whirring sound of gravel.

Gibbering with rage, Harriet ate a large piece of walnut cake, and then another piece, and was just embarking on a third, when she heard a step and nearly jumped out of her skin as two hands grabbed her round the waist and a familiar voice said, 'Guess who?'

Leaping away, choking over the walnut cake, she swung round and looked up through streaming eyes into a handsome, decadent face. There was something familiar about the dark eyes, which were now narrowed to slits with laughter.

'Hullo, darling,' he said. 'I'm Kit Erskine.'

'Goodness, you surprised me.'

'Oh, I'm full of surprises. Where's Cory?'

'Out, gone to Leeds.'

'That's good. We're alone at last.'

'Mrs. Bottomley's upstairs,' said Harriet hastily, backing away.

'How is old Botters?'

'On the scurry — sweeping under carpets. Mrs. Erskine and Ronnie Acland are coming to lunch tomorrow, so there's a lot to do.'

Kit whistled. 'They are? What a carve-up. That cake looks good.' He cut himself a large piece. 'I'm starving. Where shall we have dinner?'

'I can't,' said Harriet. 'I've got to . . .'

'Wash your hair,' said Kit. 'Don't worry. You can give Noel a good ten years.'

At that moment Mrs. Bottomley walked in with a feather duster.

'Master Kit!' she squeaked. 'Whatever are you doing here?'

'Botters! Darling!' He gathered her up as though she were light as a feather, and carried her round the room.

'Put me down, Master Kit!' she protested, half laughing, her legs going like a centipede.

The kitchen was large, but with Kit's arrival, it seemed to shrink. He polished off three double whiskies and most of the walnut cake, and exchanged gossip with Mrs. Bottomley, but all the time his eyes were wandering lazily over Harriet.

She tried to decorate a pudding for tomorrow, but found, in her nervousness, she was decorating far more of the table.

Kit picked up a handful of crystallized violets and scattered them higgledy piggledy on the top of the mousse.

'It's got to look nice for Mrs. Erskine,' wailed Harriet.

'No one bothers about her,' said Kit. 'You should have the courage of your confections.'

'How's Cory?' he asked Mrs. Bottomley.

'I've never known him as bad as this,' said Mrs Bottomley disapprovingly. 'I made that walnut cake this morning. You know it's his favourite and he wouldo't touch it. Like a bear with a sore head. Ever since he heard she was bringing that Ronald Acland. What's he like? He looks a smart fellow.'

'Ronnie Acland? Well, he calls himself an actor but, frankly, I wouldn't have him on my side playing charades. But his father is dying, which means any moment dear Ronnie will become Lord Acland, and that's what Noel finds attractive. She's spent all her life waiting for Lord Right to come along.'

Harriet giggled. You couldn't help liking Kit. Kit sensed weakness. 'I say Botters . . .'

'Don't call me that. It's rude.'

'Will you baby-sit so I can take Harriet out to dinner?'

Mrs. Bottomley looked dubious. 'She needs a break. Mr. Cory's been nagging her terrible but he won't like you both swanning off the moment his back's turned.'

'He won't know. I'll get her back early. Please, darling Botters?'

'Well, if I weren't fumigating with Mr Cory, I wouldn't do it.'

Kit took Harriet to a small dimly-lit club where they both talked and drank a great deal.

Kit shook his head. 'So Noel's really coming tomorrow. I suppose Botters told you Noel and I once had a walk-out.'

'It sounded more like a stay-in to me,' said Harriet.

Kit grinned. 'So the kitten had claws, after all. The odd thing is that Cory's never held it against me. "How can I blame you," he said to me afterwards, "when I'm incapable of resisting her myself".'

'Oh poor Cory,' said Harriet. 'Why doesn't he find some-one else? He's so attractive.'

'He's bewitched,' said Kit. 'He's burnt himself out in the idiotic hope that one day, after a year, maybe five years, ten years, a lifetime, he'll suddenly crack the rock, and conquer that shallow, dried-up heart.'

'I hate her,' Kit went on savagely, 'for her damn narcissism, and yet when you first meet her she's so dazzling, you can't see anything else. It's like looking straight into the sun. Anyway.' He stretched his legs so one of them brushed against Harriet's. 'Enough of other people's worries. What about yours? What made you keep the baby? Hung up on the father are you?'

'Yes — I suppose I still am.' She flaming well wasn't going to tell him anything about Cory.

Kit took her hand. 'I'm realistic about love. What's the point of eating your heart out for someone who doesn't love you? The answer is to find an adequate substitute.'

'Yes?' said Harriet, taking her hand away. 'And where do I find that?'

'Right here, darling. What could be more adequate than me?'

Harriet looked at him. Yes, he was adequate all right. Everything about him, the deep, expensive voice, the sexy eyes, the mocking mouth, the thick blond hair, the broad, flat shoulders, the long muscular thighs one of which was rubbing against hers again.

'I think we'd better go home,' said Harriet.

He stopped the car halfway up the drive and switched off the engine. Suddenly he reached forward and took hold of the ribbon tying back her hair.

'Don't touch me,' she spat, springing away.

'My, but you're jumpy,' he said, pulling off the ribbon, so her hair rippled down thickly over her shoulders.

'That's better,' he said. 'You must stop hiding the fact that you're a very attractive girl.'

'I don't want to attract men,' she said in a frozen voice.

'Listen, darling, you've had a bad knock, but it's like falling off a horse. The longer you take to ride again, the more difficult you're going to find it.'

Bending his head, he kissed her very gently on the lips.

'There,' he said, as though he were soothing a frightened animal. 'Not so bad, was it?'

Not bad at all, thought Harriet. Very pleasant, in fact. And

149

when he kissed her again, she kissed him back.

'God,' he whispered, 'We're going to be great together.'

He opened his fur coat and pulled her inside, so she could feel the length of his hard muscular body against her.

Oh dear, oh dear, she thought. Here I go again. I mustn't be so loose.

'Come on,' he said softly. 'Relax, I'm not silly enough to let you get pregnant again.'

Pregnant. If he had jabbed a branding iron on her back, nothing could have brought her to her senses more quickly. Panic stricken, she wrenched herself away from him, opened the car door, and tore up the drive.

'Hey, wait a minute!' She heard Kit laughing behind her. 'Take it easy, darling. Don't be in such a hurry to get me into bed.'

Panting, she pushed open the front door, and fled into the house, slap into Cory.

'Harriet! Thank God you're back. Are you all right?'

Her hands shot to her face, rubbing mascara from beneath her eyes, smoothing her hair, tucking in her shirt.

'I'm fine,' she stammered. 'I've been having a drink with Kit.'

'You've been out with Kit?' The voice changed, became so brutally icy that Harriet drew back as though she'd been struck. For a second she saw the blaze of contempt in his eyes, as he took in her dishevelled condition, then the shutters came down, and his face resumed it's normal deadpan expression.

'I might have guessed you'd run true to type,' he said. 'William's been yelling his guts out for the past hour. If you can't have a more responsible attitude towards the children, you'd better pack your bags and get out in the morning!'

For a minute Harriet gazed at Cory appalled. Then she jumped as a voice behind her said, 'Do I hear the sound of high words?' and Kit wandered through the front door, straightening his tie, and ostentatiously wiping lipstick off his face.

'Hullo, Cory,' he went on. 'You look a bit peaky, my dear. What you need is a few late nights.'

150

Harriet didn't wait for Cory's reply. She fled upstairs, scalded by remorse and humiliation. Surely he couldn't sack her for something so trivial.

She found William scarlet in the face, his eyes piggy from crying for so long.

'I'm sorry, darling, so sorry,' she whispered, as she picked him up and cuddled him. Gradually his sobs subsided and, as she waited for his bottle to heat up, she shivered with terror at the thought of the future — bleak, salary-less, with no Chattie and Jonah, no Cory even when he was being nice. In just a few weeks, she thought miserably, I've come to regard this rambling house as home.

As she gave William his bottle, however, there was a knock on the door. It was Cory.

'Don't get up,' he said, looking at William. 'Is he all right?'

'He's fine,' stammered Harriet. 'I'm sorry about going out.'

'It wasn't a very good idea going out with Kit. He's only interested in easy lays — and that's the last thing you need.'

Harriet hung her head. 'Then you don't hate me?'

Cory smiled faintly. 'When my horses do stupid wilful things, I beat the hell out of them. It doesn't mean I love them any the less.'

'Then you w-won't send me away?'

Cory shook his head. 'The children would be desolated. Anyway, it's me who ought to apologize, I've behaved like a bastard the past few days.'

He picked up Simon's photograph by Harriet's bed.

'I've been so bound up in my own private hell. I've been impervious to anyone else's. Poor little Harriet.' He touched her cheek gently with his hand. 'Do you still miss him so much?'

Harriet flushed

'Yes . . . no, I don't know. Why don't you tell your wife not to come tomorrow? It's not too late,' she blurted out.

'I've got to see her and Ronnie Acland together some time,' he said, going towards the door.

In the doorway, he paused and turned. 'And please tie your hair back again when Noel comes tomorrow. You look

151

far too pretty like that, and I don't want her to start cross-petitioning.'

The moment he'd gone, Harriet, carrying a protesting William, raced to the mirror. He'd called her pretty. Cory had actually called her far too pretty! He'd never paid her a compliment before. She put her hand to her face where Cory had touched it, and just for a second wondered what it would be like to be loved by him, to see the haughty, inscrutable face, miraculously softened, to hear the detached voice, for once passionate and tender. Then the great shadowy owl of shame at her own presumption swooped down to overwhelm her.

Even so, after she had put William to bed, she washed her hair, and was just drying it, when a note was thrust under the door.

On it was written ten times in huge childish scrawl: 'I must not try and seduce Harriet.' Then the writer had reverted to normal handwriting. 'Darling Harriet, Cory wants me to write this line a thousand times, but my hand is aching and I want to go to bed. So please forgive me. Love, Kit.'

Harriet giggled. You couldn't be angry with Kit for long.

CHAPTER NINETEEN

Noel and Ronnie Acland arrived at least an hour late the next day, by which time the children were frenzied with frustrated excitement, and Harriet had run upstairs at least a dozen times, to re-tie her ribbon and powder her nose.

But when she saw the figure smothered in squashy blond furs getting out of a large Rolls-Royce, she realized that her efforts had been to no avail. For Noel Balfour was undoubtedly the most beautiful woman she had ever seen. She had a gold, breath-taking, erupting beauty, and she swooped down on the family with a rasping cry of love like a bird of paradise.

'Cory, darling, you've lost far too much weight! Chattie, baby, what a beautiful dress! Jonah, my angel, how tall and handsome you've grown!'

When Harriet had recovered from the shock, she made out that Noel's face was thin and oval, her skin of a thick magnolia creaminess, her eyes tawny, clear and restless, and the impression of gold came from her marvellous mane of hair. She was tall — almost as tall as Cory — but her body was as supple as silk. Underneath her furs, she wore a saffron wool dress which clung to every curve.

As soon as she had hugged the children, she turned her dazzling smile on Harriet. 'We're horribly, horribly late. There's no excuse. Well, let's all go and have an enormous drink,' she said, putting her arm through Harriet's. 'I can't tell you how relieved I am you're looking after the children — I've heard such marvellous reports about you. After lunch I want to come and see your little baby, and you must tell me all about yourself.'

Harriet, expecting indifference, hauteur, antagonism,

153

was completely disarmed by such friendliness. In the drawing-room, they found Ronnie Acland talking to Cory about shooting.

Harriet was further surprised to find herself liking Ronnie Acland, who was a tall, handsome, rather florid man in tweeds, with a loud voice and excellent teeth. He seemed to be smiling all the time, probably from embarrassment.

Cory had completely regained his sang-froid. He gave the impression of being slightly bored by this intrusion. Not once did the aloof, unsmiling face betray the turmoil that must have been raging within.

God, he's cool, thought Harriet in admiration. I could never behave like that if I suddenly had to face Simon.

Noel took her drink from Cory, running a caressing finger along his hand as she did so, and then wandered round the room moving ornaments and straightening pictures.

'When did this fire start smoking?' she asked Cory, kicking a log with a blond suede shoe.

At that moment, Kit wandered in, wearing obscenely tight strawberry pink trousers.

For a moment Noel stiffened. She hadn't bargained on Kit.

'Whatever are you doing here?' she said, trying to keep the hostility out of her voice.

Kit stared at her insolently for a minute, then yawned so hard that Harriet thought he was going to dislocate his jaw.

'I'm visiting my brother Cory — your husband, if you remember. And laying siege to this steaming girl,' he said, putting an arm round Harriet's shoulders and kissing her on the cheek. 'But you've put that bloody bow back on again,' he added.

And once again he pulled off the ribbon that tied back Harriet's hair, letting it spill in a dark cloud over her shoulders. Leaving her scarlet with confusion, he turned and smiled at Ronnie Acland.

'We haven't met,' he said amiably, 'but I gather you're going to be Mr. Noel Balfour Number Two. Or is it Three? I can never keep track.'

Harriet escaped to the kitchen to find Mrs. Bottomley red-faced over the duck.

'Whew, it's tense in there,' she said. 'Do you think I have to have lunch with them?'

'Yes,' said Mrs. Bottomley. 'Mr. E'll expect you to keep an eye on the children. She's very hot on manners, Mrs. E.'

'Oh God,' said Harriet. 'By the way, I put some more salt in the soup.'

'So did I,' said Mrs. Bottomley.

Lunch for Harriet was a nightmare. Beneath the idle chatter, the tinkle of glasses, the exclamations of pleasure over the food, the ultra-civilized behaviour, lay the jungle.

She was amazed that these people could act as though nothing was the matter, that they could discuss friends, swap gossip, with such apparent amicability.

Noel never stopped talking — the rich, husky voice flowing on and on, about Paris and parties given in her honour and the film she'd been shooting in Africa, and what the man at Cartier's had said about the ring Ronnie had bought her.

Kit, having downed three large dry Martinis on an empty stomach before lunch, was thoroughly enjoying himself.

'Marvellous soup,' he said to Harriet. 'I always think there are two things a woman should do instinctively. And one of them's cooking!'

Noel took a mouthful and immediately asked for a glass of water.

'That's a soup spoon, not a trowel,' she said sharply to Chattie. 'Why do my children always eat as though they were gardening? I suppose it's the influence of television.'

'What a clever woman you'd have been, Noel, if you'd have been to University,' said Kit.

'I hear you hunt a lot,' said Ronnie hastily to Cory, before Noel could think up a crushing reply.

Her beautiful tawny eyes had taken on a dangerous smouldering look, which increased as Ronnie and Cory got into a discussion about different packs. She obviously didn't like to be out of the limelight for a second. When the duck

155

JILLY COOPER

arrived, she took a mouthful and this time immediately asked for the salt and then rained pepper down on to her plate.

Next moment a diversion was caused by the arrival of Sevenoaks, straight from the stream at the bottom of the garden. He greeted Harriet rapturously and then bounded up to Noel. She drew away from him in horror.

'Where did that dreadful beast come from? Look at the mess he's making on the carpet.'

'It's Harriet's dog,' said Cory.

'He needs a bath,' snapped Noel.

'He needs a psychiatrist,' said Cory.

'Is there any orange salad?' Noel asked Harriet, after Sevenoaks had been forcibly removed.

'Quit upstaging, Noel!' said Kit sharply.

Noel glared at, him, pushed the food to the side of her plate and lit a cigarette.

'Did I tell you I spent a week in Israel last month?' she said to Cory. 'I've never seen anything like the wild flowers around the Sea of Galilee. And I actually saw the place they fed the five thousand.'

'If you'd spurned your fish and loaves the way you've treated Harriet's much more miraculous duck you'd have been excommunicated, darling,' said Kit.

'It's a pity you're not staying longer, Mummy. You won't see Daddy riding in the point-to-point,' said Chattie.

Noel turned her tawny eyes on Cory.

'But, darling, that's wonderful!' she said. 'You're racing again, after all this time! Might you win?'

Cory shook his head. 'Not a chance. She's only a baby, and it's her first race.'

Noel's eyes lit up. 'Do you remember that race you won the day we got home from our honeymoon? Goodness, how excited we were, and how we celebrated.'

'And what appalling hangovers we had the next day,' said Cory dryly.

'Harriet had a hangover this morning,' said Chattie. 'And she always does when Daddy takes her out, too.'

Noel's face hardened. She looked from Cory to Harriet.

156

'Come on, Cory, open another bottle,' said Kit. 'The drink's flowing like concrete.'

'What was that marvellous Beaujolais we had when we dined with Jackie Onassis, the night the Aga Khan was there?' Noel asked Ronnie.

'Pick up those names, darling,' drawled Kit, 'you're not impressing anyone.'

Noel flushed angrily. Ronnie turned to Chattie. 'And what are you going to do when you grow up?' he asked.

Chattie beamed at him. 'I'm not going to get married,' she said. 'I might make a habit of it, like Mummy.'

Kit and Ronnie shouted with laughter. Even Cory grinned.

'Ronnie's a fine one to laugh,' said Noel angrily. 'He's had three wives already!'

'His own or other people's?' said Kit.

Harriet felt depression descending on her. She got up to remove the plates and bring in the pudding. Kit followed her into the kitchen.

'Marvellous party,' he said.

Harriet said nothing.

'Oh, darling, relax, enjoy it. Noel's putting on a command performance.'

'And what about Cory?' said Harriet savagely, clattering plates into the sink.

'You mustn't ever forget that Cory's a writer,' said Kit. 'It's all grist to his mill. This entire lunch will appear in a screen play one day.'

Back in the dining-room, Ronnie Acland was doing his best to keep the conversation going.

'How's the latest script?' he asked Cory.

'It's not,' said Cory.

'I enjoyed your last book,' said Kit, refilling everyone's glasses. 'I came across it in a girlfriend's bedroom, and stayed up all afternoon reading it.'

Cory smiled.

'Harriet makes bloody lovely puddings,' said Chattie dreamily, making rivers of cream in her chocolate mousse. 'If you're going to marry Ronnie, Mummy, why can't Daddy

157

marry Harriet?'

There was a frozen pause, then Kit began to laugh. Harriet knocked her wine glass over.

Cory calmly dipped his napkin in the water jug and started sponging the red stain.

'I don't know where you're intending to stay tonight,' he said to Ronnie Acland, 'but a very good hotel's just opened at Bolton Abbey,' and launched into a dissertation on its merits.

Suddenly, there was a faint wail from upstairs.

'Oh, there's William crying,' said Harriet thankfully, leaping to her feet.

Upstairs, Harriet pressed her burning face against the bedroom window. How could Chattie have said that! In front of Noel, too!

Just as she finished feeding William, there was a knock on the door. To her amazement it was Noel.

'I thought I'd leave the men to their port,' she said. 'What a gorgeous baby. May I hold him?'

'He's very tricky with strangers' said Harriet dubiously.

But Noel had already gathered William up in her arms, and had soon reduced him to fits of uncontrollable giggles, tickling him and giving him butterfty kisses with her long, long eyelashes.

How beautiful she is, thought Harriet enviously.

Suddenly Noel stopped tickling William and turned her huge eyes on Harriet. 'Tell me truthfully — how *is* Cory? Did he mind my coming today?'

Harriet was caught off guard.

'Yes he did. Particularly with you bringing Mr Acland.'

'Oh I know I shouldn't have done that,' said Noel. 'But Cory's so off-hand with me these days and, somehow, I felt I wanted to jolt him. I expect you think I'm wicked, but you've no idea how difficult it was being married ten years to a man who's married to his typewriter. And yet, you know, I don't really find other men lastingly attractive.' Noel went on. 'Every affair I've had has really been an attempt to shake Cory into loving me more.'

'But he adores you!' said Harriet amazed.

'Maybe he does in his fashion — but that didn't stop him switching off for hours on end when he was married to me, bashing out those bloody scripts. And he's horribly arrogant. All the Erskine family are the same. You must admit he's tricky to live with.'

She looked at William who snuggled his head against her. 'I wish they were all as easy to cope with as you,' she sighed. 'If only I could be certain I was doing the right thing divorcing Cory and marrying Ronnie. What do you think I should do?'

'I don't know,' muttered Harriet. She shouldn't talk to me like this, she thought desperately. I don't want to discuss Cory with her.

But Noel hadn't finished turning the screw. 'Do you really think Cory does love me and nobody else?'

Harriet thought for a minute. 'Yes, I do. I think he's being torn in pieces.'

Noel put William down and, smirking slightly, wandered over to Harriet's dressing table. For a minute she examined herself in the mirror, then her eyes lighted on Simon's photograph.

'My, he's pretty. Good God, it's Simon!' She looked at William and, in a flash, put two and two together. 'He's your baby's father?'

Harriet nodded, unable to speak.

'But I know him!' said Noel. 'Very well. He's doing brilliantly. There's even talk of him doing a film with me this summer. And he's this baby's father? Well! Does he know?'

'I wrote to him,' said Harriet.

'Well, he can't have got the letter. He adores children. He's always saying he wants at least ten of his own.'

Harriet's eyes filled with tears. 'Tell me how he is,' she said.

Later, Kit went to sleep on the sofa, Noel and Ronnie took the children out to tea up the valley, Cory shut himself in his study, and Harriet was thankful to be left with the washing-up and her own tangled emotions.

When Noel returned she went into Cory's study, but after

JILLY COOPER

a few minutes came out looking like a thundercloud and went upstairs to change. She and Ronnie were going out to dinner.

Eight-thirty found Ronnie pacing up and down the drawing-room. 'I don't know if Erskine had this trouble with her,' he said to Kit and Harriet, 'but Noel's incapable of getting anywhere on time. Rather embarrassing. We're dining with friends of my father's. Shouldn't keep that generation waiting.'

Kit was eating potato crisps. 'My advice,' he said, 'is to treat her as you would a nasty boy of ten.'

Cory came in and poured himself a drink. He looked absolutely exhausted.

'How's the script going?' asked Kit.

Cory shrugged his shoulders.

'So so. I spent today crossing out most of what I wrote yesterday. I suppose it's good for the wrist.'

'What's good for the wrist?' came a mocking voice, and Noel walked in.

Harriet heard Cory's sharp intake of breath. Ronnie choked over his cigar.

'Christ!' said Kit.

Noel was wearing a transparent black dress. Only her hips were concealed by a thin layer of ostrich feathers. The rest of her body, including the magnificent breasts, gleamed pearly white through the thin, black material. Her blonde hair was piled up on top of her head, diamonds glittering round her throat, in her ears, on her wrists. She looked staggering.

Kit was the first to recover.

'You look just like a picture I saw outside Raymond's Revue Bar the other day. I didn't know you'd gone into cabaret,' he said.

Ronnie Acland looked dazed. 'Very simple friends of my father's we're going to see, Noel, darling. Is it quite the thing, do you think?' Noel just shrugged.

Kit poured himself another drink. 'I shouldn't worry, Ronnie,' he said. 'That generation expect actresses to look unbelievably tarty.'

160

Noel's lips tightened. 'Go and fetch my coat, would you, Ronnie?'

She turned to Cory, who was still standing as if turned to stone.

'What do you think of me, my darling?' she said softly.

Cory walked over and stood in front of her, looking her over very slowly. His hands were clenched, a muscle was leaping in his cheek. Only the ticking of the grandfather clock broke the intolerable silence. Then he put out his hand. 'Goodbye, Noel,' he said.

'You don't really mean that,' she said slowly, her yellow eyes blazing.

'Yes, I do, I do, I do,' he said wearily, as though he was trying to convince himself.

'Come on, darling,' said Ronnie Acland, bustling in and knocking over a small table in his haste to get something more substantial round Noel's body. 'We're embarrassingly late as it is.'

In the hall, Jonah's face was putty-coloured, the tears kept well back. Chattie, in a scarlet dressing-gown, had no such reserve. 'Please don't go, Mummy!' she cried, flinging her arms round Noel's legs and bursting into tears.

'I must go,' said Noel, detaching herself gently. 'Careful, or you'll ladder my tights.'

'Oh, Mummy, Mummy,' whispered the choked little voice. 'I can't bear it. When will you come back?'

'I can't say, bebé. You must make the best of it.'

She didn't say another word to Cory, but as she climbed into the huge Rolls-Royce, she turned to Harriet. 'Goodbye, I'll certainly tell Simon I've seen you.'

Chattie began to howl in earnest as soon as Noel had gone.

'Hush darling,' said Harriet, picking her up. 'You'll see her again soon.'

Cory went into his study and slammed the door behind him.

I wish I could comfort him as easily as Chattie, thought Harriet.

Kit left soon after Noel. He handed her his telephone

161

number and address in London. 'If you get into any diffi-
culties, ring me. I'm worried about Cory, but you're a
warm, lovely girl and I've a feeling you're going to be the
one to get hurt the most.'

Cory refused any supper, and Harriet, feeling exhausted,
went to bed early, but found she couldn't sleep. She tried to
work out exactly what she felt about Simon. But he seemed
to have become a shadowy figure, and her thoughts kept
straying back to Cory, and the hell he must be going
through.

Oh, why can't I fall for straight-forward men who fall in
love with me, she thought miserably.

About midnight, the storm broke. Lightning brighter than
day, followed immediately by great poundings of thunder.
Wandering down the landing to see if the children were all
right, Harriet heard the sound of crying coming from
Jonah's room. She went in and turned on the light.

'It's only thunder, darling,' she said taking him in her
arms. He was such a reserved child that it took several minutes before she discovered it wasn't the storm that was upsetting him. He was sick with misery about Noel and Cory.

'I know it's beastly,' said Harriet. 'Of course, it doesn't
matter a scrap about crying. Everyone cries about things like
this, and you've been terribly brave up till now.'

Jonah gave a sniff. 'You think so?'

'Yes, I do. You're like your father. He's very brave, too.'

'Then why does my mother want to marry that awful
man? What's my father done wrong that my mother doesn't
like him any more?'

'He hasn't done anything wrong. People just stop loving
people sometimes, like you cooling off people you've been
very friendly with the term before at school, and now you
can't see what you saw in them.'

Jonah looked dubious. 'Is it the same?'

'In a way. It happened to me with William's father. I loved
him so much, but he still stopped loving me. But not because I'd done anything wrong.'

'*You* won't go away, will you?' said Jonah.

Harriet shook her head.

'Perhaps you could marry Daddy, like Chattie suggested,' he added hopefully.

'He doesn't want to, and the same thing would probably happen all over again. People should only marry people they love.'

A shadow fell across the bed. Harriet looked up in embarrassment to see Cory standing there.

'Hullo,' said Jonah.

'I'll go and get some hot chocolate to make you sleep,' said Harriet, fleeing from the room. When she got back upstairs, Jonah was nearly asleep.

'Don't go,' he muttered drowsily. 'Both stay, Harriet's not very happy either, Daddy. I think you should look after her.'

Harriet suddenly felt the tears trickling down her cheeks. She sat down on the bed, and turned her face away so Jonah shouldn't see her. Then she felt Cory's hand, warm and dry, over hers.

She didn't move, breathlessly aware of how close he was to her. And she was filled with a brazen, shameless longing to be closer still. She looked away, dumb and stricken, afraid that he might read the lust in her eyes.

'He's asleep,' said Cory.

Harriet got clumsily to her feet and, without speaking went out of the room. Cory caught up with her outside his bedroom, put his hand on her shoulder and pulled her round to face him. The light from the bedroom lit up his face, and Harriet noticed how old and tired he looked suddenly.

Oh, poor, poor Cory, she thought.

'It's so bloody for you,' she said in a choked voice.

'And for you, too,' he said gently and, quite naturally he pulled her into his arms.

'Don't cry, little Harriet.'

She melted.

'Don't cry,' he went on. 'It's crazy to go on like this, when we both need each other. Come on, little one. You'll see, I'll make everything all right for you.'

And Harriet knew with a sudden, blinding intensity of

163

grief how much she loved him.

But I can't take it again, she told herself in panic. It's no good falling again for a man who doesn't love me, who this time, is absolutely mad about someone else.

For a second she trembled violently in his arms, then she moved away.

'It's no good,' she gasped, 'You can't just take me like aspirin to deaden your pain for a few hours. It'll come back worse than ever afterwards.'

'Not always. Sometimes you wake up and find the pain's gone altogether.'

But she bolted down the passage to her room, and cried until dawn, because she realized she'd failed him when he needed her most, and that being Cory he'd never lower his guard again.

CHAPTER TWENTY

The atmosphere in the house was so highly charged that it was almost a relief when Cory got a cable next day from MGM to fly out to the States at once. Tadpole drooped when he saw the suitcases coming out, and went and sat in one of them looking utterly miserable. Harriet knew how he felt. At least Cory was unlikely to be gone more than a fortnight, as he wanted to get back in time to ride Python in the point-to-point.

Once he'd gone, Harriet missed him terribly. She had got so used to having him around, to turn to for help and advice; she felt completely lost. For the millionth time, she kicked herself for rejecting him.

Chattie soon cheered up after Noel had left. Cory had finally relented and bought her a bicycle, and all her energies were employed in learning to ride it. Jonah on the other hand seemed very pulled down; he refused to eat, and complained of headaches.

The day after he left was Mrs. Bottomley's day off.

'I must put something in the *Craven Herald*,' she said, walking into the kitchen in her purple turban and musquash coat.

'Whatever for?' said Harriet listlessly.

'It's ten years now since Mr. Bottomley passed on,' said Mrs. Bottomley solemnly. 'I always put something in the *In Memoriam* column. It seems fitting.'

'Of course,' thought Harriet. 'Loving remembrances to dear Gran, who certainly wasn't an also ran, from Dad and Mum and all the family.'

'Mr. Cory usually writes it for me,' grumbled Mrs.

Bottomley, 'but he went off in such a hurry.'

'Is Mr. Bottomley staying in God's spare room now?' inquired Chattie, who was very interested in death.

'I expect so,' said Harriet hastily.

'Lucky thing. He'll have biscuits in a tin by his bed. D'you think one has to clean one's teeth in heaven?'

'Perhaps you could put in the same verse you used last year,' said Harriet.

'Folk would notice,' said Mrs. Bottomley, 'I'll have to think up something myself. Cheerio everyone,' and, humming Rock of Ages, she set out for the bus stop.

Harriet picked up a pile of ironing and went upstairs. She'd have to get William up in a minute. Suddenly she heard a terrible moaning from Jonah's room. Dropping the ironing and rushing in, she found him lying on the bed, white faced, clutching his head.

'I've got these terrible, terrible pains,' he moaned.

Harriet took his temperature. It was 103, he was pouring with sweat.

The doctor came at lunchtime and said there was a lot of 'flu about, and prescribed antibiotics.

'Sponge him down if he gets too hot. He should be better tomorrow.'

Jonah, in fact, seemed better by the afternoon. His headache had gone and he was hungry. He wolfed all the boiled chicken, mashed potato and ice-cream Harriet brought him.

'You wouldn't, no I'm sure you wouldn't,' he said as she took the tray away.

'What?' said Harriet.

'Play a game of Monopoly.'

'Sevenoaks has eaten Old Kent Road and Mayfair.'

'I'll make some new cards,' said Jonah. 'Can we play for 10p?'

Then, just as they were about to start playing, Jonah was violently sick. By the time Harriet had cleaned up and changed the sheets, he was much worse; his temperature had shot up to 106; he was burning hot and screaming about the pain in his head.

At that moment William chose to wake up from his afternoon rest, and Chattie, as usual wandering round without shoes, stubbed her toe on the corner of Jonah's bed, and burst into noisy sobs.

'Oh please be quiet, all of you,' screamed Harriet, her nerves already in shreds.

She rushed downstairs to ring the doctor. Dr. Burnett was on his rounds, said the recording machine; if she left a message they would get in touch with her as soon as possible. She tried Dr. Rowbotham and got the same answer. It was such a lovely day, they were probably both out playing golf.

She waited half-an-hour; no one rang back. William was bellowing to be fed. Chattie charged about trying to be helpful and getting in the way. Sevenoaks, having decided it was time for a walk, lay across the landing moaning piteously. Jonah was thrashing on the bed now groaning in anguish, chattering, deliriously, about coachmen and the horses not being ready in time.

In despair Harriet rang Elizabeth Pemberton. She could hear bridge party noises in the background. She could imagine them all stuffing themselves with chocolate cake, and tearing everyone to shreds.

'Yes,' said Elizabeth unhelpfully.

'Cory's gone to the States. Mrs. Bottomley's out. I think Jonah's very ill. He's complaining of pains in his head. I can't get hold of Dr. Rowbotham or Dr. Burnett. Can you suggest anyone else?'

'I'll have a think,' said Elizabeth. 'I'm awfully tied up at the moment, Harriet.'

'Bugger you,' she was saying thought Harriet.

'Try Dr. Melhuish in Gargrave,' said Elizabeth. 'He's old-fashioned but very reliable. Ring back later if you need any help.'

Dr. Melhuish was also on his rounds. She could hear Jonah screaming with pain. Harriet took a deep breath and dialled 999.

'I'm stuck in the house with a baby and two children, and the boy's seriously ill. I think he's got brain damage or something. Please can you help?'

167

She was trying so hard not to cry, she had great trouble telling them the address.

'Don't worry, luv,' came the reassuring Yorkshire accent, 'we'll be over in a minute.'

She was just getting down Jonah's suitcase, trying to dress William, comfort Chattie and not fall over Sevenoaks, when the telephone rang again.

It was Sammy.

'What's happening?'

'Jonah's ill. I've rung for an ambulance.'

'Good for you. I'll come straight over. We'll take Chattie and William. Yes, of course we can. We'll manage. You must go with Jonah.'

'What will Elizabeth say?'

'She can stuff herself,' said Sammy. 'She won't be looking after them anyway. Keep smiling. I'll be right over.'

Harriet charged round gathering up pyjamas, toothpaste, an old teddy bear, Jonah's favourite *Just William* book. She wanted to write a note to Mrs. Bottomley, but she couldn't find a biro. Cory always whipped them all to write with.

Sammy arrived with the ambulance, her round face full of concern.

'I got away as soon as I could, the unfeeling bitch and her bridge parties. I'll sort out the bottles, the nappies, and Mrs. Bottomley. Don't you worry about a thing.'

Two ambulance men, who had camp voices and left-of-centre partings, came down the stairs with Jonah on a stretcher.

He was quieter now. Sammy smiled down at his white pain-racked face.

'Poor old love, you do look poorly. Never mind, the nurses'll make you better. I'll bring you a present tomorrow.'

'Can I sleep in the same bed as Georgie?' said Chattie.

'How old is Cory?' said the doctor at the hospital.

'Thirty-four,' said Harriet.

The doctor raised his eyebrows.

'Oh I'm sorry. Cory's only his first name. We call him

Jonah. He's eight.'

The doctor underlined the word Jonah with a fountain pen and went on to ask her a lot of questions — when did Jonah first sit up and walk? Had he had all his injections? — none of which she could answer.

Then they were taken down endless passages into a room with one bed. Everything was covered in cellophane; the nurses came in in masks.

'Just a precaution until we find out what it is,' said one of the nurses.

It was a nice little room. On the blind was painted a village street with dogs and cats and people buying from a market stall. The church clock stood at three o'clock; a chimney sweep was cleaning an immaculate chimney; children looked out of the window. Harriet gazed mindlessly at it as she waited for the results of Jonah's lumbar puncture.

Thoughts of typhoid, smallpox, polio chased themselves relentlessly round her head. Oh God, don't let him die.

Jonah's blond hair was dark with sweat but he seemed calmer. Harriet bent over him, sponging his forehead.

'Your tits are too low in that blouse,' he said with a weak grin.

'I didn't have time to put on a bra,' said Harriet.

Half an hour later, the nurses took off their gowns and masks. Much later a specialist arrived. He was a tall man with untidy grey hair, scurf all over his collar, who stank of body odour.

'We think it's early meningitis,' he said. 'We've found far too many white corpuscles in the fluid, but that's not too much to worry about unless there's a growth. But I think you should notify the boy's parents.'

Then followed the hassle of trying to find where Cory was in America.

Harriet tried very hard not to show Jonah how panicky she felt. The only thing that sustained her was the thought of talking to Cory on the telephone. Never had she needed him so badly.

She was frustrated, however, at every turn. Cory's agent in London had closed his office for the weekend and couldn't be found at home. She hadn't enough money to dial the number Cory left her in New York. Noel's agent said she'd gone to Paris for the weekend, was due back on Tuesday but had left no forwarding address. A queue of large swollen ladies in quilted dressing-gowns from the Maternity Ward were waiting to use the telephone and starting to mutter. In desperation she rung Elizabeth Pemberton, who promised rather unwillingly to see what she could do. Afterwards Harriet had a word with Chattie. Her heart was wrung listening to the choked little voice:

'Elizabeth asked me if I used a dry brush or a wet brush to do my teeth. I wasn't thinking, I said dry. It was horrid. Everyone's gone away, Daddy, Mummy, Jonah, you. I do miss you, Harriet.'

As the night-nurses came in Jonah grew increasingly worse; his temperature shot up to 106 again. He couldn't keep any of the antibiotics down. He kept asking for water, but every time he drank he was violently sick. Soon he became delirious, crying for Noel, for Cory, shouting out about the black coachman who was coming to get him. Harriet kept hoping he'd gone to sleep, then his eyes would open and he'd groan. On other occasions he'd drop off, then wake up, be all right for a few seconds, and the pain would take over.

Harriet clung on to his hot dry hand and wondered how she'd get through the night.

CHAPTER TWENTY-ONE

The noise of the floor-polisher was like sandpaper on her brain; the bleep of a doctor's walkie-talkie made her jump out of her skin. After twenty-four hours in hospital with no sleep, she seemed to have Jonah's head — even the slightest sound, running water, the air conditioner, seemed to be magnified a thousand-fold.

Jonah was no better. He had kept nothing down. In between bouts of delirium he complained of a stiff neck.

'No one's trying to make me better,' he groaned. 'You're all trying to kill me.'

Harriet was very near to breaking. She had been unable to locate Cory or Noel. She had not slept at all, and she had taken against the new day nurse, Sister Maddox, who was a snooty, good-looking redhead with a school prefect manner. I've got twenty-five other children to see to in this ward, so don't waste my time, she seemed to say.

'We've seen much worse than Jonah, I can tell you,' she said briskly as she checked his pulse.

'Dying, dying, dying,' intoned Jonah like a Dalek.

'Now pull yourself together, young man,' she said. 'We're trying to make you better.'

She looked out through the glass partition at a group that was coming down the passage. Hastily she patted her hair and straightened her belt. Harriet understood why when the Houseman Dr. Williams entered. He was by any standards good-looking: tall, dark, with classical features, and cold grey eyes behind thick horn-rimmed spectacles. Nurse Maddox became the picture of fluttering deference as he examined Jonah and looked at the temperature charts.

He glanced at Harriet without interest, making her

acutely aware of her shiny unmade-up face, sweat-stained shirt and dirty hair.

'Hasn't kept anything down,' he said. 'Probably have to put up a drip soon.'

'Can't he have anything to stop the pain?' protested Harriet.

'Not till we can locate what's causing it,' said Dr. Williams in a bored voice. 'He'll have to sweat it out.'

Harriet followed him into the passage. 'He's not going to die, is he?' she said in a trembling voice, 'I mean, how ill is he?'

'Well, he's seriously ill,' said Dr. Williams, 'but he's not on the danger list yet.'

Harriet went off and cried in the lavatory. Sister Maddox was talking to Dr. Williams as she came out.

'I'll see you at eight o'clock then, Ruth,' he was saying.

'Handsome, isn't he?' said a junior nurse.

Yes, thought Harriet, and he knows it.

When she got back, Jonah was awake and screaming with pain.

'Everyone's gone away. You left me, you left me. Where's Daddy? I want to *see* him.'

Suddenly she had a brain wave. She would ring Kit. The next time Jonah fell asleep, she went and called him. He took so long to answer she nearly rang off.

'Were you in bed?' she said.

'Naturally,' said Kit. 'It's lunchtime!'

She told him about Jonah's meningitis and that she still couldn't raise Noel or Cory. She tried to be calm, but hysteria kept breaking through her voice.

'I wouldn't bother about Noel darling; she's not likely to be of help to anyone, but I'll get hold of Cory for you, don't worry. If I can't find him by tomorrow, I'll drive up myself. Jonah'll pull through The Erskines are a pretty tough bunch.'

Another day and night limped by. Jonah woke at 1.30 in the morning screaming for Noel. Harriet felt her self-control snapping as the nurse trotted out the same platitudes about having to get worse before he got better.

He woke again at five and at seven. Another day to get through, thought Harriet, as the sun filtered in through the blind. It seemed like midnight. She must know every inch of that village scene now. She was weak with exhaustion; her eyes were red and felt as though they were full of gravel. Neuralgia travelled round her head, one moment headache, then toothache, then earache.

It was impossible to keep Jonah quiet. Reading aloud was too loud, sponging his head was too painful.

'Where's the doctor, where's the doctor?' he screamed.

'He'll be here soon,' said Harriet soothingly, but the very word 'soon' had become meaningless. Mrs. Bottomley popped in to see him, and went away looking shattered.

'Poor little lamb, lying between death and life,' she said, telephoning Sammy when she got home. 'Still where there's life . . .'

She brought Harriet a change of clothes — a tweed skirt, which Harriet hated, a brown jersey that sagged round the waist, and a cream shirt that had no buttons.

Might as well stay in jeans, thought Harriet.

Eventually at mid-day Dr. Williams rolled up, yawning and rubbing his eyes. Too much Sister Maddox, thought Harriet.

'You've got to do something,' she pleaded in desperation. 'I don't think he can take much more.'

Jonah started to scream out about the pain killing him.

'Hush, darling,' said Harriet. 'The doctor's here.'

'And you can shut up,' said Jonah, turning round and bashing her in the face with his hand, 'Shut up! Shut up! You're all trying to kill me.'

'He's losing faith in all of you,' said Harriet with a sob.

Dr. Williams drew her outside.

'The child is getting too demanding,' he said. 'He's playing you up and you're overreacting. He senses your panic and it panics him too. I suppose his parents will turn up eventually. How long is it since you ate?'

'I don't know,' said Harriet.

173

JILLY COOPER

'Well, go downstairs and have something.'

Down in the canteen, Harriet spread marmalade on toast the consistency of a flannel. Allround her nurses were gossiping and chattering about their lives. They all ought to be upstairs making Jonah better. Sister Maddox and Dr. Williams obviously felt she was hopeless and hysterical and were trying to keep her away from Jonah. She mustn't get paranoiac. She mustn't build up a hatred.

Upstairs she found Jonah having his temperature taken, the thermometer sticking out of his mouth like a cigar. With his slitty eyes and his hair brushed off his forehead, he suddenly looked very like Cory. Oh, I love him, I love him, she thought.

As the afternoon wore on he grew more and more incoherent, and difficult to quiet, now semi-conscious, now screaming with pain.

'Daddy, Daddy, I want Daddy. I don't want you, I want Mummy,' he shouted. 'Why can't I have a Mummy? Everyone else at school does.' He struggled free from the blankets. 'I want Daddy.'

'You shall have him very soon. Kit's finding him.'

'I want him *now*.'

Oh so do I, thought Harriet.

She hoped Jonah was falling asleep, but just as she tried to move away, she found him gazing at her in horror, trying to bring her face into focus.

'Harriet! Oh it's you. Don't leave me!'

'Of course I won't.'

'I'm so thirsty.' The hands clutching her were hot, dry and emaciated.

'This isn't my room. Why am I here? I want to go home.'

Dr. Williams came back in around six. He looked even more bored.

'We're going to put up a drip now. He can't take anything orally and obviously isn't responding to treatment.'

A junior nurse popped her head round the door.

'There's a Kit Erskine on the telephone for you in Sister's office,' she said to Harriet.

'Darling Harriet, are you all right?' said Kit. 'I gather

174

from the nurse Jonah's not too bright. Don't worry, I got a message through to Cory. He's on location, but he's flying back tonight. He should be with you tomorrow afternoon. I've left a message for Superbitch too. All that rubbish about a weekend in Paris was absolute crap. She's been frantically losing weight at a health farm, so she may descend on you too, I'm afraid.'

Harriet didn't care about Noel. That Cory was coming back was all she could think about.

The drip was up when she got back, a great bag of liquid seeping into Jonah's arm. He was delirious most of the time now, his cheeks hectically flushed, his pulse racing. In the end they had to strap his arm down, as the needle kept slipping and blood came racing back down the tube.

Sammy arrived next with Chattie. 'It's long past her bedtime but she wanted to come.' Sammy brought Jonah a book about Tarzan, Chattie a balloon she'd bought out of her own pocket money.

'William's fine,' said Sammy. 'Chattie and I've been looking after him, haven't we?' Harriet felt guilty yet relieved they hadn't brought him; her well-springs of affection seemed to have dried up. 'Elizabeth's been the last straw,' Sammy went on, 'telling all her friends how she'd taken the baby and Chattie in to help Cory out.'

Chattie seemed quite cheerful, but she hugged Harriet very tightly. 'Can I see Jonah?'

'Yes, of course,' said Harriet, 'but whisper and don't worry if he's not quite himself.'

Unfortunately, just as Chattie was walking into the room, the balloon popped. Jonah woke up with a start and, not recognizing any of them, started raving incoherently about monsters coming to get him.

'I'll stay with him,' said Sammy. 'You take Chattie down to the canteen for an ice-cream.'

Chattie charmed everyone, her long blonde hair swinging as she skipped about the canteen talking to all the nurses. Then suddenly she clung to Harriet, her eyes filling with tears.

'He's not going to die, is he?'

175

'Of course he isn't,' said Harriet, hugging her, but feeling inside a sickening lack of conviction.

'I heard Mrs. Bottomley telling Sammy it could go either way. What does that mean?'

'Nothing really,' said Harriet.

'If he died he'd go to heaven wouldn't he?' said Chattie.

'Of course he would,' said Harriet, 'but he's not going to.'

'Then I'll never see him again,' said Chattie, 'because I'm so naughty, I'll go straight to hell.' She broke into noisy sobs.

Harriet cuddled her, trying to keep control of herself. 'Darling, of course you'll go to heaven.'

'I don't really believe in heaven anyway,' sobbed Chattie. 'I've been up in the sky in an aeroplane, and I didn't see it.'

Harriet sat biting her nails watching two very young nurses fiddling with the Heath Robinson equipment constituting the drip. Bubbles were streaming down the tube, as they tapped away and the needle kept slipping out of the proper place. Jonah lay in a rare moment of consciousness, the tears pouring down his cheeks.

Harriet turned to the nurses, her control snapping 'Why the bloody hell,' she snapped, 'can't one of you make it work?'

As a result, Dr. Williams gave her a talking-to.

'We're going to give you a Mogadon tonight,' he said. 'We know you feel responsible with both the parents away, but you *must* pull yourself together. You only upset him by screaming at the nurses; they're doing their best.'

'But why can't he have proper pain killers and sedatives? If he felt you were doing something to make him better, I know he'd relax and stop fighting you.'

'Jonah's a very brave child, Miss Poole,' said Dr. Williams coldly. 'It's you who can't take the pain, not him.'

'He's very very ill, isn't he?' said Harriet. She had heard the nurses talking about the intensive care unit.

'He's certainly not a well child,' said Dr. Williams, 'but where there's life there's hope.'

By midnight Jonah had gone into a coma. Harriet had pretended to take her Mogadon, but had thrown it down

176

the lavatory. She sat hour after hour fighting exhaustion and despair, listening to his heavy breathing, holding his hand and praying. Through the glass panel, she could see the black nightnurse moving round the wards, adjusting blankets, checking pulses. In a minute she'd be coming into Harriet's room to change the drip. This time tomorrow Cory would be here. How could she face him if anything happened to Jonah? She put her head in her hands and wept.

She must have fallen asleep. When she woke up it was nearly light. Jonah lay motionless in bed. For a terrifying moment, Harriet thought he was dead. She felt his forehead; it was cold; he was still breathing faintly.

Getting to her feet, she ran into the passage to the sister's office.

'Jonah, he's breathing so quietly now,' she stammered. 'He looks so peaceful, as though he was d-dying.'

The black nurse got up and took Harriet's arm. 'I'll come and see.' She felt his pulse, and took his temperature. She turned to Harriet, a great white toothy smile splitting her face.

'I think he's over the crisis,' she said. 'He's breathing quite normally and his pulse rate's coming down.'

Harriet turned away, her shoulders shaking.

'There, there,' said the nurse. 'I'll get you a cup of tea, then you can get some sleep.'

Harriet didn't trust doctors and nurses; she knew they lied. For all she knew Jonah was still in danger. She sat by his bed until breakfast time, as plastic bag after plastic bag dripped into his arm, listening to the heavy breathing getting slower and more even, the restless movements growing quieter.

Sister Maddox came on at eight, looking as ice-cool and elegant as ever.

'Good Morning. How's the patient?' she said briskly. 'I expect you had a nice sleep with that Mogadon. I envy you. I didn't get to bed till four o'clock.'

She picked up Jonah's chart. His temperature and pulse ratings were right down.

177

'Well, that is better,' she said. 'I hope you appreciate Dr. Williams a bit more now.'

'Jonah hasn't come round yet,' said Harriet sulkily. She knew she was being ungracious.

'He's getting a much-needed rest,' said Sister Maddox. 'I wouldn't fuss him any more if I were you. I'd go and have some breakfast.'

Instead Harriet tried to concentrate on an old copy of *Reader's Digest*. It pays to improve your word power, she said to herself. She felt absolutely all in. She hardly recognized her grey face in the mirror. She wished she could wash her hair and have a bath before Cory came, but she was too scared to leave Jonah until she knew he was out of danger.

The specialist arrived at eleven and didn't appear altogether happy. 'He's not out of the woods yet,' he said. 'Let me know when he regains consciousness.'

Back came the panic, the terrifying fears. Oh don't let him die, prayed Harriet.

Quarter of an hour later came Dr. Williams, even more unreceptive than usual, as Harriet bombarded him with questions about Jonah's condition.

'But he is going to get better, isn't he?' she said in desperation.

'Really, Miss Poole,' said Sister Maddox, 'Dr. Williams has got a hundred and one other people to look after.'

'I'm sorry,' insisted Harriet, 'but Jonah's father's due after lunch and he'll want to know exactly what the score is.'

'Oh, he rang ten minutes ago,' said Sister Maddox.

Harriet went white. 'What did he say? Why didn't you let me speak to him?'

'You were in the loo or making a cup of coffee,' said Sister Maddox. 'I didn't think it was that important.'

'But you could have got me. You must have known I'd want to talk to him.'

'And you must realize that Sister Maddox has better things to do than acting as a switchboard for all the patients' relations. You must realize Jonah isn't the only child in the hospital,' snapped Dr. Williams.

178

'But he's the only child here belonging to me,' shouted Harriet.

'Have I come to the right place,' said a deep throbbing voice. They all turned round. There in the doorway making the perfect stage entrance smothered in a huge black fur hat stood Noel Balfour.

'Oh yes, I have,' she said seeing Jonah, and walked quickly towards the bed.

'Oh my precious, precious darling,' she said with a break in her voice.

And suddenly exactly on cue, Jonah stirred, sighed and opened his eyes, for a moment he looked at Noel incredulously.

'Mummy,' he croaked weakly.

Harriet felt once more the explosion of jealousy as Jonah's pale face lit up.

'Mummy, is it really you?'

'Yes it is, my darling. What a dreadful, dreadful time you've had.' She brushed the dank blond hair back from his forehead.

'My arm's sore,' muttered Jonah.

'I know, darling,' said Noel, 'it's that horrid drip, but it's making you so much better every minute, so I know you'll be brave about it. Because these kind nurses and doctors have been working so hard to make you well.'

'I feel better,' said Jonah, 'but my head's still sore,' and, sighing, he drifted back to sleep. Noel bent and kissed him on the forehead, aware that she made a most touching sight. Hardly a dry eye in the room, thought Harriet. Everyone was gaping in admiration.

Noel stood up and looked round. Pulling off her fur hat and running a careless hand through her blonde hair, so that it fell perfectly into shape, she smiled with dazzling wistfulness at the nurses, then turned her headlamp stare on Dr. Williams who was blushing like a schoolgirl.

She held out a hand. 'My name's Noel Balfour,' she said, as if everyone didn't know it.

'We didn't know you were his mother,' said Sister Maddox, looking rather shaken.

'I don't expect Harriet thought it important,' said Noel. 'Not when Jonah's life was at stake. How is my son, Doctor?'

'Well it's been touch and go, but it looks as though he'll pull through now.'

'How long has he been here?'

'Four days now.'

'*Four days*! Why wasn't I told before?' Noel collapsed on a chair, and got out a cigarette with a trembling hand, letting her fur coat fall open to display her magnificent bosom.

Dr. Williams leapt forward with a lighter.

'We tried to find you,' protested Harriet. 'They said you were in Paris, but they didn't know where.'

'It was the studio trying to protect me,' said Noel. 'I escaped to Paris to learn a part. And you've been all by yourself, poor Harriet. What you must have been through! I'm sure she's been wonderful.'

Dr. Williams gave a chilly smile. 'Miss Poole takes her responsibility as a nanny very seriously.'

Noel, instantly detecting tension, looked from one to the other.

'Where's Cory?' she asked Harriet.

'He's on his way back from the States,' said Harriet.

'He rang to say he'd be here this afternoon,' added Sister Maddox.

'Oh thank God,' said Noel, 'thank God we can give him good news. Let me sit with him for a bit, Harriet,' she went on. 'Go and have a cup of tea and get some rest. You look so tired.'

Dropping with fatigue, black-ringed beneath the eyes, greasy-haired, and wearing the wrong length skirt, Harriet was only too well aware of the contrast she must make to Noel.

As she went listlessly down to the canteen she knew she'd been outmanoeuvred. No doubt at this moment Dr. Williams was telling Noel how stroppy she'd been with the nurses, and what a bad influence she was on Jonah. And this afternoon Cory would be back, and the first thing he'd find was Noel looking stunning by the bedside. Suddenly she felt twitchy and threatened.

CHAPTER TWENTY-TWO

Noel, like all charming people, was totally dependent on the approval and admiration of others. When she sensed disapproval, she merely moved on to fresh conquests. She only liked to live in the sunshine. Her effect on the hospital was dramatic. Suddenly every doctor and nurse in the building seemed to find an excuse to pop in and check Jonah's condition. The passage outside was like Paddington Station.

'The poor little lad took a turn for the better the moment his mother arrived.' Harriet heard one nurse saying to another as they added ice-cream scoops of potato to the roast lamb on the supper trays.

'Isn't she lovely, and so natural?' said the other. ' "Nurse you must be so tired," she said, "Thank you for saving my baby's life." Which is more than the complaints we got from that . . .' They stopped abruptly when they saw Harriet.

'Did you see her shoes?' said one.

'Weren't they lovely? And her hair. And did you see the way her face lit up when she heard her husband was coming? Such a shame they're splitting up. She's obviously still in love with him. Perhaps this'll bring them together again.'

The most dramatic change was in Dr. Williams's behaviour. Usually one couldn't see him for dust the moment he'd done his rounds, but now Noel was ensconced, he was looking in every five minutes. Harriet knew he was off duty that day at three o'clock, but he was still hanging around at five. The compelling, cold, surgical grey eyes were quite moony now, the bored voice husky and caressing. Harriet even caught a waft of aftershave.

He was very concerned that Noel hadn't had any lunch. But there was no suggestion that she might go down to the canteen for a cup of tea, Irish stew and carrots. A quarter of an hour later, smoked salmon sandwiches and iced white wine appeared.

'Isn't he wonderful?' Noel said to Harriet. 'So considerate and so concerned about Jonah.'

'It's only since you've been here,' said Harriet sulkily. 'He's been a pig up till now.'

One of the day nurses popped her head round the door.

'I was just going off duty, Miss Balfour. I wondered if I could have your autograph.'

'Tell me your name,' said Noel, taking the piece of paper.

'Nurse Rankin,' said the nurse.

'No, I know you're Nurse Rankin. I mean your christian name.'

Nurse Rankin giggled. 'Actually it's Dorothy. But everyone calls me Dotty.'

'To Dotty with great pleasure, love and gratitude,' wrote Noel in her huge scrawl. 'I think Dotty's a lovely name. Imagine what it was like being christened Noel. People were always making jokes about the first Noel.'

'I've seen all your pictures,' said Nurse Rankin, a slave to sudden passion. 'I think you're absolutely wonderful.'

'And I can never thank you enough for what you've done for my little boy.'

Lay it on with a trowel, thought Harriet in disgust.

'Everything all right?' It was Dr. Williams popping in again.

'Absolutely marvellous,' said Noel, turning her startling tawny eyes on him. 'You are a saint, David.'

David now, thought Harriet. He was looking exactly like Sevenoaks when Mytton's bitch was on heat.

'I haven't managed all the sandwiches,' said Noel. 'I'm feeling too upset to eat, but the wine is delicious. Won't you have some?'

'Not when I'm on duty,' he said, 'but I'd love one later.'

Harriet's only comfort was that Sister Maddox was looking absolutely furious.

When Noel heard that Chattie and William were staying at

the Pembertons', she went off and had a long telephone conversation with Elizabeth.

When she returned her attitude was distinctly less friendly towards Harriet. Oh God, I bet Elizabeth mentioned something about my being wrapped round Cory at the Hunt Ball, thought Harriet.

Noel's main preoccupation now seemed to be to get her out of the hospital before Cory came back.

'I really don't feel we can dump William and Chattie on Elizabeth any longer,' she said, 'particularly when William's teething and keeping them up every night. I think you should go and collect them, and take them home.'

'Sammy really doesn't mind looking after them,' said Harriet. 'I would like to stay here with Jonah, just another night.'

'Are you quite sure you're the best person?' said Noel gently. 'People here seem to think you're rather — well— overemotional.'

'I l-love him,' stammered Harriet. 'I was worried.'

'I quite realize that, but you must remember you're well only . . .'

'The nanny.' Harriet felt herself going very red in the face.

'Exactly,' said Noel, pouring herself another glass of wine. 'And it's your duty to go home and look after Chattie and William, so I'd like you lo pack your things at once, and my driver will take you home, and you can collect the children on the way.'

'But Mr. Erskine left me in charge of the children. I'm sure he'd want me to stay.'

Noel lost her temper.

'I've been married to Cory for ten years. I think I know him slightly better than you. The thing he'll like best when he arrives is to find me here with Jonah.'

Harriet was beaten. She went next door and began to gather up her things. She heard Jonah waking up again and complaining that his head ached, and could he have some iced water. Noel poked her head through the door.

'Could you just pop down and get me some ice,' she said.

Running the tray under the tap to get out the ice cubes, Harriet suddenly thought she'd burst if she didn't see Cory. I hate Noel, I hate her, I hate her.

Then soon she heard a quick step in the passage and there was Cory walking past. Her heart lurched. She tried to call out to him, but her voice stuck in her throat. She went out into the passage. It required the greatest control of her life not to run after him.

As it was, she reached the door in time to see Noel leaping to her feet. The next moment Cory had taken her in his arms and was comforting her as she sobbed with great restraint, but not enough to spoil her make-up. I can't bear it, thought Harriet, her nails digging into her hands.

She saw Cory let Noel go, and move forward to speak to Jonah. She tiptoed forward trying to hear what he was saying.

But Sister Maddox was too quick for her. The faster Noel transferred her attentions to Cory and got her claws out of Dr. Williams the better.

'I think the family would all like a little time on their own,' she said firmly. 'The porter downstairs has just rung up to say the car's waiting for you.'

Harriet went into the side room, and mindlessly put the rest of her things into the canvas bag Mrs. Bottomley had brought.

Then she heard Jonah say, 'Where's Harriet?' And Cory saying, 'Yes where is she?'

'I'm here, said Harriet, pushing open the door.

Cory was sitting on the bed holding Jonah's hand. Harriet expected him to be pale and drawn. But he was tanned dark brown by the Los Angeles sun. Never had he seemed more handsome — or more beyond her reach. He looked up quickly, full of concern. 'My God, what you must have been through! I'm sorry I wasn't here.'

'I'm so glad you've come now,' she muttered, fighting back the tears.

'All I can say is thank you,' he said. 'Sit down. You look absolutely knackered. Are you up to telling me something about it?'

184

'My driver's waiting to take her home, Cory,' said Noel in icy tones. 'She's been here for four days. She needs a break. And she's going to collect Chattie and William. Elizabeth's looking after them but we can't leave them with her for ever.'

Cory didn't turn round.

Jonah, still drowsy, suddenly said, 'Where's Mummy?'

'Here darling,' said Noel, going towards the bed.

'Where's Harriet?' muttered Jonah.

'She's going home, darling.'

'No,' said Jonah, sitting bolt upright, suddenly hysterical, 'I don't want her to go home. I want her to stay. I want Harriet! I want Harriet!'

'But *I'm* here,' snapped Noel, her lips tightening.

'But you won't stay,' he screamed in desperation, 'You only say you'll stay, then you go. Harriet stays all the time.'

He started to cry.

Cory took him by the shoulders, and gently eased him back on the pillow. 'It's all right, old boy. Harriet's not going anywhere.'

He turned to Noel. 'I took the precaution of getting Kit to find us a temporary nanny. She came up in the plane with me. She took the taxi home. She's going to look after William and Chattie. I thought as you'd seen the whole thing through you'd probably want to stay with Jonah,' he added to Harriet.

'Oh, yes please,' she whispered.

'But Cory,' began Noel. 'Can we have a brief word?'

Harriet retreated into the side room shutting the door. She was shaking like a leaf. No doubt Noel was telling Cory what a disaster she'd been with all the nurses and doctors. She caught the word 'hysterical' several times, and then Noel was saying in acid tones,

'She complained about Dr. Williams, but honestly he couldn't have been kinder, popping in every five minutes, solicitude and kindness itself. She's obviously the sort of girl that gets people's backs up.'

Harriet couldn't hear Cory's reply. She collapsed on the bed, holding her clenched fists against her forehead in a desperate attempt to gain control.

A minute later Cory came in, shut the door behind him and sat down on the bed. Her whole body was shaken with sobs.

'It's all right, little one,' he said gently, stroking her hair. 'I know what you've been through.'

'And I know I'm bad for Jonah at the moment,' she sobbed. 'I'm overreacting, but I love him so much, and I thought he was going to die, and no one would take any notice, and they wouldn't give him any pain killers, and bloody Dr. Williams was so bored with the whole case it wasn't true. And then she, I mean Noel, turns up this morning, and suddenly everyone rolls up, and starts paying attention to the case, and giving Jonah VIP treatment, and he's been getting better all day. I know I should be h-happy. I prayed to God, if he m-made Jonah better, I'd never be unhappy again. I c-can't think why I'm so miserable.'

'I can,' said Cory, his hand over hers. 'You're absolutely played out. What I want you to do now, is not to argue, but to go and have a bath and wash your hair, have a little gentle supper, and then go to bed and have a decent night's sleep. Then you'll be fresh to look after him in the morning.'

'But he gets such frightful nightmares. You think he's better, and suddenly he gets worse. Will someone sit with him tonight?'

'I will,' said Cory.

He went back into Jonah's room.

'Well,' said Noel icily. 'Have you finished consoling her?'

'For the time being,' answered Cory in a level voice. 'She must have been through hell and back. I'm absolutely appalled by her appearance.'

'She's obviously one of these people who go to pieces in a crisis,' said Noel.

Cory was about to reply when Noel added quickly, 'Where can one eat round here?'

'There's a good restaurant in Skipton,' said Cory.

'As soon as Jonah's asleep, I thought we might go there. In fact I've asked Dr. Williams to join us. He's charming and I thought he could give you the low-down on Jonah.'

'No thanks,' said Cory. 'I didn't come four thousand miles to go out to dinner.'

Jonah in fact made very good progress and was out in five days. Harriet hardly recognized the nursery and the children's rooms when she got home, they were so tidy. All the playing cards and jigsaw puzzles had been sorted out, the children's clothes lay in serried ranks, beautifully ironed in the drawers. William's nappies were all fluffy and as white as snow, even the old table in the nursery coated with generations of poster paints, gripfix, pentel, and coca cola, had been scrubbed and was now gleaming like a furniture polish ad. Miss Hanbury, the temporary nanny, was a miracle, and Noel took every opportunity to point out the fact.

Noel stayed at the Wilderness and only left at the end of a week because she had to be in London to go on the Parkinson Show. It was one of the worst weeks of Harriet's life. William was teething and, like Cherubim and Seraphim, continually did cry, which gave Noel plenty of excuse for more bitchiness. Jonah, having had undivided attention for so long, displayed all the despotism and capriciousness of the convalescent. Chattie, from lack of attention, was very jealous and playing up. She was only just stopped from giving two of Noel's minks to a woman collecting jumble, and one afternoon Harriet came into the kitchen and found her and Sevenoaks both looking sick and extremely sheepish. They had consumed a whole tin of Good Boy Dog Choc Drops between them.

Chattie burst into tears when Harriet ticked her off. 'I was only trying to turn Sevenoaks into a Good Boy,' she wailed.

The worst part was having Noel about the place, looking gorgeous, getting in the way, and interfering with the running of the house.

'I can't call my kitchen my castle any more,' grumbled Mrs. Bottomley.

Nor did the telephone ever stop ringing. It was either Noel's agent, or the people on the Parkinson Show, or the *Yorkshire Post* wanting to interview her, or Ronnie Acland, or Dr. Williams. Then, if people weren't ringing her, she was making long distance telephone calls herself, or getting Harriet to run errands for her, or wash her shirts, or sew on her buttons. Then there were the interminable discussions about her choosing the right thing to wear on Parkinson.

When one has passed through a time of great anxiety, relief and happiness do not immediately follow. Harriet found herself subject to fits of depression, inclined to be crotchety. She told herself she was very run down. She was fed up with seeing Noel's peach-coloured silk underwear on the line, of smelling her wafts of scent everywhere.

Dr. Williams called every day, which Harriet was sure was quite unorthodox. Looking out of the window, while making beds one day, Harriet saw Noel sitting girlishly on the old swing under the walnut tree, with Dr. Williams pushing her, totally infatuated. The next moment she was called inside for a ten-minute drool with Ronnie Acland. Wedging her options open, thought Harriet.

One lunchtime, Dr. Williams rang up, and after a brief conversation Noel disappeared in Cory's car. She returned five hours later, flushed and radiant, and came into the kitchen to regale Mrs. Bottomley and Harriet with a long spiel about the impossibility of finding the right pair of shoes in Leeds for her television appearance.

'Did you try Schofields?' said Mrs. Bottomley.

'I tried everywhere. I must have visited twenty shoe shops,' sighed Noel.

At that moment, Sevenoaks wandered over to her big bag which lay open on a chair, and before she could stop him, plunged his face inside and drew out a pair of frilly peach-coloured pants.

'I'm surprised you didn't find anything at Dolcis,' said Mrs. Bottomley.

Harriet had to go out of the room to stop herself from laughing. She would have given anything to have told Cory.

She suspected, however, that Dr. Williams and Ronnie were pure dalliance, and Noel's big guns were aimed at getting Cory back. Cory avoided opportunities to be alone with her and slept in the spare room. He buried himself in a load of work he'd brought back from America, and in getting

Python ready for the point-to-point on Saturday. Occasionally Harriet saw his eyes resting on Noel, but she could not read their meaning. How did that beauty affect him now? He was kind to Harriet, but detached, as though his mind was somewhere beyond her reach. One thing she was certain of. If Noel came back, she would be straight out of a job. It made her very uneasy.

On the last evening before Noel went South, she and Cory stayed up talking. Harriet, coming down to get some Ribena for William, heard raised voices. The door was ajar and she stopped to listen:

'You've been content to leave the children entirely to me,' Cory was saying. 'Now you have the effrontery to say you want them back.'

'Ronnie and I have a house in France now as well as one in London,' said Noel. 'They'd be proper bases for the children to live. Be honest, Cory, children need a mother. A man can't really bring up children on his own.'

'I haven't managed too badly so far,' snapped Cory. 'You know perfectly well there is only one set of terms on which I'm prepared for you to have the children and as you're quite incapable of complying with them, there's no point in discussing it.'

He means her coming back to him and chucking all the others, thought Harriet miserably.

'How do you know I'm incapable of complying with them?' said Noel huskily.

The next moment the door shut.

Harriet fled upstairs. It's going to happen, she thought in anguish. But five minutes later she heard Cory come upstairs and the spare-room door open and shut. It was as though a great spear had been drawn out of her side.

CHAPTER TWENTY-THREE

Harriet never forgot the day of the point-to-point — the bookies shouting, the county in their well-cut tweeds, the children sucking toffee apples, the crowds pressing around the paddock and the finishing post, the circling horses with their glossy coats.

She stood in the paddock trying to hold on to an impossibly over-excited Chattie — poor Jonah hadn't been allowed out — watching Python being saddled up. The black mare's coat rippling blue in the sunshine.

Cory came over to them. He was wearing a pink and grey striped shirt, and carrying a pink and grey cap. They had hardly spoken since Noel left. He picked up her hand and gave her his watch.

'Look after it for me,' he said, curling her fingers over it.

'Good luck,' she whispered.

'Good luck, Daddy,' said Chattie.

They watched him feel Python's girths, clap a hand on the ebony quarters, put a foot in the stirrup and he was up, riding slowly round the paddock.

Two men beside Harriet in the crowd were discussing them.

'Grand looking beast. Bit young, bit light, though.'

'Erskine can ride her.'

'Oh it's Erskine is it? That's worth a fiver each way.'

Harriet's heart swelled with pride. Oh, please let him win. He needs this small, unimportant victory so much to cheer him up.

There were nine horses in the race. Acceptance, the favourite, a tall rangy bay, had been heavily backed to win. Harriet and Chattie climbed to the top of the hill, so they

190

could see nearly all the way round the course and also hear the commentator. Harriet was so nervous she could hardly bear to watch.

At last they were off. For the first time round, Python was lying sixth for most of the way, but as the field started to jump the fences for the second time, she slowly began moving up.

'And now they've only got eight fences to jump,' said the commentator. 'And it's still Snow Moss from Acceptance, then Lazy Lucy and Tragedy Queen. Python is going very well and making ground all the time. Now they're coming up to the seventh from home and it's still Acceptance and Snow Moss. But Acceptance jumped that crooked and someone's down. I can't see exactly who it is . . . yes, it's Python! Python's down, I'm afraid.'

The crowd gave a groan. Harriet felt an agonizing pain shoot through her. But she was only conscious of fear — that Cory might be hurt, badly hurt.

Chattie started to cry.

'He'll be all right,' said Harriet in a shaking voice.

The microphone crackled. 'I'm sorry,' said the commentator. 'I made a mistake. It wasn't Python, it was Lazy Lucy who fell at the last fence — they've got similar colours. Python's there and still making ground.'

Tears pricked Harriet's eyes. Relief streamed over her.

As if in a dream, she watched Cory's figure crouched over the little black mare, coaxing her, urging her on. Slowly the distance between him and the leaders shortened. Only one more fence to go, and then Snow Moss had fallen, and it was only a tiring Acceptance between Cory and victory.

'Come on,' shrieked Harriet. And now Python was drawing level. For a split second, it looked as though Acceptance was going to hold on, then Python drew ahead by a nose as they passed the post.

How Harriet and Chattie hugged each other!

'I've won 50p,' screamed Chattie.

Everyone cheered as Cory rode in. For once, a broad grin was spread across the impassive features, as he patted the sweating mare.

'Oh, clever, clever Daddy!' screeched Chattie.

Cory's eyes met Harriet's. 'Well,' he said, 'we did it.'

He dismounted and then, Harriet never remembered afterwards how it happened, a golden figure smothered in furs suddenly pushed her way through the crowd, and flung her arms round Cory's neck. It was Noel.

'Oh, darling, darling,' she cried. 'I'm so proud of you.'

'Mummy! Whatever are you doing here?' said Chattie.

'I'm not going to marry Ronnie,' cried Noel. 'I've come back, back to Daddy. We're all going to be one happy family again.'

Suddenly the paddock seemed to be full of photographers.

'This is the most wonderful day of my life,' said Noel, smiling at them radiantly.

Cory's face was quite expressionless.

In a daze, Harriet watched Chattie pulling at Noel's coat.

'Mummy, Mummy! Did you bring me a present?'

'Yes, of course I did, darling.' She turned round to Harriet with a mocking smile on her beautiful face. 'I even brought a little *cadeau* for Harriet.'

Harriet looked round and gave a gasp. She hadn't noticed the slender, elegant figure in the black fur coat and dark glasses.

'Hullo, Harriet, darling,' said Simon.

'Simon! Oh, my God,' whispered Harriet. 'What are you doing here?' Her hand flew to her cheek. Then Chattie gave a shriek. 'Look at Harriet! She's hurt herself.'

Looking down, Harriet realized that blood was pouring from her hand. Then the horrified faces in front of her started going round and round, and she lost consciousness.

Darkness, sickness, throbbing pain engulfed her. The sound of different voices drummed in her ears.

A wail from Chattie: 'She's not dying, is she?'

Noel's voice, steel-tipped with irritation: 'Of course not, she's only fainted.'

Cory's voice like gravel, harsh with anxiety: 'Get back all of you ! Can't you see she needs more air?'

Another voice, tender, caressing, languid. Could it really be Simon's?

'Everything's going to be all right, darling, I'm with you now.'

Then great whirling clouds of darkness coming down again, then slowly clearing and, suddenly, she opened her eyes and saw a face looking down at her, pale against the sable coat, a face she was only used to seeing in dreams, or disappearing in nightmares.

'Oh, Simon,' she croaked weakly, 'is it really you?'

'Hullo, baby. Yes, it's me, but you mustn't try to talk.'

'I'm not dreaming, am I?'

He smiled, but there were tears in his eyes. 'Not dreaming. Feel.' He touched her cheek with his hand but, as she turned her head to kiss it, he said, 'Lie still.'

'Where am I?'

'In a draughty ambulance. A bossy old fag's been bandaging up your hand. You cut it breaking the glass on Cory's watch in your pocket. Must have been the shock of seeing me. Flattering, I suppose, that I still have that affect on you.'

That wasn't quite right, but Harriet was too dazed to work out why.

'Where's Cory? And the children and everyone?'

'Stop worrying about other people,' he said soothingly.

'Oh, Simon, you do look lovely,' she sighed.

It was exactly the right thing to have said. He smiled and dipped a lavender silk handkerchief in a mug of water beside her, and gently began to sponge the blood from the side of her face.

'When you're feeling up to it, I'm going to drive you to the hospital to have some stitches put in your hand.'

Harriet watched him light a cigarette and insert it carefully in a dark blue cigarette holder.

'Simon, Noel didn't force you to come up here?'

He looked mortified. 'Oh, darling! Do you think I'm that much of a bastard? Borzoi and I broke up just after I saw you last. I've been trying to trace you ever since. No one knew where you were — your old boss, your landlady, even your parents. I didn't know a thing about the baby until

Noel rang me this morning. I was completely poleaxed — half knocked out at finding you, half horror at what you'd been through.'

He took her hands. 'From now on I'm going to make the decisions, and I'm never going to let you go again.'

At that moment, Cory came into the ambulance, and Harriet was furious to find herself snatching her hands away. He was wearing a battered sheepskin coat over his pink and grey silk shirt, and had to stoop in order to avoid banging his head.

'Hullo, how are you?' How austere it sounded, after Simon's gushing tenderness.

She struggled to sit up. 'I'm all right. I'm sorry about your watch.'

'Doesn't matter at all, you only smashed the glass.'

'I'm so pleased you w-won the race.'

He smiled briefly. 'Bloody good, wasn't it? When you're feeling stronger, I'll run you over to the hospital.'

'I'm taking her to the hospital,' said Simon in his languid voice tipping ash from his cigarette on to the floor just by Cory's feet. The gesture was curiously insolent. 'And then I thought we'd drive back to your place. I'm quite anxious to see my son.'

Then Noel came into the ambulance. 'I'm giving Harriet the weekend off, Cory,' she said. 'It won't do Mrs. Bottomley any harm to do some work for a change. She can easily take care of the children and William.'

'Don't be ridiculous!' snapped Cory. 'Harriet's lost a lot of blood. She's going straight home to bed after she's been to hospital.'

'Cory,' said Noel patiently, 'these children haven't seen each other for absolutely ages. They ought to be on their own together.'

'Rubbish,' said Cory brusquely. 'They've got nothing to say to each other. It was all over years ago.'

Harriet took no pleasure that these people were fighting over her. She felt a bit like a hostess with no drink in the house, invaded by a crowd of people. The mixture of heavy scent, antiseptic and French cigarettes was making her dizzy.

Noel's cold yellow eyes were boring into her.

'I think I'd better go with Simon,' she said.

Harriet only remembered isolated incidents about the rest of the day. 'I've booked in at a hotel down the valley,' Simon said as he drove her back from the hospital. He put his hand on her thigh. 'I hadn't realized how much I'd want you; I've never met anyone who took to sex like you did.'

Harriet felt overwhelmed by a great weariness. She was in no mood for a sexual marathon.

Neither was Simon's meeting with William the success she had hoped. William, woken from sleep, was red-faced and bad-tempered. Simon, after initial cooings and ravings, had no idea what to do with him. Holding him at arm's length like a bomb about to explode, fearful he might be sick over the beautiful fur coat, he handed him back to Harriet almost immediately.

She had fantasized about them meeting for so long, the joy, the incredulity, it was bound to be an anticlimax. Simon couldn't be expected to be as good with babies as Cory.

She tried to shake off her depression as she threw clothes into a small suitcase, but she was gripped with the same feeling of menace she'd always had when packing to go back to school. She felt rather ashamed that she put in three novels she wanted to read and the remains of the sleeping pills Cory had made her get from the doctor. Sevenoaks and Tadpole sat around looking miserable at the sight of suitcases.

'I'll see you both tomorrow,' she said hopefully.

Just as she was combing her hair in front of the mirror Cory walked in without knocking.

'You're mad to go off with Simon,' he said harshly, speaking directly to her haggard reflection. 'He's a spoilt, corrupt little-boy with no guts and no backbone. He's ditched you once, he'll ditch you again.'

Harriet put her head in her hands.

'Don't bully me,' she said in real anguish. 'I'm in such a muddle.'

'I'm sorry,' he said in a much gentler voice, putting his hands on her shoulders. 'But just because he's William's father, you mustn't feel you ought to marry him.'

For a second, Harriet leant against him, then she stood up.

'I've got to talk to Simon, and try to sort out what I feel.'

For a minute they stared at each other. Then he buttoned her coat up as if she was a little girl.

'Be careful,' he said.

Later, she remembered being impressed by the cool way Simon had written Mr. and Mrs. Villiers in the hotel visitors' book, as though he'd done it a hundred times before. He'd booked them into a luxury three-room suite.

He was at his most winning too, remorseful at his previous conduct, gazing into her eyes, telling her how beautiful she had become, beguiling her with bitchy stories about film stars he had met, speaking of his future with her and William. All perfect, yet Harriet had the feeling she'd got on to the wrong bus and was desperately hurtling in a direction she didn't want to go.

He had changed too. He had all the sheen and glitter of the star now. When he talked to her, she felt he was playing to an audience.

'I want to know everything that's happened to you since we split up,' he said.

But when she started telling him, despite the intent look on his face, she knew his thoughts were miles away, so she changed the subject. 'It's wonderful you've done so well, Simon.'

He spread his hands out. 'Just luck, really. I had mild success with a couple of television plays I did, and I made this film abroad; just a small part, but everyone's raving about the rushes. And in May I'm going to make a film with Noel, with a really meaty part in it. She's been terribly kind.'

Harriet wondered what form Noel's kindness had taken.

'You haven't been having an affair with her?' she asked idly.

'Dar-ling! Be reasonable. She's old enough to be my mother.'

'She could hardly be your mother when she was ten.'

'I wouldn't even put that past her! Anyway, I don't go for

these busty, earthmother types — I like my women slim.
You've got the most gorgeous figure since you lost all that
weight.'

Harriet smiled, but she found her thoughts wandering
back to Cory and how he and Noel were getting on at this
moment, and then she realized it hadn't been the shock of
seeing Simon that had made her cut her hand, it must have
been the sharp, ignored pain that shot through her when
she thought Cory's horse had fallen in the race.

Simon was still talking about his new film. Concentrate on
his beauty, she kept telling herself. He's far better looking
than Cory. The champagne was beginning to make her feel
sick.

He got to his feet and came towards her with that sudden
seductive smile that he could use as a weapon or a caress.
The brilliant blue-green eyes wandered over her body —
hard eyes now, endlessly craving distraction. She felt mes-
merized like a small bird before a snake

'Darling,' he murmured. 'It's stupid to try and communi-
cate with words. Let's go to bed.'

And he pulled her into his arms and kissed her, but it
wasn't the same as before — no turning of the entrails, no
weakness at the knees, no black turgid drowning tide of passion.

For a minute she remembered the evening when Cory
had kissed her, and she shivered as she re-lived the swooning, helpless ecstasy.

'No,' she cried wriggling away. 'I don't want to now. You
must give me more time.'

Simon's face darkened. 'What's the matter? Gone off me
since the old days?'

'I don't feel well,' she whispered. 'Would you mind if I lay
down for a few minutes?'

Now he was all contrition. 'Darling, why didn't you tell
me?'

Later she was lying in the dark, her head thrashing from
side to side in an agony of indecision, when the telephone
rang. She heard Simon lift the receiver. Then there was a
pause as he shut the bedroom door.

197

In some blind hope that it might be Cory ringing, she picked up the extension by her bed. Then she stiffened as she heard Noel's voice: 'How's it all going, precious?'

Then Simon's voice, petulant. 'All right, but she's not going to be the pushover you predicted.'

'Well, you've got plenty of time. If you can't have her eating out of your hands in twenty-four hours, you're not the man you were last night.'

Simon laughed and growled wolfishly. 'Good, wasn't it? But then it's always good with you. You — er — spur me on to greater endeavour.'

'Well, close your eyes and pretend it's me.'

'God that it was! I do miss you, darling. You won't get so hooked on Cory again so that you'll forget me, will you?'

'Darling,' Noel's deep voice was like a sedative. 'I wouldn't have angled you that part so I could spend all that time with you this summer, if I hadn't been a tiny bit smitten, now would I?'

'I suppose not.'

'What do you think of your son and heir?'

'Oh, pretty horrific. But then I'm not mad about babies. I thought you said he looked just like me.'

Noel started to laugh. Harriet put down the receiver and went into the bathroom and was violently sick. Then she stood trembling, leaning against the bathroom door, icy cold and sweating, wondering what the hell to do next.

She washed her face and went into the sitting-room. Simon was lounging across the armchair.

'Hello, beauty,' he said amiably. 'You look as though you've seen a ghost.'

'I've been listening in on the extension. I heard all your conversation with Noel.'

Simon sighed. 'Oh dear, you shouldn't have done that. Surely you know by now that eavesdroppers never . . .?'

'Simon,' she interrupted furiously. 'Stop it! Stop it! Why can't you be serious for once? How long have you been in love with Noel?'

'I'm not in love with her.'

'Well, how many times have you slept with her?'

'Once, twice. What the hell does it matter? I don't love her. It's you I love.'

'You couldn't love me, the way you were talking to her.'

'Oh, darling, haven't you heard the expression "sleeping your way to the top"? Well, I want that film part, and if it means chatting up an old prima-donna like Noel that's okay by me.'

Harriet stared at him appalled.

'And you were prepared to try and make a go of it with me, while still carrying on an affair with Noel? I don't understand you, Simon.'

He looked at her for a minute, mocking, his head on one side, his hands in his pockets.

'Well, then, I can't help you, can I?'

Then he started to laugh. 'Oh come on darling, see the funny side of it.'

Harriet shook her head. 'I don't think it's funny. I want to go home.'

It was a clear night, the stars shone electrically blue, the moon came over the crags and reflected milkily in the river. As he drove, Simon turned to look at Harriet.

'You're making a mistake going back, darling. Noel fights very dirty — and, however much Cory likes you as a plaything, he'll kick you out the moment she wants it.'

When they arrived at the house, Harriet let herself in and met Noel coming out of the drawing-room.

'Hullo, darlings,' she said. 'Had a lovers' tiff already?'

Harriet took a deep breath. 'I overheard your conversation with Simon on the telephone. I want to see Cory at once.'

Not a flicker of an eyelid did Noel betray her surprise. 'My dear, he's not here. He went out half-an-hour ago. I don't know when he'll be back. I think we'd better have a little chat together. Simon, angel, would you excuse us a minute?'

Shepherding Harriet into the drawing-room, she shut the door behind them.

Harriet sat down on the sofa. Her knees wouldn't stop trembling. Noel started pouring herself a drink.

199

'How can I make you understand,' she began, 'that I really love Cory? I admit I behaved badly in the past. But now it's different. I know he's the only person for me, and I'll do anything to get him back.'

'Like bringing your latest lover up here to lure me away and offering him the bait of a big film part?'

Noel banged the whisky bottle down on the metal tray.

'Oh, God!' she shouted. 'Grow up! I know you're nuts about Cory, but he doesn't give a damn about your stupid passion. I tried to let you out easily by getting Simon up here. He's ambitious as hell, that boy. He needed a bit of incentive. But if you honestly think I'm intending to have a prolonged affair with him and give him the lead in my next film, you need your head examined!'

She spoke as though Simon was a nasty mark on a new dress that the dry cleaners would have no trouble removing.

Harriet ran a dry tongue over her lips. 'I know Cory loves you, but he also likes me here looking after the children.'

'Darling,' Noel's eyes were huge now and strangely gentle. 'I did want to let you down easily. I admit I was the tiniest bit jealous of you. The children are wild about you, and so was Kit; and even Cory, who's notoriously hard to please, regarded you with something close to approval. But I got a letter from him this morning, which really convinced me I've got nothing to worry about.'

She opened her bag and took out a sheet of thick azure writing paper and handed it to Harriet. The black, almost illegible writing was unmistakable.

'Oh, darling,' she read. 'I'm totally destroyed. Ever since you left yesterday, I know that it's impossible for me to live without you any longer. I give in. Please, please come back, on any terms. I don't care. The thought that you could feel jealous of that zombie who looks after the children would be ludicrous, if it weren't tragic that something so trivial could keep us apart. I've got no complaints about her work, but she'll leave tomorrow if it means your coming back any sooner.'

If you walk into a torture chamber and ask to be tortured, Harriet reflected, you can't complain of the pain. Very carefully she folded Cory's letter and put it on the table, and sat still for a minute.

'And you'd like me to go now?' she said numbly.

Noel nodded. 'I think it would be better in every way. There's no need to say goodbye to the children. It'll only upset them. They need a mother and, from now on, I shall stay at home and look after them.'

'May I leave a letter for Cory telling him I'm going?'

'Of course you may,' said Noel kindly.

Before Harriet left, Noel gave her a cheque for £100. 'We wouldn't want you to starve.'

Harriet wished she were in a position to refuse.

CHAPTER TWENTY-FOUR

Harriet sat watching the smouldering log fire. She had been home with her parents a week now, and all was forgiven. But the peace and resignation she craved had not come. If it hadn't been for William, she would never have had the strength to go on living. What's going to happen to me? she thought in panic. I can't lump a broken heart around for the rest of my life.

None of the loose ends seemed to tie up either. Why had Cory come to her bedroom that last evening and tried to persuade her not to go off with Simon? Why hadn't he been home when she and Simon had returned later? One would have thought he'd be so delirious to have Noel back he'd never have left her side.

But as the days passed, it became increasingly obvious that she couldn't go on without news of him, until she knew that he and the children were all right. And what about Sevenoaks? She had put a PS on her letter asking Cory to look after him till she found a job where she could keep him. But how long would it be before Noel persuaded Cory that Sevenoaks was too much of a nuisance? But how could she find out how things were going? If she rang Mrs. Bottomley Noel might easily answer the telephone. Then she remembered Kit. Of course. He would certainly have news of Cory. The number was permanently engaged when she rang. He must have taken the telephone off the hook.

'I'm going up to London,' she said to her mother, as she went into the kitchen. 'I'll take William with me.'

Upstairs she glared at her worn reflection in the mirror.

'I'm almost beyond redemption,' she sighed sadly. But she brushed her hair until it shone, put on the grey dress

Cory had given her, and tried, without much success, to paint the circles out from under her eyes.

Kit's studio was in Islington. There was no answer when Harriet rang the bell. He must be out, she thought despairingly. It was nearly half past four and the milk hadn't been taken in. She rang again. Still no answer. Heavy-hearted, she started down the steps when the door opened and Kit, a golden giant, dishevelled and naked to the waist, stood blinking down at her. Then he gave a bellow of rage like an apoplectic colonel, which sent her even further down the steps.

'Harriet!' he shouted. 'Where the bloody hell do you think you're going?'

He bounded down the stairs, grabbed her by the scruff of the neck and pulled her inside the house. Then slammed the door and leant his huge shoulders against it.

'You little bitch!' he swore at her. 'After all your cant about loyalty. God, you make me sick!'

'W-what's the m-matter?' she faltered.

William had started to howl. Harriet herself was close to tears, when a ravishingly pretty coloured girl wandered out of a bedroom, wearing a scanty orange towel.

'What is all this noise, Keet?' she said yawning.

'Tangie, darling,' said Kit, taking the howling child from Harriet and handing him to her. 'Take this sweet little baby away and keep him quiet for a minute or two.'

The coloured girl's eyes flashed.

'Oh, no,' said Kit hastily, 'he's not mine, scout's honour! Nothing to do with me. Nor is she either, thank God. She's got herself mixed up with my unfortunate brother, Cory.'

William looked dubiously up at the sleek black face, but he stopped crying.

'Give him back to me,' protested Harriet.

'Shut up!' snarled Kit and, propelling her into the nearest room, shut the door behind them.

'Well?' he said, towering above her like some avenging angel. 'What made you do it? Swanning off with lover boy without a word of explanation.'

203

'It wasn't like that!' protested Harriet.

'Go on then,' said Kit coldly. 'Amaze me.'

'I didn't go off with Simon, and I left a letter for Cory with Noel.'

'The great postmistress,' said Kit acidly. 'You're even more stupid than I thought.'

He got up and poured himself a drink. 'I suppose you'd better tell me the whole story.'

When she had finished, he said, 'Noel seems to have over-reached herself this time. I told you never to believe a word she says. She must have torn your letter up and told Cory you'd done a bunk with Simon. He's still divorcing her. The case comes up next week.'

'It is?' Harriet whispered incredulously. 'But what about that letter from Cory Noel showed me, begging her to come back?'

'He probably wrote it years ago. She's always made a fuss about every nanny they had, and she hoards all her love letters. Did you notice the date?'

Harriet shook her head

'Well then. I had dinner with Cory last night. He's in a pretty bad shape.'

'He's in London?' asked Harriet, turning red then white 'Did he mention me?'

Kit conceded a grin. 'I've never known Cory really boring before. He's convinced he messed everything up by trying to pull you, then letting you go off with Simon.'

'Oh, God!' said Harriet with a sob. 'What am I going to do?'

Kit got to his feet. 'You'd better go round to his house at once and ask him to take you back.'

'I can't! What can I say to him?'

'I should tell him the truth — that you love him. I'll get you a taxi. Don't worry about William. We'll look after him for an hour or two.'

CHAPTER TWENTY-FIVE

In the taxi, she desperately tried to keep her hands steady as she re-did her face, spilling scent and foundation all over her bag. Now they were entering Chiltern Street; there was the familiar dark blue house. Oh wait, she wanted to say, I haven't put any mascara on. Then she thought, how silly to worry about mascara at a time like this!

She rang the bell and waited, hands clammy, throat dry, her heart pounding like surf. When Cory opened the door he seemed about to tell her to go to hell, then he realized who she was and just stared at her in amazement. She stared back unable to speak. For a moment, she thought he was going to take her in his arms, then he stood back to let her come in. They went upstairs to the room where he'd first interviewed her. He seemed to have grown taller and thinner, paler too — the haughty, inscrutable face heavily shadowed and tired. There was an embarrassed silence; then he said, 'Sit down How are you?'

Harriet perched on the edge of one of the yellow silk armchairs. Her legs wouldn't hold her up any longer.

'I'm all right.'

'And William?'

'He's lovely.'

She refused when he offered her a cigarette, her hands were shaking too much.

'How's it going, you and Simon?' he asked in a matter-of-fact voice, as he concentrated on lighting his own cigarette.

'I'm not with Simon, I never have been — only for a couple of hours that Saturday night. I realized then we were completely washed-up. Didn't Noel give you my letter?'

He shook his head slowly. He didn't seem interested in

205

explanations. 'Where are you now?'

'At home.'

'Made it up with your parents? That's good.'

'I came up to London to look for a job,' she lied.

'Why don't you come back?' He paused. 'The children are desolate without you.'

'And you?' she wanted to cry.

He was playing with a green glass paperweight on his desk. 'If you were to come back,' he said carefully, 'there wouldn't be any funny business. I shall be abroad for most of the rest of the year.'

'No!' she interrupted him with a violence that brought her to her feet, face-to-face with him. 'I couldn't come back on those terms.'

'I see,' he said in a flat voice.

She went over to the window and looked out at the young leaves of the plane tree, glinting white in the setting sun. Her throat felt like sand. She was trying to summon up courage to do the most difficult thing she'd ever done in her life.

'For someone who's too clever by three-quarters,' she said in a shaking voice, 'you're awfully dumb, where women are concerned. Don't you see, if I were living in the same house, and you were away all the time, and never laid a finger on me, I'd die of frustration?'

Cory looked up — the weary eyes suddenly alert.

'Don't you understand,' she went on slowly, 'that I only ran away because Noel said she was coming back to you, and I just couldn't take it?'

'Go on, go on,' he said, his face as white as hers.

'Don't you understand,' she sobbed, 'that I love you? Love you more than anything else in the world. And I can't live without you!'

She didn't need to say any more. He was across the room, the great arms she had been waiting for closed round her, and he was kissing her so fiercely she almost lost consciousness.

Then he said despairingly, 'Oh, darling Harriet. I love

you. But it wouldn't work. I'm too old and tired and bitter for you.'

'You're not,' she jibbered. 'Just thinking about you turns me to jelly,' she went on. 'I've never been crazy over anyone as I am over you.'

Cory stared down at her, at the parted lips, the burning eyes, the flushed cheeks, the dishevelled hair.

'Hey,' he said wonderingly. 'You do love me, don't you? What the hell am I going to do about it?'

'You will do something, won't you?' she said nuzzling against him, so he could feel the frantic beating of her heart.

'Be careful,' he said, trying to smile.

'What do you mean?'

'I'm beginning to feel as though I can be consoled,' and he kissed her forehead, and then her cheeks, salt with tears, and then her lips.

'Oh, darling,' he muttered. 'Don't give me time to be ashamed of what I'm doing. I'm going to keep you. What else can I do, when you're so adorable? But you don't know what you're in for. I shall make a bloody awful husband.'

Harriet leapt away in horror. 'I didn't mean that! You don't have to marry me.'

Cory smiled. 'You're not the only one who's allowed to dictate terms. You've just said you'll never come back to Yorkshire unless I devote every minute of the day to laying fingers on you.'

Harriet blushed. 'I never said that.'

'So if I take you, it's for good. For ever and ever.'

She was trembling now, really perturbed.

'But I forced you into it.'

He sat down and pulled her on to his knee.

'Sweetheart,' he said very gently. 'I know what a shy, re-served person you are, except when you get sloshed at Hunt Balls and I know what it cost you to come here and tell me you loved me. But if you knew what it meant to me, for the first time in ten years, the miracle of hearing the girl I love tell me she loves me, and really mean it.

'It's strange,' he went on, pushing her hair back from her forehead. 'I can't even place the moment I started loving

207

you. It's so mixed up with convincing myself I was acting for your own good — dragging you away from Billy, bawling you out for going out with Kit, because he was a wolf, trying to persuade you not to go off with Simon, because he'd make you a rotten husband, but all the time I must have been eaten up with jealousy because I wanted you for myself. I got so used to being hung-up on Noel, I never believed I could love anyone else, and then you ran away and the house was like a morgue. I knew I ought to give you and Simon a chance, but after five days I couldn't stand it any longer, so I came South. And . . . look.'

He pulled a packet of cigarettes out of his pocket, on which was scribbled a telephone number.

'That's Simon's number,' said Harriet

He nodded. 'I was going to ring up and try to persuade you to come back.'

And then Harriet realized that this awkward, difficult, beautiful man really did love her.

'Oh, I'm so happy, so happy,' she said, bursting into tears and flinging her arms round his neck. 'You're really over Noel?'

'Really, really. She's like measles — you don't catch her twice.'

Harriet giggled. 'That sounds more like Kit. Where is she now?'

'I don't know. Conserving her energies somewhere for her appearance in the divorce courts next week.' His face hardened. 'I'm afraid it's going to be very nasty. She'll probably cite you.'

'I don't care,' and she began to kiss him.

'Are the children really all right?' she said later. 'God, I've missed them so much.'

'They've missed you — if I hadn't come down here, they were threatening to get on a train to London and fetch you themselves. We'll ring them up and give them the good news in a minute. Christ, it is good news.'

Only one thing was nagging Harriet. 'How's Sevenoaks?' she said.

'Well actually he's here,' said Cory, 'I thought he'd have withdrawal symptoms if we both abandoned him, so I brought him with me.'

'Oh, you *are* sweet. Can I see him?'

'Sure, he's in my bedroom, down the passage.'

He followed Harriet to the door, adding, 'he's greatly improved by the way. In your absence, I took the opportunity of teaching him a few manners. In actual fact he's quite trainable if one's firm. He sits and stays now, and comes when he's called. And at least I've stopped him climbing on to beds and chewing everything up.'

'That's amazing,' said Harriet, opening the bedroom door, and looking inside.

On the bed sprawled Sevenoaks, his shaggy grey head on the pillow, snoring loudly. Beside him, chewed to bits, lay the remains of a pair of suede shoes.

'Oh doesn't he look sweet lying there?' said Harriet.

Sevenoaks opened an eye, and suddenly saw Harriet.

'Stay,' thundered Cory, 'Stay.'

Sevenoaks took a flying leap through the air, and landing at Harriet's feet threw himself on her in ecstasy, nearly knocking her sideways, moaning with joy.

'Stay,' howled Cory.

Sevenoaks gave Cory an old-fashioned look and took no notice at all.

Harriet caught Cory's eye and went off into peals of laughter.

'Oh, darling,' she said, 'are you sure you really want to marry me? You won't get fed up?'

'Of course I will, but not for very long,' said Cory, pulling Sevenoaks off. 'I mean we're virtually married already. We've got three children and a problem dog between us. We've spent long evenings discussing their education and what we feel about life, you've cooked and washed and kept house for me. The only thing we haven't done is slept together, and I don't have any major hangups about that.'

'We've eaten all the gingerbread,' said Harriet ecstatically, 'and now we can enjoy the lovely, lovely gilt.'

'Exactly,' said Cory, and he began kissing her . . .

209

Octavia

For Emma Renton with Love

CHAPTER ONE

The moment I set eyes on Jeremy West I knew I had to have him. I was sitting in Arabella's, watching a crowd of debs and other phonies undulating round the floor and thinking they were dancing, when suddenly the bamboo curtain was pushed aside and a blond man walked in and stood looking around for a waitress.

Even in the gloom with which Arabella's conceals its decor I could see that he had class — tall and lean, with one of those beautiful high cheek-boned faces with long, dreamy eyes like Rudolph Nureyev.

As the waitress came up to him, I watched to see if he'd leer down her exposed jacked-up bosom. He didn't. She led him to a table next but one to ours. He was obviously waiting for someone. Then a plump girl came through the bamboo curtains and stood blinking round with short-sighted eyes. He stood up and waved to her, and her face broke into a smile that was faintly familiar. Then I recogNized her. It was Gussie Forbes; we'd been at school together. How on earth had she managed to land a havoc-maker like that?

'Look,' I said, nudging Charlie. 'That's Gussie Forbes, we were at school together.'

Charlie peered over his very dark glasses, which he only wears to emphasize his Mafia-like appearance.

'She doesn't seem to have recovered from it as well as you have,' he said. 'She obviously skips the features on slimming, when she reads women's magazines, and concentrates on the ones about "three dimensional charm". I suppose you want to rush over and reminisce about the "dorm" and the French mistress's beard?'

But I wasn't listening any longer.

'Do look,' I said. 'He's ordering champagne. Do you suppose they're celebrating?'

'Can't be much to celebrate, getting lumbered with a bird that looks like that,' said Charlie, beckoning the waitress and ordering more whisky.

Charlie is immensely successful, newly rich, young and, like me, rootless. He is not interested in anyone unless they're likely to advance his career or improve his image. At that time, just as I was getting bored with him, he was beginning to fall in love with me. This irked rather than worried me. I was used to men falling in love with me. When I gave Charlie the push, he would nurse his hurt pride for a fortnight, change the colour of his Ferrari and move on to the next affaire.

I couldn't take my eyes off the man who was buying champagne for Gussie Forbes. She was raising her glass to him now, and he was holding her hand and smiling at her. He had a beautiful smile, gentle and creasing his face in all the right places. Now he was running a hand down her cheek. It was really most mystifying.

Charlie was rabbiting on about the chic men's clothes shop he owns, who had been in, how difficult it was to get the right staff. Gussie and her man were getting up to dance. He moved easily, with the grace of some jungle cat. Gussie bounced around, wiggling her arms and her large bottom. She resembled a baby elephant taking a dip in the pool. Charlie took out a gold cigarette case, lit two cigarettes and handed one to me. He is full of these self-consciously sexy gestures which only work if you're Cary Grant.

Gussie was now writhing and pushing her hair about in utter abandon.

'They never taught your girlfriend to dance at school,' Charlie said, watching her in appalled amusement.

'She was taller than most of us then, so she always had to dance man.'

The floor had filled up now and Gussie and her man were dancing close together. He pressed his cheek against her hair, but his eyes wandered lazily around the room. Her eyes were closed in ecstasy and she had a fatuous smile on her face. God, she was just as wet as she had been at school!

Charlie put his hand on my thigh and drained his glass. 'Shall we go?' he said.

'In a minute. Let's have one more drink.'

The music had stopped, and they were coming off the floor right past our table. I ran my hand through my hair to loosen it and pulled the front piece over one eye.

'Hullo Gussie,' I said loudly.

'For God's sake,' whispered Charlie.

Gussie peered through the gloom, blinking.

'Over here,' I said.

Suddenly she saw me and gave a shriek of schoolgirl excitement.

'Goodness, it can't be, Octavia! Is it really you?'

'Yes, really me. Come and have a drink.'

Gussie pushed through the tables, pink face shining with excitement, bosom heaving from her exertions.

'How lovely to see you.' She kissed my proffered cheek. 'And looking so stunning too!'

She dragged the blond man forward. 'This is Jeremy West. It's a very special evening for us, we've just got engaged!'

Engaged! Hence the champagne. At least they weren't married yet!

'Congratulations,' I said, and gave Jeremy West one of my long, hard, smouldering looks. 'How very exciting.'

He smiled back at me. 'Yes, isn't it?'

'Jeremy darling,' said Gussie. 'This is Octavia Brennen. We were at school together, in the same form, but not for very long. Octavia did something perfectly dreadful like eating one of the harvest festival apples in church, so they sent her away. Life was very dull after that.'

'I can imagine it was,' said Jeremy West. Oh, how heartbreaking that smile was.

'This is Charles Mancini,' I said.

Charlie nodded enigmatically. With his Mexican bandit's face, pink suede suit and dark grey shirt, he looked both sinister and glamorous. No girl could be ashamed of being seen with Charlie.

215

'Why don't we all have a drink?' I said, ignoring a vicious kick on the ankles from Charlie.

Gussie looked up at Jeremy. 'Why not?' she said.

He nodded. 'Charlie, get the waitress to bring some more chairs,' I said.

'What were you drinking?' said Charlie sulkily.

'Champagne,' I said. 'It's a celebration.'

'I've had quite enough to drink, I'm already getting giggly,' said Gussie. 'Can I have some orange squash?'

I told you she was wet.

'But you'll have champagne?' Charlie said to Jeremy.

'I much prefer whisky. Let me buy this round.'

Charlie shook his head and summoned the waitress.

'You actually got engaged today?' I said.

'Well, yesterday,' said Gussie, hauling a bra strap up a fat white shoulder.

'Have you got a ring?'

'Yes. Isn't it lovely?' She held out a short stubby hand that had never seen a manicure in its life. On the third finger glowed an antique ring — rubies and pearls surrounded a plait of hair.

Of course he would choose something as subtly pretty as that. All the guys I knew would have given me solitaires or sapphires as big as a gull's egg.

'It's gorgeous,' I said looking through my hair at Jeremy. 'You are lucky, Gussie. Really beautiful men with exquisite taste into the bargain are at a premium these days.'

Charlie, busy ordering drinks, missed that remark. Jeremy blushed slightly.

'Yes, he is beautiful, isn't he,' sighed Gussie. 'I have to keep pinching myself to prove it's not a dream that he should have chosen an old frump like me.'

'When you've both finished discussing me like a prize bull . . .' said Jeremy, but he said it gently and, taking a loose strand of Gussie's hair, smoothed it behind her ear.

The drinks arrived.

'Gosh, thanks awfully. It's terribly kind of you,' said Gussie, beaming at Charlie. I remembered of old how ridiculously grateful she'd always been about the smallest things.

'And that's a beautiful suit,' she added wistfully. 'Jeremy would look divine in clothes like that, but he's such an old square.'

I waited for Charlie to wince, but he didn't and was soon telling her all about the shop. That was another thing about her, she always managed to make people talk about themselves, and gave the impression she was really interested.

I gave Jeremy a long speculative look. He dropped his eyes first and took a gulp of whisky.

'That's better. I've never been wild about champagne.'

'I only like it for elevenses,' I said. 'When are you getting married?'

'November, we thought.'

'Not before! But that's light years away! Why on earth wait so long?'

'I've got a large overdraft already, and I don't relish the idea of living off Gussie.'

Gussie, I remembered, had a bit of money of her own.

'What do you do?'

'I'm in publishing, as an editor. I write a bit myself as well.'

'What sort of things?'

'Oh, poetry, a bit of criticism, the odd review, nothing likely to make any money.'

He looked like a poet with those dreamy blue eyes and long blond hair, *yet* it wasn't a weak face; there was a strength about the mouth and chin. I got out a cigarette; he lit it for me. I held his hand to steady the flame, looking up at him from under my lashes. Surely he could feel the electricity between us? He put away his lighter.

'Why are you called Octavia?'

'I was born on October the 25th. My mother'd gone off my father by then and was mad about someone else, and she couldn't have been less amused by my arrival, or be bothered to think of a name for me. So she called me after the month. It's a damn silly name to be saddled with.'

'It's a beautiful name. It suits you. Did your mother marry the man she was mad about?'

'Oh no, someone quite different, and then someone else, and then someone else. My father was married twice too, but he's dead now. I've lost count of my stepbrothers and sisters.'

'It can't have been very easy for you. I come from a broken home myself, but not one that's in smithereens. Do you see your mother?'

'Occasionally, when she's sober, or comes to London. I hardly ever go down to the country to see her. I hate scenes. She's rather sad now. Her looks are going and she gets terrible maudlin fits reminiscing about my father, which drive her present husband mad.'

How gentle and compassionate his eyes were now, and how ridiculously long his eyelashes.

'I'm sorry,' I said, putting a husky little break into my voice that I'd perfected over the years. 'I didn't mean to bore you with family history. I never talk about it usually.'

That was a lie. It was Act I in the Octavia Brennen seduction routine — make them feel I need looking after.

'I'm flattered you told me,' he said.

'How did you two meet?'

'Gussie came and did temporary typing for me while my own secretary was skiing. She wasn't wildly efficient, every letter had to be typed over again, and she kept putting things in the wrong envelopes, but she was so sweet that when my own streamlined secretary came back and restored order, I realized I was missing Gus. I telephoned the agency, started taking her out and that was that.'

'I'm not surprised; she's so lovely.' I hoped he couldn't detect the whopping ring of insincerity in my voice. 'She always protected me from all the bullies when we were at school.'

'Yes, she grows on you.'

She was evidently growing on Charlie.

'Once I tried to diet faithfully,' she was saying. 'Day after day, week after week, not eating a thing but lettuce and steamed fish. But all I'd lost after six weeks was half an inch in height!' She shrieked with laughter. So did Charlie and Jeremy.

They were playing the Rolling Stones latest record. I leaned forward, pressing my elbows together to deepen my

218

cleavage. I saw Jeremy glance down at it and quickly glance away.

'I'm mad for this tune,' I said.

'What are we waiting for?' said Charlie, getting up.

Dancing is the thing I do best in the world. It seems to release all the frustrations from my body, all the evils from my soul.

I was wearing a long, gold, semi-transparent tunic, exactly the same colour as my hair, with a mass of gold chains round my neck. I felt like a piece of seaweed streaming with the tide of the music, flowing now this way, now that. I knew everyone in the room was watching me, the women with envy, the men with lust.

Charlie dances superbly too; his body seems to turn to rubber. I never fancy him so much as when we're on the dance floor. Through a sheet of gold hair I saw Jeremy was watching me. He turned and said something to Gussie; she smiled and looked in my direction. The music stopped; hand-in-hand Charlie and I wandered back to our table.

'We're off,' I said, deciding this was the ideal exit note.

'Going home?' said Gussie.

'No, we're going to another place,' said Charlie. 'It's just been opened by a mate of mine. Want to come?' He *had* changed his tune.

Jeremy looked at Gussie; she shook her head.

'We've both got to get up early in the morning, but do give me your telephone number, Octavia. We must keep in touch.'

'We must,' I said, staring shamelessly at Jeremy. 'You must both come to dinner.'

'Yes, we'd like to,' he said, emphasizing the 'we'.

Even when we finally got home, I was still walking on air, unable to keep the Cheshire cat grin of exultation off my face. As the lift shot up to the penthouse flat I had the feeling it might take me through the roof straight up to the stars.

My flat was beautiful. Alexander, my brother, who is an expert at interior decorating, had helped me do it up. Everyone gasped when they first saw it. Huge fleshy potted plants, banked at each end of the long drawing room, gave the effect of a jungle. The fourth wall was all window, looking out onto the lamp-lit plane trees of Green Park. Kicking off my shoes, I felt my feet sink into the thick, white carpet.

Almost immediately the telephone rang.

'Answer it, would you?' I said to Charlie.

'Yeah?' said Charlie, picking up the receiver. 'It's someone called Ricardo,' he added. 'He sounds a long way away.'

'Crackling with lust,' I said, taking the receiver. 'Go and get a bottle out of the fridge, darling,' I said to him loudly, so Ricardo could hear.

'Hi, my darling,' I said to Ricardo.

When I had taken my time over the telephone call, I wandered into the bedroom. Charlie was lying naked on the blond fur counterpane, drinking champagne and looking beautiful and sulky. On the wall above his head hung my favourite picture: a 16th century Italian oil painting of Adam and Eve in the garden of Eden, surrounded by hundreds of animals and birds.

'It's vital,' my brother had insisted, 'to have something pretty to look at over one's bed to while away the excruciating boredom of sexual intercourse.' I knew that picture pretty well.

Ignoring Charlie, I undressed unhurriedly and sat down at my dressing table, admiring my reflection in the triple mirror. I liked what I saw. My body was as warm as an apricot in the soft light, my breasts, in contrast with the extreme slenderness of the rest of my body, had a heavy golden ripeness. Voluptuously I began to brush my hair.

'Who's Ricardo?' said Charlie, trying to appear cool.

'A rather persistent bit of my past,' I said. 'You know I never let a dago by.'

Charlie laughed. 'I hope he is past.'

He got up, crossed the room and stood behind me, his hands caressing my shoulders. His body was dark brown from the Marbella sun as he bent his head to kiss me. I could see the gold streaks growing out of his dark hair.

We made a stunning picture, like a Fellini film.

'Come on, Narcissus,' he said. 'It's time for bed.'

Afterwards he reached out for the champagne and gave me a glass.

'Christ, you were sensational tonight,' he muttered sleepily, as I examined my now tousled but not unpleasing reflection in the mirror opposite. 'What got into you?'

'You did,' I said, and laughed softly. There was no need to tell him the whole time we had been making love I had been practising every trick in the trade, imagining he was Jeremy West.

He fell asleep almost immediately, with his arms around me. It was terribly hot. I soon wriggled out of his embrace, and lay on my back, thinking about Jeremy, memorizing every angle of his face and every word he'd spoken to me. The fact that he was engaged to Gussie didn't worry me a bit, made it more of a challenge.

Eventually I got up, went to the bathroom, removed every scrap of make-up, then luxuriously massaged skin food all over my body. Then I took a couple of sleeping pills, switched off the telephone and fell into a dreamless sleep.

CHAPTER TWO

When I awoke at two o'clock in the afternoon Charlie had gone, leaving me a note on the pillow, saying he loved me, and to ring him when I was conscious. I switched on the telephone, it rang almost immediately. "Ullo, this is the Moroccan Embassy,' I said.

'Octavia, you *are* dreadful; it's Gussie here,' came the breathless, eager voice.

'Gussie, how lovely!'

'I thought I'd ring straightaway, before we lost touch.'

'You must come to dinner,' I said.

'We'd love to, but actually we've got a plan. Are you doing anything the weekend after next?'

'I'm supposed to be going to France, but it's a fluid arrangement.'

'Well, I expect you'd find it awfully boring, but Jeremy shares a boat with another chap, and we've got it next weekend. We wondered if you'd like to come too.'

'I might get seasick,' I said, trying to keep the excitement out of my voice.

'Oh you couldn't! It's a barge, and all we do is drift up and down the canals, going through the locks and tying up where it takes our fancy. Would you like to bring Charlie?'

'He'll be away,' I lied. 'It's not a big thing, Charlie and me, we're just mates.'

'You haven't got someone special you'd like to bring?'

'I did have. We were going to get married, but he was killed in a car crash earlier this year.'

'Oh, poor, poor Tavy,' she said, unconsciously lapsing into the nickname of schooldays. 'Oh God, I'm sorry.'

There was a pause.

'Well, anyway,' she floundered on. 'If you didn't want to bring someone, Jeremy had thought . . . do you know Gareth Llewellyn?'

'No, should I? The name sounds faintly familiar.'

'He's a great friend of Jeremy's. We've been trying to persuade him to come on the boat for ages, but he works so hard, he can never get away. I think you'd like him; he's awfully attractive.'

I didn't care if he were. My mind was already jumping ahead, dreaming of a long weekend, drifting up and down the canals, lounging on the deck in my bikini by day, my hair gleaming pale in the moonlight by night — how could I not hook Jeremy?

'It sounds great,' I said. 'I'd love to come. Why don't you and Jeremy come to dinner on Monday and we can talk about it?'

I planned Monday's dinner like a military operation. As I'm a rotten cook and can be guaranteed to louse up even fake mashed potato, I arranged for the food to be sent up from the restaurant around the corner, so I could pass it off as my own efforts.

Gussie had obviously given Jeremy the impression that I was a frivolous social butterfly and I was determined to dispel it. I scoured the shops until I found a dress that made me look both demure and sexy, and I bought all Jeremy's books — two slender volumes of poetry and a book of criticism of John Donne's poems. I found Jeremy's poems quite incomprehensible. The long, rather self-admiring introduction written by Jeremy himself made me understand them even less.

The doorbell rang as I was spraying scent round the flat. Gussie stood in front of Jeremy, clutching a huge box of chocolates.

'For you,' she said, giving me a bear hug. 'You're the only friend I have who doesn't need to diet. Goodness, that blue looks stunning!'

I couldn't say the same for her. She was wearing a scarlet dress which clashed horribly with her flushed face. We went into the drawing-room and I poured everyone stiff drinks.

'How delicious to have a flat like this all to oneself,' said Gussie, collapsing on to the sofa.

'I can't wait to get out of London on Friday,' I said.

'Nor can I,' said Gussie, shovelling nuts into her face like a starved squirrel. 'My office is like a furnace. Gareth *is* coming, by the way. I lured him by telling him what a knockout you were.'

'Well then, he's doomed to bitter disappointment,' I said with a sidelong glance at Jeremy.

'Not in your case,' he said, staring back at me until I demurely dropped my eyes.

Oh Good-ee, I thought, it's beginning to work. I sat on the sofa, stretching long brown legs in front of me. I saw Jeremy looking at them surreptitiously. I didn't blame him, they were a far prettier sight than Gussie's tree trunks, displayed almost in their entirety by a rucked-up skirt.

'Gareth wants us to go round after dinner for a drink,' she said. 'He says he can't wait until Friday.'

'Do you like him?' I asked Jeremy, as though it were only his opinion that mattered.

'Yes, I do. He's one of my oldest friends. We were at Oxford together. His father was a Welsh miner, and he was a scholarship boy with a chip as big as a plank on his shoulder. Then he ended up with a first.'

'He's got a mind like a steel trap but he's not at all academic,' added Gussie. 'All he's ever wanted to do is make masses of money. He's got his own company now, with thousands of little men working for him putting up sky-scrapers. He's the most energetic man I've ever met.'

'He sounds exhausting,' I said, filling Jeremy's drink.

'Not really,' said Jeremy. 'You occasionally feel you want to add water, but on the whole he's fine.'

'Won't he get bored on the boat?'

'Not with you around. He loves girls.'

'He has time for them?'

'Oh, yes,' sighed Gussie. 'He's awfully attractive. He makes you feel all body, somehow.'

Dinner was a success. Luigi's had surpassed themselves.

Both Jeremy and Gussie were extremely impressed.

Over coffee, I opened Gussie's chocolates.

'Oh, we oughtn't to,' said Gussie, rootling round for a soft centre. 'We bought them for you.'

It was then that I played my trump card. Turning to Jeremy I said, 'You never let on you were the Jeremy West. You've been a god of mine ever since I can remember. I've got all your books.'

How sweet he looked when he blushed.

'And you've actually read them?'

'Of course. I know most of your poems by heart. I like the one about Victoria Station late at night best.' I reeled off a few lines.

After that nothing stopped him. The occasional murmur from me was all he needed. I didn't listen to what he was saying, I was too busy gazing hypnotically into his eyes. It was Gussie who finally halted him, when she'd finished the chocolates.

'Dar-ling, if we're going to Gareth's, it's gone ten o'clock.'

He was all contrition. 'Sweetheart, I am sorry. When I get on my hobby horse, it's like crossing a motorway in the rush-hour, trying to stop me.' He took her hand. 'It's so rare meeting someone who actually understands what I'm trying to say.'

'Unlike me,' said Gussie, without rancour. 'Let's quickly do the washing-up.'

'Absolutely not,' I said firmly. I wasn't going to have her finding Luigi's take-away carrier bags in the kitchen.

'Oh, well, if you insist. Can I go to the loo?'

Jeremy and I went into the drawing-room.

'There you are,' I said, pointing to his books on one of the bottom shelves. I'd taken the jackets off and dirtied them up a bit.

He looked at me for a second. 'You're very unexpected, you know.'

'I am?'

'Yeah. When we met last week I thought you were one of those impossibly beautiful girls, incapable of doing anything but look glamorous. Now I find you know how to make a flat look wonderful, you cook like an angel, and you seem to know more about books than any woman I've ever met!'

'I aim to please,' I said. 'Have you got a cigarette?'

'Of course.' He lit one for me.

'Gussie seems determined to get me off with this Gareth man.'

'Gussie's a romantic; she longs for everyone to be as happy as she is. I'm sure you'll like him. Most women do.'

'I'm choosy,' I said carefully. 'I prefer to do my own hunting.'

For the first time we really looked at each other, slowly, lingeringly, exploring each other's faces, unable to tear our eyes away.

'Stop it,' he said, but quite gently. 'Gussie'll be back in a minute.'

The hot June night blazed with stars. We drove through London with the roof down and the wireless blaring, in wild spirits. We were all a bit tight. As it was only a two-seater I had insisted on sitting in the luggage compartment on the right side so I could catch Jeremy's eye in the driving mirror. When we swung round corners I let my fingers rest lightly on his shoulder.

Suddenly I felt a pang. Perhaps it was a bit much trying to nick him from Gussie. Then I saw Gussie put her hand on his thigh, not in a very sexy way, just in a friendly gesture of togetherness, and I was shot through with jealousy. The pang disappeared. Any girl who let herself get as fat as Gussie deserved to lose a man like Jeremy anyway.

I managed to show as much leg as possible as I got out of the car. In the row of large white, elegant Kensington houses, Gareth Llewellyn's stood out like a sore thumb. It was painted violet, with a brilliant scarlet door. How ostentatious can you get, I thought.

Unexpectedly, the door was answered by a girl with long red hair, eyes the colour of greengages and endless legs.

'Mr. West,' she said, giving Jeremy a pussy-cat smile. 'Come in. Mr. Llewellyn is upstairs; perhaps you'd follow me.'

On the third floor, standing in the doorway, stood a tall, thickset man, smoking a cigar. Jeremy collapsed into his arms, clutching at his shirt and gasping out some story about having become separated from the main party with which he had scaled all but the final peak. 'Brandy,' he croaked and, staggering past the man with the cigar, collapsed onto a pile of cushions. Gussie shrieked with laughter.

'I think he's a bit tight. Hullo Gareth darling,' she said, kissing him. 'This is Octavia Brennen. Isn't she a knockout?'

'How do you do?' I said, putting on my society voice because I was embarrassed.

'Very well, thank you,' he mimicked me, looking me over very slowly, like a judge examining a show hack.

He turned and smiled at Gussie. 'She's beautiful, Gus. For once you haven't exaggerated.'

'Are you sure you two haven't met before?' said Gussie. 'I should have thought you would have, being jet-setters and all that.'

Gareth Llewellyn examined me a bit more and shook his head.

'No, I never forget a body. Did she really come up the stairs? I thought girls like that only came down the chimney at Christmas time.'

His voice was low in both senses of the word, with a soft but very discernable Welsh accent. I had the feeling he was laughing at me. Gussie shrieked with more giggles; she was beginning to get seriously on my nerves.

We joined Jeremy in a room which looked like the sunset people walk hand-in-hand into, at the end of technicolor films — brilliant pink walls, covered in books and paintings, scarlet curtains, parquet glimmering in pools round flamingo-coloured longhaired rugs, piles of white fur cushions and a long orange sofa. It was vulgar, but it worked. Papers were scattered over the floor and the girl who'd let us in started picking them up.

'I love your cushions,' said Gussie, collapsing onto a pile beside Jeremy.

'I took my hangover to Habitat last Saturday and bought

227

them. At least they keep everyone horizontal,' said Gareth, winking at me and moving towards a bookshelf of leather-bound volumes. The next moment he'd pressed a button and the entire works of Walter Scott slid back to reveal a vast cocktail cabinet.

'Now,' he said. 'What would anyone like?'

He was absolutely *not* my type. His face was heavy with a powerful butt of a jaw, big crooked nose, full sensual mouth and wicked black eyes which seemed to be continually laughing at some private joke.

His skin was swarthy, and his thick black hair, prematurely streaked with grey, grew over his collar and in long sideboards down his cheeks. He was wearing light grey corduroy trousers and a dark blue shirt, open at the neck to show a mat of black hair. His height and massive shoulders didn't entirely draw the eye away from a thickening waist-line.

He handed me a drink. 'There you are, baby. It's a real L.O.'

'L.O.?'

'Leg opener. Never fails to work.'

Blushing angrily, I turned away.

By the time he had fixed us all drinks, the beautiful red-head had collected all the papers from the floor.

'You haven't met my P.A., Mrs. Smith, have you?' said Gareth. 'Now, in her case the 'A' stands for Aphrodisiac. Do you want a drink, lovely?'

She shook her head and gave him her pussy-cat smile.

'I ought to be getting home. My poor husband will be wondering what the hell's happened.'

'I'll see you out,' said Gareth. 'I won't be a minute,' he added to us.

'Isn't he gorgeous?' said Gussie.

'Great,' I replied, unenthusiastically.

There was a crude power about him. I could see why certain women might go for him — but not me. I detest those big, hunky aggressively sexual men; they make me feel claustrophobic. I like my men gentle, reticent, subtle. Gareth Llewellyn was about as subtle as a steam roller in overdrive.

I wandered round the room examining objects and giving Jeremy the opportunity to admire my figure. I avoided looking into an adjoining room, after glimpsing one of the biggest double beds I'd ever seen. I half expected to see a blond in gold lame pyjamas revving-up beneath the sheets.

A slight breeze swayed the curtains, bringing a scent of mignonette and tobacco plants from the window box outside. I looked out of the window. Down below Gareth Llewellyn was talking to Mrs. Smith. Suddenly he pulled her into his arms and kissed her very thoroughly. After a minute, he let her go and opened the car door for her. She patted his cheek with her hand.

As he turned to come back into the house, he looked up and caught me looking at him, and grinned.

The telephone rang. Gussie picked up the receiver.

'Hullo, yes. He's downstairs. Hang on a minute. Gareth,' she yelled, 'telephone.'

He grimaced apologetically at us as he came in and took the receiver.

'Vinnie, baby, how are you? Yeah. I've missed you too. Sweetheart, I haven't a hope this evening. I'm knee-deep in people, and later I've got to work. I've got one hell of a day tomorrow. Listen, darling, what about Wednesday evening?' God, that Welsh voice could turn it on.

Trying not to listen, I turned to Jeremy. He smiled at me reassuringly.

'What other writers do you like?' I said.

'Keats, of course, Thomas Campion, some of A. E. Housman.'

'What do you think of Robert Browning?' I asked.

'Why?' said Gareth, coming off the telephone. 'Is he marrying anyone we know?'

Gussie giggled. 'You mustn't mob them up; they've been having high-powered intellectual conversations all evening. Don't you think, Tavy, that the colours of Gareth's curtains would be ideal for my bridesmaids?'

After that I was forced to listen to her rabbiting on about her wedding. I lounged on the floor, propped against the sofa, lacing my fingers behind my head to show off my bust, and rucking up my skirt. With my other ear, I listened to Jeremy's conversation with Gareth.

'Is that bird really your secretary?'

'Mrs. Smith?' said Gareth. 'Quite a doll isn't she?'

'Doesn't she mind working at this hour?'

'Mr. Smith is an in-work actor; irregular hours suit her. So stop eating your heart out, you'll never get your spoon into that pudding.'

The telephone rang. It was South America on the line. Gareth, claiming it was business, took it into the bedroom. Jeremy and I helped ourselves to more drink.

'Does he always carry on like this?' I said.

'With girls? Usually, not always. He isn't trying to prove anything, he's just a glutton. He can't pass anyone up.'

'He ought to get married,' said Gussie. 'He needs the love of a good woman.'

'He'd need the love of four good mistresses as well to keep him going,' I said. 'Are you installing a telephone on the boat?'

'No, that's one of the conditions of his coming down, no telephones,' said Gussie. 'I'm going to make some coffee.'

She wandered out of the room. I got to my feet and strolled over to the fireplace to examine the pile of invitations — parties, dinners, business functions. Jeremy came over and stood beside me. I looked up at our reflections side by side in the huge mirror above the fireplace.

'How odd,' I said slowly. 'Have you noticed how alike we are, both blue-eyed and blonde? We could be brother and sister. I've always felt incest has the edge on all other relationships.'

Jeremy's breath was coming rapidly and his eyes had gone almost glazed with lust.

'You must know I don't feel remotely brotherly towards you.'

I looked up at him, running my tongue slowly along my bottom lip.

'How *do* you feel?' I said softly.

'Bloody disturbed — and I'm not amused by sleepless nights either.'

OCTAVIA

'Oh, nor am I, nor am I. We can't do anything about it, you know.'

'Of course we can't, but that doesn't stop me being obsessed with you. You're the most beautiful girl I've seen in my life.' He paused. 'I suppose lots of men have told you that.'

'A few. Not many of them meant it.'

'Well I do,' he said angrily.

'Do you *not* want me to come on the boat?'

'Of course I want you to . . . and, well . . . Gussie would be so disappointed.'

'You realize how difficult it's going to be, being thrown together all the time.'

'We shall probably both go mad, but rather that than you staying away because of me.'

I took a step towards him. 'We shall both have to rely on self-control, that's all.'

'Oh, I shouldn't do that,' said a voice from the doorway. 'It's not infallible in my experience . . .'

We spun around, appalled to find Gareth watching us. His eyes weren't laughing now. There was a calm, bland, dangerous look about him, but all he said was, 'Your glass is empty, Octavia.'

Then Gussie came bustling in with the coffee. How much had he heard? I bit my lip with vexation.

After that we talked about plans for the weekend, who should bring what, what route we should take. I didn't contribute much. I was too shattered. I couldn't look at Jeremy.

'When are you planning to drive down?' Gareth asked.

'Lunchtime on Friday. And you?'

'I've got meetings all day. I won't be able to make it much before five.' He turned to me. 'When do you knock off work?'

'I don't work,' I said haughtily.

'No, I should have realized that. Your private life must be a full-time activity. I'll give you a lift down.'

'No,' I said, much too quickly. 'I want to go down early with Jeremy and Gussie; then I can help them get the boat cleaned up.'

231

Suddenly his swarthy face was a mask of malice. 'Don't you think the young lovers should have some time on their own? Three's a crowd and all that.'

'Yes, you go with Gareth, Tavy,' said Gussie, pleased that her match-making was working out. 'It'll be nice for him to have someone to drive down with. It's a rough old job getting the boat ready, but it'll be all beautiful by the time you both arrive.'

'I'm not afraid of hard work,' I snapped.

'No, of course you're not,' she said soothingly. 'You can do the cooking on board, if it makes you any happier.'

It didn't. There wouldn't be any Luigi's restaurant to take food away from, on the backwaters of the Thames. I started to yawn.

'Octavia's tired,' said Jeremy. 'We must go.'

As we were going down the stairs, the telephone rang again. Gareth took it on the first floor.

'Charlotte, darling, great to hear you. Hang on love, I'm just seeing some people out.' He put his hand over the receiver. 'I'll see you all on Friday.' He turned to me. 'What's your address?'

'Eleven Mayfair Street.'

'I'll collect you about half-past five.'

'Isn't he a scream?' said Gussie, as we went out into the street.

'Oh blast, I've forgotten that list of houses he gave me.'

She charged back into the house.

Jeremy and I looked at each other. His eyes showed as two black patches in the pallor of his face.

'Do you think Gareth caught the gist of what we were saying?' I said.

'I expect so. Doesn't matter. Did you fancy him after all that?'

'He's not my type. He looks like a lorry driver.'

'What is your type?'

'You are,' I said.

CHAPTER THREE

Next day the weather soared into the eighties. London wilted, but I blossomed. I felt absurdly and joyously happy, and spent most of the day lying naked on my balcony, turning brown and gazing up at a sky so blue that it reminded me of Jeremy's eyes.

I refused to go out with anyone that week, and made sure of ten hours' sleep every night by taking too many sleeping pills. I spent a fortune on clothes for the weekend. I was only faintly disappointed Jeremy didn't ring me. But I was ex-directory and he could hardly have got the number from Gussie.

On Thursday morning I had my recurrent nightmare — more terrifyingly than ever before. The dream always started the same way; my father was alive still, and although I was grown-up, I was paralysed with childish fears of the dark, creeping down the stairs, hearing the sound of my parents' quarrelling getting louder and louder, not daring to turn on the light because I knew my mother would shout at me. As I reached the bottom of the stairs, I could distinguish what my mother was saying in a voice slurred with drink.

'I've had enough, I'm leaving you, and I'm taking Xander with me.'

Then my father started shouting back that she'd take Xander over his dead body. Then my mother screaming, 'Well you can keep Octavia then.' And my father saying, 'I don't want Octavia. Why the bloody hell should anyone want Octavia when you've completely ruined her?'

'Someone's got to have her,' yelled my mother.

JILLY COOPER

'Well, it's not going to be me.'

Then I started to scream, pushed open the door, and there was my mother, her beauty all gone, because she was drunk and red in the face. She and my father were both looking at me in guilt and horror, wondering how much of the conversation I'd heard. Then suddenly my father turned into Jeremy, shouting, 'I don't care how much she heard, I still don't want her.'

I woke up screaming my head off, the sheets were drenched with sweat. For a few minutes I lay with my eyes open, gulping with relief, listening to the diminishing drumbeats of my heart, feeling the horror receding. Then I got up, took a couple of Valium and lit a cigarette with a shaking hand. I had to talk to someone, just to prove that someone wanted me. If only I could ring Jeremy, but it was too early in the relationship to show him how vulnerable I was. Nor could I talk to Charlie. It would only start the whole thing up again. I caught sight of the silver framed photograph on the dressing table and realized with relief that Xander must be back from Bangkok. At that time Xander was the only person in the world I really loved and trusted; not that I trusted him to behave himself or not do the most disgraceful things, but because I knew he loved me and that that love was intensified by guilt because he realized our parents had adored him and never loved me. Xander, four years older than me, had always fought my battles in the nursery. He had protected me from the succession of nannies that my mother never got on with, and later from the succession of potential and actual stepfathers who thundered through the house.

I looked at my watch; it was 10.45. Even Xander — not famous for getting to the office on time — might just be in. I dialled Seaford-Brennen's number.

'Can I speak to Alexander Brennen please?'

Xander's secretary was a dragon, trained to keep the multitudes at bay, but she always put me through. Xander answered.

'Octavia darling, I was going to ring you today,' he said, in the light, flat drawling voice, which I always liked to think

234

became gentler and less defensive when he talked to me.

'How was Bangkok?' I asked.

'Like a fairy tale — literally — I stayed in Pat Pong Street which was nothing but gay bars and massage parlours.'

I giggled.

'Do you want something?' said Xander, 'or are you just lonely?'

'I wanted a chat,' I said.

'A chap?'

'No, silly, just to talk to you.'

'Listen, I don't want to be unfriendly darling, but I'm a bit tied up at the moment. I've just got in and several people are trying to hold a meeting in my office. What are you doing for lunch?'

'Nothing.'

'O.K., I'll meet you at Freddy's at one o'clock.'

I lay back feeling better; the Valium were beginning to work. Soon I should feel strong enough to get down to the daily pastime of washing my hair.

Because of my grandfather, Henry Brennen, I didn't have to work for a living. After the First World War he came out of a fashionable regiment and, realizing he had no money left to support a wife and three children, the eldest of which was my father, joined forces with a fellow officer, William Seaford, to form a company, Seaford-Brennen, in the unfashionable field of electrical engineering. Both men were tough, astute and ambitious, and by dint of hard work and good luck, soon had factories turning out transformers, switchgear, generators and electric motors. Business prospered and survived the next war. After that, two rival heirs apparent joined the company—my father, who'd covered himself in glory as a Battle of Britain pilot, and William Seaford's far less dashing son Ricky, who'd spent most of the war in a routine staff job. My father had the additional kudos of having a new and ravishingly beautiful actress wife who promptly gave up work and produced a Brennen heir, while poor Ricky Seaford married a plain, domineering Yorkshire girl who, despite her capabilities on local committees and the golf course, only provided him with daughters.

My father, however, while appearing to hold all the cards, found it extremely difficult to settle down to a nine-to-five job after the excitement of the war. His restlessness increased as the years passed, and he discovered that my mother — who found him far less glamorous out of uniform — had started drinking too much, and launched herself on a succession of very indiscreet affairs.

By the time I was born in I950, the marriage was well into injury time and my father even expressed grave doubts that I was his child which, I used to fantasise, explained his indifference to me. Despite such setbacks, he and my mother staggered on together for another six years, by which time old Henry Brennen had died of a heart attack and William Seaford had retired, having made his pile, leaving my father as chairman and Ricky as managing director. Ricky, meanwhile, the tortoise to my father's hare, had put his head down and spent the postwar years building up Seaford International, a vast empire of which Seaford-Brennen soon became only a subsidiary.

In I956, my mother left home with my brother Xander and one of her lovers. A few months later she had a pang of guilt and sent for me and the nanny to live with her in France. My father was disconsolate for a short time, then moved in with his secretary whom he married as soon as he could divorce my mother. The marriage was extremely happy, and enabled my father to concentrate on work, and when he died, very young, of throat cancer, in 1971, he was able to leave huge blocks of Seaford-Brennen shares to Xander and me, which should have guaranteed us private incomes for life.

Alas, no income would have been enough for my brother Xander. Sacked from school for smoking grass and seducing too many new boys, he was also sent down from Cambridge after two terms for riotous living. Being artistically inclined, he would have been happier editing an art magazine or working in a gallery, but as the only existing Seaford-Brennen heir, he automatically went into the family firm. Here he survived — after my father was no longer alive to protect him — by the skin of his beautifully capped teeth, and by his immense personal charm. Three years ago, when Ricky Seaford was on the brink of sacking him, Xander redeemed himself by selling an Arab a power station worth millions of pounds in a deal carried out across the roulette table. Eighteen months later when things had again looked really dicey, Xander had played his trump card by running off with Ricky's elder daughter, Pamela, to the horror of both her parents. Even Ricky, however, didn't want to have the reputation in the city as the man who'd booted out his son-in-law. Xander was made export sales manager, which gave him access to vast expenses.

In his new, exalted position Xander had managed to fiddle the renting and redecorating of my flat on the firm. After all, he said, one must have somewhere nice to take overseas clients. The firm also paid my rates, telephone, electricity and gas, and provided me with a car which I'd just smashed up. On the whole Xander and I did pretty well out of Seaford-Brennen.

While I was waiting for the conditioner to soak into my hair, I flipped through my wardrobe deciding what to take on the weekend. I'd bought so many new clothes this week, my cheque book had run out, but after the nasty letter I'd got from my bank manager, I didn't dare order another one. American Express and Access had also cut off their supplies. I still had to get another bikini and a glamorous dress to float around on deck. I'd have to borrow from Xander.

The doorbell rang. I peered through the spy hole looking out for creditors or unwelcome suitors, but all I could see were flowers. They turned out to be a huge bunch of pink roses in a plastic vase, filled with green spongy stuff, into which was stuck a mauve bow on a hatpin. I hoped for a blissful moment they were from Jeremy and felt a ridiculous thud of disappointment when the note in loopy florist's handwriting said: 'Don't cut me out of your life altogether, all love, Charlie.'

Charlie, I reflected as I rinsed and re-rinsed, was going to be as hard to get out of my hair as conditioner. I wondered how the hell I was going to survive the next 30-odd hours until I saw Jeremy again. I felt a restlessness like milk coming up to the boil, an excitement sometimes pleasurable, but far more often, painful.

CHAPTER FOUR

The heatwave had set in relentlessly. The traffic glittered and flashed in the sunshine as it crawled up Piccadilly. The park was full of typists in bikinis, sliding off the deckchairs as the park attendant approached with his ticket machine. I could feel the tarmac burning through the soles of my shoes as I crossed the road to Freddy's. I nipped into the Ladies first to tidy my hair and take the shine off my nose. I was wearing new pale pink dungarees with nothing underneath. I toyed with the idea of wearing them when I travelled down with Gareth tomorrow.

'Thank you very much,' I said in a loud voice to the cloakroom attendant as I left, just to draw her attention to the 50p I'd put sop in the saucer. Since I'd met Jeremy, sheer happiness made me overtip everyone.

Freddy's was packed as usual and giving off the same my-dear-punctuated roar as a smart wedding. Along the bar sat advertising executives with brushed forward hair and romantic looking young men wearing open-necked shirts. Chatting them up were beautiful girls, their streaked hair swinging, their blusher in exactly the right place, their upper lips painted a perfect crimson double circumflex. As they sat, fingers tapping on their slim thighs, eyes flickering over each other's shoulders to see who had just come in, they constantly checked their appearance in the mirror above the bar. Freddy's was the current favourite haunt of trendies and showbusiness people, anyone in fact who was important enough to get in, and rich enough to get out.

Freddy, a mountain of a man with a face as red as a dutch cheese, was serving behind the bar.

'Hullo, ugly mug,' he bawled at me. 'How the hell did you

get past the doorman?' Nearby drinkers looked at me in admiration. Only favourites and the famous got insulted. Freddy leaned over and pumped my hand vigorously.

'Where the hell you been anyway, Octavia? Sneaking over to Arabella's, I suppose. Can't say I blame you, I eat there too. The prices here are too high for me.' He bellowed with laughter, then added, 'Your no-good brother's already at the table upstairs drinking himself stupid.'

I followed the smell of garlic, wine and herbs up to the dining-room, waited in the doorway until I had everyone's undivided attention, then sauntered across the room. The pink dungarees definitely had the desired effect; the front flap only just covered my nipples.

Xander was sitting at a window table, flipping through a Sotheby's catalogue. He looked up, smiled, and kissed me on both cheeks. 'Hullo, angel, you look positively radiant. Have I forgotten your birthday or something?'

Waiters immediately rushed up, spreading a napkin across my knees, pushing in my chair, getting a waiting bottle of Poully Fuissé out of an ice bucket, and filling up my glass. Xander ordered another large whisky.

Perhaps it's because he *is* my brother that I always think Xander is the best looking man in the world. He is slim and immensely elegant, with very pale patrician features, brilliant grey eyes, fringed by long dark lashes, and light brown hair, the colour mine was before I started bleaching it. Even on the hottest day of the year he gives the impression of a saluki shivering with overbreeding. As usual he was exquisitely dressed in a pale grey suit, grey and white striped shirt, and a pink tie.

Impossibly spoilt, with all the restlessness that comes with inherited wealth, he moved through life like a prince, expecting everyone to do exactly what he wanted, and capable of making himself extremely disagreeable if they did not. Few people realized how insecure he was underneath, or that he employed a technique of relentless bitching to cover up his increasing black glooms. He was always sweet to me, but I was very glad he was my brother and not a boyfriend. Part of his charm was that he always gave one his undivided

240

attention. He didn't need to look over your shoulder, because he was always the one person people were looking over other people's shoulders to see.

On closer examination that day, he looked rather ill, his eyes laced with red, his hands shaking. He had placed himself with his back to the window, but still looked much younger than his thirty years.

'How are you?' I said.

'A bit poorly. I ran into a bottle of whisky last night. Later I landed up at Jamie Bennett's. We smoked a lot of grass. I'm sure it had gone off. There was a case of stuffed birds in the corner and Jamie started cackling with laughter, saying they were flying all over the room, then suddenly he was sick in a wastepaper basket.'

'What happened to you?'

'I started feeling frightful too, and decided I must get home, so I drove very slowly to Paddington, but it wasn't there, so I came back again.'

I giggled. 'So you never got home?'

He shot me a sideways glance. 'Can I tell Pamela I spent last night at your place?'

'Of course,' I said lightly. 'It's only another point she'll notch up against me.'

Pamela had never forgiven me for slashing my wrists the day she and Xander got married, taking all the attention from her.

'How's our dear mother?' I said.

'Absolutely awful! You've no idea how lucky you are not being the apple of her eye. She rings up every day. Gerald is evidently threatening to walk out if she doesn't stop drinking, so she has to restort to having quick swigs in the lavatory.'

'Does she ever say anything about me?' I asked. Even now I can't mention my mother's name without my throat going dry.

'Never,' said Xander. 'Do you want to order?'

I wasn't hungry, but I hadn't eaten since yesterday lunchtime, and the wine was beginning to make me feel dizzy.

'I'll have a Cobb salad and a grilled sole,' I said.

JILLY COOPER

'You really do look marvellous,' said Xander. 'What's up? Someone must be. Who's he married to?'

'No one,' I said, grooving four lines on the table cloth with my fork.

'There must be some complication.'

'He's engaged,' I said.

'I didn't know anyone did that any more. Who to?'

'An eager overgrown schoolgirl; she's so fat, wherever you stand in the room she's beside you.'

'Unforgiveable,' said Xander with a shudder. 'What's he like?'

'Tall and blond — almost as beautiful as you, and so gentle and sympatico.'

'Rich?'

'I don't know. I haven't asked him; not particularly.'

'Well that's no good then.' Xander broke a roll impatiently with his fingers, then left it. He watched his figure like a lynx. Then he sighed, 'You'd better tell me about him.'

Conversation was then impossibly punctuated by waiters laying tables, asking who was having the smoked trout, giving us our first courses, brandishing great phallic pepper pots over our plates, and pouring us more wine. A quarter of an hour later I was still picking bits of bacon out of my avocado and chopped spinach.

'Am I boring you?' I said.

'Yes,' said Xander gently. 'But it really doesn't matter. You have got him bad. What about Charlie?'

'Charlie who?' I said.

'Like that, is it? Who's going to be the other guy on the boat?'

'A friend of Jeremy's called Gareth Llewellyn.'

Xander looked up. 'He's supposed to be rather agreeable.'

'If you like jumped-up Welsh gorillas,' I said.

Xander laughed. 'He's phenomenally successful — and with birds too, one hears.'

'Oh, he's convinced he's got the master key to everyone's chastity belt,' I said. 'But I've had the lock changed on mine. He doesn't like me very much. He caught me swapping ex-

242

travagant pleasantries with Jeremy. He knows something's up.'

'Well, I'd get him on my side, if I were you,' said Xander. 'He sounds pretty formidable opposition.'

Now we were into the rat-race of the second course. Waiters kept butting in, asking if I wanted my sole on or off the bone, offering vegetables and salads, more wine and more phallic pepper and tartare sauce.

'Everything all right, sir?' said the head waiter, hovering over us a minute later.

'Yes, perfect, if you'd go away and leave us alone,' snapped Xander.

'There's only one thing,' I said, pleating the table cloth with my fingers. 'Can you possibly lend me £200?'

'What for?' said Xander.

'I need some clothes for the weekend.'

'You've got quite enough,' sighed Xander. 'As it is, Covent Garden comes to you every time they want to dress an opera.'

'Just £200,' I pleaded. 'I promise, once I hook Jeremy I won't ask you for another penny.'

'Darling, you don't seem to realize that things are frightfully tight at the moment. There's a little thing called inflation which neither you nor Pamela seem to have heard of. We're all going to have to pull our horns in. My dear father-in-law's been on the warpath all morning, bellyaching about my expenses. I gather this year's accounts are pretty disastrous too.'

'For the whole group or just Seaford-Brennen?'

'Well Seaford-Brennen in particular. Everyone's very twitchy at the moment. Something's obviously up! Directors going round after dark piecing together one's torn-up memos. Every time you go down the passage, you're subjected to a party political broadcast on behalf of the accounts department. Both Glasgow and Coventry look as though they're going to come out on strike — the shop stewards so much enjoyed appearing on television last time.'

'Things'll get better,' I said, soothingly.

'Bloody well hope so,' said Xander. 'I've borrowed so

243

JILLY COOPER

much money from the company they'll have to give me a
rise so I can pay them back. Thank God for Massingham, at
least he's on my side.'

Hugh Massingham was managing director of Seaford
Brennen, a handsome, hard-drinking Northerner in his late
forties, who liked Xander's sense of humour. They used to
go on the tiles together, and bitch about Ricky Seaford.
Hugh Massingham liked me too. When my father died six
years ago he had looked after me, and eventually we'd
ended up in bed. The affair had cooled down but we'd remained friends, and he still spent odd nights with me.

'He sent his love,' said Xander. 'Said he was going to come
and see you next week.'

I wondered, now I'd fallen for Jeremy, if I'd be able to
come up with the goods for Massingham any more. Never
mind, I'd cross that bridge party when I came to it.

Depression suddenly seemed to encompass the table. I
could feel one of Xander's black glooms coming on, probably caused by my tactlessly rabbiting on about Jeremy —
which must only emphasize the stupid mockery of his marriage.

I took his hand.

'How's Pamela?' I said.

'Not awfully sunny at the moment. She's spending the
weekend at Grayston with Ricky and Joan, and I've refused
to go. I have to put up with my dear father-in-law five days a
week, I need a break at weekends. And I can put up with
Joan even less, the great screeching cow. No one can accuse
me of marrying Pamela for her Mummy.'

I giggled. 'What's she done now?'

'Alison's pregnant.'

'Oh God, I'm sorry.'

Alison was Pamela's younger sister, only married this year.

'And dear Joan never stops subtly rubbing Pammie's nose
in it that she isn't,' said Xander.

'What does the gynaecologist say?'

'He can't find anything wrong with her. Joan wants her to
have a second opinion — nice if she had an opinion at all. So
the onus falls firmly on me. Pamela takes her temperature

244

every morning, and when it goes up I'm supposed to pounce on her, but I always oversleep, or have debilitating hangovers, or don't get home like last night. But I've a feeling nothing's going to happen while I lie on one side of the bed reading Dick Francis, and she lies on the other poring over gardening books.'

He was rattling now. His hand shook as he lit a cigarette. I could sense his utter despair.

'Is it absolute hell?' I asked.

He shrugged. 'I suppose prep school was worse, but at least one had longer holidays then.'

'Don't worry,' I said. 'She'll get pregnant soon.'

Xander was busy ordering coffee and brandies and I was easing a piece of bacon out of my teeth, when I looked up and saw a boy of about twenty-three standing in the doorway. He had dark Shelley-length hair, huge languorous dark eyes, and a Mediterranean suntan. He wore navy blue pinstripe trousers and was carrying his jacket slung across his shoulders. His pale blue shirt was open at the neck to reveal a jungle of gold medallions nestling in a black hairy chest. He looked like a movie star. For a second I felt a flicker of unfaithfulness to Jeremy.

'Look at that,' I breathed to Xander.

'I'm already looking,' said Xander, and suddenly there was a touch of colour in his pale cheeks, as the dark boy looked round, caught Xander's eye, waved, and wandered lazily towards us.

'See a pinstripe suit, and pick him up, and all the day you'll have good luck,' murmured Xander.

'Hi,' said the dark boy. 'I was worried I'd missed you. The traffic is terrible.'

He had a strong foreign accent, and was shooting me an openly hostile look, which became distinctly more friendly when Xander said,

'This is my sister, Octavia. Darling, this is Guido. He comes from Florence, I must say I learnt more on my first trip to Florence than during my whole time at Radley.'

Guido sat down and said he would have expected Xander to have such a beautiful sister. Xander had completely shed

245

his black gloom now. He seemed greatly exhilarated.

'Guido works at the Wellington Gallery,' he said. 'He's in disgrace at the moment because he put his foot through a Sisley yesterday, stepping back to avoid the attentions of the gallery owner. Another large brandy and some more coffee,' he added to the waiter.

Guido was staring openly at Xander. His glance had flickered over me and passed on in that dismissive way a man would by-pass the woman's page in a newspaper, knowing it had nothing to offer him.

'How is your dear wife?' he said.

'Dear,' said Xander. 'She's busy putting in a swimming pool. You must come down for a weekend.'

Suddenly I felt *de trop,* and got to my feet.

'I must go,' I said.

'Must you?' said Xander, but without conviction.

Then he suddenly remembered. 'I was going to get you some money, wasn't I? Come on, we'll go and chat up Freddy, I'll be right back,' he said to Guido.

We found Freddy in the bar.

'Now,' said Xander, making sure he looked Freddy straight in the eye. 'Can you cash me a small cheque?'

'Of course. How much?'

'£200.'

Freddy didn't bat an eyelid. He pulled a thick pile of notes in a money clip out of his pockets, and laid twenty tenners on the bar.

'I'll have to date the cheque sometime after the first of the month; is that O.K.?'

'Sure,' said Freddy, soothingly. 'I can always sue you.'

Xander gave me the money and escorted me to the door. I thanked him profusely.

'Don't give it a thought,' he said. 'Now have a ball with Jeremy Fisher. But keep your options open and your legs shut, and don't rule out Gareth Llewellyn altogether; he could keep us both in a style to which we're totally unaccustomed. Don't you think,' he jerked his head in the direction of the dining room, 'that that is quite the most ravishing thing you've seen in years?'

'Yes, he is,' I said with a sinking heart, 'but for God's sake be careful, Xander.'

'And the same to you, darling. Give me a ring when you get back.'

And he was gone, trying to appear not to be in too much of a hurry to get upstairs.

I felt curiously flat and decided to wander along to Hatchards and buy some highbrow books to impress Jeremy on the boat.

CHAPTER FIVE

By Friday evening I was golden brown all over and ready for action. I decided Xander was right, my best tack was to charm Gareth and get him on my side, and at five-thirty I was waiting for him with my three suitcases packed. I was wearing a wickedly expensive pink and white striped blazer with nothing underneath, white trousers, and cherry red boots. The blazer and boots were really both too hot to wear but I was only going to be driving in a car. I felt entirely satisfied with my appearance.

The minutes ticked by. Six came and went, half-past six, a quarter to seven. I vacillated between seething temper that Gareth was late on purpose, and worry that he might have lost my address.

At half-past seven the telephone went. 'This is Annabel Smith,' said a husky voice. 'I'm ringing for Mr. Llewellyn.'

'Where the hell is he?' I snapped.

'I'm afraid his meeting is going on longer than expected. Could you possibly jump in a taxi and come over here? The address is Llewellyn House, Great Seaton Street. I'll meet you on the ground floor and reimburse you for the taxi.'

Oh, the hateful, horrible, utterly bloody man! Why the hell had I piled up my car? No taxis were free when I telephoned, all the mini cabs were booked for the next hour. My make-up was beginning to run in the heat. It was no joke having to hump three huge suitcases into the street and wait half-an-hour for a taxi. My blazer was too hot, my new boots killing me. By the time I reached Llewellyn House I was gibbering with rage.

Mrs. Smith, in green, looking as cool as an iced gin and lime, was there to meet me.

'Come upstairs; you must be exhausted. Someone will put your luggage in Mr. Llewellyn's car. What a perfect weekend for going on the river,' she said as we climbed in the lift to the fifteenth floor. I had a feeling she was amused.

I was ushered into an office as modern as the hour. There were some good modern paintings on the wall, leather arm-chairs with chrome legs, one wall covered in books and fac-ing it a vast window, a cinemascopic frame for St. Paul's and the city. How could anyone work with a view like that? Gareth evidently could. He was lounging behind a huge black leather-topped desk, on the telephone as usual, talk-ing execrable French.

He grinned and jabbed a paper in the direction of one of the armchairs. I ignored him and went over to the window. Buses like dinky toys were crawling up Fleet Street.

Mrs. Smith came in with a tray. 'Would you like a drink?'

I didn't want to take anything of Gareth's but I needed that drink too badly.

'Gin and tonic, please.'

She mixed me one with ice and lemon, and then poured a large whisky for Gareth.

He put down the receiver and smiled at me.

'Hullo, lovely. I'm sorry I've messed you about.' There wasn't a trace of contrition in his voice. 'You look stunning. It's as good as a day in the country just to see you.'

'I've been waiting nearly three hours,' I spat at him. 'Shall we go?'

He wandered towards the door taking his whisky with him. 'I'm going to have a shower first; make yourself at home.'

Mrs. Smith brought me some magazines. I thumbed through them furiously, not taking in a word.

It was nine o'clock by the time he came back, looking more like a lorry driver than ever, in jeans and a red shirt. He kissed Mrs. Smith very tenderly before we left.

'I see you believe in mixing business with pleasure,' I snapped as we went down in the lift.

'But of course. You wouldn't expect me to sit looking at some top-heavy frump in basic black all day, would you?

249

That's a nice blazer you're wearing. Did you think we were going to Henley?'

'Oh this, it's as old as the hills.' I was damned if I was going to admit I'd bought it that morning.

He reached out his hand towards the back of my neck and pulled something off my collar.

'Don't touch me,' I hissed.

He handed me a price tag with a hundred pounds on it.

'If this is a cleaning ticket, darling, I'm afraid you've been robbed.'

I was furious to find myself blushing.

Outside the vulgarest car I've ever seen stood waiting for us, a vast open Cadillac sprayed a brilliant shade of peacock blue. I was surprised he hadn't hung nodding doggies from the driving mirror.

I had to admit he was a good driver, threading that huge car through the traffic in no time. We were soon out on the M4 speeding towards Oxford.

The sun had set. In the west were great masses of crushed-up rose-coloured clouds. Broad beams of light shone down, reminding me of an old biblical picture. If God were up there this evening dispensing justice, I hoped He'd give Gareth his come-uppance. And He might grant me Jeremy at the same time.

The needle on the speedometer registered a hundred m.p.h.

'Let me know if you're frightened and I'll go a bit faster,' said Gareth.

I stared stonily ahead.

'Oh pack it in, lovely; stop sulking. We've got to spend the weekend together, we might as well call a truce.'

'Why didn't you let me go earlier with the others?'

'Because I couldn't resist it — I wanted to annoy you. Never mind, I'll buy you a nice dinner.'

'I don't want any dinner.'

'All right, then, you can watch me eat.'

He pulled in at an hotel beyond Henley. It was obviously very expensive. Waiters were flambee-ing ducks all over the place and the menus had no prices on them. I suddenly realized I hadn't eaten all day and found my mouth was watering.

Gareth grinned at me. 'Come on, eat; you might as well.'

'Oh, all right,' I said.

Reluctantly I had to admit the food was excellent.

'I always eat well,' he said.

'So I notice,' I said, looking at his waist line.

He roared with laughter. 'I suppose you like little mini boys with hip measurements in single figures, but as Freddie Trueman once said, it takes a big hammer to drive a big nail.'

'Don't be disgusting,' I snapped.

His table manners were atrocious. Somehow he managed to eat very fast and talk at the same time. Now he was draining butter out of his snail shells with a sound like water running out of the bath. God, it was hot in the restaurant. I was pouring with sweat but I could hardly take my blazer off.

'I had lunch with Jeremy, yesterday,' he said, wiping butter off his chin.

'Oh, I'm surprised you found the time.'

'I always find time for things that matter. I think I've found them a house.'

'That's clever of you,' I said coolly. 'Whereabouts?'

'Kensington, round the corner from me.'

'How can they afford it? Jeremy hasn't got that kind of money.'

'But Gussie has. She's going to buy the house.'

'Jeremy'd loathe that.'

'Not now, he doesn't. I've managed to persuade him how sensible it is. They can let out the bottom floor which will pay off the mortgage, and it means they can get married next month instead of waiting until November.'

His face had that dreamy far-away look of a volcano that has just devastated entire villages. I wanted to kick his teeth in but I was determined not to betray any emotion.

'They must be thrilled,' I said.

'Yes they are. I expect Gussie'll ask you to be a bridesmaid.'

I couldn't speak for rage. I was glad when the pretty wait-

251

ress came over. 'Everything all right sir?' She smiled at him admiringly.

'Marvellous.' He looked her over in a way that made me even angrier.

'How much further have we got to go?' I asked as we got back into the car.

'Twenty, thirty miles, not more.'

The stars were of Mediterranean splendour now, the newly cut hay smelt sweet, feathery moths were held prisoner in the beams of the powerful headlights. The air, cool at fast speeds, grew hot again whenever Gareth slowed down to take a corner. We were driving past the Reedminster flyover now.

'Look,' said Gareth, pointing upwards. On a huge floodlit placard was written the word 'Llewellyns'.

'You?' I said, in surprise.

'Me. I'll be bigger than Taylor Woodrow one day.'

'Quite the boy wonder. Why do you go on working so hard? You've made your packet. Why's it so important to make more money?'

'Oh lovely, you must be weak in the head. For heaven's sake, if you play a game, even if it's only scrabble, you want to win don't you?'

'And it matters so much to you, the winning?'

'Of course it does, why not have a Lamborghini and a Rolls Royce and a nice house in London, and a villa in France? And if you can throw in a few good paintings, a string of race horses, the odd yacht in the Med, well bully for you.'

'It's status symbols that really matter to you don't they?'

'And to you too,' said Gareth. 'More than anyone, you need a sybaritic existence with different guys to take you to trendy restaurants, buy you fur coats, fly you to all the smart places. It wouldn't amuse you at all to be shackled to a poor man.'

I opened my mouth to protest, but he went on.

'Jeremy's the same. He's lucky to be marrying Gus, who's got some bread.'

'Jeremy'll make money out of writing,' I said quickly.

'Nuts ! He can't write "bum" on a wall. I bet you don't understand a word of those poems of his you claim to be so fond of, and do you know why? It's because there isn't anything in them *to* understand.'

'I can only assume you must be jealous of his talent,' I said furiously.

'Oh, don't be pompous, sweetheart. There's far more poetry in those blue eyes of his than there is in any of his verse.'

'I thought you were supposed to be a friend of his?'

'So I am, but I believe in doing practical things for him like getting him somewhere to live, rather than swooning over his tin-pot poetry.'

I didn't trust myself to speak. Gareth said, 'We'll be there in ten minutes.'

I started to do my face.

He flicked on a spotlight to help me, then said, 'Go easy on the warpaint.'

'Why?' I asked, painting a more seductive curve on my bottom lip.

'Because Jeremy belongs to Gussie.'

'And?'

'You've come down with the sole purpose of getting him away from her.'

'I don't know what you mean.'

'Oh yes you do. That performance you two were putting on the other night, not speaking to each other when anyone else was around, rushing together as soon as you were alone. I heard you both: "Oh darling, we shall have to rely on self-control." '

It was a brilliant imitation of my voice.

'Gussie is an old friend,' I said evenly.

'That's the trouble, you're jealous of her.'

'Jealous. Me jealous of Gussie? You must be joking!'

'Because, despite your looks, people love her more than they do you.'

'That's not true,' I said through gritted teeth. 'Gussie is a friend and I couldn't be less interested in Jeremy.'

'Good,' said Gareth amiably. 'Keep it that way then. Here we are.'

253

He turned off the road down a long woody tunnel. Clenching my hands, I choked back the torrent of rage and fury that was ready to pour out of me. Jeremy's mad for you, I said to myself, keep calm. Gareth's just trying to bug you. Gareth stretched.

'What a marvellous prospect, three whole days of sleep, sex and sun.'

'It isn't very likely,' I hissed, 'that you'll get any sex from me.'

'Not likely at all, unless I ask you for it,' he said.

Just as I was groping for a really crushing reply, we emerged out of the tunnel and found ourselves almost at the water's edge. The sky unfurled like a banner cascading with stars. Black hulks of barges darkened the water. Behind, the murky towers and pinnacles of Oxford rose indistinctly.

Jeremy emerged from the nearest boat to meet us. I'd never felt more pleased to see anyone. I wanted to throw myself sobbing into his arms.

'Hullo,' he said. 'You made it okay? Let me help with the cases.'

'I'm desperately sorry we're so late,' I said.

'Doesn't matter. Gareth rang this afternoon and said you wouldn't be here much before midnight.'

In the headlamps of the car I could see the barge was painted scarlet and decorated in brilliant blues, yellows and greens, like a gypsy caravan. The brasswork glinted, the red curtains glowed behind the saloon windows. In gold letters edged with blue was written her name, *The Lady Griselda*.

'Isn't she lovely?' I said.

Jeremy helped me across the gangplank, but he didn't squeeze my hand, nor answer when I whispered that it was heavenly to see him again.

Gussie was in the kitchen. She was wearing old jeans and an oil-stained shirt. I suddenly realized how stupid I must look bringing three suitcases.

'Tavy,' she hugged me. 'How lovely. Have you been having fun?'

'Yes, marvellous,' I lied, disengaging myself from her. I didn't want oil stains all over my new blazer.

'You must be exhausted. Come and see your cabin, and then I'll give you a huge drink.'

We went through a cabin with two bunks in it.

'This is Jeremy and me,' she said, and then opening another door, 'This is you and Gareth.'

Oh, my God, I thought, I'm going to have to spend the whole weekend fighting him off. Our suitcases were already deposited on one of the bunks. On a ledge stood a glass jam jar which Gussie had filled with meadow sweet, buttercups and already wilting roses.

'The heads and the washbasin are next door. I'm afraid they're a bit primitive, and the saloon's beyond that,' she said. 'Come through when you're ready.'

I washed and put on more scent and make-up to give me confidence. In the saloon I found them all gathered round a portable television set.

'Look at Gareth's toy,' said Gussie.

'Trust him to bring the twentieth century with him,' I said and looked at Jeremy, but he looked quickly away.

'Have a drink?' said Gussie.

'I'll get her one,' said Gareth, getting a glass out of a cupboard in the corner and filling it with wine.

'Isn't this gorgeous?' I said, looking round at the oil lamps, the panelling and the gleaming brass.

'Very sexy too,' added Gareth approvingly. 'Octavia and I are waking at the crack of dawn to do PT.'

'PT?' said Gussie in surprise. 'That doesn't sound Octavia's line of country.'

'Some people call it sexual intercourse,' said Gareth.

He raised his glass to me, his wicked lecherous eyes moving over me in amusement.

Gussie went off into peals of laughter.

'You mustn't tease, Gareth. Poor Tavy won't know if she's coming or going.'

'Coming, hopefully,' said Gareth.

'I hear you've found a house,' I said to Jeremy. 'I'm so pleased.'

For a moment he looked up and our eyes met, then he looked quickly away. A muscle was going in his cheek; he was obviously in a state.

'Yes, it's great, isn't it?'

'Great!' said Gussie, 'it's marvellous! Most couples can't afford a house for years. Gareth fixed us a mortgage and found us the ideal place in a few days. You must come and help me choose curtains and carpets, Tavy. I'm so hopeless.'

They started talking about the house and wedding plans until I couldn't stand it any more. 'Does anyone mind if I go to bed?' I said.

'Of course not,' said Gussie. 'I'll come and see everything's all right.'

'You'll see me anon,' said Gareth.

'No doubt,' I said, turning to Jeremy, 'Goodnight, it's such a treat to be down here.'

Just for a moment I was comforted by a flicker of misery in his eyes, then the shutters came down.

'Goodnight, sleep well,' he said.

In my cabin, Gussie was plumping pillows.

'It was a good thing Gareth rang Jeremy and said you were going to be late, or we'd have been in an awful shambles. Jeremy and I spent all afternoon in bed,' Gussie confided with a little giggle, then went on, 'I hope you don't mind sharing a cabin with Gareth. I'm sure he won't pounce on you unless you want it.'

'What on earth do you mean?' I snapped.

'Oh well,' she stammered. 'I mean, I thought you might want it, perhaps, if you found him attractive.'

'I don't,' I said.

'Oh dear,' her face fell. Realizing it was a bad move, I added, 'I like him very much, but not in that way.'

Once I was alone, I couldn't stop shaking. What had that snake Gareth been saying to Jeremy to change him so much? Had he just done it out of sheer bloodymindedness or did he want me for himself? When I was in my nightie (which was apricot silk, clinging and, ironically, bought to inflame Jeremy) I found to my horror that I had left my sleeping pills behind. In the state I was in I'd never sleep without them.

I put all my suitcases on the floor, and crept into the top

bunk and lay there, tense and trembling, waiting to fend off the inevitable assault when Gareth came to bed. All I could hear were shouts of laughter from the other room.

An hour went past; they were coming to bed; there were shouts of 'goodnight', then silence, broken only by the sound of water lapping against the boat.

The door opened, and Gareth slid quietly into the cabin. Hoping he would not hear the terrified thudding of my heart, I tried to breathe slowly and evenly.

'Only five out of ten,' came the soft Welsh voice. 'People who are really asleep breathe much faster than that.'

Then, to my amazement, I heard him getting into the bottom bunk. He must be trying to lull me into a feeling of false security. I lay frozen for ten minutes, but suddenly my terror turned to fury. Unmistakably from the bottom bunk came the sound of gentle snoring.

I lay there spitting with rage until eventually I decided it was no use working myself up into a state. Gareth might have temporarily chucked a monkey wrench into the romantic works, but if he intended to fight dirty, he would find that no one could fight dirtier than me when I put my mind to it. Whatever he had told Jeremy — that I was a spoilt bitch, a parasite, an opportunist — would make no difference in the end. Jeremy was mad for me, try as he might to fight it.

Time was on my side. In this heat, cooped up together for three days, Jeremy's self-control was bound to desert him. All I had to do was look stunning and wait. *Festina lente*. But how could I be expected to look stunning if I couldn't sleep? I wanted to go up on the moonlit deck and cool off. But although Gareth was now snoring like a warthog, I had a feeling that as soon as I tried to climb out of my bunk, his hand would shoot out and grab me by the ankle. Why, oh why, had I forgotten to bring my sleeping pills? The hours crawled by, and only when a misty dawn began to filter through the porthole, did I fall asleep.

CHAPTER SIX

When I woke the boat was moving. Through the porthole I could see shiny olive-green water, a tangle of rushes and brilliant blue sky. I could hear voices and the crash of footsteps above me. I pulled the sheets over my head and tried to go back to sleep again, then gave up and looked at my watch. It was nearly twelve o'clock.

When I pushed open the door of the loo I was confronted by a huge brown back and tousled black hair. Gareth, wearing only a towel around his hips, was cleaning his teeth.

'You're up with the lark,' he said grinning. 'You must have slept well.'

'Don't you ever wear any pyjamas?' I snapped.

'Never, never. I always sleep in the raw. I like to get really close to people. Shall I run you a bath, or would you prefer a shower? I'll see if Gussie's got any Badedas.'

Knowing there was only a cracked wash basin, I ignored this and flattened myself against the wall to let him pass. He paused in front of me and once again I was overwhelmed by the claustrophobia I always felt when he was close to me. As I bolted past him and locked the door behind me, I could hear him laughing.

He'd gone, thank goodness, when I got back to the cabin. I couldn't decide what to wear, all my clothes looked so new. In the end I settled for a dark green towelling jump suit with a red and green striped leather belt.

Gussie was in the kitchen, cooking and pinkfaced. 'Hello,' she said. 'How are you? Did you sleep all right?'

She was obviously dying to know if I'd slept with Gareth or not, and was on the look out for signs of ravage in my face.

258

'I fell asleep the moment my head touched the pillow,' I said blithely. 'Can I do anything to help?'

'No, don't bother. Do you want some breakfast?'

'Only a cup of coffee.'

'You ought to eat something, you know,' she insisted.

'I can't even look a fried egg in the face in the morning.'

She began boringly explaining to me the merits of eating a proper breakfast, so I made a cup of coffee and a quick exit up on deck.

A beautiful burning day had soared out of the mist. On either side white cornfields slanted down to the water, ahead on the left bank a clump of copper beeches glittered purple in the sun. The water ahead was so smooth, it was as though we were gliding over an old mirror. Jeremy, wearing only a pair of jeans, was at the wheel. He looked all tawny and golden haired, like a young lion, but his dark blue eyes were tired.

'Everything all right?' he said.

'Yes, thank you, everything's wonderful.' I gave him a smile of pure happiness. Let him sweat, I thought, let him have a few nasty moments wondering if I really have been screwed by Gareth.

'You look very pleased with yourself,' said a soft Welsh voice. Gareth sat hunched up on the roof, his arms round his knees, smoking and reading the *Financial Times*.

'How the hell did you get hold of that?' I asked.

'From the last lock-keeper, a man of property like myself.'

'Anything up?' asked Jeremy.

'My shares are, by 10p,' said Gareth.

'Don't you ever let up?' I said.

'Only in the mating season.'

'Jeremee,' called Gussie from the kitchen.

'Yes love?'

'You haven't kissed me for at least a quarter-of-an-hour.'

Jeremy looked at us and blushed.

'Get on with it, you fleshmonger,' said Gareth, getting to his feet. 'I'll take the wheel.'

'We'll be coming up to Ramsdyke Lock in half-an-hour,' said Jeremy. 'I'll come and take over then.'

He went dutifully down into the kitchen.

'In a few years' time,' I said savagely, 'they'll be calling each other "Mummy" and "Daddy".'

I enjoyed going through the lock. The lock-keeper's little house was surrounded by a garden of flowers as gaudy as the front of a seed packet. A goat looked over the fence, a golden retriever sat lolling its tongue out in the heat. When Jeremy sounded the horn a fat woman in an apron came out and opened the first lot of gates for us. Then the boat edged its way into the dark green cavern with dank slimy walls and purple toadflax growing in the crevices, and the gates clanged behind us. Suddenly water poured in from the other end, gradually raising our boat to the new level of the river.

'Very phallic, isn't it?' said Gareth, who was waiting on the shore to open the gates at the other end.

I looked up at him with loathing. 'Do you keep your mind permanently below your navel?'

We tied up for lunch under a veil of green willows, and I changed into my favourite bikini, which is that stinging yellow which goes so well with brown skin and blonde hair, and very cleverly cut to give me a cleavage like the Grand Canyon.

'Hickory dickory dock, the mouse ran up the drink bill,' said Gareth, pouring himself a quadruple whisky. 'This weekend is fast degenerating into an orgy.'

He looked up and whistled as I walked into the saloon.

'Despite your obvious limitations, Octavia, I must admit that you're very well constructed. Really, it's a sin for you to wear any clothes at all. Don't you agree Jeremy?'

Jeremy was devouring me, as a starved dog might look at a large steak. His hand shook as he lit a cigarette, that muscle was going in his cheek again.

'Oh these engaged men never look at other women,' I said lightly. 'Pour me a drink, Gareth darling.'

We all got tight at lunch. It was far too hot to eat but as Gussie had spent all morning making a fish mayonnaise, we had to make half-hearted efforts. She'd even cut the tomatoes into little flowers. As usual she ended up by guzzling most of it herself.

Afterwards, as Jeremy and Gareth cast off, I curled up in a sunbaked corner on deck. A few minutes later Gussie joined me — not a pretty sight in a black bathing dress, her huge white bosom and shoulders spilling over the top. She immediately started boring me making lists for her wedding.

'There's so much to do with only a month to go,' she kept saying. How many double sheets did I think she'd need, and was it absolutely essential to have an egg beater? But her fond dreamy gaze rested more often on Jeremy than on her lists.

'Isn't he beautiful?' she said, then giggled. 'Gareth's given me this fantastic sex instruction book. I can now see why so many people end up with slipped discs. The things they expect you to do, and it's a bit tricky when you have to hold the book in one hand in order to learn how to do it,' and she went off into shrieks of laughter.

'How are you getting on with Gareth?' she went on.

I admired my reflection in her sun glasses. 'Well I'm not getting off with him, if that's what you mean.'

'Ah — but the weekend is still in its infancy,' said that hateful Welsh voice and Gareth lay down on the deck between us, cushioning his dark head on his elbow, the wicked slit eyes staring up at the burning sky.

'I've just been telling Tavy about your fantastic sex book,' said Gussie.

'I wouldn't have thought she'd need it,' said Gareth. 'She must have taken her "L" plates off years ago.'

A large white barge was cruising towards us on the other side of the river. A middle-aged man in a yachting cap was at the wheel, addressing two fat women with corrugated hair up at the front of the boat, through a speaking trumpet. Another man with a white moustache and a red face was gazing at us through binoculars. They all looked thoroughly disapproving. Gareth sat up and waited until they drew level with us.

'Have a good look, sir!' he shouted to the man with the binoculars. 'I've got two lovely young girls here, whose

261

knickers are bursting into flames at the sight of you. Only fifty quid each, satisfaction guaranteed. We even accept Barclay Cards.'

The man with the binoculars turned purple with rage and nearly fell off the roof.

'It's young men like you who ought to be turned off England's waterways!' bellowed the man with the speaking trumpet.

'We even take luncheon vouchers!' Gareth yelled after them.

'I'll ask you along instead of a conjurer next time I give a children's party,' I said.

Gussie, who was doubled up with laughter, got to her feet.

'I'm going to see how Jeremy's getting on,' she said.

I buried my face in my biography of Matthew Arnold.

'Still on the culture kick?' said Gareth in amusement. 'There's only one poem, lovely, you should read, learn and inwardly digest.'

'What's that?'

"'Who ever loves, if he do not
        propose
    The right true end of love, he's one
        that goes
    To sea for nothing but to make
        him sick." '

'Who wrote that?'

'Your alleged favourite, John Donne.'

'He must have been having an off day,' I said crossly.

Another boat passed us with a pretty brunette sunning herself on deck. Gareth wolf-whistled at her; she turned round and smiled at him, showing big teeth. Gareth smiled back.

'Don't you ever knock it off,' I snapped. 'Haven't you ever heard of the law of diminishing returns?'

A dark green world slid past my half-shut eyes. The darkness of the trees over-arched the olive shadows and tawny lights of the water. On the bank was a large notice: 'Danger. Keep Away from the Weir.'

'It's not the weir that some people should keep away

from,' said Gareth.

Beyond the weir, the surface of the river was smothered in foam, a floating rainbow coloured like gossamer.

'Oh how pretty it is !' I cried.

'Detergent,' said Gareth.

I shot him a venomous glance and started fiddling with my wireless. I'd given up listening to pop music since I'd met Jeremy, but suddenly I hit upon some grand opera, a soprano and a tenor yelling their guts out. I was just about to switch over when Gareth looked up. 'For Christ sake turn that caterwauling off. You'll wake up all the water rats.'

So I kept it on really loud to annoy him, absolutely murdering the peace of the afternoon. After an agonizing three-quarters of an hour, the opera came to an end.

'What was that?' bellowed Gussie from the wheel.

'Don Carlos,' I said.

'Oh how lovely! That's your favourite, isn't it, Gareth? How many times have you seen it?'

The rat! The snake! Smiling damned villain! I couldn't trust myself to speak. I turned over and pretended to go to sleep.

I was lying half drugged with sun when I heard Jeremy's voice. 'Octavia, are you asleep?'

I opened my eyes; the sky was shimmering with heat. I smiled lazily up at him. From the ribald laughter I could hear, Gareth and Gussie were obviously up at the other end of the boat.

Jeremy sat down beside me.

'You must watch the sun. With fair skin like yours, you could easily burn.'

'Oil me then,' I said softly, turning over on my front and handing him a bottle of Ambre Solaire.

He put a dollop on his hands and began to rub it into my back.

I squirmed voluptuously. 'Oh, how blissful. I wish I had a tame slave to do it all the time. Put lots on the tops of my thighs,' I went on mercilessly. I heard him catch his breath.

When I had made him spin it out as long as possible, I added, 'And could you possibly undo my bikini strap. I don't

263

want a white line across my back.'

His hands shook so much he had the greatest difficulty with the clasp.

'Thank you,' I said when he had finished, turning my head and looking at him. He was breathing very fast, and his eyes were almost opaque with lust.

The afternoon was perfect now. The water was plumed with alders and willows, and in the distance two or three pink farm houses dozed among the apple trees. The white spire of a village church appeared behind a hill and a plane sailed silver across the sky.

'How remote everything seems,' I said. 'I can't believe that this time next week I shall be in Marbella.'

Jeremy sat up on his elbow, chewing a piece of grass.
'You will?'

'And Sardinia the week after, and then I think I shall probably take off for Bermuda for the summer.'

'Bermuda? Whatever for?'

I was taunting him now.

'Oh, because a guy with whom I'm just good friends is mad for me to join him out there. He was even generous enough to send me my air ticket.'

'Doesn't it worry you at all? Living off men all the time?'

'Who said I'm living off men? I give as good as I get. Anyway it's only normal if one's father rejects one early in life, to go round looking for other daddies, preferably sugar daddies and playing them up until they're forced to reject you too.'

'Don't you ever want to settle down with one man?'

'Not any more,' I paused, making my voice quiver slightly. 'Not since Tod was killed earlier this year.'

'Gussie told me about that. I'm terribly sorry.'

A yellow butterfly shimmered over us. 'That's me,' I said, pointing to it. 'Always on the loose.'

'So you're really committed to the fleshpots,' said Jeremy bitterly. 'Drifting from one rich playboy to another. Dropping your knickers so you don't have to drop your standard of living.'

'That sounds exactly like Gareth,' I said through my

264

teeth. 'It's neither funny nor true.'

'Maybe not. Now you can have as many minks and gold bracelets as you like, but what happens when your looks go and you can't get men any more? Do you know how women like you end up, unless they're very careful? They start making concessions in order to escape from their loneliness, then more and more concessions until they turn into a raddled old harridan that everyone laughs at.'

'Why do you tell me these things?' I hissed at him.

'It's only natural,' he said in a low voice, 'that I should try and run down all the things I could never afford to give you.'

'Gareth could give them to me,' I said.

'What happened between you two last night?' he said sharply.

'Oh, you know Gareth's reputation, and you think mine is totally beyond redemption, I'm surprised you ask.'

'What happened?' he said, seizing my wrist.

'Stop it, you're hurting me!'

'Did you or did you not sleep with Gareth?'

'No I didn't, but it's no thanks to you,' I stormed. 'Ignoring me when we arrived last night, avoiding my eyes whenever I looked at you. If anything was calculated to throw me into Gareth's arms that was.'

Jeremy put his face in his hands.

'I know, I know. Christ I'm in such a muddle. A month today I'm getting married, and I feel as though I'm going into hospital for a major operation.'

'Well, that's your problem, isn't it?' I said, fastening my bikini strap and getting to my feet. 'I'm going to get a drink of water.'

I found Gussie in the kitchen eating biscuits and talking up at Gareth who was steering.

'Gussie and I were just saying how much we were looking forward to sampling some of your famous cooking,' said Gareth maliciously.

'There's a chicken in the fridge,' said Gussie. 'I wish you'd do that marvellous thing you did when Jeremy and I came to dinner.'

'It's a very complicated recipe,' I said quickly, 'and needs lots of special things I'm sure we haven't got.'

'We can get them,' said Gussie. 'Gareth and I have got a yen for Pimms tonight, so we thought we'd stop off at the village shop at the next lock. We'll buy everything you need at the same time.'

I hope my dismay didn't show on my face. While Gareth and Gussie were shopping, I had a good wash to get off all the sun-tan oil and sweat. I was just wandering into the kitchen to get another glass of water when I felt something furry run across my feet. I gave a scream. Jeremy came racing down the passage.

'What's the matter?'

'Look,' I screamed. A huge spider ran across the floor and disappeared under the sink.

'It's only a spider,' he said. 'It won't hurt you.'

'They terrify me,' I sobbed. He took a step towards me and then the next moment I was in his arms. As his lips touched mine, we both began to tremble. The warmth, the dizziness, the taste of that kiss lasted a long, long time. Then he buried his face in my hair.

'Oh my God, Octavia, you're driving me mad. What am I going to do?'

'Nothing for the moment, except go on kissing me,' I whispered, taking his face in my hands.

CHAPTER SEVEN

The crimson sun was sinking, the pink water darkening as we tied up for the night alongside a bank of meadowsweet. The air throbbed with the formless chattering of birds, and all along the bank water rats and owls began to come out on night duty. I managed to postpone cooking by saying the chicken would take too long to make.

I put on a pale grey semi-transparent mini-dress. I didn't need the cracked looking glass to tell me how marvellous I looked. Gussie was looking hideous in white. She was scarlet from the sun.

'She looks like a great red lobster,' I thought with a giggle. 'All she needs is a dollop of mayonnaise.'

Gareth handed me a Pimms. It was afloat with apple, cucumber and oranges.

'Is this dinner as well?' I asked coolly.

'It's utterly divine,' said Gussie. 'Try it.'

I took a sip and smirked at Gareth. 'It tastes exactly like cough mixture,' I said.

Jeremy, sitting at the table shelling broad beans, looked fantastic. His skin was tanned to the colour of dry sherry; he was wearing a white shirt. I surreptitiously lowered the zip of my dress a few inches, then caught Gareth looking at me and pretended I was fanning myself because of the heat.

'Jeremy darling,' cooed Gussie fondly, 'you're putting all the pods in the pan and the beans in the muckbucket. You *are* abstracted today.'

'His mind's on other things,' said Gareth.

'Like this bloody review I've got to write for the *Statesman*,' said Jeremy. 'I've got to file copy on Tuesday. I simply can't get beyond the first chapter.'

267

'Well say so, then,' said Gareth.

'I can't,' said Jeremy. 'It was written by the editor's wife.'

'That's a gorgeous dress,' said Gussie, looking at me enviously. 'I'd love something really sexy like that.'

'You've got Jeremy,' I said, smiling at him.

'Yes, and don't let any of us forget it,' said Gareth.

'Broad beans are disappointing,' grumbled Gussie, raking her thumb nail down the furry inside of the last pod. 'They always look as though they're going to produce far more than they do.'

'Like someone else I could mention,' muttered Gareth as he filled up my glass.

A smell of mint drifted in from the kitchen.

'I'm starving,' said Gussie.

For dinner Gareth fried some huge prawns in garlic and parsley and we ate them with broad beans and new potatoes.

'Our new house has a little garden,' said Gussie with her mouth full. 'Just think Jeremy darling, we'll be able to grow our own vegetables. You're a fairy godmother, Gareth, finding us this house.'

'I'm neither a fairy nor a godmother,' said Gareth, forking a large new potato out of the dish and putting it straight into his mouth.

'These prawns are fantastic,' said Jeremy. 'Have some more, Octavia.'

'No thanks,' I said. 'I'm surprised to see Gareth cooking at all. With your pithead upbringing I'd have thought you'd have been dead against men in the kitchen.'

There was a slightly embarrassed pause.

'My father spent his time in the kitchen when he was home,' said Gareth. 'It was the only room we had downstairs.'

'How amazing,' I said, my lips curling. 'Did you all sleep in the same bed?'

'I liked your father,' said Jeremy hastily.

'So did my mother,' said Gareth. 'If you're a miner you're a real man — and women like that.'

Gussie sensed that I was about to make some crushing

remark.

'Whatever happened to your glamorous brother?' she said. 'I remember him coming down to take you out at school and watching a lacrosse match, and no one scoring any goals at all. They were far too busy gawping at him.'

'He went into the family business,' I said. 'But he hates it. He's export sales manager now and has to spend his time swapping filthy stories with reps.'

'Who did he get married to?' said Gussie.

'Ricky Seaford's daughter, Pamela.'

'That was a good dynastic match,' said Gareth. 'Aren't Seaford-Brennen's in a bit of trouble at the moment?'

'Of course not,' I said, scathingly. 'They've had a terrific year.' I always say that.

'Oh well, you should know,' said Gareth. 'I just heard rumours of strike trouble.'

'All firms have to cope with strikes from time to time.'

'I don't,' said Gareth, grinning. 'My men know they've got the best boss in the world, so why should they strike?'

'Modesty certainly isn't your strong point,' I snapped.

'Of course it isn't. I'm much better at being immodest.'

God, he irritated me. I wanted to throw my drink in his face. Gussie went off to bring in some strawberries and cream, so I stretched out my foot towards Jeremy and started rubbing it against his leg. The pressure was immediately returned. And when Gareth started quizzing him about publishing, he obviously had great difficulty in concentrating.

'These are the first strawberries of the year, so you must all make a wish,' said Gussie, doling out great platefuls.

I wriggled down a bit further under the table, and ran my leg up and down Jeremy's thigh. The next moment I could feel his hand stroking my foot, gently caressing the instep. It felt fantastically sexy. I wiggled my toes against his hand voluptuously.

'Did you know that buggery was legal after 90 days on board?' said Gareth. 'So we've only got 89 days to go, boyo.'

'Oh darling,' sighed Jeremy, 'I never knew you felt that way.'

That warm hand was still stroking my ankle. Then suddenly I looked across the table, and froze with horror as I realized that Jeremy was squashing up his strawberries with both hands. Before I could whip my foot away, the hand had closed round my ankle like a vice.

'What big feet you've got Grandma,' said Gareth, his eyes glinting with laughter. I tugged frantically for several seconds before he let me go.

After dinner he turned on the television. It was an old film, *Carmen Jones.*

'*You go for me, and I'm taboo,*' sang Dorothy Dandridge, shaking her hips, '*But if you're hard to get I go for you . . . and if I do, I'll tell you baby, that's the end of you.*'

'Oh, turn it off, I've seen it twice already,' said Gussie.

We took our drinks out on deck. The trees on the edge of the river were as dark as blackberries. A little owl swooped by noisily. A slight breeze wafted the strong soapy scent of the meadowsweet towards us. In the distance we could hear the sensual throb of pop music, and see the dark sky florid like a great bruise.

'It's a fair,' said Gussie in excitement. 'Oh, please let's go.'

The red and yellow helter-skelter rose like a fairy tower out of the pale green chestnut trees, the lights of the big wheel turned like a giant firework. I listened to the beat of the music, the roar of the generators and the thwack of balls on the canvas at the back of the coconut shies. I'm always turned on by fairs.

Gareth had just loosened every tooth in my head, driving like James Hunt round the dodgem car track. My only consolation was that Jeremy and Gussie, now clutching a Gary Glitter poster, a china Alsatian and a huge mauve teddy bear, had been watching our progress. Next to them had stood a group of youths who had wolf-whistled and whooped in admiration every time we crashed past them, as my hair whipped back and my skirt blew up to reveal an expanse of brown thigh. This was the kind of corporate approval that wouldn't do Jeremy any harm. Now Gareth was wasting a fortune at the shooting range, and Jeremy and I stood side by side watching Gussie riding on a merry-go-round horse with red nostrils. Grasping the brass rod with both hands, her handbag flying on her arm, her eyes shining, she smiled at us every time she came past. We smiled dutifully back.

The sensual beat of the music was eating into my soul. It was now or never. Out of the corner of my eye I saw the big wheel pause to take on more passengers. Gussie's merry-go-round would stop in a minute.

'Let's go on the big wheel,' I said to Jeremy.

'Won't you be scared?'

'Not with you.'

'We must be careful. Gussie'll start suspecting something.'

'I want her to,' I said.

With almost indecent haste, we slid into the bucket seats. At that moment Gussie clambered off her horse and looked round.

'Over here,' shouted Jeremy.

She looked up and grinned. 'Take care,' she shouted.

Up and up went the wheel. At the top we could see for miles. The moon had broken free from its moorings and was sailing up in the sky. Below us lay lit-up villages, dark woods, pale hayfields, and to the right, the distant gleam of the river.

'Oh isn't it beautiful?' I said, moving my leg against his.

'Beautiful,' he said, not looking at the view.

Then down we plunged; with that dreadful stomach-stealing, heart-dropping fall. Screaming like a peacock, I clutched Jeremy's arm.

'Are you all right?' he said, as we swooped upwards again.

Then suddenly, fate came to our rescue. The wheel stopped to drop off some passengers, leaving us at the top, miles from everyone.

For a second we gazed at each other.

'What are you so frightened of?' I said softly. 'Gareth's disapproval or hurting Gussie?'

'Both. Gus doesn't deserve to be hurt, and I feel guilty bringing Gareth down here, laying on a bird for him, then trying to lay on her myself.'

271

'You'd be insane with rage if I'd got off with Gareth.'

'I know I would.'

'Well then, is it fair to Gussie to marry her when you feel like this?'

'I think I'm more frightened of you than anything else,' he muttered. 'Like Carmen Jones on the box tonight, I'd be like that poor sod Don José. Once you got me away from Gussie you'd get bored with me. Then I'd find myself totally hooked on you, and not capable of holding you.'

'Oh darling,' I said, putting a little sob in my voice, 'don't you realize, I'm only playing the field because I'm unhappy? When I find the right guy, I'm quite capable of sticking to him. I was never unfaithful to Tod.'

'Not at all?'

'Not at all. You've got to learn to trust me.'

Jeremy looked up at the sky.

'I could reach up and pick you a bunch of stars,' he said. 'I wish we could stay up here forever and never go back to reality.'

The wheel started moving again.

'We've got to talk,' I whispered. 'Wait till Gussie's asleep and then creep up on deck.'

'It's too risky. Gareth's got a nose on elastic.'

'He's drunk so much this evening, he'll go out like a light.'

'Anyone want a drink?' said Gareth when we got back to the boat.

'I'm going to hit the hay,' said Jeremy. 'I've got a bloody awful headache from the sun.'

'I've got some pain killers in my suitcase,' said Gareth. 'I'll get them.'

He went out of the room. Gussie was rootling around in the kitchen. I moved towards Jeremy.

'Have you really got a headache?' I said.

He smiled slightly and shook his head: 'I ache in rather more basic parts of my anatomy.'

'Painkillers won't cure that,' I said softly. 'The only remedy is to come up on deck later.'

'How long shall I leave it?'

272

'Well I certainly can't hold out for more than an hour,' I said, running my tongue over my lips.

At that moment Gareth returned with the pills.

'I really don't like taking things,' said Jeremy.

'You take three,' said Gareth firmly. 'That should do the trick.'

I'd have given anything to have a long scented bath. As it was, I stood barefoot on the rushmatting, soaping my body, and then dried myself with an old towel, the consistency of a brillo pad. I didn't even dare scent my body with bath oil, in case Gareth thought I was giving him the come on. But luckily when I went back to the cabin, he was already in bed, snoring away like Tommy Brock. I waited half an hour, then very slowly eased myself out of bed, groping for the wall and then the doorway. I had my alibi ready — I was just getting a drink of water — but I didn't need it. Gareth didn't stir. I tiptoed out of the cabin and up onto the deck.

The sullen heat of the torrid afternoon had given way to a blissful cool. Through the overhanging willows, the stars shone like blossom. I lay stretched out on the deck, listening to the soft gurgling of the river, the drowsy piping of birds, and the chatter and rustlings as the animals of night plied their trades. Half an hour passed in blissful expectation, then another half-hour when I knew he'd be here any minute.

What was that poem that always made us giggle at school?
He is coming, my dove, my dear:
He is coming, my life, my fate;
The red rose cries, 'He is near, he is near';
And the white rose weeps, 'He is late.'

Well it seemed the white rose had got the message all right. Another hour limped by, by which time the deck was harder than a board, and fire was beginning to come out of my nostrils. It was obvious I was going to get no chance to play deck coitus. Anger gave way to misery and exhaustion, and I crept back to bed.

273

CHAPTER EIGHT

I was woken by the din of church bells. The cabin was already like an oven, the day far sunnier than my mood. I lay for a few seconds sourly wallowing in the bitterness of rejection. Master Jeremy, it had to be faced, had displayed thighs of clay. It was possible Gussie had had an attack of insomnia or intense amorousness last night, which had prevented him sneaking up on deck to find me, but it seemed unlikely. I had been convinced I could extract him from her as easily as a Kleenex from its box. But I had plainly miscalculated. He must prefer the security of her prop forward arms to my more subtle embraces. They were, after all, engaged, and he more accustomed to behaving like a gentleman than a full-blooded male. All the same, I wasn't going to give up without a fight; it would give old Torquemada Llewellyn too much satisfaction. I'd just have to find a chisel and prise Jeremy away like a barnacle.

The boat was also beginning to get on my nerves. My hair hadn't been washed for two days and was losing its slippery sheen. I was desperate to have a bath, and fed up with not being able to admire myself in a long mirror.

Gussie was in the kitchen — I'm surprised she didn't put up a camp bed there — simultaneously washing up breakfast, cooking lunch, eating cold new potatoes and making out wedding lists.

'Hullo,' she said, beaming. 'Did you sleep well?'

'Brilliantly,' I said. 'It must be all that fresh air.'

'Don't the church bells sound lovely?' she said, 'I adore country churches — all that soft brick, and sermons about crops, and rosy-cheeked choirboys scuttling in late.'

'Because the vicar's been pinching them in the vestry. It'd

274

be worth going to church to get cool. It's like a sauna on board.'

Gussie looked a bit shocked.

'I don't believe in God,' I said lightly. 'Or rather I've never had any evidence that He believed in me.'

'I didn't think about Him that much,' said Gussie, 'until I found Jeremy, and then I just felt I ought to be saying thank you for my incredible luck all the time.' She bent over to empty the sink tidy, displaying a vast stretch of blue-jeaned bottom. Wranglers must sew up their trousers with underground cables to stand that kind of strain.

'I hoped Jeremy'd wake up in time to go to Matins with me,' she went on, 'but he's still out like a light. Mind you, it's good for him. He's been working so hard at the office, and I often think the strain of getting married is even worse for men.'

She glanced at her list again, absent-mindedly breaking off a bit of celery and putting it in her mouth.

'Do you think I'll need a Mac in my trousseau?'

'Well, I've always preferred men with cars,' I said. 'But I suppose you could wear a black plastic one with nothing underneath for the bedroom. Do you need any help?' I added, unenthusiastically, taking an orange from the fruit bowl.

'Oh no,' she said, 'I want you to enjoy yourself.'

'I'll go and sunbathe then.'

I took a lilo and my incredibly boring biography of Matthew Arnold out on deck. I had put on a new black bikini, composed only of four black triangles, held together by bootlaces, with not really enough triangle to go round. The sun was already high in the sky and boring down on the boat. Snaky brown tree roots gleamed below the surface of the oily water. Meadow-sweet was spread thick as cream on the lush green banks. The birds were still being shouted down by the church bells. It was far too hot for clothes. I took off my bikini top and lay down. Within twenty minutes sweat was pouring in rivulets down the ridges of the lilo. I was just about to retreat inside for a towel and a drink of water when I heard a wolf whistle. I flicked open my eyes, straight into the highly unacceptable face of capitalism, and quickly flicked them shut again. It was Gareth — already after two days tanned dark brown by the sun — carrying the Sunday papers, a large gin and tonic, and a wireless playing Mozart.

'Morning, lovely,' he said. 'You're overdressed. Why don't you take off the bottom half as well?'

I ignored him, feigning sleep.

The next moment Gussie joined us.

'Oh Tavy,' she said. 'Do you think you should? Someone might see you from the bank.'

'Don't be a spoilsport,' said Gareth. 'Here's the *News of the World,* and shut up. I won't give you a paper, Octavia, as I know you're finding that biography of Matthew Arnold quite unputdownable. Bags I borrow it next.'

I gritted my teeth. For a few minutes they read in silence. I got hotter and hotter, like a chicken on a spit.

'Why do they always write about the emphasis being on the hips this year, when one's just had a huge breakfast?' sighed Gussie.

'That's nice,' said Gareth, showing her the *Sunday Times.* 'They've given us a good write-up, recommending their readers to buy our shares, which is more than they're doing for Seaford-Brennen.'

'How many people work at Seaford-Brennen, Tavy?' said Gussie.

'About a quarter of them,' said Gareth, taking a huge swig at his gin and tonic.

Gussie giggled.

'You don't know anything about them,' I hissed at him. 'Why don't you stick to underpasses, which you seem to know all about?'

'There's a most interesting thing here about schism in the Catholic church,' said Gussie, hastily. 'Do you think priests should marry, Gareth?'

'Only if they love each other.'

Gussie shrieked with laughter.

There was only one single bell tolling now, hurrying people to church.

276

'They always ring out of tune back home in Wales,' said Gareth. 'One of the bellringers is a very pretty girl given to wearing mini skirts. All the men bellringers are in love with her, and every time she lets her bell go up, they pull their bells down to have a good look. Christ it's hot. It must be in the nineties.'

'I'm going to get a drink. Do you want one, Tavy?' said Gussie.

'I do,' said Gareth, handing her his glass.

'I hope Jeremy wakes up soon. It'll be much cooler once we get going,' said Gussie.

I turned over on my side, pretending to be asleep. Through the rails I could see the elm trees full of a blue darkness, and a heat haze shimmering above the hay fields. I must have dozed off, for the next thing I heard was Jeremy's voice saying, 'What the hell did you give me last night?'

'Mogodon,' said Gareth.

'Mogodon!' said Jeremy in horror. 'Three of them! Christ, you bastard! That's almost an overdose. No wonder they knocked me out like a sledge hammer.'

'It was for your own good,' said Gareth. 'Kept you out of mischief and Miss Brennen's bed.'

'I wish you'd bloody well stop playing Anti-Cupid,' snapped Jeremy.

'Hush,' said Gareth softly, 'you'll wake Octavia.' Jeremy lowered his voice, 'God she looks fantastic.'

'Like a Ming vase,' said Gareth. 'Beautiful, but empty. Why don't you write one of your famous poems about her? "Oh lovely Octavia, How I'd like to make a slave of ya."'

'Oh, put a sock in it,' said Jeremy angrily.

'Have you got a copy of Shakespeare on board?' asked Gareth.

'Somewhere in the bookcase in the saloon. What do you want to look up?'

'*The Taming of the Shrew*,' said Gareth, 'I thought I might pick up a few tips on how to handle Octavia.'

Jeremy lost his temper. 'Will you stop jumping on that poor girl?'

277

'Why, are you jumping on her already?'

'I am *not*. Why the hell don't you go and start the boat?'

'Why don't you?' said Gareth. 'I've come here on holiday. It's the first break I've had in months, and I'm enjoying the view far too much. I can't decide if Octavia's glorious knockers remind me more of the Himalayas or the Pyramids.'

'Jeremy,' called Gussie — she obviously didn't like Jeremy admiring the view either — 'do come and start the boat.'

'All right,' he said, reluctantly; then more softly to Gareth, 'if you don't get off Octavia's back, there'll be trouble.'

'Her back is not the part of her anatomy uppermost in my mind at the moment.'

I was nearly expiring with heat and rage by now. I was also worried about my tits burning. My hair was ringing with sweat. I shook it out of my eyes and glared at Gareth.

'Do you want me to oil you?' he said.

'No thank you,' I hissed.

'Why don't we have a cease-fire. It is the sabbath after all?' he said, looking down at me with amused and lascivious pleasure.

'You're disgusting,' I said, furiously turning over on my front.

There was the sound of engines, and the boat started. Even when we were on the move the heat didn't let up. As we sailed into a long stretch of open river with no shade, Gareth got to his feet and stretched.

'I'm worried you'll overcook, Octavia.'

And the next moment he'd dived into the river with a huge splash, sending a tidal wave of filthy oily water all over me. I leapt up, screaming, grabbing my bikini top.

'Will you stop hounding me,' I howled as he surfaced, laughing, shaking his hair out of his eyes.

'I thought you needed cooling down,' he said, and, scooping a great handful of water in my direction, soaked me again.

Gibbering with rage, I rushed into the kitchen.

'That sod's just drenched me.'

Gussie giggled. 'Oh poor Tavy! Here, have a towel.'

'It's soaked my hair,' I stormed, 'I must wash it at once.'

278

'You can't really,' said Gussie, sympathetically. 'There simply isn't enough water. I'm sure it'll dry all right.'

I caught sight of my face in the mirror. There was a great red mark on my cheek where I'd lain on Matthew Arnold. It looked as though Gareth had socked me one, and doubled my ill temper.

'But normally I wash my hair every day,' I screamed. 'It's crawling off my head. I've never been on anything as primitive as this bloody boat.'

Then I made the most awful scene. None of Gussie's bromides could soothe me.

'No one goes out of their way deliberately to hurt people,' she said finally.

'I do,' said Gareth, coming in dripping river water and seizing the towel from me. 'I'm like a leopard, I kill for the hell of it.'

'You shouldn't have soaked her,' said Gussie, reproachfully.

'I'm going back to London,' I said.

'Splendid,' said Gareth. 'There's a fast train on the hour from Reading. Next time you come down we'll arrange QE2 facilities.'

'What's the matter?' said Jeremy, shouting down the stairs.

'We've got a mutiny on our hands, Mr. Christian,' said Gareth, 'Able seawoman Brennen wants to desert. Shall we keelhaul her or give her 1000 lashes?'

Gussie — God rot her — started to laugh.

Jeremy came down the stairs and took in the situation in a swift glance.

'Go and steer,' he said angrily to Gareth. 'You've caused enough trouble for one morning. I own this boat, and what I say goes.'

'Sorry Captain Bligh, I mistook you for Mr. Christian,' said Gareth, grinning and filling up his glass, he disappeared up the stairs, shouting, 'Ahoy, Ahoy, my kingdom for a hoy.'

Jeremy poured me a stiff drink, and took me into the saloon.

'I'm sorry about Gareth,' he said, gently, 'he's being dia-
bolical. I think he must be going through the change of life.'

'He's probably irritated I haven't succumbed yet,' I said.

'Hell knows no fury like a Welshman scorned.'

There was a pause. Jeremy put some books back on the
shelf.

'Did you wait very long last night?' he said in an undertone.

'Not very,' I said. 'I was disappointed, that's all.'

'Oh Christ,' he said. 'Gussie was yapping and yapping
away about soft furnishings and the next thing I knew it was
morning. Bloody sleeping pills. I'm terribly sorry, you must
think me such a drip.'

I laughed, suddenly I felt much happier.

'You couldn't do much on three Mogodons.'

'If you're really desperate for a bath,' he said, 'we'll stop at
the next lock and see what we can do.'

'Where are we anyway?' I said.

'About half a mile from Grayston.'

'That's where Ricky Seaford lives,' I said in excitement.
'I'll give him a ring at the next lock and we can go and swim
in his pool.'

'I'll come ashore with you,' said Jeremy.

'Behave yourself, Octavia,' Gareth shouted after us as we got
off the boat, 'or we'll get The Rape of the Lock Keeper, and
Jeremy'll be forced to write a long poem about it afterwards,
in heroic couplets.'

Scarlet geraniums blazed in pots on the window-ledges;
the whitewashed stone of the lock-keeper's cottage assaulted
the eye. The quay scorched my bare feet. Inside the cottage
it was dark and at least cooler. Jeremy tactfully stayed outside while I telephoned. The butler answered. Mrs. Seaford
was not back from church, but Mr. Seaford was in, he said.
That was a relief.

Ricky was a long time coming to the telephone. I watched
the flypaper hanging from the ceiling, black with desperate,
writhing insects, and examined the coronation mugs and
framed photographs of children with white bows in their

hair on a nearby dresser.

'Hullo Octavia,' said Ricky's familiar, plummy, port-soaked voice. It sounded more guarded than usual. 'What can I do for you?'

'I'm only a quarter of a mile away,' I said. 'Roughing it on a barge.'

'I can't imagine you roughing it anywhere.'

'Can we come and see you this afternoon?'

There was a pause. I could imagine his bull-terrier eyes narrowing thoughtfully. He probably had business friends staying the weekend. It would impress them to invite a sexy bit of crumpet like myself over but would it be worth incurring Joan's wrath?

Then he said, 'We're going out to dinner, but come over and have tea or early drinks or whatever. Who's on the boat with you?'

'Oh, a sweet engaged couple, you'll absolutely adore them, and a ghastly jumped-up Welshman, who's convinced he's Charlie Clore. I wanted to show him a real Captain of Industry in the flesh. That's why I rang you.'

Ricky laughed. I could tell he was flattered.

'Do put him down if you get the chance,' I said.

'Talking of Captains of Industry,' said Ricky, 'there's a great fan of yours staying here this weekend.'

'Oh, who?'

'Wait and see. We'll see you later.'

Things were decidedly looking up. Gareth and Jeremy were already at each other's throats, and this afternoon I would not only have the pleasure of seeing Ricky take Gareth down a few pegs, but also have an old admirer to spur Jeremy on to greater endeavour. Smiling to myself, I went out into the sunshine. Jeremy was leaning over the back-door gate, gazing moodily at the sweltering horizon. Above a pair of much faded pale blue denim shorts, his back was tanned a gleaming butterscotch gold. Suddenly I thought what ravishing children we'd have. No one could see us from the boat. I put a hand on his shoulder.

'Stop all-in wrestling with your conscience,' I said. 'It's too hot.'

281

The next moment I was in his arms.

After a second I pulled away.

'Didn't you know it was dangerous to exceed the stated dose?' I whispered, gazing blatantly at his mouth.

By the time we got back, Gareth had taken the boat through the lock.

'You *have* caught the sun,' said Gussie, gazing at me in admiration. She was obviously pleased I was in a good mood again.

'What's worrying me,' said Gareth, grimly, 'is whose son she's caught.'

CHAPTER NINE

Great fans of overhanging willow trees crashed against the roof as we drew up at Ricky Seaford's newly painted blue and white boathouse. Hayfields rose pale and silver towards a dark clump of beech trees, surrounding a large russet house, which was flanked by stables, sweeping lawns, and well kept fruit and vegetable gardens.

'Goodness, how glamorous,' said Gussie, standing on the shore and tugging a comb through her tangled hair. 'I hope we don't look too scruffy.'

I certainly didn't. I was wearing a pale pink shirt over my black bikini, and the heat had brought a pink glow to the suntan in my cheeks.

'Ricky Seaford's a frightfully big noise, isn't he?' said Gussie.

'Well, he makes a lot of noise,' I said, admiring my reflection in the boathouse window.

'It'll be so useful for Gareth to meet him,' said Gussie.

'Oh he's right out of Gareth's league.'

'Never mind,' said Gareth equably. 'I may pick up a few tips.'

We walked up the slope, past hedges dense and creamy with elder flowers and hogweed. Under huge flat-bottomed trees, sleek horses switched their tails deep in the buttercups. We came to a stile. Jeremy went over first, and helped Gussie and then me. For a second I let myself rest in his arms.

We let ourselves in through a wrought iron gate, walking across unblemished green lawns, past huge herbaceous borders luxuriating in the heat.

'These are Joan's pride and joy,' I said. 'She's very good in flower bed.'

'Is she nice?' said Gussie.

'Well, let's say I prefer Ricky. She's a perfectly bloody mother-in-law to poor Xander.'

At that moment, several assorted gundogs and terriers poured, barking, out of the French windows, followed at a leisurely pace by Ricky Seaford. He was a tall man, who had grown much better looking in middle age, when his hair had turned from a muddy brown to a uniform silver grey. This suited his rather florid complexion which had been heightened, year by year, by repeated exposure to equal quantities of golf-course air and good whisky. Beneath the bull-terrier eyes the nose was straight, the mouth firm. A dark blue shirt, worn outside his trousers concelaed a middle-aged spread. The general effect was pro-consular and impressive.

'Hullo, chaps,' he said in his booming voice, kissing me on the cheek. 'Joan's down at the pool.' He was always more friendly to me when she was out of earshot.

'This is Gussie Forbes and Jeremy West,' I said.

'Nice to see you,' said Ricky, giving them the big on-off smile that gave him such a reputation for having charm in the city. 'You've certainly picked the right weather.'

Suddenly he saw Gareth who had lingered behind to talk to the dogs. For a minute Ricky looked incredulous, then his face lit up like a Christmas tree.

'Why Gareth,' he bellowed. 'You do pop up in the most unexpected places. What the hell are you doing here?'

'Cruising down the river on a Sunday afternoon,' said Gareth. 'I must say it's a nice place you've got here, Ricky.'

'Well, well, well, I didn't realize you were going to see it so soon.'

Ricky now seemed terribly pleased with everything. 'Fancy you meeting up with this lot. Now I expect you'd like a drink. Come down to the pool. Joan's been so looking forward to meeting you.'

'You know each other?' said Gussie, looking delighted. 'What a coincidence; you never said so, Gareth.'

'No one asked me,' he said.

'Is this all of you?' said Ricky. 'I thought you mentioned some tiresome little parvenu who needed putting in his place, Octavia?'

'That was probably me,' said Gareth drily.

If I'd had a knife handy, I'd certainly have plunged it into him. I moved away, kicking a defenceless-looking petunia when no one was looking.

The pool, which was of Olympic size and always kept at 75 degrees, lay in an old walled garden, overgrown with clematis, ancient pink roses and swathes of honeysuckle. At one end, in a summerhouse, Ricky had built a bar. Joan Seaford, a 15 stone do-gooder, most of it muscle, lay under a green and white striped umbrella, writing letters. She glanced up coldly as we approached. She always looks at me as though I was a washing machine that had broken down. As is often the case, the people who married into the Seaford-Brennen clan were the ones who felt the family rivalry most strongly. The violent jealousy Joan had always displayed towards my mother was now transferred to me and intensified by the resentment she felt towards Xander.

'Hullo Octavia,' she said. 'You're looking very fit.'

Her voice had that carrying quality developed by years of strenuous exercise bawling out gundogs, and terrorizing charity committees. Drawing close I could see the talcum powder caked between her huge breasts, and smell the Tweed cologne she always used.

I introduced Gussie and Jeremy. Ricky had dropped behind, showing the new diving boards to Gareth.

'I've never seen such a beautiful pool,' raved Gussie. 'And your herbaceous borders are out of this world. How on earth do you grow flowers like that? My fiancé and I have just got a house with a tiny garden. We're so excited.'

Joan looked slightly more amiable; her face completely defrosted when Ricky came up and said, 'Darling, isn't this extraordinary? Guess who's on the boat with them — Gareth Llewellyn.'

'Oh, I've heard so much about you.'

'And Octavia's been telling us lots about you, Mrs. Seaford,' said Gareth, taking her hand.

285

Joan shot me a venomous look, then turned, smiling, back to Gareth.

'My dear, you must call me Joan. I gather you and Ricky have been doing a lot of business together.'

'Well, yes,' said Gareth, the lousy sycophant, still holding her hand. 'We hope to. I must say you've done this pool beautifully.'

'Well what's everyone going to have to drink?' said Ricky, rubbing his hands.

Gussie was putting an awful flowered teacosy on her head.

'I'd love to have a swim first,' she said.

I sat down on the edge of the pool. One of the Seaford setters, sensing my ill-humour, wandered, panting, over to me and shoved a cold nose in my hand. The dogs had always been the only nice people in the house.

My temper had not improved half an hour later. Everyone had swum and Gareth, having totally captivated Joan Seaford, had been taken off to the house to talk business with Ricky. Ricky, having learnt from Gareth that Jeremy was in publishing, had invited him to inspect the library which dripped with priceless first editions that no one had ever read. Gussie was still gambolling round in the shallow end like a pink hippo, rescuing ladybirds from drowning. I was left with Joan.

'Where's Pamela?' I said.

'She's gone off to lunch with some friends — the Connolly-Hockings. He's prospective candidate for Grayston. Xander finds them boring. We were rather surprised he couldn't make it this weekend. You'd think after three weeks in the Far . . .'

'He was exhausted by the trip,' I said. 'It's his first weekend home. I expect he had a lot of things to catch up on.'

'Ricky thought it rather odd he used pressure of work as an excuse,' said Joan. 'He must confine all his industry to the weekends.'

'What do you mean?' I said sharply.

Joan wrote the address of some Viscountess on the envelope in her controlled, schoolgirl hand. Then she said,

'Xander doesn't seem to understand that office hours run more or less from 9.30 to 5.30 with one hour for lunch. He shouldn't spend quite so long every day pouring drinks down young men who ought to be back in their offices at the Stock Exchange.'

Despite the white heat of the day I suddenly felt as though ice cold water was being dripped down my neck. Had Ricky and Joan got wind of Xander's proclivities? God help him if they had.

'Xander does most of his deals over lunchtime drinks,' I protested.

At that moment Gussie joined us.

'Are you talking about Xander?' she said, ripping off her petalled tea cosy. 'I always did think he was the most glamorous man ever — after Jeremy that is.'

Joan gave a wintry smile.

'I gather from Tavy that Pamela is divine too,' said Gareth, having gathered no such thing. 'But I can't believe you've got married daughters, you look so young.'

Joan patted her sculptured blue curls. 'I'm going to be a grandmother soon.'

'How exciting,' shrieked Gussie. 'You didn't tell me Xander was having a baby, Tavy.'

'No, my other daughter,' said Joan. 'She only got married in March, but they don't believe in waiting, unlike Xander and Pammie who've been married two years.'

'Oh that's not long,' said Gussie, soothingly. 'I know she'll get pregnant soon.'

'She might,' said Joan, 'if Xander spent more time at home.'

I flushed and was about to contradict her, when Gussie said, 'Alison was only married in March? Then you must be an expert on weddings. I bet it was lovely.'

'It was rather a success. Poor Ricky had to sell a farm to pay for it. Perhaps you saw the photographs in *The Tatler*?'

'I believe I did,' lied Gussie.

And they were off: Searcy's, The General Trading Company, Peter Jones, soft furnishings and duvets, and cast iron casseroles, and 'weren't lots of little bridesmaids in Laura

287

Ashley dresses much sweeter than grown up ones'. Gussie really ought to cut a disc.

'Alison's husband, Peter, is an absolute charmer,' Joan was saying, 'we like him awfully. They spent their honeymoon in the Seychelles.'

The bitch! God how I wanted to hold her underneath her horrible, chlorinated, aquamarine water, until her great magenta face turned purple.

I watched the Red Admirals burying their faces in the buddleia. I wished Jeremy would tear himself away from the first editions. A great wave of loneliness swept over me.

'If you're in a hurry for a wedding dress,' said Joan, 'I've got a little woman who can run up things awfully quickly. Shall I give her a ring?'

I knew she was only handing out largesse to Gussie like nuts at Christmas to emphasize her disapproval of me.

'Would you mind if I washed my hair, Joan?' I said, getting to my feet. 'I've brought my own shampoo.'

'Of course not; help yourself. Use my bedroom; there are plenty of towels in the hot cupboard.'

And arsenic in the taps, I muttered, walking towards the house, feeling her hatred boring into my back. She was probably glad of an excuse to question Gussie about me and Gareth. As I crossed the lawn I deliberately didn't look into the library to see if I could see Jeremy.

Suddenly a voice with a slight foreign accent said, 'Hullo, Octavia.'

I gave a shudder of revulsion as I looked up into the coarse, sensual face of Andreas Ratz, porn-king and multi-millionaire.

'What are you doing here?' I said, not bothering to keep the hostility out of my voice.

'Staying here.'

So this was the old admirer Ricky was talking about.

'Let me monopolize you for a minute,' he said, taking my arm. I felt his fingers, warm and sweaty, enveloping it. I moved away, but his grip tightened.

'Come and look at Joan's rose-garden,' he said. 'I gather it's quite exceptional.'

I could see the line on his forehead where the man-tan ended and the gunmetal grey hair began. He was a man who seldom ventured out of doors. His eyes were so dark the pupils were indistinguishable from the iris, and always looked so deeply and knowingly into mine, I felt he knew exactly the colour my pants were. He was wearing a black shirt and silver paisley scarf which blended perfectly with the gunmetal hair. I supposed he was handsome in a brutal, self-conscious way, but I could never look at him without realizing what a really evil man he was. I was surprised Joan allowed him into the house. Inflation makes strange bed fellows.

As well as owning strip clubs and half the girly magazines in London, he also produced a prestigious semi-porno-graphic magazine called *Hedonist* which ran features by intellectuals alongside photographs of naked girls with Red Indian suntans lying on fur counterpanes. It was regarded as the English answer to *Playboy*. For a number of years now he had been chasing me in a leisurely fashion, offering me larger and larger sums to be photographed. I always refused him. I didn't fancy a staple through my midrift. I felt towards him that contempt with which one regards a bath rail in an hotel bathroom, convinced one will never be old and frail enough to need it.

I stopped to admire a purple rose. Andreas admired my figure, which, in its sopping wet bikini, left nothing to the imagination.

He pressed a clenched fist gently against my stomach.

'When are you going to come and pose for me?' he asked.

'I'm not. I don't need the bread.'

'You never know,' he said. 'Nothing's gilt-edged any more. Not even your beautiful hair. Roots cost money to be touched up.'

'It's natural,' I snapped.

'I hear Seaford-Brennen's are in a spot of bother,' he went on. I could feel his hot breath on my shoulder.

'Oh for God's sake, why does everyone keep telling me this? Of course they're all right. They've been all right for over fifty years.'

Andreas splayed his fingers out and caressed my rib cage. He was the only man I knew who gave me that horrible squirming feeling of excitement. I imagined the hundreds of girls and the millions of grubby girly pictures those fingers had flicked through. I moved off sharply and buried my face in a dark red rose. He lit a cigar with a beautiful manicured hand, holding it between finger and thumb like a workman. I could feel him watching me.

'Why don't you stop staring?'

'A Katz can look at a Queen.' He'd made that joke a hundred times before. 'You're a very beautiful girl, Octavia, but not a very bright one. I'll pay you fifteen hundred for one photographic session. Why don't we have dinner next week and discuss it? And that wouldn't be the end, you know. I could give you everything you want.'

'Well, I certainly don't want you,' I said, turning and walking back. 'And if people saw the goods displayed so blatantly across your gatefold, they might not be interested in purchasing them any more.'

Andreas smiled the knowing smile of a crafy old animal.

'I'll get you in the end, baby, and by then it'll be on my terms. You wait and see. By the way, what's Gareth Llewellyn doing closeted with Ricky?'

'He's spending the weekend with us on the boat.'

Andreas laughed. 'So he's your latest. No wonder you're not interested in bread at the moment.'

I looked towards the house, the wistaria above the library was nearly over and shedding its petals in an amethyst carpet over the lawn. Out of the library window I caught sight of Jeremy watching us. I turned and smiled warmly at Andreas.

'There's a beautiful girl down at the pool, talking to Joan. Why don't you go and sign her up instead of me?' I said and, patting him on the cheek, ran laughing into the house.

Joan Seaford must have got the most sexless bedroom in the world, with its *eau de nil* walls, sea green carpet, and utterly smooth flowered counterpane tucked neatly under the pillows so they lay like a great sausage across the top of the bed. On the chest of drawers stood large framed Lenare photographs of Pamela and Alison, looking mistily glamorous in pearls. There were also a large photograph of Peter, Alison's husband, and one of Alison and Peter on their wedding day, knee deep in little bridesmaids in Laura Ashley dresses, but not even a passport snap of Xander, who was a hundred times more handsome than the whole lot put together. I was tempted to take the picture of him out of my wallet and stick it on top of Peter's smug, smiling, square-jawed face, but it wouldn't have done Xander any good.

I felt better after I'd had a bath, washed my hair and rubbed quantities of Joan's bottle of Joy over my body. I hoped she wouldn't recognize the smell on me. Anyway, she deserved to be Joyless, the old bag.

Combing my wet hair, I looked out of the window. Two girls — the kind who open their legs like airport doors whenever a man approaches — wearing white bikinis, stiletto heels and about a hundredweight each of make-up, were teetering across the lawn. They must have been brought down by Andreas. He always carried a spare. Suddenly Jeremy came out of the door leading to the swimming pool and walked past the tarts without even noticing them. They, on the other hand, swivelled round, gazing at him in wonder, watching him avidly as he loped with lazy animal grace towards the house. I can't say I blamed them.

Bring me my beau of burning gold, I muttered, as, wrapped only in a huge fluffy blue towel, I curled up on the floor to dry my hair. I didn't wait long. There was a quick step outside, and a knock on the door.

'Come in,' I said huskily.

He closed the door behind him. I let the towel slip slightly.

'Why are you here?' I said. 'I'm amazed you could tear yourself away from those first editions.'

'You're why I'm here,' he said. 'Who was that repulsive man you were talking to?'

My heart sang. It had worked.

'Andreas Katz. I've known him for years.'

'How well?'

I went on drying my hair.

'How.well?' persisted Jeremy. 'Oh for God's sake, turn

that bloody thing off.'

'Not as well as he would like,' I said, but I turned off the dryer.

He put his hands down, pulled me to my feet and kissed me passionately, his hands moving down to my breasts and over my hips. Just for once, I thought, the millpond smoothness of Joan's flowered counterpane is going to be ruffled. Then suddenly Jeremy pushed me away and went over to the window.

It took him a few seconds to get himself under control. I picked up the dryer.

'No,' he said. 'For Christ's sake don't turn it on yet. Look, you must understand how crazy I am about you.'

'You've got a funny way of showing it.'

He knelt down beside me, took my face in his hands, began stroking it very gently, as though he wanted to memorize all the contours.

'Gus doesn't deserve to be hurt, you know that as well as I do. Not now anyway, when Gareth's around to fuck everything up as well. If you and I have got something going for us, and I believe we have, let's wait until we get back to London.'

For a minute I looked mutinous. But I knew it wouldn't further my cause to tell him that part of the charm of hooking him would be to upset Gussie and Gareth.

'It's only tonight and Monday to get through,' he went on. 'On Tuesday we go back to London and we can meet on Wednesday and decide what the hell to do about it. You're so important to me, I reckon it's worth waiting for.'

I nodded, picking up his hand and planting a kiss in the palm. 'All right, I'll try,' I said.

With the tips of his fingers he traced a vein on the inside of my arm, down to the scar that ran across my wrist.

'How did you get that?'

'With a razor. The day Xander married Pamela. I felt the only person in the world who really loved me was being taken away from me.'

He bent his head and kissed the scar.

'You do need looking after, don't you? Be brave and trust

me, little one. It isn't long to wait.'

After he was gone I finished drying my hair, and went downstairs, experiencing a great and joyous calm. The road was clear now, there was nothing Gareth could do.

Down at the pool the two tarts were swimming, holding their made-up faces high out of the water, encouraged by Gareth, who was sitting on the edge talking to Ricky and Andreas, and drinking a Bloody Mary. He'd been swimming again and his black hair fell in wet tendrils on his forehead.

'I certainly don't want yes-men around me anymore,' said Ricky.

'I certainly want "yes" women around me,' said Gareth. 'I suppose we'd better go in a minute. Oh, there you are Octavia, cleansed in mind and body I hope.'

The three men looked at me. Together they made a nerve-racking trio.

'Octavia has so far refused to cook a single meal on board,' said Gareth. 'So no doubt I'll be slaving over a hot tin opener again tonight. I really don't approve of role-reversal.'

'The only time any role-reversal takes place in our house,' said Ricky, laughing heartily, 'is when Joan reverses the Rolls into the gateposts.'

'Who's taking my name in vain?' said Joan, coming through the gate, followed by Gussie and Jeremy, absolutely weighed down with loot from the vegetable garden.

'Look,' screamed Gussie. 'Isn't Joan angelic? We can have asparagus for supper tonight, and strawberries.'

'At least we won't get scurvy,' said Gareth, smiling at Joan. 'Thank you very much.' He got up. 'We must go.'

'You'd better go and change darling,' said Ricky. 'I'll walk down to the boathouse with them. It'll give the dogs a run. I won't be long.'

He bustled into the house.

'Such a pity we're going out to supper,' Joan said, kissing Gussie. 'Do send me a postcard when you know what your telephone number's going to be. And I'll get Alison and Peter to give you a ring. I know you'll get on.'

'Goodbye, Octavia.' She gave me the usual chilly peck.

'You must bring Mrs. Smith down one evening,' she said to Gareth. 'I hear she's the most gorgeous gel.'

She'd only started saying 'gel' since Pamela came out.

Ricky returned with the visitor's book. 'You must all sign before you go.'

He always does this so he can remember who to claim on expenses. I didn't dare look at Jeremy when Gussie signed them both under their new address.

'We won't be actually living there for a month or two,' she said, beaming round.

Andreas abandoned us at the edge of the hayfields. He was not cut out for country walks.

'Goodbye Octavia,' he said. 'Think about what I've said. We can't go on not meeting like this.'

'That man's a shit,' said Gareth, as soon as we were out of earshot.

'I know,' said Ricky, 'but an extremely clever one.'

CHAPTER TEN

After the thrill of my recent encounter with Jeremy I behaved atrociously for the rest of the day. As we were sailing
towards evening through low fields of buttercups and overhanging trees, I made Jeremy teach me how to steer the
boat. I insisted on driving it towards the bank all the time, so
he had to keep putting his hands over mine in order to
straighten up. Gussie seemed to see nothing wrong. She
beamed at us both. Gareth was making Pimms.

After dinner Gussie dragged a very reluctant Jeremy
across the fields to look at a Norman church, and Gareth
and I were left on the boat together drinking brandy. The
night was very hot and still. An owl hooted in a nearby spin-
ney. The first star flickered like a white moth in a dark blue
sky. Gareth smoked a cigar to keep off the midges. The wireless was playing Beethoven's Third Piano Concerto. If only
it was Jeremy sitting there, I thought. Nevertheless, I'd
made such good progress that day. I felt nothing could dim
my happiness.

Gareth got up, flicked his cigar into the water and strolled
over to the other side of the boat to stand looking at the
darkening horizon.

'How's your weekend of sun, sex and sleep going?' I
asked.

'Not quite as eventfully as yours,' he said.

He came and stood over me, looking down at me, huge
against the sky. Suddenly my heart began to thump un-
pleasantly, perhaps at last he was going to try his luck with
me after all.

'I want another drink,' I said, getting quickly to my feet
and wandering into the saloon.

Gareth followed me. 'Aren't you beginning to wonder why I haven't made a pass at you?'

I turned round. 'Since you seem quite incapable of passing anyone up, it had crossed my mind.'

He looked at me for a minute and then grinned.

'Because I don't like bitches, and you're the biggest bitch I've ever met.'

Wham! I let him have it, slap across the cheek. He didn't flinch, he didn't even put his hand up to his face.

'And that seems to substantiate my theory,' he said, pulling a packet of cigarettes out of his hip pocket and offering me one. I shook my head dumbly, appalled at what I had done. He selected a cigarette carefully and then lit it.

'You're not really my type,' he went on. 'I like my women gentle and loving, soft and tender. Women so vulnerable I want to protect them just as I'd look after a kitten or a little girl lost in the street. Women who don't automatically expect me to love them more than they love me. Maybe once upon a time before everyone started spoiling you you were like that, but not any more. You're so hard now, lovely, they could cut a diamond on you.'

'How dare you speak to me like that!' I said furiously.

'Because I'm probably the first man you've ever met who's been left completely cold by you. I've met your sort before; you're just a prick teaser or what the French call an "allumeuse", more anxious to inflame men than gratify them once they're well and truly hooked. You give off so much promise with that marvellous body and that great bright mane of hair falling over your eyes. And you've got the most beautiful face I've ever seen. But it doesn't add up to a thing, because you're so much in love with yourself that there isn't room for anyone else.'

'Shut up,' I said in a choked voice. 'I don't want to listen.'

'And another thing,' he went on, pouring a couple of fingers of brandy into his glass, 'although you've probably seen more ceilings than Michaelangelo, I guess you've never got any pleasure out of all those men you've slept with, and that troubles you a bit, because you've read somewhere that sex is supposed to be rather enjoyable and you can't understand why it doesn't work for you.'

It was like a nightmare.

'Stop it, stop it!' I screamed. 'You don't understand anything. I was going to get married but he was killed in a car crash only a few months ago.'

'I know all about that,' he said softy. 'Tod was never going to marry you.'

I clutched the table for support; my legs seemed to give way.

'You knew him?' I whispered. 'I don't understand. Then you knew . . .'

'. . . All about you long before I met you?' said Gareth. 'Yes, of course I did. Tod was living with an old girl friend of mine, Cathie Summers. They were fantastic together until you came along and broke it up.'

'I didn't break it up,' I whispered.

'Oh yes you did, lovely. You waited until Cathie'd gone to the States for a week and then you moved in. But it wasn't any good. Tod was fallible like most men, but he saw through you pretty quickly.'

'You're wrong. You're wrong. He loved me far more than he did her! He was with me the night he was killed.'

Gareth turned to me, his eyes suddenly stony with contempt.

'I know he was. But as usual Miss Brennen — Myth Brennen I ought to call you — you're bending the facts. Tod and I had a drink in the Antelope that night. Cathie was due back the next day, and Tod was in a panic about what she'd say if she found out about you. He was steeling himself to come round and tell you it was all off. I told him not to bother, just to let you stew. But Tod, being an ethical sod, insisted on going through with it.'

'That's right,' I stammered. 'And the moment he saw me he realized it was me he loved, not Cathie, and he was going to give her up.'

'You're a bloody liar,' said Gareth. 'Tod left me in the pub at five to eleven. He must have been with you by eleven o'clock. He was killed at ten past eleven — driving like the devil to get away from you.'

297

For a second I couldn't move or tear my eyes away from his. Then I gave a sob and fled out of the saloon down the passage to my cabin and, throwing myself down on my bunk, broke into a storm of weeping. I couldn't stand it. Gareth knew Tod, he knew all about me. He'd looked into my mind and seen everything — the aridity, the desert, the emptiness — and he'd brought to light terrible things I'd never admitted, even to myself, disproving lies that even I had begun to believe were the truth. I cried and cried, great tearing sobs until I thought there were no more tears inside me, then I just lay there, my face buried in my sodden pillow, trembling with terror.

Much later I heard Jeremy and Gussie come back. Oh God, I thought in agony, I expect Gareth's giving them a blow-by-blow account of the whole incident. They must have stayed up to watch the midnight movie, because it was half-past two before Gareth came to bed.

'Octavia,' he said softly.

I didn't answer. I ached for Jeremy. I wanted him to take me in his arms, to caress and console me and reconcile me with myself.

I didn't sleep all night. Great waves of anguish kept sweeping over me. I toyed with the idea of creeping off the boat before anyone was up and going back to London. But how would I get there? There wasn't a railway station for miles. I suppose I could ring one of my boyfriends and ask them to drive down and collect me. But would they? I'd never doubted I could get a man back at the drop of a hat. Now, suddenly, I wasn't sure.

I was feeling so paranoid I could hardly get myself out of bed. Thank God I'd brought the biggest pair of dark glasses in the world with me. In the kitchen Jeremy and Gussie were cooking breakfast.

'If you've got a hangover like the rest of us,' said Gussie, 'there's some Alka Seltzer in the cupboard.'

'No, I haven't actually.' Gussie poured me out a cup of coffee.

'Do you take sugar?'

298

'Of course she doesn't, she's quite sweet enough as it is,' said Jeremy, smiling at me. He was so used to getting the come-on sign from me, he seemed amazed I didn't crack back, and when he handed me my cup, his fingers closed over mine for a second. Yesterday I would have been certain he was trying to make contact with me; now my self-confidence had taken such a bashing, I felt it must be accidental.

I took my coffee up on deck. Three vast pairs of pants and the biggest bra in the Western Hemisphere were dripping from the railing. Gussie had obviously been doing some washing. A silver haze lay over the countryside. Pale green trees rose tender as lovers from the opposite bank. I couldn't stop shaking. Amidst all this beauty and sunshine, I felt like an empty shell.

A minute later Gussie came and joined me.

'What a beautiful shirt that is,' she said. 'I do envy you, Tavy. It doesn't matter if you've got a hangover or feel off colour, you've got such a lovely figure and such marvellous hair, people still thing you're a knock-out. But with me, my face is the only thing I've got — and that isn't all that great — and when that looks awful,' — she squinted at herself in the cabin window — 'like today, with this spot, I've got nothing to offer.'

She looked down at her left hand and flashed her engagement ring in the sun.

'Jeremy's wild about you,' she said wistfully. 'He was teasing me yesterday, saying that I was lucky I'd got his ring on my finger before he met you, or heaven knows what would have happened.'

I suddenly wondered what Jeremy was playing at.

'He's got no right to say that,' I said crossly. 'He adores you. You've only got to see the way he looks at you when you don't know he's looking.'

She looked at me, delighted.

'Do you really think so? Oh that does make me feel so much better. You don't think me silly?'

I shook my head and she went on. 'I was convinced Jeremy'd fallen for you. I was really screwed up about it. That's why I've been eating so much lately. Not that I thought for a moment you'd lead him on. I mean, you're one of my best friends — at least you were at school, I hope you still are. But you're so beautiful I didn't see how he could help it. And somehow you look so good together.

'That's why when he suggested asking you down for the weekend, I persuaded him to ask Gareth as well. Gareth's so attractive, I thought you were bound to fancy him and that would put Jeremy off.'

God, how naive she was! I concentrated on lighting a cigarette. Oh why were my hands shaking so much?

'I like Jeremy enormously,' I said slowly. 'He's extremely attractive too, but I also think he's perfect for you.'

'I'm not sure he's perfect for me at all,' said Gussie. 'I think he'll probably be wildly unfaithful to me, but that's because underneath he's not very sure of himself, and he'll need to make passes at women from time to time, just to boost his ego. But I hope so long as I make him happy enough, he'll always come back to me in the end.'

I looked at her round earnest face, appalled.

'But you can't marry him, Gus, not thinking that!'

'Oh yes I can. I love him so much it hurts sometimes. And I know it'll kill me when he is unfaithful, but at least I can try and make him more secure by loving him.'

I looked at her in awe. This was the sort of girl Gareth was talking about last night. Friday's child, loving and giving, prepared to give far more than she took.

Jeremy came up on deck. His blond hair gleamed almost white from the sun. Instinctively I turned my head away.

'I wish Gareth would step on it,' he said.

'Where's he gone?'

'To ring up some friends of his who live a few miles up the river,' said Jeremy. 'He thought we might take a drink off them. He must have run out of 2ps by now.'

'Here he comes,' said Gussie.

Gareth walked up the path, whistling. He grinned when he saw us, wicked gypsy eyes narrowed against the sun. He bounded up the bank and, scorning the gangplank, jumped across onto the boat. He looked up at Gussie's underclothes on the line.

'Is that a signal?' he said. 'England expects every man to do Octavia?'

'Did you get through?' snapped Jeremy.

Gareth nodded. 'We've timed it very well. They're giving a party tonight. They want us all to go. The land at the back of their house slopes straight down to the river. They suggested we tie up there about teatime. Then you two girls can have baths and tart up at your leisure.'

'How super,' said Gussie. 'But I haven't got anything to wear. Will it be very smart?'

'I don't expect so. Anyway they can lend you something if it is.'

I turned away. My palms were damp with sweat. The thought of a party terrified me. Drinks and noise and people I didn't know. They would be Gareth's friends too, probably as tough and flash and sarcastic as Gareth himself. He must have warned them about me already — the tart with the heart of ice.

'We'd better get moving,' said Jeremy. 'I'll start up the engine.'

'I'll wash up,' I said, diving into the kitchen.

No one had washed up last night's plates and, as we were running short of water, I had to wash everything in the same grey, greasy liquid.

'Hi,' said a voice. Gareth was standing in the doorway. I stiffened and concentrated hard on the bubbles of yellow fat floating on top of the washing-up water.

'Hullo,' I said with studied lightness. I was determined to show him that yesterday's showdown hadn't bothered me in the least.

He came and put his hand on my shoulder. I jumped away as though he'd burnt me.

'Easy now,' he said. 'I only wanted to apologize for last night. Not for what I said, because it needed saying, but I should have put it more tactfully.'

'If you think anything you said last night had any effect on me, you're very much mistaken,' I said in a stifled voice. 'Damn ! We're out of Quix.'

With a swift movement he took off my dark glasses.

301

'Don't! Don't you dare!' I spat at him. I didn't want him to see how red and puffed my eyes were with crying.

'All in good time,' he said. He had me cornered now. God, he was big. His very size in that kitchen was stifling, overpowering. I backed away against the draining board, looking down at my hands, trembling with humiliation.

'Why do you keep bullying me?' I whispered.

I'd done that trick before, letting my breasts rise and fall very fast in simulated emotion, but now I found I couldn't stop myself.

Gareth put his hand under my chin and forced it upwards. For an insane, panicky moment, I wondered whether to bite him, anything to drive him away, to destroy this suffocating nearness. Then he let go of me, and handed me back my dark glasses.

'You can actually look ugly,' he said, in surprise. 'I don't know why, but I find that very encouraging.'

'Gareth,' shouted Jeremy, 'can you come and open the lock gates?'

'Just coming' Gareth shouted. He turned as he went up the steps. 'Don't forget it's your turn to put on the chef's hat and cook us lunch.'

That was *all* I needed. I opened the door of the fridge and the baleful eye of a huge chicken peered out at me. How the hell did one cook the beastly thing?

Gussie popped her head through the door.

'Gareth says you're going to cook lunch. How lovely. I'll truss the chicken for you if you like, and then you can make that thing you made us the other night. There's masses of cream and lemon juice in the fridge.'

She'd only just had breakfast and her mouth was watering already.

'Thank you,' I said weakly. Why, oh why, had I been so foolish as to pass Luigi's *haute cuisine* off as my own last week?

I go hot and cold every time I remember that lunch. I got in such a muddle that we didn't eat until three o'clock, by which time the others were absolutely starving. I shall never forget their hungry flushed faces turning gradually to dismay as they sat down to eat and realized the chicken was burnt to a frazzle, the sauce was curdled past redemption and the spinach boiled away to a few gritty stalks. But the potatoes were the worst disaster. Because I hadn't realized you had to roast them longer than twenty minutes, they were hard as bullets.

'It's a pity we haven't got a twelve bore on board,' said Gareth. 'Then we could have spent the afternoon shooting pigeons with them.'

'It's absolutely delicious,' said Gussie, chewing valiantly away at a piece of impossibly dry chicken.

Jeremy said nothing. Gareth laughed himself sick. He didn't even make any attempt to eat, just lit a cigar, blew smoke over everyone, and said at last he understood why Gussie was always going on about the importance of having a good breakfast.

I escaped on deck and sat there gazing at the pink rose petals drifting across the khaki water. The panic and terror of the morning were fast hardening into hatred against Gareth. Once and for all I was going to get even with him.

Jeremy came and sat down beside me.

'What's the matter?' he asked gently.

'Nothing,' I said. 'I get these blinding migraines some-times, they make me completely stupid. I'm sorry I loused up lunch.'

'Hell, that doesn't matter. We should never have let you do all the cooking. Why didn't you tell us you were feeling awful?'

I smiled up at him. 'It'll go soon. Do we have to go to this party tonight?'

'Of course not, if you don't want to. I rather fancy going, just for the sake of going into a room with you, and every-one thinking you belong to me.'

'You win,' I said.

He took my hand. 'Do you still dislike Gareth that much?

'Is it that obvious?'

He nodded. 'A bit.'

He caught at a leaf of an overhanging tree. 'Gus gets some funny ideas. She thinks you're very mixed up beneath the panache and the sophistication. She says you need someone like Gareth to sort you out.'

'How kind of Gussie to be so concerned with my welfare,' I said, trying to keep the tremble of anger out of my voice.

There was a burst of laughter from the other end of the boat. Such was my paranoia, I was convinced Gussie and Gareth were talking about me.

'Would you make me any different?' I asked, looking deep into Jeremy's eyes.

'I'd just like to make you,' he said. 'Let's not bother about irrelevancies.'

It's the same old story, I thought, as I did my face before we went ashore. Now he's really pursuing me, I don't want him so much. The intensity and lust in his eyes had me frightened. I had a feeling I might have got a tiger by the tail.

My thoughts turned to Gussie and Gareth.

'Insecure, unhappy, mixed-up, frigid, hard enough to cut a diamond on.' They were having a field-day passing judgements on me. How dare that fat slob Gussie patronize me, how dare Gareth take it upon himself to tell me so many home truths? The chips were down. If they thought I was a bitch, all right, I was going to behave like one.

CHAPTER ELEVEN

Later in the afternoon as we went across water meadows into a large orchard, we could see a Queen Anne house through the trees.

'What are these people called?' asked Gussie.

'Hamilton,' said Gareth. 'Hesketh and Bridget. They've got hordes of children, but I don't know if any of them are at home.'

Gussie picked a scarlet cherry up from the long grass. 'And they're nice?'

'Nice, but perfectly crazy,' said Gareth. 'Hesketh has madness on one side of the family and a Rumanian grandmother on the other, so you never know what to expect.'

'I bet they're hell,' I whispered to Jeremy.

But they weren't hell. They were a gently unworldly middle-aged couple. Hesketh Hamilton was tall and thin with spectacles on the end of his nose. He had been gardening and was wearing faded blue dungarees and a kind of mauve and white striped baseball cap on his head to keep off the sun. His wife had straggly pepper and salt hair, drawn back into a bun, and eyes the colour of faded denim. She was wearing odd shoes and an old felt skirt covered in dog hairs. They were both obviously delighted to see Gareth.

The house was beautiful but terribly untidy, with books and papers everywhere. It didn't look as though anyone could possibly be giving a party that night. The afternoon sun slanting through the drawing-room window showed thick layers of dust on everything. Assorted dogs lay on the carpet panting from the heat.

'We'll have tea in the garden,' said Bridget Hamilton. 'You can come into the kitchen and help me carry the tray,

305

Gareth. I want you to tell me if Hesketh's got enough drink for this evening. We seem to have asked rather a lot of people.'

Out in the garden the lawn sloped down to a magnificent herbaceous border. Through an iron archway swarming with red roses, deckchairs and a table were set out under a walnut tree.

Gussie as usual went berserk, gushing like an oil well.

'What a fantastic garden! My mother would be green with envy! Look at those roses and those fabulous blue hollyhocks!'

'They're delphiniums,' said Hesketh Hamilton gently.

'Oh yes,' said Gussie unabashed. 'And that heavenly catmint. I love the smell.'

'It always reminds me of oversexed tomcats,' Hesketh said, smiling.

'It's so kind of you to let us all come to your party,' said Gussie, sitting down and putting a very severe strain on a deckchair.

She ought to be re-christened Gushie, I thought savagely.

Gareth came across the lawn carrying a tray, his eyes slanting away from the smoke of his cigar.

'You've got enough drink in, Hesketh, to float the QE2,' he said.

Bridget Hamilton, her hands still covered in earth from gardening, poured black tea into chipped mugs and handed sandwiches round.

'How many of the children are home?' asked Gareth.

'Only Lorna, and she doesn't know you're all coming. She's taken her new horse out. Absolute madness in this heat. She's not such a child now you know, Gareth. She'll be eighteen in August.'

Gareth grinned. 'I know. I hope you've been keeping her on ice for me.'

He helped himself to a cucumber sandwich as big as a doorstep.

'I'm starving.' He gave an unpleasant smile in my direction. 'I don't know why but I couldn't eat a thing at lunchtime.'

Bridget Hamilton turned to me. 'And what do you do in London? You look like a model or an actress or something.'

'She's quite unemployable,' said Gareth.

Bridget looked reproving. 'I see you're as rude as ever, Gareth.' She smiled at me. 'I never worked in my life until I got married. Anyway, I expect you meet lots of interesting people.'

'Yes I do,' I said.

She sighed. 'The one I'd like to meet is Britt Ekland — so charming looking. Wouldn't you like to meet Britt Ekland, Hesketh?'

'Who's he?' said Hesketh.

Inevitably there was a good deal of laughter at this and Bridget Hamilton was just explaining, 'He's a she, Hesketh, he's a she,' when a door slammed and there was a sound of running footsteps and a girl exploded through the French windows. She was as slim as a blade, in jodhpurs and a red silk shirt, with a mass of curly hair and a freckled, laughing face. Her eyes lighted on Gareth and she gave a squeal of delight.

'Gareth! What are you doing here? How lovely to see you!'

Gareth levered himself out of the deckchair and took both of her hands and stared at her for a long time.

'But you've grown so beautiful, Lorna.'

She flushed. 'Oh Golly, have I really turned into a swan at last?'

'A fully-fledged, paid-up member,' he said, bending forward and kissing her smooth brown cheek. There was not much more he could do with us all watching him, but I had the feeling he wanted to take her into his arms and kiss the life out of her.

'You might acknowledge someone else, darling,' grumbled her mother.

'Oh I'm sorry!' The girl beamed at the rest of us. 'I'm Lorna. It's just that I'm so pleased to see Gareth. You will stay for the party, won't you?' she added anxiously.

'I suppose we ought to think about washing a few glasses and rolling up the carpet,' said Hesketh Hamilton.

'I must wash my hair,' said Bridget. 'It's the only way I'll get the garden out of my nails.'

'Aren't they complete originals?' said Gussie, as she and I changed later. She was wandering around in the nude trying to look at her back. Between her fiery red legs and shoulders, her skin was as white as lard.

'I'm not peeling, am I?' she asked anxiously. 'It itches like mad.'

'Looks a bit angry,' I said, pleased to see that a few tiny white blisters had formed between her shoulders. It'd be coming off her in strips tomorrow.

'Isn't that girl Lorna quite devastating?' she went on. 'You could see Gareth wanted to absolutely gobble her up.'

'She's not that marvellous,' I said, starting to pour water over my hair.

'Oh but she is — quite lovely and so natural. Think of being seventeen again, all the things one was going to do, the books one was going to write, the places one was going to visit. I must say when a girl is beautiful at seventeen she gets a glow about her that old hags like you and I in our twenties can never hope to achieve.'

'Speak for yourself,' I muttered into the washbasin.

I knew when I finally finished doing my face that I'd never looked better. My eyes glittered brilliantly blue in my suntanned face; my hair, newly washed and straight, was almost white from the sun. Gussie, I'm glad to say, looked terrible. She was leaning out of the window when there was a crunch of wheels on the gravel outside.

'Oh look, someone's arriving. It's the vicar.'

'We're obviously in for a wild evening,' I said.

'We'd better go down. Shall I wait?'

'No. I'll be ready in a minute. You go on.'

I was glad when she'd gone. I thought she might kick up a fuss at the dress I was going to wear. It was a short tunic in silver chain mail — the holes as big as half-crowns. High-necked at the front, it swooped to positive indecency at the back. Two very inadequate circles of silver sequins covered my breasts. I didn't wear anything underneath except a pair of flesh-coloured pants, which gave the impression I wasn't wearing anything at all.

Slowly I put it on, thinking all the time of the effect it would have on Jeremy when I walked into the sedate country living room. I gave a final brush to my hair and turned to look in the mirror. It was the first time I'd worn it with all my party warpaint, and the impact made even me catch my breath. Oh my, said I to myself, you're going to set them by their country ears tonight. I was determined to make an entrance, so I fiddled with my hair until I could hear that more people had arrived.

There was a hush as I walked into the drawing-room. Everyone gazed at me. Men's hands fluttered up to straighten their ties and smooth their hair, the women stared at me with ill-concealed envy and disapproval.

'Christ!' I heard Jeremy say, in appalled wonder.

But I was looking at Gareth. For the first time I saw a blaze of disapproval in his eyes. I've got under his guard at last, I thought in triumph.

There seemed to be no common denominator among the guests. They consisted of old blimps and tabby cats, several dons from the University, and their ill-dressed wives, a handful of people of Lorna's age, the girls very debbie, the boys very wet, and a crowd of tough hunting types with braying voices and brick red faces. It was as though the Hamiltons had asked everyone they knew and liked, with a total disregard as to whether they'd mix.

I wandered towards Jeremy, Gussie and Gareth.

'I see you've thrown yourself open to the public,' said Gareth, but he didn't smile. 'I suppose I'd better go and hand round some drinks.'

'You shouldn't have worn that dress, Octavia,' said Gussie in a shocked voice. 'This isn't London, you know.'

'That's only too obvious,' I said, looking round.

Bridget Hamilton came over and took my arm. 'How enchanting you look, Octavia. Do come and devastate our local MFH. He's dying to meet you.'

He wasn't the only one. Once those hunting types had had a few drinks, they all closed in on me, vying for my at-

tention. Over and over again I let my glass be filled up.
Never had my wit been more malicious or more sparkling. I
kept them all in fits of braying laughter.

Like an experienced comedian, although I was keeping
my audience happy, I was very conscious of what was going
on in the wings — Jeremy, looking like a thundercloud because I was flirting so outrageously with other men, Gareth
behaving like the Hamilton's future son-in-law, whether he
was coping with drinks or smiling into Lorna's eyes. Every
so often, however, his eyes flickered in my direction, and his
face hardened.

About ten o'clock, Bridget Hamilton wandered in, very
red in the face, and carrying two saucepans, and plonked
them down on a long polished table beside a pile of plates
and forks.

'There's risotto here,' she said vaguely, 'if anyone's hungry.'

People surged forward to eat. I stayed put, the men
around me stayed put as well. The din we were making increased until Gareth pushed his way through the crowd.

'You ought to eat something, Octavia,' he said.

I shook my head and smiled up at him insolently.

'Aren't you hungry?' drawled the MFH who was lounging
beside me.

I turned to him, smiling sweetly, 'Only for you.'

A nearby group of women stopped filling their faces with
risotto and talking about nappies, and looked at me in horror. The MFH's wife was among them. She had a face like a
well-bred cod.

'The young gels of today are not the same as they were
twenty years ago,' she said loudly.

'Of course they're not,' I shouted across at her. 'Twenty
years ago I was only six. You must expect some change in
my appearance and behaviour.'

She turned puce with anger at the roar of laughter that
greeted this. Gareth didn't laugh. He took hold of my arm.

'I think you'd better come and eat,' he said in even tones.

'I've told you once,' I snapped, 'I don't want to eat. I want
to dance. Why doesn't someone put on the record player?'

The MFH looked down at the circles of silver sequins.

'What happens to those when you dance?'

I giggled. 'Now you see me, now you don't. They've been known to shift off centre.'

There was another roar of laughter.

'Well, what are we waiting for?' said the MFH. 'Let's put a record on and dance.'

'All right,' I said, looking up at him under my lashes, 'But I must go to the loo first.'

Upstairs in the bathroom, I hardly recognized myself. I looked like some Maenad, my hair tousled, my eyes glittering, my cheeks flushed. God, the dress was so beautiful.

'And you're so beautiful too,' I added and, leaning forward, lightly kissed my reflection in the mirror.

Even in my alcoholic state, I was slightly abashed when I turned round and saw Gareth standing watching me from the doorway.

'Don't you know it's rude to stare?' I said.

He didn't move.

'I'd like to come past — if you don't mind,' I went on.

'Oh no, you don't,' he said, grabbing my wrist.

'Oh yes I do,' I screamed, trying to tug myself away.

'Will you stop behaving like a whore!' he swore at me and, pulling me into the nearest bedroom, threw me on the bed and locked the door.

'Now I suppose you're going to treat me like a whore,' I spat at him. 'What will your precious Lorna say if she catches us here together?'

Suddenly I was frightened. There was murder in his eyes.

'It's about time someone taught you a lesson,' he said, coming towards me. 'And I'm afraid it's going to be me.'

Before I realized it, Gareth had me across his knee. I've never known what living daylights were before, but he was certainly beating them out of me now. I started to scream and kick.

'Shut up,' he said viciously. 'No one can hear you.' The record player was still booming downstairs. I struggled and tried to bite him but he was far too strong for me. It was not the pain so much as the ghastly indignity. It seemed to go on

311

for ever and ever. Finally he tipped me on to the floor. I lay there trembling with fear.

'Get up,' he said brusquely, 'and get your things together. I'm taking you back to the boat.'

The moon hung over the river, whitening the mist that floated transparent above the sleeping fields. Stars were crowding the blue-black sky, the air was heavy with the scent of meadowsweet.

Aching in every bone, biting my lip to stop myself crying, I let Gareth lead me across the fields. Every few moments I stumbled, held up only by his vice-like grip on my arm. I think he felt at any moment I might bolt back to the party.

Once we were on deck I said, 'Now you can go back to your darling teenager.'

'Not until you're safe in bed.'

I lay down on my bunk still in my dress. But when I shut my eyes the world was going round and round. I quickly opened them. Gareth stood watching me through cigar smoke.

I shut my eyes again. A great wave of nausea rolled over me.

'Oh God,' I said, trying to get out of bed.

'Stay where you are,' he snapped.

'I ought to be allowed to get out of my own bed,' I said petulantly. 'I agree in your Mary Whitehouse role you're quite entitled to stop me getting into other people's beds but a person should be free to get out of her own bed if she wants to.'

'Stop fooling around,' said Gareth.

'I can't,' I said in desperation, 'I'm going to be sick.'

He only just got me to the edge of the boat in time, and I was sicker than I've ever been in my life. I couldn't stop this terrible retching, and then, because Gareth was holding my head, I couldn't stop crying from humiliation.

'Leave me alone,' I sobbed in misery. 'Leave me alone to die. Gussie and Jeremy'll be back in a minute. Please go and keep them away for a bit longer.'

'They won't be back for hours,' said Gareth, looking at his

watch.

'Can I have a drink of water?'

'Not yet, it'll only make you throw up again. You'll just have to grin and bear it.'

I looked up at the huge white moon and gave a hollow laugh. 'It couldn't be a more romantic night, could it?'

In the passage my knees gave way and Gareth picked me up, carried me into the cabin and put me to bed as deftly as if I'd been a child. He gave me a couple of pills.

'They'll put you to sleep.'

'I wasn't actually planning to meet Jeremy on deck to-night.'

I was shivering like a puppy.

'I'm sorry,' I said, rolling my head back and forth on the pillow. 'I'm so terribly sorry.'

'Lie still,' he said. 'The pills'll work soon.'

'Don't go,' I whispered, as he stood up and went to the door.

His face was expressionless as he looked at me, no scorn, no mockery, not even a trace of pity.

'I'm going to get you some more blankets,' he said. 'I don't want you catching cold.'

That sudden kindness, the first he'd ever shown me, brought tears to my eyes. I was beginning to feel drowsy by the time he came back with two rugs. They smelt musty and, as I watched his hands tucking them in — powerful hands with black hairs on the back — I suddenly wanted to feel his arms around me and to feel those hands soothing me and petting me as though I were a child again. In a flash I saw him as the father, strict, yet loving and caring, that all my life I'd missed; someone to say stop when I went too far, someone to mind if I behaved badly, to be proud if I behaved well.

'Getting sleepy?' he asked.

I nodded.

'Good girl. You'll be all right in the morning.'

'I'm sorry I wrecked your party.'

'Doesn't matter. They're nice though, the Hamiltons. You should mix with more people like them; they've got the right values.'

'How did you meet them?'

He began to tell me, but I started getting confused and the soft Welsh voice became mingled with the water lapping against the boat; then I drifted into unconsciousness.

CHAPTER TWELVE

When I woke next morning I felt overwhelmed with shame. In the past when I'd got drunk, I'd just shrugged it off as part of the Octavia Brennen image. Now I curled up at the thought of last night's performance — barging in on those people half naked, behaving atrociously, abusing their hospitality, and then the humiliation of Gareth putting me across his knee and, worst of all, throwing up in front of him and having to be put to bed.

Oh God, I groaned in misery, as I slowly pieced the evening together, I can't face him. Yet, at the thought of slipping off the boat unnoticed, it suddenly hit me that if I did I might never see him again. It was like a skewer jabbed into my heart.

Oh no, I whispered in horror, it can't have happened! I couldn't hate someone so passionately, and then find overnight that hatred had turned into something quite different — something that looked suspiciously like love.

I couldn't love him, I couldn't. He despised me and thought I was the biggest bitch going, and the nightmare was that, if we had been starting from scratch, I could have pulled out the stops, knocked him over with my looks, even fooled him into thinking I was gentle and sweet. I'd done it often enough before. But now it was too late. He'd seen me, unashamedly pursuing Jeremy, knew so many adverse things about me that I hadn't a hope where he was concerned. It was funny really, the biter bit at last.

Finally I dragged myself out of bed. A shooting star was erupting in my head, waves of sickness swept over me. My face was ashen when I looked in the mirror. I was still wearing last night's make-up, streaked with crying; my mouth

315

felt like a parrot's cage.

I staggered down to the horrible dank loo which reeked of asparagus pee and wondered whether to be sick again. Even cleaning my teeth was an ordeal. Somehow I got dressed, and crawled along to the kitchen. Gussie was cooking kippers of all things.

'Hullo,' she said. 'You disappeared very suddenly last night. Gareth said you felt faint from the heat, so he brought you home. You're not pregnant or anything awful?'

I smiled weakly and shook my head. That was one problem I was spared.

'What did the rest of you get up to?' I asked.

'Nothing much. We stayed up very late dancing on the lawn, it was so romantic in the moonlight. Then Lorna came back and had a drink on the boat. You were fast asleep by that time. Later Gareth took her home. We didn't hear him come in.'

I felt sweat rising on my forehead. The thought of Gareth and Lorna wandering back through the meadowsweet with that great moon pouring light on them drove me insane with jealousy. The smell of those kippers was killing me. Suddenly I saw a pair of long legs coming down the steps.

'I'm going on deck,' I said in a panic, and bolted back through my cabin and the saloon, out into the sunshine at the far end of the boat.

I sat down, clutching my knees and gazing at the opposite bank. A water rat came out, stared at me with beady eyes and then shot back into its hole. Lucky thing, I thought. I wish I had a hole to crawl into. The wild roses which had bloomed so beautifully yesterday were now withered by the sun and hung like tawdry party decorations that had been up too long.

I heard a step behind me and my heart started hammering. I was appalled by the savagery of my disappointment when I realized it was only Jeremy.

'Hullo,' he said sulkily, sitting down beside me. 'Are you feeling better?'

'Yes thank you.'

'Gareth gets all the luck. Why don't you feel faint when

I'm around? I wouldn't have minded bringing you back here on your own and putting you to bed.'

Something in his voice pulled me up sharply. 'I felt faint,' I snapped.

'And I'm sure Gareth made you feel better. His restorative powers are notorious, you know.'

'It wasn't like that,' I said angrily. 'If two people absolutely don't fancy each other, it's Gareth and me.'

'So you keep telling me,' he said. 'I'm wondering if the lady isn't protesting a bit too much.'

'Breakfast's ready,' said Gareth, appearing suddenly in the doorway.

'I don't want any,' I said, blushing scarlet and wondering how much of our conversation he'd heard.

Jeremy got to his feet.

'I'll come back and talk to you when I've had mine,' he said, following Gareth down the steps.

Two minutes later Gareth reappeared.

'Here's your breakfast,' he said, dropping four Alka Seltzers into a glass of water. He waited until the white discs had completely dissolved, then handed me the glass.

'Thank you,' I muttered, quite unable to meet his eyes. 'I'm sorry about last night.'

'Skip it,' he said. 'Everyone makes a bloody fool of themselves from time to time.'

'But you stopped everyone else finding out. I thought . . .'

'. . . I'd go back and tell everyone you'd puked your guts out. I'm not that much of a sod.'

I looked at him for the first time. He looked very tired; there were dark rings under his eyes. I wondered what he and Lorna had been up to last night. It was as though he'd read my thought.

'Lorna's coming over for lunch,' he said. 'She's dying to meet you again. She's still at the age when she's immensely impressed by beautiful women.'

Wow, that was a backhander.

'I'll attempt not to disappoint her,' I said, trying to keep the resentment out of my voice.

He laughed. 'Don't pout, it doesn't suit you.'

317

JILLY COOPER

The Alka Seltzers eased my headache to a dull throb. I wished it could have as easily cured my heart.

Lorna arrived about twelve-thirty. She'd taken a great deal of trouble with her appearance and was wearing a rust coloured T-shirt which matched her hair. She looked very pretty, but somehow I thought she'd looked more attractive when she'd roared in on us unawares the day before.

'Hullo,' she said, sitting down on the deck beside me, 'I'm sorry we didn't have time to talk yesterday and that you felt horrible. Mummy always forgets to open any windows. Everyone was so disappointed you went. All the men were wild about you, and everyone who rang up to thank us this morning wanted to know who you were.' Her voice was suddenly wistful. 'The country hasn't seen anything as gorgeous as you in a hundred years.'

Suddenly I found myself liking her. I realized there was no bitchy motive behind her remarks, just genuine admiration.

'I'm afraid my dress was a bit *outré* for the country,' I said. 'I hope your parents didn't mind?'

She shook her head violently. 'Oh no, they thought you were wonderful. It's typical of Gareth to turn up with someone like you. I always knew he would in the end. I've had a crush on him for years, you see. I'd always hoped he'd wait for me, but now he's got you.'

'Oh no he hasn't,' I said quickly. 'There's nothing between us at all. We'd never met before this weekend. I'm Gussie's friend. We were at school together.'

'You were?' Her face brightened. 'Then you and Gareth aren't . . .?'

'Not at all. He just discovered I was feeling bloody and brought me home.'

'Oh,' she said happily. 'That does cheer me up. I do wish I could do something romantic like fainting when he's around, but I'm far too healthy.'

I laughed wryly. She wouldn't have enjoyed what I'd endured last night.

'Mind you,' she went on confidingly, 'he did kiss me on the way home last night. But then I expect he kisses most girls.'

318

The sun was making me feel sick again. I moved into the shade. She asked me endless questions about my life in London and the people I knew.

'Do you actually know Mick Jagger?' She couldn't hear enough about it.

'I'm coming to London soon. I've just finished a typing course, and I've got to look for a job.'

'Come and stay,' I was amazed to find myself saying. 'My flat's huge. You can have a bed for as long as you like.'

'Goodness,' she went all pink. 'May I really? It'd be marvellous, just for a few days until I find somewhere. And I wonder, could you tell me the best place to buy clothes? I mean my mother's super, but she's never been much help in that way.'

A moment later, when we were joined by the others, she immediately told Gareth I'd asked her to come and stay. I expected him to discourage her, but he merely said, 'Good idea, why not?'

Why had I done it, I wondered, as I escaped to help with lunch. Was I trying to prove that I could be nice occasionally, or was I unconsciously trying to impress Gareth by getting on with one of his friends, or was it merely that I wanted to keep some link with him, however tenuous, after tonight?

I had a great deal of difficulty forcing anything down at lunch. I couldn't even smoke, which is a sign of approaching death with me. I was paralysed with shyness by Gareth's presence. Every time he looked at me I jerked my eyes away. Why couldn't I bring any of the old magic into play? Glancing sideways from under my lashes, letting my hair fall over my eyes, pulling up my skirt to show more leg, leaning forward so he could see down my shirt, which would always be buttoned a couple of inches too low. Overnight I'd suddenly become as gauche as a teenager. I didn't even know what to do with my mouth — like the first time one wears lipstick.

To make matters worse, Jeremy was watching me like a warder. He no longer held any charm for me; he was so anxious to please, he'd lost all the lazy, take-it-or-leave-it manner that I'd found so irresistible a week ago. Immediately we'd finished eating, I leapt up to do the washing up. Any-

JILLY COOPER

thing to get away from that highly charged atmosphere.

'Leave it,' said Jeremy. 'For goodness sake, Octavia, relax.'

'What a bore we're going back to London tonight,' grumbled Gussie. 'It's been such a lovely restful weekend.'

A smile flickered across Gareth's face.

'You must have so much planning to do for the wedding,' Lorna said. 'I love weddings.'

Jeremy's leg suddenly pressed against mine. I moved it away.

'Your hair's gone a fantastic colour in the sun,' he said.

'Is it natural, I can't remember?' said Gussie.

I was about to say 'yes' — I'd never admitted to anyone before that it was dyed — when I caught Gareth's eye and, for some strange reason, changed my mind.

'Well, let's say my hairdresser helps it along a bit.'

Gussie picked up a daisy chain she'd been making. The threaded flowers were already wilting on the table. Lorna looked out of the port-hole at the heat-soaked landscape. Any moment one felt the dark trees might move towards us.

'It's like one of those days people remember as the end of something,' she said, 'The last before the war, the day the king died.'

Gussie split another daisy stalk open. 'Don't frighten me, you make me think something frightful will happen tonight.'

A mulberry-coloured cloud had hidden the sun.

'I think it's going to thunder,' said Jeremy.

Gussie put the daisy chain over his head. It was too small and rested like a corona on his blond hair. He pushed it away irritably.

'Oh, you've broken it,' wailed Gussie.

I couldn't stand the tension any longer. I got to my feet and stretched.

'Where are you off to?' said Gussie.

'I'm going to wander up-stream.'

'We'll come with you,' said Jeremy standing up.

'No!' I said sharply, then tried to make a joke of it. 'I like walking by myself. I feel my Greta Garbo mood coming on.'

'We're going to Lorna's parents for tea,' said Gussie.

320

I didn't join them. As I wandered through the meadows I tried to sort out what I really felt. It's the heat and the proximity I kept telling myself. You've fallen for Gareth because he's the first man to pull you up. It's a challenge because he doesn't fancy you — just as Jeremy was a challenge until you'd hooked him. But it was no good. Wanting Jeremy had been but a child's caprice for a forbidden toy, nothing compared with the desperate need I felt for Gareth.

I wandered for miles and then sat down under a tree. I must have dozed off, for the shadows were lengthening when I woke up. I couldn't face tea with the Hamiltons, tea-cups balanced on our knees, having post mortems about the party; so I went back to the boat. No one was about. I packed my suitcases, tidied the saloon and washed up lunch. I was behaving so well, I'd be qualifying for my girl guide badge at this rate.

Then I heard footsteps, and someone jumping on to the deck. I gave a shiver of excitement as a tall figure appeared in the doorway. But it was only Jeremy. Once more I felt that crippling kick of disappointment.

'Why didn't you turn up for tea? I've been worried about you.'

There was a predatory look in his eyes that suddenly had me scared and on my guard.

'I fell asleep and when I woke up I realized it was late, so I came back here.'

'And by telepathy I knew and followed you,' he said.

'Are the others coming?'

'Not for ages. Gussie's discovered a grand piano, so she's happy strumming away. Gareth and Lorna have gone off for a walk together.'

My nails were cutting into the palms of my hands. Last night Gareth had kissed her. God knows what else he might get up to on a hot summer afternoon. I picked up some glasses.

'Where are you going?' asked Jeremy.

'Putting these away.'

For a second he barred my way, then stood aside and followed me through into the saloon. Very slowly I stacked the glasses in the cupboard. When I turned round he was standing just behind me. He put his hands on my arms.

'No,' I said sharply.

'No what? I haven't done anything yet.'

'Then let me go.'

'The hell I will!'

His fingers tightened on my arms.

'I want you,' he said. 'Ever since I first saw you, I've been burning up with wanting you.'

'What about Gussie?' I asked feebly. 'We were going to wait till we got back to London.'

'Oh come *on* now. You, of *all* people, don't give a damn about Gussie, and at this moment in time, neither do I.'

He bent his head and kissed me, forcing my mouth open with his tongue.

'No !' I struggled, completely revolted. 'No ! No ! No !'

'Shut up,' he said. 'Don't play the little hypocrite with me. We all know your reputation, darling. You wanted me, don't pretend you didn't, and now you're going to get me, hot and strong.'

Desperately, I tried to pull away from him.

'Let me go !' I screamed.

But he only laughed and forced me back on to one of the bench seats, shutting my protesting mouth with his, tearing at the buttons of my shirt.

Suddenly a door opened. 'Knock it off you two,' said a voice of ice.

Jeremy sprang away from me. 'What the fuck . . .'

'For God's sake pull yourself together. Gussie's just coming,' said Gareth.

But it was too late, Gussie came bouncing into the saloon.

'Darling love, I missed you. Hullo Tavy, did you get lost?'

Then, with agonizing slowness, she took in the situation, looking at my rumpled hair and torn shirt, the buttons of which I was frenziedly trying to do up, the smeared lipstick on Jeremy's face, the chair knocked over, the papers strewn all over the floor.

There was a ghastly pause.

322

'Octavia,' she whispered in horror. 'You of all people, how could you? You swore you weren't interested in Jeremy. I thought you were a friend of mine. And as for you!' She turned to Jeremy, 'Don't you think I want to marry you after this.'

She tugged at her engagement ring but it wouldn't come off. Finally she gave a little sob and fled out of the cabin.

'Go after her!' said Gareth. 'Say you're sorry, that it didn't mean anything — at once,' he rapped out at Jeremy.

I collapsed into a chair, my heart pounding, my face in my hands. 'Oh my God, how terrible!'

'And you can belt up,' Gareth snarled at me. 'You've done enough damage for one afternoon.'

'I tried to stop him, really I did.'

'Don't give me that. There's no need to explain yourself. You were just running true to form.' And he walked out of the saloon, slamming the door behind him.

The awful thing was that we still had to pack up the boat and Lorna had to drive us to the original mooring twenty miles away, where Jeremy and Gareth had parked their cars. Gussie insisted on sitting in the back with Gareth and sobbing all the way. Jeremy and I, loathing each other's guts, had to sit in front with Lorna.

When we finally got to where the cars were parked, Gussie refused to drive back to London with Jeremy. Gareth didn't even say goodbye.

God, how ironic, I thought miserably, it's worked out exactly as I planned it should. Gussie and Jeremy breaking up and Jeremy driving me back to London. But instead of being in each other's arms, we were at each other's throats. Jeremy looked grey beneath his suntan, all the bravado and panache seemed to be knocked out of him. The trees by the roadside fell away and rushed back in clumps.

'You've got to talk to Gussie,' said Jeremy. 'Tell her it was all your fault. All right, I admit I tried to pull you this afternoon, but my God, I had provocation.'

'I know you did,' I said listlessly. 'I'm sorry. I thought I wanted you so much; then when it came to the crunch, I found I didn't after all.'

'Yeah well, it's the same with me. I was crazy about you, but now I realize I'm in danger of losing Gus, it all seems a terrible mistake. It's the ill-wind department, I suppose. Takes a jolt like this to make you realize how much you really need someone. She's so straight, Gus.'

I'd seldom seen a man more shattered.

'Tell her it was your doing,' he pleaded. 'Tell her how much you led me on. It's no skin off your nose.'

'All right,' I said, 'I'll talk to her. But it's no good trying to see her until tomorrow.'

CHAPTER THIRTEEN

On the day after we got back to London, I tried to ring Gussie several times at the office. Finally they admitted she hadn't come in, so I went round to her flat. It was a typical girl's flat — unwashed cups and overflowing ashtrays everywhere and three half-unpacked suitcases in the drawing-room. I removed a grubby white bra and a brown apple core from one of the armchairs and sat down.

'What do you want?' asked Gussie. She was still in her dressing gown and her face was swollen with crying.

'To explain about Jeremy,' I said.

'I don't want any of your lies,' she said.

'But you've got to listen. It was all my fault, you see, from the beginning. I took one look at Jeremy that first night at Arabella's and he was so beautiful I decided I must get him away from you at all costs. I never wanted anyone so much in all my life so I pulled out all the stops — making eyes at him, admitting to his face that I fancied him, wandering round with only a towel falling off me, arranging to meet him on deck after you'd gone to sleep. He didn't stand a chance.'

She looked at me in horror. 'You actually went out of your way to get him?'

I nodded. 'I made an absolutely dead set that evening at the Hamilton's party,' I went on, lying now. 'When I got drunk and behaved so badly, it was only because I was furious with Jeremy, because he wasn't reacting at all.'

'But what happened yesterday?'

'I was sulking by myself on the boat, when Jeremy turned up, worried I'd been gone for such a long time, and well, I sort of tried to seduce him.'

325

'And that's when Gareth and I came in?'

'That's right.' I got up and wandered over to the window. 'Any man would have been flattered by being pursued so relentlessly. It was just the heat and being cooped up on the boat together. Hell, he only kissed me, anyway. He loves you, he does really. He was absolutely demented on the way home last night.'

Gussie pulled at a wispy bit of hair.

'He was?' she said dully.

'Anyway,' I went on, 'you said the other day on the boat, that you expected him to be unfaithful to you and you'd always forgive him.'

'I know I did,' said Gussie with a sob, 'but one says such stupid things in theory, and they're so horrible when they happen in practice.'

I went over and put my arm round her. 'Please don't cry, Gussie.'

'Don't touch me,' she hissed. 'I was thinking about you all last night. You're wicked, you've always been wicked. Ever since we were at school together, you've resented my friends and tried to take them away from me. And now you've stolen the most precious thing I ever had. Why do you do it? You're so beautiful you can have any man you choose.'

'Because I've always been jealous of you,' I said slowly, echoing Gareth's words. 'Because, in spite of my yellow hair and my long legs, people have always liked you more than they liked me.'

There was a pause.

'I suppose it was kind of you to come and tell me all this,' she said in a set little voice. 'It does make a difference. I had a long talk to Gareth last night.'

'What did he say?' I tried to keep my voice expressionless.

'That Jeremy was basically a lightweight, that I'd do better to cut my losses and pack him in. He said you may have encouraged Jeremy in the beginning, but on reflection he guessed that he was only too ready to be distracted and that it was Jeremy who forced the pace yesterday. He said marriage to Jeremy would be one long string of infidelities, and he was only marrying me for security and for my money.'

OCTAVIA

'But that's brutal!' I gasped.

'Isn't it? But that's the thing I like about Gareth, he tells the truth about things that matter.'

'Did he say anything else?' I said numbly. 'About me, I mean.'

'Not much. He agreed with me that if you really set your cap at someone, it would be almost impossible to resist you.'

I bit my lip. 'I'm sorry.'

'It's not so easy for me,' Gussie said, playing with the tassel of her dressing gown. 'I don't get boyfriends very easily. Jeremy was the first man who ever said he loved me. I can't go to a party tomorrow like you can, and pick up a new man just like that. I can't walk down the street and be caressed and comforted by the admiration in men's eyes. You haven't a clue what it's like not having any sex appeal. With you it's only a question of time. I may never meet another man who wants to marry me.'

I felt a flash of irritation. Why the hell didn't she go on a diet? Then I felt guilty.

'Will you ever be able to forgive me?'

'I don't know, not now. Perhaps in a few weeks I shall feel differently.'

I went towards the door.

'Will you see Jeremy if he turns up here?'

She burst into tears. 'Oh yes, of course I will.'

It was only when I left her that the full desolation of my situation hit me. Since we'd left the boat I had been numb with misery, as though I'd put my heart in deep freeze until I had straightened the account with Gussie and Jeremy. Now I had to face up to the future — to the agony of loving a man who hated and despised me — who would despise me even more once he heard what I had told Gussie.

For the next few days I was on the rack. I never believed it was possible to suffer so much. Pride, despair and longing chased each other monotonously around my head. I cried all night and, at the slightest provocation, during the day. Over and over again I wandered down to the river and wondered whether to jump in. A thousand times I started letters to Gareth, pleading my case, but each time I tore them up.

327

My case was so hopeless, I couldn't even take refuge in day-dreams.

Most evenings I borrowed my landlord's car, drove it across London and lay in wait outside Gareth's house, but there were never any lights on and I used to turn the engine off and cry uncontrollably.

CHAPTER FOURTEEN

The blistering hot weather continued to grip London by the throat. Outside my flat Green Park was fast losing its greenness, the plane trees were coated in thick grey dust, the grass bleached to a lifeless yellow. Commuters wilted silently at the bus stops.

Two Mondays after we got back from the boat, I was woken by the doorbell ringing on and on. Wrapping a towel round me, I waded through the post, which was scattered over the carpet and consisted entirely of brown envelopes. I peered through the spy-hole, in a blind hope it might be Gareth. But it was only a thin youth with a moustache, and ears like the F.A. cup, wearing a crumpled suit and a battery of fountain pens in his breast pocket. He obviously had no intention of getting off that bell. I opened the door. He looked at me wearily.

'Miss Brennen?'

'No,' I said. I knew the tricks of old.

'But Miss Brennen lives here?'

'Sure she does, but she's abroad at the moment. Can I help you?'

'It's about her income tax returns. We've written to her repeatedly. The matter is getting rather urgent.'

'Oh dear,' I said sympathetically. 'I'm sure she's not avoiding you deliberately. She's just rather vague where income tax is concerned.'

'Lots of people become very vague when it's a matter of paying it,' he said, his weary eyes travelling over my body, 'When are you expecting her back?'

'She's gone to the Bahamas,' I said. 'After that I think she's flying on to New York. She's got a lot of friends there. She didn't say when she was coming back.'

'We're interested in a sum of money she earned doing a commercial for Herbert Revson.'

Thank God he was looking at my legs, or he would have seen how green I'd gone.

'But that was three years ago,' I stammered, 'and in America.'

'Yes, but she was paid by their English subsidiary, who, of course, declared it.'

'Poor Octavia,' I said faintly. 'Have you any idea how much she owes?'

'Well,' he said, confidingly. 'We don't usually disclose figures' (he was obviously crazy for me to disclose mine) 'but I think it wouldn't be much under five figures. She didn't by any chance leave a forwarding address, did she?'

'No she didn't. There's the telephone. I must go and answer it,' I said firmly, shutting the door in his face.

Ten thousand pounds ! Where the hell was I going to get that kind of money? Bleating with terror, I ran to answer the telephone, crossing my fingers once again that by some miracle it might be Gareth. But it was Xander. I'd only talked to him briefly since I got back. He'd been busy, so I hadn't told him about Gareth. I was sure I wanted to, I couldn't bear for him not to take it seriously.

'Oh how lovely to hear you,' I said.

'You probably won't think so when you hear the news,' he said. 'Hugh Massingham's dead.'

'What!' I sat down on the bed.

'Heart attack at the weekend. He'd been playing tennis,' said Xander.

'Oh God, how awful.' Kind, handsome, indolent, sensual, easy-going Massingham — Xander's patron and boss, my friend. He's always been so generous to both of us — and taken care of all my bills. It didn't seem possible.

'I can't bear it,' I whispered, the tears beginning to roll down my cheeks.

'Terrible, isn't it. I really loved that guy. But darling, I'm afraid that isn't all. There's trouble at mill. Ricky's been going through the books with a toothcomb and smelling salts, and the skeletons have been absolutely trooping out of the cupboard. This year's figures are catastrophic, shares have hit rock bottom, orders are right down; unfortunately expenses, particularly yours, and mine, are right up.'

He sounded in a real panic.

'Ricky's called an emergency department head meeting for tomorrow at three o'clock. He wants you there as well.'

'Whatever for?'

'Well, there's a bit of aggro over your flat, and all the bills we've run up between us, and there's the car too. I think we'd better have a session tonight, and see how many bills we can rustle up,' he went on, trying to sound reassuring.

'All right,' I said. 'Come round after work.'

It seemed hardly the time to tell him about my income tax bill.

'Actually,' Xander went on, 'it's a good thing poor Hugh did kick the bucket when he did, Ricky'd already made plans to replace him.'

'Did Hugh know?'

'Don't think so, but it's certainly made Ricky's task easier. He's bringing in this new whizz kid over everyone's heads to get us out of the wood.'

'Do you think he'll be able to?'

'You should know, darling. It's your friend, Gareth Llewellyn.'

I lay back on my bed, holding my burning face in my hands — all thoughts of Massingham, ten grand tax bills and fiddled expenses forgotten. Why, why, why had Gareth done it? He'd got far too much on his plate as it was. Why should he take on another directorship? Was it for power, or financial gain, or just to get his fingers into another industrial pie? Could it just possibly be that he wanted to see me again? Or, much more likely, that he'd got it in for me and wanted to cut me to ribbons. Whatever the reason, in just over twenty-four hours I'd see him again.

In the evening Xander and I spent two fruitless hours trying to sort out our expenses — then gave up. I set my alarm clock for eleven the next day, to give me plenty of time to get ready. Even so I panicked round trying on one dress after another. It's strange how one's wardrobe tells the story of one's past. There was the cornflower blue midi I'd bought to ensnare Jeremy, the backless black that had inflamed Ricardo, the gold pyjama suit that had brought Charlie literally to his knees with a proposal, and lying on the cupboard floor, spurned, and never worn again, was the grey dress that had failed to detach that French racing driver from his wife at a ball in Paris last winter.

What could I possibly wear to win over Gareth? He'd said he liked his women gentle, unspoilt and vulnerable. I put on a white dress, bought for Ascot last year, but never worn. It was very garden party, with a full skirt, long sleeves and a ruffled low-cut neckline which showed off my suntan and I hoped made me look innocent and fragile. I had to make a hole in the material to do the belt up tight enough. My eyelids, after a fortnight's crying, were the only part of me that hadn't lost weight. I hid them behind tinted spectacles.

I arrived at Seaford-Brennen's head office to find everyone in a jittering state of expectancy. Yesterday's shock over Massingham's death had given way to excitement over Gareth's arrival. The secretaries had seen his picture on the financial pages. They knew he was rich, successful, attractive and, most important of all, single. They had all washed their hair and tarted themselves up to the nines. The offices, as I walked through, smelt like Harrods' scent department; not a paper was out of place. I encountered some hostile stares. Why did I have to come swanning in to steal their thunder?

The Seaford-Brennen boardroom, with its dove grey carpet, panelled walls and family portraits, was discretion itself. Xander was the only person in there, sitting halfway down the huge polished table, directly beneath the portrait of my father. Their two bored, handsome restless faces were so much alike. Xander was chewing gum, and drawing a rugger player on his pad.

'Hullo angel,' he said in a slurred voice as I slipped into the seat beside him. 'The condemned board is still out eating a hearty lunch. This place is in an incredible state of twitch, even the messenger boys are on tranquillizers.

Ricky's already been on to me this morning breathing fire about expenses. You must keep bills. I said I'm already keeping a Pamela, what would I want with a Bill.'

Oh God, I thought, he's smashed out of his mind; he must be chewing gum to conceal the whisky fumes.

'What happened after you left me?' I said.

'I went out and dined, not wisely, but too well, with a friend, and things escalated from there.'

'Did you get to bed?'

'Well not to my own bed, certainly.' He tried to rest an elbow on the table, but it slid off.

The door opened and Miss Billings, the senior secretary, came in, fussing around, moving memo pads, straightening pencils. A great waft of Devon violets nearly asphyxiated us.

'You ought to put a bit more Pledge at the top of the table,' said Xander reprovingly, 'and I'm rather surprised you haven't laid on a red carpet and a band playing "Land of my Fathers". Mr. Llewellyn is used to the best of everything you know.'

Miss Billings clicked her tongue disapprovingly and bustled out, beads flying. Next moment she was back, with Tommy Lloyd, the sales director.

'Do you think we ought to put flowers in the middle of the table?' she asked.

'A bunch of leeks would be more appropriate,' said Xander.

Tommy Lloyd gave him a thin smile. He tolerated Xander but didn't like him. An old Wellingtonian with a bristling grey moustache, ramrod straight back, and clipped military voice, he had been in next succession after Massingham. His red-veined nose must be truly out of joint at Gareth's arrival. He was followed by Peter Hocking, who was in charge of production and just about as inspiring as a flat bottle of tonic, and old Harry Somerville his false teeth rattling with nerves, who'd been with the firm since he was sixteen, and was still treated by everyone as though he was a messenger boy.

Gradually the rest of the chairs were taken up by departmental heads, flushed by lunch, who greeted me with a good deal less enthusiasm than usual, a far cry from the fawning sycophancy when my father was alive.

There was desultory talk of our chances of winning the Test match. Peter Hocking was boring Harry Somerville with a recipe for home-made wine. But on the whole everyone was strangely quiet, and kept glancing at their watches or the door.

'When all else fails, go to Wales,' said Xander. 'I feel exactly as though I'm about to go over Niagara Falls in a barrel. Have you got a cigarette? I seem to have run out.'

I gave him one and, having opened my bag, took the opportunity to powder my nose and put on some more scent. My hand was shaking so much, I put on far too much. The smell of Miss Dior wafting through the room, clashed vilely with the Devon violets.

'Never mind,' said Xander. 'At least it will cover up the smell of congealed blood and rotting corpses.'

He seemed strangely elated. He'd always liked novelty. There were little red patches along his cheekbones.

The waiting got worse. Everyone's shirt collars were getting too tight. Miss Billings sat on the right of the top of the table, flicking the elastic band which held back the pages on which she had already taken shorthand that day. We all jumped when the telephone rang.

Tommy Lloyd answered.

'Downstairs are they? Good. Well no doubt Ricky'll bring them up. Miss Billings, will you go and meet them at the lift.'

'The enemy are at the gates,' said Xander, still drawing rugger players on his memo pad. 'The Barbarian Hoards are coming. I suppose we'd better lie back and enjoy it.'

There was a spurt of nervous laughter round the room, which died quickly away as the door opened. They came in like the magnificent four, Ricky smirking as though he was carrying a very large bone, followed by Gareth, and a huge, massive shouldered wrestler of a man in a white suit. Bringing up the rear was Annabel Smith. She was wearing a very simple black suit, and her conker-coloured hair was drawn back in a chignon. The dead silence that followed was a tribute to her beauty. Suddenly I felt silly in my white dress, like

334

a deb who'd been left out in the rain.

I was so wraked with longing and shyness, it was a second before I could bring myself to look at Gareth. He was wearing a light grey suit, dark blue shirt and tie. I'd never seen him so formally dressed. His heavy face had lost most of its suntan, and looked shadowed and tired. He didn't glance in my direction.

Everyone sat down except Ricky, who stood for a minute looking silently round the table, as if counting the house.

'Shall I bring in coffee now?' said Miss Billings fussily.

'I don't think we need it, thank you,' he said. 'And you needn't bother to stay either, Miss Billings. Mrs. Smith is going to take the minutes.'

Displaying the same sort of enraged reluctance as a cat shoved out in a rainstorm, Miss Billings was despatched from the room. Any minute I expected her to appear at the window, mewing furiously.

Ricky cleared his throat.

'Gentlemen, I just want to introduce Mr. Llewellyn whom I'm sure you all know by repute. He's brought with him his right hand man, Mr. Morgan,' — the massive wrestler nodded at us unsmilingly — 'and his very charming personal assistant, Mrs. Smith, who together have been responsible for so much of Mr. Llewellyn's success.'

Mrs. Smith gave everyone the benefit of her pussy-cat smile. Round the table a few faces brightened. Mrs. Smith's legs were a much better reason for staying awake in meetings than Miss Billings'.

'Although Mr. Llewellyn has come in at very short notice,' Ricky went on, 'as your new', he paused on the word, 'overall director, he has, as you know, many other commitments, so we mustn't expect to monopolize too much of his time. He has, however, been examining the structure of Seaford-Brennen's for some weeks, and has come up with some very useful suggestions, but nothing for anyone to get alarmed about.'

'What about Hugh Massingham?' said Xander's slurred voice. Everyone looked round in horror, as though one of the portraits had spoken. There was an embarrassed pause.

335

Xander went on carefully putting the stripes on a rugger shirt. I didn't dare look at Gareth.

'I was just coming to that,' said Ricky, with a slight edge in his voice. 'I know how upset you must all be over Hugh's death. As a close personal friend and a colleague for many years, I know how much I'm going to miss him, and how our sympathy goes out to his widow and family. I hope as many of you as possible will go to the memorial service on the 5th. In the meantime,' he said, going into top gear with relief, 'it was vital to restore public confidence immediately and prevent a further fall on the stock market, so we invited Mr. Llewellyn to join the board.'

To avoid any further interruption from Xander, he hastily started introducing Gareth round the table. Tommy Lloyd shook hands, but was obviously bristling with antagonism, nor did any of the older department heads look particularly friendly. Poor Gareth, he was obviously in for a rough ride. It seemed an eternity before they came to me. I was sure the whole room could hear my heart hammering.

'You know Octavia,' said Ricky.

Gareth's eyes were on me. They were hard and flinty, without trace of the former laughing gypsy wickedness.

'Yes, I know Octavia,' he said grimly.

The flinty glance moved on to Xander.

'And this is Octavia's brother, my son-in-law, Alexander,' said Ricky, as though he was daring Xander to speak out of turn.

Xander got to his feet. 'Heil Hitler,' he said with a polite smile, hiccoughed and sat down.

'Xander!' thundered Ricky.

'I know that in welcoming Mr. Llewellyn,' said old Harry Somerville, his Adam's apple bobbing furiously, 'I speak for everyone in saying how pleased we all are.'

'Balls,' said Xander.

'Xander,' snapped Ricky, 'if you can't keep a civil tongue in your head you'd better bugger off.'

. All the same I had a chilling feeling that he was delighted Xander was playing up, so that Gareth could see what provocation he normally had to put up with.

'Well, I think it's over to you now, Gareth,' he added, sitting down.

Gareth got to his feet, still unsmiling, but completely relaxed. For a second he upended a memo pad on the table, swinging it reflectively between finger and thumb, then he looked round like a conductor waiting until he had everyone's attention.

'I'd like to kick off by examining the structure of the company,' he said. 'As Mr. Seaford has already indicated, I've been studying your outfit for a few weeks, and I've come to the conclusion — and I'm going to be brutal — that your whole organization needs to be restructured from top to bottom, and that some people, particularly those at the top, are going to have to pull their fingers out.'

He then proceeded to launch a blistering attack on Seaford-Brennen's managerial hierarchy, its distribution of assets, and its work in progress, which left everyone reeling. Tommy Lloyd was looking like an enraged beetroot, the rest of the table as though they were posing for a bad photograph. There was no doubt that Gareth could talk. He had all the Welsh gift of the gab, the eloquence, the magnetism, the soft cadences. You might hate what he said, but you had to listen.

'I called this meeting in the afternoon,' he went on, 'because with your track record, I didn't think you'd all manage to make it in the morning. Half of you seem to feel it's only worth putting in an hour's work before going to lunch. One can never get any of you before 10.30 or after 5.0, not to mention the three hours you all spend in the middle of the day, roughing it at the Ritz.'

Tommy Lloyd's lips tightened. 'While we rough it at the Ritz, as you so politely call it,' he said coldly, 'most of the company business is done.'

'Not on the evidence of the order books,' said Gareth. 'You've got to wake up to the fact that the old boy network is dead — all that palsy walsy back-scratching over triple Remy Martins doesn't count for anything any more, and you've got to stand on your own feet too. You've got too used to relying on government subsidies or massive loans from the parent company, and when they run out you squeal for more.' He looked round the table. 'When did any of you last go to the factory?' he said, suddenly changing tack.

There was an embarrassed shuffling silence.

'We're in frequent telephonic communication,' said Peter Hocking in his thick voice.

'That's not good enough,' said Gareth banging his hand down on the table so loudly that everyone jumped. 'I know, because I've been up to Glasgow, *and* Coventry *and* Bradford in the last few days and morale is frightful. No wonder you're crippled by strikes.'

'You should know, of course,' said Tommy Lloyd, thoroughly nettled. 'I was forgetting you're one of the new establishments without roots or responsibility.'

'Do you think I've got 50,000 employees,' Gareth snapped, 'without any kind of responsibility? Sure, I did my stint on the factory floor, so I happen to know men work, not just for a pay packet, but because they're proud of what they produce, and because the people they work for care about them. You lot think as long as you give the staff a gold watch after fifty years' hard grind, and a booze-up at Christmas, and then forget about them, it's enough. In my companies,' he went on, the Welsh accent becoming more pronounced, 'we tell everyone what's going on. We have a policy of employee participation. We even have someone from the shop floor in on board meetings. A blue print of the company's future is regularly circulated to all staff. It brings them in, makes them feel they belong. Every worker can ask the management a question and feel sure of getting an answer.'

He was stunning. There is nothing more seductive than seeing the person one loves excelling in a completely unexpected field. I wanted to throw bouquets and shout 'Bravo'.

Tommy Lloyd's lips, however, were curling scornfully.

'Good of you to give us your advice, Mr. Llewellyn,' he said. 'That kind of Utopian concept may work in the building industry, but I don't get the impression you know much about engineering. We've been running our own show very successfully, you know, for fifty years.'

'That's the trouble. Seaford-Brennen's was a first class family firm, but you've been living on your reputation for the last twenty years.'

'We've got the finest, most advanced research department in the country,' said Tommy Lloyd, stung, but still smiling.

'That's the trouble again,' said Gareth. 'Lots of research, and none of it applied. Two months ago I came back from a world trip. The Brush Group and British Electrical were everywhere, you were nowhere. I'm sorry, but it's the truth.'

Tommy Lloyd picked up a cigar and started paring off the end.

Gareth turned to Kenny Morgan who handed him a couple of sheets of paper.

'Kenny's been looking into your books,' said Gareth.

'He's no right to,' said Tommy Lloyd, turning purple.

'He calculates you won't even make a profit next year, certainly not £8 million as you forecast. That's a lot of bread.'

'I consider that a gross breach of security,' said Tommy Lloyd, addressing Ricky directly.

Ricky ignored him and continued looking at Gareth, who went on softy:

'And if anything, Kenny's estimate is still too high. All I'm saying is you need help in running your business, and I intend to make it what it's never been — efficient. You've got to face up to international competition: Americans, Germans, Japs, Russians. Last year I saw some industrial complexes in Siberia running at a fraction of our costs. If we're going to beat the Russians at their own game, there's no room for companies with a purely domestic market.

'And your domestic figures aren't very pretty, either,' he added. 'You all know they've sagged from 15.2 per cent of the home market four years ago to 4 per cent today.'

He paused, stretching his fingers out on the table, and examining them for a minute.

'Now, what is the solution?' he said, looking round the table.

Xander drew the bar across a pair of rugger posts.

'I think we'd all better start practising the goose step,' he said.

There was an awful silence. All eyes turned once more on Xander, but this time more with irritation than embarrassment. A muscle was going in Gareth's cheek.

'When I need a funny man,' he said sharply, 'I'll hire Morecambe and Wise. Do you personally have the answer to the problem?'

Xander leaned back for a minute to admire his artwork.

'Well, not right here in my pocket,' he said, and hiccoughed gently.

'Well shut up then,' snapped Gareth.

He got out a packet of cigarettes. Several lighters were raised, but he used his own, inhaling deeply, then said briskly:

'To get you out of the wood, Ricky and I suggest the following measures. To start with Seaford International is going to write off their £15 million loan as a loss, and give you a further £10 million over the next four years for a new model programme, and for modernizing the factories. Secondly, the existing products need more stringent tests. Practically everything you've produced recently has been blighted by poor reliability. Thirdly, I intend to re-jig the production operation. It's got to be speeded up. Waiting lists are so long, buyers have been forced to go elsewhere. I'd like to have the new engines rolling off the assembly by January at the latest. And you're not producing enough either, so instead of laying off men at Glasgow and Bradford, we're going to initiate a second shift system. There are enough men up there who need work. Then it's up to you to sell them. That's your baby, Tommy.'

Tommy Lloyd turned puce at the casual use of his Christian name.

'We've got to completely re-think the export market too,' Gareth went on. 'The appetite in the Middle East and in Africa for your sort of stuff, particularly power stations, should produce thumping big orders.'

'You talk as though we've been sitting round since the war doing F. . . all,' said Tommy Lloyd stiffly. 'Anyone can put up proposals.'

'Exactly,' said Gareth. 'So let's get the ball rolling early

340

tomorrow. Over the next fortnight Kenny and I plan to have talks with all of you individually. I won't be here all the time, but Kenny's going to put in a four-day week for the moment. Kenny,' he added, turning and looking at his manager's battered lugubrious face, 'I can assure you, is much tougher than he looks.'

A tremor of sycophantic laughter went through the room.

Gareth stood for a minute, looking cool, almost indifferent, but his left hand was squeezing the back of a chair so hard I could see the whiteness of his knuckles.

'I'm looking forward to working with you,' he said softly, 'but I'd like to add that I find it impossible to breathe or conduct business in a taut, patched-up regime; so you're either for me, or against me.'

And except for Xander, who was gazing blankly into space, and Tommy Lloyd, who was still looking livid, everyone seemed to be eating out of his hand. For a minute he glared at them grimly, then suddenly he smiled for the first time, the harsh, heavy features suddenly illuminated. The contrast was extraordinary; you could feel the tension going out of the room, as though you'd loosened your fingers on the neck of a balloon.

'I'm sorry I've been so blunt, but these things had to be said. You're in a hell of a mess, but frankly, I wouldn't have taken you on if I didn't think you could get yourselves out of it.'

When he sat down there was even a murmur of approval.

Ricky rose to his feet, oozing satisfaction like an over-ripe plum.

'Thank you, Gareth. I'm sure you can count on 100 per cent support. Now gentlemen, I believe that will be all today.'

There was a shuffling of feet. Everyone started to file out looking shell-shocked.

'I'll leave you then,' said Ricky. 'Again, many congratulations. We'll talk later today.'

I was dying to tell Gareth how great he'd been. But Annabel Smith was already doing it, speaking in an under-

341

tone, smiling warmly into his eyes, the predatory, self-possessed bitch.

Oh please at least let him say goodbye to me, I prayed, as I started towards the door.

Gareth turned. 'I want a word with you, Alexander, and you, Octavia,' he said shortly.

'Oh dear,' sighed Xander, 'I was afraid you might. Are we going to get a thousand lines, or is birching the only answer?'

CHAPTER FIFTEEN

As the last person shut the door behind them, Xander very slowly counted Mrs. Smith, me and Gareth with a shaking finger. Then he looked down at the long polished table.

'If we could find a net,' he said confidingly, 'we could have a ping-pong four.'

I giggled. Gareth and Mrs. Smith didn't. Xander pinched another of my cigarettes and went over to the window. We could hear the clunk of his signet ring as his fingers drummed nervously on the radiator. Gareth looked worn-out. I realized now what a strain the meeting had been.

'I wonder what's happening in the Test match,' said Xander to Mrs. Smith. 'You don't like cricket? Perhaps you had to play it at school like I did? Terrible for breaking one's finger nails.'

'That's enough,' snapped Gareth. 'I want to talk about your expenses.'

Xander and I sat quite still, not looking at each other. The temperature dropped to well below zero. My stomach gave a rumble like not so distant thunder. I'd only drunk cups of coffee since yesterday.

Gareth took a bit of paper from Mrs. Smith. 'We'll start with you, Alexander. Your U.K. expenses for the last month alone were well over two grand,' he said.

Xander removed his chewing gum reflectively, and parked it underneath the table.

'Arabs are dreadfully expensive to amuse,' he said.

'What Arabs?' asked Gareth. 'Not a single order has come from the Middle East to justify expenses like this.'

'Well it's in the pipeline,' said Xander. 'These things take time, you know.'

'I don't,' said Gareth brusquely. 'In most of these cases, initial meetings were never followed up, some of them never took place at all. Mrs. Smith has been doing a bit of detective work. You claim to have taken a certain Sheik Mujab to the Clermont three times, and to Tramps twice over the past two months, but he says he's never heard of you.'

'He's lying,' blustered Xander. 'They all do.'

'And Jean-Baptiste Giraud of Renault's,' Gareth ran his eyes down the page, 'appears to have had nearly £400 spent on him during the last four weeks, being wined and dined by you and Octavia.'

'Octavia's a great asset with customers,' said Xander.

'I can well believe that,' said Gareth, in a voice of such contempt I felt myself go scarlet with humiliation. 'Unfortunately for you, Jean-Baptiste happens to be an old Oxford mate of mine. It took one telephone call to ascertain he only met you once over lunch at the Neal Street where he paid, and he's never met Octavia at all.'

'He must have forgotten,' said Xander.

'Don't be fatuous,' said Gareth. 'I don't hold much brief for your sister, but she's not the sort of girl an old ram like Jean-Baptiste would be likely to forget.'

I bit my lip. Annabel Smith was loving every minute of it.

'And so it goes on,' said Gareth. 'God knows how much you've cheated the shareholders out of — old ladies who've gambled their last savings, married couples with children who've hardly got a penny to rub together, and all the time you two've been treating the company like a bran tub, helping yourself as you choose.'

Xander started to play an imaginary violin. Gareth lost his temper.

'Can't you be fucking serious about anything? Haven't you any idea what an invidious position you've put Ricky in? He can't give you the boot because you're his son-in-law, but at the moment you're about as much good to him as a used tea bag.'

He walked over to the window, squinting at the traffic below, his huge shoulders hunched, his broken nose silhouetted against the blue sky, black and silver badger's hair curling thickly over his collar. I suddenly felt absolutely hollow with lust.

We all waited. As he turned round his expression hardened.

'I don't suppose I've ever come across a more greedy couple,' he said, speaking with swift curious harshness. 'I guess Massingham let you get away with it. I gather he was quite a fan of Octavia's.'

'Don't you dare say a word against Hugh,' I hissed. 'He was worth a million of you.'

Xander slumped in his chair. Suddenly to my horror I saw the tears pouring down his face. I put my arm round his shoulders.

'It's all right darling,' I said.

Once again Gareth changed tack and, with one of those staggering *volte faces,* said very gently,

'You were fond of him. I know. I'm sorry.'

Xander pushed back his hair and blinked two or three times.

'He was my friend, faithful and just to me,' he said slowly. 'But Ricky says he was incompetent. And Ricky is an honourable man, so they are all honourable men. Oh Christ, I should have had breakfast,' he added in a choked voice, groping for a handkerchief.

'Can't you leave him alone?' I screamed, turning on Gareth. 'Can't you see he isn't in any state for one of your bawlings out?'

'I'm sorry,' said Xander. 'When people call me Alexander, I always know they're cross with me.'

Gareth opened the window and threw out his lighted cigarette, seriously endangering the passers-by in the street below. Then he slammed the window shut and said to Xander in a businesslike tone,

'As I see it we have two alternatives. We could send you to prison for what you've been doing, or we can cart you onto the Board, which'll give you more money and enable you to start paying back some of the bread you've borrowed from the firm. It'll also mean we can keep a closer watch on your activities. You're bloody lucky you've got a rich and loyal wife.'

'The son-in-law also rises,' sighed Xander. 'I don't think I can accept your offer.'

'Don't be wet,' said Gareth brutally. 'I want you in the office by nine o'clock tomorrow, so we can re-jig the export schedule. In the meantime you'd better take a taxi home and sleep it off.'

'All the way to Sussex?' said Xander.

'You've got plenty of mates who'll put you up for the afternoon. Now beat it.'

Xander walked very unsteadily towards the door, cannoning off the table, the wall and two chairs. At the doorway he paused, looking anxiously at me, clearly about to say something in my defence, but was baulked by Gareth saying again, 'Go on, get out.'

There was an agonizing pause after he had gone. My stomach gave another earth-shattering rumble. I could feel my early morning cup of coffee sourly churning round inside me. I licked my lips.

'Now,' said Gareth grimly, 'what about you?' And he looked me over in a way that made me feel very small and uncomfortable and miserable.

'Can I go too?' I said, getting to my feet.

'Sit *down*.'

I sat.

'Annabel, can I have those other figures?' he said.

Annabel Smith handed him a pink folder at the same time putting a new tape in the machine. God, she was enjoying this.

'You should go cock-fighting next time,' I said to her. 'You'd find that even more exciting.'

'At the moment,' said Gareth, glancing down at the figures, 'you're living in a flat that's paid for by the firm. I also gather that, when you moved in three years ago, the firm coughed up at least seven grand to have it re-decorated. Since then Seaford-Brennen has not only been paying your 'phone bills and rates, but also the gas and electricity. And recently Massingham gave you the Porsche on the firm which is costing a fortune to be repaired at the garage.

There's also £3,500 worth of unspecified loans to be accounted for.'

There was another dreadful pause. All you could hear was the hiss of the tape-recorder.

'It wasn't just *my* flat,' I protested. 'Directors and clients often stayed there.'

'And you, I suppose, provided the service.'

'I bloody did not,' I said furiously. 'What d'you think I am — a flaming call girl?'

I was shaking with anger. I could feel my whole body drenched with sweat. Annabel Smith gazed out of the window and re-crossed her beautiful legs.

'Does she have to be here?' I went on. 'I suppose it's customary to have a woman cop present if you're going to beat up the prisoner. And can't you turn that bloody tape-recorder off?'

I imagined them playing it back to each other in bed, drinking Charles Heidsieck and laughing themselves sick. Gareth leaned forward and switched it off. Then he said:

'Annabel baby, go and get us some coffee, and see that Xander's safely put into a taxi.'

She smiled and left us, quietly closing the door behind her. I noticed with loathing that there wasn't a single crease in her black suit.

For a minute Gareth's fingers drummed on the table. Then he said,

'For the last three years you've been conducting your jet set existence entirely on the firm. Even if we write off your joint junketings with Xander, you owe nearly £6,000. I want you out of that flat by the end of the month and I want the keys to your company car tomorrow. Here are your last quarter's bills, electricity, telephone for £425 — all discovered unpaid in Massingham's desk. I want those settled up. They're all final reminders. And the loan to the firm must be paid off as soon as possible.'

I felt icy cold. I wasn't going to cry, I wasn't. I dug my nails into the palms of my hands.

Gareth walked down the table until he was standing over me. Against my will, I looked up. His eyes were as hard and

347

as black as the coal his forefathers had hewn from the mines. In them I could read only hatred and utter contempt, as though he was at last avenging himself for all the wilful havoc I'd created in the past, for breaking up Cathie and Tod, for jeopardizing Gussie and Jeremy.

'You're nothing but a bloody parasite,' he said softly. 'I'm going to make you sweat, beauty. No more helping yourself to everyone's money and their men too. The party's over now. You're going to get a job and do an honest day's work like everyone else.'

I couldn't look away. I sat there, hypnotized like a rabbit by headlights.

'As your creditor,' he went on, 'I'd quite like to know when you're going to pay up.'

'I'll get it next week,' I whispered.

'How?'

'I'll sell shares.'

He looked at me pityingly.

'Can't you get it into your thick head that unless I can put a bomb under them Seaford-Brennen aren't worth a bean any more? We've also had enquiries from the Inland Revenue; you owe them a bit of bread too.'

The Debtor's Prison loomed. I gripped the edge of the table with my fingers. Then I lost my temper.

'You bloody upstart,' I howled. 'You smug, fat, Welsh prude, walking in here and playing God. Well God's got a great deal more style than you. You're nothing but a bully and a thug. They'll all resign here if you go on humiliating them. See if they don't, and then you'll look bloody silly after all your protestations about waving a fairy wand, and turning us into a miracle of the eighties. God, I loathe you, loathe you.' My voice was rising to a scream now. 'Marching in here, humiliating Xander and Tommy Lloyd, with that fat slob Ricky lapping it all up.'

I paused, my breath coming in great sobs. Then suddenly something snapped outside me. It was my bra strap, beastly disloyal thing. I felt my right tit plummet. Gareth looked at me for a second, then started to laugh.

'You should go on the stage, Octavia; you're utterly

348

wasted on real life,' he said. 'Why not pop down to Billingsgate? I'm sure they'd sign you up as a fishwife.'

'Don't bug me,' I screamed, and groping behind me, gathered up a cut glass ash tray and was just about to smash it in his face when he grabbed my wrist.

'Don't be silly,' he snapped. 'You can't afford to be done for assault as well. Go on, drop it, *drop* it.'

I loosened my fingers; the ashtray fell with a thud on the carpet.

I slumped into a chair, trembling violently. Gareth gave me a cigarette and lit it for me.

'I'll pay it all back,' I muttered, through gritted teeth. 'If I do some modelling I can make that kind of bread in six months.'

'Things have changed, beauty. You can't just swan back to work and pull in ten grand a year. There isn't the work about. You're twenty-six now, not seventeen, and it shows. Anyway, you haven't the discipline to cope with full-time modelling, and it won't do you any good gazing into the camera hour after hour; you'd just get more narcissistic than ever. For Christ's sake get a job where you can use your brain.'

My mind was running round like a spider in a filling-up bath, trying to think of a crushing enough reply. I was saved by the belle — the luscious Mrs. Smith walking in with three cups of coffee. She put one down beside me.

'I don't want any,' I said icily.

'Oh grow up,' said Gareth. 'If you give Annabel a ring she'll help you to get a job and find you somewhere to live.'

I got to my feet.

'She's the last person I'd accept help from,' I said haughtily, preparing to sweep out. But it is very diffcult to make a dignified exit with only one bra strap, particularly if one trips over Mrs. Smith's strategically placed briefcase on the way.

'I expect Annabel's even got a safety pin in her bag, if you ask her nicely,' said Gareth.

I gave a sob and fled from the room.

CHAPTER SIXTEEN

From that moment I was in a dumb blind fury. The only thing that mattered was to pay Seaford-Brennen back, and prove to Gareth and that over-scented fox, Mrs. Smith, that I was quite capable of getting a job and fending for myself.

I went out next day and sold all my jewellery. Most of it, apart from my grandmother's pearls, had been given me by boyfriends. They had been very generous. I got £9,000 for the lot — times were terrible, said the jeweller but at least that would quieten the income tax people for a bit, and pay off the telephone and the housekeeping bills. A woman from a chic second-hand-clothes shop came and bought most of my wardrobe for £600: it must have cost ten times that originally. As she rummaged through my wardrobe I felt she was flaying me alive and rubbing in salt as well. I only kept a handful of dresses I was fond of. There were also a few bits of furniture of my own, the Cotman Xander had given me for my 21st and the picture of the Garden of Eden over the bed. Everything else belonged to the firm.

In the evening Xander rang:

'Sweetheart, are you all right? I meant to ring you yesterday but I passed out cold. And there hasn't been a minute today. How was your session with Gareth?'

'You could hardly say it was riotous,' I said. 'No one put on paper hats. How did you get on this morning?'

'Well that wasn't exactly riotous either. He certainly knows how to kick a chap when he's down. I thought about resigning — then I thought why not stick around and see if he can put us on the map again. He is quite impressive, isn't he?'

'*Oppressive*, certainly.'

'Well tell it not in Gath or the Clermont, or anywhere

350

else,' said Xander. 'But I must confess I do rather like him; he's so unashamedly butch.'

'Et tu Brute,' I said. 'Look, how soon can I put my two decent pictures up for auction at Sotheby's?'

'About a couple of months; but you can't sell pictures — it's blasphemy.'

It took a long time to persuade him I had to.

I spent the next week in consultation with bank managers, accountants, tax people, until I came to the final realization that there was nothing left. I had even buried my pride and written to my mother, but got a gin-splashed letter by return saying she had money troubles of her own and couldn't help.

'You can't get your thieving hands on the family money either,' she had ended with satisfaction. 'It's all in trust for Xander's children, and yours, if you have any.' The only answer seemed to be to get pregnant.

When everything was added up I still owed the tax people a couple of grand, and Seaford-Brennen's £3,400. Both said, with great condescension, that they would give me time to pay.

The heatwave moved into its sixth week. Every news bulletin urged people to save water, and warned of the possibilities of a drought. Cattle were being boxed across the country to less parched areas. In the suffocating, airless heat, I tramped the London streets looking for work and a place to live. I never believed how tough it would be.

Just because one doting ex-lover, who'd put up with all my tantrums and unpunctuality, had directed me through the Revson commercial, I was convinced I could swan into acting and modelling jobs. But I found that Equity had clamped down in the past two years, so I couldn't get film or television commercial work, even if ten million starving out-of-work actresses hadn't been after each job anyway. Modelling was even more disastrous. I went to several auditions and was turned down. I seemed to have lost my sparkle. Gareth's words about not being seventeen anymore, and it showing, kept ringing in my ears. The first photographer

351

who booked me for a job refused to use me because I arrived an hour late. The second kept me sweltering for four hours modelling fur coats, expecting me to behave like a perfectly schooled clothes horse, then threw me out when I started arguing. The third sacked me because I took too long to change my make-up. I moved to another agency, and botched up two more jobs. After that one of the gossip columns printed a bitchy piece about my inability to settle down to anything, and as a result no one was prepared to give me work. Gareth was right anyway — it *was* no cure for a broken heart, gazing into the lens of a camera all day.

I tried a secretarial agency. I asked them what they could offer me. What could I offer them, they answered. Gradually I realized that I was equipped for absolutely nothing. I took a job as a filing clerk in the city. Another catastrophe — within two days I'd completely fouled up the firm's filing system. Next the agency sent me to a job as a receptionist.

'All you have to do, Miss Brennen, is to look pleasant and direct people to the right floor.'

I thought I was doing all right, but after three days the Personnel woman sent for me.

'Receptionists are supposed to be friendly, helpful people. After all, they are the first impression a visitor gets of the company. I'm afraid you're too arrogant, Miss Brennen; you can't look down your nose at people in this day and age. Everyone agrees you've got an unfortunate manner.'

Unfortunate manor — it sounded like a stately home with dry rot. It was a few seconds before I realized she was giving me the boot. The third job I went to, I smiled and smiled until my jaw ached. I lasted till Thursday; then someone told me I had to man the switchboard. No switchboard was ever unmanned faster. After I'd cut off the managing director and his mistress twice, and the sales manager's deal-clinching call to Nigeria for the fourth time a senior secretary with blue hair and a bright red face came down and screamed at me. My nerves in shreds, I screamed back. When I got my first pay packet on Friday morning, it also contained my notice.

Which, all in all, was great on character building but not

too hot for morale. One of the bitterest lessons I also learnt was that beauty is largely a matter of time and money. In the old days when I could sleep in until lunchtime, and spend all afternoon sunbathing or slapping on face cream, filing my nails and getting ready to go on the town, it was easy to look good. But now, having to get up at eight o'dock to get to an office by nine-thirty, punched and pummelled to death by commuters on the tube, scurrying round all day with not a moment to do one's face, not getting home till seven absolutely knackered, it was a very different proposition. I lost another seven pounds and all my self-confidence; for the first time in my life I walked down the street and no one turned their heads to look at me. In a way it was rather a relief.

After the secretarial agency gave me up, I rang up a few old friends who owned boutiques. Their reactions were all the same. They were either laying off staff, or told me kindly that their sort of work would bore me to death, which really meant they thought I was totally unreliable.

In the evenings I went and looked for flats which was even more depressing. Living on my own, I couldn't afford anywhere remotely reasonable, and in my present mood I couldn't bear to share with other girls. All that cooking scrambled eggs, knickers dripping over the bath, and shrieking with laughter over last night's exploits. It wasn't just that I couldn't face new people, I was feeling so low I couldn't believe they'd put up with me.

I was also fast running out of Valium — only six left, not even enough for an overdose. I couldn't go to my doctor; I owed him too much money. At night I didn't sleep, tossing and turning, eating my heart out for Gareth, worrying about leaving my darling flat, my only refuge. At the back of my mind, flickering like a snake's tongue, was the thought of Andreas Katz. If I took up his modelling offer, it would get me off the hook, but I knew once Andreas had something on me, or in this case, everything off me, I'd never escape. I'd be sucked down to damnation like a quicksand. Even Xander had deserted me; he hadn't called me for days. Gareth must be working the pants off him.

I was due to move out on the Saturday. The Thursday before, I sat, surrounded by suitcases, poring over the *Evening Standard,* trying not to cry, and wondering whether 'Bedsitter in Muswell Hill with lively family, £15 a week, some baby sitting in return, was worth investigation, when the telephone rang. I pounced on it like a cat. I still couldn't cure myself of the blind hope it might be Gareth. But it was only Lorna asking if she could come and stay the night. It was the last thing I wanted, but I had a masochistic desire to find out what Gareth was up to.

'You'll have to camp,' I said, 'I'm moving out the day after tomorrow.'

'Well, if it's not too much bother, I'd so adore to see you again.'

She arrived about six o'dock in a flurry of parcels and suitcases.

'I've gone mad buying sexy clothes,' were her first words. 'Gareth's taking me out tonight.'

I couldn't stand it, sitting in the flat and seeing her get all scented and beautiful for him.

I showed her to her room and then went into my bedroom and telephoned my ex-boyfriend, Charlie, and asked him to take me out.

He was enchanted. 'God, it's great to hear you baby. Mountain's come to Mahomet at last. I won a monkey at poker last night so we can go anywhere you want. I'll pick you up about nine.'

'Can't you get here any earlier?'

'I'll try, sweetheart.'

I wandered along to Lorna's bedroom. She was trying on a new orange dress she'd just bought.

'Do you think Gareth will like me in this?' she said, craning her neck to see her back in the mirror.

'Yes,' I said truthfully. 'You look ravishing. I'm going out too by the way, at about nine.'

'Oh, Gareth's coming at a quarter to, so you should see him.'

While she was in the bath, the telephone rang. Trembling, I picked up the receiver. Somehow I knew it was going to be

Gareth.

'Lorna's in the bath,' I said quietly. 'Can I give her a message?'

'Yeah, tell her I'll be a bit late, around nine-thirty.'

'All right,' I said.

'How are you?' he asked brusquely.

'I'm fine,' I stammered. 'And you?'

'Tired, I've been working too hard. I'm off to the Middle East with your brother next week, which should be enlightening if nothing else. Have you found somewhere to live?'

'Yes thanks,' I said. 'I'm moving out tomorrow.'

'What about a job?'

'That's fine too. I must go,' I went on, fighting back the tears. 'I've got so much to do. Goodbye.' And I put down the receiver.

I can't stand it, I can't stand it, I thought in agony.

Lorna walked in, wrapped in a towel, pink from her bath.

'Oh I feel so much better. I used your Badedas. I hope you don't mind.'

'That was Gareth,' I said. 'He's going to be late — about nine-thirty.'

'Oh goodee, that'll give me more time to tart myself up.'

Suddenly she looked at me.

'Octavia, you look awfully pale. Are you all right?'

Tears, embarrassingly hot and prickly, rose to my eyes. I began to laugh, gasped hysterically, and then burst into tears.

'Octavia! Oh poor love, what is it?'

'N-nothing. Everything,' I couldn't stop now.

'What's wrong? Please tell me.'

'Oh, the usual thing.'

'You're mad for someone?'

'Yes.'

'Well you're so stunning, he must be mad for you.'

'He isn't. He hardly knows I exist.'

'He couldn't know you properly then. Here, take my handkerchief.'

'I'd better go and get ready,' I said. 'I've got to go out in a minute.'

I put on a black trouser suit with a high mandarin collar and huge floppy trousers. It hung off me. I tied my hair back with a black bow. Were those dry lips and red swollen eyes really mine? Charlie wouldn't recognize me.

Lorna answered the door when he arrived. She came rushing into my bedroom.

'He's *absolutely* gorgeous. The campest thing I've ever seen,' she said excitedly. 'I'm not surprised you're wild about him.'

It was too much effort to explain to her he wasn't the one.

'Can you give him a drink?' I said. 'I'll be out in a minute.'

I hung around, fiddling with my make-up, trying to summon up enough courage to face him. I'd lost all my confidence. Finally I realized if I didn't get a move on I'd go slap into Gareth.

Charlie looked exquisite, and to me, absurd. He had already helped himself to a second whisky and was settling down on the sofa to chat up Lorna.

He got to his feet when I came in and pecked me on the cheek.

'Hullo baby. Playing it in the minor key for a change,' he said, taking in the black suit, the dark glasses, the drawnback hair. 'I like it, it's great.'

'Shall we go?' I said, going towards the door.

'Already?' said Charlie. 'I haven't finished my drink.'

'I want to go now,' I snapped.

'The lady seems to be in a hurry, so I'll bid you goodnight,' said Charlie, theatrically, bowing from the waist to Lorna. 'I hope you'll come into the shop one day now you're in London.'

'You've got a key, haven't you?' I said to her. 'Have a good evening. I'll see you in the morning.'

'Hey, what's bitten you?' said Charlie, as we went down in the lift.

It was a hideous evening. In three short weeks I seemed to have grown a world apart from Charlie and his flash trendy friends, waiting round in Tramps all night for something to happen, only interested in being the first ones to latch on to

356

the latest fad. Suddenly their values seemed completely dis-
located.

We went to Annabel's and I couldn't stand it, then we
moved on to the Dumbbells, then on to somewhere else and
somewhere else. Finally Charlie took me back to his flat and
we played records.

I have to hand it to Charlie; he seemed to realize instinctively that I was at suicide level and didn't attempt to pounce
on me in his usual fashion. Perhaps it had something to do
with his having a new girlfriend who was off modelling in
Stockholm for a couple of days. I looked at my watch. It was
three o'clock.

'What's the matter baby?' he asked. 'Have you fallen for
some bloke at last? I've never seen you so *piano*, you're not
even bitching how bored you are by everything this evening.
You look different too.'

He took off my dark glasses.

'Boy; you do look different. I must say I rather go for the
Ave Maria look.'

It would have helped if I could have cried on his shoulder,
but I'd gone beyond that stage now, I was just numb with
misery.

'Take me home, please Charlie,' I said.

Next day, life picked up about half an inch. For an hour I
endured the torture of listening to Lorna babbling on at
breakfast about the marvellous time she'd had with Gareth.

'After dinner, we went up to the top of the Hilton for a
drink, and looked out over the whole of London, it was so
romantic,' she said, helping herself to a third piece of toast
and marmalade. Her mascara was still smudged under her
eyes. I hoped it wasn't sex that had given her such an appetite.

Then she started to ask me awkward questions about the
new job I'd lied to Gareth that I'd got.

'It's in Knightsbridge,' I said.

'Well you must give me the telephone number because
you'll be moving out of here.'

'I'll be travelling a lot,' I said hastily. 'And they're always a bit dodgy about personal calls to start off with. I'll write and tell you.'

'It sounds marvellous,' said Lorna, selecting a banana. 'But if by chance it doesn't work out, Gareth says there's a marvellous new agency started up in Albemarle Street called Square Peg. They specialize in placing people who want to branch out in completely new fields.'

'I'll take the address just in case,' I said.

As soon as she'd gone, pleading with me to come and spend the weekend soon, I had a bath, painted my face with great care, took my last two Valium, and set out for Square Peg. They turned out to be very friendly and businesslike, and dispatched me straightaway to a public relations firm in the City.

The firm's offices were scruffy, untidy, and terribly hot. The secretary who welcomed me looked tired out, and her hair needed washing, but she gave me the sort of smile that all those personnel bitches I'd worked for were always banging on about.

'It's been a hell of a week,' she said. 'The air conditioning's broken and the heat's been terrible. It's crazy hard work here, but it's fun.'

The boss was a small dark Jew called Jakey Bartholomew, who seemed to burn with energy. His foxy, brown eyes shone with intelligence behind horn-rimmed spectacles. He had to lift a lot of files, a box of pork chops, and a huge cutout cardboard of a pig off a chair before I could sit down.

'We've just landed the Pig Industry account,' he said grinning. 'I'm trying to persuade them to produce kosher pork. We've been going for nine months now, and we're taking on new business all the time because we provide the goods on a shoestring. Do you know anything about public relations?'

'No,' I said.

'Just as well. You haven't had time to pick up any bad habits.' He ripped open a couple of beer cans and gave me one.

'We're a small outfit, only ten people in the firm, and we can't afford passengers. We need a girl Friday — you can see this place is in shit order — to keep it tidy, make decent coffee, and chat up the clients when they come. Then you'd have to do things like putting press releases into envelopes, taking them to the post, organizing press parties, and probably writing the odd release. It's very menial work.'

'I don't care,' I said, trying to keep the quiver of desperation out of my voice. 'I'll do anything.'

'If you're good we'll promote you very fast.'

Suddenly he grinned, reminding me of Gareth.

'All right, you're on, baby. Go along to the accounts department in a minute and get your P.45 sorted out. We'll start you on a three months trial on Monday.'

I couldn't believe my luck; I hardly concentrated as we discussed hours and salaries, and he told me a bit more about the firm. He was very forceful. It was only when I stood up to go that I realized I was about four inches taller than he was.

'The agency was right,' he said. 'They insisted you were a very classy looking dame.'

I didn't remember the agency saying any such thing when they telephoned through. They must have rung again after I'd left.

I then took a long 22 bus ride out to Putney where the *Evening Standard* had advertised a room to let. Everywhere I could see the ravages of the drought, great patches of black burnt grass, flowers gasping with thirst in dried-up gardens. As I got off the bus, a fire engine charged past, clanging noisily. Although it was only the end of July, a bonfire smell of autumn filled my nostrils.

The house was large and Victorian on the edge of the common, the front rooms darkened by a huge chestnut tree. A stocky woman answered the door. She had a tough face like dried out roast beef, and muddy, mottled knees. She was wearing a flowered sleeveless dress that rucked over her large hips. Rose petals in her iron grey hair gave her an incongruously festive look. At present she was more interested in stopping several dogs escaping than letting me in.

'I've come about the room,' I said.

'Oh,' she said, looking slightly more amiable. 'I'm Mrs. Lonsdale-Taylor. Come in, sorry to look such a mess, I've been gardening. Come here Monkey,' she bellowed to a small brown mongrel who was trying to lick my hand.

'Mind the loose rod,' she said as we climbed the stairs. In front of me her sturdy red legs went into her shoes without the intervention of ankles. Her voice was incredibly put on. I was sure she'd double-barrelled the Lonsdale and Taylor herself.

The room was at the top of the house; the sofa clashed with the wallpaper, the brass bed creaked when I sat on it, rush matting hardly covered the black scratched floorboards. On the wall were framed photographs cut out from magazines and stuck on cardboard. The curtains hung a foot above the floor like midi skirts. It would be a cold and cheerless room in winter.

I looked outside. In spite of the drought Mrs. Lonsdale-Taylor had been taking great care of her garden. The mingled scent of stocks, clove carnations and a honeysuckle, which hung in great honey-coloured ramparts round the window, drifted towards me. A white cat emergd from a forest of dark blue delphiniums and, avoiding the sprinkler that was shooting its rainbow jets over the green lawn, walked towards the house at a leisurely pace. It was incredibly quiet.

'It's beautiful here,' I said. 'You're lucky to be so countrified living so near London.'

I bent to stroke the little brown mongrel who'd followed us upstairs. He wagged his tail and put both his paws up on my waist.

'Get down, Monkey,' said Mrs. Lonsdale-Taylor, aiming a kick at him. 'He was my late husband's dog, I've never really taken to him. My husband passed on last year, or I wouldn't be taking people in.'

'Of course not,' I murmured.

'I prefer a pedigree dog myself,' she said, wiping her nose with her hand, and leaving a moustache of earth on her upper lip.

'Well, if you like the room, it's £15 a week all in, but you've got to pay for your own telephone. I've installed a 'phone box downstairs. You can use the kitchen when I'm not using it, as long as you clear up afterwards, but no food in the bedroom. I don't mind you having friends in if they behave themselves, but no gramophones, or young gentlemen after nine o'clock. And I'd like the first month's rent when you arrive. I like to get these things straight.'

CHAPTER SEVENTEEN

Looking back, I shall never know how I got through the next few weeks. I hadn't realized that the journey from Putney to the city would take two hours in the rush-hour, or in this heat, the bus would be like a Turkish bath. My second day working for Jakey Bartholomew I didn't get in till quarter to ten, and received such a bawling out I thought I'd blown the whole thing. But gradually as the days passed I began to pick up the job. I learnt to work the switchboard and skim the papers for anything important and stick press cuttings into a scrap book. The work was so menial that sometimes I did scream. But Jakey was a hard taskmaster, and came down on any displays of sulks or ill-temper like a ton of concrete slabs. In the same way, he picked me up for any stupid mistakes.

Gradually too, I got to know the other girls in the office, and learnt to grumble with them about the lateness of the second post, and the failure of the roller towel in the lavatory, and have long discussions about Miss Selfridges and eye make-up. The days were made bearable by little unimportant victories — one of the typists asking me to go to the cinema; Miss Parkside, the office crone, inviting me to supper at her flat in Peckham; a client ringing up asking if I could be spared to show some V.I.P. Germans round London.

I soon discovered, however, that I'd never be able to pay Seaford-Brennen back on my present salary, so I took another job waitressing in Putney High Street. Here, for six nights a week, and at lunchtime on Saturdays, I worked my guts out, earning £40 a week by looking pleasant when drunken customers pinched my bottom, or bollocked me

because the chef had had a row with his boyfriend and forgotten to put any salt in the Chicken Marengo. At the end of
each week I sent my £40 salary in a registered envelope to
Mrs. Smith, and received a polite acknowledgement. Gareth
was still in the Middle East with Xander so at least I didn't
worry all day about bumping into him.

Every night I fell into bed long after midnight, too
knackered to allow myself more than a second to dream
about him. But his face still haunted my dreams and every
morning I would wake up crying, with the sun beating
through the thin curtains, and the little mongrel Monkey,
curled up on my bed, looking at me with sorrowful dark
eyes, trying to lick away my tears. He was a great comfort. I
couldn't understand why Mrs. Lonsdale-Taylor preferred
her fat Pekineses. I realized now how much my mother had
deprived me of, never letting me have animals.

August gave way to September; the drought grew worse;
it hadn't rained for three months; the common was like a
cinder; the leaves on the chestnut tree shrivelled and turned
brown. People were ordered not to use their hose-pipes.
Mrs. L-T panted back and forth with buckets of water, grumbling.

On the Tuesday of my eighth week, Jakey Bartholomew
sent for me. I went in quaking.

'You can't send this out,' he said.

He handed me a photograph of a girl with very elaborate
frizzled curls, one of the dreadful styles created by our hairdressing client, Roger of Kensington. Turning it over I saw
I'd captioned it:

'Sweet and sour pigs trotters' — one of the Pig Industry's
equally dreadful recipes.

'Oh God, I'm sorry,' I said.

Jakey started to laugh.

'I thought it was quite funny. Have a beer, get one out of
the fridge.'

I helped myself and sat down.

Jakey leaned back. 'Our advertising associates want to
borrow your legs on Friday week.'

'They what?'

'They're pitching for a stocking account. All the guys reckon you've got the best pair of legs in either office. They want you to model the tights for them during the presentation.'

I felt myself blushing scarlet. I never realized any of the men in the office had even noticed me; they'd certainly kept their distance.

'They want to take some photographs this afternoon,' said Jakey, 'and get them blown up by next week.' I said that was O.K. by me. 'If they land the account, we'll probably get the P.R. side. And if the client likes the idea, they may use you in ads, which could make you quite a lot of bread.'

'Thank you so much,' I stammered. I felt I had conquered Everest.

'Are you feeling all right?' he said, as I went out. 'You're looking knackered.'

'I'm fine,' I said quickly.

'Well bring me the Roger of Kensington file then.'

He was right of course. Gradually I was coming apart at the seams. In the last week or so I had noticed a growing inability in myself to make decisions, even small ones. The problem of where to find the file suddenly began to swell like a balloon in my head. The familiar panic began to surge inside me. I'm going crazy, I whimpered. I put my hands on my forehead and waited. Keep calm, it'll go in a minute, don't panic.

I felt as if I were trying to get out of a dark slimy cavern, and my nails kept grating down the inside. My mind raced from one fear to the other, in search of a grip to secure myself from the blind horror that swirled around me. I leant against the wall, trying to take deep breaths, praying no one would come out into the passage. Gradually the panic ebbed away. I went into the general office. It was empty. With shaking hands I dialled the number of the psychiatrist who'd been recommended to me in the old days. I made an appointment for Thursday lunchtime.

The first visit wasn't a conspicuous success. The analyst was middle-aged, handsome, well-dressed, with teeth as white as his shirt-cuffs, a soothing deliberate manner, and a photograph of a beautiful wife and child on the desk. I was too uptight to tell him very much, but he gave me enough tranquillizers to last a week, on condition that I returned again next Thursday lunchtime.

'It's very kind, but I can't afford it,' I muttered.

I felt a totally doglike gratitude when he waved my protestations airily away and said:

'Don't give it a thought, Miss Brennen. In exceptional circumstances I take National Health patients, and your case interests me very much.'

The tranquillizers got me through another week. My legs were photographed in every conceivable type of stocking, and the advertising department professed themselves delighted with the result.

The following Thursday morning, just as I was setting out for the doctor, Xander rang, just back from the Middle East, and absolutely raving over his trip. He and Gareth had pulled off some fantastic deals he said, and Gareth was a star.

'I simply adore him,' he went on. 'I'm thinking of divorcing Pammie and asking him to wait for me, and darling, he can sell *absolutely anything*, even a pregnant rabbit to an Australian sheep farmer, if he felt so inclined. We had a terrible time to begin with. I didn't realize the Middle East was dry. For twenty-four hours we didn't have a drink, then the pink elephants started trooping into my bedroom, and Gareth had a quiet word with the resident Sheik. From then on we had whisky pouring out of our ears.'

'Was it terribly hot?' I said.

'Terrible, and if I see another belly dancer, I'll go bananas.'

'Did Gareth have lots of birds out there?' I said, suddenly feeling my voice coming out like a ventriloquist's dummy.

'No, actually he didn't. I think he's got some bird in England he's hooked on.'

'Any idea who?'

'Well, this ravishing redhead met him at the airport, bubbling over with excitement, flinging her arms round him.'

'Mrs. Smith?' I said in a frozen whisper.

'No, much younger. Laura, I think she was called.'

'Lorna Hamilton?'

'Yes, that's it. Gareth was supposed to be giving me a lift into London, but I left them to it.'

Almost sleep-walking, I got myself to the analyst. On the way I passed a church; the gutter outside was choked with confetti. Gareth and Lorna, Gareth and Lorna, a voice intoned inside me — they sounded like a couple by Tennyson.

The analyst had darkened his waiting room. After the searching sunlight it was beautifully cool. His receptionist got me a glass of iced water, and then I heard him telling her to go to lunch. I lay down on the grey velvet sofa. This time I found myself able to talk. I didn't tell him about Gareth, but raved on about my childhood.

'I wasn't allowed to be loving as a child,' I sobbed. 'My mother didn't love me. She never kissed me goodnight or tucked me up. Neither of my parents loved me, they fought like cats to have custody of my brother, Xander, but they fought equally hard not to have me . . .'

'Go on,' said the analyst noncommitally. I could feel his pale blue eyes watching me, smell the lavender tang of his aftershave.

'I know what happens to people who aren't loved enough,' I went on. 'They just close up, and love or hate themselves too much. They're incapable of getting it together with anyone else . . .'

After three-quarters of an hour of my ramblings, he glanced at his watch.

I got up to go.

'I'm sorry, I must have bored you to death. You can't possibly put me on the National Health.'

'I thought we'd dispensed with all that,' he said gently. 'You'll come again next week?'

'Oh please, if you can spare the time.'

He scribbled out a prescription. 'Here's another week's supply of Valium.'

He turned towards me, the prescription suddenly trembling in his hand. He was trying to smile; his blue eyes glazed, his face pale, he was sweating and there was a tic in his cheek. Then he walked round the table, stood in front of me and put a wet hand on my arm.

'I was wondering,' he said, that tic was going again, 'if I might see you — outside consulting hours. I am sure I could show you there was no need to be so lonely.'

Behind him, smiling sunnily, was the photograph of his wife and children. I had trusted him implicitly.

'I d-don't think it'd be very wise,' I said, backing away from him, I've never found married men very satisfactory.'

I wrenched open the door behind me, amazed to find it unlocked. I saw fear start in his eyes, the Medical Council passing judgment. Then he squared his shoulders.

'Of course,' he pressed the bell on the desk, magicking up the instant receptionist to show me out.

I ran down the street prescriptionless and sobbed help-lessly in the nearest garden square.

By some miracle I got back to the office just before Miss Parkside, the office crone. She arrived grumbling that she couldn't find a 16 size skirt to fit her anymore, and bran-dishing a large Fuller's cake to distract everyone's attention from her lateness.

'I suppose I ought to have worn my all in one,' she said, plunging a knife into the hard white icing, 'but it's too hot in this weather. It must be well up in the nineties. Come on, Octavia, you need feeding up.'

She handed me an enormous piece. In order to save money, I'd trained myself to go without lunch and breakfast. I usually had something to eat free in the evening at the restaurant while I was waitressing. Every mouthful of the cake seemed like sand in my throat. All the typists looked sympathetically at my reddened eyes, but said nothing.

My task for the afternoon was to ring up the papers and chase them to come to a press preview the next morning. I found it distasteful and embarrassing. In the middle Xander suddenly rang me. He sounded drunk.

'I know you don't like personal calls, darling, but this is a very special one. You're going to be an aunt.'

'A what?'

'An Aunt! Pammie's pregnant.'

I gave a scream of delight that must have echoed through

367

the whole building.

'Oh Xander, are you sure?'

'Quite, quite sure, she's even being sick, poor darling.'

'How long's she known?'

'Well, just after I went to the Middle East, but she wanted to be quite sure before she told anyone.'

I'd never known him so chipper.

'Good old Pammie, isn't it marvellous,' he went on, 'Ricky rang me up just now and was so nice, he even congratulated me about work, said the Middle East trip had been a great coup. Look, darling, I mustn't keep you, I know you're busy, but come over and celebrate at the weekend.'

I put the telephone down feeling utterly depressed. I knew I ought to be delighted, but all I could think was Xander was getting so far ahead of me in life, with a job that was going well, and a baby on the way. I felt sick with jealousy. I wanted a baby of my own. Listlessly I finished making my telephone calls, and started stapling press releases together for the preview tomorrow. The afternoon sun was blazing through the window. I could feel the sweat running down my back. Miss Parkside and the typists had already started grumbling about the prospects of the journey home.

The telephone went again. Miss Parkside picked it up.

'For you,' she said, disapprovingly. 'Make it snappy.'

It was Lorna. I could recognize the breathless, bubbling schoolgirl voice anywhere. This time she was jibbering with excitement and embarrassment.

'Octavia, I must see you.'

I felt my hands wet on the telephone.

'Where are you?' I said.

'At home.'

Memories came flooding back, the white house deep in the cherry orchards, Gareth beating the hell out of me, then putting me to bed, Jeremy trying to rape me.

'But I'm coming to London tomorrow,' she went on. 'Could we have lunch, I've got something I must tell you.'

'Nice or nasty?' I asked.

'Well, heaven for me, but I'm not sure . . .' her voice trailed off.

'Tell it to me now.'

'I can't, I'm in such a muddle,' she said. 'Please, let's meet for lunch. I'll come and pick you up.'

'I've got a very heavy day.'

'You can slip out just for a drink. I'll pick you up at one o'clock. And please Octavia, don't, don't be furious with me.'

The telephone went dead. I stood for a second, then just made the loo in time, and threw up all the Fuller's cake. For a second I crouched, wracked by retching and sobbing. So it was true about Gareth and Lorna, it must be what she was trying to tell me. With agonizing slowness, I pulled myself together. You must finish those press releases, I said over and over again, as though it was really me that needed stapling together. I splashed water over my face and rinsed out my mouth. God, I looked terrible. My suntan had turned yellow. My eyes were red and puffy. My hair, filthy and dark mouse at the roots because I couldn't afford to have it re-streaked, was bleached like straw at the ends. One of the secretaries poked her head round the door.

'Parkside's on the warpath,' she said. 'Some V.I.P.'s just arrived. Can you make him a cup of coffee and take it into Jakey's office?'

I couldn't find my dark glasses. The wretched V.I.P. would have to put up with reddened eyes. I knocked on Jakey's door and walked into his office. The next moment the cup of coffee had crashed to the ground, for sitting behind the desk was Gareth. He leapt to his feet.

'Are you O.K. lovely? You haven't burnt yourself?'

'I'm fine,' I muttered. 'But it'll ruin the carpet.'

I grabbed a drying-cloth that was lying on top of the fridge and, kneeling down, started frenziedly mopping up the coffee. Anything for Gareth not to get a glimpse of my face. I hadn't seen him for over two months; he'd have a fit to catch me looking so awful.'

'Leave it,' he said. 'It'll dry in a minute.'

He put a hand under my elbow and pulled me to my feet.

'I'll get you another cup of coffee,' I said, making a bolt for the door.

But he got there first, standing in front of me, shutting the door firmly. As usual his presence made the room shrink.

'Sit down,' he said, tipping a pile of files off a chair. 'I want to talk to you.'

'What are you doing here anyway?' I said. I still hadn't looked him in the eyes.

'Visiting my old mate Jakey Bartholomew.'

'You know him?' I said sharply. 'But I didn't, I mean . . .'

'You should read your own company notepaper,' said Gareth. He handed me a sheet that was lying on Jakey's desk. Sure enough in the middle of the list of directors was printed G. Llewellyn.

'T-then you fiddled me this job,' I blurted out. 'I thought I g-got it on my own . . .'

'Merits, yes of course you did,' he said gently. 'Jakey'd have never employed you if he hadn't liked you.' He held up one of the blown-up photographs of my legs.

'I must say I like these. I'd recognize those pins any-where.'

Everything was moving too fast for me. I was trying to work out what influence Gareth must have had over my working at Bartholomews.

'How are you enjoying it anyway?' he said.

'It's fine. How was the Middle East trip?'

'Hell,' said Gareth. 'And bloody hot and exhausting. Your brother was the only redeeming feature.'

'He's nice, isn't he?'

'He overreached himself one night. He charmed one sheik so much that later the sheik insisted that only Xander should have the culinary *piece de resistance* at dinner.'

'What was it?' I said.

'A sheep's eyeball,' said Gareth.

I started to giggle.

'He's over the moon about the baby,' I said, trying to keep the trace of wistfulness out of my voice.

'Yep, it's a good thing. It'll patch up things between him and Ricky, too.'

There was a pause. The room was suffocatingly hot. I still

hadn't looked at him. A schoolgirl embarking on her first love affair couldn't have behaved with more gaucheness. I felt hollow with longing and misery.

'It's very hot isn't it?' I said.

'Very,' said Gareth.

This wasn't getting us very far. I got to my feet, edging towards the door.

'I must get you some coffee.'

'I don't want any.'

'I-I've got some work I've got to finish.'

He followed me into the general office, passing Miss Parkside on the way out, bearing her floral sponge-bag off to the Ladies.

'It's going-home time,' he said.

'I've got to finish these,' I said, picking a page off the four separate piles of paper until they shook in my hand as though they were being fluttered by an electric fan.

Gareth looked at me for a minute.

'You're getting them all out of order,' he said, taking them from me, and restacking them. He shoved them between the stapler and banged it down with one hand. Nothing happened.

'Bloody thing's run out,' he said. 'Come on, you can do them in the morning. I'll buy you a drink.'

The bar was crowded with commuters who couldn't face the journey home yet. Gareth found me a bar stool, I curled my feet round one of the legs, trying to control the hammering in my heart. In a minute I knew I'd wake up from a dream, and be crying back in bed in Putney. He handed me a gin and tonic and shot soda into his whisky. I took a slug of my drink at once, gripping it with both hands to stop them shaking.

I glanced up at the smoked mirror behind the bar; my eyes met Gareth's. For a second we gazed at each other with a steady fascination, as though we were two quite different people, in another world for the first time. I felt if his sleeve touched mine the whole bar would burst into flames.

I tugged my eyes away and took another gulp.

'You've lost a lot of weight,' he said.

'Have I?'

'Too much.'

'It's the heat.'

He glanced at the beige sausage rolls and curling sandwiches in the glass case.

'D'you want something now?'

I shook my head. A fire engine clanged past the door, followed by another.

'D'you think it'll ever rain again?' I said.

I noticed for the first time how tired he looked, the black rings under his eyes, almost as dark as his eyebrows.

'Is Seaford-Brennen too much of a sweat?' I said.

'Well it's not exactly a day trip to Llandudno,' he said. 'Jakey's very pleased with you, by the way.'

I felt myself blushing. 'He is?'

'Yep, and so am I. You haven't just turned over a new leaf, Brennen, it's a bloody great tree.'

He looked at me reflectively for a minute.

'Why have you been crying your eyes out all afternoon?'

I took a hasty swig of my drink, the glass was too deep and it ran all over my face.

'I'm trying to get my head sorted out,' I said, frantically. wiping gin away with my sleeve. 'So I started going to a shrink.'

'Jesus, you don't need a shrink.'

'H-he thinks I do. He pounced on me today.'

I started to tremble again. For a moment Gareth's hand tightened on my arm, then he said,

'The bastard. Report him to the Medical Council.'

'I don't think you can report shrinks, but it was a shock. I sort of trusted him.'

'You give me his name and address, and I'll get him kicked out,' said Gareth. He was really angry. God, he was being so nice, any minute I'd start crying again. I took a bite of my lemon peel.

'Lorna rang me this afternoon,' I said. 'She was in the country.'

Suddenly he looked evasive and shifty. He got out a packet of cigarettes, and when I refused one; lit one for himself.

'She said she had something special to tell me,' I went on, 'but she wouldn't tell me over the telephone in case it upset me.'

Gareth shook his ice round in his glass.

'Do you want another drink?'

I shook my head, the lump was getting bigger and bigger in my throat.

'She sounded over the moon, like Xander,' I continued. 'I guess she was trying to tell me she was getting married.'

'Yep,' said Gareth. 'That's about it.'

'Soon?' I said.

'Pretty soon. Lorna's one of those girls who wants to keep her virginity for marriage. She's worried she can't hold out much longer.'

'Bully for her,' I whispered.

'She feels terribly guilty,' he went on. 'She's worried stiff about upsetting you, and she knows Hesketh and Bridget are going to say she's too young.'

'You can't win them all,' I said in a choked voice.

'Look Octavia, you're a beautiful, beautiful girl. There are plenty of other guys in the sea, and masses on land for that matter.'

'Sure,' I said numbly, the tears beginning to course down my cheeks.

He took my hand; it was all I could do not to fling myself into his arms.

'I'm really sorry,' he went on. 'Look I've got nothing to do tonight. I'll buy you dinner and we can talk about it.'

'No you won't. It's very kind, but no thank you,' I said, wiping away the tears with the back of my hand. 'I've already got a date,' and breaking away, I slid off the bar stool and fled out of the bar.

'Octavia, wait,' I heard his voice calling after me. Then I plunged down into the Underground.

CHAPTER EIGHTEEN

When I got back to Putney, Monkey threw himself on me, yelping with ecstasy, taking my hand in his mouth, and leading me up the path. I found Mrs. Lonsdale-Taylor grumbling about the heat and the greenfly and pouring boiling water on a plague of ants who were threatening to enter the house. The dustmen were on strike and hadn't collected for two weeks; the stench of Jeyes fluid in the dustbins was almost worse than yesterday's smell of rotting food and vegetation.

Mrs. Lonsdale-Taylor straightened up, scarlet in the face.

'There's a young man waiting for you upstairs,' she said with a sniff, 'he says he's your brother.'

I bounded upstairs, I couldn't wait to tell someone how miserable I was. Xander loved Gareth too; he would understand how suicidal I felt. I found him in my bedroom, his face had a luminous sickly tinge, as though he was standing under a green umbrella. A muscle was going in his cheek. The ashtray beside him on the table was piled high with half-smoked cigarettes.

'Thank God you've come,' he said. 'I'm in dead trouble.'

His light brown hair, almost black from sweat, had fallen in a fringe over his forehead, emphasizing the brilliant grey eyes. He looked absurdly young. I ran across the room and put my arms round him.

'What's happened? Tell me. It's not the baby?'

He shook his head.

'I'm sorry,' I said. 'I haven't got anything to drink. Tell me what's the matter.'

'I've got to get £2,000 by tomorrow.'

'God, whatever for?'

'I'm being blackmailed.'

'Then you must go to the police at once.'

'I can't,' he said with a groan. He was near to tears. I realized I was the one who had to stay as calm and cool as a statue.

'You must go to the police; they'll keep your name out of it. What on earth have you done? It can't be *that* bad.'

The door suddenly opened, making us both jump, but it was only Monkey. He trotted over and curled up at Xander's feet. I kicked the door shut.

'Who is it?' I asked.

'It's Guido,' said Xander in a dead voice.

'Guido?'

'The Italian boy, the good-looking one you met that day we had lunch at Freddy's, before you went on the boat with Gareth and Jeremy.'

'Oh yes, I remember,' I said.

'That weekend you were away I refused to go and stay with Ricky and Joan.'

'Yes.'

'I went down to Devon with Guido — to a gay hotel.'

Oh God!

'Well one of his mates turned up, another pretty boy, also Italian, and we all got stoned of course, and started taking polaroid photographs in the bedroom. Some of them went pretty far. Now Guido and his pal want a couple of grand for a start, and if I don't cough up tomorrow, they're going to send the photos to Pammie and Ricky.'

I thought for a minute. The scent of tobacco plants was almost sickening outside. I could hear the outside tap water plummeting into Mrs. L-T's watering can.

'Don't you think Pammie twigged long ago?' I said. 'She's not stupid.'

'She can't admit it, even to herself.'

'Wouldn't it be better to tell her?'

Xander's voice broke. 'Not when she's pregnant. She was so happy about the baby, and suddenly everything's going so well at work, and we're getting on so much better at the moment.'

There was no point in reminding him he'd only been back from the Middle East twenty-four hours.

'Ricky'll throw me out, and so will Pamela, and I know it sounds wet, but I really want that baby. You've got lots of rich friends.'

'What about Gareth?' I said. 'He'll help you.'

'I'm getting on so well with *him* too,' said Xander fretfully.

'If you give in to Guido this time, he'll only be back for more bread in a week or two.'

'If I get a breathing space,' said Xander, 'I can think of a way to hammer him, I just need time. Oh for God's sake Octavia,' his voice rose, almost womanish, 'I've helped you out enough times in the past.'

It was true.

'All right, I'll get you the money,' I said.

'How?'

'I've got a friend who's offered me £1,500 to do some modelling,' I said, 'I guess I can push him up to £2,000.'

As soon as Xander had gone I went out to a telephone box and dialled Andreas's number.

I imagined him pushing aside a blonde, and climbing over a huge pair of tits to answer the telephone.

'Hullo,' said the husky, oily, foreign voice.

'Andreas,' I said. 'This is Octavia.'

There was a pause.

'Octavia Brennen.'

'I know,' he said softly. 'Just let me turn this redhead down. I was expecting a call from you.'

'You were?' I said sharply. 'What d'you mean?'

'Well, the grapevine said you were having rather a lean time, and you'd left the flat. Pity. It was a nice situation, that flat. Anyway, what can I do for you?'

I swallowed. 'Do you remember what you said about photographing me for *Hedonist*?'

'Sure do.' He had difficulty keeping the triumph out of his voice.

'You were talking in terms of £1,500,' I said.

'I must have been crazy.'

'Could you make it £2,000?'

'Inflation's clobbered everyone, baby.'

'Not that much. Your circulation's booming. I read it in *Campaign* last week.'

'Well, if you make yourself available for — er — dinner and other things afterwards, I might consider it.'

He waited. I could almost feel him writhing like a great snake in anticipation. What the hell did it matter? Gareth was caput as far as I was concerned. What did anything matter?

'All right,' I said, 'that would be nice. But can I have the cash tomorrow?'

'Greedy, aren't we? I hope there's nothing the matter with you, Octavia. I've never known you haggle before. Take it or leave it, that's the sort of duchess you always were. I wouldn't like you to be any different. It'd make me think things had a certain impermanence.'

'I need the bread,' I said.

'All right.' His voice suddenly businesslike. 'Cy Markovitz is in London at the moment. I've booked him all day tomorrow. Come along at two.'

In utter misery I realized I would have to cut the presentation. But getting the money for Xander had to be more important than anything else.

'All right,' I said.

He gave me the address and then added softly.

'And don't wear anything tight. We don't want crease marks all over you. Till tomorrow, darling. You won't regret it, I promise you.'

After that I had to go and waitress. When I got home I washed my hair and made pathetic attempts to get my body into some sort of shape to be photographed. I then spent hours writing and tearing up letters of explanation to Jakey. Even the final result didn't satisfy me. I was so much on the blink, I could hardly string a word, let alone a sentence, together and nothing I said could change the fact I was doing the dirty on him. Monkey lay on the bed, dozing, unsettled by the change in routine. Every so often he gave a yawn which turned into a squeaking yelp. I refused to go to bed, it was too hot to sleep anyway, and if I did sleep I would have to wake up and face afresh the truth about Gareth and Lorna.

Nothing — not even the truth — prepared me for the horror of the photographic session with Andreas. I felt as though I was hurtling on a fast train towards Dante's Ninth Circle, the one where the treacherous are sealed in ice and eternally ripped apart by Satan's teeth. But I'd betrayed Jakey, so I deserved to be ripped apart.

I sat in a little side room in front of a mirror lined with lit bulbs, wearing only an old make-up-stained dressing gown. The wireless claimed it was the hottest day of the year. It was impossibly stuffy in the huge Wimbledon studio Cy Markovitz had hired for the afternoon, but I still couldn't stop shivering. I knew I looked terrible. I had covered my yellowing suntan with dark-brown make-up, but it didn't stop my ribs sticking out like a Belsen victim. I had poured half a bottle of blue drops into my eyes but they were still red-veined and totally without sparkle.

In one corner of the studio, an amazing faggot called Gabriel with very blue eyes and streaked strawberry blond hair, clad only in faded kneelength denim trousers and a snake bracelet, was whisking about supervising two sulky, sweating minions into building a set for me. It consisted of a huge bed with a cane bedhead, silver satin sheets, and a white antique birdcage. One minion kept staggering in with huge potted plants, the other was pinning dark brown patterned Habitat wallpaper to a huge rolled-down screen. Gabriel was arranging a Christopher Wray lamp, a silver teapot and glass paper weights on a bedside table.

'Andreas asked for something really classy to set you off, darling. I've never known him to take so much interest.'

In another corner of the studio to an accompaniment of popping flashbulbs and Ella Fitzgerald on the gramophone, Cy Markovitz was photographing a spectacular looking black girl with 44-20-44 measurements. She was wearing red lace open crotch pants, heels with nine inch spikes, and was writhing against a huge fur rug which was pinned against the wall.

'It's to make her black boobs fall better,' explained Gabriel with a shudder. 'In the pix, it'll look as though she's lying on a bed.'

I turned back to the mirror, sweat already breaking through my newly applied make-up. Then I heard the noise of men laughing; my mouth went dry, my shivering became more violent. Next moment the curtain was pushed aside and Andreas came in reeking of brandy and after-shave, a big cigar sticking out of his mouth. Even heat and drink hadn't brought any flush of pink to his man-tanned cheeks. He was carrying a bottle of Charles Heidsieck and two glasses which he put on the dressing table. I clutched the white dressing gown tighter round me. For a long time he stood behind me looking into the mirror, his eyes as triumphant as they were predatory. Then he said in his oily, sibilant voice,

'You look a bit rough, baby. Been up against it, have you?'

'I've been working hard.'

Andreas laughed.

'You're not cut out for a career, I always warned you. And Gareth Llewellyn's ditched you; I knew he would. You must listen to Uncle Andreas in future.'

He seemed to revel in my utter desperation.

'Never mind,' he went on soothingly. 'I'll see you right. A few weeks of cushy living and you'll soon get the ripe peachy look you had at Grayston.'

He ran his hands over me, lingeringly and feelingly, like a child trying to gauge the contents of a wrapped Christmas present. I gritted my teeth, trying to suppress the shudder of revulsion. He let go of me, and started to take the gold paper off the top of the champagne bottle. I watched his soft white hands in horror. God knows what they wouldn't be doing to me later this evening.

I took a deep breath. 'Can I have the cash now?'

Andreas shook his head. 'Uh-uh. You get the cash when you deliver the goods, and they'd better be good.'

The top shot off the bottle into the rafters. Andreas filled a

JILLY COOPER

glass and handed it to me.

'That should relax you,' he said. 'Make you feel nice and sexy.'

I took a belt of champagne, wondering if I was going to throw up.

'Come in boys,' shouted Andreas over the curtain, and we were joined by a couple of Andreas' hood friends, flashing jewellery, sweating in waisted suits. They were the sort of guys who'd give even the Mafia nightmares.

'Meet Mannie and Vic,' said Andreas.

He must have brought them along to show me off. They were obviously disappointed I wasn't as fantastic as Andreas had promised but were too wary of him to show it.

'You wait till she's been with me for a bit,' purred Andreas, pinching my cheek. 'You won't recognize her.'

'Fattening her up for Christmas, are you?' said Mannie, and they all laughed.

Cy Markovitz, having finished with the black girl, wandered over and said he was almost ready. He was a tall, exhausted and melancholy man in his late forties, wearing army trousers, sneakers, and a khaki shirt drenched with sweat.

'Come and meet Octavia,' said Andreas, re-filling my glass. 'She's a bit nervous, first time she's done anything like this, so treat her with care. Lovely isn't she?' he added, smoothing my hair back from my forehead.

Cy Markovitz nodded — he was, after all, being paid vast sums by Andreas — and said the camera would go up in smoke when it saw me.

'You needn't worry about the pix,' he went on. 'We'll shoot through a soft-focus lens with the emphasis on the face and the direct gaze, very subdued and elegant.'

Oh God, what would Gareth say if he ever saw the results. I imagined him suddenly stumbling across them as he flicked through magazines on some foreign news-stand, his face hardening with disapproval, then shrugging his shoulders because he'd always known I was a bad lot. Was it really worth going through with it to help Xander? Was blood really thicker than water?

380

'Ready when you are darlings,' said Gabriel, popping his golden head round the curtain.

Andreas gave me a big smile. 'Come on baby, you'll enjoy it once we get started.'

I sat on the silver satin sheets, gazing in misery on the forest of potted plants. The studio seemed to be very full of people, all watching me with bored appraising eyes. I huddled even deeper into my dressing gown.

Cy Markovitz came over to me.

'You're not going to need that,' he said gently.

As I took it off, even Markovitz caught his breath. Andreas' thug friends were trying to preserve their poker faces, but their eyes were falling out.

'I told you she was the nearest thing to a Vargas girl you were ever likely to see,' said Andreas smugly.

Cy was gazing into the viewfinder. His assistant took some polaroid pictures, peeling them off like a wet bikini. Andreas and Cy poured over them.

'We'll need the cold blower to stiffen her nipples,' said Cy.

Andreas was determined to get his 112 lbs of flesh. Two agonizing hours later, I had been photographed in every conceivable position and garment, including a white fox fur with a string of pearls hanging over one breast, a soaking wet cheesecloth shirt, black stockings and a suspender belt, and nothing but an ostrich feather.

Gabriel, who was fast losing his cool, had been sent out to hire a Persian cat for me to cuddle, but after 30 seconds of popping flash bulbs the poor creature, having lacerated my stomach with its claws, wriggled out of my clutches and took refuge in the rafters.

Now I was stretched out on the satin sheets, wearing a sort of rucked up camisole top. Cy Markovitz clicked away, keeping up a running commentary.

'Lovely, darling, just pull it down over your right shoulder, look straight into the camera. A bit more wind machine, Gabriel, please. Come on Octavia, baby, relax, and let me have it, shut your eyes, lick your lips and caress yourself.'

'No,' I whispered. 'I won't do that.'

381

Markovitz sighed, extracted the roll of film from the camera, licked the flap, sealed it up and, taking another roll from the assistant, replaced it.

'Turn over,' he said. 'Bury your face in the sheets, stick your ass in the air, and freeze in that position.'

'I can't freeze when I'm absolutdy baking,' I snapped.

'Hold it,' said Markovitz, 'hold it. That's fan-bloody-tastic. Come over and have a look, Andreas.'

Andreas joined him. They conferred in low voices, then Andreas came and sat down on the bed beside me, filling up my glass.

'You're too uptight baby,' he said. 'You're not coming across.'

'How can I when you're all here gawping at me?'

It was like the times when I was a child and my mother insisted on being present when the doctor examined me.

'You'll have to try.' And once again I realized how much he was enjoying my utter humiliation, paying me back for all the times I'd put him down in the past. I lay back on the bed.

'Open your legs a bit further, open wide, that's lovely,' said Cy, clicking away. Any moment he'd ask me to say 'ah'. After this was all over, I supposed I could go out and throw myself over Westminster Bridge.

Gabriel was still whisking about, adjusting plants, his bronzed, hairless pectorals gleaming in the lights.

'Why don't we dress her up as a nun and let Angelica seduce her?' he said. 'Then it wouldn't matter her looking so uptight.'

'That's an interesting thought,' said Andreas.

There was a knock on the door. One of the assistants unlocked it, and let in a girl in a red dress with long black hair, and a pale, witchy, heavily made-up face. She looked furious and vaguely familiar. Perhaps miraculously she was going to take over from me.

'Hi, Angelica,' said Markovitz. 'Go and get your clothes off. We'll take a break for ten minutes.'

'She was on the gatefold of *Penetration* this month,' said one of Gabriel's minions. 'The blurb said Daddy was a regular soldier and that Angelica was reading philosophy at university, and spent the vacation pottering round ruins.'

'You could hardly call Andreas a ruin,' said Gabriel.

Andreas opened another bottle of champagne.

'I've booked a table at Skindles' tonight,' he said, caressing my shoulder with a moist hand. 'I thought in this heat it'd be nice to get out of London.'

He took a powder puff from one of Cy's assistants, and carefully took the shine off my nose. Tears of utter despair stung my eyelids.

'If you could find a horse,' said the other of Gabriel's minions, 'she'd make a stunning Godiva.'

'Shut up,' hissed Gabriel. 'There's a riding school round the corner. I've had enough hassle getting that bloody cat.'

A few minutes later Angelica emerged from behind the curtain, wearing only a red feather boa and a corn plaster. She walked sulkily up to the bed, looking at Andreas with the mixture of terror and loathing such as a lion might regard a sadistic ringmaster.

'You've already met Angelica Burton-Brown, haven't you Octavia?' said Andreas. He seemed to be laughing at some private joke.

'I don't think so,' I began, then realized that she was one of the tarts Andreas had brought down to Grayston. She was now glaring in my direction. Clytemnestra could hardly have looked more blackly on Agamemnon.

'Come and lie down, Angelica,' said Andreas, patting the bed.

She stretched out beside me, her black-lined eyes not quite closed. Underneath each false eyelash was a millimetre of dark venomous light raying straight in my direction. Trust Andreas to set up a scene that tortured both past and intended mistress.

'How's that?' he said to Cy. 'They make a good contrast, don't they? Profane and not-so-Sacred Love.'

I got to my feet and reached under the bed for the dressing gown. 'You've finished with me then?'

Andreas put a heavy hand on my shoulder, pressing me down again.

'On the contrary,' he said, 'we're only just beginning. Put the Nun's headdress on Angelica,' he said to Gabriel.

She looked so utterly ridiculous — talk about sour Angelica — that I was hard put not to giggle with hysterical laughter. But not for long; the next moment Andreas had hung a cross round my neck.

'Kneel beside her, Angelica,' he went on. 'That's right, as close as you can.'

I felt as though great toads were crawling all over me. I gazed down at the cross hanging between my breasts. Perhaps if I held it up to Andreas, he would suddenly age hundreds of years and shrivel into dust like Count Dracula.

'Now put your hand on Octavia's shoulder,' he said. I jumped away as I felt her fingers.

'No!' I screamed. 'No! I won't do it, I won't!'

'Cut it out,' said Andreas. 'Do you want two grand or not?'

I looked at him mutinously; then I remembered Xander and nodded.

Angelica looked about as cheerful as a cat with toothache. She'd obviously never had bread like that from him.

Andreas ruffled the sheets round us, and gazed into the viewfinder.

'Very nice,' he said softly. 'A bit more amiable, both of you.' Cy took over again.

'Put your hand on Octavia's throat, Angelica,' he said.

I steeled myself, feeling the tense hatred in her fingers. The sweat was glistening on her black moustache.

'Lovely,' said Cy. 'Now slide your hand down a bit Angelica, and down a bit further.'

I couldn't bear it, even for Xander, I couldn't take any more. I shot a despairing supplicating glance at Andreas and was appalled by the expression of suppressed excitement on his face. I felt the tears coursing down my cheeks.

Then suddenly there was a tremendous crash outside. Everyone jumped, as someone started pummelling on the door.

'It's the fuzz,' squeaked Gabriel in excitement, patting his curls.

'You can't go in there,' screamed a female voice. 'The stu-

384

dio's booked.'

'Oh yes I bloody can,' shouted a voice.

There was another tremendous crash, the door seemed to tremble, then suddenly caved in. I gave a gasp, half of relief and half of horror, for in the doorway, fierce as ten furies, terrible as hell, stood Gareth. Slowly he looked round the room, taking in first Cy, then Andreas and his hood cronies, then finally me on the bed with Angelica. With a whimper I pulled one of the satin sheets round me.

'What the bloody hell's going on?' he howled, walking across the studio towards me. 'You whore, you bloody cheap whore! I might have known you'd end up like this. Get your clothes on.'

Andreas moved towards him.

'Take it easy, big boy,' he said softly. 'Don't get so excited.'

Gareth turned on him.

'You lousy creep,' he hissed. 'I know how long you've been scheming to get your dirty hands on her. I'll get you for this. Go on,' he added, out of the corner of his mouth, to me. 'For Christ's sake, get dressed.'

I stood up, still too frightened to move.

'How on earth did you know she was here?' asked Gabriel, looking at him with admiration.

'Andreas shouldn't go round boasting in restaurants,' said Gareth. 'These things get overheard.'

'Look, wise guy.' Andreas was talking slowly and patiently now, as though he was dictating to an inexperienced secretary. 'You're gatecrashing a very important party. Cy's booked for the day, and so's Octavia, and neither of them for peanuts. She needs the money, don't you Octavia?'

Gareth glanced in my direction. I nodded miserably.

'So you can't come barging in here making a nuisance of yourself,' said Andreas.

'Oh, can't I?' said Gareth with ominous quiet.

There was a long pause; then, suddenly, he went berserk. Turning, he kicked Cy's camera across the room, then he smashed his fist into Cy's face, sending him flying after the camera. The next moment he'd laid out Cy's assistant with a punishing upper cut. Then Vic the hood picked up a rubber

385

plant and hurled it at Gareth, who ducked just in time and, gathering up another plant hurled it back.

Screaming like a stuck pig, still in the Nun's headdress, Angelica dived under the bed, followed immediately by the two minions and Gabriel.

'Oh dear,' sighed Gabriel as two more plants sailed through the air. 'Burnham Wood came to Dunsinane, now its going back again.'

Ducking to avoid more flying vegetation, I shook off the silk sheets, ran across the room, dived behind the curtain and started to pull on my clothes. By the sound of it Gareth was still laying about him like a maddened bull. As I looked out he was having a punch-up with Mannie who wrong-footed him and sent him crashing to the ground. The next moment Gareth had got to his feet and thrown Mannie into the middle of the remaining potted plants.

'Oh my poor jardiniere,' wailed Gabriel's voice from under the bed. 'What *will* the plant shop say?'

As I crept out from behind the curtain, a silver teapot and two glass paperweights flew across the room, none of them fortunately hitting their target.

Gareth paused; he was breathing heavily. Cy was still nursing his jaw in the corner. Mannie was peering out of the plants like a spy in L'Attaque. Vic was shaking his head and picking himself up. Cy's assistant got to his feet. As he started edging nervously towards the door, Gareth grabbed him by the collar.

'No you don't,' he said. 'Where are those rolls of film? Come on or I'll beat you to a pulp.' His fingers closed round the boy's neck.

'Over there on the trolley,' choked the boy in terror.

Gareth pocketed the rolls. As I sidled round the wall towards him, he glanced in my direction and jerked his head towards the door. He was just backing towards it himself when Vic moved in, catching him off guard with a blow to the right eye. Gareth slugged him back, sending him hurtling across the room, then, trying to right himself, tripped over one of the light wires and cannoned heavily into a pile of tripods. It was getting more like Tom and Jerry every minute.

Next minute, Andreas, who'd been watching the whole proceedings without lifting a finger, picked up the champagne bottle and, cracking it on the underneath of the bed, moved with incredible speed across the room towards Gareth. Cornered, Gareth scrambled out of the tripods, shaking his head. His right eye was beginning to close up. His forehead, just above his eyebrow, was bleeding where Vic's gold ring had gashed it.

He backed away from Andreas until he reached the wall.

'Now then big boy,' murmured Andreas, his voice almost a caress. 'I'll teach you to get tough with me.' He brandished the jagged edge of the bottle in Gareth's face. 'Give me back that film.'

Gareth stared at him, not a muscle moving in his face.

'You lousy cheap punk,' he said.

Then I froze with horror as I saw that Mannie had extracted himself from the potted plants and, armed with a flick knife, was moving relentlessly in from the right. Without thinking, I picked up the Christopher Wray lamp and hurled it at him, slap on target. Just for a second Andreas' concentration flickered, giving Gareth the chance to leap on him, knocking him to the floor. Over and over they rolled like Tommy Brook and Mr. Tod, yelling abuse at each other. Then finally Gareth was on top smashing his fists into Andreas' head. For a minute I thought he was going to kill him; then he got up, picked Andreas up and threw him through the Habitat wallpaper like a clown through a hoop.

There was another long pause. Gareth looked slowly round the room. Everyone flattened themselves against the wall or the floor. Then suddenly there was the sound of clapping, and Angelica emerged from under the bed, her Nun's headdress askew.

'I've been waiting three years for someone to do that,' she said.

Blood was pouring from Gareth's arm. He must have jagged it on Andreas' bottle.

'You'll bleed to death,' I moaned, gathering up a peach silk petticoat that was lying on the floor.

'Well, bags I give him the kiss of life,' said a little voice from under the bed. Gareth grabbed my wrist. 'Come on, let's get out of here.'

CHAPTER NINETEEN

I hoped Gareth had worked off his rage breaking up Cy's studio, but as we stormed up Parkside towards London, with Wimbledon Common on our right, the full storm of his fury broke over me.

'I tried to help you,' he yelled. 'We all did. Jakey's nursed you like a baby through the last eight weeks, and then you have to pick this afternoon to blow the whole thing just when Jakey needed you. I don't understand you, Octavia. Have you got some sort of death wish? Don't you care about anyone?'

He overtook another car; you could have got fag paper between them. Thank God we were going against the traffic. Home-going commuters crawling in the other direction stared at us in amazement. Some of them were stopping to put their hoods up. The stifling heat hadn't let up, but an ominous, bilberry dark sky had replaced the serene unclouded blue of the morning.

'Why did you do it?' said Gareth, overtaking yet again. 'Go on, I want to know.'

'I can't tell you.'

'Sure you can't. Well I'll tell you; you're so bloody idle you can't resist making a quick buck from Andreas. But my God, you'd have paid for it. He'd have broken you in a couple of months.'

We were passing Wimbledon Windmill now. I gazed stonily at the dried-up-pond and the great sweeps of platinum-bleached grass, blackened everywhere by fires.

Gareth warmed to his subject:

'I guess you're turned on at the thought of all those men on news-stands slobbering over your photograph, misting

389

up windows in Soho to get a second glance at your tits, not to mention the ones in bedsitters wearing raincoats . . .'

'They'd hardly keep their macs on in the bedroom,' I protested.

'Don't be flippant,' he howled.

We had reached the roundabout at Tibbet's Corner now, but he was so incensed he kept missing the turning off to Putney and had to go round three times, which didn't improve his temper.

'Don't you give a fuck about your reputation?'

'I don't care,' I snapped. 'I needed the bread in a hurry, that was all. But you're so well-heeled you wouldn't understand things like that.'

Gareth turned on me, enraged.

'Haven't you any idea how poor we were when I was a child?'

'I don't want to hear,' I said, putting my hands over my ears. 'I've read D. H. Lawrence, I know quite enough already about poverty at the pithead. I'm just fed up with you going round censoring my behaviour. Who the hell do you think you are, Mary Whitehouse, you great Welsh prude?'

'You've called me that already,' he said.

'What !' I shouted, my hands still over my ears.

'Don't bug me,' he shouted back and, seizing my arm, yanked my hand away from my ear.

I sat very still, watching the white marks left by his fingers slowly turning red. Then out of the corner of my eye I noticed the peach silk petticoat I'd tied round his arm completely drenched in blood, and a red stain creeping down his blue check shirt. He'd gone very white. Suddenly the fight went out of me.

'For God's sake let's call a truce and go to Roehampton Hospital. You need stitches in that arm,' I said.

'I don't want any stitches,' he said, screeching to a halt at the top of my road. Leaning across, he opened the door.

'Now get out, or I'll throw you out, and don't come grovelling back to Jakey either. You're on your own from now on.'

And, swinging the car round, he drove off in a cloud of dust.

As soon as he'd gone I began to shake again. How the hell was I going to tell Xander I hadn't got the money? I hadn't got the rent either. Mrs. Lonsdale-Taylor was sure to sling me out. The trauma of the afternoon had left me in a state of total shock. Numbly I walked towards the river, kicking my shoes off, when I came to the Common, not even noticing the sharp dry grass cutting into my feet.

A large drop of rain fell on the path in front of me. Perhaps at last the drought was at an end. The poplar trees by the bowling green clattered their leaves in a sudden gust of wind. The light was curious, as though one was swimming under water. Picnickers and dog-walkers hurried home, looking anxiously up at the sky; even the rooks were silent. The river bank was covered with coke tins, bottles and old ice-cream cartons. Two dogs were splashing about in the water, cooling off. I wished I had Monkey for company.

A large drop of warm rain splashed on my face, then on my hand; the discoloured sky was suddenly veined by lightning, followed three seconds later by an earth-shattering clap of thunder. The whole valley seemed to be boiling, the rain was coming down faster now, pattering on the leaves above me, pitting the river with rings, bouncing off the iron-hard ground. Another flash of lightning unzipped the sky, followed by another, far more brilliant, which seemed to snake down the centre of a huge elm tree only fifty yards away, and rip it apart. Then the whole sky exploded with rain.

I didn't care. I wanted to be struck down. I put back my head, feeling the drops dripping down my neck, cascading on my face, washing away all the horrible stage make-up. In two minutes I was drenched. The lightning was coming at the same time as the thunder claps now; it sounded like Gareth up in heaven breaking up another studio.

I don't know how many hours I wandered round, half crazy with grief I felt like Lear: 'poor naked wretches, whereso'er you are, that bide the pelting of this pitiless storm.'

Then suddenly it was getting dark, and the storm was moving away, grumbling like a drunk turned out of the pub. The rain was letting up, night was falling. In the distance I could see the orange lights on the roads around the common. It must be nearly ten o'clock.

Xander, Mrs. Lonsdale-Taylor and the music had to be faced. Listlessly I started to walk home. I was frozen and drenched. The temperature had probably dropped to the seventies, but after weeks up in the nineties, it felt like midwinter. My pink smock, worn on Andreas' instructions, had instructions of its own on the label about being only dry cleaned. Wet-cleaned, it had shrunk drastically, risen to mini skirt level, and was now clinging to every inch of my body. My hair was hanging in dripping tendrils. People giving their dogs last runs before bedtime looked at me strangely as I wandered barefoot past them. The whole common was steaming now like a crocodile swamp.

I walked listlessly up the street, the drenched gardens bowed down under their great weight of water. The gutters ran like millstreams, the street lamps reflected in the wet pavement. I paused outside my digs, trying to screw up enough courage to go in, rubbing the rain from my eyelashes. The iron gate was ice-cold beneath my touch.

The next minute Monkey hurled out of the front door and threw himself on me, yelping hysterically, licking my hands, scrabbling at my bare legs with his claws. I tried to creep up the stairs past Mrs. Lonsdale-Taylor, but she shot out of the kitchen, her tough roast beef face rigid with disapproval.

'Damn storm's snapped off half the delphiniums,' she said.

'Oh, I'm sorry. What a shame, after the way you've nursed them through the drought,' I said, sidling up the stairs, but she was not to be deflected.

'Where on earth have you been? Your office has been ringing all day. People have been calling in. You're not in any trouble are you? I hope you've remembered the rent.'

'I'll get it by tomorrow.' I had reached the bend in the stairs now.

'The agreement was every fourth Friday in the month,' she called after me, 'so I'd like it now; and there's someone waiting for you upstairs. I told you I won't have men in after nine o'clock. He must go at once.'

With a heavy heart I climbed the next flight. It must be Xander, waiting for the cash. I opened the door. The room was in darkness. Then my heart gave a lurch. A man was standing against the window. No one could mistake the width of those shoulders. It was Gareth.

'What are you doing here?' I whispered.

'Looking for you,' he said.

'I don't understand.'

'I love you,' he said simply, 'and I can't go on anymore.'

I ran towards him: 'Oh please, hold me.'

He put his arms round me and, as he kissed me, I felt the strength and warmth and love flowing out of him.

'Oh darling,' he muttered into my hair. 'Christ, I'm sorry. I was so angry this afternoon, but I was so jealous and I didn't understand what was going on.'

'I couldn't help it,' I said, starting to sob hysterically. 'It was the only way I could get the cash.'

'I know it was. Hush, sweetheart, hush. I've been with Xander since I left you. I was so miserable, I had to talk to someone. He told me everything.'

'Oh God, what's he going to do?'

'He told Pamela, then he went to the Police. It was the only hope. I took him to the station and held his hand for the first half hour. He'll be all right.'

'But what did Pamela say, and Ricky?'

'Darling, I really couldn't care less.'

'I couldn't let Xander down,' I muttered. 'He's always looked after me.'

'I know, I know, you're a bloody star, I just wish you'd come to me, instead of Andreas. Now for God's sake get out of those wet clothes.'

He let go of me and switched on the light. My legs wouldn't hold me up any longer so I sat down on the bed, gazing dumbly at him. His right eye had closed up completely now. He was still wearing the same blood-stained shirt but at least someone had bandaged up his arm. The next moment he'd pulled my suitcase down from the top of the wardrobe and, taking my dresses off the hangers, started throwing them in.

'What are you doing?'

'Packing. You're getting out of here.'

'I haven't got anywhere else to go,' I whispered.

'You're coming home with me.'

'But I can't. Lorna wouldn't like it.'

'What's she got to do with it?' He picked up my cornflower blue dress. 'You were wearing that the first time I met you. Put it on now.' He put it on the bed.

'But you and Lorna,' I was gagging on the words. 'Aren't you going to get married?'

He stopped for a second, his hands full of my underwear.

'What on earth gave you that idea?'

'She did. She said, you and she.'

'Not *me*, *Charlie*!'

'Charlie,' I said stupidly. '*Charlie*! But how on earth?'

'They met at your place,' said Gareth. 'The night she stayed with you, he asked her to come along to the shop, started taking her out, and bingo. She said you said you were crazy about someone that night. She assumed it was Charlie. That's why she felt so awful about telling you.'

'Oh God,' I said. 'It was you all the time. I never stopped loving you for a moment since that evening I was sick on the boat. God, what a stupid muddle!' And I started to laugh, but it went wrong in the middle and I started to cry again. Gareth chucked the rest of my underclothes into the suitcase and put his arms round me, holding me so tight I thought my ribs would crack.

'Now for Heaven's sake get that dress off or I'll strip it off you myself.'

I started to blush. 'I can't while you're looking.'

He grinned. 'After that matinée earlier, I can't see much point in false modesty.'

Then he must have seen something in my face because he turned his back and started talking to Monkey who was sitting shivering in the suitcase.

I'd just peeled off my wet smock when there was a loud knocking on the door. I grabbed a towel as Mrs. Lonsdale-

Taylor walked in.

'Miss Brennen,' she spluttered. 'I've told you I won't have men in my house. You must leave at once,' she added to Gareth.

'She'll be out of here in five minutes,' said Gareth curtly, 'so beat it.'

'Don't you dare address me like that, young man,' said Mrs. Lonsdale-Taylor. 'What about my rent? She owes me £60.'

Gareth put his hand in his pocket and pulled out a wad of notes. He counted out six tenners and gave them to her. Then he looked at poor little Monkey still shuddering in the suitcase.

'How much d'you want for the dog?'

'He's not for sale. He belonged to my late husband.'

'Ten quid,' said Gareth.

'Well, it doesn't seem right.'

'Twenty,' said Gareth, thrusting the notes into her hand. 'Now get out, you fat bitch, and bully someone your own size.'

Three quarters of an hour later, Gareth and his two waifs had reached home, and were sitting in the drawing-room. Although I was wearing one of his sweaters and nursing a large glass of brandy, I was assailed once again by a terrible fit of shaking. The tension was unbearable. The only sound was Monkey gnawing ecstatically on the remains of a leg of mutton which Gareth had found him in the fridge.

'He's happy,' said Gareth. 'Now it's my turn, come here.'

'I can't,' I said in a stifled voice.

'All right, I'll come to you.'

He sat down on the sofa about a foot away from me. I gazed desperately at my brandy.

'I'm now going to give you a short lecture,' he said. 'If you had any idea what I've been through since we got back from the boat, wanting you so fucking badly I thought I'd go up in smoke. I know I showed it in a funny way, fighting it because I didn't want to betray myself, because I couldn't see any way that you could possibly feel the same way about me.

395

The reason I finally agreed to take over Seaford-Brennen was because it gave me a chance to keep in touch with you, and that wasn't the only length I went to, sucking up to your degenerate brother, Xander, in the hope he might put in a good word for me, ringing Jakey every evening to see you were O.K. Why do you suppose none of the guys there ever laid a finger on you? Because I'd have fired them if they had.'

'I don't b-believe you,' I said incredulously.

'Don't interrupt,' he said. 'You're also right about my being a Welsh prude. I couldn't stand anyone coming near you. I nearly went spare over Jeremy and Charlie. This afternoon, as you saw, I flipped my lid.'

'You were wonderful,' I breathed, putting a hand up to touch his poor bruised eye.

He grinned, imprisoning my hand against his cheek:

'There's something to be said for being brought up in the valley. Then I talked to Xander. He told me about your childhood, and your parents and what a lousy deal you had all along. But that's all over now.'

And, kneeling beside me, he took me in his arms. I started to cry.

'What's the matter?' he whispered.

'It's no good,' I sobbed. 'I love you more than anything else in the world. I'm crucified with longing for you, but that's just in my heart. You were right from the beginning, I am frigid. I've been to bed with so many men I can hardly remember, but I hated it with all of them. I can put on a good act, but inside I just freeze up.'

'Hush lovie, hush.' He was stroking me in that soothing way you might gentle a horse.

'I'm telling you this because I love you, I'm no good to you.' 'I'm the best judge of that,' he said. 'You've never been properly loved in your life, just spoilt, and told to push off and play somewhere else, and produced to show off when grown-ups came to tea because you're so beautiful. Come on,' he went on, pulling me to my feet and leading me towards the bedroom. 'Let's not muck about any more.'

'No.' I shrank away from him. 'You'd be disappointed. I

396

couldn't fake it with you.'

'I won't, because I don't expect anything. We've got to get used to each other.'

In the bedroom he switched on a sidelight, illuminating the vast double bed, and drew back the fur counterpane. As he undressed me with undeniable deftness, I thought of all the women he must have laid on that bed before me . . . I felt like a novice horse entering the Horse of the Year Show for the first time, with the jumps up to six feet and all the previous competitors having had clear rounds.

Once we were in bed he just held me very gently until the horrors of the day began to recede. Then he said:

'I'm not going to lay a finger on you tonight. You're too tired.'

I felt a stab of disappointment.

'At least I don't think I am,' he went on, putting a warm hand on my tits, spanning both nipples with finger and thumb.

'Look,' he whispered, 'I can stretch an Octavia.'

I giggled.

'That's better. Come on lovely, remember, from now on I've got custody, care *and* control of you — and I'm not going to leave you, like your bloody mother did, ever again.'

And with infinite tenderness he kissed me, until I felt the waves of lust begin to ripple through me.

'It's Friday,' he said, as his hand edged downwards. 'We've got the whole weekend ahead. We needn't get up at all.'

Then later he said, 'Relax sweetheart, don't try so hard, there's no hurry. I actually *like* doing these things for you.'

Then later, more harshly, 'Stop fighting me; we're on the same side.'

Then suddenly it happened — like a great, glorious, whooshing washing machine — it's the only way I can describe it — leaving me shuddering and shuddering with pleasure at the end, like the last gasps of the spin-dryer. And afterwards I cried some more because I was so happy, and he held me in his arms, telling me how much he loved me until I fell asleep.

A few hours later the dawn woke me. We'd forgotten to draw the curtains. All I could see were huge windows framing the plane trees of Holland Park. I blinked, turned and found Gareth looking at me. I must be dreaming.

I put my hand out to touch his cheek.

'Are you real?' I said incredulously.

He smiled. 'I am if you are.'

His eye had turned black, his chest was covered in bruises.

'I think I'm in bed with Henry Cooper,' I said. 'I never dreamt he'd make such a sensational lover. Do you think we could possibly do it again?'

And we did, and it was even better than the last time, and I screamed with delight and joy because I'd been so clever.

When I woke again he wasn't there. I looked round in panic; then I found a note pinned to the pillow.

'Gone shopping with Monkey. Back about eleven. I love you, G.'

Still overwhelmed with wonder at what was happening to me, I got up, wrapped myself in a towel and, wandering into the kitchen, found a pile of unopened mail. I flipped through it. Three envelopes were written in distinctively female hands. I turned them over. One was from someone called Michelle in France, another from a Sally in the Middle East, another hadn't put her name on the back, but it was post-marked Taunton, and she'd written 'private and confidential' on the bottom.

I stood, overwhelmed with terror. Gareth had had millions of women before me. What was to stop him having millions in the future? Last night's protestations might have been just a ruse to get me into bed. I couldn't bear it. I went back into the bedroom and sat shaking on the bed, feeling myself pulled down into the familiar black slimy cavern of horror.

'Keep calm,' I kept saying to myself. 'It's all right.'

Suddenly I jumped out of my skin as the telephone rang. It was Mrs. Smith.

'He's not here,' I said. I could feel myself bristling.

'Well that's all right. Just give him a message that everything's O.K.'

'I'll tell him,' I said stiffly.

Mrs. Smith laughed, 'I'm so glad you two have finally got it together,' she said. 'He's been absolutely insufferable since he came back from that boat trip. It'll be nice working for a human being again.'

'Oh,' I stammered, feeling myself blushing all over. 'Do you mean to say — was it that obvious?'

'Yes,' she said. 'He's a very dear man. I think you're very lucky, and if you look behind the drawing-room door you might find something else to convince you.'

She dropped the receiver.

I ran to the drawing-room. Behind the door were two canvases stacked against the wall. I turned them over and gave a gasp of delight. One was my Adam and Eve picture, the other the Cotman. I looked at them incredulously, tears filling my eyes.

Then I heard a key in the door, and a scampering of feet. Monkey, rushing up the stairs, reached me first, but the next moment I was in Gareth's arms, with Monkey frolicking and frisking round our feet.

'I was worried some of Andreas' hoods might have got you. Annabel Smith says you've been like a bear with a sore head since the boat trip,' I gabbled incoherently. 'And you bought back my pictures; it's the nicest thing anyone's ever done for me, I can't believe it. When did you do it?' I added as we went upstairs.

'Last week sometime. I didn't hang them. I thought you could decide where you want to put them. But I'm not having Adam and Eve over the bed to distract you whenever we have sex.'

I went scarlet. 'I suppose bloody Xander told you that.'

He stopped in the doorway of the kitchen and kissed me on my bare shoulder.

'Christ, you're beautiful Octavia. Do you feel you can really put up with a jumped-up Welsh gorilla for the rest of your life?'

Then he kissed me on the mouth.

'Xander ought to be shot,' I said when I could speak,

blushing even more furiously.

He laughed. 'I'm only teasing you.'

The telephone rang. 'If that's Mrs. Smith again, she said you weren't to worry about anything,' I said.

It was Xander.

Gareth listened for a minute; then he said, 'That's great. Talk to Octavia.'

'Hullo darling,' said Xander. He sounded very cheerful. 'Are you all right?' I said.

'Well things have been pretty heavy. Ricky made the most awful scene, and I hoped very much Joan was going to have a coronary, but Pammie was staunchness personified; she told them both to get stuffed. And the police have pulled in that little snake, Guido, so all in all things haven't turned out too badly. And I must tell you,' he lowered his voice, 'I do fall on my feet. There is the most enchanting constable in the C.I.D. here who's been too marvellous to me.'

'Xander, you are *awful*.'

'Well since you've taken Gareth away, I had to find some compensation. Look, I'm terribly sorry, I'd no idea you'd have to take your clothes off to get me that money.'

Gareth was frying bacon and eggs when I came off the telephone. Stroking Monkey, I told him about the police constable.

'He's quite incorrigible,' said Gareth. 'All the same he'll be nice as a brother-in-law.'

My hand stopped in mid-stroke.

Gareth turned the bacon thoughtfully, then he shot a sideways glance in my direction.

'What did you say?' I whispered.

'I said I was looking forward to having him as a brother-in-law.'

'You shouldn't tease,' I stammered.

'I'm not teasing. I told you I'd been shopping this morning.'

He extracted a dark blue leather box from his pocket, his hand shook slightly as he handed it to me. So did mine as I opened it. I had terrible trouble with the clasp. Inside was the biggest sapphire I'd ever seen.

'Oh,' I breathed, 'is it really for me?'

'No one else.' He switched off the bacon and slid it onto my finger.

'W-what about your harem of girls, Annabel Smith and co?'

'I'll give them up if you will.'

'You don't have to marry me,' I said.

'Oh yes I do,' he said. 'I'm not a Welsh prude for nothing. I want to regularize things, particularly for Monkey, make him feel more secure.'

I giggled.

'I'm going to put my mark on you, so no one else can get near you,' he went on, his eyes suddenly serious. 'But I warn you, baby, even if we have to fight like cats, I'm going to wear the trousers. You're going to do what I tell you, and if you start upstaging me, I'll put you down. The boys in the Valley are like that. We keep our women in the background and we beat them if they give us any trouble, but we know how to love them.'

Suddenly I felt my knees giving way with lust.

'Could we possibly do it again just very quickly before breakfast?' I asked.

We never made it to the bedroom, but the kitchen floor proved perfectly satisfactory.

Imogen

For Lyn Adams with Love

CHAPTER ONE

The little West Riding town of Pikely-in-Darrowdale clings to the side of the hillside like a grey squirrel. Above stretches the moor and below, in the valley, where the River Darrow meanders through bright green water meadows, lies Pikely Tennis Club. In the High Street stands the Public Library.

It was a Saturday afternoon in May. Miss Nugent, the Senior Librarian, put down the mauve openwork jumper she was knitting and helped herself to another Lincoln Cream.

'I've never known it so slack,' she said to the pretty girl beside her, who was dreamily sorting books into piles of fiction and non-fiction and putting them on a trolley. 'Every one must be down at the tournament. Are you going, Imogen?'

The girl nodded. 'For an hour or two. My sister's raving about one of the players — some Wimbledon star. I promised I'd go and look at him.'

'I'm sorry you had to work this afternoon,' said Miss Nugent. 'You're always standing in for Gloria. I wonder if she really was "struck down by shellfish". I'm going to ring up in a minute and see how she is.'

'Oh, I wouldn't do that,' said Imogen hastily, knowing perfectly well that Gloria had sloped off to Morecambe for the week-end with a boyfriend, 'The — er — telephone in her digs is in the hall, and I'm sure she's feeling far too weak to stagger down two flights of stairs to answer it.'

Feeling herself blushing at such a lie, she busied about stacking up leaflets entitled *Your Rights as a Ratepayer* and *What to do in Pikely*. Bugger all, Gloria always said, in answer to the latter.

Miss Nugent burrowed inside her cream rayon blouse,

and hauled up a bra strap.

'Decided where to go for your holiday yet?'

'Not really,' answered Imogen, wishing some reader would come in and distract Miss Nugent's attention. 'My father's swapping with a vicar in Whitby in September. I might go with him.'

She dreaded discussing holidays; everyone else in the library seemed to have planned trips to exotic places months ago, and talked about nothing else. She extracted a romantic novel called *A Kiss in Tangier* from books destined for the Travel Section and put it on top of the Fiction pile. On the front was a picture of a beautiful couple embracing against a background of amethyst ocean and pale pink minarets. Oh dear, thought Imogen sadly, if only I could go to Tangier and be swept off my size seven feet by a man with a haughty face and long legs.

The library was certainly quiet for a Saturday. In the left-hand corner, where easy chairs were grouped round low tables, an old lady had fallen asleep over Lloyd George's letters, a youth in a leather jacket was browsing through a biography of Kevin Keegan, his lips moving as he read, and little Mr Hargreaves was finishing another chapter of the pornographic novel he didn't dare take home, for fear of his large wife's disapproval. Apart from an earnest young man with a beard and sandals flipping through the volumes of sociology and a coloured girl who got through four romances a day, desperately trying to find one she hadn't read, the place was deserted.

Suddenly the door opened and two middle-aged women came in, red-faced from the hairdressers opposite, smelling of lacquer and grumbling about the wind messing their new hair-dos. Imogen took money for a fine from one, and assured the other that Catherine Cookson really hadn't written another book yet.

'Authors have to write at their own pace you know,' said Miss Nugent reprovingly.

Imogen watched the two women stopping to browse through the novels on the returned books trolley. Funny, she thought wistfully, how people tended to look there first rather than at the shelves, how a book that appeared to be going out a lot was more likely to be in demand. Just like Gloria. Three boys had been in asking for her already that day, and had all looked sceptical on being told the shellfish story. But Imogen knew they'd all be back again asking for her next week.

You learnt a lot about the locals working in a library. Only this morning Mr Barraclough, who, unknown to his wife, was having a walk-out with the local nymphomaniac, had taken out a book called *How to Live with a Bad Back*. Then Mr York, reputed to have the most untroubled marriage in Pikely, had, with much puffing and blowing, rung in and asked Imogen to reserve *Masters and Johnson on Sexual Inadequacy*. And after lunch Mrs Bottomley, one of her father's newest parish workers and due to do the flowers for the first time in church next week, had crept in and surreptitiously chosen four books on flower arrangement.

'Vivien Leigh's going well,' said Miss Nugent, 'and you'd better put David Niven aside for repair before he falls to pieces. When you've shelved that lot you can push off. It's nearly four o'clock.'

But next minute Imogen had been accosted by a dotty old woman with darned stockings asking if they had any dustbin bags, which led to a long explanation about how the old woman's dog had been put down, and she wanted to throw its basket and rubber toys away as soon as possible.

'The dustmen don't come till Wednesday, and I'll be reminded of him everytime I see them int' dustbin.'

Imogen's eyes brimmed with tears. 'Oh, I'm so sorry,' she said. After devoting five minutes to the old woman, she turned to two small boys who came up to the desk looking very pink.

'Any books about life?' asked the eldest.

'Whose life?' said Imogen. 'Biographies are over there.'

'You know, facts'a life — babies and things,' said the boy. His companion started to giggle. Imogen tried to hide a smile.

'Well the biology section's on the right,' she said.

'Don't be daft,' snapped Miss Nugent. 'Run along, you

JILLY COOPER

lads, and try the children's library next door. And hurry up and shelve those books, Imogen.'

She watched the girl pushing the squeaking trolley across the library. She was a nice child despite her timidity, and tried very hard, but she was so willing to listen to other people's problems, she always got behind with her own work.

Imogen picked up a pile of alphabetically arranged books in her left hand — so high that she could only just see over them — and started to replace them in the shelves. The collected editions were landmarks which made putting back easier. *Sons and Lovers* was replaced at the end of a milky green row of D. H. Lawrence. *Return to Jalna* slotted into the coral pink edition of Mazo de la Roche.

Even working in a library for two years had not lessened her love of reading. There was *Frenchman's Creek*. She stopped for a second, remembering the glamour of the Frenchman. If only a man like that would come into the library. But if he did, he'd be bound to fall in love with Gloria.

A commotion at the issue desk woke her out of her reverie. A man with a moustache and a purple face, wearing a blazer, was agitatedly waving a copy of Molly Parkin's latest novel.

'It's filth,' he roared, 'sheer filth. I just came in here to tell you I'm going to burn it.'

'Well you'll have to pay for it then,' said Miss Nugent. 'A lot of other readers have requested it.'

'Filth and written by a woman,' roared the man in the blazer. 'Don't know how anyone dare publish it.' Everyone in the library was listening now, pretending to study the books on the shelves, but brightening perceptibly at the prospect of a good row.

Imogen returned *The Age of Innocence* to its right place and rolled the trolley back to the issue desk.

'Let me read you this bit, madam,' shouted the man in the blazer.

'Run along now, Imogen,' said Miss Nugent, hastily.

Imogen hesitated, embarrassed, but longing to hear the outcome of the row.

'Go on,' said Miss Nugent firmly. 'You'll miss the tennis. I

408

won't be in on Monday. I'm going to Florrie's funeral, so I'll see you on Tuesday. Now, sir,' she turned to the man in the blazer.

Why do I always miss all the fun, thought Imogen, going into the back office where Miss Illingworth was clucking over the legal action file.

'I've written to the Mayor five times about returning *The Hite Report*,' she said crossly, 'You'd think a man in his position . . . '

'Maybe he thinks he's grand enough to keep books as long as he liked,' said Imogen, unlocking her locker and taking out her bag.

'Twenty-one days is the limit, and rules is rules, my girl, whether you're the Queen of England. Have you seen Mr Clough's PC? It's a scream.'

Imogen picked up the postcard of blue sea and orange sand and turned it over.

I wouldn't like to live here, the deputy librarian, who was holidaying in Sardinia, had written, *but it's a horrible place for a holiday. The pillows are like bags of Blue Circle cement. Wish you were here but not queer. B. C.*

Imogen giggled, then sighed inwardly. Not only had one to find somewhere smart to go on holiday, but had to write witty things about it when you got there.

She went into the Ladies to comb her hair and wash the violet ink from the date stamp off her hands. She scowled at her reflection in the cracked mirror — huge grey eyes, rosy cheeks, too many freckles, a snub nose, soft full lips, long hair the colour of wet sand, which had a maddening tendency to kink at the first sight of rain.

'Why do I look so young?' she thought crossly. 'And why am I so fat?'

She removed the mirror from the wall, examining the full breasts, wide hips and sturdy legs which went purple and mottled in cold weather, and which fortunately today were hidden by black boots.

'It's a typical North Country figure,' she thought gloomily, 'built to withstand howling winds and an arctic climate.'

During her last year at school she had been unceasingly

409

ragged for weighing eleven stone. Now, two years later, she had lost over two stone, but still felt herself to be fat and unattractive.

Her younger sister, Juliet, was waiting for her as she came out of the library. Far more fashion-conscious than Imogen, she was wearing drainpipe pedal pushers, brilliant coloured glove socks, and a *papier mâché* ice cream cornet pinned to her huge sloppy pink sweater. A tiny leather purse swung from her neck, and her blonde curls blew in the wind as she circled round and round on her bicycle like a vulture.

'There you are, Imogen. For goodness' sake, hurry! Beresford's on court already and he's bound to win in straight sets. Did you bring *Fanny Hill*?'

'Blast! I forgot,' said Imogen, turning back.

'Oh, leave it,' said Juliet. 'It doesn't matter.' And she set off down the cobbled streets, pedalling briskly.

'What's his name again?' said Imogen, panting beside her.

'I've told you a million times — Beresford. N. Beresford. I hope the 'N' doesn't stand for Norman or anything ghastly. Mind you, *he* could get away with it. I've never seen anyone so divine!'

Last week, Imogen reflected, Juliet had been distraught with love for Rod Stewart, the week before for Georgie Best.

Although a pallid sun was shining, afternoon shoppers, muffled in scarves and sheepskin coats, scuttled down the street, heads down against the wind. Imogen and Juliet arrived at the Tennis Club to find most of the spectators huddled for warmth round Court One.

'I can't see, I can't see!' said Juliet in a shrill voice.

'Let the little girl through,' said the crowd indulgently and, in a few seconds, Juliet, dragging a reluctant Imogen by the hand, had pummelled her way through to the front.

'There's Beresford,' she whispered, pressing her face against the wire. 'Serving this end.'

He was tall and slim, with long legs, smooth and brown as a conker, and black curly hair. His shoulder muscles rippled as he served. His opponent didn't even see the ball. A crackle of applause ran round the court.

'Game and first set to Beresford,' said the umpire.

'He plays tennis champion,' said a man in the crowd.

'Isn't he the end?' sighed Juliet.

'He looks okay from the back,' said Imogen cautiously.

But as Beresford turned round and sauntered back to the baseline for the next game, she caught her breath.

With his lean brown features, eyes bluer than delphiniums, and glossy black moustache above a smooth curling, sulky mouth, he was the embodiment of all the romantic heroes she'd ever dreamed of.

'You win,' she muttered to Juliet, 'he's devastating.'

In a daze, she watched him cruise through the next three games, without conceding a point. Then — she could never remember afterwards exactly how it happened — he was strolling back to the wire netting to retrieve a ball, when suddenly he looked up and smiled at her. He just stood there smiling, his brilliant blue eyes burning holes in the netting.

The crowd was becoming restless.

'Beresford to serve!' snapped the umpire for the third time. Beresford shook himself, picked up the ball and went back to the base line. He served a double fault.

'At the first sight, they have changed eyes,' crowed Juliet, who was doing *The Tempest* for 'O' Level. 'Oh, Imogen, did you see him look at you? And he keeps on looking. Oh, it's too unfair. Why, oh, why, aren't I you?'

Imogen wondered if she had dreamed what had happened. She glanced round to see if some beautiful girl, the real object of Beresford's attentions, was standing behind her. But there was only a fat woman in a purple trilby and two men.

His game had certainly gone to pieces. He missed several easy shots and every time he changed ends he grinned at her.

'He'd better stop fooling about,' said Juliet, 'or he's going to lose this set.'

As if by telepathy, Beresford seemed to pull himself together. Crouching like a tiger, he played four games of rampaging brilliance to take the match without dropping a set.

How the crowd — particularly Imogen — thundered

their approval. Beresford put on a pale blue blazer and gathered up his four rackets. As he came off court, he stared straight at Imogen. Suddenly she felt frightened, as though the tiger she'd been admiring at the zoo had just escaped from its cage.

'Let's go and find Daddy,' she said.

'Are you mad?' said Juliet. 'Stay put and Beresford'll know where to find you.'

But Imogen, seeing Beresford pause to satisfy the demands of a group of autograph hunters, had already bolted into the tea tent.

They found their father talking to the Club Secretary.

'Hullo,' he said, 'have some tea.' And went back to his conversation.

A savage example of the Church Militant, the Reverend Stephen Brocklehurst had one great secular passion — sport. He was now giving the Club Secretary a blow by blow account of why Beresford had played so badly.

'The boy was overconfident, of course; thought he had the whole thing sewn up.'

Juliet giggled and applied herself to the cucumber sandwiches. Imogen sat in a dream, until Juliet nudged her. 'Beresford's just walked in,' she hissed.

Imogen choked over her tea. Everyone was hailing him from all corners.

'He's seen you,' whispered Juliet. 'He's working his way in this direction.'

'Hullo Nicky,' said the Club Secretary. 'Whatever happened to you?'

Beresford laughed, showing very white teeth. 'I saw something I fancied on the other side of the netting,' he said, looking at Imogen.

'You ought to play in blinkers,' said the Club Secretary. 'Come and join us. Have you met our vicar, Mr Brocklehurst, and his daughters, Imogen and Juliet?'

'No, I haven't,' said Beresford, shaking hands and holding Imogen's hand far longer than necessary before he sat down between her and the vicar.

'Brocklehurst,' he said reflectively, as he dropped four

lumps of sugar into his tea. 'Brocklehurst? Weren't you capped for England just after the war?'

Mr Brocklehurst melted like butter in a heatwave.

'Yes indeed. Clever of you to remember that.'

After talking to the vicar about rugger for five minutes, and having wangled himself an invitation to lunch next day, Beresford turned his attention to Imogen.

'Well, you certainly threw me,' he said softly. 'It's a good thing there weren't any Davis Cup selectors about.'

'I'm so pleased you won,' stammered Imogen.

'And I'm pleased,' he looked straight into her eyes, 'that you're even more beautiful close up.'

So was he, thought Imogen. Far more beautiful, with dark smudges under his eyes, and damp tendrils curling round his forehead. His voice was low and confiding as though she were the only person in the world he wanted to talk to.

And although he asked the usual questions — What did she do for a living? Did she enjoy it? Did she ever come to London? — his smoky voice, and the way his eyes wandered over her body and her face, made even those familiar phrases sound significant.

A pale youth with long mousy hair, wearing a v-necked sweater with reindeers round the border, came up and cleared his throat. Nicky looked up without enthusiasm.

'Yes?'

'I'm from Yorkshire Television,' said the youth. 'I wonder if we could have a few words with you?'

'When?' said Nicky.

'Well now?'

'I'm busy.'

'It won't take long.'

'I'll talk to you after the doubles. Now beat it,' said Nicky curtly, and turned back to Imogen.

She gazed at him, bewildered by such perfection. Perhaps it was the black rim round the iris or the thickness of the lashes that gave his blue eyes their intensity. His suntan was so even, it looked painted on. And he'd actually called her beautiful. Later that night she would bring out the remark like an iced cake saved from tea murmuring it over and over

to herself, trying to remember exactly the husky smouldering overtones of his voice.

'Where d'you play next?' she asked. The thought of him
going away was already unbearable.

Nicky grinned. 'Rome on Monday, Paris the week after,
then Edinburgh, Wimbledon, Gstaad, Kitzbühel, and then
the North American circuit, Washington, Indianapolis, Toronto, finally Forest Hills, if I don't die of exhaustion.'

Imogen gasped. Scotland was the most abroad she'd ever
been to.

'Oh, how lovely,' she said. 'Think of the postcards one
could send.'

Nicky laughed. 'I could face it if you came with me,' he
said, lowering his voice.

Imogen blushed and gazed into her tea cup.

They had been so engrossed, they hadn't noticed the arrival of a stocky, grinning young man. He was chewing gum
and wearing a gold ear-ring, a pale blue tracksuit top and a
blue towelling headband to keep his blond hair from flying
about.

'I came to see the reason you dropped three games in the
singles,' he said.

'This is it,' said Nicky.

Once more Imogen felt herself colouring painfully.

'Congratulations,' said the young man, giving Imogen a
comprehensive once-over and shifting his gum to the other
side of his face. 'You always had good taste, Nicky.'

'This is Charlie Painter,' said Nicky. 'My doubles partner.
Fancies himself as a tough guy.'

'I don't take anything lying down, except pretty girls,'
said Painter, winking at Juliet. 'Look, if you can bear to tear
yourself away, we're on court in a minute.'

'I can't,' said Nicky, turning his steady, knowing smile on
Imogen again. 'You don't need me. You can thrash those
two creeps with your hands behind your back.'

'The light's terrible. It's going to be like playing in a coal
cellar,' said Painter, peering out of the tent.

'Well, appeal against it,' said Nicky. 'You know I'm frightened of the dark and I want to go on chatting up Miss

414

Brocklehurst.'

Imogen shot a fearful glance at her father, but happily he was still nose to nose with the Club Secretary, rhapsodising over Hancock's try.

The loudspeaker hiccupped and announced the finals of the men's doubles. Reluctantly Nicky got to his feet.

'There's a party here this evening, I wonder if you — and your sister, of course,' he added smiling at Juliet, 'would like to come?'

'Oh, yes please,' began Imogen, but the vicar promptly looked round.

'Good of you to ask them,' he said blandly, 'but I'm afraid they've already been booked to help at the Mothers' Union whist drive. We shall look forward to seeing you at lunch tomorrow, any time after half past twelve.'

Both Imogen and Juliet opened their mouths in protest, then shut them again. They knew their father. Just for a second Nicky's eyes narrowed. Then he smiled.

'I shall look forward to it too,' he said, and followed Painter out of the tent.

'Sod the Mothers' Union,' muttered Juliet.

'I know you like them below the age of consent,' said Painter, as they walked towads the No. 1 Court, 'but isn't she a bit wet behind the ears?'

'Older than she looks, left school two years ago,' said Nicky, pausing to sign a couple of autographs. 'And very nice, don't you think?'

'Sweet,' agreed Painter, signing them too.

'And entirely untouched by human hand,' said Nicky, 'which makes a change.'

'We were the first that ever burst into that sunless sea,' said Painter and laughed. 'All the same, you'll never get your spoon into that pudding. Bet the old Rev locks them both in chastity belts every night.'

'He's asked me to lunch.'

'So what? He'll still never let you get near enough to pull her.'

'Want to bet?' said Nicky, taking a racket out of its press, and making a few swipes with it. 'Bugger, my shoulder's playing up again.'

'A fiver,' said Painter, taking off his blue jacket.

'Make it a tenner,' said Nicky, flexing his shoulder,

'All right, you're on.'

As he and Painter took the first set 6-0, Nicky was aware of the vicar and his daughters watching him. He was glad his first serve went in each time, and for once volleys, smashes, lobs, drop shots, everything, worked. He was getting to the ball so quickly he had time to examine it for bugs before he hit it. This was the kind of barnstorming form he'd got to maintain for the rest of the season. He flashed his teeth at Imogen and saw she was about to go.

Nicky had reached the age of twenty-six without ever falling seriously in love. He had had affairs by the score — there were endless temptations on the tennis circuit. If you were superbly fit, you didn't just go to bed and read a book in the evenings. If you won, you wanted to celebrate, if you lost you needed cheering up. But on the whole his heart was more resilient than his self respect. From broken affairs he recovered rapidly without any need of convalescence. They left no scars and no regrets and sometimes he was sorry they didn't, thinking he was missing out on something other people had and seemed to value, although it caused them anguish at the time.

Recently, too, he had felt a vague dissatisfaction with his life. There had been trouble about his knocking off another player's wife, a Mexican beauty, whose insanely jealous husband had rumbled them. The reason Nicky was playing in Pikely this week rather than Hamburg was in the hope that the whole thing might blow over. Then last week an offer of an advertising commercial which would have brought him in several thousand a year had suddenly gone instead to another British player, who, although less glamorous than Nicky, had reached the finals of the big tournaments more often than Nicky had the preceding year. Finally, the night before he'd driven up to Pikely, his Coach had taken him out to dinner.

'What are you playing at, Nicky boy?' he had asked after the second bottle, with his usual mixture of bluntness and concern. 'You've got everything going for you, but you're not getting any younger, and you'll never make it really big unless you cut out the birds and the booze and the late nights. Haven't you ever thought of settling down?'

Nicky had replied that he had too much trouble settling up in life to think of any permanent commitment. His debts were crippling at the moment, he said, and they had both laughed. But the Coach's remarks had stung and Nicky had not forgotten them.

As the crowd clapped approvingly at the end of the set, Mr Brocklehurst dragged his protesting daughters away, saying they mustn't be late for the whist drive. Nicky had looked so sensational on court that Imogen could hardly believe their *tête-à-tête* in the tea tent had ever taken place, but as she left he had waved his racket at her, so it must be true.

As they drove home to the vicarage with Juliet's bike perched precariously on the roof rack, they passed a school friend of Juliet's riding home from a gymkhana festooned with rosettes, who gave them a lordly wave with her whip.

'Just showing off, silly bitch,' muttered Juliet.

'10p in the swear box,' reproached the vicar, but mildly, because he doted on his younger daughter.

As he crossed the River Darrow and took the road up to the moors, he, too, felt a faint dissatisfaction with life. Watching Beresford today had reminded him of his youth on the rugger field. He had been good looking too, and had experienced the same adulation from women and hero-worship from men.

'Having achieved the ultimate glory of playing rugger for England,' said an unkind fellow clergyman, 'Steve Brocklehurst spent the rest of his life in exhausted mediocrity.'

Mr Brocklehurst was also only too aware that another great athlete, David Shepherd, had made bishop. But no such promotion had come his way. No doubt he would be left to moulder away the rest of his life in Pikely, where the adoration of the spinsters of the parish was no substitute for

the stands rising at Twickenham. In his more gloomy moments the vicar thought there was a great deal to be said for
an athlete dying young, cut off in his prime, rather than
growing paunchy and rheumaticky.

Life, however, had its compensations. He was well re-
spected in the district; no local committee was complete
without him; he loved his garden and his games of golf, and
his vague, charming wife, probably in that order. His two
sons, both at boarding school and costing the earth, were
shaping up as excellent athletes. Michael was already in the
fifteen. Juliet, adorable, insouciant, the baby of the family,
could twist him round her little finger.

But as a man of God, it had always nagged his conscience,
like a bit of apple core wedged in one's teeth, that his elder
daughter, Imogen, got on his nerves. In the beginning he'd
resented her not being a boy; as she grew up he was irritated
by her clumsiness, her dreaminess, her slowness, her tender
heart (how easily he could reduce her to tears, her inability
to stand up to him, and her complete lack of athleticism.He
still remembered a humiliating gym display at her school a
few years ago, when Imogen had been the only one in her
class who totally failed to get over any of the apparatus. He
had also been deeply ashamed of her lumpiness, but at least
she'd slimmed down a bit lately, and she'd kept her job in
the library, which helped out with the housekeeping.
(Money was very tight, with three children still at school.)
But why did she have to agree with everything he said, like
one of those nodding doggies in the back of cars?

There was no doubt, though, that young Beresford
seemed taken with her, and needed keeping an eye on. The
vicar might not love his elder daughter, but he wouldn't let
her come to any harm. He had been a bit of a lad himself in
his day and, like most reformed rakes, he veered towards
repressive puritanism where his daughters were concerned.
He was only too aware of the lusts of young players after too
much beer.

Next moment he caught sight of his curate on his new
red racing bicycle, with its drop handlebars which the vicar
thought both undignified and far too young for him. He

waited until they were only a few yards behind the curate, then sounded his horn loudly, which made the poor young man nearly ride into the ditch. The vicar chuckled to himself and turned up the drive.

The vicarage was one of those draughty Victorian houses made only slightly less forbidding by the creepers and rambler roses surging up its dark grey walls, and the wallflowers and purple irises in the front flower beds. At the back of the house was a lawn long enough for a cricket pitch, where Imogen bowled endlessly to her younger brothers when they were home. On either side were herbaceous borders, and at the end long grass and bluebells growing round the trunks of an ancient orchard.

As they opened the front door, Homer, the golden retriever, his eyes screwed up from sleep, greeted them, singing with pleasure, looking frantically round for something to bring them and settling for a pair of socks lying on the floor.

Going through the hall, with its old coats hanging on a row of pegs and a pile of parish magazines waiting to be delivered, Imogen found her mother in the drawing-room, looking rather pious and virtuously sewing buttons on one of her father's shirts. She knew perfectly well that her mother had been reading a novel and had shoved it under the shirt the moment she heard wheels on the gravel.

'Hullo, darling,' she said vaguely. 'Had a nice time at the tennis?'

'Yes, thank you,' said Imogen, kissing her. She knew there was no point in saying any more; her mother wouldn't listen to the answer.

'I suppose we ought to get changed for the whist drive,' said Mrs Brocklehurst with a sigh. 'What time does it begin?'

'Eight o'clock,' said the vicar, coming through the door. 'Hullo, darling. Just time for me to plant out my antirrhinums.'

'Well, of all the blooming cheats,' said Juliet to his departing back, as he went out of the french windows. 'We could have stayed and watched the last set after all. I hope his rotten snapdragons never come up.'

The whist drive seemed to last an eternity, but eventually the final chair had been stacked in the church hall, and the last *vol-au-vent* crumb swept away.

'Don't you sometimes wish Daddy had been an engineer?' said Juliet, as she and Imogen trailed home.

'Yes,' said Imogen, listening to the lambs bleating in the field behind the house, and praying that Nicky wasn't enjoying his party too much. 'I say, Juliet,' she felt herself blushing, 'it did happen, didn't it? This afternoon I mean.'

'Course it did,' said Juliet. 'Even Daddy got the wind up\and whisked you home. Normally he'd never leave in the middle of a match.'

When she got home Imogen washed her hair, undressed and got into bed. Then she filled the rest of May and the whole of June in her diary ecstatically describing her meeting with Nicky, shivering with excitement and wonder at the imperious way he'd dismissed Yorkshire Television, and told his partner to appeal against the light to give him more time with her.

Why me? why me? she kept saying over and over again, burying her hot face in her pillow, and squirming with delight. She must get some sleep or she'd look terrible in the morning. But it only seemed a few seconds later that she was woken by Homer barking at the paper boy and the church bell tolling for Holy Communion, and the Sunday morning panic of her father calling from the depth of the hot cupboard that he couldn't find a clean shirt.

CHAPTER TWO

Imogen sat clutching a cup of black coffee at breakfast. The vicar, mopping up egg yolk with fried bread, was deep in the sports pages of the *Sunday Times,* while Juliet, who was eating toast and marmalade, peered across at the headlines.

'What a dreadful world,' she sighed. 'I don't think I shall ever live to see twenty-one.'

'What are we having for lunch?' asked Imogen.

'Macaroni cheese, plum tart and custard and then, I suppose more cheese,' said her mother vaguely.

'But we can't give him that!' said Juliet aghast. 'I mean he's famous. Can't we have a joint?'

'I'm afraid the shops aren't open on Sunday,' said her mother. 'I'll try and persuade Daddy to open a bottle of wine.'

Imogen wondered how on earth she could last through the morning. But in the end there seemed to be lots to do, frantic hoovering and dusting, bashing lilac stems and arranging them with irises in a big bowl in the drawing-room, laying the table, trying and failing to find matching wine glasses, making a crumble top to liven up the plums, mixing a dressing for the salad, and praying that the vicar, who disapproved of frivolous culinary refinements, wouldn't notice the addition of garlic. Then she had to go to Matins. It was a beautiful day. The cuckoo was calling from the beech wood beyond the churchyard, and the trees were putting out acid green leaves against a heavy navy blue sky, which promised rain later.

'Defend us with thy mighty power, and grant that this day we run into no sin,' prayed the vicar, addressing the congregation in a ringing voice.

Juliet grinned and nudged Imogen, who went pink and gazed straight in front of her. She had already prayed fervently to God to grant her Nicky, but only, she added hastily, if *He* thought it was all right.

Her father was getting to his feet. A hymn and a sermon and another hymn, thought Imogen thankfully, and they would be out in the sunshine again. She mustn't forget to pick up the cream for the crumble from the farm.

Then she gave a gasp of horror, for she saw that her father, with what seemed a suspiciously malicious glance at their pew, was walking over to the Litany desk.

'Oh, no,' groaned Juliet. 'We had the Litany last week. Beresford will have come and gone by the time we get out of here.'

'And what about my pie in the oven?' muttered Mrs Connolly, their daily woman, who was sitting in the pew behind. The congregation knelt down sulkily.

Never had Imogen found it more difficult to concentrate on her imperfections.

'From fornication, and all other deadly sin; and from all the deceits of the world, the flesh and the devil,' intoned the vicar.

'Good Lord, deliver us,' Imogen chorused listlessly with the rest of the congregation. Oh, why hadn't she had a bath beforehand?

'From lightning and tempest; from plague, pestilence and . . . '

The sun was shining outside the church, but inside it was freezing. The vicar, who never felt the cold, insisted on turning off the radiators in April. It was twenty past twelve by the time she got home, and Nicky was due at a quarter to one. To warm herself up, she had far too hot a bath.

Having tried on every dress in her wardrobe, and hating them all, she settled for a black sweater and skirt which at least slimmed her down a bit. Her legs looked red and fat through her pale stockings. If only she'd got out of the bath sooner. There was no doubt, she thought sadly, if there was less of you, people thought more of you.

Going out of her room, she nearly fell over Juliet who was

lying on the floor in the passage pulling up the zip on her jeans.

'How do I look?' said Juliet, scrambling to her feet.

'Familiar,' said Imogen. 'That's my shirt.'

Juliet looked her over critically.

'You look nice, but I think you should tone down some of that rouge.'

'It's not rouge,' sighed Imogen, 'it's me.'

It was five to one. Imogen checked that everything was all right in the kitchen and went into the drawing-room to wait. She picked up the colour magazine. There was a long piece on Katherine Mansfield, which she vowed to read later, but knew she never would. She had read the report of a tournament in Hamburg three times at breakfast, particularly the bit about 'The British contribution being severely weakened by the absence of Beresford, who was playing at Pikely, where he triumphed in the singles, doubles and mixed doubles, as was to be expected.' Nicky was so illustrious, it was as though the sun was coming to lunch. Once more she got her compact out of her bag, and powdered her pink cheeks with more energy than success. Oh, to have been born pale and interesting.

It was five past one now. Perhaps he wasn't coming after all, perhaps after all that winning he'd forgotten or met someone at the party last night. She put down the magazine and wandered nervously round the room rearranging the lilac, plumping cushions, straightening Juliet's music which was littered over the top of the piano.

The clock that had dawdled all morning suddenly started to gallop; it was edging towards a quarter past one now. Her father always kicked up a fuss if lunch was late. It was quite obvious Nicky wasn't coming. I can't bear it, she thought in anguish. Then suddenly she heard the rattle of a car on the sheep track and Homer barking.

Next minute her hands went to her face in terror and excitement, then frantically she smoothed her hair, pulled down her sweater and put on more scent, most of which went over the carpet. In a panic, she rushed into the hall and locked herself into the downstairs lavatory. Next moment Juliet was shaking the door.

'Come out quickly. Nicky's just rolled up in a Porsche looking too fantastic for words. Go and let him in.'

'I can't,' squeaked Imogen. 'You go.'

'I'm putting on the broccoli, and Mummy's still tarting up. Go *on,* he's your lover.'

Imogen came out wiping her sweating hands on her skirt. She could see a man's figure through the bubbly glass panel of the front door. The bell rang.

'Anyone for tennis players?' cried Juliet.

'Oh, shut up,' said Imogen.

'Go *on.* He'll think we've forgotten and go away.'

With a trembling hand Imogen opened the door. Nicky was bending down to pat Homer, who was wagging his blond plumy tail and carrying a stick.

'You're not much of a watchdog,' said Nicky, rubbing his ears. 'Hullo, angel.' He straightened up and smiled at her. 'Sorry I'm late. I took a wrong turning and got stuck behind a convoy of Sunday motorists.'

'Doesn't matter. It's lovely to see you,' said Imogen.

She had wondered if he'd look less glamorous out of tennis things, like sailors out of uniform, but he looked even better, wearing a scarlet shirt which set off his suntan, and jeans which clung to his lean muscular hips even more tightly than Juliet's.

'Come in here,' she muttered, going towards the drawing-room. Nicky stepped forward to open the door for her, reaching the handle the same time as she did, letting his hand linger on hers far longer than necessary.

'Would you like a glass of sherry?' she said. 'It's quite dry.'

'I'd prefer beer, if you've got some. I'm supposed to be in training.'

'I'll go and get it. Won't be a second.'

'Don't be, I'll miss you,' said Nicky, picking up the paper and turning to the sports page.

Imogen rushed into the kitchen. Fortunately there were six Long Life in the fridge.

'How's it going?' said Juliet, dropping broccoli spears into boiling water.

'I don't know,' said Imogen rushing out, nearly falling over Homer. 'Promise you won't leave me alone with him too long.'

'What I like about this house is its relaxed atmosphere,' said Juliet.

'Nastase won at Hamburg,' said Nicky, putting down the paper and taking the can and a glass from Imogen.

'Do you know him?'

'Yes, he's a great mate of mine.'

He walked over to the french windows.

'This is a lovely house.'

'It's a bit scruffy,' said Imogen, acutely aware of the worn carpets, the cat-shredded armchairs and the faded red curtains, which had shrunk in the wash and hung three inches above the window ledge.

Nicky, however, used to the impersonality of hotel bedrooms, only noticed the booklined walls, the friendly dog, the fat tabby cat asleep on the piles of music on top of the piano, the *Church Times* scrumpled up under the logs in the fireplace, waiting to be lit on a cold night, and the apple trees snowed under with blossom at the end of the garden.

'It's a family house,' he said. 'My father was in the army so I spent my childhood being humped from one married quarter to another. I always longed for a real home.'

He glanced across at Imogen, gazing at him with such compassion. He had also seen how deeply moved and delighted she'd been when he arrived. He was touched. He liked this solemn little girl with the huge eyes.

'You smell marvellous,' he said, moving towards her.

'It's not me, it's the carpet,' confessed Imogen.

There was a pause. What could she say next? If only she had the badinage and ready-made phrases like Juliet or Gloria.

'Lunch won't be long,' she stammered, as Nicky sat down on the sofa. 'Would you like some peanuts?'

'No thank you,' said Nicky softly, 'I want five minutes alone with you. Come and sit beside me.' He patted the sofa.

Imogen sat down. There was another pause. She stared at her hands, aware that he was watching her. Then they both

425

jumped out of their skin as the large tabby cat leapt off the Beethoven Sonatas on to the treble keys of the piano, and proceeded to plink plonk his way down to the bass clef, and walk with dignity out of the french windows.

They both burst out laughing. It broke the ice.

'Was it a nice party, last night?' asked Imogen.

'How could it be? You weren't there,' said Nicky. 'I drank too much cheap wine, and nearly came and broke up your whist drive.'

'I wish you had,' said Imogen wistfully. 'When d'you go to Rome?'

'Tonight. I'm driving straight to Heathrow from here. Might reach the quarter finals this year. I've got an easy draw.'

And a friend of Nastase's too, thought Imogen.

'Doesn't it frighten you, so much success so early?' she asked.

Nicky laughed softly with pleasure. She'd fed him the right cue.

'I don't frighten easily,' he said, taking her hand and spreading the fingers out on his thigh.

She heard a step outside and, terrified it might be her father, snatched her hand away, but it was only her mother in a crumpled flowered dress, smelling faintly of mothballs, which she'd obviously just got out of the drawer. There was also too much powder on one side of her nose.

'Mr Beresford, how nice to see you,' she said, teetering forward on uncomfortable and unfamiliar high heels. 'Has Imogen given you a drink? She's awfully forgetful.'

Oh God, thought Imogen, I do hope she's not going to be too embarrassing.

'She's looked after me beautifully,' said Nicky, as Mrs Brocklehurst helped herself to a glass of sherry, 'and I love your house.'

She was followed by Juliet, who sat on the piano stool, patting Homer and grinning at Nicky.

'Hi,' she said.

'That's a nice dog,' said Nicky. 'What's his name?'

'Homer,' said Juliet. 'Short for Homersexual. He's always

mounting male dogs.'

'Really darling, that's not true,' said Mrs Brocklehurst mildly.

'Who plays the piano?' asked Nicky.

'I do,' said Juliet. 'I'm thinking of taking up the cello as my second instrument.' And next moment she was bombarding Nicky with questions about tennis stars. Was Nastase as difficult as everyone made out, and Stan Smith as dead-pan as he looked, and did Borg have lots of girls?

To have a better look at Nicky, Mrs Brocklehurst removed her spectacles, leaving a red mark on the bridge of her nose. Goodness, she thought, he really is a very good looking young man, and he seems nice too.

'What's Connors like?' said Juliet.

'Darling, poor Nicky,' remonstrated her mother. 'Give him a chance and go and mash the potatoes. Daddy'll be in in a minute. When did you first decide to become a tennis player?' she said to Nicky.

'When I was a child I used to go down to the courts at seven o'clock in the morning, hanging around hoping for a chance to play. Every time I seemed to get a rapport with a coach my father was posted somewhere else. I used to spend hours playing imaginary matches with myself hitting a ball against the garage door.'

'How splendid! I suppose if one wants to do anything badly enough in life, one usually does.'

'I like to think so,' said Nicky, shooting an unashamedly undressing glance in Imogen's direction, and rubbing his foot against hers behind the safety of an occasional table.

The vicar came in, rubbing his hands and looking quite benevolent, spectacles on his nose.

'Ah, good morning Nicholas. Lunch not ready yet? Preaching's thirsty work, you know.'

'It won't be a minute,' said his wife soothingly. 'Juliet's just doing the potatoes.'

'Is there time for a quick look round the garden?' asked Nicky.

'Of course,' said the vicar with alacrity. 'Bring your drink out.'

'What a nice young man,' said her mother.

'Unbelievable,' sighed Imogen.

There was an embarrassing moment before lunch.

'I expect you'd like a wash,' said the vicar, pointing to the door of the downstairs lavatory. He always liked male visitors in particular to go in there so they could admire his old England and Harlequin Rugger groups hanging on the wall.

'I'm not sure there's any loo paper,' said Mrs Brocklehurst.

'There wasn't,' said Juliet, crossing the hall with the macaroni cheese, 'so I tore some pages out of the parish mag.'

Lunch, however, was a success. Nicky had two helpings of macaroni cheese which pleased Mrs Brocklehurst, talked at length to the vicar about the British Lions and regaled them with gossip about tennis players and the various celebrities he'd bumped into on the circuit.

'I'm afraid I'm talking too much,' he said.

'No, no,' said Mrs Brocklehurst eagerly. 'We lead such sheltered lives in Pikely. Fancy Virginia Wade reading Henry James between matches!'

'Have you really met Rod Stewart!' sighed Juliet.

The vicar surprisingly opened a second bottle of wine.

'I wish we could have wine at the Mothers' Union,' said Mrs Brocklehurst. 'It would make things so much less sticky.'

'What about hash rock cakes?' said Juliet, taking a slug of wine.

'Eat up, Imogen,' snapped the vicar. She was still struggling with her first helping. The food seemed to choke her.

'Picking away like a sparrow,' went on the vicar, his voice taking on a bullying tone, 'or more like a crow in that colour. I do wish young people wouldn't wear black.'

Imogen bit her lip.

'Bastard,' thought Nicky. He turned to the vicar. 'How d'you think England'll do against the West Indies?' That should keep the old bugger gassing for a few minutes. Out of the corner of his eye, he examined Imogen, mentally undressing her. He would take her later in the heather, and be very gentle and reassuring. He was certain she was a virgin.

'They ought to bring back Dexter,' the vicar was saying.

'Don't bother to finish, Imogen,' whispered her mother. 'I should clear if I were you.'

Thankfully Imogen gathered up the macaroni cheese and the plates. As she took Nicky's he stroked the back of her leg, the one farthest away from the vicar.

She went into the kitchen and, licking macaroni cheese off her fingers, dumped the plates in the sink. She picked up a drying-up cloth, bent down and opened the oven door. As she was just easing out the plum crumble, she heard a step behind her.

'Isn't he the most utterly fantastic man you've ever seen?' she murmured from the depths of the oven.

'Glad you think so,' said a husky voice behind her. Appalled, she swung round. Nicky, holding a vegetable dish in each hand, was standing, laughing, in the doorway. The crumble was burning her through the drying-up cloth. She shoved it down on the kitchen table. Nicky put down the dishes and ran a finger caressingly down her cheek.

'Sweetheart, you must learn not to blush. It's terribly pretty, but it'll give you away to your unspeakable father.'

Imogen, terrified he'd try and kiss her when she tasted of macaroni cheese, hastily handed him the plates.

'We must go back.'

But Nicky waited in the doorway, holding the plates and still grinning at her. Imogen stared fixedly at the door hinge, where generations had cracked the paint screwing off the tops of refractory bottles.

'It'll get cold,' she stammered.

'I won't though,' said Nicky, and brushed her cheek with his lips as she scuttled past him.

'You've forgotten the plates,' snapped her father.

'I've got them,' said Nicky. 'Must say, I'm dying to sample Imogen's — er — pudding.' He winked at Juliet who giggled.

'Don't you get nervous before a big match?' she said.

'No.' He shot a glance in Imogen's direction, 'The suspense turns me on.'

'What's Goolagong like?' asked Juliet.

'Sweet; much prettier in the flesh.' Nicky poured cream thickly over his crumble. 'Always humming to herself and laughing if she does a good shot. She never knows what the score is.'

He then told them a story about one of the linesmen falling asleep in a big match. 'He'd had too good a lunch,' he went on. 'The crowd were quite hysterical with laughter.'

His eyes are as dark as pansies now, thought Imogen, trying to memorise every feature of his face. His hands were beautiful too, so brown and long-fingered. She suddenly felt quite weak with longing. Then she felt a gentle pressure against her ankle. It *must* be Homer rubbing against her, but he only begged during the meat courses. He was now stretched out in the sun under the window, twitching fluffy yellow paws in his sleep.

Nicky continued to talk quite calmly to her father, but the pressure against her ankle became more insistent.

'Good congregation?' he asked, draining his wine glass.

'Pretty good,' said the vicar.

He looks sensational in those jeans, thought Imogen. In spite of their tightness and, although he was sitting down, not an ounce of spare flesh billowed over the top. Her mind misted over; she didn't even hear Nicky asking her father what he had preached his sermon about, or her father replying:

'Ask Imogen, she was there.'

'What *was* it about?' asked Nicky, smiling wickedly at Imogen.

'What, sorry,' she said, startled.

'Wake up,' said her father.

'I'm sorry, I was thinking about something else.'

'Nicky wants to know what my — er — sermon was about.' There was a distinct edge to the vicar's voice.

She felt the blood rushing to her face; they were all looking at her now.

'Nicodemus,' muttered Juliet.

'Oh, yes,' stammered Imogen gratefully. 'The wind blowing where it listeth, and people who believe in God having everlasting life.'

With a shaking hand, she reached out for her wine, praying the storm was over.

Nicky looked at his watch.

'Good God, it's nearly quarter to three.'

'I've missed Gardener's Question Time,' said the vicar.

'I hope I haven't gone on too much,' said Nicky modestly, in the sure knowledge that he hadn't. 'If you care about something, you tend to bang on about it.'

'Oh no,' said Mrs Brocklehurst. 'It's been fascinating, hasn't it, Stephen? We shall all enjoy Wimbledon so much more, having met you.'

'I must drive back to London soon,' said Nicky. 'But I wouldn't mind a walk on the moor first.' He increased the pressure of his foot on Imogen's ankle.

'I must write my Evensong sermon,' said the vicar regretfully, 'and someone's coming at four to borrow a dog collar for the Dramatic Society's play.'

'I must bath Homer,' said Juliet.

'Imogen will take you,' said Mrs Brocklehurst.

'That's what I hoped,' said Nicky, smiling at Imogen.

'Why has Imogen painted her eyelids bright green to go walking on the moors?' asked the vicar, as he helped his wife with the washing-up.

'I'm afraid she's fallen in love,' said Mrs Brocklehurst.

'She's for the moors and martyrdom,' muttered Juliet.

The wind had dropped since yesterday and, as they climbed up the moor, the hot sun had set the larks singing and was drawing them up the sky. The bracken uncurled pale green fingers. Lambs ran races and bleated for their mothers.

'Bit of a sod to you, your pa, isn't he?' said Nicky.

'He was disappointed I wasn't a boy,' said Imogen.

'Jesus, I'm bloody glad you're not.'

He slid an arm round her about six inches above the waist,

'Very, very glad,' he repeated, as his fingers encountered the underside of her breast. Imogen leapt away; they could still be seen from the house.

'Don't know if you're more frightened of me or him,' said Nicky.

'Oh, I don't feel at all the same way about you,' protested Imogen. 'It's just that I've never met a famous person before.'

Nicky laughed, 'I'll introduce you to lots more if you promise not to fancy them.'

Imogen, not nearly as fit as Nicky, was soon puffing. Fortunately, he did most of the talking. 'It's a lonely life being a tennis player. Here today, gone tomorrow — thousands of acquaintances, very few friends. Never in one place long enough to establish a proper relationship.' He gave a deep sigh.

Imogen, her perceptions a little blunted by wine at lunch, did not smile. She looked at him sympathetically.

'Will you think of me occasionally when you're beavering away in your little library?'

'Oh yes, all the time.'

'That's nice,' he said, taking her hand and pulling her down beside him in the heather. Close to, she smelt of toothpaste and clean shining hair·— rather like his little nieces when they came downstairs after their baths to say goodnight, thought Nicky sentimentally. He raised Imogen's hand to his lips.

Across the valley, the khaki hillside was latticed with stone walls, the fells glowed a misty violet. You could just see the mill chimneys, a dingy shadow in the distance.

'Isn't it beautiful?' said Imogen, desperately trying to remain calm.

'Not nearly as beautiful as you are,' said Nicky. 'And your pulse, my darling,' he added, feeling her wrist, 'is going like the Charge of the Light Brigade. Do you believe in love at first sight?'

'I don't know,' stammered Imogen truthfully.

'Well, I do. The moment I saw you yesterday — pow — it happened, as though I'd been struck by a thunderbolt. I don't know what it is about you. But it's something indefinable, quite apart from being beautiful.' He put his arm round her, holding her tightly so she couldn't wriggle free. After a minute she ceased to resist and lay back.

All the sky seemed concentrated in those blue eyes and, as he kissed her, she felt the stalks of the heather sticking into her back. It was all so smooth, so practised, so different from the grabbing and fumbling of the few local boys who had made passes at her, that it was a few seconds before Imogen realised what was happening. Suddenly his hand had crept under her sweater and snapped open her bra, and her left breast fell warm and heavy into his other hand.

'No, no, Nicky! We mustn't.'

'Why not, sweetheart? Don't you like it?'

'Oh, yes ! Yes, I do. But . . .'

'Well, hush then.'

He was kissing her again, and his free hand was inching up her thigh. Paralysis seemed to have set into her limbs. She was powerless to fight against him. Then suddenly a tremendous crashing in the bracken made them jump out of their skins. Rescue had appeared in the form of a large black labrador, which stood lolling its pink tongue, its tail beating frantically.

'Heavens,' said Imogen in a strangled voice. 'It's Dorothy!'

'Who's Dorothy?'

'The churchwarden's dog.'

'Which means the churchwarden must be in the vicinity,' said Nicky, smoothing his hair. The dog charged back into the bracken.

Horrified, Imogen wriggled back into her bra, which had ridden up, giving her four bosoms like a cow, and went and sat on a moss-covered rock a few yards away, gazing down into the valley. Beneath them, the churchwarden was taking his afternoon stroll. Far below she could see her father walking back and forth in the orchard memorising his sermon.

'I must be crazy,' she said, and buried her face in her hands. Nicky came over and put his arms round her.

'It's all right, love. All my fault. I just want you too much, and you want me, don't you?'

She nodded dumbly.

433

'But not in front of the whole parish, eh? We'll have to find somewhere more secluded next time.' He looked at his watch. 'I must go now.'

'You will write to me, won't you?' he said as he slid into his sleek silver car.

Imogen didn't know if she could bear so much happiness and unhappiness in one day. Against the joy of his wanting her was the utter misery of his going away. Look thy last on all things lovely, she thought, her eyes filling with tears. Nicky rummaged about in the glove compartment. 'I've got something for you.' He handed her a small box and watched her bowed head and the incredulous smile on her pale lips as she opened it. She took out a red enamel bracelet, painted with yellow, blue and green flowers.

'But it's beautiful,' she gasped, sliding it on to her wrist. 'You shouldn't — I can't believe — no one's ever given me I'll never take it off except in the bath. It's like a gipsy cara-van,' she added, moving her wrist so the painted flowers flashed in the sunshine.

'That's because it's a present from a gipsy,' said Nicky, turning on the ignition. 'See you when I get back from Paris.' And, kissing her lightly on the lips, he drove off with a roar of exhaust which set the cat leaping in horror out of its comfortable bed of catmint on the edge of the drive.

Imogen, Nicky reflected without a flicker of conscience as he headed for the A1, had been far more delighted with the bracelet than his Mexican beauty, who, after a few shrieks of pleasure, had asked Nicky to keep the trinket for her, in case her husband noticed it and kicked up a fuss.

CHAPTER THREE

Imogen couldn't wait to get to the library next morning and tell Gloria all about Nicky. Fortunately Miss Nugent had gone to the funeral, Mr Clough, her deputy, was still on holiday, and the only other senior, Mr Cornelius, was busy making a display of fishing rods, nets and flies in the main entrance to encourage readers to take out some of the new sporting books, so Gloria and Imogen more or less had the place to themselves.

'This is him,' said Imogen, opening the *1977 World of Tennis Annual* and showing Gloria a photograph of Nicky stretching up, muscles rippling, to take a smash.' And here he is again coming off court after beating Mark Cox.'

'Oh, I know him,' said Gloria, peering at the book. 'Seen him on telly playing at Wimbledon. Wasn't there some row because he threw his racket at a linesman?' She turned the book round to the light. 'He's certainly fantastic looking.'

'But so much better in the flesh,' said Imogen, dreamily putting a pile of romances on the non-fiction pile. 'He's got this way of looking at you, and the husky way he drops his voice and says things that no one but you can hear. And then we went for this heavenly walk on the moors, and he said when he saw me it was like being struck down by a thunderbolt.'

'Did he try anything?' said Gloria.

Imogen blushed. 'Well he couldn't do much, because the churchwarden suddenly came round the corner walking his dog.

Gloria looked at the photograph again, and then incredulously at Imogen, who was so unsophisticated. How could a man like Nicky possibly fancy her? She felt slightly irritated too — *she*, Gloria, was the one who had the adventures, Imogen the one who listened in awed amazement. She wasn't too keen on such role reversal.

'When are you going to see him again?' she said, picking out a Catherine Cookson novel and putting it aside to be repaired.

'Well, he's playing in tournaments most of the summer, but he said it'd be soon and in a more secluded place this time,' said Imogen, fingering her red bracelet. She was disappointed that Gloria wasn't more enthusiastic. Then she added humbly, 'But just think, Gloria, if you hadn't gone to Morecambe,' she looked round nervously, 'I mean, been struck down by shellfish, you'd have come down to the Tennis Club with me, and it would have been you he'd have fallen for instead.'

She suddenly felt faint with horror at the thought.

'Don't talk so daft,' said Gloria, patting her curls and cheering up because, secretly she agreed with Imogen.

'Anyway he's promised to write to me,' sighed Imogen. 'Oh, Gloria, you've no idea how beautiful he is.'

In fact Nicky proved an extremely bad correspondent. He sent her one postcard from Rome saying he wished she were there. Imogen wrote back by return of post, a long passionate letter which took her hours to compose, pouring her heart out with the aid of the *Oxford Dictionary of Quotations*.

The Rome tournament ended, and Imogen glowed with pride as she read in the paper that Nicky had reached the quarter finals, and then only been knocked out after a terrific fight. Then he moved on to Paris, working his way steadily down the singles draw, and even reaching the semifinals of the men's doubles. Every paper commented on his improved game, but no letters arrived.

He'll ring you when he gets back to England,' said Juliet soothingly. But Imogen was in despair. It had all been a dream, probably her last letter had been too soppy and put him off. What right anyway had anyone as dull and fat as she to expect Nicky to fancy her?' She couldn't eat, she couldn't sleep, and mooned around in her room playing the gramophone and reading love poems. Nicky had turned out her heart as one might scrabble through an old chest of drawers throwing everything into confusion.

On the third Monday after their first meeting, Imogen walked to work in despair. There had been no letter on Saturday and, after an interminable 48 hours' wait, no letter this morning. She daren't ring up home to see if anything had arrived mid-morning in case she got her father yet again. She was on until eight this evening; she wondered how she'd ever get through the day. Her black gloom, if anything, was intensified by the beauty of the day. A slight breeze had set the new grass waving and catching the light; cow parsley frothed along the verges, white candles still lit the darkening chestnuts, and the hawthorns, exploding like rockets, gave off a soapy sexy smell in the warm sun. It was all so bridal, rioting and voluptuous. She was glad to reach the narrow streets of Pikely with their blackened houses and dingy mill chimneys, and escape into the cool gloom of the library.

She was met by Miss Nugent in a maroon dress and a foul temper.

'You're ten minutes late. There's two trolleys of books to be shelved. You didn't finish half those withdrawal forms on Saturday, and you sent the Mayor an overdue notice when he returned the books weeks ago. It's not good enough, you know. There are plenty of others who'd like your job.'

'Can't say I know any,' muttered Gloria, whisking up in yellow shorts and a tight chocolate brown sweater and dumping a pile of books on the trolley. 'The old bag's on the warpath this morning,' she whispered to Imogen. 'No one can do a thing right. Old Cornelius should have been back from his holiday, but he sent her a cable saying: "Stranded in Gib." I expect he's fallen for one of the monkeys. Did you get a letter?'

Imogen shook her head.

'That's a shame,' said Gloria, with all the enthusiasm of the secretly relieved. 'Don't fret, all men are lousy letter writers. I went to a terrific party on Saturday night. Tony Lightband was there; he really fancies you. He wants me to fix up a foursome.'

'That's nice,' said Imogen, failing to sound enthusiastic.

Tony Lightband was five foot three, wore spectacles thick as the bottom of beer bottles, and was inflated with his own importance.

'Clough's back from his hols, looks lovely and brown,' said Gloria.

'Will you girls stop gossiping?' snapped Miss Nugent, bustling out of the inside office. 'And turn off the lights, Imogen, or Mr Brighouse will be over in a flash complaining about his rates.'

The day got progressively worse. Imogen didn't seem to be able to do a thing right. Even the sky began to cloud over.

It was early afternoon. Imogen was on the request desk, answering queries, finding books for people. Miss Nugent had also given her the least favourite task in the library of chasing up unreturned books.

'Lady Jacintha's had the new Dick Francis six weeks,' she said, handing Imogen the list, 'and Brigadier Simmonds has still got the Slim biography, and you must get on to Mrs Heseltine at once. She's got twelve books out, including *The Wombles in Danger* and *Andy Pandy*. I want the whole lot dealt with today. Tick them off as you telephone.'

'Yes, Miss Nugent,' said Imogen listlessly.

Miss Nugent relented a little. The last thing she wanted was to bully Imogen into giving in her notice.

'I only keep on at you because I think you're worth taking trouble with,' she said, offering Imogen a Polo. 'There's no point bothering with Gloria. She'll just go off and get married. But you've got the makings of a good librarian. Have you thought any more about taking the library diploma? You'll miss it this year if you don't sign on soon. It's always a good idea to have a training if you can't bank on finding a hubby.'

Imogen knew Miss Nugent meant it kindly, but it only made her feel more depressed.

'How's it going?' said Gloria half an hour later.

'Awful,' said Imogen. 'Brigadier Simmonds would like to

438

court-martial me; Mrs Heseltine keeps pretending to be the Spanish *au pair* and not understanding, and Lady Jacintha's butler obviously has no intention of passing on the message.'

'Nugent always gives you the lousy jobs. Look, why don't we go to the pictures tomorrow night?'

This was a great concession, Imogen realised. Gloria didn't believe in wasting evenings on girlfriends.

'I can't. I've got to go to my first aid class,' she said gloomily.

'Don't say Nugent's pressganged you into that.'

Imogen nodded. 'We're doing the kiss of life tomorrow. I do hope Mr Blount doesn't use me as the model. Finish me off altogether.'

'I say,' said Gloria, lowering her voice, 'Judy Brighouse's just been in and taken out *Understanding Cystitis*. She only came back from her honeymoon last night. Bet they've been at it all the time. Oo, look, he's back.'

A good-looking man in a green velvet jacket came through the swing doors and up to the desk. 'I think I left Richard Strauss behind,' he said.

'You did,' said Gloria, giving him the book and the benefit of one of her hot stripping glances, which sent him crashing back against the doors, nearly falling over the fire bucket on the way.

'It says pull, not push,' said Gloria, smirking at the effect she'd had on him. 'Wish he'd try and pull me. He's lovely.'

'No good to you, lass,' said Mr Clough, on his way to a NALGO meeting. 'He's on his third marriage, and he's already got four children to support.' He turned to Imogen. 'Tell your Dad I've just got that gardening book in. If he'd like a quick look before we put it into circulation he can keep it until Wednesday.'

'There's something rather attractive about Cloughie,' said Gloria, shoving a couple of requested books into a side shelf. 'Here's just the thing for you, Imogen: *How to Stop Feeling Depressed and Inadequate*.'

'I *am* inadequate,' sighed Imogen..

'Oh come on,' said Gloria. 'Do cheer up. We don't want you dripping over everyone like a Chinese water torture all week.'

A man in dungarees came reeling up to the desk. 'Where can I find books on starting one's own business?' he said.

'Over there,' said Gloria, adding in an undertone, 'Absolutely reeked of drink, didn't he?'

'Expect he's just been fired,' said Imogen. 'Oh look, Mr Passmore's fallen asleep over the *Financial Times*.'

'No one's allowed to sleep in a library,' said Gloria. 'It's in the by-laws. Go and wake him up.'

'Telephone, Gloria,' said Miss Nugent, bustling up. 'Reader with a query. It's come through in my office. Can you go and man the issue desk, Imogen? Miss Hockney's gone to tea and there's a queue waiting.'

Gathering up her papers, Imogen went and sat down at the desk at the entrance of the library and began to check people's books in. Once she'd dealt with the queue she went back to her overdue list. Susan Bridges had kept *Colloquial German* and *Scaling the Matterhorn* out since February, when she met that Austrian ski instructor. She picked up the telephone and dialled Miss Bridges's number, but there was no answer — probably at work. She looked at the pile of cards in front of her. '*If you have returned the books in the last few days, please ignore this letter.*' The words blurred before her eyes. Outside the sky was darkening. Oh Nicky, Nicky, she thought desperately, will I ever see you again? She looked at the red bracelet on her wrist, tracing the pattern of the flowers with her finger, shivering at the memory of that day on the moor.

'Thus have I had thee, as a dream doth flatter,

In sleep a king, but, waking, no such matter,' she whispered sadly. Nicky was the black Rowntree's fruit gum everyone wanted. How ridiculous to think that he could ever have fancied her for more than a moment.

She was so deep in thought she didn't see a large bad-tempered woman in a trilby with a snarling boxer on a lead, until they'd come pounding through the door.

Imogen steeled herself for a fight.

'I'm terribly sorry, you can't bring dogs in here.'

'Where am I supposed to leave him?' snapped the woman.

'There are dog hooks provided outside the door. You could tie him to one of those.'

'He'd howl the place down and break his lead. It's not safe in this traffic. I've come all the way from Skipton. I'll only take five minutes.'

'I'm sorry,' said Imogen nervously. 'Shall I hold him for you?'

She advanced towards the dog, which bared its teeth and growled ominously. She backed away.

'Have your hand off,' said its owner. 'Now are you going to let me in, or do you want me to go over your head?'

Imogen had a lunatic vision of the woman and dog taking off and flying over her head through the room.

'I'm sorry. Dogs simply aren't allowed,' she repeated.

'I need the books for my work. I'll complain to the council. I've got fines on all these books.'

Imogen looked hopelessly round for help. Miss Nugent had disappeared, Gloria was on the telephone, Miss Hockney was surreptitiously making wedding lists on the request desk.

'If we allowed one dog in, we'd have to let the whole lot,' she said firmly.

'That's what's wrong with this country,' snapped the woman, straightening her trilby and storming through the doors. 'Bloody civil servant,' she shouted back at Imogen.

'I must not cry,' said Imogen, gritting her teeth. 'I must not drip like a Chinese water torture.'

'I say,' said Gloria, rushing up and patting her hair, 'that Richard Strauss man in the velvet jacket's just phoned up from a call box and asked me out. Goodness, what's up with you?'

'A woman with a boxer just called me a bloody civil servant.'

'Old cow, she's not allowed to swear in a library, it's in the by-laws too, and anyway we're not civil servants, we're local government officers.' She switched back to the Richard Strauss man. 'He didn't even know my name, just asked for the "glamorous one",' she said, squinting at her reflection in the glass door. 'Didn't think I was looking very good today either.

Imogen went wearily back to her overdue postcards, laboriously filling in the computer number of each book.

'I say,' breathed Gloria, 'get a load of him.'

'Don't bother me,' said Imogen. 'I've got to finish these beastly things. Anyway I'm not interested in men any more.'

'You'll be interested in this,' said Gloria faintly.

'No I won't ever again. My life is over,' said Imogen. Then a familiar husky voice said very softly:

'Have you got a book called "*Would the Assistant Like to Come out to Lunch*"?'

Imogen looked up and gave an unbelieving cry. For there, resplendent in a white suit and dark blue shirt, was Nicky. She gave a whimper and a gasp and, getting clumsily to her feet, ran round her desk and crashed into him, burying her face in his shoulder.

'I can't believe it,' she said, her voice thick with tears.

'Hey, hey,' said Nicky, lifting her chin with his finger, and smiling down at her. 'There's no need to cry, little one. I said I'd come back, didn't I?'

'I didn't think I'd ever see you again.'

'Didn't you get my postcard?'

'Yes, I did. It was lovely.'

Nicky shook his head. 'Oh ye of little faith,' he said gently and, well aware that there was now a gaping audience, including Miss Nugent, watching him, he bent his head and kissed her lingeringly.

'But what are you doing here?' said Imogen, wiping away her tears with the back of her hand, 'I thought you were in Edinburgh.'

'Got a walkover. Chap I'm playing pulled a muscle. Wants to rest it for Wimbledon. I don't have to play till tomorrow afternoon. Can I have a bed for the night, preferably yours?'

Imogen laughed joyfully, 'Of course you can. I'll ring Mummy. The only problem is the boys have been home for half term, so the place'll be in a bit of a shambles.'

Nicky was stroking her face now, tenderly smoothing away a smudge of mascara with his thumb. 'Can you get out for some lunch now?' he said softly.

Imogen eyed a disapproving and approaching Miss Nugent.

'Not really. I've already eaten and I'm on till eight. Oh, isn't it a drag?'

'Well, that works out quite well,' said Nicky. 'I'll go and have a work-out down at the club, and then I've got to do a short interview for Yorkshire Television. This afternoon seemed a good opportunity. I'll be through by eight. I'll come and pick you up and we'll go and have dinner somewhere.'

'But I'm not dressed for it,' wailed Imogen, conscious of her old grey sweater and jeans.

'You look beautiful,' said Nicky who only noticed how her grey eyes shone at the sight of him and how the stitches of the old sweater gaped over her bosom and how, with no make-up on, she looked about fourteen. 'You could never look anything else.'

There was a disapproving cough behind them. Nicky turned a dazzling smile on Miss Nugent.

'You must be Imogen's boss,' he said. 'I've heard so much about you.'

He was so lovely to everyone thought Imogen as she introduced him. Miss Nugent was now patting her crenellated curls, and simpering like a schoolgirl. Even Miss Hockney had put down her shopping list. Gloria was smouldering so hard she'd burst into flames any minute.

'Would you like a cup of tea?' she said.

Nicky shook his head. 'I must get down to the club.'

Outside the swing doors he kissed Imogen again.

'It's been a very long three weeks,' he said. 'I'm glad you're still wearing my bracelet.'

Funny, he thought, as he drove down the High Street, how pleased he was to see her. If Painter hadn't nagged him about not winning his bet, he doubted if he'd have bothered to look her up again. But now he had he was glad. He felt all the satisfaction of a dog with a number of bones buried round the garden, who suddenly unearths one unexpectedly and discovers it's matured much better than he had hoped.

He'd liked to have taken her straight up on to the moors and screwed her now, but he didn't particularly want to cover his new suit with grass stains before the interview. Anyway, there'd be plenty of time tonight, and it'd be more of a turn on pulling her under the old vicar's nose.

It was quite an achievement washing oneself from top to toe with gritty soap and a face towel in the Ladies at the library but Imogen managed it. She also nipped across the road and bought a new pair of black pants which cut into her. And now she was sitting in the Dog and Duck enveloped in a cloud of Gloria's *Babe* being eyed by Pikely locals, drinking champagne with Nicky and wondering if she'd ever been happier in her life.

'This is the first champagne I've had this year,' she said.

'Then you must wish,' said Nicky.

Imogen shut her eyes, and took a gulp. 'Oh please,' she wished silently, 'give me Nicky.'

Nicky laughed and kissed her cheek. 'You'll get me if you play your cards right,' he said.

'How did you know what I was wishing?'

'You're totally transparent. That's what I like about you.'

'Did you think Gloria was pretty,' said Imogen wistfully.

'Who's she?'

'The sexy one in yellow shorts who offered you a cup of tea.'

'Didn't notice her, but then I only have eyes for you.' He filled up her glass. As they worked their way down the bottle he told her about Rome and Paris, but she was so longing and longing to have his arms round her again, and yet panicking where it would all lead to, she could hardly concentrate.

'And what have you been up to?' he said, ordering another bottle.

'Nothing really.'

She told him about Juliet having to write out the 23rd Psalm ten times for saying bugger. But she didn't really think he'd be very interested in hearing about the second-hand book stall she had to organise for the church fête in aid of a new spire, and even spires seemed so phallic at the moment.

'How is your dear father? Still on the one day week?' said Nicky.

Imogen giggled and knew she shouldn't.

'Oh come on, darling, you know he's a pig.'

'Only to me,' said Imogen.

Nicky emptied the remains of the first bottle into her glass.

'Who's at home this evening?' he said carefully.

'No one,' said Imogen without thinking. 'Juliet's staying the night with a friend, and Mummy and Daddy are taking the boys back and stopping for dinner with the vicar of Long Preston.'

Nicky picked up the unopened bottle of champagne.

'Let's go then.'

Outside it was pouring with rain, street lamp reflections quivering in the cobbled streets. People huddled in the doorway of the fish shop. The smell of frying fat wafted towards them.

'Are you hungry?' asked Nicky.

'No,' said Imogen.

The powerful headlamps of his car lit up the cow parsley flattened by the deluge. The rain rattled against the windscreen. In the light from the dashboard she could see Nicky's profile.

'I went for that drop shot at the right moment,' he was saying. 'I was beginning to get the right length, and make friends with the ball again.'

A vast pile of unopened letters and cables were scattered on the back seat. 'Goodness, you get a lot of post,' said Imogen. 'It's last week's fan mail,' said Nicky.

As he swung up the moorland road leading to the vicarage, he put his hand on her thigh, caressing her through the thick stiff material. She lifted her legs slightly off the seat, hoping to make them seem thinner.

The house was dark and empty except for Homer who welcomed them ecstatically, charging off upstairs and, returning with a pair of old grey pants Imogen had been wearing yesterday, deposited them at Nicky's feet.

'Extraordinary pants,' said Nicky. 'Not yours, are they?'

'Goodness, no,' lied Imogen. 'They're probably jumble.'

'Look as though they belonged to your grandmother,' said Nicky. 'Go and get a couple of glasses, sweetheart.'

As Imogen threw the offending pants into the dustbin, she heard the champagne cork pop. She felt like a gas fire that had been left on unlit for too long — Nicky's touch would be like a lit match, making her explode in a great gushing blue flame, singeing everything around including Homer's eyebrows.

They sat drinking on the sofa. Nicky had turned off all the lights except one lamp in the corner. She was shaking with nerves again, quite unable to meet his eye.

'It's been awfully wet the last few weeks,' she said.

'It's been awfully dry abroad,' said Nicky, picking up the bottle.

'No,' squeaked Imogen putting her hand over her glass.

'Don't be silly,' said Nicky, so the champagne trickled through her fingers, and spilled icy cold down her sleeve, meeting the rivulets of sweat that were coming the other way. Desperate for something to do, she drained her glass and felt slightly dizzy.

'Let's get down to business,' said Nicky and took her in his arms. 'You like me, don't you?'

'Oh, yes,' she stammered, 'I haven't thought about anything else for a single minute since we met.'

She was achingly aware of him, his mouth over hers, his hands in her hair.

'Come on,' he whispered. 'Let's go upstairs, much more comfortable. We've got hours of time. Homer will bark if anyone comes.'

'Not at Daddy and Mummy, he won't.'

'They won't even have started dinner yet.'

Imogen gazed up at Nicky with huge troubled eyes,

'It'd kill my father.'

'Hooray,' said Nicky. 'I'll come and sell tickets at his funeral.'

Imogen tried and failed to look shocked. He put his hands round her waist. She came towards him, dissolving into him. He moved his hand under her sweater, and closed it over her breast.

Imogen started to struggle.

'It'd be so awful,' she muttered, 'if I got pregnant.'

'You're not fixed up?' he asked sharply. 'When are you due?'

Imogen swallowed. She'd never discussed things like this with a man. 'Tomorrow or the next day.'

'No problem,' said Nicky, relaxing, launching into the attack again. 'That's why your tits are so fantastic at the moment.'

She was glad to be able to hide her embarrassment in his shoulder. Now she felt his hand on her back. She'd never known anyone with such warm hands. Next moment he'd slipped it under her jeans, and was stroking her bottom.

'You must stop,' gasped Imogen as he pushed her back on the sofa, and removed her sweater. 'I've never done it with anybody before,' she said, emerging from the fluff.

'I'm not just anybody,' said Nicky. 'And you can't stop, sweetheart, any more than I can.' Oh, help, thought Imogen, what's happening to me. But next minute she froze with horror as the back door opened and Homer bounded out with a crash.

'Yoo hoo,' said a voice. 'Anyone at home ?'

'*Ker-ist*,' said Nicky, then with incredible presence of mind he seized Imogen's sweater, turned it rightway out and pulled it over her head.

'Keep cool,' he murmured, kicking her bra under the sofa and tucking in his shirt.

'We're in here,' he called.

'Hullo Nicky,' said her mother walking into the room carrying a large marrow. 'Hullo darling, what a beastly night. Isn't it a shame, poor Mrs Westley's got shingles? They tried to ring us but we'd already left. We didn't stop to dinner, and came straight home. They gave us this.' She waved the marrow. 'Daddy's putting the car away.'

'Well, have some champagne to cheer you up,' said Nicky.

Imogen rushed off to get more glasses, her heart hammering, feeling quite faint with horror. Just think if her father had found her and Nicky at it on the floor, in front of Homer too, she thought with an hysterical giggle. Thank God it was her mother who'd come in first.

As she went back into the drawing-room she heard her mother asking Nicky, 'Do you think there's any hope of Virginia Woolf winning Wimbledon?'

The rest of Nicky's visit was disastrous. They'd all gone to bed early and Nicky had whispered to Imogen on the stairs, '*Courage, ma brave*. As soon as all's quiet on the West Riding Front, I'll creep along to your room.'

But alas, the vicar, suffering from one of his periodic bouts of insomnia, had decided to sleep — or rather not sleep — in his dressing-room, which was equidistant between Imogen's room and the spare room. There he lay with the light on and the door ajar, pretending to read Donne's sermons, but actually brooding on former glories, a row of silver cups on the chest of drawers and framed pictures of muscular men with folded arms round the wall.

Imogen lay shivering with terror in bed. And every time Nicky tried to steal down the passage, the vicar, who had ears on elastic, called out, 'Is that you, my dear?' So Nicky had to bolt into the lavatory. By one o'clock, mindful that he might rot up his chances in the Scottish Open tomorrow, he gave up and fell into a dreamless sleep. Imogen, who didn't sleep at all, could hardly bear to look at his sulky face next morning.

'Well that was a lead balloon, wasn't it?' he said, getting into his car. Tears filled Imogen's eyes. This was obviously good-bye for good. Then, noticing the violet shadows under the brimming eyes, Nicky relented. It wasn't her fault. If the vicar hadn't come home unexpectedly, she'd have dropped like a ripe plum into his hands. 'You couldn't help it. I shall be much freer once the American Open's over. Would your parents ever let you come away for a weekend?'

Imogen shook her head. 'I doubt it.'

'Have you got any holiday left?'

'A fortnight in September.'

'Anything planned ?'

'No — nothing really.'

How few girls would have admitted it, thought Nicky, taking her hand. She was as transparent and as wholesome as Pears Soap.

'Well the only answer's to go on holiday together then.'

All heaven seemed to open. 'Oh, how lovely!' gasped Imogen. Then it closed again. 'But my father would never allow it.'

'H'm . . . we'll see about that.'

CHAPTER FOUR

A fortnight later, during Wimbledon week, Nicky had a drink with his friend Matthew O'Connor in Fleet Street. He had known O'Connor on and off for a number of years. They bumped into each other abroad — Nicky playing in tournaments, O'Connor covering stories — and they had got drunk together and been slung out of more foreign nightclubs than they cared to remember.

'Are you going to France this year?' said Nicky.

'In September. Why?'

'Any room in your car?'

The big Irishman looked at him shrewdly. 'Depends who you want to bring.'

Nicky grinned. 'Well, I met this bird in Yorkshire.'

'What's she like?'

'Got a pair of knockers you can get lost in.'

'What else?'

'Well she's adorable, like a puppy. You want to pick her up and cuddle her all the time. But terribly naïve. Dad's a vicar and a bloody tartar — like that Mr Barrett of Walpole Street.'

O'Connor grinned. 'And you see yourself as Robert Browning?'

'Well something of the sort. Anyway, I can't get within necking distance on home ground.'

'Green is she? So you fancy an away fixture?'

'An away fixture is what I fancy.'

O'Connor ordered another round of drinks.

'I've always believed,' he said, 'that if a bird's worth doing, she's worth doing well. But a fortnight's a hell of a long time. Don't you think you better take her away for a week-

450

end first?'

'I've got tournaments every week-end for the next two months. Besides I doubt if the old vicar would let her.'

'Well, he's not likely to let her go on holiday, is he?'

'He might. I can say we're going in a large party. Parents seem to have some totally mistaken idea that there's safety in numbers.'

'Will she fight with Cable?' asked O'Connor.

'You've never allowed me to meet Cable.'

'No more I haven't. Come and have a drink with us this evening.

The next day Nicky wrote to Imogen's parents. He was planning to go to France for a fortnight in September with a couple of friends who were engaged, and there would also be another married couple in the party taking their own car. He'd thought Imogen was looking tired last time he'd stayed. She needed a holiday. Could she join their party?

To Imogen's joy and amazement her parents agreed. Even her mother had noticed how down she was, and her father, who was looking forward to his three weeks exchange stint in the North Riding in September (the golf course was excellent there), had no desire to have his elder daughter slopping around with a February face spoiling the fun.

'I'll never, never be unhappy again,' vowed Imogen. She dialled Nicky's number in London to give him the good news.

All the same, it was a very trying summer. Wimbledon fortnight came, and Imogen and Gloria spent most of it with the transistor on or with a pair of binoculars surreptitiously trained on the television in the Radio Rentals shop opposite the library. Nicky was in coruscating form, reaching the last eight of the singles and only being knocked out after a marathon match, and the semi-finals of the doubles with Charlie Painter. Everyone commented on his improved game. And whenever he appeared on the television screen, clothed in white tennis clothes, mystic, wonderful, whether he was uncoiling like a whiplash when serving or jumping from foot to foot as though the court were red hot beneath his feet, waiting to whistle back a shot, he seemed a god infinitely beyond Imogen's reach.

She had also seen him in the players' stand, laughing with some of the more beautiful wives. Nor could she miss the way the tennis groupies (pert little girls with snake hips and avid eyes) made every match he played a one-sided affair by screaming with joy whenever he did a good shot, even cheering his opponent's double faults, and mobbing him every time he came off court. Could this really be the man who'd eaten her mother's macaroni cheese and wrestled with her on the sofa?

After Wimbledon he moved on to ritzy places all over the world and Imogen found that a diet of almost illiterate postcards and occasional crackling telephone calls were not really enough to sustain her. Oh ye of little faith, she kept telling herself sternly, but found herself increasingly suffering from moodiness and then feeling desperately ashamed of herself.

Even worse, everyone at work, having glimpsed Nicky and learnt they were going on holiday together, had turned the affair into a sort of office *Crossroads*. Not a day passed without someone asking her if she'd heard from him, or how long was it until her holiday, or how was he getting on in Indianapolis. Gloria's attitude was ambiguous too. On the one hand she liked to boast, when out, of how her greatest friend Imogen was going out with a tennis star, and let slip crumbs of tennis gossip passed on by Imogen. But on the other she was wildly jealous, particularly when the word got round and several of the local wolves started coming into the library asking Imogen for dates.

'They ought to provide wolf hooks as well as dog hooks outside,' Gloria said, with a slight edge to her voice. 'Then they wouldn't be able to come in here pestering you.'

Stung by Gloria's sniping (You shouldn't put all your eggs in one basket. I bet Nicky's playing round with all those foreign birds), Imogen gritted her teeth and went out with one or two of the wolves. But when the evening ended,

452

remembering Nicky's beautiful curling mouth, and the caressing deftness of his touch, she couldn't even bear to let them kiss her; then felt mean when they stormed off into the night.

Finally, the weather had been terrible. Throughout July, August and early September, it deluged without stopping. The River Darrow flooded the water meadows and the tennis courts, and endangered the lives of several flocks of sheep. Imogen's hair crinkled depressingly, and she had absolutely no chance to brown her pallid body before her holiday. And the vicar, whose garden and golf had been almost washed away, was in a permanently foul mood and vented most of his rage on Imogen.

At last September arrived. By scrimping every penny, she'd managed to save a hundred pounds. Nicky had told her not to worry about money, that he'd take care of everything, but she knew France was terribly expensive, and she wanted to pay her way. As most of her wages went towards the housekeeping, it didn't leave much for her wardrobe.

'What am I going to do about beach clothes?' she said.

'You won't need much in a small fishing village,' said her mother. 'Which reminds me, Lady Jacintha sent a lovely red bathing dress for jumble. Red's in this year, isn't it? It's perfect, except for a bit of moth in the seat.'

The jumble was also deprived of two of Lady Jacintha's wide-bottomed cotton trousers, which didn't really fit, but Imogen thought she could pull long sweaters over them. Her mother bought her two kaftans in a sale in Leeds.

'This phrase book isn't much good,' said Juliet, lounging on Imogen's bed the night before she left. " 'My coachman has been struck by lightning." "Please ask the chambermaid to bring some more candles." I ask you!'

Imogen wasn't listening. She was trying on Lady J's red bathing dress for the hundredth time and wondering if it would do.

'My legs are like the bottom half of a twinset and pearls,' she sighed.

JILLY COOPER

'You ought to get a bikini. Bet it's topless down there,' said Juliet. 'I think Mummy and Daddy are so funny.'

'Why?' said Imogen, folding up a dress.

'Thinking you'll be safe because you've got a married couple in the party to chaperone you. Ha! Ha! To egg you on more likely. I hope you're on the pill!'

'What on earth do you mean?' snapped Imogen.

'Well, you won't be able to hold off a man like Nicky once he gets you in France.'

'Don't be ridiculous,' said Imogen, storming out of the room.

But it was all too near the knuckle. Nicky's last letter — the only one he hadn't written on a postcard — had ended *. . . and, darling, for goodness sake go and get yourself fitted up. We don't want to spoil the whole fortnight worrying about you getting pregnant.*

Time and again during the past month Imogen had walked up and down in front of Dr Meadows' surgery, and each time she had funked it. Dr Meadows was one of her father's oldest friends and well over sixty. How *could* she ask him?

In the end, once more egged on by Gloria, she had gone to a family planning clinic in Leeds on the pretext of looking for holiday clothes. Unfortunately her two brothers, Michael and Sam, still home for the holidays, had insisted on coming with her, in the hope of catching a Gillette Cup match at Headingley. But this, predictably, had been rained off, and Imogen had great difficulty shaking them off, even for a couple of hours.

'I've got to buy lots of boring things like underwear,' she said.

'We'll come too,' said Sam, who at fourteen had only recently become interested in girls. 'We might be able to see into some of the changing rooms.'

'I don't like people hanging round when I'm buying clothes,' said Imogen quickly. 'It muddles me. Look, here's a fiver. Why don't you go and see the new James Bond? I'll meet you at the barrier at five o'clock,' and, blushing violently, she charged through the glass doors of Brown and

454

Muff. Rushing straight through and out the other side, she set off at a trot towards the clinic.

'Where's old Imo really going?' said Sam, as they shuffled off to the cinema

'F.P.A.,' said Michael, who was concentrating on lighting a cigarette in the rain.

'Blimey, is she pregnant?'

'Course not, just getting fixed up before her holiday.'

'How d'you know?'

'Left the address lying around in her bedroom.' He began to cough. The cigarette went out.

'Hope to Christ Dad doesn't find it,' said Sam. 'Fancy old Imo getting round to sex at last.'

'Just as well she's taking precautions. They're randy buggers these tennis players, even worse than rugger players.' Michael's cigarette, sodden now, obstinately refused to be lit. 'I hope she'll be all right, won't get hurt I mean,' he went on, throwing it into the gutter.

'Do her good to grow up,' said Sam, who was staring at a couple of giggling typists who, under one umbrella, were teetering by on high heels, heading towards the pub. 'I say, shall we skip James Bond and go and have a drink instead?'

'They'd never serve us.'

'It's pretty dark in there; you'd pass for eighteen anywhere. Fancy old Imo going on the pill.'

'Buy anything good?' said Sam innocently, as Imogen came rushing up to the barrier with only a few minutes to spare.

'I'd forgotten the sales were on. There's nothing nice in the shops,' stammered Imogen, failing to meet either of her brothers' eyes.

'Got your ticket?' said Michael, waving his. 'We'd better step on it; they're closing the doors.'

'Oh goodness,' said Imogen, 'I've got it somewhere.'

And, as she was nervously rummaging, her shaking hands slipped, and the entire contents of her bag, including 6 months supply of the pill crashed on to the platform.

'I wonder if scarlet women are called scarlet because they

blush so much,' said Sam, bending down to help Imogen pick everything up.

And now on the eve of her holiday, the mauve packets of the pill were safely tucked into the pocket of her old school coat hanging at the back of her wardrobe. She'd been taking it for eight days now, and she felt sick all the time, but she wasn't sure if it was side effects or nervousness at the thought of seeing Nicky. It was such ages since their last meeting she felt she'd almost burnt herself out with longing. Then she was worried about the sex side. She'd been taking surreptitious glances at *The Joy of Sex* when the library was quiet, and the whole thing seemed terribly complicated. Did one have to stop talking during the performance like a tennis match, and wouldn't Nicky, accustomed to lithe, beautiful, female tennis players, find her much too fat?

She put her hot forehead against the bathroom window. In the garden she could see her father talking to the cat and staking some yellow dahlias beaten down by the rain and wind.

'That's what I need,' she thought wistfully. 'I'll never blossom properly in life unless I'm tied to a strong sturdy stake.'

She wondered if Nicky was really stake material. Her father was coming in now. He looked tired. He'd been closeted with members of his flock all afternoon.

She went back to her room and found Homer dispiritedly pulling her underwear out of her suitcase. He hated people going away. 'I'll be back soon,' she said, hugging him.

She also packed a pile of big paperbacks she'd never got round to reading, *Daniel Deronda*, *Lark Rise To Candleford*, Scott Fitzgerald and *Tristram Shandy*. On the bed lay a box of tissues (they don't have the kind of loo paper you can take your make up off with in France, Miss Hockney had told her), a cellophane bag of cotton wool balls and a matching set of Goya's *Passport* she had won in the church fête raffle. They didn't look very inspiring as beauty aids. She imagined Nicky's other girlfriends with the whole of Helena

Rubinstein at their disposal.

There was a knock on the door. It was her mother.

'Hullo darling, how are you getting on? Daddy wants a quick word before he goes down to the jumble sale pricing committee.'

As she went into the vicar's study, Imogen started to shake. He was sitting behind his huge desk, lighting his pipe, a few raindrops still gleaming on his thick grey hair. All round him the shelves were filled with Greek and theological books, which the vicar never looked at, and gardening and sporting works which were much more heavily thumbed. On one ledge were neatly stacked volumes of the *Church Times* and the parish magazine. On the wall the vicar allowed himself one modest photograph of himself surrounded by the England team. On the desk was a large inkwell. He despised Biros.

Now he was looking at her over his spectacles. Was his jaundiced air due to the fact she'd been wearing the same skirt and sweater all week to save her best clothes for France, or was he remembering all the countless times he'd called her in to lecture her about inglorious reports, or misbehaviour at home?

'Sit down,' he said. 'Are you looking forward to your holiday?'

'Yes,' said Imogen.

'Wish I'd been lucky enough to gallivant off to the sun when I was your age,' he went on heavily, 'but times were harder then.'

Oh God, thought Imogen, he's not going to start on that one.

But instead her father got to his feet and began to pace the room. 'I don't think your mother and I have ever been oppressive parents — we've always tried to guide you by example rather than coercion.' He gave her the chilly on-off smile he used for keeping his parishioners at a distance. His flock-off smile Michael and Juliet always called it.

'But I can't let you depart without a few words of advice. You are going to a foreign country — where there will be temptations. I trust you follow me, Imogen.'

'Yes,' she whispered.

'We are letting you go because we trust you. We know Nicky is an attractive young man, and a celebrity, used to getting his own way in life, but we still trust you.'

He stopped by the window, absent-mindedly stripping yellow leaves off a geranium on the ledge, testing its earth for sufficient moisture.

'It's been a trying afternoon,' he went on. 'Molly Bates and her daughter Jennifer were here for over an hour. Poor Molly. Jennifer suddenly revealed she was three months pregnant and the young man concerned has disappeared. Of course every attempt will be made to trace him and persuade him to marry the girl, but if not, she will spend the next months in an unmarried mothers' home — not the most attractive of dwelling places — but Molly Bates feels, as a member of the Parochial Church Council, that Jennifer cannot have the child at home. Whatever the outcome, the girl's life is ruined. She is second-hand goods now.'

Poor Jennifer, thought Imogen, perhaps she'll be sent off to the jumble sale.

'When you're in the South of France,' said her father, 'remember the fate of poor Jennifer Bates and remember you're a clergyman's daughter, and they, like Caesar's wife, must be above suspicion.'

Imogen had a momentary fantasy that the packets of purple pills must at this moment be burning a hole in her old coat pocket, that her father's outrage was like the sun on glass. Fortunately he construed her crimson face as embarrassment at the topic of conversation rather than guilt.

He sat down and moved the inkwell on the desk. 'Remember the words of Milton,' he said in sepulchral tones, 'She that has chastity is clad in complete steel.'

Imogen suddenly had a vision of herself clanking around the beach in the South of France in a steel suit of armour. Her father, she decided, must have been very much like Milton. She also suspected that he was rehearsing his sermon for next Sunday. She had a horrible feeling that he was going to make her kneel down and pray over her.

'You are entering the school of life,' he said, dropping his voice dramatically. 'All I can do is pray for you night and day. Now go back to your packing and have a wonderful holiday in the sun. I must away to the jumble pricing committee.'

The contrast between her gadding, sybaritic existence and his modest, selfless toil was only too obvious. Imogen went out of the room, closing the door quietly behind her. She went upstairs feeling hopelessly depressed. Her father had brilliantly succeeded in taking all the excitement out of her holiday. Sex with Nicky would be even more of a moral battlefield than ever. Whatever she did, bed or not, her father would be standing at the bottom of her bed in spirit, shaking his finger at her.

Oh hell, it was time to have the pill, lying in its little capsule like one of the lights round an actress's mirror. She felt like Persephone about to take her pomegranate seed and be condemned to an eternity in Hades.

She shut her bedroom door and started groping through her half-empty wardrobe to find the thickness of her old tweed coat at the back. She couldn't find it. She pushed aside the rest of the clothes; it wasn't there, not even slid off its hanger on to the floor. She burrowed frantically through the landing cupboard, then ran downstairs. Her mother was peeling potatoes and reading a novel at the same time.

'My old school coat, it's gone,' gasped Imogen.

'Surely you're not taking that to France?' said her mother.

'No, but where is it?'

'I gave it to the jumble, darling. As we'd taken out Lady Jacintha's bathing dress and those trousers I thought it was the least we could do.'

But Imogen had gone, out of the house like a rocket, belting down the garden path, slipping on the wet pavement, tearing along the moorland path, bracken slapping against her stockings, twigs scratching her face.

The coat had her name in it, the pocket contained the pills and Nicky's last letter, the one about getting fitted up and telling her most explicitly all the delicious things he was going to do to her when he got her to France. Visions of what her father would do swept over her. He'd stop her going. Suddenly the thought of not seeing Nicky again filled her with such horror she thought she'd faint. Her breath was coming in great sobs.

There was the church hall, light, laced with raindrops, streaming from its uncurtained windows. Inside Imogen found scenes of tremendous activity and was nearly knocked sideways by the smell of moth balls, dust and none too clean clothes. Ladies of the parish in felt hats stood round laden trestle tables, rooting through other people's cast-offs, searching for possible bargains, subtly pricing down garments they pretended they didn't know had been sent in by fellow sorters.

'I don't think she's even bothered to launder these corsets,' said the butcher's wife, dropping them disdainfully into the nearest bin. 'And this hostess gown is quite rotted under the armpits.'

'Lady Jacintha has sent in a fox fur without any tail,' said the local midwife. 'Rats, rats,' she added, waving it at the caretaker's cat, who, giving her a wide berth, leapt on to a pile of old books and records.

'Hullo, Imogen love,' said the butcher's wife. 'Come to lend a hand? I thought you were off on your holidays to-morrow.'

'I am,' said Imogen, frantically searching round for the piles of coats.

'If you're looking for your Dad, he's over there.'

Imogen peered through the dusty gloom and froze with horror. In the far corner, in front of a long freckled mirror, Miss Jarrold from the Post Office was trying on Imogen's school coat, which came down to her ankles, and being encouraged on either side by Mrs Connolly, her mother's daily woman, and the vicar.

'There's still some wear in it,' Miss Jarrold was saying. 'I could get my sister from Malham to turn it up.'

'Oh very becoming, Miss Jarrold,' the vicar was saying jovially. He had his hearty 'flock-off' smile on again.

'Not sure about the colour, Elsie,' said Mrs Connolly. 'It

never did anything for Miss Imogen either.'

'I'm only going to use it for gardening and walks, seems a bargain for 50p,' said Miss Jarrold, and turning back to the mirror, she adopted a model girl's stance shoving her hands into the pockets. 'Oh look, there's something inside.'

Imogen was across the room in a flash, just as Miss Jarrold pulled the purple packets and Nicky's letter out of the pockets.

'What ever's all this?' she went on.

'They're mine,' said Imogen, snatching them from her.

Miss Jarrold was so startled she stepped back with a resounding crack on some 78s of the Mikado.

'Imogen,' thundered the vicar, 'where are your manners, and what have you got there?'

'Nothing,' she muttered, going as red as a GPO van.

'Love letters and photos,' said Mrs Connolly calmly, who disliked the vicar intensely, and had seen exactly what was inside the pocket. 'No girl likes to lose those, do they, love? Oh look, there's Lady Harris at the door. I expect she wants to discuss the refreshments with you, vicar.'

'Ah, yes, indeed. Welcome, welcome,' said Mr Brocklehurst in a ringing voice, finishing off the Mikado altogether as he went towards the door.

For a minute Imogen and Mrs Connolly looked at each other.

'Thanks,' stammered Imogen. 'That was terribly kind.'

'Better to be safe than sorry,' said Mrs Connolly. 'My Connie's been on them things for years. I'd beat it if I were you, before your Dad has second thoughts. Have a nice time. 'Spect you'll come back brown as a little nigger.'

'Seems in a hurry,' said Miss Jarrold innocently. 'Is she courting?'

'Happen she is,' said Mrs Connolly, who knew perfectly well Miss Jarrold read all the cards that came through the Post Office. 'She hasn't told me owt about it at any rate.'

The last few hours were a torment, but at last Imogen was on the train to London, her small suitcase on the rack. Her mother, Juliet and Homer, drooping and looking gloomy, stood on the platform. Suddenly Imogen felt a great lump in her throat. 'I'm sorry I've been so awful and boring the last few weeks. I'll make it up to you, really I will,' she said, leaning out of the window. 'I wish you were coming too.'

'We'll all miss you,' said her mother.

'Don't forget to send me a card,' said Juliet.

'Be careful about drinking the water,' said her mother.

'Remember chastity begins and *ends* at home,' said Juliet. 'Here's something to read on the train,' handing her a parcel as the train drew out. In it were copies of the *Kama Sutra* and *The Sun is my Undoing*.

Gradually the dark stone walls, the mill chimneys, the black-grimed houses, the rows of washing and dirty white hens in the garden wer left behind. She was on her way.

CHAPTER FIVE

An hour and a half from London she started doing her face. Half an hour away she decided she looked awful and took all her make-up off and put it on again. The new, very cheap dress, ivy green with a white collar, which had looked so pretty when she'd tried it on in the shop, was now crumpled like an old dishcloth. Her new tights were making spiral staircases round her ankles. The train drew into King's Cross. Imogen was one of the first off, pushing her way through the crowd, radiant smile at the ready like a British Railways' Ad. She had lived this moment so often in her mind. People rushed forward to kiss people and gather up their suitcases. No one came forward to claim her. The kissers dispersed and still no Nicky. She was sure she'd told him she was arriving on the eight-thirty train.

The station clock jerked agonisingly round to nine-ten. Two drunken sailors lurched up to her and lurched away when they saw the frozen expression on her face. She struggled not to cry.

Then, like an Angel of Mercy, loping across the station, in the same white suit and an orange shirt, came Nicky. 'Darling, sweet love! God, I'm sorry. What can I say? There's the most God-awful traffic jam in Piccadilly. Are you all right? Has half London been trying to pick you up?'

'Oh,' said Imogen, half-laughing, half-crying, 'I'm so, so pleased to see you.'

As he kissed her, he smelt of drink and, she thought, of scent. Perhaps it was her own scent, new yesterday, which she wasn't yet used to.

'Come on,' he said, picking up her suitcase.

In the taxi he took her hand. Imogen was too besotted to

JILLY COOPER

realise the roads were quite clear.

'We're going straight to Matt and Cable's, the people we're going to France with. You'll like them. He's a lunatic Irish journalist and she's a model.'

'A model?' Imogen tugged surreptitiously at her wrinkled stockings. She hoped she wasn't too glamorous. Then she remembered with relief, 'Oh, but they're the engaged couple.'

'Well, not engaged exactly, just co-habiting. But I had to bend the facts a bit to reassure your father.'

They arrived at a huge block of flats. Imogen was disappointed Nicky didn't kiss her. There would have been plenty of time as the lift climbed to the tenth floor. Instead he smoothed his hair in the lift mirror. There was no answer when he rang the door bell, so he pushed open the door and shouted, 'Anyone at home?'

Footsteps came from the back of the flat, a waft of scent flooded the hall. 'Darlings! You've arrived,' said a girl in a light drawling voice. 'How are you?'

Her red dress was slit to the thighs. Her lips were as crimson as her painted toe nails, which peeped out of high black sandals. She had delicate cat-like features, sly, slanting eyes the colour of watercress and carefully tousled inky-black hair snaking down her back. Except for her suntan she might have stepped out of a Beardsley drawing. There was something serpentine, too, in the way she coiled herself round Nicky, kissing him on the cheek and murmuring:

'Darling, marvellous to see you.'

'Imogen, this is Cable,' he said, disengaging himself too slowly for Imogen's liking. The girl stared at Imogen incredulously for a minute and then a slow smile spread over her face. 'Welcome to London,' she said. 'Did you have a good journey? I've been packing since dawn and I'm completely exhausted. Where's your luggage?'

Nicky held up Imogen's dog-eared suitcase.

'Heavens,' said Cable. 'Is that all? Matt will adore you. I've filled three suitcases already and he's griping about my taking a fourth. Come and have a drink.'

'Can I go to the loo?' said Imogen, who didn't want to, but

464

was desperate to repair her face before Nicky could compare her any more with this ravishing creature.

'Down the passage on the left,' said Cable. 'We'll be in here. Do you think five bikinis will be enough, Nicky?'

What price Lady J's motheaten red bathing dress now? thought Imogen savagely as she combed the tangles out of her hair. Her face was all eyes in a for-once pale face. She pinched some of Cable's rouge, but it made her look like a clown so she rubbed it off again.

She found Nicky and Cable in a room where everything seemed scarlet — carpet, curtains, and every inch of wall that wasn't covered by books and pictures. Even the piano was painted red, and in one corner stood a huge stuffed bear wearing a scarlet regimental jacket.

'Oh, what a heavenly room,' sighed Imogen.

Cable looked at her with surprise. 'Do you think so? Matt's taste — not mine. He'd been here a year when I moved in, so the damage was done. It's hell to keep tidy,' she added, pointing to the papers billowing out of the desk, and the piles of books and magazines on every available surface.

In one chair sprawled a basset hound who thumped his tail but made no effort to get up, and on the sofa, snoring gently, lay a very big, very long man.

'He was playing poker all night,' said Cable sourly. 'He's been lying there since he came in at half-past eleven this morning.' She kicked him, none too gently, in the ribs. 'Come on, Sloblomov, wake up.'

The man groaned and pulled a cushion over his face.

'He even sleeps standing up,' said Cable. 'I've seen him at parties propped on one leg like a horse, patiently waiting to be led home to his stable.'

The man removed the cushion and opened a bloodshot eye. 'Stop beefing for God's sake. I'm on my holiday. I'm entitled to kip if I want to.'

'Not when we've got company,' said Cable.

He opened the other eye. 'Hullo, kids,' he said, and yawned without bothering to put his hand over his mouth.

Imogen was astounded that such a beautiful girl should go for such an ugly man. He had battered features, a very sallow skin, dark heavy-lidded eyes that turned down at the corners, and a streaky blond mane, much in need of a cut. He got up and shook himself like a dog. Beside Nicky's gleaming beauty he looked thoroughly seedy. She also had a vague feeling she'd seen him before.

'How are you, Nicky boy?' he said.

'He needs a drink,' said Cable. 'We all do.'

'Well, run along and get me some Alka Seltzer.'

'You do look a bit rough,' said Nicky. 'Did you make a killing last night?'

Matt drew a large wad of notes out of his hip pocket.

'It'll buy us a few snails,' he said.

Nicky grinned. 'I'll go and help Cable with the ice.'

'Bring the evening paper with you,' Matt shouted after him. 'I want to see what won the three-thirty.'

He turned to Imogen, looked her over lazily and gave her a surprisingly attractive smile. 'Just come from Leeds, and covered in coal-dust are you? I went there once, a terrible dirty place it was. I thought I'd been misrouted to Hell.'

Imogen giggled. 'The part where we live is very pretty. I like your flat.'

'Come and look at the view.' He went over to the window and drew back the curtains. All London glittered before them.

'There's Big Ben, Westminster Abbey, the Shell Building. On a clear day you can see Margaret Thatcher.' He had a nice voice, too, thought Imogen, leisurely, with a faint trace of Irish. Perhaps he wasn't so ugly after all — just different looking from other people. She was still trying to work out where she'd seen him before.

'Now, what are you drinking, beauty? Whisky, gin, anything you like.'

'Oh, whisky, please, with masses of water.' She sat on the arm of the dog's chair and stroked his ears. 'What's his name?'

'Basil. Never get a basset hound; they rule your life.'

'You can say that again,' said Cable, coming in with Nicky and the ice tray. 'There's a ton of rump steak for him in the fridge while we're away.'

466

'It's not his stomach that bothers me,' said Matt, dropping five Alka Seltzers into a glass of water and watching them fizz, 'it's his soul. I think I'll get Father O'Malley to visit him while we're away. Did my proofs arrive?' he added to Cable.

'About an hour ago. They're over there on the table. They said you could telephone any corrections through tonight.'

Matt half-emptied his glass and grimaced. Then he picked up some long narrow sheets of newsprint from the table and began to examine them.

'Who've you taken apart this week?' said Nicky.

'The medical profession,' said Matt, 'and they're not going to like it.' He picked up a biro, added one word and crossed a couple out.

Suddenly Imogen twigged. 'You're not *the* Matthew O'Connor?'

Matt looked up. 'I'm not entirely sure today.'

'But you're marvellous,' stammered Imogen. 'I loved your book on Parnell. There's still a waiting list at the library. And I always read your pieces in the paper. We all do — even my father thinks you're funny.'

'And that really is saying something,' said Nicky. 'Not given much to giggling is our vicar.'

'Well, that is nice,' said Cable with a slight edge to her voice. 'You've got a fan at last, Matt. Aren't you lucky?'

'Very,' said Matt, seeing Imogen flush and giving her a reassuring smile. 'It's manna to my ears, darling.'

'I suppose you two'll be rabbitting on about Proust all the way to Provence,' said Cable.

'It'd make a nice change,' said Matt.

Imogen couldn't believe it. Nicky and Matthew O'Connor in the same party as her. Any moment she expected Jackie Kennedy or Mick Jagger to pop out of the grandfather clock.

'What time do we leave tomorrow?' asked Nicky.

'The boat sails at eleven. We ought to leave the house by eight,' said Matt.

For a while they discussed arrangements; then Imogen's stomach gave a great rumble and Nicky said that he was hungry.

'I could cook something,' said Cable, as though it were a rare occurrence.

'I'm not having you slaving over a hot tin opener all night,' said Matt, who had picked up the evening paper. He gave an exclamation of pleasure.

'The little darling — she won by three lengths, romped all the way home like a child off to a party. Come on, my angels, on the strength of that, I'll buy you all dinner.'

They piled into a large, incredibly dirty, white Mercedes.

'You might have had it cleaned before we left,' grumbled Cable. Imogen found she was sitting on a bridle. They ate in a little Italian restaurant and drank a good deal of wine. Nicky talked about his tennis exploits, grumbling how political the game was getting these days. Matt asked the questions; he had a journalist's ability to get an incredible amount of information out of people without their realising it. Every place Nicky had played at, Cable seemed to have been there too, filming or modelling, which produced the inevitable questions about 'Did you meet the so-and-so's?' and 'Have they split up yet?'

Imogen didn't say much; she was too busy taking it all in. But there was a bad moment when Nicky suddenly put his hand on her thigh and she jumped so much that her fork fell on to the floor, taking most of her spaghetti with it. Nicky was insane with irritation, but Matt just laughed and ordered her some more. He was very funny throughout dinner and Imogen found herself liking him more and more.

Cable she was less sure of — sitting there picking at her food, examining her reflection in her spoon, looking at Nicky with those sly green eyes.

'Sophia Loren was in here last week,' she said, 'just sitting over there, wearing the most incredible plunging neckline.'

'I went to the Gents fifteen times during dinner, just so I could look down it,' said Matt. 'I'll get the bill,' he said, seeing Imogen was nearly falling off her chair with exhaustion.

'It's only midnight,' said Cable. 'Can't we have some brandy?'

'Some of us who do a decent week's work get tired on Friday.'

468

'I work,' snapped Cable. 'I went to two cattle markets yesterday.'

'Any good?' asked Nicky.

'Second one might be. They're launching a new chewing gum. The bread's terrific. My agent's going to ring me in France and let me know.'

Matt handed the waiter what seemed an inordinate number of notes. 'A cattle market is a model's audition,' he explained to Imogen. 'Very appropriate, too, when you see some of the cows that turn up. Come on, let's go.'

There was another bad moment when they got back to the flat. Cable had opened the door of one of the bedrooms, and said, 'You and Nicky are in here.'

Oh, my goodness, thought Imogen, her mind racing like a weasel in a trap. Did Matt see her expression of dismay? Five minutes before he had been yawning his head off; now he suddenly asked Nicky and Cable if they wanted a nightcap.

'I wouldn't mind,' said Nicky. He ruffled Imogen's hair. 'Go to bed, love. I'll be with you in a minute.'

But an hour and a bottle of brandy later, when he went to bed, he found Imogen fast asleep with the light on, *Tristram Shandy* still open on the pillow and Basil sprawled beside her.

'Bloody dog,' he said, trying to push Basil off. The dog gave an ominous growl.

'Foiled again,' said Matt sympathetically. 'You'll never shift him now he's pitted down for the night. I'll give you an eiderdown and you can kip on the sofa.'

CHAPTER SIX

A gale was lashing the rain against the windows when they woke next morning. Nicky was moaning about his hangover and the rotten night he'd spent. Matt and Cable were having a row.

'Next time you shave your legs with my razor for God's sake wash it out. Now for the fourth time, may I take the cases down to the car?'

'I'm not ready,' snapped Cable, putting on a second layer of mascara.

'Look, baby, it's ten past eight. I'm leaving in five minutes, with or without you!'

'Oh, don't go on,' said Cable, her voice rising. 'Have you hidden my jewellery?'

'Yes — in the window box.'

'Well, take these three cases down — at least it'll give you something to do.'

The front door slammed.

'Nick!' called Cable.

'Yes, love?'

'I can't shut my suitcase.'

Imogen, who had been sitting about feeling spare for the last half hour, wandered along to Cable's bedroom to see if she could help.

Nicky and Cable, who was wearing the most ravishing pink suede suit, were sitting side by side on the suitcase.

'That's it,' said Nicky, leaning across Cable and clicking the second flap down.

Imogen froze in the doorway as she saw Cable put her hand over Nicky's. Nicky looked up at Cable and smiled. 'You'd better lock it,' he said slowly. 'I wouldn't like you to

470

lose anything valuable — to anyone else!'

'I'm so glad you're coming with us,' purred Cable. 'It makes everything so much more — well — exciting.'

Imogen didn't know which of them jumped the most when Matt's voice behind her said, 'A quick worker, isn't she? She'll have you tied in knots if you're not careful, Nicky.'

For a minute Cable glared at Matt, and then, to Imogen's amazement, she burst out laughing.

'Darling Sloblomov,' she said, wrinkling her nose at him. 'You don't let me get away with a thing, do you?'

In that pink suit, thought Imogen wistfully, she was so lovely she could get away with murder. Matt grinned reluctantly, picked up the long khaki scarf that was lying on the bed and wound it round Cable's neck, pulling it tight and pretending to throttle her. 'So sweet were ne'er so fatal,' he said. 'Come on, Circe, let's go.'

'Bloody English weather,' grumbled Nicky.

'At least it might wash the car,' said Matt.

They had only been driving ten minutes when Cable gave a shriek.

'My night cream. It's still in the fridge!'

'Well, I expect Basil will be having it on his strawberries,' said Matt calmly.

'Don't be bloody silly,' snapped Cable. 'We must go back.'

'Look, baby, you've kept us hanging about for twenty minutes already.'

'But my skin will dry up.'

'Why don't you dry up?'

Imogen gazed in trepidation at Cable's rigid profile. Was Nicky really keen on her, or just flattered by her attentions? As if in answer Nicky put an arm round Imogen's shoulders. 'All right, sweetheart? Excited?'

When he looked at her like that, she was incapable of answering. She just nodded and snuggled against him.

'Who are the couple we're joining at Dover?' he asked Matt.

'Cable's chums,' said Matt. 'I disclaim all responsibility.'

'Very funny,' said Cable, darting a venomous glance at

him. 'Actually, they're an awfully sweet couple.'

'Which puts the kiss of death on them,' said Matt.

'Will you shut up! They're called Edgworth, James and Yvonne Edgworth. James is very straight and does something with shares in the City. She's a very well known model. You'll recognise her face.'

Oh God, sighed Imogen, another model. I hope she doesn't run after Nicky too.

The weather grew worse and worse. The traffic was appalling too. They nearly missed the boat and were the last to drive into the vast cellar at the bottom of the boat which housed all the cars.

'Why are you looking so sour, Matt?' asked Cable petulantly.

'As we were last on we shall be last off. And as we're booked into an hotel a hundred miles south of Paris, you're unlikely to get any dinner tonight.'

A sailor advanced on him waving a chamois leather.

'No, I don't want my car washed,' he said and stalked upstairs. Cable grinned at Nicky. 'We're meeting James and Yvonne in the bar,' she said. Unable to see in her dark glasses she stumbled over a step. Nicky caught her elbow, stopping her falling, and leaving his hand on her arm far too long for Imogen's liking.

'God, the English dress badly,' he said, as they walked along the deck. Imogen pulled her sweater further down over her ill-fitting trousers.

'Cable, darling!' shrieked a voice, as they went into the bar.

'Yvonne, angel!'

'We thought you'd missed the boat!'

'We nearly did!'

'Terrific hat!'

'Fantastic shoes!'

'Stunning suit!'

'You've changed your hair!'

After screeching at each other for some minutes like a couple of parakeets, they remembered the rest of the party. Yvonne, Imogen decided with relief, wasn't half as dangerous as Cable. It must be the inspired ordinariness of her features — china blue eyes, curly red hair and dimples — that made her such a success as a model. She would automatically have the creamiest margarine, the whitest wash and the steaming hot milk drink ever on the boil for the homecoming husband. She was wearing a grey trouser suit and a spotless white blouse, with an embroidered '30s couple tangoing over her bosom.

'You must be Matt,' she said, flashing her teeth at Nicky. 'Cable's told me so much about you, but she never said how good-looking you were.'

Cable looked put out. 'This is Nicky Beresford,' she said sharply.

'Of course,' giggled Yvonne. 'How silly of me. I've seen you playing at Wimbledon.'

'This is Matt,' said Cable.

'Oh,' said Yvonne, looking up at Matt rather dubiously. 'Awfully pleased to meet you. This is my Jumbo.'

James Edgworth had the rosy complexion, puffed out cheeks and curly hair of cherubs that blow the wind at the corner of old maps. He was small, plump, and wore a yachting cap and a look of eager expectancy.

'Let's have a drink,' said Nicky.

'Tomato juice for me,' said Yvonne.

'Pity to waste it when it's duty free,' said Nicky, giving her one of his hard, sexy looks.

'Oh, well, if you twist my arm I'll have a Babycham,' said Yvonne.

Everyone else had double brandies.

'This is jolly, just like going on an away match,' said James Edgworth.

'How many bikinis did you bring, Cable?' asked Yvonne.

Nicky was busy converting English money into francs on the back of a sick bag.

'You're going to need that bag,' said Matt, 'when you realise how low the rate of exchange is.'

Two giggling teenagers sidled up to Nicky. 'Could we possibly have your autograph?'

Everyone was gaping at them. Not surprising, thought

Imogen, they were easily the noisiest, most glamorous group on the boat. She hoped she wasn't letting the side down.

'I say,' said James happily, 'it's beginning to get choppy.' The boat, having left the harbour, was bucking like a bronco. Every few minutes the windows were entirely covered by angry grey water. Imogen's stomach began to heave. All the chairs in the bar, she noticed, were chained to the floor. On her right, James, Cable and Nicky were talking about people she didn't know, so she idly listened to Yvonne attempting to chat up Matt.

'You write for the papers, don't you? Rather fun, I should think. I was rather good at English at school. They all said I should take up writing.'

Matt looked at her. 'It would have been tragic to deprive the modelling world,' he said drily.

Imogen suppressed a smile.

'That's what I thought,' said Yvonne. 'Now I just write Jumbo's speeches.'

'His speeches?'

'Didn't you know?' She bared her teeth like the wolf in Red Riding Hood. 'James is prospective candidate for Cockfosters. He's awfully busy at the moment, but if you ask him nicely, I'm sure he'd spare the time to give you an interview for your paper.'

'I'll remember that,' said Matt.

'Mind you,' said Yvonne, 'I do think the articles you write are rather — well — exaggerated.'

'In what way?' said Matt, his eyes narrowing.

'Well that piece last week on Northern Ireland. I mean I didn't finish it, and I know all journalists sensationalise things for the sake of circulation . . . '

'Go on,' said Matt, an ominous note creeping into his voice.

'Well I do think it's rather disloyal to write things like that.'

'Disloyal to whom? Those men had been tortured. One young boy committed suicide rather than take any more.'

'These things happen,' said Yvonne. 'But surely it's better

not to make too much fuss? It only stirs up hatred and makes things difficult for the poor soldiers. To be quite honest, I can't stand the way you Irish come over here and take our jobs and use our Health Service, and then say beastly thing about us.'

'Whenever I come across atrocities I write "beastly things" about them,' snapped Matt.

'Now, you mustn't get uptight,' said Yvonne reprovingly. 'I bet you didn't have any breakfast. Why not have a matchstick?' she added, producing a polythene bag of cut up carrots from her hold-all. 'Veggies don't put on an ounce of weight. Do have one.'

Imogen didn't stay to hear Matt's reply.

'I must get some air,' she gasped, staggering across the bar. It was better outside. She clung to the rails and the spray lashed her face. Down below, the sea was writhing and foaming. Two minutes later Matt joined her. His face was olive green.

'God ! Cable does pick them,' he groaned.

'She thought she was bringing you out.'

'In a nervous rash most likely.'

'I'm sure she's awfully good as a model.'

'Forces grey in, you mean. The only thing she could sell is packaged nausea.'

'Are you all right?' asked Imogen anxiously. The olive green was now tinged with grey.

'I'll manage. Be back in a second,' and he practically hurled himself over the edge of the boat.

'Oh, poor, poor thing,' she said, when he came back.

He grinned weakly. 'There goes yesterday's dinner and tea. At least I've ruined their rotten boat.'

Imogen was amazed at his stoicism, particularly when he added a moment later, 'You mustn't let Cable upset you.'

Imogen flushed. 'I wasn't! I mean, I like her very much.'

'She's only flirting with Nicky to annoy me,' he said. 'She does it with any attractive man who comes along.'

'But whatever for?'

'She's trying to pressure me to marry her.'

'Don't you want to?'

He shrugged his shoulders. 'I'm a Catholic, if somewhat lapsed. I'm supposed to try to marry for good. I can put up with a free range mistress, but not a free range wife:

'She'd probably settle down once you married her,' said Imogen.

'Perhaps. Oh, my God,' he muttered, turning green again. 'Here goes yesterday's breakfast.'

She had never known anyone could be so seasick. Each time he returned, more white and shaking, to her side. In the middle Cable had the gall to saunter up and put a proprietorial hand over his: 'We're going to have some lunch, darling. See you later. Isn't Yvonne nice?'

'Adorable,' said Matt. 'I'm just wondering how I'm going to kill her.'

At last they sighted Boulogne, hanging in a mist of seagulls, its cranes jabbing the sky. They were now joined by the rest of the party, bumptious from duty-free drink, and clutching their packets of duty-free cigarettes.

'Hullo,' said Cable. 'You do look peaky, darling. Do you like my new scent?' and she thrust her wrist under Matt's nose.

The skies were overcast as the boat drew in and it was still raining. A few fat Frenchmen in blue overalls and berets were waiting on the quay. Goodness, they look very English, thought Imogen, and the weather's just like Yorkshire.

'Shall I drive?' asked Nicky as they got back into the car.

Matt shook his head. 'It'll take my mind off my stomach.'

'Imogen looks rather grey. She'd better go in the front,' said Cable, nipping into the back beside Nicky.

The Mercedes was soon eating up the miles. So this is France, thought Imogen. Great avenues of poplars, cornfields stretching to infinity, incredibly ugly towns with their peeling Dubonnet posters and gaudy gardens like seed packets. There was no one in the streets. Perhaps they were all making fantastic French love behind those closed shutters.

'The First World War was fought all over here,' Matt told her. 'Most of the old houses were razed to the ground. That's why the villages are so new and hideous. Have you read *Goodbye to All That*?'

Imogen shook her head.

'Marvellous book. I've got a copy in my case. I'll lend it to you.'

'I couldn't get beyond the first page,' said Cable.

'Too many long words for you,' said Matt, 'and no pictures.'

'Oh, don't be so effing superior,' snapped Cable.

'There are still plenty of unexploded bombs in the fields,' said Matt, ignoring her.

And plenty inside the car too, thought Imogen. Nicky and Cable chattered away, the names dropping like autumn leaves. But finally even they fell quiet. Glancing round, Imogen saw that Cable was asleep, her head on Nicky's shoulder. She looked away quickly, trying desperately not to mind. If Matt saw anything through the driving mirror he took no notice.

The rain had stopped and a few stars were trying to peer through the veil of cloud as they reached their hotel. It stood on the edge of a river, festooned with bright pink geraniums and creepers trailing down into the water. The attractive mademoiselle behind the desk seemed delighted to see Matt again. But she looked aghast when James and Yvonne came through the door. There was much hand-waving and shoulder-shrugging, and Matt came over looking rueful.

'Sorry, loves, my crazy secretary's only booked two double rooms instead of three.'

'That's okay,' said Cable. 'We're all whacked. Yvonne and Imogen and I can shack down in one double bed. You three can have the other.'

Matt looked relieved. 'If that's all right with everyone else?'

Imogen nodded. Another day's reprieve — she wasn't up to a sexual marathon with Nicky tonight.

'Rather a lark,' said James Edgworth. 'Just like the dorm at school.'

Yvonne's face, however, was working like milk coming up to the boil.

'But that's absurd. Jumbo and I are married.'

'We all know that, baby,' said Matt.

'Don't call me "baby"!' Yvonne stamped her foot. 'I've had an exhausting day. I don't see why I should suffer merely because you've made a hash of things.'

Her eyes brimmed with tears. James patted her shoulder gingerly. 'Don't cry, dear. Matt, would you mind awfully if we had one double room?'

Matt looked at Nicky, who nodded.

'Right you are, James; anything to oblige. Nicky and I can kip in the car. Dinner in quarter of an hour then.'

'I'm not going to change if I've got to use these clothes as pyjamas,' said Nicky.

Up in the bedroom Cable got out her heated rollers.

'I don't think Matt and Yvonne are going to hit it off,' she said happily. 'Do you know, she's filled a whole suitcase with packets of All-Bran to keep James regular?'

478

CHAPTER SEVEN

Imogen felt absolutely knackered. She longed to soak in a hot bath, and spend ages tarting up and putting on something sensational. But she had nothing sensational to put on, and she felt far too fat and cumbersome to undress and change in front of Cable. With all Cable's suitcases and bottles of make-up, there wasn't really room enough for them both anyway. Besides, if she got down early she might snatch a few moments alone with Nicky, so she contented herself with a quick wash and brush-up.

'If Matt's belly-aching, tell him I won't be long,' said Cable who was now wandering about the bedroom totally naked, except for a green silk scarf holding her rollers in.

Imogen averted her eyes and fled. Was modesty perhaps a question of fatness, she wondered. If she looked as marvellous as that, perhaps she'd wander around with no clothes on. On the landing she found Yvonne, wearing a pink plastic cape round her shoulders to protect her clothes from makeup, and brandishing a hairdryer at a nervous looking maid.

'You speak English, don't you?'

'Oui, Madame.'

'Then why don't you speak it, instead of standing there talking in a foreign language? I want the plug on this dryer exchanged at once.'

Imogen slunk past them. No one was about in the hall. She looked at the menu in the glass case, her mouth watering. The kitchen was wafting beguiling smells of garlic, wine and herbs from its warm interior. She went into the lounge and sat down with *Tristram Shandy*. An English family nearby whispered as though they were at a funeral, and gloomily

479

lifted the brass hats on their *café filtrés*. On her table a vase of mauve and salmon pink gladioli clashed horribly with each other and even worse with the tartan table cloth. Odd that the French, who were supposed to be so chic, should have so little colour sense.

She tried to read. It was really awful the way her concentration had gone to the wind since she met Nicky. She gazed out of the window where an orange street lamp lit up the poster of a forthcoming circus.

We're a bit like a travelling circus, she thought. James is one of those eager perky little dogs that jumps through hoops, and Yvonne is a trapeze artist, tough but dainty, tripping around with her feet turned out, and Nicky and Cable were like sleek beautiful wild animals, panthers or tigers, who kept escaping from their cages and disrupting the local community, and she was a small fat shaggy pony trying desperately to keep up with everyone. She was just trying to work out what Matt was, something large and friendly, when she jumped as she heard his voice saying, 'You'll never get yourself a drink that way, sweetheart. We're in the bar. What are you reading?' He picked up her book. 'Oh that, never managed to get through it myself.'

They found Nicky sitting on a bar stool.

'Hullo, pet, what d'you want? Matt and I are drinking pernods.'

'That'd be lovely,' said Imogen, not having a clue what it was, some kind of alcoholic pear juice perhaps.

Matt ordered another round and dropped a packet of crisps into her lap.

'You must be starving.'

'You looked bushed too,' said Nicky, pouring water into the pernod so it went cloudy like dettol. 'Probably a good thing you're going to get a decent night's sleep tonight, but there'll be no holding me tomorrow,' he added, lowering his voice.

Imogen went pink, took a great slug of her drink, and nearly spat it out. It was unbelievably disgusting, like distilled liquorice allsorts. And she needed a drink so badly. She took another cautious sip and almost threw up.

480

Matt picked up a copy of *Le Figaro* that was lying on the bar.

'I say,' said Nicky, 'have you heard the one about the Irishman who tried to swim the channel?'

'No,' said Matt, not looking up.

'He tried to swim it "lenktways".'

Imogen giggled. Nicky put a warm hand over hers. 'At least someone thinks I'm funny.'

'Jesus,' said Matt. 'Braganzi's in Marseilles only a few miles from where we're staying.'

'With the Duchess?' asked Nicky.

'So it says here.'

'Never understand that,' said Nicky, peering at the paper. 'Beautiful classy bird throwing everything up to run off with a little wop runt like Braganzi.'

'Hush,' said Matt looking round in mock alarm. 'The Mafia are everywhere. Anyway he's probably more enterprising in bed. According to Fleet Street, the old Duke was a bit of a stately homo, one pretty valet after another.'

'Every valet·shall be exalted,' said Nicky.

'Didn't the Duchess have Braganzi's baby?' asked Imogen.

'Yeah,' said Matt. 'Must be 18 months now. They've been together nearly three years. Perhaps she enjoys living with a hood. Women are. always turned on by power, and Braganzi's got the whole of the Midi sewn up.'

Nicky squinted at his reflection in the smoked looking-glass behind the bar. 'All the same he is an oily little runt.'

Matt grinned. 'Once she hears you're in the area, Nicky baby, she'll promptly abandon Braganzi.'

'I've never had a Duchess,' mused Nicky, as though it was a matter of surprise to him. 'Can't you imagine her gliding downstairs in one of those red robes lined with ermine, and nothing on underneath, saying, "Would you prefer the West Wing or the East Wing, Mr Beresford?"'

'Then she'd probably hand you over to the National Trust,' said Matt, catching sight of Imogen's stricken face. 'Anyway, you'd just be getting down to business when the door'd be flung open and you'd have some guide showing a coachload of large ladies on a Mothers' Union mystery tour all over you.'

'I'd like that,' said Nicky. 'I'm turned on by crowds.'

Imogen, who was feeling quite sick at the thought of Nicky and the Duchess, took another slug at her drink, and felt even sicker, and had to have three potato crisps to take the taste away.

'Hullo, you chaps, what's anyone going to drink?' said a jolly voice. It was James, wearing a pale blue corduroy coat, his light brown curls smoothed flat to his head. Perhaps Yvonne insisted on 100 brushes a day — like Nanny.

'It's my round,' said Nicky.

'I'll have whisky then, a large White Horse please, *un grand cheval blanc*,' said James and giggled, looking furtively round. 'You'd better make it snappy. Yvonne doesn't approve of spirits.'

'Make it two,' said Matt, and, picking up Imogen's pernod, emptied it into his own glass. 'You're not enjoying that much, are you, sweetheart?'

'Oh thank you,' stammered Imogen, touched that he'd noticed.

'D'you know the story of the white horse going into a pub and sitting down on the bar stool and ordering a large whisky?' said James.

'No,' said Nicky, who didn't like other people telling jokes.

'The barman gave the horse his drink, and said "Did you know there's a whisky named after you?" "Really," said the white horse, "I didn't know there was a whisky called Eric."'
'

James laughed so hard that in the end everyone joined in. He's really rather nice, thought Imogen, taking a thankful gulp of her whisky.

The head waiter was hovering with a menu, *chat du jour* at the ready.

'Was Cable or your wife looking within a million years of being ready?' asked Matt. 'They're getting a bit restless in the kitchen.'

'No,' said James cheerfully.

Imogen's stomach gave a thunderous rumble.

'Hear, hear,' said Matt. 'I'll keel over if I don't eat soon.'

'You chaps didn't have any lunch, did you?' said James sympathetically.

'Jesus,' said Nicky, looking at the bill for the round of drinks. 'It's even gone up since I was here in May.'

'Exactly,' said Matt. 'That's why we're not staying in four star hotels. We'll have to put Imogen on the streets as it is.'

'They say vicars' daughters are always the worst,' said James.

The whisky was making Imogen perk up. It was nice being just her and the three men. The conversation moved on to Northern Ireland. Imogen ate her crisps and let the world flow over her. Nicky held her hand and occasionally stroked her hair. James was caught red-handed buying another round of large drinks by the arrival of Yvonne.

'I'm not late, am I?'

'Yes,' said Matt. 'What d'you want to drink?'

'Tomato juice, please,' said Yvonne. 'No thanks, Imogen, I won't have any of your crisps. They're so fattening and it's more than my life's worth to exceed my calorie count.'

She looked rather disapprovingly at Imogen's thighs splayed out on the bar stool. Imogen blushed, let the large crisp already in her mouth melt like a communion wafer, and gazed at Yvonne in admiration. There wasn't a chip of varnish off the long coral nails, nor a newly curled red hair out of place, and the white silk blouse with the couple tangoing over the bosom was still spotless from that morning.

Having got her way over the room, Yvonne was also prepared to be conciliatory. The vibes sizzling between Nicky and Cable had not been lost on her. Cable mustn't be the only one with a holiday admirer. Yvonne decided to charm Matt.

'Are you feeling better?' she asked. 'Mind you, I always suspect seasickness is psychosomatic.'

'I agree,' said Matt. 'So's bloody-mindedness.'

The irony was quite lost on Yvonne.

'I do envy you coming from Ireland,' she went on. 'I did a butter commercial there once. It was all so green and unspoilt. Where do you live, Matt?'

'In Moone.'

'Is it pretty?'

'Well, it's very good hunting country.'

'I think hunting's rather cruel,' said Yvonne, 'but I suppose people in the country have to occupy their time somehow.'

'Indeed they have,' said Matt. 'The Irish haven't discovered the infinite possibilities of sexual intercourse yet.'

'The men in the Moone always came too soon,' said Nicky.

Matt laughed. Yvonne hastily changed the subject. 'I don't always agree with what you say, but I do admire your ability to do it week in week out.'

'Do what?'

'Write your amusing articles. Where do you think up your ideas?'

'In the bog,' said Matt. 'I'm thinking of doing a piece on bitches next week.'

'Oh, I can help you with that,' said Yvonne enthusiastically. 'One meets so many in the modelling world. It's the price you have to pay for being at the top,' she added, draining her tomato juice. The head waiter was hovering again, looking bootfaced.

'Where is Cable?' said Yvonne disapprovingly? 'You haven't trained her very well, you know.'

'She knows people'll wait for her,' said Matt.

'So inconsiderate to keep the kitchen staff waiting. I must say I am looking forward to my meal. You can't beat French cuisine,' Yvonne retorted.

At that moment Cable sauntered in, looking quite unrepentant in khaki jeans, and a tight olive green T-shirt with 'I'm Still A Virgin' printed in large letters across the front. The colour gave a warm dusky glow to her brown face and neck, and intensified the greenness of her eyes. The barman nearly dropped the glass he was cleaning, the head waiter stopped in mid-grumble. Nicky's hand slid out of Imogen's and his presence seemed to slip away from her too, as he examined the lettering on Cable's bosom.

'Matt's just been telling us the Irish haven't discovered sex yet. Here we have the proof,' he said.

'You'll get clobbered under the trade descriptions act,' said Matt.

'I'd better give it to Imogen, then,' said Cable. 'She's the only one entitled to wear it.'

Everyone glanced at Imogen, who blushed crimson and looked down at her hands speechless with embarrassment. Nicky *must* have told Cable. How *could* he?

'Sorry,' said Cable. 'That *was* below the belt.'

'Your mind's never anywhere else,' said Matt sharply. 'Let's go and eat.'

'Let me have one drink,' said Cable, smiling witchily at the head waiter. 'Surely we've got time?'

The head waiter promptly melted and said there was all the time in the world, and why didn't they have a round of drinks on the house?

'I thought you weren't going to change, Cable,' said Yvonne. 'No, thank you, *garçon*, I won't have another drink, and you've had enough, Jumbo,' she added to James who was still gaping at Cable. 'You know I hate you drinking spirits.'

'Don't be silly,' said Matt, accepting large glasses of whisky and handing one to James. 'Never look a gift White Horse in the mouth.'

At last they went in to dinner. Most people had reached the coffee stage. After a quick calculation, Imogen posted herself next to where she thought Nicky would be. But at the last moment Cable sat down beyond Matt, and Nicky moved in opposite her, with Yvonne next to him, leaving James and Imogen on the outside.

'We can play footy footy,' said James.

His fat little legs would never reach me, thought Imogen. At least she was next to Matt, which was a comfort. He promptly began to guide her through the menu.

'Have that and that if you're starving,' he said. 'This place really deserves every flicker of its three stars.'

'I'm going to have a large steak,' said Nicky. 'I'd better make some attempt at keeping fit.'

485

'Oh good, they've got crudities. Can I have mine undressed?' said Yvonne to the waiter.

Undressed crudities! thought Imogen. Perhaps Yvonne was going to whip off her clothes and tango naked on the snow white table cloth. It must be all the whisky, it was beginning to make her feel fuzzy and irresponsible.

Everyone, except Cable and Yvonne, fell on the bread.

'What's *cervelles*?' said James, unpacking a square of butter.

'Brains,' said Matt.

'Ugh,' shuddered Yvonne. 'I can't stand brains.'

'That's patently obvious,' said Matt to Imogen in an undertone.

'Shall we all drink red?' he added, looking round the table.

'I want white,' said Yvonne. 'Much less fattening, don't you agree, Cable?'

'What?' said Cable, who was smouldering at Nicky. 'Oh yes I'm sure.'

Yvonne decided it was high time to break them up.

'I've just been telling Matt how much I love Ireland, Cable, it's so wonderfully primitive.'

'You'd enjoy our hovel then,' said Matt, taking another piece of bread. 'Chickens in the parlour, me granny shacked up with the donkey in the best bedroom, and my mither entertaining gentlemen friends, while the pig waits at table.'

'Now you're teasing me,' said Yvonne, her eyes crinkling, 'I bet your family are charming, aren't they, Cable?'

'I haven't been allowed to meet them,' snapped Cable.

Suddenly the temperature seemed to have dropped below zero.

'I'm frightened she might go off me,' said Matt lightly.

There was an awkward pause, broken fortunately by the arrival of the wine. James, who was oblivious of any undercurrents, started to tell a stock-exchange joke, waving a large radish around as he talked. With his pale blue coat and his puffed out cheeks, he suddenly reminded Imogen of Peter Rabbit.

486

'Don't crunch, Jumbo,' said Yvonne irritably. 'You know how it gets on my nerves. The service is awfully slow here.'

A moan of greed escaped Imogen at the sight of her first course, a sort of chicken rissole, stuffed with foie gras, and surrounded by bright orange sauce flecked with black. Opposite her James was smacking his lips over smoked salmon and a shiny green sauce. Matt was eating snails. Yvonne was chewing grated carrot 20 bites a mouthful. Nicky and Cable had skipped a first course and were smoking.

The wine, even to Imogen's uneducated palate, was spectacular, thick and sultry with grapes.

'You can almost taste the peasants' feet,' said Matt.

'What are the black bits?' she asked him, as she used her fourth piece of bread to mop up the sauce.

'Truffles,' said Matt. 'Bloody bad luck for pigs, really. They rootle round for days, and the moment they find some marvellous delicacy, it's snatched from under their nose.'

Like Nicky from me, thought Imogen wistfully.

Cable and Yvonne were talking shop.

'They sacked her from a bikini feature because she was too fat,' said Yvonne.

'That pale lipstick makes her mouth look like a rubber tyre,' said Cable.

'It's her own fault. She's in Wedgies or Tramps every night, and after all the client is buying your face, not your ability to drink in the right places till four o'clock in the morning.'

'Who are they talking about?' muttered Imogen.

'Obviously someone extremely successful,' said Matt.

'I got the Weetabix commercial,' said Yvonne patronisingly, starting on strips of green pepper. 'You were after it weren't you, Cable? The producer told me you were too overtly sexy for the part.'

'That's obviously why he tried to take me to bed,' snapped Cable, lighting one cigarette from another.

Nicky suddenly glanced across at Imogen, his eyes swivelling from Cable to Yvonne, then raising them to heaven. Imogen giggled with relief.

'No more bread, Jumbo,' said Yvonne, still chewing everything 20 times. 'You've already had quite enough.'

Everyone else had finished except her. The waiters were hovering to take the plates and putting silver dishes over blue flames.

'I should go on,' Matt told them. 'We can't hang around all night.'

Imogen's second course, boeuf bourgignon, rich, dark, aromatic and pulsating with herbs, was almost better than her first.

'I've never tasted anything so heavenly in my life,' she said to Matt.

'Good,' he said, filling her glass and looking across at Cable, who was picking imaginary bones out of her trout. 'Nice change to have someone around who enjoys eating.'

'These quenelles are very disappointing,' grumbled Yvonne.

'What d'you expect from upmarket fish cakes?' said Nicky.

'I always thought a quenelle was something the dog slept in,' said James, and roared with laughter.

'No more wine for you, Jumbo,' said Yvonne sharply.

'How long have you two been married?' asked Matt.

'Forty-eight weeks exactly,' said Yvonne, with what she thought was an engaging smile. 'We still count our marriage by weeks not months.'

'Weekiversaries,' said Matt drily. 'How touching.'

Cable shot him a warning glance.

James started to tell Imogen a long complicated joke about a parrot, upon which she found it impossible to concentrate because at the same time Yvonne turned to Nicky, saying:

'How did you and Imogen meet?'

'In Yorkshire.'

'Oh, I love Yorkshire, it's so unspoilt.'

'Like Imogen,' said Nicky.

'They tied a handkerchief over the parrot's eyes,' said James.

'Have you been going out long?' said Yvonne,

'No,' said Nicky.

'And another one round its beak,' said James.

'She looks awfully young. I'm surprised her father let her go away with you.'

'So was I.'

'What does she do?'

'Sits and dreams in a library.'

'And then they both got into bed,' said James.

'That's nice,' said Yvonne. 'She and Matt'll be able to have a lot of good talks about books.'

'They already have,' said Cable. She put her hands behind her head and leant back against the wall, her breasts jutting out dramatically. The effect was not lost on a handsome Frenchman drinking brandy with a plain wife at the next table. He and Cable exchanged a long lingering eye-meet. The Frenchman dropped his eyes first, then, after a furtive glance at his wife who was still spooning sugar into her coffee, looked at Cable again. Cable smirked and looked away. Even the cook had come out of the kitchen to have a look at her and was standing open-mouthed in the doorway with a lobster in his hand.

Suddenly Imogen was brought back to reality by James roaring with laughter and saying, 'And the parrot said Kama Sutra is a liar. Get it? Kama Sutra is a liar.'

Imogen, realising he'd reached the punchline, roared with rather forced laughter too. Matt filled up James's glass. Yvonne glared at Matt.

'Please don't. I don't want him to have any more. You won't be jogging every day in France you know, Jumbo.'

'Have some more,' said Matt, ladling more beef and potatoes on to Imogen's plate.

'Oh I shouldn't.'

'You should. Do you good to have a blow out on your first night. No one else will but us,' he went on, emptying the casserole dish on to his own plate.

Yvonne smiled at Imogen brightly.

'I hear you work in a library.'

Oh God, thought Imogen, she's going to bring *me* out now.

'Yes,' she muttered with her mouth full.

'I used to love reading,' Yvonne went on, 'but I don't get the time now. I have to read a lot of papers from Central Office for James. I've got an aunt who reads though, four novels a day. We all call her the book worm.'

She then proceeded to launch into a long and unutterably boring description of her aunt's reading habits and literary tastes.

'Someone ought to put a green baize cloth over her,' muttered Matt as he leant across to fill Imogen's glass.

Having finally exhausted her aunt, Yvonne said, 'You're so lucky not having a job where you have to watch your figure.'

Imogen blushed and put down the potato she was about to to eat.

'I'd be very happy to watch Imogen's figure all the time,' said Matt evenly.

'Me too,' leered James.

The head waiter came up and put his hands on Matt's shoulders.

'Everything all right, Monsieur O'Connor?'

'*Formidable*,' said Matt, breaking into fluent French.

'My trout was simply delicious,' said Cable, who'd left most of hers.

Imogen's waistband was biting into her stomach. She wished she hadn't eaten so much.

The restaurant was empty except for their table. Matt ordered coffee.

'Not for me,' said Yvonne. 'It keeps me awake, and we've got a long drive tomorrow.'

'I'd like an enormous brandy,' said James defiantly.

'Bravo,' said Nicky.

'Mustn't squander all our money at once, Jumbo. Night, night all,' said Yvonne, getting to her feet and dragging the reluctant James off to bed.

'Got to get her ugly sleep,' said Matt.

'God, she's a bitch,' said Nicky.

Matt ordered Marcs all round.

'If you go away in a party,' he said, 'it's essential to have a

490

holiday scapegoat, so that everyone can gang up and work off their spleen bitching about her. Mrs Edgworth fits the bill perfectly.'

After dinner they wandered round the village. The sky glimmered with stars now, and down by the river the air was heavy with the musty scent of meadowsweet.

Imogen and Nicky dawdled behind the others.

'Lovely moon,' sighed Imogen.

'Seen it before,' said Nicky.

He put a protective arm round her shoulders. She could feel the warmth of his body through her sweater. Suddenly he paused. Perhaps at last he might be going to whisk her off down some side road and the primrose path. She felt weak with abandon. But he was only pausing to read a poster giving details of a forthcoming tennis match.

'They wanted me to play in that,' he said. 'Didn't offer enough bread though, and the L.T.A. get very uptight if one does too many exhibition matches.'

Imogen felt overwhelmed with humility. What right had she got to be here at all with such a star? Ahead of them Matt's blond hair gleamed in a street lamp.

'How are you getting on with Matt?' said Nicky.

'Oh, very well. He's so nice.'

'He is, isn't he ? She's a funny girl.'

'In what way?' said Imogen carefully.

'You never know what she'll do next. Unlike you, my angel, who are totally predictable.'

'I do love you,' she murmured, like a child touching wood.

'Well that's nice, except that we seem to be frustrated at every turn. Never mind, we've got a whole fortnight ahead of us.'

He dropped a kiss on top of her head. The night was really very warm. Imogen tried to suppress the thought that back in June, when he'd been mad to pull her, he'd certainly have whipped her off to some discreet corner of a foreign field, and made passionate love to her, and not given a damn about the others.

491

'I have observed a faint neglect of late,' she thought sadly, then felt furious with herself. In Yorkshire she'd never stopped panicking and bellyaching because he was trying to pull her, now she was in a state because he wasn't. Her father would be delighted by such circumspection anyway. Perhaps Nicky was playing a waiting game so as not to frighten her.

In front she could see Cable's hips undulating langorously as she walked beside Matt. She wished she hadn't eaten so much. She wished she was as tall and as slim as her shadow.

Outside the hotel, quite without self-consciousness, Matt had taken Cable into his arms and kissed her very thoroughly. Nicky had followed suit with Imogen but when she opened her eyes in the middle, he was gazing over her shoulder at Cable and Matt.

'Sweet dreams, darling,' said Matt, reluctantly, relinquishing her. 'And I'd love to be away by ten — we've got a long drive.'

Up in their room, Imogen undressed quickly and jumped into bed. It was long after midnight, but she'd never known anyone take so long to get into bed as Cable, removing her make-up several times, massaging skin food into her face, brushing her hair, touching up her nail varnish, doing long, complicated exercises and chattering all the time.

'Such a relief not to have Matt beefing at me to hurry up,' she said, rubbing vaseline into her eyelashes, and because there were no men present giving Imogen the benefit of her enchanting wicked smile. 'In fact it's rather a relief to have a night off sex as well.'

Imogen snuggling down in the coarse sheets, fought sleep, tried to concentrate on *Tristram Shandy* and not stare at Cable too hard.

'God the bed's hard,' said Cable, finally getting in beside her. 'I hope you're not finding this trip too alarming.'

'No it's lovely,' said Imogen timidly, touched that Cable should be concerned.

Cable, however, immediately got the subject back to herself. 'I remember the first time I came to France on an ex-change scheme when I was fifteen. I was absolutely terrified. I travelled by train overnight, 3rd class can you believe it? And there was this repulsive man who had little finger nails longer than the rest, and put on a blue hair net after he got into his couchette. The moment we dimmed the lights, he tried to fiddle with me, and there were two nuns in the bot-tom couchettes. I bit him so hard, he nearly pulled the com-munication cord. What d'you think of that?' She laughed to herself.

But before Imogen could think up a suitable answer, she realised Cable had fallen asleep like a cat. Having fought sleep for so long, Imogen now felt wide awake. Thank goodness Yvonne was not sharing the bed too, or she'd be a model sandwich. Every man in the hotel would give a mil-lion francs to be in my place, she thought as, petrified she'd touch Cable, she perched on the edge of her side of the bed. She hoped she'd dream of Nicky, but she didn't.

CHAPTER EIGHT

Imogen went down to breakfast next morning and found Nicky and Matt dirty and unshaven like a couple of bandits.

Matt smiled at her and asked her if she had slept well.

'Marvellously,' lied Imogen.

'I'm glad someone did,' said Nicky sulkily. 'The Royal Philharmonic of tomcats started caterwauling around five o'clock.'

'We abandoned all hope of sleep and invented tortures for Mrs Edgworth,' said Matt.

At that moment Yvonne bustled in wearing a dress and a pink headscarf.

'Good morning,' she said briskly. Matt and Nicky looked at her stonily.

'I didn't sleep a wink,' she grumbled. 'What with the cats and the clocks striking. Do remember to book rooms at the back in future, Matt. And the beds were awful.'

'Surprised you didn't use James as a mattress,' said Matt.

'Why are you all done up like a dog's dinner?' said Nicky.

Yvonne's lips tightened as she pulled on white gloves. 'I'm off to Mass, where you all should be!' she said.

The next stage of the journey was a disaster. Cable took so long to pack and get ready that she and Matt had another blazing row.

'They ought to hold sheepdog trials for people like me,' said Matt as he finally rounded the three of them up into the car. James and Yvonne had already gone on ahead. Nicky and Imogen sat in the front, Cable and Matt in the back, Matt reading a French Sunday paper, Cable looking stonily out of the window.

Nicky, whose turn it was to drive, was determined to notch up more miles an hour than Matt had yesterday, but Imogen spoilt everything by reading the map all wrong. The countryside they passed through had been so beautiful — old mills covered in reddening Virginia creeper, tender green poplar groves rising out of lush grass, and huge golden chateaux at the end of long shining lakes. Then suddenly she realised to her horror that she'd missed an important turning. As a result Nicky had to spend the next three-quarters of an hour disentangling them from the tentacles of a large industrial town. He got more and more angry, which was not helped by Imogen out of sheer nerves telling him he could overtake three times when he couldn't, directing him slap into oncoming traffic.

Cutting short her stream of apologies, Nicky had turned on the car wireless. They could still get Radio 3. Patricia Hughes was announcing a performance of Handel's Little Organ Concerto.

'I didn't know Handel had a small prick,' drawled Cable.

Nicky grinned round at her. 'Probably couldn't Handel it,' he said.

They both giggled and started swapping more anecdotes about mutual acquaintances, ostentatiously excluding Matt and Imogen.

Imogen wished she could amuse Nicky like that. But we've only got my family and Homer in common, she thought dolefully, and we can't really talk about them for a fortnight. She noticed that each time they reached the end of a village, its name was signposted with a diagonal red line through it. She had a gloomy vision of Nicky taking a ruler and calmly drawing a red line through her name to signify the affair was over.

Later, tempers were not improved by no one being able to decide on the right picnic place, which at 110 miles an hour on the motorway was admittedly quite hard to find. James, who had been obliged to stop for Yvonne several times, was driving just behind them now. Imogen could see his eager pink face, with Yvonne beside him, wearing dark glasses, her mouth opening and shutting in a constant stream of chat.

Cable meanwhile was driving Matt insane by sitting with a red Michelin Guide in her hand, saying every time they came to a village, 'There's a fabulous restaurant here. It'd be so much nicer to stop here than have a rotten picnic.'

'And five times more expensive,' snapped Matt. 'I'm buggered if I'm going to fork out 100 francs for something you won't eat. I'm fed up with providing expensive leftovers for restaurant cats all over England and France.'

'Oh, shut up,' said Cable.

Eventually they stopped high up in the mountains, with a deep green valley falling away from them, richly dotted with herds of golden cattle, and russet farm houses. Despite the height it was appallingly hot. A heat haze danced above the rocks. Cheese, pâté and garlic sausage were soon sweating and melting in the blazing sun, ham curled and turned brown, the acid red wine was as warm as tea.

Yvonne perched on a rock, still looking as though she'd been wrapped in tissue paper, daintily eating cottage cheese with a pink plastic spoon, and grumbling about the insects.

'Doesn't the silly cow remind you of little Miss Muffet?' said Matt to Imogen. 'Pity a big spider can't roll up and put the frighteners on her for good.'

Nicky, having wolfed a couple of pieces of bread and pâté, had annexed a bottle of wine, and was further punishing Imogen by dancing attendance on Cable. Lying on the grass beside her, he alternately fed her swigs of wine from the same paper cup, or dropped green grapes into her mouth. Occasionally, after shooting a venomous glance in Matt's direction, Cable would whisper something in his ear, sending them both into fits of laughter.

Yvonne looked disapproving, and unpacked yet another polythene bag of carrot matchsticks. Ignoring them both, Matt stretched out and fell asleep among the wild flowers like Ferdinand the Bull. Imogen, incapable of such *sang-froid*, miserably ate her way through five pieces of bread and garlic sausage and then felt sick.

James had positioned himself so he could look up Cable's skirt. As she writhed on the ground with Nicky, her pink dress rode up further and further to reveal black *broderie anglaise* bikini pants, threaded with scarlet ribbon.

Suddenly a car drew up on the road below and three Frenchmen got out, quite unselfconsciously unzipped their flies and relieved themselves against the grass verge

'How disgusting,' spluttered Yvonne, going scarlet with disapproval.

'How lovely and uninhibited,' said Cable, sitting up and putting a cigarette in her mouth. In a flash James' lighter was out, the flame shooting into the air, nearly singeing Cable's hair and eyelashes.

'Overeager, like its master,' said Nicky pointedly.

James went slightly pink and helped himself and Imogen to more wine.

'That's enough, Jumbo,' snapped Yvonne. 'You know what I feel about drinking and driving.'

She got off the rock and started to tidy up the picnic, exclaiming over the ants that had already crawled into the pâté, neatly tidying the rubbish into a polythene bag and stacking it in the boot.

'Don't work so hard,' said Cable lazily. 'You're making us feel so guilty.'

'Someone's got to do it,' said Yvonne. 'I, for one, like things ship-shape.'

Imogen got back into the car, wincing as the sun-baked seat burnt her skin.

'Everyone's awfully prickly today,' she said to Matt.

'That's why it's called a holly day,' said Matt.

And now it was late afternoon. Imogen sat in the back feeling car sick, homesick, cooped up and uncertain where life was taking her. After the long hours of travelling, she felt sluggish and weighed down, as though all the pieces of bread she'd eaten in the last twenty-four hours were lying in a leaden lump at the bottom of her stomach.

And now the shadows were lengthening and Matt was driving again, sweat darkening his shirt, an old panama hat pulled over his nose to keep his dark blond mane out of his eyes. All the windows were open; the heat was coming in great waves; the windscreen was coated with dead flies.

The road was curling now through pine woods and burning red rock, the crickets were going like rattles, the air was getting clearer and clearer. Up and up they went, round and round, until it seemed their car would touch the sky. Then, suddenly, like a sheet of metal glinting in the evening sun, sparkled the Mediterranean.

Imogen caught her breath. Cable got out her make-up case. Imogen wished she had some of those little cleansing pads which Cable and Yvonne whipped out on every occasion. Even her flannel was packed in her suitcase in the boot.

'There's Port-les-Pins,' said Matt.

Imogen craned her neck. Down below, the hill was thick with little white villas with red roofs and green shutters. Shops, cafés, casinos and pale pastel houses jostled for position along the sea front. A fleet of fishing boats and yachts tossed in the harbour. Some tiny fishing village, thought Imogen.

Another shock awaited her. She had always believed the French were an ugly race, dumpy with incipient moustaches. But as they drove along the front, she had never seen so many beautiful girls, trailing back from the beach, with their waistlength hair, long limbs and brown faces. No wonder Cable had spent three-quarters of an hour on her face. No wonder Nicky looked like a small boy let loose in a sweet shop.

Their hotel, La Reconnaissance, was at the far end of the front. Drying bathing dresses and towels hung from every balcony. The fat Madame, accompanied by an even fatter poodle, came waddling out gabbling with excitement and kissed Matt on both cheeks. Imogen was relieved to discover that she and Nicky had a room each.

Madame combined respectability with avarice, Matt explained in English as they climbed the red-tiled staircase. She got more money for two single rooms than a double, but as long as appearances were kept up, she didn't mind who slipped into whose room after lights out.

Imogen's room was extremely small with a large single bed, no soap, no coat-hangers, no drawer space and the tiniest of face towels. A piece of plastic holly was tucked behind the only picture. Five pink, lurex bullrushes stood in a vase beside the bed. If she leaned right out of the window she could just see the sea.

She sat down overwhelmed by another desperate wave of homesickness. Her hair felt stiff with dust, her body ached with the inactivity of the long day's drive. Outside, Yvonne was complaining bitterly that baths cost 10 francs each and Cable was bullying Matt to go downstairs and get the plug changed on her Carmen rollers. I must pull myself together, thought Imogen. She was on holiday, after all, and she must try and enjoy herself. She washed as best she could in stone cold water and put on one of her new voluminous orange kaftans. She wore stockings and high-heeled shoes to make herself look taller and slimmer and took a lot of trouble over her face, before joining the others in the bar on the front.

Immediately she was conscious of wearing quite the wrong clothes. Most people were in trousers and shirts in soft pastel shades. Girls in dresses wore them fitted or tightly belted, with Greek sandals on their bare feet. She was aware of brown faces laughing at her all around.

Nicky looked at the kaftan in ill-concealed disapproval.

'Expecting a baby, darling?' said Cable in her cool, clear voice.

'She looks lovely,' said Matt, who was filling in the brown identification forms.

He patted the chair beside him. 'Come and sit here, baby, and let me take down your particulars. Is your room all right?'

'Oh yes, it's fine,' she said gratefully.

'Ours isn't,' said Yvonne, 'I haven't got a bedside lamp.'

'With all those raw carrots you eat,' said Matt, 'I would have thought you could see in the dark.'

'It is rather a dump,' snapped Yvonne. 'I had expected something a bit better — like that for instance.' She waved in the direction of the huge white Plaza Hotel which, with its red and white umbrellas, dominated the bay.

'You can stay there if you're prepared not to eat or go out in the evening,' said Matt. 'One night at the Plaza'll cost you as much as a fortnight at La Reconnaissance.'

'Well perhaps not the Plaza,' conceded Yvonne, 'but there must be somewhere a little less primitive.'

Matt went on filling in Imogen's form. For her occupation he put *bibliothecaire* which sounded very grand.

'Madame was good to Matt in the old days,' said Cable defensively.

'When I was an undergraduate she let me stay for practically nothing,' said Matt. 'She used to be in the Resistance. I'm sure she'll lend you her revolver if it comes to a shoot out with the cockroaches.'

Imogen gazed at the Prussian blue sea which glittered and sparkled in the sinking sun.

'What's the French for "Model"?' said James trying to bridge an awkward silence and fill in Yvonne's form at the same time.

'*Catin*,' said Matt.

Cable stifled a giggle and James solemnly wrote it down.

A party of Germans sat down at the next table and started banging the table for waitresses.

'This place is awfully touristy,' grumbled Yvonne.

'Well, you're a tourist, aren't you?' said Matt.

A slim brunette went by in a lace shirt with the tails tied under the bosom to reveal a beautiful brown midriff.

'Everyone seems to be wearing those this year,' said Cable. 'I must get one.'

'What does *catin* really mean?' said Imogen to Nicky later, as they strolled along the front.

'Prostitute,' said Nicky.

They had dinner in a restaurant overhung with vines. Below, the sea was a wash of blue shadow, sparked by the lights of the fishing boats putting out for the night's catch. Everyone was hungry and they ate garlicky fish soup and cassoulet. The wine flowed freely. Even Yvonne seemed more cheerful when suddenly she put on her wolf in Red Riding Hood smile and turned to Matt.

'Isn't it time you and Cable named the day?'

Everyone stopped talking. Matt looked at Yvonne steadily and said, 'What day?'

She waved a playful finger at him. 'Now don't be evasive.

You and Cable have been going out for nearly two years now. It's only fair to make an honest woman out of her.'

Cable flushed angrily, 'It's none of your damn business, Yvonne.'

'Darling — I was only interested in your welfare.'

Matt took Cable's hand and squeezed it. Then he turned to Yvonne and said softly, 'Let's get three things straight. First, I have Cable's welfare very much at heart; secondly, I agree with her, it's none of your damn business; and thirdly, you've got butter on your chin.'

There was a frozen pause, then everyone burst out laughing, except Yvonne who went as red as her hair with rage.

Nicky yawned. 'God, I'm so tired I could sleep on a clothes line.'

Matt was gently stroking Cable's cheek. 'Early bed, I think, darling, don't you?'

She looked at him and nodded gratefully. He's a nice man, thought Imogen, a really nice man. She was beginning to feel sick. Perhaps that garlic soup hadn't been such a good idea. Nicky was eyeing a sumptuous blonde at the next table.

'Don't forget to sleep on the right side of the bed,' said Cable mockingly to Imogen as she climbed the stairs to her room. She felt sicker and sicker. White-faced, white-bodied, she looked at herself in the mirror. Oh, fat, white woman who nobody loves, she thought sadly, as she put on her nightdress and jumped into bed.

There was a knock on the door. It was Nicky in a violet dressing-gown and nothing underneath. His black curls fell becomingly, the gold medallions jangled on his chest, after-shave lotion fought with the sweet scent of deodorant. Imogen's heart turned over. She had never seen such a beautiful man. If only he weren't going round and round.

'Hullo, darling,' he said huskily, sitting down on the bed. ''Thank God we're alone at last. I couldn't sleep last night for thinking about you.'

Or the tomcats or the clocks, thought Imogen. He was kissing her now and his hands started to rove over her body. He put his tongue in her ear, and Imogen, who couldn't

JILLY COOPER

remember whether she'd washed her ears that morning, wriggled away, simulating uncontrollable passion.

Nicky laughed. 'Underneath the surface, you're a hot little thing.'

Great waves of nausea were sweeping over her.

'Come on,' he said. 'Let's have that stupid nightdress off.'

'Nicky, I feel sick,' she said, leaping out of bed and rushing to the bidet.

'You can't be sick here,' said Nicky in horror.

'Can't I?' said Imogen, and was. And all night long, like the Gadarene swine, she thundered down the passage to the black hellhole of a lavatory.

Nicky, foiled yet again, went back to his room in an extremely bad temper.

CHAPTER NINE

Next morning, feeling pale and sickly, Imogen staggered down to the beach. The sea was blue and sparkling, the sand hot and golden. Umbrellas stretched six deep, edge to edge, for half a mile along the beach. Bodies lay stretched out hundreds to the acre, turning and oiling themselves like chickens on a spit.

Nearly everyone, Imogen realised to her horror, was topless. Cable, as brown as any of them, was wearing the bottom half of the briefest bikini — two saffron triangles, held together by straps of perspex. Her small perfect breasts gleamed with oil. Her hair hung black and shiny over the edge of her lilo. Nicky lounged beside her, slim, lithe and menacing. He totally ignored Imogen when she arrived. Matt lay on his back, his eyes closed, his powerful chest curved in an arch above his flat heavily muscled stomach. Having sallow skin, he was already going brown.

He opened a lazy eye and grinned at Imogen. 'Come and join the oppressed white minority.'

As she struggled into Lady Jacintha's red bathing dress, she tried to protect herself with a small face towel.

'There's masses of room on my towel if you need it,' said Matt who had been watching her struggles with unashamed amusement. He rolled over and went back to sleep. Imogen lay in silence, bitterly ashamed of her whiteness.

'Christ,' said Nicky, who was reading a copy of yesterday's *Daily Telegraph*, 'Nastase was knocked out in the first round.'

'Damn, damn, damn!' said Matt suddenly. Everyone looked up. 'Here comes Mrs Set-your-teeth-on-Edgworth and the prospective candidate for Cockfosters.'

Yvonne was picking her way daintily across the miles of

tangled brown flesh. Behind her staggered James weighed down by towels, lilos, snorkel masks, picnic baskets, a large parasol and Yvonne's make-up case, but still managing to cast excited glances at the naked bosoms around him.

'They look as though they're going on safari,' said Cable. 'There's something rather prehistoric about James's shorts.'

'He looks as though he's crossing the foot hills,' said Nicky.

'What a crowd,' sighed Yvonne. 'You get such lovely deserted beaches in the Bahamas. No, put the lilo there, Jumbo, with the towel spread over it. I don't want to perspire. And put the parasol so it keeps the sun off my face. Can you move just a fraction of an inch, Imogen? Yes, that's lovely. When you've finished, James, just pop over to the café and get me some orange squash. Such a funny thing's just happened,' she added to Cable. 'A little French girl came up to me and asked me for my autograph. She'd seen one of my commercials when she was staying in England.'

Matt, looking at her with acute dislike, was about to say something, then turned over and went back to sleep.

Although she was pouring with sweat, Imogen was too ashamed of her white body to go and swim until Cable and Nicky were safely in the sea. Then how cool and sympathetically soothing the water felt to her limbs. Below the dark green surface, she could see the slow moving shape of a fish. Then suddenly someone grabbed her ankles and she was falling. She seemed to swallow half the ocean. Choking, she came to the surface to see Nicky shooting away at a flashy crawl. Later he and Cable played very ostentatiously with a yellow beach ball.

'I say, that's rather naughty,' said James, staring fascinated at a girl whose bikini pants had practically no back to them.

'I don't know why she bothers to wear anything at all,' snapped Yvonne.

'Why don't you wear a bikini?' Yvonne asked Imogen. 'I'd lend you one, but I don't think you'd get into it. I really think you ought to do something about your thighs.'

'Exercises are the best thing,' said Cable, flopping down on the lilo. 'Sally Chetwynde lost five inches by bicycling every night.'

Imogen blushed as red as her bathing dress. If Matt had been there she was sure they would never have been so nasty to her. They shut up as soon as he came back.

She watched him oiling Cable, his hands moving steadily over her slim brown body, big practised hands, as skilful at making love as keeping a large car steady on a winding road at excessive speeds.

Her heart suddenly twisted with loneliness. Her skin was already turning as pink and as freckled as a foxglove. Oh, to be as beautiful as Cable, and to be loved by a man like Matt.

She was also worried that although she'd searched her room high and low she couldn't find her pills. What on earth was Nicky going to say when he discovered she'd lost them? Perhaps she could get some from a chemist. '*Avez-vous la pilule pour arreter les bébés?*' But wasn't France a Catholic country which forbade the pill anyway? If only Yvonne or Cable were more cosy she could have asked them.

'Of course *Vogue* pay peanuts, only twenty-five quid a day,' Yvonne was saying.

'I wouldn't put on my make-up for twenty-five quid a day,' said Cable.

Matt sighed and took refuge in a tattered copy of *Brideshead Revisited*.

When Imogen looked at herself in the glass before dinner, she was scarlet. Her head and her eyes ached; she had obviously overdone it. Her hair was stiff with oil, sand and sea water. Sand also seemed to have got into everything: towel, comb, bag, clothes; the floor of the room was just like the Gobi Desert. She lay on her bed and wondered which would be the worst evil, her baggy trousers or her other kaftan. She decided on trousers, which would at least hide her legs. After she had dressed and had another fruitless search for her pills, she wandered into Cable's room and found her busy combing out newly washed ebony curls.

'Goodness, you're red,' said Cable. 'Good thing you kept yourself well oiled. Try some of my green face powder. Guess what? James Edgworth's just made a pass at me.

Serve Yvonne right for being so bitchy last night. I can't think why I liked her in London. And, do you know, she was Purley Carnival Queen when she was 14? James made me promise not to tell anyone!'

In spite of the green face powder, Imogen's face glowed like a furnace as the evening wore on. After dinner they went to a night club. She couldn't believe how ravishing the girls were with their smooth expressionless faces, and long, long legs. And how beautifully they danced. It was as though the sun had melted their limbs to liquid. Nicky, having drunk too much, spent most of the evening wrapped round Cable. Matt ignored them both, and gabbled away to the nightclub owner. Every so often he smiled reassuringly at Imogen through the soupy darkness.

But later, back in her room, she wondered if she had ever been more miserable in her life. Here she was on the Riviera with the handsomest man in the world — a real daydream situation come true — and she was loathing every minute of it. She winced from sunburn as she climbed into bed. Oh please, God, make him be nice to me tonight.

Much later Nicky came in wearing not the violet dressing-gown which she'd so nearly been sick over last night, but a pair of black pyjamas. His gleaming beauty, after a day in the sun, was overwhelming. Squinting slightly from so much drink, he looked like a dangerous, hungry Siamese cat. He was obviously not going to put up with any nonsense to-night. Her stomach contracted with fear and expectancy.

'Feeling bridal, darling?' he said silkily, and pulled her towards him, his fingers biting into her arms. 'It's time you stopped playing games.'

His kisses were hard and brutal and gave her no pleasure. She was nearly suffocated by the smell of Cable's scent.

'No, no, Nicky, I don't want to!'

'Well, this time you're going to have to, honey child.'

'But you don't love me,' she gasped. 'Not a bit. You've ignored me since we left England.'

'Rubbish,' said Nicky, 'I tried hard enough last night, didn't I?'

'I couldn't help it. Oh, Nicky please, please don't. I can't

506

find my pills.'

'Your what!' It was like a pistol shot.

'I've looked for them everywhere. I must have left them in that hotel on the way.'

His slit eyes were like dark thread. 'Jesus, can't you do anything right? I don't believe you ever got them in the first place.'

Imogen gave a gasp of horror. 'Oh, I did, I did. I promise.'

'Crap,' said Nicky. 'You just pretended you had. We can't do anything to upset Daddy, can we?'

'I *did* get them,' said Imogen, bursting into tears. 'Oh, why won't you believe me?'

Nicky, mean with drink inside him, rattled her like a cat shaking a mouse, calling her every name he could think of until someone banged on the wall and told them to shut up in German. Nicky swore back in German and pushed Imogen back against the pillow.

'I'm s-s-sorry, Nicky,' she sobbed. 'I do love you.'

'Well, I don't love you,' he snarled. 'Get that straight. Nor do I like prissy little girls who string men along just for the sake of a holiday in the sun.'

And he stormed out of the room, slamming the door behind him.

There were four church clocks in Port-les-Pins, and Imogen counted each one chiming the quarter hours through the night, until the crowing cocks brought the morning sun streaming through the shutters.

As she was going downstairs next morning, dark glasses covering her reddened eyes, Cable popped her head out of the bedroom door. 'I just found these at the bottom of one of my espadrilles,' she said. 'I do hope you weren't looking for them.' And, laughing, she thrust the mauve card holding the pills into Imogen's hand.

Laughter, thought Imogen, is the most insidious sound in the world. Cable and Nicky lay on the beach slightly out of earshot from the rest of the party, heads together, laughing and talking in low caressing voices.

The heat of the sun was as fiery as yesterday's. But a fierce wind was raging. It tore the parasols out of the ground, blew sand in everyone's faces, and ruffled the green feathers of the palm trees along the front.

'It's called a mistral,' Matt told Imogen. 'It makes everyone very bad-tempered. Have you noticed how the nicest people became absolute monsters with too much spare time on their hands?'

Yvonne was moaning at James, who was hiding his pink burnt body under a huge green towel. Cable was as snappy as an elastic band with Matt, and Nicky didn't deign to recognise Imogen's existence.

A black poodle with a red collar came scampering by, scattering sand. James whistled and made clicking noises with his hand.

'Don't talk to strange dogs, Jumbo,' snapped Yvonne. 'They might easily have rabies.'

Cable, in an emerald green bikini with a matching turban to keep the sand out of her hair, had never looked more seductive. Matt retired behind *Paris Match*. Yvonne put on a cardboard beak to protect her nose from the sun, which made her look like some malignant bird. James got out his Box Brownie and went on a photographic spree which consisted mainly of front approaches on large ladies. Nicky went off to hire a Pedalo.

Three handsome muscular Frenchmen playing ball edged nearer Cable, then one of them deliberately missed a catch, so the ball landed at her feet. With laughter, and voluble apologies and much show of interest, they all came to retrieve it. Cable gave them a smouldering look. They smiled back in admiration. Next moment another catch was missed and the ball landed on her towel and, with a flurry of '*Pardons*', was retrieved again. Cable smirked. Matt took no notice and went on reading. Imogen suddenly thought how infuriating it must be for Cable that he appeared so unjealous. Maybe it was an elaborate game between them. She picked up a copy of *Elle* that Cable had abandoned which said '*une vrai beauté sauvage*' would be fashionable this autumn. The glamorously dishevelled mane of the model on the front cover bore no resemblance to Imogen's awful mop of hair which was now going in *'toutes directions'*. The heat was awful. Imogen, who was burning, picked up a tube of sun lotion and began plastering it over her face.

Yvonne gave a squeal of rage and snatched it away from her. 'How dare you use my special lotion!'

Matt lowered *Paris Match*. 'Stop beefing,' he said sharply. 'One oil's the same as another.'

'This one was specially made for me at great expense, because of my sensitive skin,' said Yvonne. 'Because I'm a model, it's absolutely vital I don't peel. This stuff is . . . '

Matt got up and went down to the sea leaving her in mid-sentence.

'He's the rudest man I ever met,' Yvonne said furiously as she re-adjusted her cardboard beak. 'I don't know why you put up with him, Cable.'

Cable rolled over and looked at Yvonne, her green eyes glinting. 'Because, my dear,' she drawled, 'he's a genius in bed.'

'What a disgusting thing to say,' said Yvonne, looking like an enraged beetroot.

'Once you've had Matt,' said Cable, 'you never really want anyone else.'

'Then why are you fooling around with Nicky Beresford?' Imogen caught her breath.

Cable grinned wickedly. 'Because Nicky's so pretty, and I must keep Matt on his toes or, shall we say, his elbows.'

'You're going about it the wrong way,' said Yvonne. 'You should occasionally sew a button on his shirt or cook more. Modelling's not a very stable career, you know.'

'Neither's marriage,' snapped Cable. 'Your husband made the most *horrendous* pass at me last night.'

And getting up in one lithe movement, she made her way down to the sea to join Nicky on a pedalo.

Yvonne turned on Imogen as the only available target. 'I don't know why you came out here with Nicky and then let him get away with it,' she snapped, and, spluttering with fury, went off to find James.

Imogen got some postcards out of her bag. She had bought them to send home to the family and the office, but what on earth could she say to them? They had all been so excited about her going. How could she tell them the truth?

Dear everyone, she wrote very large. *How are you all? I arrived safely. None of the gardens here are as good as ours.* Suddenly she had a vision of the vicarage and Pikely. Juliet and the boys would be at school now, her mother would probably be getting ready to go down to the shops, flapping about looking for her list while Homer waited for her, impatiently trailing his chain lead around like Marley's ghost. At such a distance even her father seemed less formidable. A great wave of homesickness overwhelmed her.

Matt strolled lazily up from the sea, water dripping from his huge shoulders, heavy-lidded eyes squinting against the sun. There was poor little Imogen in that awful bathing dress, surrounded by other people's possessions. He'd never seen anyone so woebegone. Today she was red-eyed, covered in bruises. Nicky must have put her through hell last night. Those pale-skinned English girls always translated badly to the South of France for the first few days. Her clothes were frightful, her hair a disaster. Once she turned brown, however, she might have possibilities. I could teach her a thing or three, he thought. He lay down beside her and put his arm round her shoulders.

'I declare National Necking Week officially open,' he said.

She turned a woeful face to him and held up an arm covered in bites.

'I don't seem to attract anything but mosquitoes,' she said, her lips trembling.

'Has Yvonne been bullying you? Listen baby, don't let her get you down. I know how she comes on, like she owns this beach personally and everyone has to act like a vicarage tea party, but you've just got to ignore her.'

Poor little thing, he thought, she really is miserable. Something will definitely have to be done about it.

CHAPTER TEN

'I feel lucky tonight,' said Matt after dinner, I'm off to the Casino.'

'To blow all our French bread, I suppose,' said Cable sourly.

As they went into the Roulette Room, Imogen was over-whelmed by the smoke, the glaring lights, and the fever the place itself generated. Gambling was obviously taken very seriously here. Round the table sat women with scarlet nails and obsessive faces. None of the pale, hard-eyed men be-hind them betrayed a flicker of interest in Cable. Huge sums of money were changing hands.

Matt went off to the Cashier and returned with his big hands full of counters.

'Fifteen for Cable, fifteen for Imogen, and the rest for me because I'm good at it. The others are fending for themselves.'

To Imogen, her fifteen counters suddenly became of cru-cial importance, and the green baize table a fearsome battle-ground. If she won, she would get Nicky back; if she lost, then all was lost. She would play number twenty-six, Nicky's age. But twenty-six obstinately refused to come up, and gradually her pile dwindled away, until she had only one counter left. She put it on number nine. It came up. Relief flooded her. She backed it again, and again it came up.

'Good girl,' said Matt, who was steadily amassing chips beside her.

But something compelled her to chance her luck and go on playing, and this time she lost and lost until she only had two counters. In desperation, she put them both on Noir. Rouge came up.

Tears stinging her eyes, she escaped to the Ladies.

'Oh God, I look hateful,' she moaned. Her face was still bright scarlet. The mistral had played even worse havoc with her hair, whipping it into a wild mop like a Zulu warrior. She couldn't even get a comb through it.

She didn't recognise the couple locked together in the passage when she came out a few minutes later. But she stiffened as she heard the familiar purr of Nicky's voice.

'Darling, you're so lovely,' he was saying. 'And I can feel your heart going like the Charge of the Light Brigade.'

Cable gave a husky laugh, and wound her arms round his neck.

'Do you believe in love at first sight?' he went on. 'I didn't until I met you. Then — pow! Suddenly it happened, as though I'd been struck by a thunderbolt. I don't know what it is about you — something indefinable, apart from being so beautiful.'

Imogen couldn't believe her ears. He was using exactly the same words he'd used when he'd tried to seduce her that first time on the moor. Words that were irrevocably signed on her heart.

'What about old purple sprouting Brocklehurst?' said Cable softly.

Nicky laughed. 'I knew it was a mistake the moment I met you, but I couldn't let her down. She's not much trouble and anyway it gave me a chance of being near you.'

'I feel a bit mean. Can't we find some arresting Provençal fisherman to bed her down?'

'Never get near her,' said Nicky and started to kiss Cable again.

They were so preoccupied they didn't notice her stumbling past.

She met Matt coming out of the Roulette Room. He was looking pleased with himself.

'I've just won nearly three thousand francs,' he said.

'How much is that?' said Imogen, desperately trying to sound normal.

'About £300. I've been good and cashed it in.' He looked at her closely.

'Hey, what's the matter?'

'Nothing, I'm fine,' she said.

'Cable and Nicky, is it?'

She nodded — impossible to keep anything from him.

He took her arm. 'I think you and I had better have a little talk.'

He led her to a deserted corner of the beach. They sat down on the warm sand. A huge white moon had turned the sea to gunmetal; the waves were idly flapping on the shore.

Matt lit a cigarette. 'All right lovie, what happened?'

Stammering, she told him.

'I don't mind him kissing her so much,' she said finally. 'I mean she's so lovely anyone would want to. But it's just his using the same words.'

'Cliché, cliché, cliché,' said Matt scornfully. 'But then you can't expect someone who hits a white ball across a net year in year out to have a very extensive vocabulary, can you?'

Imogen had a feeling he was laughing at her. 'But Nicky's clever. He speaks five languages,' she said defensively.

'A sign of great stupidity, I always think,' said Matt. 'Hell, I'm not trying to put Nicky down. I've nothing against people with I.Q.s in single figures. I just think you should know some home and away truths about him. I bet I know how he picked you up.'

'We were introduced,' said Imogen stiffly.

'No, before that. Wasn't he playing in a match, and he suddenly picked you out in the crowd, and acted as though he'd been turned to stone? Then, I suppose, he missed a few easy shots, as though he was completely overwhelmed by your beauty, and flashed his pretty teeth at you every time he changed ends.'

'He must have told you,' said Imogen in a stifled voice.

'No such luck, sweetheart. It's standard Beresford pickup practice in tournaments, all round the country. Quite irresistible, too, when combined with those devastating good looks. He never does it if there's any chance he might lose the match.'

'Then why did he bother to bring me on holiday?'

'For a number of reasons, I should think. Because you're very pretty, because he's got a jaded palate, and you're different from his usual run of scrubbers. Because he couldn't make you in Yorkshire, and he always likes to get his own way and, finally, because he hadn't met Cable then.'

'And what chance have I got against her?' sighed Imogen.

'You still want him, after hearing all that?'

Imogen nodded miserably. 'I'm a constant nymph,' she said.

Matt sighed. 'I was afraid you were. Well, we'll have to get him back for you, won't we?'

Outside her bedroom he took her key and unlocked the door.

'Now baby, lesson one. Don't cry all night. It'll only make you look ugly in the morning. And if you're still smarting about the purple sprouting Brocklehurst bit, remember that Cable's real name is Enid Sugden.'

He smiled, touched her cheek with his hand, and went. Imogen undressed and lay on her bed for a few minutes in the moonlight. Fancy Cable being called Enid. She giggled, then her thoughts turned to Matt.

Was it Jane Austen who said friendship was the finest balm for the pangs of despised love? She got up, locked her door and fell into a deep sleep.

It was after ten o'clock when she woke next morning. She found Matt drinking Pernod on the front, surrounded by newspapers, his long legs up on the table.

'You're going brown. Isn't it a pity one can't have the first drink of the day twice?' he said, ordering her a cup of coffee.

'How is everyone?' she said.

'Grimly determined to enjoy their fortnight's holiday. Yvonne running herself up as usual, Cable in one of her moods — I'm not sure which one. They've all gone water skiing.'

'Didn't you want to go?' said Imogen anxiously. It was bad enough that Nicky should annexe Cable without Matt being left with Nicky's boring girlfriend.

'After my performance on the boat coming over — you must be joking. You and I are going to take a trip along the coast.'

It was a perfect day. The mistral had retired into its cave. The air was soft. And as they drove along the coast road, the smell of petrol mingled with the scent of the pines. She still felt upset about Nicky, but for today she was determined not to brood.

'Where are we going?' asked Imogen.

'St Tropez,' said Matt.

Oh, God, thought Imogen, as the wind fretted her hair into an even worse tangle. Everyone will look like Bardot there.

Matt parked the car on the front. In the yachts round the Port, the rich in their Pucci silks were surfacing for the first champagne of the day. Matt steered Imogen through a doorway, up some stairs, into a hairdressing salon.

'To kick off, we're going to do something about your hair,' he said.

Imogen backed away in terror. 'Oh, no!' she said. 'They'll chop it all off.'

'No they won't,' said Matt, explaining to the pretty receptionist exactly what he wanted them to do.

'It'll look great,' he said, smiling at Imogen reassuringly, 'I'll pick you up later.'

'*Il a beaucoup d'allure,*' sighed the pretty receptionist to one of the assistants, who nodded in agreement as she helped Imogen into a pink overall.

When Matt came back, he didn't recognise her. He gave her one of those hard, appraising sexy looks that men only give to very pretty girls. Then he said, 'My God!' and a great smile spread across his face.

Her hair hung in a sleek bronze curtain to her shoulders, parted on one side and falling seductively over one eye.

'Very pretty, little one,' he said, walking round her. 'You don't look like Judge Jeffreys after too much port any more.' But the expression in his heavy-lidded eyes belied the teasing note in his voice.

'Let's go and have some lunch,' he said, tucking his hand underneath her arm.

He led her down a labyrinth of alleys smelling of garlic, abounding in cats and washing, to a tiny dark restaurant,

JILLY COOPER

which was full of fishermen. The food was superb.

Imogen watched Matt slowly pulling leaves off his artichoke.

'What does *beaucoup d'allure* mean?' she asked.

Matt looked up. 'Lots of sex appeal. Why?'

Imogen blushed. 'I just heard someone saying it about someone.'

As always he drew confidences out of her, as the sun brings out the flowers. Under that exceptionally friendly gaze, she was soon telling him about the vicarage, and her brothers and sisters, and what hell it had been to be fat at school, and how difficult it was to get on with her father. He's a journalist, she kept telling herself, he's trained to ask questions and be a good listener. He'd do the same to anyone. But she found herself noticing that his eyes were more dark green than black, and there was a small scar over his right eyebrow.

'You're not eating up,' he said, stripping one of her langoustine, dipping it into the mayonnaise and popping it into her mouth.

'I was wondering what the others were doing,' she lied.

'Bitching I should think. Yvonne told me this morning that it takes all sorts to make a world. Really someone should write all her sayings down in a book so they're not forgotten.'

He ordered another bottle of wine. Two of the fishermen were staring fixedly at Imogen now. She wondered if she'd got lipstick on her teeth, and surreptitiously got out her mirror.

Matt grinned at her. 'They're staring at you because you look beautiful,' he said.

The musky treacherous fires of the wine were stealing down inside her. She was beginning to feel wonderful. Matt asked for the bill. Imogen got out her purse.

'Let me pay, please let me.'

Matt shook his head. 'This is on me.'

As they went out into the fiery sunshine, she swayed slightly, and Matt took her arm.

'Come on, baby, we've got things to do.'

Imogen kept catching reassuring glimpses of her sleek reflection in shop windows. The rich in their yachts and their Pucci silks held no terrors for her now. She was walking on air.

'I think I'm a bit tight,' she said.

'Good,' said Matt, turning briskly into a boutique.

In a daze, she watched him rifling through a tray of bikinis.

'If it's for Cable,' she said, 'that red one would look lovely.'

'Not for Cable,' he said, piloting her into one of the changing rooms, 'for you.'

'Oh I couldn't! I'm too fat.'

'I'm the best judge of that,' said Matt handing her a pale blue bikini and drawing the curtain on her.

'Oh, what the hell,' thought Imogen, hiccuping gently.

She put on the bikini, and then stood gaping at herself. Except for her midriff which was still pale, there, smiling back at her in the mirror, was one of those beautiful shapely blondes who paraded up and down the beach at Port-les-Pins. Could it really be her? She gave a squeal of delight.

Matt pulled back the curtain and gave a low whistle,

'That's not bad for a start,' he said.

'But I'm practically falling out of it,' she said.

'Disgusting.' He ran a leisurely hand over her midriff, 'You'll have to put in some overtime here. Try these on.'

Everything he handed her — dresses, trousers, shirts, beach shifts — was in pale greens, blues and pinks, calculated to take the last tinge of red out of her suntan.

The record player was pounding out old pop tunes.

'You're just too good to be true,
Can't take my eyes off you . . .' sang Andy Williams.

'Took the words out of my mouth,' said Matt. Still the same teasing note in his voice. But in his eyes once again, she read approval and something else which made her heart beat faster.

As she struggled into an apple green dress covered in white daisies, wondering how he should so instinctively know what suited her, she suddenly heard a commotion outside.

'Matthieu, mon vieux!'

JILLY COOPER

'*Antoine, mon brave!*' followed by a torrent of excited French.

Imogen put her head round the curtain to find Matt talking nineteen to the dozen to the wickedest-looking Frenchman she had ever seen. He was wearing an immaculately tailored suit in brilliant yellow pinstripe, with a grey shirt and a green carnation in his button hole. Rings flashed from his fingers, gold rings in his ears. He reeked of scent and was smoking a large cigar, and although he had a young dark gipsy face, his hair was already quite grey.

Suddenly his black eyes lighted on Imogen.

'She come with you, Matthieu? What a beautiful girl.'

'This is Imogen,' said Matt.

'Beautiful,' murmured Antoine, fingering the green dress. 'You look like a meadow, Mademoiselle. May I come and roll in you some time?'

'Imogen, baby,' sighed Matt, 'I'm afraid this is Antoine de la Tour, playboy of the Western world. In between bouts of debauchery, he makes films.'

'We are old friends,' said Antoine. 'We were at Ox-fawd together.' He spoke English fluently with a strong Yorkshire accent.

'My Nanny come from Yorkshire,' he explained to Imogen. 'She taught me English, and much else besides. Ever since Nanny, I've a *tendresse* for Yorkshire girls.'

'Keep your hands off her,' said Matt. 'She's not mine to lend. I only borrowed her for the day. Tell me, do you know anything about Braganzi?'

'I've seen him in Marseilles once,' said Antoine. 'And the Duchess, what a beautiful woman.'

'How do I get to see him?' asked Matt.

'You don't,' said Antoine. ' 'is house is like a fortress.'

At that moment a redhead came undulating across the room with a pile of silk shirts over her arm. She was of such massive proportions, she made Imogen feel like Twiggy.

'This is Mimi,' said Antoine. 'Good girl, but spik no English.'

He handed her his wallet and, after smiling ravishingly at him, she undulated to the cash desk.

518

'Look at those 'ips,' sighed Antoine, 'but then I always prefer quantity to quality. Her father is biggest bidet manufacturer in France. 'E finance my next film.'

'What is it?' asked Imogen, wondering where Matt had disappeared to.

'I mek story of 'annibal and the Halps. We import one hondred elephants from Africa. Mimi will 'ave small part as 'annibal's slave girl.'

'She'll be splendid,' said Imogen.

Matt appeared and handed her a bulging carrier bag. She peered inside, aghast. 'But Matt, I can't. I thought we were just fooling about. All these things must have cost a fortune. You can't give them to me!'

'All in a good cause,' said Matt. 'Consider that they come with the compliments of Port-les-Pins Casino. Let's go and see Antoine off,' he added before she could argue any more.

Outside, deep in onlookers, was a huge pale mauve Rolls Royce with smoked glass windows. Mimi, two Great Danes and a goat were watching television in the back.

A tall sleek Negro in a white suit and dark glasses was opening the door for Antoine.

'This is Rebel,' said Antoine. 'My bodyguard and friend. I want him to play Caesar in my film. But he say it against Black Power principles to play white dictator. We'll come over to Port-les-Pins this evening. *Au revoir, mes petites,*' and he joined Mimi and the menagerie in the back.

'He certainly has great style,' said Imogen, still giggling as she and Matt stretched out on the beach later. 'I mean that grey hair with that young face.'

'It's dyed,' said Matt. 'You may laugh, but he's absolutely lethal where women are concerned. You should have seen him at Oxford, bowling them over with his Cartier watches and his dinner jacket with green facings. Any girl worth her salt in those days claimed to be educated at Roedean, Lady Margaret Hall, and Antoine de la Tour. So watch it, mate.'

Although everyone else on the beach was sunbathing topless, Imogen jumped out of her skin as she felt Matt's fingers undoing the clasp of her bikini.

'No, I can't,' she gasped.

'Don't be silly,' said Matt. 'Turn over. I'll oil you.'

Imogen shut her eyes and turned over. The hot sun beat red through her lids. Hastily she covered her breasts with her folded arms.

'Come on,' said Matt. 'I want to look at you.'

'Oh please don't,' muttered Imogen. 'I'm so awful.'

'Shut up,' he said, gently pulling down her arms.

'You've been hiding your finest asset for far too long. Nicky was absolutely right about your tits.'

As his hands began to move luxuriously over her stomach, she felt her throat tighten and her mouth go dry. She opened her eyes to find him smiling lazily down at her, the heavy olive lids almost shutting out the dark green eyes. Her heart was going bump-bump like an overloaded spin dryer. Suddenly the beach had become a tiny room.

'I'll oil the rest of me,' she stammered, snatching the tube of *ambre solaire* from him and hastily smothering her tits.

Matt laughed. 'Fear no more the heat of the sun,' he said.

'It's not the heat of the sun I'm scared of at the moment,' muttered Imogen, frantically reaching for her bikini top. 'I'm going for a swim.'

'Uh, uh,' he held her down. 'Not when I've just oiled you. Concentrate on getting brown.'

He picked up the evening paper. 'Bugger,' he said. 'Braganzi and the Duchess went to the theatre in Marseilles last night. Jesus, if only I could get in there.'

If he's totally unmoved by my lying beside him half naked, perhaps it's all right, thought Imogen, looking timidly around. A few yards away a handsome German was lasciviously rubbing oil into his companion's enormous breasts. Goodness, I am seeing life, she thought as gradually the tension seeped out of her.

Much later, when Imogen's bosom and the sea were turning a deep rosy gold, Matt glanced at his watch. 'Christ it's late. We'd better get back.'

They drove back in a manic mood. The wireless was roaring out the Fifth symphony. Matt was waltzing the car round the hairpin bends. He was wearing that battered

Panama hat to keep the sun out of his eyes. His thick tawny hair was now extravagantly bleached and streaked by the sun, his teeth gleamed white in his brown face.

God, he's divine. How could I ever have thought he was ugly? she wondered.

'Such a lovely day,' she said, stretching luxuriously. 'And all my heavenly clothes. You are good to me, Matt.'

He looked round and smiled approvingly.

'Nicky won't be able to keep his hands off you now.'

Nicky! That brought her up with a jerk. How awful, she hadn't given him a thought for hours.

CHAPTER ELEVEN

Sulky faces greeted them as they drove up to the hotel.

'Where the hell have you been?' snapped Cable.

'Exciting each other on the beach at St Trop,' said Matt.

Nicky and James were gaping at Imogen, who had got out of the car and was standing in the street in her bikini, her hair streaming down her back.

'Gosh,' said James in awe. 'You look like one of the girls at the Motor Show.'

'Matt seems to have been playing Pygmalion,' said Cable frostily.

'Rather successfully, don't you think?' said Matt, looking at Imogen.

'She looks tremendous,' said James. 'Have a drink?'

'We bumped into Antoine de la Tour, mad as ever. He's coming over this evening. How was the water skiing, darling?' said Matt to Cable. He bent over to give her a peck on the cheek, but she jerked her head away and spat a remark at him which only he heard.

He straightened up and looked at her.

'It's those loving things you do that make me grow so close to you,' he said in an undertone.

'Yvonne's ill,' said Nicky, who was still staring at Imogen. 'She's been stung by a jellyfish.'

'Oh dear,' said Matt in concern. 'Is the poor jellyfish expected to live?'

James tried, but failed, to look affronted.

'She wants me to sit by her bedside all night,' he said plaintively. 'I'd get her some pills to ease the pain, but I can't make the beastly chemist understand.'

'I'll get her something,' said Matt. 'Order us a drink. I'll be right back.'

'First she says I stink of garlic, and then I mustn't touch her because of her sunburn, and now this. What a holiday.' James looked as though he was going to cry.

Nicky turned to Imogen. 'You look sensational,' he said, and began to tell her about the water skiing, his eyes wandering over her body as of old. Cable looked so thunderous, Imogen was glad when Matt came back.

'Here you are,' he said, handing James a phial of green pills. 'But tell Yvonne not to take too many. They're absolute knockouts.'

'Thanks awfully,' said James, bolting into the hotel. He came back five minutes later, his face wreathed in smiles.

'What on earth were they?' he asked. 'She went out like a light.'

'Smarties,' said Matt. 'I got them from the sweet shop round the corner. We extracted the green ones.'

Cable was the only person not to join in the shouts of laughter.

'I'm going to change,' she said.

'So am I,' said Matt grimly.

Imogen, at a discreet distance behind them, saw Matt follow Cable into their room.

'When are you going to stop buggering up every one else's holiday?' she heard him say.

'Male chauvinist Pygmalion,' thought Imogen.

Dinner was decidedly stormy. The collision of wills in the bedroom had obviously escalated into a major row. Cable was in a murderous mood, her jaw set, her green eyes glittering. She kept ordering the most expensive things on the menu, and then sending them back untouched.

She was drinking heavily. And although Nicky was listening to her feverish chatter, every so often he cast discreet glances in Imogen's direction.

Imogen was feeling beautiful in one of the dresses Matt had bought her. She had noticed the way men's heads had turned and looked at her and stayed looking, as she came into the restaurant. It was a completely new experience. Even Cable couldn't destroy her mood of euphoria. James, delirious to be off the matrimonial lead, was getting thoroughly overexcited. Matt appeared outwardly unruffled, but he was lighting one cigarette from another.

No one was sorry when Antoine and Mimi arrived and bore them all off to a disco outside the town.

On the way they passed a large turreted house, strewn with creeper, set back from the road behind high walls and huge iron gates.

'That's one of Braganzi's 'ide outs,' said Antoine. 'It go straight down to a private beach.'

Above the burglar alarm trill of the cicadas, they could hear the faint baying of guard-dogs.

'I 'ave made the enquiries, Matthieu,' Antoine went on. 'If you go along to Le Bar de la Marine tomorrow lunchtime and ask for a Monsieur Roche, 'e might be able to help.'

The disco was called Verdi's Requiem. Imogen was almost knocked sideways by the brush-fire smell of pot, Alice Cooper thundering out of the stereo and a mass of writhing bodies. Antoine promptly ordered champagne all round and installed them at the best table.

Immediately Nicky asked Imogen to dance.

'You look simply terrific,' he said as soon as they were out of earshot of the others. 'I hardly recognised you when Matt brought you back this evening. I'm afraid I've been a bit offish lately. But when you kept hustling me out of the bedroom and then losing your pills.'

'It seemed as though I was deliberately rejecting you?'

'A deliberate rejection was exactly what it seemed.'

'I'm sorry, Nicky. I didn't mean it.'

'I'm sorry too. No hard feelings?'

They smiled at each other. His eyes are like velvet, thought Imogen, but was shocked to find herself adding that his forehead was too low, and his smile like a toothpaste commercial. He laid his smooth brown cheek against her hair and drew her closer to him, but her heart didn't thump in the usual way; she even felt very strong at the knees.

'Did you have a nice day with Matt?' he said.

'Yes, thank you. Did you have a nice day with Cable?'

'It's rather like looking after a two year old,' said Nicky. 'You have to keep her amused all the time and she's into everything, particularly boutiques. I can't think how Matt can afford her. She needs a play pen.'

The moment they got back to the table James swept her on to the floor. It was as though he had hitherto proceeded gingerly through life like a sports car towing a huge cumbersome trailer. But now suddenly the trailer had been detached (or rather stung by a jellyfish) and the sports car was careering off joyfully into the unknown.

'Jolly handsome chap, Antoine,' he said as his hands roved eagerly over Imogen's body. 'I wonder if I could get away with wearing earrings.'

'Would it be quite the thing for a Tory candidate?' shouted Imogen above the din of the music. 'You'd have to have your ears pierced.'

'My ears are pierced every day by the voice of my dear wife,' said James petulantly.

Imogen giggled. She realised she'd had a great deal too much to drink. Oblivious that James was breathing down the front of her dress, and caressing her back, she tried to unravel her confused emotions. Whatever had happened to that undying love she had sworn to Nicky last night?

She looked across the room at him, talking earnestly to Cable, as though he was placating her for dancing so long with Imogen. She was alarmed that she felt no pang of jealousy. What price the constant nymph now?

'*Many a tear has to fall but it's all in the game,*' sang the record player.

'That Mimi's a bit of all right, isn't she?' said James, squeezing Imogen ever tighter. 'How do you say, "Do you bop?" in French?'

A few minutes later James and Mimi had taken the floor.

James, just about coming up to Mimi's shoulder, happily buried his pink face in her magnificent bosom.

Imogen meanwhile was having a long dance with Antoine, who divided his time between flirting outrageously and telling her how awful he thought Cable was. 'She is a nighthorse,' he said finally.

'Nightmare,' giggled Imogen. But she was surprised.

She had thought Antoine and Cable would get on. Perhaps they were both too fond of the limelight.

'This is a very nice place,' she said.

'I own it,' said Antoine simply, looking like the devil himself, swaying in front of her, all in black with his diamonds flashing gaudily, and his white teeth gleaming tigerish in his dark gipsy face. Any moment she expected him to disappear through a trapdoor in a puff of smoke.

'Oim jolly well pleased to see you,' he said.

'Mimi goes to Paris at the week-end. I come over and see you. I have villa just behind the village. We might go riding or sailing together. I have been sailing in England, at Calves.'

'Calves?' said Imogen, puzzled.

'Yes, in the Island of Wight.'

'Oh, Cowes!' She went off into peals of laughter. She found it impossible to take him seriously.

'I love England, but I think your countrymen behave atrocious abroad.'

He was looking at James, who, with Mimi's help was energetically lowering his country's prestige on the other side of the floor.

'Mimi make the distress signals,' he said. 'I must salvage her. *A bientôt, ma cherie,*' and kissing Imogen fondly on both cheeks, he delivered her back to the table.

James asked her to dance, and then Nicky again and then James. Cable, refusing to leave the table and the champagne, was looking absolutely thunderous, and didn't even cheer up when Nicky made the disc jockey play one of her favourite tunes.

Fate is conspiring against me, thought Cable bitterly. For the first few days of the holiday, everything had gone so well; she had succeeded in enslaving Nicky and James, irritating Yvonne, utterly overshadowing stupid naïve Imogen, and finally most important of all continually keeping Matt on the jump. She knew how upset he had been beneath that apparent imperturbability. She had felt the whole time as though she'd been driving a coach and five with complete success. But tonight, suddenly, she felt the reins slipping out of her hands. Matt had obviously enjoyed his day with Imogen and brought her back looking quite passable — at least Nicky and James and Antoine obviously thought so and were all over her. Men always went for anything new. Cable was further irritated that Antoine hadn't reacted to her charms.

She'd always heard what a wolf he was and he wasn't even flickering in her direction. As for that blousy overweight Mimi, even in the gloom of the disco everyone was turning their heads and staring at her in admiration.

In the same way, Cable supposed people would stare at an elephant if it came through the door. And then Nicky wasn't being as tractable as usual. That very afternoon she'd caught him exchanging surreptitious but no less smouldering glances with a blonde nymphette at the water-skiing club. She'd have to give him some concessions soon. She drained her glass of champagne and banged it imperiously on the table.

'Get another bottle,' she ordered Matt.

Totally ignoring her, Matt turned towards Imogen, who was coming off the floor with James. Her hair was tumbled from dancing, her cheeks flushed, her breasts rising and almost falling out of the low cut dress.

'My turn I think,' he said, getting to his feet.

'Beautiful, beautiful girl,' said Antoine. 'How I love York-shire girls.'

Nicky was about to agree with him, and claim responsibility for discovering her, then, glancing at Cable's face, thought better of it.

'Isn't that Bianca Jagger over there?' said James, peering through the gloom. 'I'm going to ask her to dance.'

Imogen had been waiting to dance with Matt all evening. There was a thrill of excitement in the pit of her stomach, as, loose-jointed, he swayed in front of her, his lazy triangular eyes amused yet approving.

'You're having a good evening, darling. They've been after you like wasps round a water melon.'

'It's entirely due to you,' she said. She looked across the

room at Nicky and Cable who were deep in conversation. Nicky was holding Cable's hand and apparently trying to calm her down.

'I'm sorry it didn't work — getting Nicky off Cable, I mean.'

Matt shrugged his shoulders. 'I'm not losing any sleep,' he said. The music accelerated, the colours were shifting like a kaleidoscope. The floor was filling up and they were constantly thrown together. Matt put his hands on her shoulders to protect her. She was finding it difficult to breathe.

Suddenly, he buried his face in her neck. Her body turned to liquid.

'You've been pinching Cable's scent,' he said.

'Oh, goodness, I'm sorry,' said Imogen, blushing crimson in confusion.

'I don't mind. Pinch away. It doesn't suit you, that's all. Too clinging.' Imogen was about to say she *felt* clinging when Nicky came over.

'Antoine's off, James is about to be duffed up by the husband of a girl he's convinced is Bianca Jagger, and Cable says she's bored.'

'And I'm in absolutely no hurry. Cable can do the waiting for a change,' said Matt.

Imogen didn't dare look in Cable's direction, and tried not to feel elated, as they danced on for another two records by which time the table had emptied.

Outside they found Rebel, the black chauffeur, bearing a heavily embracing Antoine and Mimi away in the huge Rolls-Royce. Cable was crouched over the wheel of the Mercedes with Nicky beside her, an arm along the back of the seat.

'Where the hell have you been?' said Cable, furiously revving up the car.

'Keeping you waiting,' snapped Matt.

'You and your darling protegée have been doing that all day.

'I should write to *The Times* about it if I were you,' said Matt.

'Stop sending me up,' howled Cable. 'You can both bloody

well walk home,' and, jamming her foot down on the accelerator, she thundered off down the coast road.

'Oh dear,' said Imogen in horror.

'Silly bitch,' said Matt totally unmoved. 'Shall we walk? It's only a mile or two. If you're too knackered I'll go back and ring for a taxi.'

'Oh, no, I'd love to,' said Imogen, unable to believe her luck.

'Suits me,' said Matt, taking her arm. 'I want to have a closer butcher's at Braganzi's house on the way.'

After the day's relentless heat, the night was warm and sultry. Compared with the stuffiness of the disco the air was sweet and smelt faintly of dew, wild thyme and the sea. The cicadas were cawing in the trees like frogs. Port-les-Pins glittered in its cove ahead of them, and every few seconds its northern jut of rock was bathed in a white beam from the lighthouse. Far above them everything in the sky, stars, planets, southern cross, moon seemed to be out and twinkling eons away in their own heavens. And I'm so lit up they can probably see me twinkling away down here on earth too, thought Imogen. She was swaying slightly from drink and euphoria, but Matt steadied her, holding her above the elbow, gently stroking the inside of her arm with his thumb. He's probably so used to caressing Cable, he does it automatically, she thought.

'You're too good to be true, can't take my eyes off you,' hummed Matt abstractedly.

They could see Braganzi's house ghostly in the moonlight, its turrets thickly hung with creeper and silhouetted against the sky.

'Is it really necessary to get to see him?' said Imogen nervously. 'Oughtn't you to be relaxing on your holidays?'

'All journalists are the same. Once they've got on to a scent they can't let it alone, like dogs with a bitch on heat.'

They were only a hundred yards away now. There were two lights on upstairs with bars like lift gates over the windows. Perhaps one was the Duchess's bedroom. Imogen imagined her brushing out her long dark hair with silver brushes with coronets on. She longed to open all the shutters like an Advent calendar and perhaps find the little baby asleep in one room or Braganzi plotting some dastardly crime in a black shirt and a white tie in another.

Outside the main gates, they could see a figure walking up and down with an Alsatian on a lead. The dog growled, the man stubbed out his cigarette and looked around. Imogen started to tremble.

'Let's have a look round the back,' whispered Matt.

Fifteen foot high walls with another three feet of iron spikes, and rolled barbed wire on top of that, went almost all the way round the house, then divided at the back, running down to the sea and protecting Braganzi's stretch of private beach.

'The only way into the house is from the sea,' whispered Matt, 'and I bet that's guarded night and day. He's not taking any chances, is he? It's worse than Colditz.' He looked at the burglar alarms that clung like limpets to the walls of the house.

The brightness of the moonlight and the sweet heavy smell of tobacco plants and night-scented stocks made it all the more sinister.

'Do let's go,' pleaded Imogen. She was sure the guard dogs could hear the frantic hammering of her heart. They were creeping close to the wall now. Suddenly she heard a tinny sound, as her foot hit something metallic.

'Bugger,' said Matt, bending down to look. 'That's probably an alarm.'

Next moment there was a frantic barking of dogs, and sounds of a door clanging.

'They've rumbled us,' gasped Imogen.

'Come here,' said Matt, and the next moment he'd pushed her down on the ground and was kissing her, tugging down the top of her dress, baring her shoulders. She could feel the rough scrub against her back, and taste the salt and brandy on his lips.

The growling grew closer and more ferocious.

Imogen wriggled in terror.

'Lie still,' muttered Matt, putting his full weight on her. 'It's a lovely way to go.'

Next moment the area was flooded with light. The dogs charged forward. It seemed they must rip them to pieces, and then suddenly the ferocious growling stopped not six inches away. Imogen's French was not particularly fluent, but she could just make out Matt furiously asking what the bloody hell the guards thought they were doing as he pulled Imogen's dress up over her shoulders.

The guards dragged the dogs off and made her and Matt get to their feet. Matt explained that they were holiday-makers who'd got separated from the rest of the party and decided to walk home, that they were staying at La Reconnaissance in Port-les-Pins. Then the guards frisked Matt and had a look at his wallet and his traveller's cheques. Imogen nearly fainted when she saw that all four men had guns. They certainly took their time searching her, rough hands wandering into the most embarrassing places until Matt shouted at them to leave her alone.

Finally the guards conferred among themselves for a minute and then told them to be on their way, shouting something after them with a coarse laugh that Imogen didn't understand. She could feel their eyes following her and Matt like eight prongs sticking into their backs.

'Keep walking! Don't look round,' hissed Matt. 'Thank Christ I didn't have my passport on me, or they'd have rumbled us.'

After what seemed an eternity they rounded the corner, out of sight, with Port-les-Pins's friendly lights winking just below them.

Imogen started to tremble violently.

Matt put his arms round her. 'Darling, I'm terribly sorry, Are you all right?'

'I'm not sure,' she said. 'I thought our last moment had come.'

He held her close to him and stroked her hair and her bare arms until the reassuring warmth of his body made her calmer.

'But your reactions were like lightning,' she stammered. 'Pushing me on to the ground like that, then acting dumb and outraged like any old tourist caught in the act.'

531

Matt laughed and got a packet of cigarettes out of his pocket.

'I always turn into a bumpkin at midnight. Anyway I've talked myself out of much worse trouble spots than that. All the same, I'm really sorry, I shouldn't have put you through it.'

'What did they say as we were leaving?'

'Next time I brought a bird up on to the cliffs for a quick poke to choose somewhere else.'

'So they really believed you?'

Matt shrugged his shoulders. 'They won't tomorrow when they check up with the hotel.'

He was walking along with an arm round her shoulders now, and suddenly she felt choked with happiness almost to the point of tears, as it dawned on her how much, in spite of the danger, she'd enjoyed being kissed by him, and feeling the muscular weight of his body on top of her. She was still trembling, but not from fear.

'He must be terrified of something to wire a place up like that.'

'Losing the Duchess, I guess,' said Matt.

They had dropped down into the port now. Lights from the boats shivered in the black water like fallen earrings; the forest of masts swayed gently against the stars. In the distance they could hear the faint splash of the sea as it rolled over and over on the white sand.

They came to an all-night café along the front. A few fishermen were drinking morosely at the bar; a tired-looking waitress had kicked off her shoes and was polishing glasses as though in her sleep.

'What we need is immediate first aid,' said Matt, and as he was ordering black coffee and triple brandies for them both, he suddenly turned round and smiled at her. The effect of him that close was so mind-blowing that her knees gave way. She had to fumble for a bar stool and clamber on to it.

'Will you bother to go and see Antoine's contact tomorrow?' she asked, as they got their drinks.

'If that doesn't lead to anything, I'll scrub the whole thing and preserve my energies for squabbling with Mrs

Edgworth.' He took her hand and she hoped he couldn't feel the tremor that shot through her. 'Look, angel, I'm really sorry you were frightened. When one's had scraps with Provos, and white Rhodesians, and even Amin's henchmen, as I have in my time, Braganzi's hoods seem pretty small fry, but I know how terrifying it was for you.'

'Honestly, I'm fine now.' She could hardly tell him she'd never felt so happy in her life, and she thought he was the nicest man she'd ever met, and if he'd taken her in his arms, and thrown her down on the heath again, she wouldn't have minded if the entire criminal world formed a shrieking witch's coven round them. So instead she said, 'What were Amin's henchmen like?'

Then he told her about some of the trouble spots he'd been to and they had several more brandies by which time the stars were fading and the horizon was lightening to a pale turquoise. They walked back past the Bar de la Marine and the Plaza Hotel, with its striped umbrellas folded and its dozing doorman. They passed a few elderly homosexuals looking for comfort, and guitarists from the nightclubs sleepily twanging their way home.

'You're too good to be true, can't take my eyes off you,' hummed Matt.

At the reception area of La Reconnaissance with its one naked light bulb, he took down her key and extracted a dripping purple aster from the vase on the desk. Imogen ran upstairs pressing the lights and racing to catch the next switch before it went out and plunged them into darkness.

Outside her room, he stopped. 'Good-night little accomplice,' he said softly, handing her the dripping purple aster.

He's going to kiss me, she thought in rapture. But as he bent his head and touched her lips a door flew open, and out charged a fat woman in a hair net, who barged past them and rushed down the passage to the lavatory. Next minute they heard the sound of terrible retching, and both collapsed with silent laughter.

Then suddenly another door opened and there was Cable wrapped in a dark green towel, a cigarette hanging from her scarlet lips.

'And about bloody time too,' she said.

Inside her room Imogen wandered around in a daze. Matt had kissed her. She knew how casual kisses could be, and they'd both been drinking all day. But she didn't think Matt was a casual person. Port-les-Pins was teeming with beautiful girls but, unlike Nicky and James, beyond a cursory approving glance, he'd never shown much interest in any of them.

She looked in the mirror, and touched her lips where he'd kissed off all her lipstick, then ran her hands over her body with a shiver of excitement — a genius in bed Cable had said. But it wasn't just the bed she wanted.

Wipe that silly grin off your face, she kept telling herself, you're banking on too much. She lay down on the bed, but the room swung round and round, so she got up, and tried on all her new clothes, standing swaying on the bed to see them full length. Tomorrow she'd wear the pale green sundress, or perhaps the duck-egg blue shirt with most of the buttons undone like Cable did. She imagined Matt at this moment having a blazing row with Cable, saying it's all over between us, I love Imogen.

You mustn't hope, she told herself sternly, he loves Cable, he only gave you those clothes to get Nicky off her back, but the words made no sense to her.

I love him, I love him, she said, pressing her burning face in the pillow. Then she carefully put the purple aster between the pages of her diary, which wouldn't shut now because of the yellow centre bit, and lay for a long time watching the sky lighten, listening to cocks crowing and cars starting up, and children shouting, before she fell asleep.

CHAPTER TWELVE

She was woken by the sun on her body, the same delicious feeling of happiness spreading through her like a rosy glow. She put on the new pale blue sundress and went downstairs to find the rest of the party in various stages of disintegration, having breakfast on the front and reading the papers.

Yvonne was displaying a black and blue foot on a chair for everyone to see. Having had no dinner last night, she had insisted on James ordering a boiled egg for her.

'This egg is as hard as a bullet, Jumbo,' she was screeching as she tried to force a buckling toast soldier into it.

'I asked for *quatorze minutes*,' said James defensively.

'That's fourteen, not four,' shrieked Yvonne. 'Why do you drink so much when you know you can't hold it, Jumbo? You know how idiotic it makes you next morning.'

James, desperately trying to disguise his hangover, was lifting his cup of coffee with both hands. He looked terrible. Matt didn't look much better. He smiled rather guardedly when he saw Imogen, and didn't quite meet her eyes as he ordered her some coffee.

Nicky, looking healthy as ever, was reading the sports page of *The Times*.

'Christ,' he said, 'Connors got knocked out in the third round.'

Imogen watched him surreptitiously move his foot forward, and rub it gently against Cable's ankle. Cable returned the pressure, then stretched her beautiful brown legs out in front of her. She was wearing a Jean Machine rugger shirt and sitting on one of Matt's knees, reading the *Daily Mail* horoscopes.

'I do hate not getting the horoscopes till the day after. Evidently I should have had a disastrous day for romance yesterday, which simply wasn't true, was it, darling?' She coiled an arm round Matt's neck, and kissed him lingeringly,

Imogen picked pieces of skin out of her coffee with a spoon, and felt happiness slowly oozing out of her like air out of a badly tied balloon.

Madame waddled out with a telegram for Matt.

'It's from Larry Gilmore,' he said, when he'd opened the orange envelope. ' "Arriving Plaza 8 p.m.," ' he read.

'Oh, that's great,' said Cable.

'Is that Larry Gilmore, the photographer?' said Yvonne. 'I thought he was supposed to be a monster.'

'He's fine as long as you don't burst into tears every time he calls you a stupid cow, and Bambi, his wife, is lovely,' answered Cable defensively.

'Bambi and Jumbo,' said Nicky. 'It's getting more like the zoo every minute.'

Everyone brightened at the prospect of new blood, it would perhaps get them off each other's backs, except Imogen who merely expected it would mean more talk about models.

'What d'you want to do today, Jumbo?' said Yvonne petulantly.

'Anything you like, darling.'

'Oh, don't be awkward. Anyway I've got to go into Marseilles to show this foot to a decent doctor.' She turned steely forget-me-not eyes on the rest of the company. 'They shoot horses you know, when they're in this kind of pain.'

'I'd like to go to the Isle of Levant and bathe nude,' said Cable. 'Have you any idea how lovely water feels on your naked body?'

'Yes, every day in the bath,' said Matt.

Nicky yawned and stretched out his legs, once again rubbing his foot against Cable's.

'I feel bloody unfit,' he said. 'I'm going to find some courts in Marseilles and have a workout. Will you be all right on the beach, darling?' he added to Imogen, who nodded with relief.

536

'I'm going into Marseilles too then,' said Cable, shooting a spiteful glance at Imogen. 'I think it's my turn to buy a few new clothes today. Are you coming too, darling?' she added to Matt, slipping a hand inside his shirt and stroking his chest.

'Can't, really. I've got to see this chap at the Bar de la Marine at twelve.'

Imogen's face lit up. Perhaps he was staying behind to be with her.

'Jesus, can't you ever stop working?' snapped Cable.

She glanced at Imogen, who was stirring her coffee and crumbling her croissant with a trembling hand, not looking at Matt and avoiding Cable's eye. She's got a schoolgirl's crush on Matt, thought Cable. It had happened before fairly often, with women friends of hers Matt had been particularly kind to, or girls who worked on the paper who came round for drinks, all tarted up, then looked at Cable with dismay, realising the competition. It was all Matt's fault for paying Imogen so much attention yesterday, as if he honestly believed that by buying her a few clothes he'd get Nicky back for her. She was a drip and Nicky didn't like drips, and a few sophisticated clothes wouldn't change that. Cable wasn't in the least jealous of Imogen. The blazing row she'd had with Matt last night had been followed by the most passionate rapturous lovemaking. But she didn't like him singling anyone out for attention. He never bothered with Yvonne like he did with Imogen.

As she and Matt went upstairs to get her some money, she said quite gently,

'Darling, you must stop leading Imogen on. She's got a terrible crush on you. She hasn't taken her eyes off you all morning.'

Matt sat on the beach beside Imogen, reading the same page over and over again. Ever since he'd woken up he'd been kicking himself, and going round saying damn, damn, damn, damn, like Professor Higgins. Admittedly he'd been smashed out of his mind last night, or he'd never have risked casing Braganzi's house and putting himself and

537

Imogen in such danger, but he never should have given her that aster, or kissed her good-night. If they hadn't been interrupted by that fat woman rushing down to the lavatory, heaven knows how far he might have gone. He had his hands full with Cable. He liked Imogen far too much to hurt her.

It was a soft day. The breathing of the sea was remote and gentle; the sky arched a perfect cornflower blue over their heads. But yesterday's easy camaraderie had vanished. Imogen didn't seem to be getting on much better with *Tristram Shandy* either. Matt shut his book.

'Let's go for a walk,' he said.

He bought her a Coke and a can of beer for himself, and they wandered along the beach, Imogen gathering shells and popping seaweed. As she popped away he could see her mouth moving — he loves me, he loves me not — and the look of desolation on her face when it came out, he loves me not.

They examined a dead jellyfish (like a striped red blister), overturned rocks so that little crabs scurried out, and when they walked over the dark wet saffron masses of seaweed covering the rocks, her hand slid into his as trustingly as a child to stop herself slipping. Oh Christ, why had he led her on? He had only meant to be kind.

They reached the end of the beach, and sat down to cool off under the indigo shadow cast by a huge red rock. He looked at her round innocent face longing to be kissed.

'Imogen, darling?'

'Yes,' she said, her eyes lighting up.

'How old are you?'

'Nearly 20.'

'And how many affairs have you had?'

'None really,' she blushed. 'Not bed anyway. I expect I would have with Nicky, but I lost my pills. But I found them again. I took three yesterday,' she added quickly.

'Well, don't tell him,' said Matt, deliberately misreading her offer. 'Nicky's no good for you. He's only interested in conquest, servicing totally *compris* in fact. He treats birds like French letters, throwing them away as soon as he's used them.'

He picked up a handful of sand, letting it drift through his fingers.

'Do you know what you should do after this holiday? Get away from your father and the family and Yorkshire and get a job in London. The paper's got a terrific library; they sometimes have a vacancy. Would you like me to see if I could get you a job?'

'Oh, yes, please,' she gasped. 'Oh, yes.' To have a chance to see him every day, to cut out his stories every week and file them under 'O'Connor, Matt', to do telling research for him whenever he needed help with a story.

'But I don't really know anyone in London,' she stammered.

Matt smiled. 'You know me and Basil — and Cable.'

Her fingers, which seemed to be sleepwalking towards his hand, suddenly stopped at the mention of Cable. She took a hasty swig from her tin, leaving a moustache of Coke on her upper lip.

'You should live a little,' he said very gently. 'Get more experience. Play the field. Break a few hearts, and have fun. You'll soon grow out of men like Nicky.'

'I don't want to play the field,' she said dolefully.

'Cable and I have been together a long time. We understand each other.'

He was trying to tell her something, however gently, and she didn't want to hear it. Keep out of Ireland. Hands off O'Connor. In the heat, he had pushed his damp blond hair back from his sweating forehead, showing the thick horizontal wrinkles, and the laughter lines round his eyes, which were bloodshot from drinking and lack of sleep, the heavy lids swollen. He looked thoroughly seedy and hung over, and every bit of his thirty-two years. But gazing at the battered sexy face she wondered how she could ever have loved anyone else in her life.

Matt sighed. He wasn't finding this at all easy. 'Look, sweetheart,' he said, 'I shouldn't have kissed you last night. I was extremely drunk and I enjoyed it, but I shouldn't have done it. You've had enough flak from Nicky without my putting the boot in.'

Imogen watched a speedboat shooting by, rearing up thirty degrees out of the water. The noontide sky was the same colour as the sea now; you could hardly distinguish the horizon.

She leapt to her feet.

'If you're trying to pretend last night meant anything more to me than a friendly good-night kiss,' she said, 'you're very much mistaken.'

And, turning away, she ran back down the beach towards the hotel.

'Hell, hell, hell and damnation,' said Matt,

A huge pair of dark glasses over her reddened eyes had got her through lunch. She could hardly eat anything, picking away like Cable. She avoided looking at Matt, who wasn't eating much either. He announced he was going into Marseilles by himself that afternoon, to follow up a tip-off Antoine's contact had given him at the Bar de la Marine.

'I've had quite enough of Marseilles for one day,' said Cable, who'd had a successful shopping expedition. 'I'm going to sleep for a few hours. Such an exhausting night, darling,' she added, running a caressing hand inside Matt's shirt. Imogen gritted her teeth. Yvonne, looking smug and well bandaged after a trip to the doctor, said the sun was too hot for her foot, and she would like James to drive her to look over a nearby château.

'And Imogen shall come with us,' insisted James, terrified of being left on his own with Yvonne.

'That's a good idea, darling,' said Nicky, running a lazy finger down Imogen's cheek. 'I've found some passable courts about five miles from here, so I'll have a workout this afternoon. You go with James and Yvonne. You'll enjoy it.'

He was wearing a navy blue T-shirt and white shorts, and Imogen could see the muscles rippling on his thighs and his shoulders, and suddenly she was shot through with sadness, because she had adored him so much and she remembered the ecstatic admiration she had felt when she'd first watched him playing tennis. And now, although she could still appreciate his beauty, he meant nothing to her. Maybe one day she'd feel as indifferently towards Matt.

'I'm cured of Nicky,' she thought dolefully. 'Now I've got to start again and get over the cure.'

In the end, when Cable had gone up to bed and Nicky and Matt had set out, she suddenly felt she couldn't face Yvonne bitching all afternoon at James and told them she felt like a walk on her own.

It was very hot. She wandered out of the town up a hill path which began with shallow steps between red and white holiday villas, then became a rough track leading on to wilder heath above the cliffs, not unlike the moors at home. The sea sparkled below and the air had a marvellous sweetness from wild lavender and thyme mingling with the sharper tang of the sea. If only Matt were here all would be perfect, but she mustn't think of him.

The path forked. She followed a track leading steeply down. She was pouring with sweat by the time she reached the sea's edge, picking her way across the jagged red rock, feeling its heat and sharpness even through the soles of her espadrilles. She took off her dress and shoes and dropped in her bikini into the cool green water, hoping it might bring her some relief. She swam out to sea, wondering in a brief despairing moment whether to swim on and on. But they always said you saw your past life again if you drowned, and the past four months had been far too traumatic for her to want a replay.

She floated for a bit, then swam round into the next cove, climbing back on to the rocks, regaining her breath. Suddenly she could hear the sound of voices and edged her way round the cove, until she could see a beautiful stretch of beach deserted except for one family. She sat down to watch them. A dark-haired, dark-eyed child in a pink sun hat was aimlessly banging a red spade on the ground, and watching his pretty mother and father build him a huge elaborate sandcastle. The girl was wearing a red bikini, the man a shirt and black trousers. He must be baking in this heat.

Tears filled Imogen's eyes. They looked so united and happy. She had a sudden fleeting picture of herself and Matt laughing together, building a castle for their own suntanned blond baby.

The child got unsteadily to its feet and waddled off, clambering on to the rocks, about twenty yards from her. He was so beautiful and fat and brown, she longed to call to him. The parents hadn't noticed his departure, they were so intent on building their castle. The man was kneeling down tunnelling a moat round the castle, forging a hole under a bridge, keeping the sand firm with his other hand. The girl was laughing and very close to him, bending over to look. The man suddenly turned round, looked at her for a second, and then kissed her, taking her by surprise. For a second she struggled then lay still in his arms, kissing him back. Imogen looked away. The world was like Noah's ark, everyone in twos, in love with each other, except her. She looked back at the child, then gave a strangled cry of horror. He was teetering on the edge of the rocks now, looking down into the deep water, where more sharp wicked rocks lay beneath the weed below. The next minute he had overbalanced and fallen in.

Imogen gave a scream.

'He's fallen in!' she yelled to the couple, who looked round at her uncomprehendingly. 'Vite vite!' she went on in her schoolgirl French, 'Il a tombé.'

Frozen with horror, neither of them moved. The only thing to do was to plunge into the water herself, swimming round the rocks to where she could see the little pink sunhat bobbing on top of the water. The current was suddenly terrifyingly strong, tugging her in every direction. When she dived under, frantically searching around, all she could feel was thick weed, and sharp rocks jagging her legs. She surfaced gasping, to find the man swimming in her direction, followed by the hysterically screaming mother.

'Ici,' she called to them shaking her hair out of her eyes. 'He's down here.' And she plunged down under the surface again. Next time she came up for air, choking and spluttering, the father had reached her, his face ashen, the mother followed him, frantically dog-paddling, still yelling hysterically.

Over and over again, they all dived down. He can't be

still alive, thought Imogen despairingly, then suddenly between two rocks, she felt something soft, she tugged and tugged, but the object seemed wedged by the weed. She surfaced one more, her ears drumming.

'I think he's down here,' she spluttered. 'I can't shift him.'

Taking a huge breath, she plunged under once more and this time managed to catch the child's hair, and then one arm, and just as she thought her lungs would explode, she dislodged him, and lugged him to the surface. His eyes were shut, his mouth open.

The mother redoubled her sobs.

'Help me,' gasped Imogen, taking great shuddering gulps of air.

She was so exhausted now, the child felt like lead in her arms.

The father took the weight from her, and together they towed him to the shore, with the mother screaming behind them. They laid the child on the sand, and the man started pummelling and pumping at his chest.

'Let me do it,' said Imogen, frantically trying to remember her first aid classes. First you had to jerk back their heads to see if the wind pipe was blocked. It didn't seem to be. Then bending down, she put her lips to the slack little mouth, and slowly started breathing into it. He felt so cold and lifeless. She had a terrible feeling they were too late. She was so worn out by diving, it was almost impossible to keep her breathing even. She tried to ignore the hysterical ranting of the mother.

It seemed for an eternity she laboured, but it was obviously hopeless, not a flicker of response, there was no point in going on. She willed herself to continue, she could feel the sun burning into her back, then suddenly, miraculously, there was a faint flutter in the child's chest, and slowly she could feel his lungs expanding like a bellows, and gradually with agonising slowness he took up the breathing of his own accord.

Imogen knelt back on her heels, feeling dizzy, the next minute the child opened bloodshot eyes, gave a sob, and was violently sick.

'He's going to be all right,' said Imogen.

The mother's hysterics incomprehensibly increased, Imogen noticed a trickle of blood on her left leg where she had jagged it on the rocks.

'*Ferme ta gueule*,' snarled the father, still looking grey with fear. A fat lot of help, they're being, thought Imogen. She reached for a towel, cleaned the child's face, and gently began to dry him.

'He'll be O.K. honestly,' she said, wrapping another towel round him. They still seemed incapable of movement.

'You must get him home at once,' she urged them as though speaking to children, 'and keep him warm and very quiet, and call the doctor immediately.' The man began to gibber his thanks.

'Honestly, it's nothing,' she said. 'You're probably suffering from shock too,' she added to the snivelling mother. 'But he's all right, *really* he is.'

'But how did you come to be here?' said the father in very broken English. 'Didn't you know the beach was private?'

'Oh, goodness. No I didn't. I'm so sorry. But look, the important thing now is to get him home.'

'Where are you staying?' asked the father slowly.

'In Port-les-Pins.' She picked up the shivering child in his towel and handed him to the father. 'At once, go home. C'est très important.'

Only after she'd got dressed and begun the long walk home did she realise how much the incident had shaken her. She must go back to the hotel and tell someone. Her thoughts veered towards Matt and then away. Matt was out of bounds and belonged to Cable. Perhaps Madame was in; she was always good for a gossip. But when she reached the hotel, she heard the ricochet of bullets and the thunder of horses' hooves coming from Madame's room behind the reception desk — the family must be stuck into some television Western. Then she saw Nicky's key was missing from its hook; he must be back.

She ran upstairs and knocked gently on his door; there

was no answer. She knocked again. Perhaps he was asleep. She tried the handle and the door opened. The shower was going. He couldn't have heard her. Then she saw Cable lying naked on the bed, her beautiful breasts poking up in the air. She was smoking a cigarette and laughing and saying something to Nicky, who was obviously in the shower, because he shouted back something Imogen couldn't hear and Cable laughed even more.

Imogen shut the door and ran down the corridor. Her legs felt completely weak. Her body was one burning blush. Oh, poor, poor Matt; he loved Cable, and she could do this to him. And Nicky, allegedly his great friend, pretending he was going off to practise tennis. What on earth would happen if he came back from Marseilles and caught them at it?

In a state of complete shock she wandered round and round the town, then went and sat trembling on the beach. A sailing boat was putting out. She noticed how pretty its red sails looked against the darkening blue of the sea, and the soft ochre of the sand. She wished she were on that boat escaping from all the turmoil and cross-currents and the misery.

CHAPTER THIRTEEN

She was suddenly aware of a clock striking seven and, turning round, saw that the tables at the bars along the front were filling up. It was part of the Port-les-Pins ritual. Every night you sat and drank and commented on the beautiful people drifting along the street on foot or driving slowly by in open cars. Often they merely paraded to one end of the beach, turned round and walked back again, over and over again, so everyone could admire them. Reluctantly she decided she had better be getting back.

The rock that overhung the bay was turning rose red in the sunset; the cypress trees reared up stiff as cats' tails against the glowing sky; the sea was veiled in an amethyst haze.

To her horror the first people she saw were Nicky and Cable drinking vodka and tonics under a Coca-Cola umbrella which gave a faint red glow to their sunburnt faces. Cable was wearing a white lace top tied under her breasts, with matching lace Bermudas which would have made anyone else look fat. Her long expanse of midriff was as smooth and brown as mahogany. Nicky was wearing white trousers and a grey cashmere sweater, his black curls still hanging in wet tendrils from the shower. They both looked superbly indolent, replete and handsome, like two panthers after feeding time.

Blushing crimson, aware of her tousled hair and unkempt appearance, Imogen tried to creep past them, but Nicky saw her and called out:

'Where have you been? I've been looking everywhere for you: Come over here and tell us all about the chateau and the embattled Edgworths.'

546

'I didn't go in the end,' she stammered.

For a second Nicky looked wary.

'I walked along the beach,' she added quickly, 'and sun-bathed and wrote postcards instead. I must go and change.'

'Have a drink first,' said Nicky, steering her firmly into an empty seat beside him. 'You look bushed.'

Fortunately at that moment Yvonne and James arrived, both washed and changed and looking incredibly well laundered.

'The château was quite lovely. You *did* miss a treat, Imogen. The owner happened to be in residence, and took quite a fancy to me,' said Yvonne, patting her hair, 'and showed us everything. They had a wine-tasting on too, and gave us free glasses of wine. No, I'll only have a pineapple juice thank you, Nicky, and James doesn't need anything stronger.'

Nicky ordered the drinks in his rapid French, and went on eating his way through a packet of crisps.

'It's a pity you don't take more interest in culture, Cable,' said Yvonne, looking disapprovingly at Cable's stretch of midriff. 'I'm sure you and Matt would find a lot more to talk about in the evenings if you did.'

'Matt and I have got more exciting things to do in the evenings than talk,' snapped Cable.

A seagull that had been circling overhead looking for tit-bits suddenly swooped on one of Nicky's crisps that had dropped on the floor.

'Bugger off,' said Nicky, swiping at it with his foot.

'Bet you say that to all the gulls,' said Cable.

Nicky grinned. 'I don't want it to dump on me.'

'Supposed to be lucky,' said James.

'One dumped on me when I was playing in Rome. I promptly dropped the set.'

'How did the workout go?' asked James. 'Find someone good enough to play with?'

Nicky laughed. 'Surprisingly, yes. For once I was really stretched,' and in the diversion caused by the drinks arriving Imogen saw him stretch a hand out and gently stroke the underneath of Cable's thigh. She wriggled luxuriously

547

and smiled at him.

James took an unenthusiastic gulp of his pineapple juice and nearly choked.

'Must have gone down the wrong way,' he said, his eyes streaming, as Imogen thumped him on the back.

'I didn't think your hair would stay like that, Imogen, once it got wet,' said Yvonne smugly.

I hate her, thought Imogen. I'd like to take her beastly clean neck between my fingers and throttle her. Then she saw Matt coming towards the table, and her stomach dropped with love and she felt as though she was hurtling downwards in a very fast lift. He looked bug-eyed and exhausted, and collapsed into a chair next to Cable.

'Darling,' she said with unnatural enthusiasm, 'how was the tip-off?'

'Disastrous, complete bum steer. I give up. It's obviously impossible to reach Braganzi.'

'Can't say I'm sorry,' said Cable, running her hand sexily over his thigh. 'We might have the pleasure of your company for a change.'

How can she? thought Imogen, appalled. She's just got out of bed with Nicky, and in front of him she's fawning all over Matt.

Matt threw a bulging airmail envelope down on the table.

'Braganzi's cuttings. I asked the paper to send them out,' he said ruefully. 'Arrived by second post. Won't be needing them now, so I might as well get drunk tonight.'

'You did that last night, remember?' said Cable, with a slight edge in her voice. She pointedly removed her hand from his thigh.

Another large round of drinks was ordered. Imogen hadn't even finished her first. She wondered how on earth she was going to get through the evening. There seemed to be so many people in the party whose eyes she couldn't meet any more. It was as though Matt had read her thoughts.

'Gilmore'll be here any minute,' he said to the table in general, but more in her direction. 'You'll like him. He and Bambi are one of the few happily married couples I know.'

'She actually *likes* staying home and being a mother and

baking bread and polishing furniture,' said Cable.

'How nice,' said Yvonne. 'How old is she?'

'About forty.'

'I love older women,' said James, taking a hefty belt at his pineapple juice and looking very excited.

'She's happily married, Jumbo,' snapped Yvonne.

'I don't think Gilmore's ever strayed either,' said Matt.

Cable smirked as though she knew better.

'Oh, he may have pinched your bottom at the odd press party,' admitted Matt, 'but it's all show.'

'I must say it will be nice to have another wife to talk to. Once one gets married one does find single girls rather limited,' said Yvonne, getting to her feet. 'I must just pop over to the newsagents and get some more postcards. I haven't sent one to your mother yet, Jumbo.'

'Bitch,' said Cable, sticking her tongue out at Yvonne's trim departing back.

'What *did* you ask them to put in these pineapple juices, Nicky?' said James.

'Vodka,' said Nicky. 'I thought it was the least obvious. Probably disgusting.'

'At least it's alcohol,' said James. 'Thanks awfully. Let me get another round quickly while the old girl's buying postcards.'

'You're very quiet, Imogen,' said Cable. 'Are you all right?'

'The heat's probably been too much for her,' said Nicky. 'We should have taken better care of you, and not left you alone.'

They were all looking at her now. Imogen thought her face would crack with trying to smile.

'I think I'll go and change,' she said.

Upstairs she listlessly flipped through her wardrobe. In the end she put on the green dress with the white daisies, though it seemed far too frivolous for her mood of black gloom. The low-cut neck showed her shoulders and breasts, beautifully tanned now. During a day of such traumas it seemed odd that she should have turned so brown. Her hair, despite Yvonne's acid comments, fell into perfect shape when she combed it. She fiddled around a long time getting ready. She didn't want to go down; she couldn't bear to face the faces. A knock on the door made her jump. Matt, she thought with longing. But it was Cable.

'Hullo, that's nice,' she said, not looking Imogen in the eyes. 'Did Matt get it for you yesterday?'

Imogen nodded.

'He really ought to be on the women's page. We were worried about you, you took so long.'

You can talk, thought Imogen.

'I'm so pleased Larry and Bambi are arriving tonight,' said Cable as they went downstairs. 'Bambi'll be such a relief after Yvonne. She's sliding into middle age in such a happy leisurely sort of way. Makes one think getting old might not be so desperate after all. You'll love her.'

Bambi was obviously no competition, thought Imogen. From Cable's Mona Lisa smirkings earlier, Larry Gilmore was obviously an old flame of hers. With Nicky as a current admirer, James ever ready to pounce and Matt in attendance, no wonder she was in such a good temper.

When they got to the table, James wolf-whistled at Imogen and Nicky told her she was looking beautiful. Imogen went and sat next to him, as far away from Matt as possible. I've got dinner to get through, and then I'm going straight to bed, she thought. A girl a few tables down was petting a panting golden retriever. It reminded her of Homer. Suddenly she felt so homesick she could hardly see straight. She mustn't cry. She stared down at her clenched fists, fighting back the tears.

'The Blaker-Harris's are supposed to be arriving at St Syriac tonight,' said Cable. 'We must call them tomorrow.'

Conversation fortunately moved on to the rocky state of the Blaker-Harris's marriage, and Imogen was able to recover herself. Glancing up, she saw Matt was watching her. She flushed and looked quickly away. I'm an embarrassment to him now, she thought miserably.

Then, to her relief, Cable said, 'Look, there's Gilmore.'

'Over here,' yelled Matt, waving his arms at a very suntanned man of medium height with a thin hawk-like face. He was wearing a beautifully cut cream boiler suit, slashed to the waist and tucked into black boots. He was screwing his eyes up and looking round.

'He can't see a thing without his glasses,' said Cable. 'Christ, what has he done to himself?'

The suntanned man finally located them and, stopping to gawp at a sensational brunette as he crossed the road, nearly got run over by a couple of stunning blondes in a pink convertible.

'What a lovely way to go,' he drawled. 'Hullo, everyone.' He clapped Matt on the shoulder, kissed Cable and collapsed into a chair. 'Jesus, I need some first aid. Order me a quadruple whisky.' No one moved.

'What *have* you done to yourself?' asked Matt.

'You've changed your hair,' said Cable.

'It's the Mark Antony look.' Gilmore pulled the brown tendrils over his forehead.

'*And* you've been at the Grecian 2000. You're as brown as a berry.'

'It's been a very good summer in Islington,' said Gilmore, and roared with laughter.

'You've had your ear pierced. And *where* did you get that white suit from?'

'I decided my image was getting a bit dreary, I ought to jazz myself up a little.'

'A *little*,' said Cable. 'Christ Almighty, Gilmore!'

Matt started to laugh.

'Oh, shut up,' said Gilmore. 'It jolly well works anyway. How are you, Nicky? You look disgustingly healthy.'

'No more than you,' said Nicky, and introduced Imogen and James.

Matt ordered Gilmore a drink and another round for the rest of them.

'Any luck with Braganzi?' said Gilmore.

Matt shook his head. 'Not a squeak. I've tried everything; *and* he machine-guns doorsteppers.'

'Well, if you can't get in there no one can,' said Gilmore.

'They were bloody good, those beauty queen pictures of yours,' said Matt.

'Took a hell of a lot of re-touching, both beauty queens

and pix.'

'How's the paper?' asked Matt.

'Much the same when I left it.' Gilmore drained half his whisky in one gulp. 'Bruce Winter gave in his notice again; wrote a 17-page letter of resignation which no one could be bothered to read. So he's staying on after all. Our man in Jerusalem was wounded in the foot in a riot. H.E. sent his love. All he can think about at the moment is the All-Woman Everest Expedition.'

'Are we going to sponsor it?'

'Not if the finance boys have their way.'

'I picked up a good story this afternoon,' said Matt. 'All the kids have been cheating in their *Baccalaureate*. Some child got hold of the papers in advance and gave the answers to all and sundry. The authorities are completely flummoxed.

They can't fail the whole lot of them.'

'Wish that would happen in London,' sighed Gilmore.

'It's the only way my children would ever get their 'A' levels. Are you going to file any copy?'

'I might,' said Matt, 'if I can summon up the energy.'

'There's trouble blowing up in Peru,' said Gilmore. 'If it gets any worse H.E. did say you might have to cut short your lotus-eating and fly out there.'

'What sort of trouble?' said Matt.

He's happy, thought Imogen wistfully. He must have been bored out of his mind this week with the rest of us.

It was Cable who broke them up.

'Must you two talk shop all day? Where's Bambi? In the bath?'

'Er, no,' said Gilmore, wincing as he gingerly turned the ring in his ear. 'God, these things hurt! She's in Islington.'

'She's *what*?' said Cable.

'In Islington.'

'You've come on your own, then?'

'In a word, no,' said Gilmore.

'You haven't brought someone else?' said Cable suspiciously.

'In a word, yes,' said Gilmore.

The stunned silence was interrupted by a gasp of amazment from James. An incredible blonde in silver platform heels, a silver space suit, with long blonde hair was causing considerable excitement as she wended her way along the front.

'There she is,' said Gilmore, going slightly pink under his suntan. 'Over here, my cherub.'

'She looks just like Bardot. She isn't, is she?' said James in excited tones.

'Not quite,' said Gilmore. 'I call her Brigitte Barmaid actually.'

'Jesus, look at those tits,' said Nicky, smoothing his hair.

Matt was torn between laughter and disapproval.

'Where on earth did you find her?' he said.

'She came to us as a temporary,' said Larry. 'I kept bumping into her in the lift.'

'There was room for you both in the lift?' asked Matt.

'I thought she'd have a nice soothing influence on Cable,' said Gilmore. 'I know how she likes as many pretty girls around her as·possible.'

Cable was looking like the inevitable thundercloud.

'This is Tracey,' went on Gilmore, as the blonde sat down between him and Imogen, with a flurry of 'pleased-to-meet-yous'. 'And she never drinks anything else but sweet Cinzano, because she's hung up on sweet sin, aren't you, my precious?'

'Do you mind?' said Tracey. 'You're lovely and brown,' she added, beaming at Imogen. 'I always think a tan does more for a blonde than anyone else. Thank God I brown very quickly.'

'Don't you burn?' said Imogen, looking at the platinum hair.

'Never,' said Tracey. 'This colour's out of a bottle. Normally it's dark brown.'

Imogen blinked, unused to such frankness. 'Larry's a wonderful colour already,' she said.

'Oh, that's Man Tan,' said Tracey. 'It didn't work on his legs. They're all striped like a tiger.'

Imogen giggled, and suddenly felt more cheerful.

553

At that moment Yvonne arrived, weighed down with paper bags and postcards.

'I got this for our Daily,' she said, producing a lady in a crinoline made entirely of shells. 'Isn't it original? Oh hullo,' she added to Gilmore. 'You must be Larry. We've never met, but I so admire your work. And you must be Bambi?' she said turning to Tracey. 'I've heard so much about you. May I call you Bambi?'

'Well I keep doing it all the time,' said Gilmore in his lazy drawl, 'but she doesn't like it very much.'

Yvonne sat down between James and Matt.

'Where are you staying?' she asked.

'At the Plaza,' said Tracey. 'The rooms are awfully pokey.'

Yvonne looked put out. 'You should see our little hell-holes,' she said, glaring at Matt.

Tracey turned back to Imogen. 'Isn't it awful? Every time you turn on the bath in an hotel you get absolutely drenched from the shower. I got soaked tonight.'

She can't be much older than I am, thought Imogen. Cable and Yvonne were both glaring at her as though she was a particularly nasty maggot who'd appeared in their salad. Looking at her more closely, Imogen realised that underneath the heavy make-up she had a round face, huge brown eyes and a very sweet smile.

'Ta very much,' she said, taking her Cinzano from Matt. 'Who belongs to who round here?' she added to Imogen. 'Who's the little one with the pink face who looks like Ronnie Corbett?'

'That's James. He's married to Yvonne, the one with red hair. She's a model.'

'And the lovely brown one next to you? Goodness, he's handsome. He must be a coastguard or a swimming instructor or something.'

Imogen stifled a giggle. 'He's called Nicky Beresford.'

At the mention of his name Nicky looked up. 'I was just wondering what you do for a living,' said Tracey, smiling at him with luscious simplicity.

'He plays tennis,' snapped Cable, then after a pause, 'extremely successfully.'

'Oh, how lovely! I love tennis. Perhaps we could have a game tomorrow.'

'Perhaps we could,' said Nicky, smiling into her eyes. 'It doesn't have to be tennis.'

'*Encore de whisky*, shouted Gilmore, glancing round at the girls sitting at nearby tables and walking along the front. 'Christ, the standard of talent is fantastic here. Just like the King's Road used to be on a Saturday afternoon. Can't think why I brought you, Tracey darling. Rather like carrying electric logs to Newcastle.'

'You'd have to speak French to them, I shouldn't wonder,' said Tracey placidly, 'and you know how that tires you. I'm hungry. I hope the food's better than it was in Paris. We went to Maxim's last night. It was disgusting. I wanted a steak, and they gave me this charred rectangle of beef; when you put your fork in all the blood ran out. I love a nice scampi and chips.'

'I expect it can be arranged,' said Gilmore.

Yvonne was looking at Tracey in a puzzled way. 'I can't believe you're forty,' she said.

'She is round the bust,' said Cable spitefully.

'That's clever,' said Tracey, quite oblivious of either girl's animosity. 'How did you guess? I hear you're a model,' she added to Yvonne. 'I do a bit too in my spare time.'

'What kind?' said Yvonne coldly.

'Oh, nude stuff mostly. I was Penthouse Pet of the Month last July.'

'Were you indeed?' said Nicky, shamelessly undressing her with his eyes.

'They told the most terrible lies,' said Tracey. 'They photographed me cycling against a backdrop of some old university, with some pictures in these lovely silk undies and some in nothing at all.'

'Really,' said James, his eyes out on stalks.

'Then they wrote all this stuff in the paper about me being an intellectual and my father being a don. But they let me keep the undies, and they paid very well.'

'Is your father a don?' said Yvonne.

'No, he's an undertaker,' said Tracey.

Yvonne looked taken aback. 'Well, I suppose they do fill a need.'

'And an awful lot of holes,' said Matt drily.

'Do you do any nude work?' Tracey asked Yvonne.

'I couldn't do that sort of thing,' said Yvonne in a shocked voice.

'Oh, I wouldn't be discouraged,' said Tracey kindly. 'I used to be as flat as a board like you too. Then my manager said, "Tracey, why don't you get some decent tits?" He's got this doctor friend who can give you boobs like Sophia Loren. So I went and saw him. The operation was a bit of a drag, but the after-effect was terrific. These are just silicone,' she said, patting her jutting bosom fondly. 'But I've never looked back since. I'll give you the address of the doctor if you like. Pity not to be able to take your clothes off when it's so lucrative.'

For once Yvonne was completely at a loss for words.

Glancing across, Imogen saw that Matt was crying with laughter.

'Where did you really find her?' he said to Gilmore, wiping his eyes.

'Came to me as a temp. Types 30 words a minute and spells Laurence with a W all the time, but any girl with a body like that deserves to make it in life.'

'Can't think what she's doing with you.'

'She obviously wants to marry her grandfather.'

Yvonne leant across to Cable. 'I don't think that girl's married to Larry Gilmore at all,' she hissed.

'We ought to eat soon,' said Larry, lifting up one of Tracey's silver breasts which was hanging over his watch. 'It's nearly half past nine.'

'I'll get the bill,' said Matt, tipping back his chair and waving to a waitress. Then suddenly — Imogen could never remember exactly how it happened — the bustling, noisy street went absolutely quiet. Waiters stopped in their tracks with trays held aloft, a man carrying a basket of fish up from the quay dropped it with a crash on the ground and stood motionless as though hypnotised, conversations all along the front slithered to a halt, a poodle barked and was

angrily hushed, a child cried and was clouted. Everyone
had turned towards the end of the street. Somehow the fear
and anticipation had infected even the rowdiest holiday-
maker. The only sound was the swish of the waves, and faint
complaining of the seagulls. It was like *High Noon*. And then
Imogen saw him, strolling lazily down the street towards
them chewing on a cigar, a little bald man wearing dark
glasses, a black shirt and ill-fitting white trousers, and apparently in no hurry. But even in his leisureliness there was
tension.

'Braganzi,' hissed Matt.

'Christ, I wish I had a camera,' muttered Larry.

He was only a couple of tables away now, everyone smiling
sycophantically. The same poodle growled and was kicked
again.

'He's making for this table,' said Cable, shaking back her
hair and licking her lips in anticipation. 'Perhaps he's coming to say you can do a piece on him.'

'More likely to warn us off,' said Matt.

Imogen watched him, mesmerised. It wasn't often you
saw a legend that close.

He reached their table now, and paused, taking them all
in. Then he took out his cigar and ground it into the pavement.

'Good evening,' he said in a very strong Italian accent. 'I
look for Mees Brocklehurst.'

Imogen gasped in terror and threw a supplicating glance
in Matt's direction.

'What d'you want her for,' said Matt sharply.

'May I present myself,' said the little man softly. 'My name
is Enrico Braganzi.'

'We know that,' said Matt.

'I would simply like to talk to Miss Brocklehurst.' He
smiled, showing several gold stoppings.

Nicky put a protecting hand on Imogen's arm.

'This is her,' he said.

Braganzi removed his dark glasses. His eyes were
hooded, watchful, very, very dark. 'Mademoiselle,' he asked,
'were you by any chance swimming round the rocks to the

Petit Plage today?'

Imogen gazed down, hoping the ground might swallow her up.

'Were you, lovie?' said Matt gently.

She knew the whole beach was watching her.

'Yes,' she stammered. 'I'm terribly sorry. It was so pretty. I just wanted to be on my own for a bit. I didn't realise it was private.'

'Please, Mademoiselle.' Braganzi held up a beautifully manicured hand, heavy with gold rings. 'I have only come to thank you from the bottom of my heart. You saved my little boy's life.'

'I what?' said Imogen, bewildered.

'You saved him from drowning, and then bring him back to life.'

'He was *your* child?' whispered Imogen. 'But I thought he belonged to that couple.'

'That couple,' said Braganzi in a voice that sent shivers down Imogen's spine, 'were the child's nanny and one of my guards.'

So that was why the girl was sobbing so hysterically, even after the child was revived — from terror of Braganzi.

'The girl came back to the house and tried to pretend nothing had happened. Fortunately another of my men had seen everything through binoculars from the house. You were too far away for him to help. When he arrived you had gone. He said you display amazing courage and presence of mind for one so young.'

'Oh gosh, it was nothing,' muttered Imogen. 'Anyone would have done it.'

'But they did not,' he went on. 'The child would have died if it had not been for you, Mademoiselle. I owe you an eternal debt of gratitude.'

'It was nothing,' she muttered once again, scuffing the ground with her foot. 'Is he all right now?'

'Yes, thank God. The doctor's been, and a specialist. The Duchess was frantic, but they reassured her that all was well. Ricky is sleeping now. The Duchess is naturally still very shaken, but she would very much like to meet you.'

'Oh, really, she doesn't have to. I mean . . .' Imogen stammered, terrified at the prospect.

'Please, Mademoiselle. It will mean so much to her. She wishes to thank you personally. I have my car here. May I drive you up to the house?'

Imogen looked at Matt beseechingly, but he was shaking with laughter.

'You are a dark horse, darling.'

'Why didn't you tell us?' said Nicky.

'We probably didn't ask her,' said Matt.

Imogen turned to Braganzi. 'All right, I'd like to come.'

'Wonderful.' Braganzi turned and raised a hand. It was the first time Imogen had noticed the tattoos on his thick, muscular arms. Next moment a black car that seemed as long as the beach glided up to them.

A chauffeur got out and opened the door for them. As she climbed inside Imogen felt like Jonah being swallowed by the whale. She wondered if she'd ever see the others again.

'Where did you learn your first aid?' asked Braganzi as the car climbed the hill. 'Are you nurse?'

Imogen told him about working in a library, and someone having to do a first aid course. 'I grumbled like mad at the time, and I was awfully bored, but I'm very glad I did now.'

'So indeed are we, Mademoiselle. Can I please tell you something, now we are alone a few minutes? You know perhaps a little about the Duchess and me?'

Imogen nodded.

'When she leave England to come to me, she had to leave her children too. I am not considered suitable stepfather, you understand. Nor are the children allowed to visit us, although we are fighting court battle. Camilla misses the children, although she doesn't show it, so all her love has gone into little Ricky. She had him late in life. We both did. He is how you say it? — an autumn crocus. She is forty-three now. When she had Ricky she nearly died and the doctors later insisted on a hysterectomy; so it's no more children for either of us. Now you can appreciate how important Ricky is to both of us, and what you have done by saving his life.'

559

Imogen glanced up and saw that his dark eyes were full of tears, and knew that she was no longer afraid of him.

'How did you track me down?'

'I have, how you say, impeccable spy system.'

Imogen was very nervous about meeting the Duchess. But one glance at that lovely ravished face, with its brilliant grey eyes which were still red from crying, and all her fears vanished.

The Duchess walked forward quickly and took both Imogen's hands, and then kissed her on both cheeks, saying in a choked voice,

'I can never begin to thank you. I really don't know how to start.' But she was so friendly and natural and incredibly grateful that, after a few minutes, armed with a large glass of whisky, Imogen began to feel she really had done something rather good after all. They sat on the terrace, chatting twenty to the dozen together, and breathing in the heavy scent of the tobacco plants and the night-scented stock and later they went up and looked at little Ricky asleep in his cot in his pale blue bedroom, a Basil Brush on the pillow beside him. His cheeks were pinker now, his black hair flopped over his forehead. The Duchess moved round the room on tiptoe, straightening his bedclothes, adjusting the pillow, arranging toys, and checking the heat of his forehead with her hand.

'He looks much better,' said Imogen.

'He does, doesn't he? The doctor says there's nothing to worry about, but I have to keep checking.'

As they went downstairs Imogen noticed a Picasso, a Modigliani and a Matisse on the wall. Braganzi was waiting for them.

'All right, darling?' he said, taking the Duchess's hand. He must have been three or four inches smaller than her, but somehow his width of shoulder and force of personality made it seem as though he was protecting some infinitely fragile object.

'Miss Brocklehurst must be hungry. Shall we eat now?'

'Yes, of course. How awful of me.' The Duchess turned,

smiling, to Imogen. 'You will stay, won't you? We see so few people here, and there are so many things I want to ask you about your holiday and about England.'

'But you must be far too exhausted after such a terrible shock,' stammered Imogen, terrified her table manners wouldn't be ducal enough. But in the end they persuaded her and she found she was absolutely famished. All her worries about her table manners vanished when she saw Braganzi falling on his food like a starved dingo, elbows on the table, taking great swigs of wine with his mouth full, and picking away at his teeth.

They had some kind of fish mousse, then delicious chicken. If the Duchess and Braganzi both picked their bones, Imogen supposed it was all right if she did too.

'And who did you come out here with?' asked the Duchess.

'He's called Nicky Beresford.'

'The tennis player? Oh, he's frightfully glamorous. I've admired him at Wimbledon so often.'

'And he thinks you're marvellous too,' said Imogen, her mouth full of fried potatoes.

'How lovely.' The Duchess looked pleased. 'So you're both having a wonderful holiday?'

'Yes, I suppose so,' said Imogen.

'You don't sound very enthusiastic,' said Braganzi. 'What was Mr Beresford doing leaving you alone on a hot summer afternoon?'

'He — er he — it's really very boring,' faltered Imogen, but she was so longing to tell someone.

'Go on,' said the Duchess. 'Enrico and I have so little excitement.'

And then the whole awful story came pouring out. 'We came in a party,' said Imogen, 'but it was quite obvious even before we left London that Nicky had fallen for one of the other girls.'

'Did she come with a boyfriend?'

'Yes. He's called Matthew O'Connor.'

'He's a journalist, isn't he, a very good one?' said the Duchess. 'When I can face the English Sundays I always read him.'

'He's terribly nice,' said Imogen, flushing

'Then why don't you do a swap?' said the Duchess.

'He loves Cable, this other girl. He just ignores her and waits for her to come back. Occasionally they have terrible rows, but he realises she's only doing it, well, to make him keener on her.'

'How very complicated,' said the Duchess.

'O'Connor seemed quite keen on you the other night outside,' said Braganzi drily.

Imogen went crimson.

'How do you know?' she stammered.

'Enrico knows everything,' said the Duchess with pride.

Goodness, thought Imogen, darting a startled glance at Braganzi, so he knew Matt and I were casing his house all the time.

They had their coffee on the terrace. The night was black now, sprinkled with huge stars. The fireflies darted above the tobacco plants and the Duchess bombarded Imogen with more questions, about her holiday, about her home in Yorkshire and then about England in general. Imogen suddenly realised it was very late.

'I must go.'

'Not yet. Enrico will take you back. Darling, go upstairs and just check if Ricky is all right.'

When he had gone, Imogen turned shyly to the Duchess.

'What a sweet man he is,' she said. 'I never dreamt he'd be so kind.'

The Duchess's face lit up. 'You think so? I'm so pleased. People in England find it quite incomprehensible that I threw up everything to run off with him.'

'I understand it perfectly,' said Imogen stoutly. She was suddenly aware she was more than a little drunk.

'I'd give anything to go home for a few weeks,' said the Duchess, 'but Enrico would be arrested the moment he set foot in England.' Suddenly she looked very tired and shadowed under the eyes. 'I miss the children horribly. Alexander, my ex-husband, won't let me near them in case they are corrupted by Enrico. Corrupted, indeed! If the courts knew what an immoral creature Alexander was!'

'I'm so sorry,' said Imogen.

'Oh, that's enough about me,' said the Duchess lightly. 'Let's talk about you. What can we possibly do to repay you? You have some days left of your holiday. We go back to Paris on Saturday. Why not leave the coast and Mr Beresford — it's too hot anyway — and come back with us? We would love to show you round Paris.'

'Oh no, really not,' cried Imogen. Suddenly the thought of being whisked away from Matt, however little he felt about her, was more than she could bear. 'It's terribly kind,' she added to soften her outburst. 'Honestly, rescuing him was enough, knowing you're pleased.'

'There must be something you'd like.'

Suddenly Imogen's heart beat faster. 'There is just one thing,' she said. 'Matt — more than anything else in the world he wants an interview with your husband. He's been trying to get one ever since we came out here. He's really a very responsible journalist. He wouldn't . . .' Her words faltered. She was about to say 'bitch him up', then thought it seemed rude.

The Duchess looked dubious. But at that moment Braganzi returned. 'The little one is fine,' he said.

For a moment they chattered to each other in Italian, the Duchess still looking worried.

'I'm sorry,' muttered Imogen. 'I shouldn't have asked. It was horribly presumptuous.'

'It is difficult in Enrico's position,' explained the Duchess. 'He is worried that anything Mr O'Connor says about him will prejudice my chances of seeing the children again.'

'Oh well, of course. I should have thought,' stammered Imogen.

Braganzi went over to the window and threw out his cigar into the garden. Then he turned round and smiled at Imogen.

'It is a very little thing, in return for what you have done for us. Tell him to come at ten o'clock. But he *must* let me see what he is going to print. That is the only condition. He is an honourable man?'

'Oh yes, yes, of course he is. He is very honourable,' she said joyfully, thinking how pleased Matt would be. 'I can't thank you enough. I really must go now.' She couldn't wait to get back to Port-les-Pins and break the news to him.

The Duchess kissed her very affectionately, saying, 'Write to us in Paris and let me know how the holiday progresses.'

Braganzi rode back with her in the car.

'It's been a wonderful evening,' she found herself saying, 'and the Duchess is so wonderful. I think she's one of the nicest people I've ever met.'

'She is,' said Braganzi. 'She likes you too. She is very isolated now, you understand. She gave up so much when she left England for me.'

'But she gained so much.'

Braganzi sighed. 'I hope so. But you will come and stay with us perhaps next year, and we see that you have a better holiday.'

He took her address in Yorkshire. What would her father say if he could see her now, thought Imogen with a giggle, hob-nobbing with one of the most notorious criminals in France.

The chauffeur was driving along the front now. Although it was long after midnight, people were still drinking in the cafés.

Imogen wondered where the others were; probably smashed out of their minds in some nightclub, or perhaps they were at the casino. It would be awful if they'd gone to bed. It was almost as though Braganzi had read her thoughts:

'There's your friend Mr O'Connor keeping an eye out for you,' he said, as the car drew to a halt, and he leaned across and opened the door for her. Then he smiled as he saw how Imogen's face had lit up. 'That pleases you, doesn't it?'

'D'you want to meet him now?' said Imogen, as she saw Matt get to his feet and walk towards them.

Braganzi shook his head. 'Tomorrow will do, and tell him to bring Larry Gilmore with him. He can take some pictures of Camilla and Ricky.'

'But I didn't even tell you Larry was here,' said Imogen

in amazement. 'You really know everything, don't you?'

'I do my rich best,' said Braganzi modestly. 'Good-bye and once again thank you for everything,' and, taking her hand, he kissed it, and Imogen could see exactly why the Duchess had given up everything for him.

She waved as the car moved away. The next moment Matt was beside her.

'What was that hood doing mauling you like that?' he said sharply.

'Just saying good-bye.'

'Was that all he did?' His face was in shadow, so she couldn't read its expression, but his fingers were hard and painful on her arm.

'Of course it was. I had the most wonderful time.'

'You were away so long we were about to send out a search party.'

'You didn't have to. They were lovely to me.'

'Bloody well should have been, after all you did for them. What was she like?' He let go of her arm.

'Oh sweet, beautiful and well — sort of vulnerable. Where are the others?'

'Inside the bar. Gilmore's pissed out of his mind. Come and have a drink.' He put an arm round her shoulders and hugged her for a second. 'Sorry I snapped, darling. I was worried about you.'

A great surge of happiness welled up inside her; then she said 'Down, boy' to herself as she remembered Matt's 'trespassers-will-be-prosecuted' lecture on the beach that morning. He'd have been worried about anyone in the party who'd been closeted in Braganzi's fortress as long as she had.

Inside the bar Larry and Tracey were dancing round to the juke box.

'I'm Larry the Limpet,' cried Larry, shoving his hand down Tracey's dress.

'I do wish you'd stop doing rude things,' she said placidly, pulling his hand out.

They danced past the Ladies which said 'Little Girls' on the door.

565

'I want seven,' said Larry, banging on the door, 'and I want them now.'

Nicky and Cable sat watching them. Nicky was roaring with laughter, Cable wasn't. James and Yvonne appeared to have gone to bed.

'Darling,' cried Nicky, jumping up when he saw her, 'are you all right?'

Tracey and Larry immediately stopped dancing and came over and showered her with questions.

'It was wonderful,' Imogen kept saying, embarrassed yet happy to be the centre of attention. 'The house is beautiful inside and the pictures are amazing.'

'Probably got half the Uffizi and the Louvre in there,' said Larry.

'Weren't you terrified?' said Tracey.

'No, not at all; not even by the Duchess. She was so friendly and — well — un-grand.'

'Why on earth should she be?' snapped Cable. 'She was only some two-bit actress before she married the Duke. She's really as common as muck.'

'Rubbish,' said Nicky. 'She comes from a perfectly respectable family. Did they seem keen on each other?'

'Oh yes, and Braganzi's amazing. He knows everything. He knew all about . . . ' She was about to say 'last night', but she didn't know how much Matt had told Cable about their skirmish with the guards. 'He seems to know who we all are,' she added lamely. Matt came over, warming a large glass of brandy with his hands.

'Have a breath of that, sweetheart, and tell me all about it.'

'I'd like one too,' said Larry.

Imogen took the glass from Matt. 'Thanks awfully,' she stammered. 'And, oh Matt, Braganzi's promised to give you an interview.'

'I've just bought you three,' Matt was saying to Larry. Then he double-took. 'He *what*?' he said, his voice like a pistol shot.

'He's agreed to give you an interview. You're to go up there tomorrow at ten o'clock.'

'You're having me on,' he said incredulously.

'No, truly I'm not; and Larry can go too and take some pictures.'

'Holy Mother, you're a genius. How the hell did you swing that?'

'I asked him. The only condition is he wants to see copy.'

'That's all right. So should I, if I were in his shoes. Baby, you really are a beautiful, beautiful thing,' and he leant forward and kissed her on both cheeks. And this time she didn't even bother to say 'Down, boy' to the surge of happiness. She just revelled in how delighted and overwhelmed he was by the news.

'Can't I come and take pictures instead of Gilmore?' said Nicky. 'I'd love a crack at the Duchess.'

Imogen giggled. 'She thinks you're beautiful too.'

'She's heard of me?' said Nicky in surprise.

'Yes. They are capable occasionally of watching television, the Upper Classes. Some of the brighter ones can even read. Now, who's going to buy me a drink?' said Larry.

'No one,' said Matt firmly. 'You're having some coffee to sober you up, or your hand'll be shaking far too much to hold a camera straight.'

'I shall be caught with my Nikkons down yet again,' said Larry. 'Just a small brandy wouldn't hurt.'

Cable got to her feet. 'Now that she's finally deigned to show up,' she said, shooting a venomous glance in Imogen's direction, 'can we please move on to somewhere slightly more exciting?'

Matt got the envelope of cuttings out of his back pocket and threw them on the table. 'You can if you want. I've got to read this lot. Now sit yourself down, Imogen my darling girl,' he patted the seat beside him, 'and if you're not too tired, would you tell me from the rescue onwards exactly what happened?'

CHAPTER FOURTEEN

Imogen woke late the next morning to another blazing hot day. Through the open window she could see a few little white clouds ermining the serene morning-glory blue of the sky. She lay for a minute reflecting on the extraordinary events of the past forty-eight hours: first Matt transforming her in St Tropez, then meeting Antoine, who was pretty bizarre by any standards, then being threatened by Braganzi's guards, Matt kissing her goodnight and warning her off next morning, then her rescuing little Ricky, finding Nicky and Cable in bed and finally meeting Braganzi and the Duchess. Live a little, get some experience, Matt had said. Well, she'd certainly made a start. Yet, as she gazed at her smooth brown face in the mirror, she looked as young and as round-eyed as ever. She looked at the purple aster wilting in the diary and sighed.

She'd just got dressed and was wondering how Matt and Larry were getting on with Braganzi when there was a knock on the door. It was Tracey, wondering if she was ready to come down to the beach.

'It's awfully hot,' she said, as they wandered along the front. 'Even a T-shirt feels like a fur coat.'

'Did Larry get off all right this morning?'

'Yes, but he was feeling very poorly. I've never known a guy knock it back like he does. That Cable's a crosspatch, isn't she?'

'Yes,' sighed Imogen.

'I dreamt all my teeth fell out last night,' said Tracey. 'Isn't it supposed to mean something?'

'Probably that you're worried about all your teeth falling

out,' said Imogen.

She noticed that even the brownest and most blasé Frenchmen sat up, pulled in their stomachs and took notice as Tracey undulated past, her silver waterfall of hair glinting in the sun. This was going to make Cable even crosser.

They found Yvonne and James parked in the middle of the beach. Yvonne was grumbling away under the cardboard nose shield, looking like a malignant goose.

'Hullo. Did you sleep well? I certainly didn't. Far too hot. I couldn't sleep a wink, and what's more I had this terrible nightmare about a jellyfish, and when I woke up I found this huge mosquito bite, and then the water in the shower was cold this morning.'

'How did you get on last night, Imogen?' said James, who'd brightened perceptibly at the sight of them. 'I was worried Braganzi might have turned you into a Pattie Hearst.'

'It was all frightfully exciting,' said Tracey, laying out a large green towel. 'Go on, tell them, Imogen.'

Imogen's account of the events of last night, however, were slightly overshadowed by the counter-attraction of Tracey stripping down to the bottom half of a leopardskin bikini.

James, who was oiling Yvonne's back, stopped in midstroke, his eyes falling out with excitement. Every Frenchman within 200 yards appeared similarly affected.

'Get *on*, James,' said Yvonne, chattering with disapproval. 'And do lie down, Tracey, and don't draw attention to yourself. Go on, Imogen. How had the Duchess done up the lounge?'

'Oh, in pale blue silk,' said Imogen, still not feeling her audience was really captive, particularly as Tracey started to oil herself all over.

'That'll keep out the ultra-violent rays,' she said.

Twenty minutes later, by which time every man on the beach seemed to have made a detour past their little group to walk down to bathe, and then return flexing his muscles and dripping water all over them, Yvonne could bear it no longer. 'You'll burn, you know, Tracey. You really ought to cover yourself up, and those — er — bits burn much the worst.'

'Maybe you're right,' said Tracey, getting to her feet. 'I think I'll go and swim.'

'Well, on your head be it,' snapped Yvonne.

'It's not my 'ead it'll be on,' giggled Tracey, and she tripped off down to the sea, followed at a very indiscreet interval by a tidal wave of Frenchmen.

'I'm going to swim too,' said James and, before Yvonne could stop him, bounded off down the beach.

'It's disgusting the way she flaunts her bosoms,' spluttered Yvonne.

'Well, they rather flaunt themselves,' said Imogen.

'Such a bad example for James, particularly Larry turning up with her. I wondered if she knows he's married.'

Imogen buried her face in the Bodley Head Scott Fitzgerald. She had given up *Tristram Shandy*.

'She's bound to burn,' grumbled Yvonne, adjusting her cardboard beak. 'People simply don't realise you have to take it slowly in this heat. That's why I never burn.' On she moaned, until Imogen was quite glad to see Cable and Nicky walking towards them. She supposed, with Matt gone off to see Braganzi, they'd taken the opportunity to spend a couple of hours in bed — and both got out of the wrong side of it, judging by the set sullen expressions on their faces.

'Good morning,' said Yvonne, cheering up at the sight of Cable's sulkiness.

'What's good about it?' snapped Cable, throwing her flattened lilo down on the ground. 'Will you blow it up for me, Nicky?'

He shot her a look which plainly said — Blow the bloody thing up yourself — then thought better of it and crouched down by the lilo, muttering under his breath.

'I hear Matt's gone to see Braganzi,' said Yvonne to Cable. 'You must be delighted for him.'

'I am *not*! A fine holiday I'm having, with him wasting his time running after silly stories. He'd gone by nine o'clock this morning, and that'll be the last I'll see of him today most likely. He's bound to be up half the night writing the beastly thing. He even asked me to find him a typewriter. I ask you, in a god-forsaken place like this. It's getting more and more like Margate,' she added, glaring round the beach. Then, turning to Nicky, who'd nearly finished blowing up the lilo, 'Why don't we push off to St Trop for the day?'

'No,' said Nicky, suddenly catching sight of Tracey frolicking around in the shallows with James, 'we haven't got a car.'

'Well, let's hire one,' said Cable imperiously, following Nicky's glance.

'Too much hassle,' snapped Nicky, corking up the lilo and laying it at Cable's feet. 'And it's far too hot to drive.' Cable's green eyes flashed.

It was getting too hot right here, thought Imogen. 'I'm going to swim,' she announced, setting off towards the sea.

'So am I,' said Nicky, hastily following her. 'You're looking very choice today, my darling. Let's get out of the line of fire.'

'We're over here,' Tracey called to them, waving frantically, her long blonde hair trailing in the green water like a mermaid's. 'It's lovely. And how are you this morning, Nicky?'

'Admiring you breasting the waves,' said Nicky, 'or rather waving the breasts.'

They all laughed, and splashed around. Then Nicky did his spectacular flashy crawl out to the raft and back.

'Oh, I wish I could swim like that,' said Tracey.

'I'll teach you,' said Nicky. 'Just rest your stomach on my hands, now move one arm like this, and put your head down.'

Tracey emerged giggling and spluttering. 'I wouldn't call that my tummy,' she said.

'Oh well, give or take a few inches,' said Nicky, smiling down at her. Suddenly they stopped laughing and just gazed at each other. Oh my goodness, thought Imogen, nervous but pleased as well, what will Cable say?

'Come on, Imogen,' said James with a jolly laugh. 'I'll give you a swimming lesson too. Ouch,' he squeaked as he stepped forward, 'I feel a prick.'

'Again,' said Nicky.

And they all collapsed into giggles again, which was all in all not the sort of behaviour to improve either Cable's or Yvonne's tempers.

When they finally came out of the water, Yvonne promptly sent James off to the café to get her some lemonade.

'Can you get me a vodka and tonic with ice and lemon?' said Cable.

'I'll come and help you,' said Nicky. 'I could do with a snifter myself.'

'Don't forget to make the tonic Slimline,' Cable called after him.

Yvonne turned her attention to Tracey, who was sitting up combing the tangles out of her hair.

'My dear, have you known Larry long?'

'Not very.'

'Well, there's something about him I feel you really ought to know. May I be frank with you? He *is* married.'

'Oh, is he?' said Tracey, quite unmoved. 'Is she nice?'

'Very, evidently,' said Yvonne. 'And they've been happily married for seventeen years.'

'Well, I expect he needs a holiday from her then,' said Tracey. 'Then he'll go home all the keener.'

'But put yourself in his wife's place,' said Yvonne. 'How d'you think she feels at this moment, abandoned in Islington with the children, while you sun yourself on the Côte D'Azure at her husband's expense?'

A shadow fell over Imogen's book. She looked up and jumped as she saw Larry, a camera hanging from his neck. He put his finger to his lips.

'My dear,' said Yvonne, warming to her subject, 'don't you realise how physical men are? It's so easy for them to be led astray by the sight of a pretty face. If I encouraged them, I could have hundreds of men and husbands running after me, but it wouldn't be fair. Men are so animal. It's up to us girls to take a stand.'

Larry had crept round to Yvonne, and the next moment

572

he was growling furiously into her ear, making her jump so much she fell off her lilo.

'How dare you?' she screamed.

'Bow wow,' growled Larry. 'Bow wow. I'm an animal being led astray by a pretty face. Bow wow. That nose does suit you, I can't think why you ever take it off,' and picking up his camera he took a succession of quick snaps of her.

'Put that thing away,' squealed Yvonne, furiously tearing off her nose.

'Well, stop brain-washing Tracey then. Not that there's a lot of brain to wash.'

'Hullo Larry,' said Nicky, returning with James, a trayful of drinks and a cornet with two strawberry spheres of ice cream spilling out of the top. 'How did you get on?'

'Fantastic,' said Larry, seizing Cable's vodka and tonic and draining half of it in one gulp. 'What a pad they've got up there! It's a tragedy we couldn't use colour.'

'How was the Duchess?' said James.

'Sensational! Christ, what a beautiful woman. I've just been to Marseilles airport and put four rolls of film on a plane to London.'

'Where's Matt?' said Cable.

'Still up there, getting on like a château on fire. Braganzi's being amazingly free and frank.'

'He can afford to be if he's going to see copy,' snapped Cable. 'You might leave me some of my drink, Gilmore.'

'Oh, sorry, darling,' said Larry, finishing it. 'I'll get us both another one in a minute.'

'Ugh,' said Yvonne. 'You're dripping ice cream all over me. Who's it for?'

'Tracey,' said Nicky, handing it to her. 'Somehow its structure reminded me of her.'

'Do you mind?' giggled Tracey. 'Ta awfully, Nicky.'

'I'm going to swim,' said Cable, tucking her black hair into a yellow turban. 'Are you coming, Nicky?'

For a minute they glared at each other, then he laughed and said all right, and, putting an arm round her shoulders, walked down to the beach with her.

'I'm going too,' said Yvonne, still obviously put out by

Larry's presence.

Larry took off his shirt and trousers. Underneath he was wearing black bathing trunks. He had a muscular well-shaped body, already very brown. The Man-Tan, as Tracey had pointed out, had striped his legs. He laughed when he caught Imogen staring at him.

'It's terribly difficult to put on over hairy legs,' he said, sitting down beside her. 'It's a great story you got Matt, you know, and you certainly made a hit with Braganzi and the Duchess. They've been singing your praises all morning. Weren't your ears burning?'

'No, but my boobs are,' interrupted Tracey, rolling over on her front and picking up Imogen's book.

Larry looked out to sea at Cable and Nicky who had reached the raft, clambered on to it and were plainly having some kind of argument.

'Cable's being poisonous to that nice tennis player,' he said in his slow voice. 'He must be her latest.'

'Oh, they've been flirting a bit,' said James. 'Jolly pretty girl, but a bit of a handful. Suppose I'm one of the lucky ones,' he said, blowing bubbles into his drink with a straw. 'Old Yvonne's never really looked at another man.'

'I'm one of the lucky ones too,' drawled Gilmore. 'Another man's never looked at old Bambi.'

That's not right, thought Imogen quickly; both Matt and Cable said she was very attractive.

Larry drained Cable's drink. 'Who's for a refill?' he said. 'What are you having, James?'

'Vodka and pineapple,' said James. 'I'm getting quite addicted to it. But for God's sake don't tell Yvonne.'

'And what about you, Tracey?'

'I'm all right for a bit,' said Tracey, licking her ice cream, and still engrossed in Imogen's Scott Fitzgerald. She glanced at the jacket. 'She writes rather well, this Bodley Head. Has she written lots of other books?'

'I'm starving,' said Nicky as the beach emptied for lunch. 'Let's find a nice cool restaurant and have something to eat.'

'And something to drink,' said Larry.

On the way they called in the hotel, where Cable found a note for Matt.

'Hooray,' she said, opening it. 'It's from the Blaker-Harris's. There's a big party on tonight. We're all invited.'

'Will it be smart?' said Yvonne.

'Pretty,' said Cable. 'Lots of Jet Set.'

'Oh, dear,' said Larry. 'I'm getting quite pixillated by high life. The Duchess this morning, the Blaker-Harris's tonight. I must go down to the Sieffs again.'

'What does everyone want to eat?' said James, as they sat down in a little restaurant hung with fishing nets and overlooking the sea. 'Hands up for Salad Nicoise.'

'I'd like an advocado pear,' said Tracey.

'I'd like an enormous vodka,' said Larry.

He's deliberately setting out to get drunk again, thought Imogen. A waiter shot past them bearing a plate of pink langoustines to a corner table, and she suddenly felt a stab of misery, remembering last time she'd eaten them with Matt in St Tropez. She wondered for the hundredth time how he was getting on.

They'd reached the coffee stage by the time he arrived. Cable and Yvonne were discussing what to wear that evening, Nicky was making discreet eyes at Tracey and talking to James about Forest Hills at the same time, Larry was ordering another bottle, when she saw him standing in the doorway watching them.

I can't help it, she thought in misery, every time I see him, I want to bound forward like a dog and wag my tail and jump all over him.

'Matt,' shouted Larry, 'bon jour main sewer. Qu'est-que ce going on up at Château Braganzi ?'

Matt pulled up a chair and sat down between him and Cable.

'Jesus, what a story,' he said. 'It's so hot it frightens me.'

'Well, have a drink, and then it won't any more,' said Larry.

Matt shook his head. 'I'd better stay sober. Going to need all the wits I've got. I'll have some coffee. Are you all right, darling?' he said to Cable, then not giving her time to answer, turned to Imogen. 'They both sent their love. They gave me a present for you, but I left it behind. I'll bring it back when I go up this evening and show them the copy — if I ever get it together, that is.'

'You'd better get it written this afternoon,' said Cable, 'The Blaker-Harrises are giving a party tonight.'

'Well, they'll manage without me,' said Matt.

'That's ridiculous,' snapped Cable. 'It can't take you that long. You're not writing a novel.'

'Bloody nearly. I've just talked to the paper. They're going to hold the review front for it. You can't churn that out in a couple of hours.'

'There'll be a lot of talent at the Blaker-Harris's,' said Cable tauntingly. 'Rod Stewart's going to be there.'

'Well, you won't need me either.' As soon as he finished the cup of coffee he got to his feet. 'I'd better get started. Did you find me a typewriter?'

'No,' said Cable.

'Christ,' said Matt.

'I did try, but I had a lot of things to do this morning,' she added defensively.

'I've no doubt one of them was human.'

'What d'you mean?' said Cable, momentarily nonplussed.

'You should tidy up after your gentlemen friends. One of them left this on the bed this morning,' said Matt, and there was a slither of gold as he dropped Nicky's medallion on to Cable's lap.

There was an awful pause, then Cable said, 'Oh, that's Nicky's. The hot tap wasn't working in his room, so he used our shower. Perhaps you'd have a word with Madame, seeing she's a friend of yours.'

Matt looked at Nicky reflectively for a minute and then he laughed. 'I would have thought a few cold showers would have done you all the good in the world, Nicky boy,' and he was gone.

There was another long pause.

'I'm going to the hairdresser this afternoon,' said Yvonne.

'So am I,' said Cable.

Nicky turned to Tracey. 'How would you like to come for a

576

ride on a pedalo?'

Larry looked out of the window at the heat haze shimmering on the road out of the village: 'I think it's going to snow. I want another large vodka.'

Larry and Imogen and James went back to the beach and they taught her how to play poker, but before long the heat and the heavy lunch overcame James and he staggered back to the hotel for a siesta. Larry picked up his camera. 'Let's wander along the beach. I'd like to take some pictures of you.'

'Oh, please no,' stammered Imogen, 'I don't take a very good photograph.'

'Don't be silly,' said Larry. 'I'm the one who takes the good photographs.'

And certainly he was so quiet and gentle, and snapped away so unobtrusively, and flattered her so outrageously, that she was soon relaxing and posing in every position he suggested, on the rocks, paddling in the shallows, lounging against a breakwater.

'Has anyone told you what a pretty girl you are?' he said.

Imogen gazed at his thick black and grey hair, as he bent over the viewfinder.

'Yes, one or two people,' she said bitterly. 'And then they rush off with other people, telling me I'm too inexperienced.'

He looked up. 'Finding the musical beds confusing, are you? I must say we're a pretty decadent lot for you to stumble on, except perhaps Yvonne, and she's enough to put one off respectability for life, the frigid bitch. Turn your head slightly towards the sea, darling, but leave your eyes in the same place.'

'But Matt doesn't seem like that.' The temptation to talk about him was too strong.

'Matt's different,' said Larry, changing the film.

'In what way?' said Imogen, letting her hair fall over her face so Larry couldn't see she was blushing. 'I mean, when he gave Cable that medallion he must have known what she'd been up to with Nicky, but he didn't seem in the least put out. He was far more annoyed with her not getting the

577

typewriter.'

'He completely switches off when he's working. Until he's got that piece finished, and it's going to be a bugger — turn your head slightly to the left, darling — he won't notice if Cable's being laid end to end by all the frogs in Port-les-Pins.'

'It must be awfully irritating for her. She's so beautiful.'

'She's nothing special. Just a spoilt little bitch who doesn't know what she wants.'

'She wants Matt,' said Imogen.

'Et alia. But I've got a feeling each time she cheats on him, it worries him less — head up a bit, darling — and if he allows her enough rape, she'll hang herself.'

Imogen giggled, and felt a bit better, and allowed herself a tiny dream about getting a job in the library on Matt's newspaper and his taking her on a story, and then getting snowed up.

'That's enough work for one afternoon,' said Larry. 'Let's go and have a drink.' He screwed his eyes up to look out to sea. 'Where's that pedalo? I hope Nicky hasn't sunk without Tracey.'

'She is nice,' said Imogen. 'In fact it's been so much better all round since you and she arrived last night. Will it be frightfully grand this evening?'

'It'll be ludicrous,' said Larry, tucking his arm through hers. 'But we might get a few laughs.'

They turned into the first bar on the front, and sat idly drinking and watching the people coming back from the beach.

'That girl oughtn't to wear a bikini,' said Larry, as a fat brunette wobbled past them, 'she ought to wear an overcoat.'

'You should have seen the sensation Tracey caused on the beach this morning,' said Imogen. 'It was a bit like the Pied Piper drawing all the rats into the water when she went down to bathe.'

Larry didn't answer, and, suddenly turning round, Imogen saw he'd gone as white as a sheet and was gazing mesmerised with horror at a beautiful woman with short light brown hair, and very high cheek bones, who was walking hand in hand with a much younger, athletic-looking man down to the sea.

'What's the matter?' said Imogen.

He took a slug of his drink with a shaking hand.

'Please tell me,' she urged. 'I know something's wrong. You seem so — well — cheerful, but underneath I'm sure you're not.'

For a minute he was silent, his thin face dark and bitter, and she could feel the struggle going on inside him. Then he took a deep breath and said:

'That woman. For a minute I thought she was Bambi.'

'But she's in Islington.'

'No she isn't. She's down here somewhere with her lover. She left me about a fortnight ago.'

'Oh,' said Imogen with embarrassment. 'I can't bear it. You poor thing.'

'I didn't want everyone pitying me. It was my fault. I suppose I neglected her. I've been working so hard the last two years just to survive and pay the school fees. Every night I'd come home and collapse in front of the telly with a double whisky, far too zonked out with my own problems to realise she was unhappy.'

'But when did she start seeing this other man?' asked Imogen.

'Oh, last year sometime. Suddenly she started finding fault with everything I did. If the washing machine had broken it was my fault. Going home at night was like being parachuted into a fucking minefield. In retrospect I realise now she was picking fights with me to justify falling for this other bloke.'

'How did you find out?'

'Silly, really. She used to go out every Wednesday to pottery classes. I used to babysit. She was quite often late back, said she and the rest of the class had been to the pub. Then one day I met her pottery teacher in the High Street, and he said what a pity it was she didn't come to classes any more when she was so talented. I went straight home and she admitted everything. In the old days I suppose I'd have blacked her eye, but I was buggered if I was going to be accused of being a male chauvinist pig, so I just got bombed out of my skull every night.'

'And what about Tracey?'

'She's just window dressing. She's a nice girl, but with me putting back the amount I'm putting back at the moment I'm not much use to her in the sack anyway. Best thing for her is to get off with Nicky. They're well matched intellectually!'

He took her hand. 'Look, I'm really sorry to dump on you like this.'

'I like it,' said Imogen. 'I've felt so useless this holiday. But aren't you likely to bump into Bambi any minute?'

He shrugged. 'I know she and loverboy are staying somewhere on the Riviera. He's frightfully rich, so it's bound to be expensive.'

'Does Matt know?'

'Of course,' said Larry. 'He rumbled it last night.'

Back at the hotel they found Cable and Yvonne both with sleek newly washed hair drinking lemon tea with Nicky and James.

'I suppose I'd better ring the paper to see if that film's arrived,' said Larry.

'What time have we got to be on parade?' asked Imogen.

'Well it starts at eight, but I don't think we need roll up much before nine or nine-thirty,' said Yvonne.

'Must make an entrance,' muttered Nicky.

James looked at his watch. 'Five o'clock. I've just got time to ring the office to see if everything's O.K.'

After that Nicky decided he ought to go and ring his agent, and Cable and Yvonne suddenly came to the conclusion they ought to ring theirs as well.

Imogen wondered if she ought to keep her end up by ringing the library, but what could she ask them? Had the mayor returned *The Hite Report* at last? Was Lady Jacintha still clinging on to Dick Francis? She decided to go upstairs and wash her hair.

She met Cable coming downstairs looking bootfaced. 'Matt's lost his sense of humour. He simply can't get his dreary piece together. He's just bitten my head off simply because I asked for some change to telephone. I'll have to borrow from Gilmore.'

Imogen turned around and went out to a nearby café and bought six cans of iced beer and a couple of large sandwiches made of French bread and garlic sausage. She could see Cable safely squawking in the telephone box as she went through reception, so she went upstairs and knocked timidly on Matt's door.

There was no answer.

She knocked again.

'Come in,' shouted a voice. 'What the bloody hell do you want this time?'

Inside she found him sitting on a chair that was too small, bashing away at a typewriter on a tiny table that shuddered and trembled under the pressure. His blue denim shirt was drenched with sweat; he looked like a giant trying to ride a Shetland pony. His shoulders were rigid with tension and exasperation; there were scrumpled-up bits of paper all over the floor.

'Can't you leave me alone for five minutes?' he said through gritted teeth. Then he looked round, blinked and realised it was her.

'Oh, it's you,' he said.

'I thought you might need something to eat — and drink — not now but later,' she said nervously. 'You didn't have any lunch. You ought to eat.'

He looked slightly less bootfaced. 'That was very kind of you, sweetheart.'

'Is it going any better?'

'Nope.' He pushed his damp hair back from his forehead. 'It's going backwards. I've got a total brainfreeze. I can't think how to do it. It'll break soon, it's got to. I've got to show it to Braganzi before midnight. The bugger is him having to see it; it's like having to adapt de Sade for the parish mag.'

His eyes were just hollows in his suntanned face. He

581

flexed his aching back. Suddenly he looked so tired and lost and defeated, she wanted to cradle his head against her and stroke all the tension out of him.

'I wouldn't bother about what they're going to think,' she said. 'I'm sure if you get across how much they adore each other, and what a sacrifice they had to make, and how the relationship does work, and how he's not just a cheap hood, they won't mind what else you say. They're just panicking that someone might write something that might prejudice her chances of seeing the children again . . . but you know all that anyway. I used to get panicky about essays in exams,' she said tumbling over her words in her shyness.

Matt reached over and opened one of the cans of beer. 'Go on,' he said.

'So I used to pretend I wasn't doing an essay at all, just writing a letter about the subject home to Juliet, trying to make it as amusing for her as possible.'

Matt grinned for the first time. 'You think I should pretend I'm writing to Basil?'

Imogen giggled. 'Well, maybe something of the sort.'

'Are you going to the Blaker-Harris's?' he said.

She nodded.

'Well, for God's sake wear a chastity belt and a bullet-proof vest. It's bound to turn into an orgy.'

He turned back to his typewriter, dismissing her, but as she went out on to the landing, he thanked her once again.

She was just starting to wash her hair when Larry knocked on the door.

'I'm going back to the hotel to have a bath and change,' he said. 'Tracey and I'll come and pick you up about half eight. We don't want to miss valuable drinking time.'

'What shall I wear?' she asked.

Gilmore went over to her wardrobe. 'The pink trousers and that pale pink top,' he said. 'It'll look stunning now you're brown.'

'Will it be smart enough?' she asked, doubtfully.

'Perfect. I want you to downstage the others. And remember no bra.'

What was the point of dressing up for a ball, she thought listlessly, when there was no chance of Prince Charming showing up?

CHAPTER FIFTEEN

'Hey you look good enough to — ah — well good enough for anything,' said Larry when he collected her. 'You certainly do things for that sweater.'

'You like it?'

'Yes, and what's inside it even better.'

'Isn't it a bit tight?' said Imogen doubtfully. 'And are you sure trousers will be all right?'

'Perfect. Why wear expensive gear to go to a rugger scrum?'

He was wearing a pale grey suit and a black shirt, which matched his black and silver hair.

'You look lovely too,' she said.

As they went downstairs they could hear the relentless pounding of Matt's typewriter.

'That's a relief,' said Gilmore. 'Sounds as though he's getting it together at last.'

It was a stifling hot night. Tracey, James and Nicky, all in high spirits, were having a drink in the bar. Tracey was wearing a black dress, plunging at the front, slit up to her red pants at the back. Madame had presented James with one of her purple asters for his button hole.

'I've never been to a jet set party,' he was saying. 'I do hope Bianca Jagger's there.'

'Who are the Blaker-Harris's anyway?' asked Nicky.

'He made a fortune in dog food,' said Larry. 'I gather they're staying with some rich frogs called Ducharmé who are giving the party. Are Cable and Yvonne anything like ready, do you suppose? I'd much rather drink at Monsieur Ducharmé's expense than my own.'

'Well, I'm ready,' said a gay voice, and Yvonne arrived in a

584

swirl of apple green, with green sandals, and a green ribbon in her red curls.

'You look lovely, my darling,' said James dutifully.

'Like *creme de menthe* frappé,' said Larry under his breath.

'I thought you said it'd be all right to wear trousers,' muttered Imogen.

'And the most wonderful news,' went on Yvonne. 'My agent's just rung back and said I'm short listed for Jane Bennet in the new BBC *Pride and Prejudice*.'

Everyone gave rather forced exclamations of enthusiasm, and James kissed her, but very gingerly, so as not to disarrange her hair.

'When will you know?' said Nicky.

'In a day or two,' said Yvonne. 'They're starting shooting in three weeks. Isn't it exciting?' Suddenly her beady eyes fell on Imogen. 'Oughtn't you to go and change? We're going to be terribly late.'

'She's already changed,' said Larry. 'Aren't you rather miscast as Jane, Yvonne dear? She was supposed to be such a nice sweetnatured girl.'

Yvonne was saved the trouble of thinking up a really crushing reply by the arrival of Cable, looking sensational in a dress entirely made of peacock feathers. It was sleeveless and clung lightly to her figure, stopping just above the knee. Two peacock feathers nestling in her snaking ebony hair and bands of peacock blue shadow painted on her eyelids made her eyes look brilliant flashing turquoise rather than green.

Nicky whistled. James gasped. Yvonne merely glared and shut her lips tighter.

'That's the most beautiful dress I've ever seen,' said Tracey.

'I'm going to change,' muttered Imogen.

'Haven't got time,' said Larry, seizing her wrist. 'I'm surprised you haven't borrowed Yvonne's cardboard beak to complete the picture, Cable darling.'

The sun was falling into the sea as the taxi turned off the coast road.

'I'm glad it's getting dark,' said Tracey, adding another layer of mascara to her false eyelashes. 'Party make-up looks so much better at night.'

In James's spotlessly clean, pale-blue car in front Imogen could see Cable, who'd commandeered the entire back seat to herself so her feathers shouldn't be ruffled, and Yvonne getting out combs and beginning to tease their hair with the pointed ends. She wished Matt were there to look after her. She was sure as soon as they got to the party, Larry would get drunk and disappear. Nicky already had his arm along the back of the seat and was surreptitiously caressing the back of Tracey's neck, so she couldn't expect much support from him either.

The taxi turned and sped up a drive, the gravel spluttering against the wheels. Vineyards and olive groves on either side stretched to infinity. Ahead in the dusk, every window blazing with light, was a huge white house.

'It's a mansion,' said Tracey.

They could see a man in a pink suit, with red and pink hair, get out of a Rolls-Royce and ring the door bell.

'I think that's David Bowie,' said Larry.

'Oh, dear,' said Imogen faintly.

As they walked up the marble steps, a butler opened the door. Then a maid whisked Imogen and Tracey upstairs to a room with walls covered in pink satin. On the floor was a thick fur carpet, the bed was covered in fur coats, which must have been brought by guests just to show off — it was such a stifling hot night.

'Do you take cloth coats too?' said Tracey, taking off her white blazer and handing it to the maid.

Cable and Yvonne were still engaged in teasing their hair in front of the mirror.

'I'm sure I caught a glimpse of Omar Sharif,' said Yvonne.

Out of the window Imogen could see a jungle of garden, punctuated by lily ponds, aviaries full of coloured birds, two lantern-lit swimming pools and, in the distance, the sea.

Shaking with nerves, she went downstairs to find Larry waiting for her and talking in a low voice to a splendid

586

blonde covered in sequins.

'Imogen darling, this is your hostess, Claudine. Take a good look at her. She may not pass this way again.'

But before he had a chance to say anything else, Claudine had shimmered forward and seized Imogen's hands.

'Mees Brocklehurst, how wonderful to meet you. What a fantastic coincidence that you should be on holiday with Matt and Nicky Beresford,' and the next moment she had drawn Imogen into a huge room, which seemed to be seething with suntanned faces with hard restless eyes, constantly on the look-out for fresh excitement.

'Wait for Larry,' begged Imogen.

'Larry who?' screamed Claudine and, shoving a drink into Imogen's hand, she dragged her from one group to another, crying, 'This is lovely Imogen Brocklehurst.' . . . whisper, whisper . . . 'Yes, really. Braganzi's child snatched from the jaws of death.'

Everyone started oohing and aahing as though Claudine was bringing in the Christmas pudding flaming blue with brandy.

'How do you do? How do you do? Hi Imogen, glad to know you. How do you do?' People were thrusting forward to meet her.

Imogen turned to Claudine in horror. 'But what have you told them?'

'Did you really meet the Duchess? What was she like? Did she seem keen on Braganzi?' clamoured the faces.

'Oh stop,' called Imogen after a disappearing Claudine. 'Please don't tell people. Braganzi doesn't want publicity.'

Now everyone was mobbing her and introducing her. She was so breathless with answering questions, she found she'd finished her drink, which was delicious and tasted rather like coke filled with fruit salad. The moment she put her glass down another was thrust into her hand.

'How has she furnished the house?' 'Are the guard dogs as ferocious as everyone makes out?' 'Weren't you terrified to meet Braganzi?' 'Does he keep her chained up there?' 'Has she lost her looks ?' 'I hear the Duke . . . '

More people were crowding round her, asking excited

questions. Finally somebody introduced her to Larry. 'No, we haven't met,' he said, grabbing her by the arm and pulling her into a side room.

'This place is a lunatic asylum,' she gasped. 'What on earth did you tell Claudine?'

'I gave her a brief run down on your life-saving activities yesterday. You're certainly the star attraction. Have another drink.' He grabbed one from a passing waiter.

'I've had several already,' said Imogen with a giggle. 'It's delicious and so refreshing. What is it?'

'Pimms,' said Larry. 'Practically non-alcoholic.'

A vision in yellow flew out at him. 'Larry darling, where did you get to? I've been looking for you everywhere.' And she hauled him away.

Next moment a stunningly handsome man in a white dinner jacket had crept up and put his arm through Imogen's. 'I hear you know darling Camilla,' he said. 'Do give her my love next time you see her.'

A light flashed. 'Thank you,' said a photographer moving away.

The sounds of revelry grew louder, the heat grew more oppressive by the minute.

'Come and look at the garden,' said the man in the white dinner jacket. Two beautiful young men, in shirts slashed to the waist, met them in the doorway.

'At last we've found you. You must be Morgan Brocklehurst,' they chorused. 'We've been simply dying to meet you all evening.'

'I hear you had dinner with Braganzi last night,' said the first.

'Is he as butch as everyone says he is?' asked the second.

A large woman in crimson with one false eyelash hanging askew like a ladder from her bottom lid charged up to them.

'Does anyone know which Morgan Brocklehurst is?' she said, eagerly. 'I hear she's actually met Braganzi and the Duchess.'

. 'She's somewhere in there,' said the first young man, pointing back at the drawing-room, from which a hysterical rush of talk was now issuing.

'Oh dear,' said the woman in crimson, 'I've just fought my way out of there. I want to try and nail her for a beach party I'm having tomorrow.' She dived back in the mêleé.

'I'll get you another drink, Morgan,' said the man in the white dinner jacket.

'Thanks, I'd adore one,' said Imogen, who was beginning to enjoy herself.

One of the beautiful young men took her arm and led her through the gardens, past huge jungle plants with leaves like dark shining shields, and brilliant coloured birds, scarlet, turquoise, dark blue and emerald, all chirruping and fluttering about their aviary, like guests at the party. Round the corner they found two pale pink flamingos standing on one leg in a bright green pond, full of fat golden carp gliding in and out of the water lilies.

In the stifling heat Imogen was quite happy to rest on a cool stone bench with lions' heads rearing up at either end. The two young men sat at her feet, a captive audience. She was soon quite happily recounting the events of yesterday.

Soon quite a crowd was gathered round her. People kept topping up her drink. 'It really is very morish,' she said to the company at large. She kept looking around for Larry, and hoping Matt would arrive, but after a bit she stopped worrying even about them.

'Can I get you something to eat?' asked the man in the white dinner jacket.

'Oh, no thank you,' said Imogen. She seemed to have consumed far too much fruit salad already.

'Well, come and dance then,' he said, leading her back into the house. 'Claudine brought in 600 bottles of champagne for this party, plus 50 lbs of caviar, and God knows how many gallons of Diorissimo to put in the swimming pool. Of course she'll claim it all on tax.'

It was far too dark to see anyone on the dance floor.

'Morgan, Morgan, you're so fresh and unspoilt,' said the man in the white dinner jacket, drawing her to his bosom.

Oh dear, she thought, I do hope I don't leave make-up all over him. Another man cut in and danced her off into another room where he tried to kiss her. She wanted to slap his face, but he wasn't very steady on his feet, and she thought she might knock him over. Then a haughty aristocratic beauty drew her aside.

'I'm giving a party in Marbella tomorrow night. Love it if you could make it. We could easily send a plane. Bring anyone you like. Perhaps Camilla'd like an outing? Has she put on any weight since she's been living with Braganzi?'

The band was playing *Smoke Gets In Your Eyes,* the laughter and tinkle of broken glass was getting louder, a crowd was clamouring round her again. Suddenly a hand shot out and grabbed her; it was Larry, waving a full bottle of champagne.

'Doctor Livingstone,' she screamed.

'I've been looking for you everywhere,' he said, dragging her through the french windows out into the garden.

'Where are the others?'

'Well, I've just seen Nicky and Tracey come out of the library, looking rather ruffled. Nicky was wearing lipstick, Tracey wasn't any more. Mrs Edgworth's been dancing the night away with Omar Sharif, and Cable's been dividing her unwrapped attention between Rod Stewart and Warren Beatty.'

'So she's happy?'

'Not entirely. No point in being the Belle of the Ball if the guy who matters isn't here to witness it. Matt hasn't showed up yet. He can't *still* be wrestling with his copy.'

'He's probably having trouble getting Braganzi to O.K. it,' said Imogen.

'If he does get it through he'll make a bomb on syndication. Bloody well need to, to pay for Cable's peacock feathers.'

Pity someone can't lock her away in the aviary with all those coloured birds, thought Imogen. She held out her glass.

'I'd like another drink, please.'

'That's my girl,' said Larry, filling her long Pimms glass up to the brim with champagne. For a while they danced on the lawn both slightly supporting one another.

'Christ, I wish I'd brought my camera,' said Larry. 'Half

the crowned heads of Europe are frisking nude in the swimming pool. Evidently Leonard is on hand with a fleet of minions to blow dry anyone who wants it when they come out.'

Imogen listened to the shrieks and splashes from the pool, and wished she felt slim enough to bathe in the nude. She seemed to have drunk all her champagne.

'I really must go to the loo.'

'Well, don't be long,' said Larry. 'It's nearly light up time.'

Imogen realised how drunk she was when she found herself liberally pouring her hostess's scent over her bosom in the pink satin bedroom. Breaking the eighth commandment again. She put the bottle down hastily. What would her father say, and Matt? Her face, however, looked rather sparkly-eyed and pink-cheeked and much better than she'd expected after so much booze.

'Have you met Morgan Brocklehurst?' she heard two women saying as she went downstairs. 'Quite ravishing. I must ask her who does her hair. Evidently Braganzi's leaving her half of Sicily.'

As she reached the bottom step, a large brunette shot past her shrieking playfully, followed two seconds later by James, very pink in the face and emitting Tarzan howls. They both disappeared into the shrubbery.

'Why aren't you dancing, Morgan?' asked Claudine, rushing forward.

'I'll take care of that,' said a smooth voice, and the next moment she felt herself clutched to the muscular, scented hairy-chested bosom of one of the screen's greatest lovers.

'I took one look at you,' he crooned in her ear, 'That's all I meant to do, And then my heart stood still. How would you like to go to a party in Rome?'

'I'm supposed to be going to one in Marbella tomorrow,' said Imogen.

'Oh, that'll be Effie Strauss's thrash. I'll give you a lift if you like.'

They danced and danced, drank and drank, and although she was slightly missing the forehand drives of conversation he didn't seem to mind at all. Then she remembered she'd left Larry in the garden. She must go and find

591

him. As she reached the end of the lawn, she passed a couple under a fig tree locked in a passionate embrace. The girl's silver blonde hair fell below her waist.

'The moment I saw you yesterday,' the man's voice was saying huskily, 'Pow, suddenly it happened, like being struck down by a thunderbolt. I don't know what it is about you, Tracey darling, but it's something indefinably different.'

'And your pulse, my darling, is going like the Charge of the Light Brigade,' shrieked Imogen loudly, and rushed off howling with laughter as they both jumped out of their skins.

She was still laughing when she found Larry rolling a joint by the flamingo pool. 'It's light up time,' he said again.

'This is the best party I've ever been to,' she said.

'Have a drag of this,' said Larry, 'and it'll seem even better.'

'I don't smoke,' said Imogen.

'Go on. I'm a great believer in first times. There may not be another opportunity.'

He lit the cigarette, inhaled deeply two or three times, then handed it to her. She took a nervous puff and choked, then took another one; then she put the joint in the snarling mouth of the stone lion at the end of the seat, and she and Larry both laughed immoderately. Then she took another drag.

'Nice?' asked Larry.

'Yes,' sighed Imogen. 'It makes the flamingos so pink and the water so green.'

Three-quarters down the cigarette, by which time they were both cackling with laughter over anything, she turned and looked at him. He was really very attractive in a hawk-like ravaged way. And quite old enough to be her father — so that made everything quite safe.

'Larry.'

'Yes, angel.'

'Do you think I'm pretty?'

'Exquisitely so,' and he bent over and kissed her very slowly and with velvet artistry.

'And now you're even prettier.' He took a deep drag on

592

the cigarette, then kissed her again, and this time it took much longer.

Imogen got to her feet and went to the edge of the pool. The flamingos seemed to be floating above the water, the turning beam of the lighthouse revolving most erratically.

The huge stars were so near she could have reached up and plucked them.

'Don't go away,' said Larry. 'The way to heaven is paved with bad intentions.'

'I'm not going anywhere.' She could hear the throb of drums and the carnival howls of the party. 'When love comes in and takes you for a spin, Oh la la la, c'est magnifique,' played the band.

The night was so warm and beautiful, yet she felt a terrible stab of longing. If only Matt were here. Then suddenly she was filled with passion and resolve and 86 per cent proof courage.

'Larry darling,' she turned to him. 'People keep telling me I've got to grow up and live a little and get some experience with men, and catch up with Cable and Yvonne and Tracey and things. You wouldn't help me, would you, and teach me about sex?'

'Wouldn't I just? What an offer! Christ, if you want experience, I'm your man, sweetheart. *Je suis le professeur.* Now stay here and finish the joint, and I'll go and get another bottle and we'll take it down to the beach.'

Imogen collapsed back on the seat. 'When love comes in and takes you for a spin,' she sang to the flamingos. She was feeling very light-headed.

From where she was sitting, she could see some planes parked in a field. Perhaps one was waiting to whisk the screen's greatest lover off to Rome. Beyond the planes were a row of cars, mostly Rolls-Royces and Bentleys, but standing there, cleaner than any other, was James and Yvonne's pale blue Cortina. Suddenly Imogen felt an overwhelming urge. She opened her bag, scrabbling inside for a lipstick. She found one that Gloria had given her for her birthday that she'd never used. It was dark maroon and called Plum Dynasty — to make you more sophisticated, Gloria had said.

JILLY COOPER

'Jolly soppy name,' said Imogen, giggling hysterically to
herself as she ran through the trees towards the cars. 'Fancy
founding a dynasty of plums. Anyway, your hour has come,
Plum,' and she repeated 'Come Plum' several times to herself, giggling some more.

And *there* was the pale blue boot door of Yvonne's car, just
asking to be scribbled on. She unscrewed the lipstick and
wrote 'Yvonne Edgworth' in a large maroon scrawl. Then
she added 'is a stroppy cow', then crossed out 'cow' and put
'bitch' and 'henpecker'. Then she wrote 'bugger' three times
on the top of the car, and 'fuck' twice on the windscreen.
Then she rushed round to the other side and wrote 'Yvonne
Bismark — the Iron Duke', but that wasn't quite right, so
she crossed out the D and changed Duke to Puke, and
laughed immoderately at her own joke. She'd just started to
write 'Go Home Carrot Top' when the lipstick broke in half,
so she ran shrieking back to Larry, who had returned and
was swaying dangerously as he tried to balance along the
top of the stone seat with a bottle in one hand and a glass in
the other.

He jumped down, spilling some of the champagne, and
said, 'I've just seen Yvonne Edgworth asking Omar Sharif if
he'd ever bought a whole flower stall for anyone.'

The path down to the sea was quite steep and they were
both very drunk, but somehow they managed to support
each other.

'I want to get my organ into Morgan,' chanted Larry, and
they both roared with laughter.

'I seem to be going from one bad end to another,' said
Imogen. 'I do love you, Larry. Is it possible to love two people at once?'

'I think so,' said Larry, 'but it's rather expensive.'

His drawl was more exaggerated than ever. His hair was
all over the place.

They reached the beach. Imogen could feel the sand cool
and separating beneath her feet. Somewhere on the way
down she'd lost her shoes.

'When love comes in and takes you for a spin,' sang Larry.
'I want to get my organ into Morgan. So do a lot of other

594

guys at the party. I found several men in white dinner jackets looking for you when I went back to the house.'

'There was only one,' said Imogen. 'You must have been seeing quadruple.'

And they both shrieked with laughter again. Pot on a lot of drink makes the stupidest things funny.

The whole beach and the distant lights of Port-les-Pins and the lighthouse seemed to hang in a rosy glow. The waves were hissing like little white snakes on the sand. A half grapefruit moon lay on its back in the dark sky — waiting to submit like me, thought Imogen. She felt weightless like an astronaut.

Larry picked up a stick and tried to write with it, but the sand was too dry.

'Tell the sea to come nearer,' he said.

They ran whooping hand in hand down to the water's edge where he wrote Larry Loves Imogen in huge letters in the wet sand. Then he kissed her, and she could feel the warm sea washing over her feet.

'I'll give you a crash course in experience,' he muttered into her hair, 'you lovely warm thing.'

'You do realise I haven't been to bed with anyone before?'

'I said I was a great believer in first time,' said Larry, gently pulling her sweater over her head. 'Shall we swim first? One should always have a bath before sex.'

Perhaps I'm not too fat to bathe in the nude after all, thought Imogen hazily, as she ripped off the trousers and pants and threw them down on the sand. There was no shock as, shrieking with joy, she paddled ecstatically into the waves. It was almost as warm in the water as out.

'It's heavenly,' she shouted to Larry.

Next minute he was chasing after her, and she felt his hands round her waist.

'You're beautiful,' he said looking down at her. 'You look like Venus coming out of the waves.'

'Bottichilly,' giggled Imogen. 'Though actually it's not chilly at all, quite the reverse.'

'That's enough overture,' said Larry. 'Let's get down to Act One.' As he kissed her his lips tasted of salt, and Imogen was glad he was holding her; she doubted she could have stood up alone. She really felt very hazy. She asked Larry if he thought there was any point in having a crash course if she wasn't going to remember the finer points afterwards.

Larry laughed and said two of her finest points were sticking into his chest at the moment and he certainly wasn't going to forget them, and began to kiss her in the hollow of her throat.

In the distance she could still hear the sound of revellers, and shrieks from the swimming pool. Then she heard voices much nearer, angry voices, and she was gradually aware that Larry had stopped kissing her and was gazing over her shoulder.

There was a long pause, then Larry muttered, 'My God, it can't be.'

Then she heard an all too familiar voice saying, 'For Christ's sake, Gilmore.'

Imogen buried her face in Larry's neck, then slowly swivelled round. A man and a woman were standing on the sands only a few yards away from them. Both their faces were in shadow, but she could see the girl had short streaked blonde hair and was very slim, and no one could miss that height and the width of the man's shoulders.

Larry swallowed nervously. 'Hi, Matt,' he said brightly.

'Oh dear,' said Imogen, 'I'd better do a Venus in reverse,' and, giggling frantically, she slid back into the water.

'What the bloody hell have you been up to, Gilmore?' said Matt icily.

'You told me to keep an eye on her,' protested Larry.

'And so he has,' said Imogen's head, just above the water. 'Two eyes most of the time, and a lot of hands. He's been lovely. We've had such a nice time. When love comes in and take you for a spin, Oh la la la.'

'Jesus,' said Matt. 'What *have* you done to her?'

Larry now seemed to be on shore, futilely trying to tug on Imogen's pink trousers which came no higher than his knee caps.

'Imogen dear,' he said, 'you haven't met Bambi.'

'Bambi,' squeaked Imogen, looking at Matt's companion.

'Oh my goodness, how do you do? I've heard so much about you.'

'Funny,' said Bambi acidly. 'I've heard absolutely nothing about you.'

Matt picked up Gilmore's trousers and threw them at him.

'I know you've been trying to get into Imogen's pants all evening,' he snapped. 'Now try and get into your own for a change.'

'Awfully good party,' said Imogen, flipping water at them.

'Come out of there at once and get dressed. I'm taking you home,' said Matt.

In no time at all, it seemed, she was sitting beside Matt in her dripping clothes, as he belted the Mercedes down Claudine's drive. Somewhere in the distance behind them she could hear Yvonne's voice rising and falling in fury like a fire siren.

'I don't want to go home. I'd like some more champagne,' said Imogen petulantly.

'You've had quite enough.'

Imogen let her head loll back on the seat.

'You're a rotten spoilsport,' she said in a slurred voice. 'I've been having the time of my life. Everyone's been trying to get off with me — Morgan the hero, the intrepid rescuer. Stars of stage and screen have been battling for my favours. I've been smoking pot, and drinking quite a lot, and having a whole load of new experiences. In fact I was just about to embark on my first affair with a married man when you and Bambi came along so inconsiderately and put a spoke in the wheel.'

Matt gazed stonily at the road in front, and jammed his foot down on the accelerator.

'Darling Larry was giving me a crash course in experience.'

'A crash course! Larry ought to be shot.'

'I don't know why you're so cross,' grumbled Imogen. 'You don't want me. You're just being a dog in the manger. Larry was just being kind. I *asked* him to seduce me. I thought if I became a woman of the world like Cable, a few

597

more people might fancy me.'

'Well, you're going about it the wrong way.' Matt ground the gears viciously.

'When love come in and takes you for a spin,' sang Imogen tunelessly. 'Oh, la la la, it's bloody awful. Do you think Bambi'll excite me as co-respondent?'

'Probably.'

'Well, what a stupid time for her to stage a comeback, in the middle of an orgy. She must have known Larry'd be up to someone, if not me.'

Matt ignored her and lit a cigarette.

She was beginning to feel very odd. Everything like Vesuvius seemed to be erupting inside her.

'Oh well, this time in a fortnight, I'll be back in my little grey home in the West Riding,' she said fretfully, 'and you can forget all about me.'

Then suddenly out of the corner of her eye she saw he was laughing.

'You're not cross anymore?'

'Absolutely blind with rage.'

'I'm awfully sorry,' she said, her head flopping on to his shoulder, 'but I do love you,' and she passed out cold.

CHAPTER SIXTEEN

When she woke next afternoon she thought she was going to die. She'd never known pain like it, as though a nut-cracker was slowly crushing her skull in, and a lot of gnomes were hammering from the inside. For a few minutes she lay groaning pitifully, then opened her eyes, whereupon an agonising blaze of sunlight stabbed her like a knife and she hastily shut them again. Wincing, she started to piece together the events of the evening, the crazy lionising, the drinking and pot smoking, and finally the nude bathing. Someone had hung her wet trousers and jersey from the window. She wondered what had happened to her knickers and her shoes. She also had hazy memories of meeting Bambi, and Matt being very cross and bringing her home. But who the hell had undressed her? Sweat broke out, drenching her entire body. She only just made the lavatory in time and was violently sick.

On the way back to her room she passed Madame and a squeegee mop, wanting to hear all about her encounter with Braganzi and the Duchess. Muttering about shellfish poisoning, Imogen apologised and bolted back into her room, where she cleaned her teeth and then crawled miserably into bed. She tried to remember what she'd said to Matt on the way home. Oh, why had she made such an idiot of herself?

There was a knock on the door. It sounded like a clap of thunder. It was Matt wearing jeans and no shirt. He had just washed his hair and was rubbing it dry with a large pink mascara-stained towel. Imogen disappeared hastily under the bedclothes. She felt him sit down on the bed and slowly emerged.

'You're an absolute disgrace,' he said.

'Oh, go away,' she moaned. 'I know I behaved horribly. I'm quite prepared for what's coming to me, and I don't want any flowers or letters please.'

A smile so faint it was almost imperceptible touched his mouth at one corner.

'Rotten France,' she said, burying her face in the pillow. 'One spends one's time being sick for love or just sick. I feel terrible.'

'Serve you right trying to pack ten years' experience into one night, and as for scribbling obscenities in lipstick all over Mrs Edgworth's clean car.'

'Holy smoke!' She sat bolt upright, clutching her head with one hand and the sheet to her breasts with the other. 'Did I really? Does she know it was me?'

'No, thanks to me. I managed to blur the Yvonne Bismark bits, so she assumes it's some random scribbler who got lit-up at the party.'

'Oh, thank goodness!'

' "Goodness," as Mae West said, "had nothing to do with it." ' He shook his head. 'I must say the most outrageous *alter ego* emerges when you get stoned. I'm not sure your father would be very pleased by your performance last night. Not that anyone else appears to have behaved particularly well. Nicky hasn't surfaced yet and Jumbo's looking very poorly.'

'W-where's Larry?' she stammered, pleating the sheet with her fingers, unable to meet Matt's eyes.

'Gone. He sent fondest love and a letter. Bambi's taken him off to Antibes.'

'Will they be O.K.?'

'Probably, after a bit of straight talking. They're both equally to blame.'

'And Tracey?'

'Gone to a thrash in Marbella with some movie star. He wanted you to go too, but I thought you'd had enough excitement to be going on with. By the way I've got a present for you,' and out of his pocket he produced a leather jewel box. For a glorious, lunatic moment Imogen wondered if he was giving her a ring. Then he said, 'It's from the Duchess and Braganzi to say thank you. There's a letter from her, too.'

Imogen opened the box. It was a gold necklace, set with seed pearls and rubies. She gave a gasp of delight.

'Pretty, isn't it? Try it on.'

She bowed her head forward. He put his arms around her to do up the clasp, his broad brown chest was only inches away from her. She ached to reach out and touch it. She trembled as she felt his fingers on her neck. She prayed it was clean enough.

'There.' Matt leaned back. 'It looks terrific. Have a look.' He reached for a hand mirror beside the bed and held it up for her. The necklace was beautiful but the effect was slightly spoiled by a mascara smudge under one eye and a large bit of sleep in the corner of the other. Hastily she rubbed them away.

'It's so kind of them both. It was so little that I did,' she muttered. Then she gave a gasp of horror. 'But I never asked you, I quite forgot. What happened about the piece?'

'They liked it. They hardly changed a thing.'

'Oh, that's wonderful. And your paper?'

'They're pretty pleased too.'

'I'm so glad. So it was worth it after all that struggle.'

'Yes, it nearly always is. I feel sort of Christlike today. It's the best feeling in the world, or almost the best feeling . . .' he smiled . . . 'the day after you've finished something you've really sweated your guts out over.' He squeezed her thigh gently through the blanket, 'And it's all due to you, darling.'

Imogen wriggled with embarrassment. 'It was nothing,' she cast desperately around for a change of subject. 'Look, does Yvonne really not realise it was me?'

'Well, her mind's on other things today. Evidently Jumbo disgraced himself last night, and being Saturday, the beach is like Oxford Street in the rush hour, but she's forgotten all that. She got a telegram midday confirming her film part.'

'Oh dear,' said Imogen.

'Quite. She's being utterly insufferable, upstaging Cable

601

in particular; so you can imagine Cable is not in the sunniest of tempers.'

His hair was nearly dry now. Blond and silky, it flopped over his tanned forehead. Imogen longed to run her fingers through it. She was driven distracted by his nearness, but it was such heaven having him sitting gossiping on her bed, she'd almost forgotten her hangover.

He got to his feet.

'To celebrate her new starring role, Mrs Edgworth has actually offered to take us all out to dinner. I hope you'll be able to make it. I need a few allies.'

When he had gone she opened her letters. There were several invitations, addressed to Morgan Brocklehurst, asking her to parties in various parts of Europe. Someone even wanted her to open a fête in Marseilles next week.

Larry's letter was scrawled on a piece of flimsy:

'*Darling little Imogen, you were very sweet to me last night, when I needed it very badly, and you succeeded in making Bambi wildly jealous, which is all to the good, although I had great difficulty on the evidence of last night in persuading her how miserable I'd been without her. I'll send you those pictures when I get them developed. If you ever want a bed in London, come and stay with us. Je t'embrasse, Larry. P.S. I thought your piece on Mrs Edgworth's car was inspired.*'

The last letter was from the Duchess.

'*My dear Imogen, Thank you again a million times for what you did for Ricky. This little necklace is only a small way of expressing our gratitude. Do come and stay with us next time you have some time off and write and let me know how your holiday works out. I liked your Mr O'Connor and he writes very well too. I wouldn't give up hope if I were you. Love, Camilla.*'

But hope would be hope of the wrong thing, sighed Imogen, but allowed herself a daydream of having a flat in London, and giving dinner parties, asking the Duchess and Braganzi to meet Larry and Bambi, with Matt coming early to help with the drinks, and her letting him in in a black satin petticoat, and him starting to kiss her so neither of them were remotely ready when the guests arrived.

Stop it, she told herself firmly, but with the thought that

she really would ask him to help her get a job in London, she drifted off to sleep.

When she woke up around eight, she felt a bit shaky, but normal. The rest of the party, gathered in the bar, greeted her like a long lost sister. Within a few minutes she realised that they were in for a decidedly stormy evening. Yvonne, dressed in a cowl-necked sky-blue dress which could easily have been worn by the Virgin Mary, was at her most poison-ous, smiling smugly, and queening it over everyone, par-ticularly Cable, whom Imogen would have felt extremely sorry for if she hadn't been in such a filthy temper, biting people's heads off, and casting dark spiteful looks in Imogen's direction. Now Tracey had gone, she had appar-ently made it up with Nicky, and insisted on sitting next to him at dinner.

They had just finished eating. Cable had only toyed with a few asparagus tips, when the waiter put a shampoo sachet on the side of her plate.

'What's that for?' said Cable. 'Do they want me to wash my hair?'

'Cleaning your fingers,' said Nicky.

'I prefer finger bowls.'

'They'd be quite useful for apres-sex,' said Nicky, examin-ing the sachet. 'They should put them in bedrooms.'

'I prefer finger bowls for that too,' said Cable.

'Tinker, tailor, soldier, sailor,' said Imogen idly counting her olive stones.

Cable shot her an uncontrollable look of hatred. 'Pity there isn't a rhyme that includes dissolute Irish journalists. That's what you're really after, isn't it Imogen?'

'Pack it in,' said Matt, icily.

'Well it's true,' said Cable, opening her bag and getting out her lipstick. At the same time a bill fluttered out on to the table. Cable quickly reached out to retrieve it, but Matt's hand closed over it first.

'Give it to me,' hissed Cable.

Matt smoothed out the bill and looked at it for a minute. A muscle started to flicker in his cheek.

603

'What's this for?' he said quietly.

'A few things I bought in Marseilles.'

'But this is for 4,500 francs!'

That's well over £500, thought Imogen incredulously.

'It must have been your peacock feather dress,' said Yvonne, brightening at the prospect of a showdown. 'I told you it was a rip-off at the time.'

'Particularly as someone ripped it right off you at that party,' said James and roared with laughter, stopping suddenly when he realised no one else was.

'D'you mean to tell me you spent 4,500 francs on one dress?' said Matt slowly.

'I had to have something new. You couldn't turn up in any old rag to that party. Everyone noticed it. That's the way one gets work.'

'Not that kind of work. How the hell d'you think we're going to pay for the rest of the holiday?'

'You'll have to win it back at the Casino. You can always cable the paper. You must have made twice that on your precious Braganzi story already.'

They paused, rigid with animosity, as the waiter cleared away the debris, leaving only clean glasses and ashtrays.

'Anyway,' Cable went on, 'since you decided to buy her' — she glared at Imogen — 'an entire new wardrobe, I thought it was my turn to have a few new clothes. Don't you agree, Nicky?'

Nicky showed his teeth non-committally. He wasn't going to be drawn in.

'Children, children,' cried Yvonne, dimples flashing, highly delighted by the turn of events, 'please don't spoil my party. I've got something to tell you all. This is a very special night for Jumbo and me.'

'So you've already told us,' snarled Cable. She turned to Matt. 'I don't know why you've got so fucking tight with bread recently.'

'Skip it,' said Matt, 'we'll discuss it later.' His face was expressionless but his hand trembled with rage as he folded up the bill and put it in his pocket.

'That's right, kiss and make-up,' said Yvonne.

There's going to be one hell of a row later, thought Imogen, as the waiter arrived with an ice bucket and a bottle of champagne.

'What's that for?' said Nicky, as the waiter removed the cork and filled up everyone's glasses.

'Because I want to celebrate my first and last film part for a long time.'

'Your last?' asked Imogen.

'When I went to the doctor about my foot the other day, he was able to confirm that I'm expecting a baby.' Yvonne, her head on one side, looked even more like the Virgin Mary than ever.

There was a long pause. Imogen caught Nicky's eye and for a terrible moment thought she was going to laugh. She could see Matt still gaining control of himself with an effort. Then his natural good nature conquered his fury with Cable.

'That's great news. Congratulations to you both.' He raised his glass in the air. 'To Baby Edgworth.'

'Baby Edgworth,' said Nicky and Imogen dutifully.

'I must say I'm jolly excited,' said James, leaning across and giving Yvonne a great splashy kiss, which she immediately wiped away with her napkin.

Cable said nothing. She was drumming her fingers on the table. Then she got to her feet.

'I'm going to the loo.'

'Aren't you going to congratulate me?' said Yvonne.

'The prospect that there might be another replica of you in the world shortly is too horrible to contemplate,' said Cable and turned on her heel.

There was another long pause.

'How horrid of her,' said Yvonne in a choked voice, then added more brightly, 'Of course she's only jealous. As I told her this morning, she's twenty-six now, her days as a model are numbered. She really ought to think about settling down soon. I know you don't like talking about marriage, Matt, but I'm sure if she had a tiny baby of her own, she'd be a different person.'

'Even worse I should think,' said Nicky, filling up everyone's glasses. 'I can't see Cable changing nappies.'

'Oh, she could always use the nappy service, or disposable nappies, don't you agree, Matt?'

'When's it due?' asked Imogen hastily.

'May the 10th,' said Yvonne. 'I'm awfully glad it'll be a little Taurean, rather than Gemini, so much more placid. Cable's Gemini, isn't she, Matt?'

She knows exactly to the day, thought Imogen. She and James can't sleep together very much.

Yvonne was still rabbiting on about the baby when Cable came back. Imogen could catch an asphyxiating waft of her scent from across the table. She'd drawn even darker lines round her eyes. She looked like a witch. For a moment she stood glaring at them until Nicky and James rose dutifully to their feet. Matt remained seated, his eyes cold, his mouth shut in a hard line.

Cable slipped into her seat.

'Where are we going next?' she said. 'Let's drive over to Antoine de la Tour's place.'

'We're not going anywhere,' snapped Matt. 'We can't afford it.'

'Oh, don't be bloody stingy.'

'When I planned this holiday I didn't bank on you spending 4,500 francs on a lot of feathers.'

'I'm going to bed too,' said Yvonne. 'With Baby on the way, I don't want any late nights.'

'I want to go to Verdi's Requiem.'

'Well, you can't.'

'Why don't we compromise?' said Nicky reasonably. 'Let's go to the fair and win some cheap plonk at the shooting range, and have a party back in our rooms.'

Only Yvonne wanted to go to bed. It would have been like missing the last act of a thriller. After they'd been to the fair, they all congregated in Nicky's room.

James, who proved a surprisingly good shot, had won a large teddy bear, a china Alsation and two goldfish, who were swimming around in the bidet.

Imogen sat on the floor, too stunned by the hostilities at dinner to say anything. Nicky was filling tooth-mugs. Matt lounged on the bed blowing smoke rings.

Cable, who was extremely drunk by now, was pacing up and down, determined to keep everyone's attention. She tossed back one mug of wine, and was about to pour another one, when Matt got up and took away the bottle.

'You've had enough,' he said quietly.

'I have not!' she snapped back.

She rushed over to Nicky and flung her arms round his neck.

'I'm as sober as a judge, aren't I, darling?'

Nicky grinned and pulled her on to his knee.

'I don't care what you are,' he said, 'but I like you.'

'There you are,' Cable said triumphantly. 'Nicky says I'm lovely. I'm glad someone appreciates me.'

'Cable, baby,' said Matt, 'at this moment the whole neighbourhood is appreciating you, particularly the people in the next door room. Keep your voice down.'

Cable slipped off Nicky's knee and went over to the dressing table and picked up the transistor.

'Let's have some music,' she said, turning it up full blast. 'Imogen did a strip-tease last night. Now it's my turn. I'm going to do the Dance of the Seven Veils.'

She kicked off her shoes and started to sway to the music.

'There's one veil gone.'

'Atta girl,' said Nicky.

'What's the next veil ?' said James.

'My watch,' said Cable, taking it off without stopping dancing.

A muscle was going in Matt's cheek.

'Cable,' he said in a voice of ice, 'turn that transistor down.'

'Why should I?' she said. 'I'm sick of being ordered about. Veil number three coming up.' She started undoing the buttons of her blue shirt.

James's eyes were out on stalks.

Matt got to his feet, went over to the transistor and turned it off.

Cable seized his wrist. 'Why are you such a wet blanket?'

'Go to bed and stop making a fool of yourself.'

'All right,' said Cable defiantly. 'I'll find some decent music somewhere else.'

She opened the window and put a foot out.

'Oh, don't Cable,' cried Imogen. 'It's terribly dangerous.'

'I'm going,' said Cable, starting to climb down the wall.

'You mustn't let her,' said Imogen, running to the window and catching Cable's hand.

'Turn on the transistor,' screamed Cable, who was hanging from the window.

Imogen turned, pleading to Matt, 'Please stop her.'

'Leave her alone. She's just showing off,' he said.

'Oh, let her go,' said Nicky. 'I'm fed up with her tantrums.'

Reluctantly, Imogen let go of her hand.

Cable started to clamber down the wall, then missed her footing and crashed to the ground.

'Are you all right?' called Imogen, worried.

Nicky and James started to roar with laughter.

'She's sitting in the middle of the road,' said Imogen, giggling in spite of herself. 'I hope she doesn't get run over.'

'Most unlikely,' said Nicky. 'It's a very deserted road, unfortunately.'

'For goodness sake forget her,' said Matt. 'She'll get bored soon and come in.'

'But she might have hurt herself,' said Imogen.

'Cable yells her head off if she even pricks her finger,' said Matt.

James put on Cable's wig, and a pair of earrings and started to do a tango with the Teddy bear. Everyone got slightly hysterical.

'She's all hunched up,' said Imogen. 'I think she's crying. I'm going down to her.'

'Not by yourself,' said Matt, taking her arm. 'I'll come with you.'

As they turned down an alley to reach the back of the hotel, Imogen stumbled. Matt caught her and suddenly she was in his arms, her eyes wide, her heart pounding.

As if by instinct, he bent his head and kissed her, and once she started she found she couldn't stop. She was powerless to do anything but kiss him back.

It was Matt who had to prise her fingers away from his neck. 'Easy, sweetheart. We've come to look for Cable not the end of the rainbow.'

He groped for a cigarette and, as the match lit up his face, his features were expressionless. Shattered, mortified, Imogen walked beside him. How could she have let herself go like that?

They found Cable lying in a huddle in the street. She was sobbing quietly. Matt was across the road in a flash. In the moonlight Imogen could see that her ankle was grotesquely swollen. Matt dropped on his knees beside her.

'Oh, God, darling, I'm sorry. I didn't realise.' There was no mistaking the tenderness and concern in his voice.

'Please don't go,' said Cable, through gritted teeth, and as he picked her up to carry her inside, she fainted. When the doctor arrived next morning he said she had broken her ankle.

CHAPTER SEVENTEEN

And that, thought Imogen dully, was that. In the simplest, if most painful, way possible, Cable had drawn Matt back to her side again. Once more she was the centre of attention. Nicky and James — mortified at having laughed at her last night — brought her huge bunches of black grapes. Yvonne, peeved at having missed a drama and furious with James for not coming to bed, was only too keen to take Cable's part.

Cable, once her ankle was set, took every opportunity to wring every ounce of pathos out of her situation.

'The terrible thing was,' she told Yvonne, 'that when I was in such agony all I could hear was drunken laughter.'

'Disgusting!' said Yvonne. 'How could they have been so heartless?'

After last night's heartlessness Cable had gone off Nicky again, but she insisted on Matt dancing attendance on her.

'I think I could just manage a little soup. Could you possibly close the shutters a little? Is it too soon for another pain killer?'

She's got us over a barrel, thought Imogen angrily, and then felt ashamed of herself. Matt, who was looking tired and on edge, drove everyone out of the bedroom in the end.

James, as a penance, was made to clean the car. Yvonne and Nicky went water-skiing. Rather half-heartedly they tried to persuade Imogen to join them. But she said she preferred to sunbathe. In fact, she just wanted to be alone.

As she lay on the beach she wondered if she'd ever been more unhappy in her life.

After yesterday's day in bed her suntan had settled to a deep tawny brown, without any red in it. Her hair was streaked with gold. The beach was packed with week-end trippers. Man after man sidled up and asked her to come for a drink or a swim.

She was wondering how much longer she could stand it when a silky voice said, 'Your sun lotion has spilled.'

'Oh, go away,' she snapped and looked up into the wicked brown face of Antoine de la Tour.

'Antoine!' she said, her face lighting up. 'How lovely to see you.'

'And you, ma petite.' He sat down beside her, his eyes running over her body.

Imogen told him about Cable.

'Serve her jolly well right,' he said. 'And now she mangle the commiseration out of everyone. I know 'er sort. Mimi has gone back to Paris,' he added, looking at her out of the corner of his eyes. 'I am poor boy on my own. 'Ow about the two of us spending the day together.'

Imogen drew circles in the sand, and decided it didn't really matter what she did now.

'I'd like to, Antoine. Can I just tell the others?'

But for reasons best known to herself, she didn't go up and tell Matt where she was going. Instead she left a hastily scrawled note at the desk.

Hours later, she sat drinking brandy on the terrace of Antoine's villa. The moon, grown slimmer since last night, was pouring white light on to the sea. Fireflies flickered in and out of the orange trees. The Milky Way rose like smoke from the dark hillside. Antoine sprawled in a hammock, smoking a cigar.

The day had passed in a dream. They had ridden along the sand for miles. They had swum and they had dined in a four-star restaurant.

Antoine had been a constantly amusing companion. But although he hadn't lifted a finger in her direction, she knew he was playing a waiting game. And this time she was dealing with a professional, not a larky amateur like Gilmore. It was like spending the evening with a tiger.

He drained his glass of brandy, stubbed out his cigar and stood over her, very tall, very dark.

'Let's go inside,' he said.

JILLY COOPER

This isn't really happening to me, thought Imogen, as she sat down on a huge sofa, covered in leopard skins. In about two minutes he's going to seduce me and I don't give a damn.

Antoine sat down beside her. He put a warm hand on her throat and slid it very slowly along her cheek to her ear and removed an earring.

'Pretty, pretty girl,' he said. 'Would you like me to make love to you properly?' He swiftly removed the other earring. 'Improperly, I mean.'

Oh God, thought Imogen, it's like being in the dentist's waiting room! The hi-fi began to swell soft music. Antoine put her earrings on the table and began to stroke her hair.

'*You're just too good to be true,*
Can't take my eyes off you,' sang Andy Williams.

Imogen burst into tears.

'Darling, ma petite, please don't cry.' She was sobbing in his arms. 'It is Matt, is it not?'

She nodded miserably.

'I thought that was the way the gale was blowing. And what does he feel?'

'Nothing, nothing at all. He loves Cable. They fight like mad but you should have heard his voice when she hurt her ankle last night.'

Antoine nodded. 'He is strange mixture. Always he joke and give impression 'e take nothing seriously except the horses and the betting. But beneath, he care about things very deeply. And even at Ox-fawd, he was always one-woman man. Though why 'e choose that 'orrible Cable, I can't imagine. I go to Rome tomorrow,' he said. 'Come with me. I show you nice time. I make you forget.'

She shook her head sadly. 'It wouldn't work.'

'I give you part in my film.'

He picked up one of the leopard skins and draped it across her shoulders, and stood back with half-closed eyes.

'You make beautiful slave girl.'

After that they drank a lot more brandy, and Antoine got out his photograph album and showed her stills from his films, and lots of snaps of himself and Matt at Oxford.

612

'I think I ought be getting back,' said Imogen.

'Hélas,' said Antoine, ruefully. 'I'm not tired. I think I'll drive as far as Milan tonight. Just wait while I pack a luggage.'

Outside the hotel, he took her in his arms and gave her a very thorough kissing.

'Pretty girl,' he said. 'Tell Matthieu I behave with honour. The sheep in wolf's suiting, I think. Are you sure you don't want to come to Rome?'

Imogen shook her head. 'No thank you.'

As she climbed the stairs, she was surprised to see a light on in her bedroom. She pushed open the door to find Matt lying on the bed. The ashtray on the bedside table was brimming with cigarette butts.

'Where the hell have you been?' he said. It was the crack of the ringmaster's lash.

'Out with Antoine,' she faltered. 'I left a note.'

'It's nearly two o'clock,' he said, getting to his feet and towering over her. His eyes were almost black.

'Did you think I'd turned into a pumpkin too?' she said with a nervous giggle.

'You wrote that note ten hours ago. I just wondered how you filled in the time.'

'We went riding.'

'And?'

'We swum and had dinner.'

'And?'

'We talked and talked.'

Matt lost his temper. It was as though a thunderstorm had broken over her head. Seizing her by the arms, his fingers biting into her flesh, he swung her round to face the mirror.

'Just look at yourself!'

Her lipstick was smudged, her hair rumpled, the two top buttons of her dress had come undone. Hastily, she did them up.

'He was just kissing me good-bye,' she said.

'Sure he was — ten hours after he'd kissed you hullo. And your dress is covered in fur. Talk yourself out of that if you can.'

613

A slow anger was beginning to smoulder inside her.

'He draped a leopard skin over my shoulders. He wanted to see what I'd look like as a slave girl.'

'Oh boy — what you lack in morals, you certainly make up for in imagination.'

'We were talking. We were talking,' said Imogen, her voice rising.

'You're repeating yourself, kid. You really want to lose it, don't you? First you try Nicky, and he's not having any, so you switch to me. Then you try Gilmore and then when that doesn't come off you fall back on Antoine.'

'I don't,' shouted Imogen.

'You picked the wrong guy,' he said viciously. 'Antoine'll have forgotten you by tomorrow.'

Imogen saw red. 'Why won't you listen?'

'Because I've had enough of your blarney. Oh Matt, Nicky's so mean to me. Oh, Matt, I'm so unhappy. Oh, Matt I'm such a constant nymph.'

'Get out! Get out!' shrieked Imogen. 'It's nothing to do with you what I do. Just because you're tied to Cable's apron strings, you can't bear anyone else to have fun.'

'Leave Cable out of this.'

But she was quite hysterical now. All the pent-up rage and jealousy of the past few days came pouring out of her. She didn't know what she was saying — every vicious hurtful thing that came into her head.

Matt grabbed her wrist.

'Shut up, shut up, shut up!'

'Now who's repeating himself?' she said.

For a moment she thought he was going to hit her. In the long silence that followed, she could only hear his rapid breathing and the pounding of her heart. Then he turned round and went out of the room.

Imogen stood, stunned and terrified, trembling like a dog on Guy Fawkes Night. How could she have said all those terrible things? She collapsed into a chair and sat hunched up, her face in her hands. Then she gave a low moan. Her earrings were missing. They were pearls and belonged to her mother. They were still on the table at Antoine's house.

She'd have to go and get them.

Putting on a sweater she tiptoed downstairs. The moon was setting. Drunks were swaying in the streets. She had no difficulty finding the road.

But it was further than she thought. She passed two men who looked at her curiously and called out to her. But she ran stumbling on. At last there was Antoine's house gleaming like an iced cake. No windows open at the front. She ran round to the back. If she lugged one of the magnolia tubs underneath and climbed on to it she could just reach. She was wriggling inside when everything round her was suddenly floodlit. Someone seized her by the ankle and pulled her to the ground. A man grabbed her arm and started gabbling at her in French. Struggling and shrieking, she was carried to a waiting car and thrown into the back, where another man pinned her arms behind her back.

She was being kidnapped. She'd never see Matt again, never see her family. She redoubled her struggles. It was only when the car drew up outside the police station that she realised she'd been arrested.

'Je ne suis pas un burglar. Je suis friend of Antoine de la Tour,' she said to the fat gendarme who was sitting behind a desk. But he just laughed and threw her into a cell.

At first she screamed and rattled the bars. But the fat gendarme came up and leered at her. He got out his keys. His meaning was quite plain.

Imogen shrunk away. 'Oh non, non — please not that!'

'*Ferme ta gueule, encore.*'

She sat on the narrow bed trying to stifle her sobs. No one would ever find her. She would be there for years like the Count of Monte Cristo. It was suffocatingly hot. She dripped with sweat, but was too shattered to think of taking off her sweater. The blazing row with Matt, the horror of her arrest were beginning to take effect. She couldn't stop shaking.

The hours crawled by. Light was beginning to seep through the tiny window, when there was a commotion outside. She heard a familiar voice.

'Matt!' she shrieked.

JILLY COOPER

He came straight over and took her hands through the bars.

'Imogen, are you all right?' His face was ashen.

'Oh, please get me out of here. They think I'm a burglar. I was trying to climb into Antoine's villa to get my earrings.' She didn't understand what Matt was saying to the fat gendarme. But he spoke very slowly and distinctly, waving his Press card back and forward, and the tone of his voice put a chill even into her heart. She was released in two minutes. She fell sobbing into his arms.

'It's all right, you're safe. Everything's all right.'

It was light in the streets as he drove back to the hotel.

'How did you find me?' she asked in a small voice.

'As soon as I cooled down, I realised I'd come on too strong. I came back to apologise and found you'd done a bunk. I toured the town for a bit, then I tried Antoine's house and found the place seething with police and Alsatians. It was simple after that.'

She hung her head. 'I'm dreadfully sorry. You seem to have spent your holiday getting me out of trouble.'

'Skip it. I had no right to shout at you. My lousy Irish temper, I'm afraid. Yesterday was a bit trying. Cable — up-staging like nobody's business. Nicky — sulking. James and Yvonne — at each other's throats.'

'Poor Matt,' said Imogen. 'You haven't had much of a holiday, have you?'

Then she tried again. 'We weren't doing anything, Antoine and I. Truthfully we weren't.'

'It doesn't matter. What you get up to is your own affair.'

'But . . . '

'Let's drop it, shall we?'

This weary acceptance was far worse than his earlier blinding rage.

CHAPTER EIGHTEEN

As soon as she got back to the hotel she went to bed, lying for a long time in a state of coma before she fell asleep. When she woke it was afternoon.

Listlessly, she dressed and wandered along the passage to Cable's room. Chaos met her eyes. Clothes of every colour of the rainbow littered the bed. Suitcases lay all over the floor.

'What are you doing?' said Imogen, aghast.

'What does it look as though I'm doing?' snapped Cable. 'Packing, of course. Since you're here, you may as well help me. Get those dresses out of the wardrobe — take the coat-hangers too. This beastly hotel can afford them — and put them in this case. My foot is hurting so much, I can't tell you.'

She sat down on the bed.

'But where are you going?' said Imogen.

Cable gave one of her sly, malicious smiles.

'All roads lead to Rome, darling. But I'm going by way of Milan.'

Imogen looked horrified. 'But that's where Antoine is.'

'Right first time,' said Cable approvingly. 'You're getting perceptive in your old age. Rebel's collecting me in half-an-hour.'

'But I thought you loathed Antoine.'

'Did you now? Well, I'm entitled to change my mind. I never said he wasn't attractive. And he's mad for me, which is half the battle. He telephoned this morning, absolutely gibbering, my dear, and said ever since he met me on Wednesday he couldn't get me out of his mind. He knew I wasn't happy with Matt. If I came to Rome, he'd give me the best time in the world. Don't forget those bikinis hanging

617

JILLY COOPER

from the window. He's going to give me a part in his film —
as a slave girl.

'And what about Matt?'

Cable's face hardened. 'Don't talk to me about Matt,' she
said stonily. 'I'm through with him for good. If anyone deserves his come-uppance, it's that guy.'

'But what's he done?' said Imogen.

'He's impossible, that's what. He was in the most vile temper all yesterday, quite unsympathetic about my foot which,
incidentally, is absolute agony. Then he swans off for most of
the night. God knows what he was up to — that blasted Casino, I suppose. Then he comes in at some ungodly hour
this morning, just as I'd taken two more sleeping pills. Put
all those bottles in my make-up case, darling. It's that trunk
over there. Where was I?'

'You'd just taken some pills.'

'So I had. Well, I was very uptight, so I began to tell him a
few home-truths. Very gently, mind you. And do you know
what he said?'

Imogen shook her head.

'He said, "Why don't you shut up about your bloody foot.
It would have been better for everyone if you'd broken your
jaw." '

Imogen buried her face in the bottles to hide a smile.

'And then without giving me a chance to retaliate, he
charges out of the room to watch some forest fire that's broken out in the mountains.'

There was a knock on the door. Cable jumped nervously.
'Answer it, will you?' she said.

A sleek black face appeared round the door. It was Rebel.

'Oh, hullo,' said Cable with relief. 'I won't be long. Could
you take these cases down? I'm afraid you'll have to make
two journeys.'

As soon as Rebel had left the room Imogen pleaded, 'You
can't leave Matt like this. O.K. — so he blew his top. But he'll
calm down. He's worth a million of Antoine. Antoine's just a
lovely playboy.'

'And I'm a lovely playgirl,' said Cable, wriggling into a
green dress that looked faintly familiar.

618

'But Matt really loves you.' Imogen was almost in tears.

'He shows it in a most mysterious way,' said Cable.

'But he'll be shattered.'

'Won't he just!' said Cable gleefully. 'Men hate it so much more when you take off with one of their mates. Well, if he loves me so much, he can come and get me. And this time it'll be marriage or nothing.'

She got an envelope out of the chest of drawers.

'I've written him this letter telling him everything,' she said, spraying it with scent. 'Will you be sure to give it him?'

Rebel appeared at the door. 'You can carry me down this time, darling,' said Cable.

Rebel picked her up.

'Lovely,' said Cable, feeling his muscles and smiling up at him. 'I don't think we'll bother to go as far as Milan.'

Fear and desolation crept slowly through Imogen's stomach like a cold wind. She went downstairs and ordered a Coke. Madame came waddling over in carpet slippers.

' 'Ave you seen Monsieur O'Connor?' she asked, putting the Coke tin and a glass on the table.

Imogen explained about the forest fire.

'Ah,' said Madame. 'Well, I 'ave his plane tickets.'

'Tickets?' said Imogen slowly.

It was as though another layer of ice was being placed over her heart.

Madame nodded despondently. 'Tonight he go. I think 'e meant to take that one back to London for her foot, but she seems to 'ave gone already. Always Monsieur O'Connor stay for two week. But this year, I think he not happy.'

Mindlessly picking up her Coke tin, Imogen left Madame in full spate and went out into the street. She was numb with horror. It was like some terrible dream. To be suddenly faced with life without Matt. A grey drab expanse stretching to infinity. Tears streaming down her face. Oblivious of the people in the street, she walked blindly to the far end of the cove, and stood there for a long time, looking at the sea frothing like ginger beer on the sand.

A car was hooting insistently. Blasted French, why did

they always drive on their horns.

'Imogen,' yelled a voice.

She looked up as the white Mercedes drew alongside her. Matt leant across.

'Jump in,' he said. 'There's something I want to show you.'

In a daze she got in.

He looked at her closely. 'Poor little love, you look done in.'

His face and hands were grimy, and his eyes bloodshot, but otherwise he seemed in excellent spirits. But not for long, thought Imogen. Cable's letter was burning a hole in her pocket.

As he swung the car off the coast road and headed for the mountains, she said, 'Matt, I've got something to tell you.'

'And there's something,' he said, taking the Coke tin from her and helping himself to a great swig of it, 'that I must tell you. In spite of her hundred per cent guaranteed sun protection lotion, Yvonne is peeling like a New York tickertape welcome. It's coming off her in festoons.'

Imogen couldn't help giggling.

'How was the fire?' she asked.

'Raging merrily, but they expect a storm tonight, so no one's very worried about it. I got a good story, though. Port-les-Pins fire brigade spent all morning bravely fighting the fire, but come lunchtime, like all good Frogs, they downed tools and returned to the town. When they got back three hours later, they found their fire engine burnt to a frazzle.' His shoulders shook.

She'd never seen him so happy — it wrung her heart. Oh damn, damn Cable.

They drove past vineyards and olive groves shimmering like tinfoil, past Braganzi's fortress and up into the mountains. When they'd gone as far up as the car could go, Matt got out.

'Come on,' he said, taking her hand and leading her up a steep path to the top.

Below them stretched a mountainous waste of Old Testament country. The sun moved in and out of the clouds lighting up villages and farms. To the right like a judgement on an ungodly people, a great furnace was licking over the hill-side. Bits of ash fluttered like snowflakes through the air.

'It's beautiful,' breathed Imogen.

'I always make a pilgrimage up here every year,' he said. 'It's sort of insurance that I'll come back again.'

The highest rock was smothered in undergrowth. Matt pulled away the brambles and the wild lavender to reveal a plaque with a list of names on it.

'Who were they?' asked Imogen.

'The local resistance fighters in the last war,' he said. 'I ought to add your name, oughtn't I?'

'My name?' she said in a stifled voice.

'Yes, sweetheart, for resisting the advances of three of the most formidable wolves in the business. Not that you were exactly resisting Larry the other night.'

She had a feeling he was laughing at her again.

'What are you talking about?' she muttered.

He sat down in a hollow in the rocks and pulled her down beside him.

'Matt,' she said desperately, 'there's something I must tell you.'

'Tell away then.' He put his hand under her hair and was gently stroking the back of her neck.

'Don't do that,' she sobbed. 'I've got a letter for you — from Cable.' She pulled it out of her pocket and almost flung it at him.

He picked it up, studied it lazily and tore it into little pieces which the wind scattered in an instant.

'Now arrest me for being a litter-bug,' he said. 'I know what's in that letter. I don't even have to open it. Cable, driven to distraction by my appalling behaviour and lack of consideration, has pushed off to Rome with Antoine.'

Imogen looked at him in bewilderment — a faint hope flickering inside her.

'I tried not to get uptight about you and Antoine,' he said. 'But in the end I knew I'd go crazy if I didn't have it out with him. So I rang Milan. He gave me a run-down on last night, corroborating your story word for word. He said you were enchanting, but entirely preoccupied with someone else.'

Imogen blushed.

'I'm sorry I was so bloody to you last night, little one. It's that Coleridge thing about being wroth with one we love working like madness in the brain. But I'm glad it happened. It showed me how hung up on you I'd got without realising it. I never felt a fraction of that white-hot murderous rage when I caught Cable being unfaithful.'

His voice was as soft as an Irish mist, and as he took her face in his hands, they smelt of wood smoke and wild lavender.

'Funny little Imogen. You were like a little girl, running after the rest of us crying, "Wait for me," ' and he bent his head and kissed her very gently. Next moment she flung her arms round his neck.

'Oh, Matt! Oh, Matt!'

Much later she said, 'But I don't understand. I thought Antoine and Cable loathed each other?'

'Did they? Animosity as intense as that often means the other thing. Neither will trust the other farther than they can throw them, which seems a good basis for a relationship.'

'But she's expecting you to follow her.'

'She's got a long wait in front of her then. If you keep turning a light switch on and off, on and off, like Cable did, the fuse blows in the end. There's nothing left.'

A suspicion crossed Imogen's mind. 'Matt, you didn't put Antoine up to it?'

He grinned. 'Not exactly. Let's say I planted the seed.'

'And what about Nicky?'

'Rumour has it that Nicky has been casting covetous eyes at some nymphette at the water-skiing school. And Tracey's due back this evening, so I don't think he'll be inconsolable for very long. Which leaves you and me.'

Imogen looked down at her hands. 'But you're going back?'

His face became serious. 'I've got to, darling. The Foreign Desk rang me this morning. This business in Peru's going to explode at any moment. They want me to fly out tomorrow.'

Imogen went pale. 'But you might get hurt.'

'Not I. Matt the cat with nine lives. Besides I've got something to come home for now, haven't I? I got a ticket for you too. I'm sorry to rot up your holiday, but I can't leave you here alone at the mercy of every passing wolf and gendarme.'

'You're taking me back to London with you?' she asked incredulously. Everything was crowding in on her. She couldn't take so much happiness at once.

Matt picked up the Coke tin that had fallen on to the ground and wrenched off the silver ring used to open it.

'You can go home to Yorkshire if you like. Or better still,' he looked at her under drooping lashes, 'you can shack up in my flat and look after Basil and make up my mind where you want to go for a honeymoon.'

Imogen opened her mouth and shut it again.

'It's all right. Don't rush into anything. Kick the idea round for a bit. You might not like being hitched to a journalist. It's a rough life. But I warn you, I don't give up easily. Anyway, people keep telling me I ought to hang on to you — Gilmore, Antoine, the Duchess, Braganzi, Tracey. You've got a lot of fans, sweetheart.'

'I have?' she said in amazement.

'Yep, and I'm the biggest one.'

He picked up her left hand and slid the Coca-Cola ring on to her wedding-ring finger. Then he pulled her into his arms and kissed her.

'I love you,' he said softly, 'because you're gentle and good, and because I know you love me.'

He looked at his watch. 'Christ. We'd better step on it, if we're going to catch that plane.'

Imogen grumbled and snuggled up to him, wanting to be kissed some more.

'Come on,' said Matt, pulling her to her feet. 'It's a great day for the Irish, but I can't answer for my actions if we stay here necking much longer, and I can't have you getting blasé.'

As he drove back into the town, she sat, her fingers

clutched over the Coca-Cola ring, half-stunned with wonder at what was happening.

As he stopped the car outside the hotel, however, she looked at him with troubled eyes. 'Matt, are you sure you're over Cable?'

'Darling,' he said, flinging his arms out in a fair imitation of Al Jolson. 'I'd run a million miles from one of her smiles. Come here, if you don't believe me.'

It was a few seconds before they realised Yvonne was tapping angrily on the window.

'Matt! Matthew!'

Matt turned round. 'Yes?'

Yvonne looked in horror, suddenly realising it was Imogen he was kissing. 'What on earth's she doing?'

'Just getting into training.'

Yvonne pursed her lips. 'Where's Cable?'

'I'm not quite sure.' 'Well, most of my wardrobe seems to be missing . . .'